PHILIP ROTH

PHILIP ROTH

NOVELS & OTHER NARRATIVES
1986–1991
The Counterlife
The Facts: A Novelist's Autobiography
Deception
Patrimony: A True Story

THE LIBRARY OF AMERICA

Library of Congress Control Number: 2008924838
ISBN: 978-1-59853-030-8

First Printing
The Library of America—185

Ross Miller
wrote the Chronology and Notes
for this volume

Philip Roth's
Novels and Other Narratives 1986–1991
is published with support from
a friend of The Library of America

Contents

THE COUNTERLIFE

To my father at eighty-five

1. Basel

E *ver since the family doctor, during a routine checkup, discovered an abnormality on his EKG and he went in
overnight for the coronary catheterization that revealed the di-
mensions of the disease, Henry's condition had been successfully
treated with drugs, enabling him to work and to carry on his life
at home exactly as before. He didn't even complain of chest pain
or of the breathlessness that his doctor might well have expected to
find in a patient with advanced arterial obstruction. He was
asymptomatic before the routine examination that revealed the
abnormality and remained that way during the year before he
decided on surgery—without symptoms but for a single terrible
side effect from the very medication that stabilized his condition
and substantially reduced the risk of a heart attack.*

*The trouble began after two weeks on the drug. "I've heard this
a thousand times," the cardiologist said when Henry telephoned
to report what was happening to him. The cardiologist, like Henry
a successful, vigorous professional man not yet into his forties,
couldn't have been more sympathetic. He would try to reduce the
dose to a point where the medicine, a beta-blocker, continued to
control the coronary disease and to blunt the hypertension without interfering with Henry's sexual function. Through a fine-
tuning of the medication, he said, you could sometimes achieve "a
compromise."*

*They experimented for six months, first with the dosage and,
when that didn't work, with other brands of the drug, but
nothing helped: he no longer awakened with his morning erection
or had sufficient potency for intercourse with his wife, Carol, or
with his assistant, Wendy, who was sure that it was she, and not
the medication, that was responsible for this startling change. At
the end of the day, with the outer-office door locked and the blinds
down, she worked with all her finesse to arouse him, but work it
was, hard labor for both of them, and when he told her it was no
use and begged her to stop, had finally to pry open her jaws to
make her stop, she was even more convinced that the fault was
hers. One evening, when she had burst into tears and told him
that she knew it was only a matter of time before he went out and*

*found somebody new, Henry struck her across the face. If it had
been the act of a rhino, of a wild man in an orgasmic frenzy,
Wendy would have been characteristically accommodating; this,
however, was a manifestation, not of ecstasy, but of utter exhaustion with her blindness. She didn't understand, the stupid girl!
But of course he didn't either, failed as yet to comprehend the confusion that this loss might elicit in somebody who happened to
adore him.*

*Immediately afterward, he was overcome with remorse. Hold-
ing her to him, he assured Wendy, who was still weeping, that she
was virtually all he thought about now every day—indeed (though
he could not say as much) if Wendy would only let him find work
for her in another dental office, he wouldn't have to be reminded
every five minutes of what he could no longer have. There were
still moments during office hours when he surreptitiously caressed
her or watched with the old yearning as she moved about in her
formfitting white tunic and trousers, but then he remembered his
little pink heart pills and was plummeted into despair. Soon
Henry began to have the most demonic fantasies of the adoring
young woman who would have done anything to restore his potency being overwhelmed before his eyes by three, four, and five
other men.*

*He couldn't control his fantasies of Wendy and her five faceless
men, and yet at the movies with Carol he preferred now to lower
his lids and rest his eyes till the love scenes were over. He couldn't
stand the sight of the girlie magazines piled up in his barbershop.
He had all he could do not to get up and leave the table when, at
a dinner party, one of their friends began to joke about sex. He
began to feel the emotions of a deeply unattractive person, an impatient, resentful, puritan disdain for the virile men and appe-
tizing women engrossed by their erotic games. The cardiologist,
after putting him on the drug, had said, "Forget your heart now
and live," but he couldn't, because five days a week from nine to
five he couldn't forget Wendy.*

*He returned to the doctor to have a serious talk about surgery.
The cardiologist had heard that a thousand times too. Patiently
he explained that they did not like to operate on people who were
asymptomatic and in whom the disease showed every sign of being
stabilized by medication. If Henry did finally choose the surgical
option, he wouldn't be the first patient to find that preferable to*

an indefinite number of years of sexual inactivity; nonetheless, the doctor strongly advised him to wait and see how the passage of time affected his "adjustment." Though Henry wasn't the worst candidate for bypass surgery, the location of the grafts he'd need didn't make him the ideal candidate either. "What does that mean?" Henry asked. "It means that this operation is no picnic in the best of circumstances, and yours aren't the best. We even lose people, Henry. Live with it."

Those words frightened him so that on the drive home he sternly reminded himself of all those who live of necessity without women, and in far more harrowing circumstances than his own—men in prison, men at war . . . yet soon enough he was remembering Wendy again, conjuring up every position in which she could be entered by the erection he no longer had, envisioning her just as hungrily as any daydreaming convict, only without recourse to the savage quick fix that keeps a lonely man half-sane in his cell. He reminded himself of how he'd happily lived without women as a prepubescent boy—had he ever been more content than back in the forties during those summers at the shore? Imagine that you're eleven again . . . but that worked no better than pretending to be serving a sentence at Sing Sing. He reminded himself of the terrible unruliness spawned by unconstrainable desire—the plotting, the longing, the crazily impetuous act, the dreaming relentlessly of the other, and when one of these bewitching others at last becomes the clandestine mistress, the intrigue and anxiety and deception. He could now be a faithful husband to Carol. He would never have to lie to Carol—he'd never have anything to lie about. They could once more enjoy that simple, honest, trusting marriage that had been theirs before Maria had appeared in his office ten years earlier to have a crown repaired.

He'd at first been so thrown by the green silk jersey dress and the turquoise eyes and the European sophistication that he could hardly manage the small talk at which he was ordinarily so proficient, let alone make a pass while Maria sat in the chair obediently opening her mouth. From the punctiliousness with which they treated each other during her four visits, Henry could never have imagined that on the eve of her return to Basel ten months later, she would be saying to him, "I never thought I could love two men," and that their parting would be so horrendous—it had all been so new to both of them that they had made adultery *positively virginal. It had never occurred to Henry, until Maria came along to tell him so, that a man who looked like him could probably sleep with every attractive woman in town. He was without sexual vanity and deeply shy, a young man still largely propelled by feelings of decorum that he had imbibed and internalized and never seriously questioned. Usually the more appealing the woman, the more withdrawn Henry was; with the appearance of an unknown woman whom he found particularly desirable, he would become hopelessly, rigidly formal, lose all spontaneity, and often couldn't even introduce himself without flushing. That was the man he'd been as a faithful husband—that's why he'd been a faithful husband. And now he was doomed to be faithful again.*

The worst of adjusting to the drug turned out to be adjusting to the drug. It shocked him that he was able to live without sex. It could be done, he was doing it, and that killed him—just as once being unable *to live without it was what killed him. Adjusting meant resigning himself to being this way, and he refused to be this way, and was further demoralized by stooping to the euphemism "this way." And yet, so well did the adjustment proceed, that some eight or nine months after the cardiologist had urged him not to rush into surgery before testing the effect of the passage of time, Henry could no longer remember what an erection was. Trying to, he came up with images out of the old pornographic funnies, the blasphemous "hotbooks" that had disclosed to kids of his generation the underside of Dixie Dugan's career. He was plagued by mental images of outlandish cocks and by the fantasies of Wendy with all those other men. He imagined her sucking them off. He imagined himself sucking them off. He began secretly to idolize all the potent men as though he no longer mattered as a man himself. Despite his dark good looks and tall, athletic physique, he seemed to have passed overnight from his thirties to his eighties.*

One Saturday morning, after telling Carol that he was going for a walk up in the Reservation hills—"to be by myself," he explained to her somberly—he drove into New York to see Nathan. He didn't phone ahead because he wanted to be able to turn around and come home if he decided at the last minute it was a bad idea. They weren't exactly teenagers anymore, up in the bedroom trading hilarious secrets—since the death of their parents, they weren't even like brothers. Yet he desperately needed someone to hear him out. All Carol could say was that he must not even begin to think of surgery if that meant running the slightest risk of rendering fatherless their three children. The illness was under control and at thirty-nine he remained a tremendous success in every imaginable way. How could all this suddenly matter so when for years now they'd rarely made love with any real passion? She wasn't complaining, it happened to everyone—there wasn't a marriage she knew of that was any different. "But I am only thirty-nine," Henry replied. "So am I," *she said, trying to help by being sensible and firm,* "but after eighteen years I don't expect marriage to be a torrid love affair."

It was the cruelest thing he could imagine a wife saying to a husband—What do we need sex for anyway? *He despised her for saying it, hated her so that then and there he'd made up his mind to talk to Nathan. He hated Carol, he hated Wendy, if Maria were around he would have hated her too. And he hated men, men with their enormous hard-ons from just looking at* Playboy *magazine.*

He found a garage in the East 80s and from a street-corner box nearby dialed Nathan's apartment, reading, while the phone rang, what had been scribbled across the remains of a Manhattan directory chained to the cubicle: Want to come in my mouth? Melissa 879-0074. *Hanging up before Nathan could answer, he dialed 879-0074. A man answered. "For Melissa," said Henry, and hung up again. This time after dialing Nathan, he let the phone ring twenty times.*

You can't leave them fatherless.

At Nathan's brownstone, standing alone in the downstairs hallway, he wrote him a note that he immediately tore up. Inside a hotel on the corner of Fifth he found a pay phone and dialed 879-0074. Despite the beta-blocker, which he'd thought was supposed to prevent *adrenaline from overcharging the heart, his was pounding like the heart of something wild on a rampage—the doctor wouldn't need a stethoscope to hear it now. Henry grabbed at his chest, counting down to the final boom, even as a voice sounding like a child's answered the phone.* "Hullo?"

"Melissa?"

"Yes."

"How old are you?"

"Who is this?"

He hung up just in time. Five, ten, fifteen more of those resounding strokes and the coronary would have settled everything. Gradually his breathing evened out and his heart felt more like a wheel, stuck and spinning vainly in the mud.

He knew he should telephone Carol so that she wouldn't worry, but instead he crossed the street to Central Park. He'd give Nathan an hour; if Nathan wasn't back by then, he'd forget about the operation and go home. He could not leave them fatherless.

Entering the underpass back of the museum, he saw at the other end a big kid, white, about seventeen, balancing a large portable radio on one shoulder and drifting lazily into the tunnel on roller skates. The volume was on full blast—Bob Dylan singing, "Lay, lady, lay . . . lay across my big brass bed . . ." Just what Henry needed to hear. As though he'd come inadvertently upon a dear old pal, the grinning kid raised a fist in the air, and gliding up beside Henry he shouted, "Bring back the sixties, man!" His voice reverberated dully in the shadowy tunnel, and amiably enough Henry replied, "I'm with you, friend," but when the boy had skated by him he couldn't hold everything inside any longer and finally began to cry. Bring it all back, he thought, the sixties, the fifties, the forties—bring back those summers at the Jersey Shore, the fresh rolls perfuming the basement grocery in the Lorraine Hotel, the beach where they sold the bluefish off the morning boats . . . He stood in that tunnel behind the museum bringing back all by himself the most innocent memories out of the most innocent months of his most innocent years, memories of no real consequence rapturously recalled—and bonded to him like the organic silt stopping up the arteries to his heart. The bungalow two blocks up from the boardwalk with the faucet at the side to wash the sand off your feet. The guess-your-weight stall in the arcade at Asbury Park. His mother leaning over the windowsill as the rain starts to fall and pulling the clothes in off the line. Waiting at dusk for the bus home from the Saturday afternoon movie. Yes, the man to whom this was happening had been that boy waiting with his older brother for the Number 14 bus. He couldn't grasp it—he could as well have been trying to understand particle physics. But then he couldn't believe that the man to whom it was happening was himself and that, whatever this man must undergo, he must undergo too. Bring the past back, the future, bring me back the present—*I am only thirty-nine!*

He didn't return to Nathan's that afternoon to pretend that nothing of consequence had transpired between them since they were their parents' little boys. On the way over he had been thinking that he had to see him because Nathan was the only family he had left, when all along he had known that there was no family anymore, the family was finished, torn asunder— Nathan had seen to that by the ridicule he'd heaped upon them all in that book, and Henry had done the rest by the wild charges he'd leveled after their ailing father's death from a coronary in Florida. "*You killed him, Nathan. Nobody will tell you—they're too frightened of you to say it. But you killed him with that book.*" *No, confessing to Nathan what had been going on in the office for three years with Wendy would only make the bastard* happy, *prove him right—I'll provide him with a sequel to* Carnovsky! *It had been idiotic enough ten years earlier telling him everything about Maria, about the money I gave her and the black underwear and the stuff of hers that I had in my safe, but bursting as I was I had to tell someone—and how could I possibly understand back then that exploiting and distorting family secrets was my brother's livelihood?* He *won't sympathize with what I'm going through—he won't even listen.* "*Don't want to know,*" *he'll tell me from behind the peephole, and won't even bother to open the door.* "*I'd only put it in a book and you wouldn't like that at all.*" And *there'll be a woman there—either some wife he's bored with on the way out or some literary groupie on the way in. Maybe both. I couldn't bear it.*

Instead of going directly home, back in Jersey he drove to Wendy's apartment and made her pretend to be a black twelve-year-old girl named Melissa. But though she was willing—to be black, twelve, ten, to be anything he asked—it made no difference to the medication. He told her to strip and crawl to him on her knees across the floor, and when she obeyed he struck her. That didn't do much good either. His ridiculous cruelty, far from goading him into a state of arousal, reduced him to tears for the second time that day. Wendy, looking awfully helpless, stroked his hand while Henry sobbed, "*This isn't me! I'm not this kind of man!*" "*Oh, darling,*" *she said, sitting at his feet in her garter*

belt and beginning now to cry herself, "you must have the opera-
tion, you must—otherwise you're going to go mad."

He'd left the house just after nine in the morning and didn't
get home until close to seven that evening. Fearing that he was
alone somewhere dying—or already dead—at six Carol had
called the police and asked them to look for the car; she'd told
them that he'd gone for a walk in the Reservation hills that
morning and they said that they would go up and check the trails.
It alarmed Henry to hear that she had called the police—he had
been depending upon Carol not to crack and give way like
Wendy, and now his behavior had shattered her too.

He remained himself still too stunned and mortified to grasp
the nature of the loss to all the interested parties.

When Carol asked why he hadn't phoned to say he wouldn't be
home until dinner, he answered accusingly, "Because I'm impotent!" as though it was she and not the drug that had done it.

It was she. He was sure of it. It was having to stay with her and
be responsible to the children that had done it. Had they divorced
ten years earlier, had he left Carol and their three kids to begin a
new life in Switzerland, he would never have fallen ill. Stress, the
doctors told him, was a major factor in heart disease, and giving
up Maria was the unendurable stress that had brought it on in
him. There was no other explanation for such an illness in a man
otherwise so young and fit. It was the consequence of failing to
find the ruthlessness to take what he wanted instead of capitu-
lating to what he should do. The disease was the reward for the
dutiful father, husband, and son. You find yourself in the same
place after such a long time, without the possibility of escape, along
comes a woman like Maria, and instead of being strong and selfish, you are, of all things, good.

The cardiologist gave him a serious talking-to the next time
Henry came for a checkup. He reminded him that since he'd been
on the medication his EKG had shown a marked diminution of
the abnormality that had first signaled his trouble. His blood
pressure was safely under control, and unlike some of the cardiologist's patients, who couldn't brush their teeth without the effort
causing severe angina, he was able to work all day standing on
his feet without discomfort or shortness of breath. He was again
reassured that if there was any deterioration in his condition, it
would almost certainly occur gradually and show up first on the

EKG or with a change of symptoms. Were that to happen, they would then reevaluate the surgical option. The cardiologist reminded him that he could continue safely along on this regimen for as long as fifteen or twenty years, by which time the bypass operation would more than likely be an outmoded technique; he predicted that by the 1990s they would almost certainly be correcting arterial blockage by other than surgical means. The beta-blocker might itself soon come to be replaced by a drug that did not affect the central nervous system and cause this unfortunate consequence—that sort of progress was inevitable. In the meantime, as he'd advised him already and could only repeat, Henry must simply forget his heart and go out and live. "You must see the medication in context," the cardiologist said, lightly striking his desk.

And was that the last there was to say? Was he now expected to get up and go home? Dully Henry told him, "But I can't accept the sexual blow." The cardiologist's wife was someone Carol knew and so of course he couldn't explain about Maria or Wendy or the two women in between, and what each of them had meant to him. Henry said, "This is the most difficult thing I've ever had to face."

"You haven't had a very difficult life then, have you?"

He was stunned by the cruelty of the reply—to say such a thing to a man as vulnerable as himself! Now he hated the doctor too.

That night, from his study, he again phoned Nathan, his last remaining consolation, and this time found him home. He was barely able to prevent himself from dissolving in tears when he told his brother that he was seriously ill and asked if he could come to see him. It was impossible living alone any longer with his staggering loss.

Needless to say, these were not the three thousand words that Carol had been expecting when she'd phoned the evening before the funeral and, despite all that had driven the two brothers apart, asked if Zuckerman would deliver a eulogy. Nor was the writer ignorant of what was seemly, or indifferent to the conventions that ruled these occasions; nonetheless, once he'd started there was no stopping, and he was at his desk most of the night piecing Henry's story together from the little he knew.

When he got over to Jersey the next morning, he told Carol more or less the truth about what had happened. "I'm sorry if you were counting on me," he said, "but everything I put down was wrong. It just didn't work." He supposed that she would now suppose that if a professional writer finds himself stymied by what to say at his own brother's funeral, it's either hopelessly mixed emotions or an old-fashioned bad conscience that's doing it. Well, less harm in what Carol happened to think of him than in delivering to the assembled mourners this grossly inappropriate text.

All Carol said was what she usually said: she understood; she even kissed him, she who had never been his greatest fan. "It's all right. Please don't worry. We just didn't want to leave you out. The quarrels no longer matter. That's all over. What matters today is that you were brothers."

Fine, fine. But what *about* the three thousand words? The trouble was that words that were morally inappropriate for a funeral were just the sort of words that engaged him. Henry wasn't dead twenty-four hours when the narrative began to burn a hole in Zuckerman's pocket. He was now going to have a very hard time getting through the day without seeing everything that happened as *more*, a continuation not of life but of his work or work-to-be. Already, by failing to use his head and discreetly cobbling together some childhood memories with a few conventionally consoling sentiments, he'd made it impossible for himself to take his place with everyone else, a decent man of mature years mourning a brother who'd died before his time—instead he was again the family outsider. Entering the synagogue with Carol and the kids, he thought, "This profession even fucks up grief."

Though the synagogue was large, every seat was occupied, and clustered at the rear and along the side aisles were some twenty or thirty adolescents, local youngsters whose teeth Henry had been taking care of since they were children. The boys looked stoically at the floor and some of the girls were already crying. A few rows from the back, unobtrusive in a gray sweater and skirt, sat a slight, girlishly young blonde whom Zuckerman wouldn't even have noticed if he hadn't been looking for her—whom he wouldn't have been able to recognize if not for the photograph that Henry had brought along on his second visit. "The picture," Henry warned, "doesn't do her justice." Zuckerman was admiring nonetheless: "Very pretty. You make me envious." A little immodest little-brother smirk of self-admiration could not be entirely suppressed, even as Henry replied, "No, no, she doesn't photograph well. You can't really see from this what it is she has." "Oh yes I can," said Nathan, who was and wasn't surprised by Wendy's plainness. Maria, if not as astonishingly beautiful in *her* picture as she'd first been described by Henry, had been attractive enough in a sternly Teutonic, symmetrical way. However, *this* bland little twat—why, Carol with her curly black hair and long dark lashes looked erotically more promising. It was, of course, with Wendy's picture still in his hand that Zuckerman should have laid into Henry with all he had—that might even have been *why* Henry had brought the picture, to give him the opening, to hear Nathan tell him, "Idiot! Ass! Absolutely not! If you wouldn't leave Carol to run off with Maria, a woman whom you actually *loved*, you are not going into the hospital for dangerous surgery just because some broad at the office blows you every night before you go home for dinner! I have heard your case for that operation and up till now haven't said a word—but my verdict, which is law, is *no!*"

But inasmuch as Henry wasn't dead then but alive—alive and outraged that a man with his moral credentials should be thwarted in this single, small, harmless transgression—inasmuch as he had already accepted the compromise of Wendy when what he had dreamed of and denied himself was to be remade in Europe with a European wife, to become in Basel an unfettered, robust, fully grown-up American expatriate dentist, Zuckerman had found his thoughts moving more along these lines: "This is his rebellion against the deal he's made, the outlet for what's survived of brutish passion. He surely hasn't come to me to be told that life obstructs and life denies and there's nothing to do but accept it. He's here to argue it out in my presence because my strong point isn't *supposed* to be a talent for self-denial—I, in their lore, am the reckless, free-wheeling impulsive, to me they've assigned the role of family id, and he is the exemplary brother. No, a certified irresponsible spirit can't now come on in fatherly tones, gently telling him, 'You don't need what you want, my boy—relinquish your Wendy and you'll suffer less.' No, Wendy is his freedom and his manhood, even if she happens to look to me a little like boredom incarnate. She's a nice kid with an oral hang-up who he's pretty sure will never phone the house—so why *shouldn't* he have her? The more I look at this picture, the more I understand his point. How much is the poor guy asking for?"

But you reason differently so close to the coffin of your only brother that you can practically rest your cheek on the shining mahogany wood. When Nathan made the inevitable effort to imagine Henry laid out inside, he did not see, silenced, the unmanned, overheated adulterer who had refused to be resigned to losing his potency—he saw the boy of ten, lying there wearing flannel pajamas. One Halloween when they were children, hours after Nathan had brought Henry home from trick-or-treating in the neighborhood, after the whole family had long been in bed, Henry had wandered out of his room, down the stairs, out the door, and into the street, heading for the intersection at Chancellor Avenue without even his slippers on and still in his sleep. Miraculously, a friend of the family who lived over in Hillside happened to be driving by their corner as Henry was about to step off the curb against the light. He pulled over, recognized the child under the street lamp as Victor Zuckerman's little son, and Henry was safely home and back beneath the covers only minutes later. It was thrilling for him to learn the next morning of what he'd done while still fast asleep and to hear of the bizarre coincidence that had led to his rescue; until adolescence, when he began to develop more spectacular ideas of personal heroism as a hurdler for the high-school track team, he must have repeated to a hundred people the story of the daring midnight excursion to which he himself had been completely tuned out.

But now he was in his coffin, the sleepwalking boy. This time nobody had taken him home and tucked him back into bed when he went wandering off alone in the dark, unable to forswear his Halloween kicks. Equally possessed, in a Herculean trance, carried along by an exciting infusion of Wild West bravado—that's how he'd struck Nathan on the afternoon he arrived at his apartment fresh from a consultation with the cardiac surgeon. Zuckerman was surprised: it wasn't the way he would have imagined walking out of one of those guys' offices after he'd told you his plans for carving you up.

Henry unfolded on Nathan's desk what looked like the design for a big cloverleaf highway. It was the sketch that the surgeon had made to show him where the grafts would go. The operation sounded, as Henry described it, no trickier than a root-canal job. He replaces this one and this one and hooks them up here, bypasses three tiny ones feeding into the one back there—and that's the whole shmeer. The surgeon, a leading Manhattan specialist whose qualifications Zuckerman had double-checked, told Henry that he had been through quintuple bypass surgery dozens of times and wasn't worried about holding up his end; it was Henry who now had to squelch all his doubts and approach the operation with every confidence that it was going to be a hundred percent success. He would emerge from the surgery with a brand-new system of unclogged vessels supplying blood to a heart that was itself as strong still as an athlete's and completely unimpaired. "And no medication afterwards?" Henry asked him. "Up to your cardiologist," he was told; "probably something for a little mild hypertension, but nothing like the knockout drops you're on now." Zuckerman wondered if, upon hearing the marvelous prognosis, Henry's euphoria had prompted him to present the cardiac surgeon with a personally signed 8½ x 11 glossy of Wendy in her garter belt. He seemed loopy enough for it when he arrived, but probably that was how you had to be to steel yourself for such a frightening ordeal. When Henry had finally mustered the courage to stop asking for reassurance and get up and go, the confident surgeon had accompanied him to the door. "If the two of us are working together," he told him, shaking Henry by the hand, "I can't foresee any problems. In a week, ten days, you'll be out of the hospital and back with your family, a new man."

Well, from where Zuckerman was sitting it looked as though on the operating table Henry hadn't been pulling his weight. Whatever he was supposed to do to assist the surgeon had apparently slipped his mind. This can happen when you're unconscious. My sleepwalking brother! Dead! Is that you in there, really, an obedient and proper little boy like you? All for twenty minutes with Wendy before hurrying home to the household you loved? Or were you showing off for me? It cannot be that your refusal to make do with a desexed life was what you thought of as your heroism—because if anything it was your *repression* that was your claim to fame. I mean this. Contrary to what you thought, I was never so disdainful of the restrictions under which you flourished and the boundaries you observed as you were of the excessive liberties you imagined me taking. You confided in me because you believed I would understand Wendy's mouth—and you were right. It went way beyond the juicy pleasure. It was your drop of theatrical existence, your disorder, your escapade, your risk, your little daily insurrection against all your overwhelming virtues —debauching Wendy for twenty minutes a day, then home at night for the temporal satisfactions of ordinary family life. Slavish Wendy's mouth was your taste of reckless fun. Old as the hills, the whole world operates this way . . . and yet there must be more, there *has* to be more! How could a genuinely good kid like you, with your ferocious sense of correctness, wind up in this box for the sake of that mouth? And why didn't I stop you?

Zuckerman had taken a seat in the first row, on the aisle, next to Bill and Bea Goff, Carol's parents. Carol sat at the center of the row, beside her mother; on her other side she had placed the children—her eleven-year-old daughter, Ellen, her fourteen-year-old son, Leslie, and nearest the far aisle, Ruth, the thirteen-year-old. Ruth was holding her violin on her knee and looking steadily at the coffin. The other two children, nodding silently while Carol spoke to them, preferred looking into their laps. Ruth was to play a piece on the violin that her father had always liked, and at the conclusion of the service, Carol would speak. "I asked Uncle Nathan if he wanted to say anything, but he says he's a little too shaken up right now. He says he's too stunned, and I understand. And what I'm going to say," she explained to them, "isn't going to be a eulogy, really. Just a few words about Daddy that I want everyone to hear. Nothing flowery, but words that are important for me. Then we're going to take him up to the cemetery by ourselves, just Grandma and Grandpa, Uncle Nathan, and the four of us. We're going to say goodbye to him at the cemetery, as a family, and then we're going to come back here and be with all our relatives and friends."

The boy wore a blazer with gold buttons and a pair of new tan boots, and though it was the end of September and the sun had been in and out all morning, the girls were in thin pastel dresses. They were tall, dark children, Sephardic-looking like their father, with rather prepossessing eyebrows for such innocent, coddled kids. They all had beautiful caramel eyes, a shade lighter and less intense than Henry's—six eyes, exactly alike, liquidly shining with amazement and fear. They looked like little startled does who'd been trapped and tamed and shod and clothed. Zuckerman was particularly drawn to Ruth, the middle child, diligently at work emulating her mother's calm despite the scale of the loss. Leslie, the boy, seemed the softest, the most girlish, the closest to collapsing really, though when, a few minutes before they left for the synagogue, he took his mother aside, Zuckerman overheard him ask, "I've got a game at five, Mom—can I play? If you don't think I should . . ." "Let's wait, Les," Carol said, one hand lightly brushing down the back of his hair, "let's see if you still want to then."

While people were still crowding into the back of the synagogue and bridge chairs were found to seat some elderly latecomers, while there was nothing to do but sit in silence only feet from the coffin deciding whether to keep looking at it or not, Bill Goff began rhythmically to make a fist and then undo it, opening and closing his right hand as though it were a pump with which to work up courage or to drain off fear. He barely resembled any longer the agile, sharp-dressing, spirited golfer that Zuckerman had first seen some eighteen years before, dancing with all the bridesmaids at Henry's wedding. Earlier that morning, when Goff had opened the door to let him in, Nathan hadn't even realized at first whose hand he was shaking. The only thing about him that looked undiminished was the full head of wavy hair. Inside the house, turning sadly to his wife—and sounding just a bit affronted—Goff had said to her, "How do you like that? He didn't even recognize me. That's how much I changed."

Carol's mother went off with the girls to help Ellen settle for a second time on which of her good dresses was right to wear, Leslie returned to his room to buff his new boots again, and the two men walked out back for some fresh air. They looked on from the patio while Carol clipped the last of the chrysanthemums for the children to take with them to the cemetery.

Goff began telling Nathan why he'd had to sell his shoe store up in Albany. "Colored people started to come in. How could I turn them away? That's not my nature. But my Christian customers of twenty and twenty-five years, they didn't like it. They told me right out, no bones about it, 'Look, Goff, I'm not going to sit here and wait while you try ten pairs of shoes on some nigger. I don't want his rejects either.' So one by one they left me, my wonderful Christian friends. That's when I had the first attack. I sold and got out, figuring the worst was over. Get out from under the pressure, the doctor told me, so I cut my losses, and a year and a half later, on my holiday, down in Boca playing golf, I had the second attack. Whatever the doctor said, I did, and the second attack was worse than the first. And now this. Carol has been a fortress: one hundred pounds soaking wet and she has the strength of a giant. She was like that when her brother died. We lost Carol's twin brother his second year in law school. First Eugene at twenty-three, now Henry at thirty-nine." Suddenly he said, "What'd I do?" and took from his pocket a small plastic prescription vial. "Angina pills," he said. "My nitroglycerin. I knocked the goddamn top off again."

All the while he'd been mourning the loss of the store, his health, the son, and the son-in-law, deep in his trouser pockets his hands had been nervously jingling his change and his keys. Now he emptied his pocket and began to pick the tiny white pills out from among the coins, the keys, and a pack of Rolaids. When he tried dropping them back into the little vial, however, half of them fell to the flagstone floor. Zuckerman picked them up, but each time Mr. Goff tried to get them into the vial again he dropped a few more. Finally he gave up and held everything in his two cupped hands while Nathan picked the pills out one by one and deposited them in the vial for him.

They were still at this when Carol came up from the garden with the flowers and said it was time to leave. She looked maternally at her father, a gentle smile to try to calm him down. The same operation from which Henry had died at thirty-nine was in the offing for him at sixty-four if his angina got any worse. "You all right?" she asked him. "I'm fine, cookie," he replied, but when she wasn't looking, he slipped a nitroglycerin pill under his tongue.

The little violin piece that Ruth played was introduced by the rabbi, who came across as amiable and unpretentious, a large man, square-faced, red-haired, wearing heavy tortoise-shell glasses and speaking in a mild, mellifluous voice. "Henry and Carol's daughter, thirteen-year-old Ruth, is going to play the Largo from Handel's opera *Xerxes*," he said. "Talking with her up at the house last night, Ruthie told me that her father called it 'the most soothing music in all the world' whenever he heard her practicing. She wants to play it now in his memory."

At the center of the altar, Ruth placed the violin under her chin, sharply cranked up her spine, and stared out at the mourners with what looked almost like defiance. In the second before she lifted the bow she allowed herself a glance down at the coffin and seemed to her uncle like a woman in her thirties —suddenly he saw the expression she would wear all her life, the grave adult face that prevents the helpless child's face from crumbling with angry tears.

Though not every note was flawlessly extracted, the playing was tuneful and quiet, slow and solemnly phrased, and when Ruthie was finished, you expected to turn around and see sitting there the earnest young musician's father smiling proudly away.

Carol got up and stepped past the children into the aisle. Her only concession to convention was a black cotton skirt. The hem, however, was banded in some gaily embroidered American Indian motif of scarlet, green, and orange, and the blouse was a light lime color with a wide yoked neck that revealed the prominence of the collarbone in her delicate torso. Around her neck she wore a coral necklace that Henry had surreptitiously bought for her in Paris, after she'd admired it in a shop window but had thought the price ridiculously high. The skirt he'd bought for her in an open-air market in Albuquerque, when he'd been there for a conference.

Though gray hairs had begun cropping up along her temple, she was so slight and so peppy that climbing the stairs to the altar she looked as though she were the family's oldest adolescent girl. With Ruth he believed that he had caught a glimpse of the woman she'd be—in Carol, Zuckerman saw the plucky, crisply pretty college coed before she'd fully come of age, the ambitious, determined scholarship student her friends had called admiringly by her two first initials until Henry had put a stop to it and made people use her given name. At the time, Henry half-jokingly had confided to Nathan, "I really couldn't get myself worked up with somebody called C.J." But then even with somebody called Carol, the lust was never to be what it was with a Maria or a Wendy.

Just as Carol reached the altar lectern, her father took his nitroglycerin pills out of his pocket and accidentally spilled them all over the floor. Handel's Largo hadn't soothed him the way it used to soothe Henry. Nathan was able to get his arm under the seat and fish around with his hand until he found a few pills that he could reach and pick up. He gave one to Mr. Goff, and the others he decided to keep in his pocket for the cemetery.

While Carol spoke, Zuckerman again imagined Henry in his flannel pajamas decorated with the clowns and the trumpets, saw him mischievously eavesdropping from within the dark box as he would from his bed when there was a card party at the house and he left the door to his room ajar so as to hear the adults kibitz downstairs. Zuckerman was remembering back to when absolutely nothing was known in the boys' bedrooms of erotic temptation or death-defying choice, when life had been the most innocent pastime and family happiness had seemed eternal. Harmless Henry. If he could hear what Carol was saying, would he laugh, would he weep, or would he think with relief, "Now nobody will ever know!"

But of course Zuckerman knew, Zuckerman who was not so harmless. What *was* he to do with those three thousand words? Betray his brother's final confidence, strike a blow against the family of the very sort that had alienated him from them in the first place? The evening before, after thanking Carol for her graciousness and telling her that he would sit down at once to compose a eulogy, he'd located, among the loose-leaf journals stacked atop his file cabinets, the volume in which he'd kept his account of Henry's affair with the Swiss patient. Must he really go in now and plunder these notes that he'd mercifully all but forgotten—had they been waiting there all these years for an inspiration as unforeseen as this?

Scattered throughout the handwritten pages were dozens of shortish entries about Henry and Maria and Carol. Some were no more than a line or two long, others ran to almost a page, and before trying to figure out what to say at the funeral, Zuckerman, seated at his desk, had read them all slowly through, thinking as he heavily underscored the promising lines, "Here the ending began, with as commonplace and unoriginal an adventure as this—with the ancient experience of carnal revelation."

H. at midnight. "I have to phone somebody. I have to tell somebody that I love her. Do you mind—at this hour?" "No. Go ahead." "I at least have you to tell. She has nobody. I'm bursting to tell everyone. I'm actually dying to tell Carol. I want her to know how terrifically happy I am." "She can live without it." "I realize that. But I keep wanting to say, 'Do you know what Maria said today? Do you know what little Krystyna said last night when Maria was bathing her?'"

"She seems far off in the distance, the way the bedposts looked when I was a kid in our room. Remember the knobs on the top of the maple bedposts? I used to put myself to sleep by imagining them to be far far away, until actually they were, and I had to stop because I was scaring myself. Well, she seemed far away just like that, as though I couldn't possibly reach a hand out and touch her. She was on top of me, far far away, and each time she came, I said, '*More*, do you want *more*?' And she nodded her head, like a child playing bouncy-horsy she nodded yes and started off again, red in the face and riding me, and all I wanted was for her to have *more* and *more* and *more*—and all the time I kept seeing her so very far away."

"You should see what she looks like, you should see this beautiful blond girl, with those eyes, up on top of me in her black silk camisole." Maria thought she'd have to go over to New York to buy the black underwear but then she found some down in the village. H. wonders if she oughtn't to have gone to New York to get it anyway.

Saturday H. saw her husband in the street. Looks like a nice fellow. Big and handsome. Bigger even than H. Very jolly with his kids. "Will you show him the underwear?" "No." "Will you wear it when you're with him?" "No." "Only for me." "Only for you." H. feels sorry for him. Looked so trusting.

In their motel room, while he watches her dressing to go home.

H. "You really are my whore, aren't you?" Maria laughs: "No. I'm not. Whores get money."

H. has cash in his wallet—a wad to pay motel, etc., without using credit card. Peels off two crisp hundred-dollar bills and presents them to her.

She doesn't at first know what to say. Then apparently she does. "You're supposed to throw them on the floor," she tells him. "I think that's the way it's done."

H. lets them flutter to the floor. In the black silk camisole she bends to pick them up and puts them into her purse. "Thanks."

H., to me. "I thought, 'My God, I'm out two hundred bucks. That's a lot of dough.' But I didn't say a word. I thought, 'It's worth two hundred, just to see what it's like.'"

"What is it like?"

"I don't know yet."

"She still has the money?"

"She does—she has it. She says, 'You are a crazy man.'"

"Sounds like she wants to see what it's like too."

"I guess we both do. I want to give her more."

Maria confides that a woman who'd had an affair with her husband before she married him once told a friend of hers, "I was never so bored in my life." But he is a wonderful man with the children. And he holds her together. "I am the impulsive one," she says.

Maria says that whenever she can't believe that H. is real and their affair is really happening, she goes upstairs and looks at the two hundred-dollar bills hidden away in her underwear drawer. That convinces her.

H. amazed that he is not in any way guilty or tormented by being so joyously unfaithful to Carol. He wonders how someone who tries so hard to be so good, who *is* good, can be doing this so easily.

Carol spoke without notes, though as soon as she began it was clear to Zuckerman that every word had been thought through beforehand and nothing left to chance. If Carol had ever held any mystery for her brother-in-law, it had to do with what if anything lay behind her superagreeable nature; he had never been able to figure out precisely how naïve she was, and what she now had to say didn't help. The story Carol had chosen to tell wasn't the one that he had pieced together (and had decided—for now—to keep to himself); Henry's misery lived in Zuckerman's recollection with a significance and meaning entirely different. Hers was the story that was intended to stand as the officially authorized version, and he wondered while she recounted it if she believed it herself.

"There's something about Henry's death," she began, "that I want all of you gathered here today to know. I want Henry's children to know. I want his brother to know. I want everyone who ever loved him or cared about him to know. I think it may help to soften the force of this stupendous blow, if not this morning, then sometime in the future, when we're all less stunned.

"If he had chosen to, Henry could have gone on living without that horrible operation. And if he hadn't had that operation he'd be working away in his office right now and, in a few hours, would be coming home to me and the kids. It isn't true that the surgery was imperative. The medication that the doctors had given him when the disease was first diagnosed was effectively controlling his heart problem. He was in no pain and in no immediate danger. But the medication had drastically affected him as a man and put an end to our physical relationship. And this Henry couldn't accept.

"When he began seriously considering surgery, I begged him not to risk his life just to preserve that side of our marriage, much as I missed it myself. Of course I missed the warmth and tenderness and intimate affection, but I was coming to terms with it. And we were otherwise so fortunate in our lives together and with our children that it was unthinkable to me that he should undergo an operation that could destroy everything. But Henry was so dedicated to the completeness of our marriage that he wouldn't be deterred, not by anything.

"As you all know—as so many of you have been telling me during these last twenty-four hours—Henry was a perfectionist, not just in his work, where everyone knows he was the most meticulous craftsman, but in all his relationships with people. He held nothing back, not from his patients, not from his children, and never from me. It was unthinkable to a man so outgoing, so full of life, that still in his thirties he should be so cruelly disabled. I have to admit to you all, as I never did to him, that however much I opposed the surgery because of the risk, I did sometimes wonder if I could carry on as a loving and useful wife feeling so cut off from him. Over the course of our last year together, when he was so withdrawn and brutally depressed, so tormented by the damage that he felt the marriage to be suffering because of this bewildering thing that had happened, I thought 'If there could only be some miracle.' But I'm not someone who makes miracles happen; I'm someone who tends to make do with what's at hand—even, I'm afraid, with her own imperfections. But Henry would no more accept imperfection in himself than in his work. If I didn't have the courage to try for a miracle, Henry did—he had the courage, we now know, for everything life could demand of a man.

"I'm not going to tell you that going on without Henry is going to be easy for us. The children are frightened about the future with no loving father to protect them, and so am I frightened of no Henry by my side. I'd grown used to him, you know. However, I *am* strengthened by remembering that his life did not come to a senseless end. Dear friends, dear family, my dear, dear, dear children, Henry died to recover the fullness and richness of married love. He was a strong and brave and loving man who desperately wanted the bond of passion between a husband and a wife to continue to live and flourish. And, dearest Henry, dearest, sweetest man of them all, it will —the passionate bond between this husband and this wife will live as long as I do."

Just the intimate family, along with Rabbi Geller, followed the hearse to the cemetery. Carol didn't want the children riding out in one of those funeral-procession black limousines and so drove them herself—the kids, the Goffs, and Nathan— in the family station wagon. The interment lasted no time at all. Geller recited the mourner's prayer, and the children laid the chrysanthemums from the garden on the coffin lid. Carol asked if anyone wanted to say anything. No one answered. Carol said to her son, "Leslie?" He took a moment to prepare himself. "I just wanted to say . . ." but afraid of breaking down, he went no further. "Ellen?" Carol said, but Ellen, in tears and clinging to her grandmother's hand, shook her head no. "Ruth?" Carol asked. "He was the best father," said Ruth in a loud, clear voice, "the *best*." "All right," said Carol, and the two burly attendants lowered the coffin. "I'll be a few minutes," Carol told the family, and she remained alone by the graveside while the rest of them walked down to the parking lot.

Carol and the kids to Albany to celebrate her parents' anniversary. Heavy backlog of lab work prevents H. from going along. Maria parks three blocks away and walks from there to the house. Appears as requested in silk jersey dress and black underwear. Has brought her favorite record to play. She waters plants in back hallway that Carol forgot before she left—also plucks out the dead leaves. Then in bed, anal love. After initial difficulties both ecstatic. H.: "This is how I marry you, this is how I make you my wife!" "Yes, and nobody knows, Henry! I am a virgin there no longer and nobody knows! They all think I'm so good and responsible. Nobody knows!" In the bathroom with him afterwards, while arranging her hair with his brush, she sees his pajamas hanging on the back of the door and reaches over to touch them. ("I didn't realize what she'd done until that night. Then I went in and did it myself, stroked my own pajamas—to see what she'd felt." Also combed her hairs out of his brush so Carol wouldn't find them.) Sitting with her in the family room—no lights on—H., famished, ate a quart of ice cream right out of the carton while she played her record for him. Maria: "This is the most beautiful slow movement of the eighteenth century." H. doesn't remember what it was. Haydn? Mozart? "I don't know," he told me. "I don't know anything about that kind of music. But it was beautiful, just watching her listen." Maria: "This makes me think of university, sitting here like this, full of you in every way, and nothing else in the world." "You are my wife now," says H., "my other wife." Played his Mel Tormé record for her—had to dance with her while they had the chance. Glued loin to loin the way he danced in high school with Linda Mandel. Sleeps alone that night in sheets spotted with baby oil, the vibrator, unwashed, on the pillow beside his head. Took it to work with him the next day. Hidden in the office with copy of Fodor's *Switzerland* that he's bought to read, and her photograph. Also took with him the hair of hers that he combed out of the brush. All in the safe. The sheets he stuffed into a black plastic bag and dumped in a trash can at the Millburn Mall five miles from the scene of their marriage. Fodor's *Dostoevsky*.

It was early in the afternoon at the end of September; from the cold touch of the breeze and the light heat of the sun and the dry unsummery whish of the trees you could easily have guessed the month with your eyes closed—perhaps have even guessed the week. Should it matter to a man, however young and virile, to be sentenced to a lifetime of celibacy when, every

year for as long as he lives, there will be autumn days like this
to enjoy? Well, that was a question for an old guy with a beard
and a gift for impossible riddles, and amiable Mark Geller struck
Zuckerman as a rabbi of another kind entirely—consequently
he declined the invitation to drive back to the house in Geller's
car, and waited with the children and their grandparents down
by the cemetery gate where the station wagon was parked.

Ruth, looking quite drained, came over and took her uncle's
hand.

"What is it?" he asked her. "Are you okay?"

"I just keep thinking that when kids at school talk about
their parents, I'll only be able to say 'my mother.'"

"You'll be able to say your parents, plural, whenever you
talk about the past. You had thirteen years of that. Nothing
you did with Henry is ever going to go away. He'll always be
your father."

"Dad would take us alone, two times a year, without Mom,
shopping in New York. It was his treat. Just him and us kids.
We went shopping first and then we went to the Plaza Hotel
and had lunch in the Palm Court—where they play the violin.
Not very well, either. Once in the fall and once in the spring,
every year. Now Mom will have to do all the things our dad
did. She'll have to do both their jobs."

"Don't you think she can?"

"I do, sure I do. Maybe someday she'll remarry. She really
likes to be married. I hope she does do it too." Then, very
gravely, she rushed to add, "But only if she can find somebody
who'll be good to us children as well as herself."

They waited there close to half an hour before Carol, walking
briskly, emerged from the cemetery to drive everyone home.

Food had been laid out by a local caterer under the patio
awning while the mourners were still at the synagogue, and
scattered around the downstairs rooms were folding chairs
rented from the funeral parlor. The girls from Ruth's softball
team, who had taken the afternoon off from school to help out
the Zuckermans, were clearing away the used paper plates and
replenishing the serving platters from the reserves in the
kitchen. And Zuckerman went looking for Wendy.

It was Wendy actually—when she'd become frightened that

Henry was beginning to lose his mind—who had first suggested Nathan as a confidant. Carol, assuming that Nathan
hadn't the slightest authority over his brother any longer, had
urged Henry to talk to a psychotherapist in town. And for an
hour each Saturday morning—until that horrendous Saturday
expedition to New York—he had done it, gone off and spoken
with great candor about his passion for Wendy, pretending to
the therapist, however, that the passion was for Carol, that it
was she whom he was describing as the most playful, inventive
sexual partner any man could ever hope to have. This resulted
in long, thoughtful discussions of a marriage that seemed to
interest the therapist enormously but depressed Henry even
further because it was such a cruel parody of his own. As far as
Carol knew, not until she'd phoned to tell Nathan that Henry
was dead had he even been aware of his brother's illness. Scrupulously following Henry's wishes, Zuckerman played dumb
on the telephone, an absurd act that only compounded the
shock and made clear to him how incapable Henry had been
of reaching *any* decision rationally once the ordeal had begun.
Out at the cemetery, while Henry's children stood at the graveside struggling to speak, Zuckerman had finally understood
that the reason to have stopped him was that he had wanted to
be stopped. The last thing Henry must have imagined was that
Nathan would sit there and accept with a straight face, as justification for such a dangerous operation, the single-minded
urging of that maniac-making lust that he had himself depicted so farcically in *Carnovsky*. Henry had expected Nathan
to *laugh*. Of course! He had driven over from Jersey to confess
to the mocking author the ridiculous absurdity of his dilemma,
and instead he had been indulged by a solicitous brother who
was unable any longer to give either advice or offense. He had
come over to Nathan's apartment to be told how utterly
meaningless was Wendy's mouth beside the ordered enterprise
of a mature man's life, and instead the sexual satirist had sat
there and seriously listened. Impotence, Zuckerman had been
thinking, has cut him off from the simplest form of distance
from his predictable life. As long as he was potent he could
challenge and threaten, if only in sport, the solidity of the domestic relationship; as long as he was potent there was some
give in his life between what was routine and what is taboo.

But without the potency he feels condemned to an ironclad life wherein all issues are settled.

Nothing could have made this clearer than how Henry had described to him becoming Wendy's lover. Apparently from the instant she'd come into the office for the interview and he'd closed the door behind her, virtually every word they exchanged had goaded him on. "Hi," he'd said, shaking her hand, "I heard such marvelous things about you from Dr. Wexler. And now that I look at you, I think you're almost too good. You're going to be so distracting, you're so pretty."

"Uh-oh," she said, laughing. "Maybe I should go then."

What had delighted Henry was not only the speed with which he'd put her at her ease but having put himself at ease as well. It wasn't always like that. Despite his well-known rapport with his patients, he could still be ridiculously formal with people he didn't know, men no less than women, and sometimes, say, when interviewing someone for a job in his own office, seem to himself as though *he* were the person being interviewed. But something vulnerable in this young woman's appearance—something particularly tempting about her tiny breasts—had emboldened him, though precisely at a moment when being emboldened might not be such a great idea. Both at home and in the office everything was going so well that an extraneous adventure with a woman was the *last* thing he needed. And yet, because everything *was* going well, he could not rein in that robust, manly confidence that he could tell was knocking her for a loop already. It was just one of those days when he felt like a movie star, acting out some grandiose whatever-it-was. Why suppress it? There were enough days when he felt like a twerp.

"Sit down," he said. "Tell me about yourself and what you want to do."

"What I want to do?" Someone must have advised her to repeat the doctor's question if she needed time to think up the right answer or to remember the one she'd prepared. "I want to do a lot of things. My first exposure to a dental practice was with Dr. Wexler. And he's wonderful—a true gentleman."

"He's a nice guy," Henry said, thinking, altogether involuntarily, out of this damn excess of confidence and strength, that before it was over he'd show her what wonderful was.

"I learned a lot in his office of what's going on in dentistry."

He encouraged her gently. "Tell me what you know."

"What do I know? I know that a dentist has to make a choice of what kind of practice he wants. It's a business, you have to choose a market, and yet you're dealing with something that's very intimate. People's mouths, how they feel about them, how they feel about their smiles."

Mouths *were* his business, of course—hers too—and yet talking about them like this—at the end of the day, with the door closed, and the slight, young blonde petitioning for a job —was turning out to be awfully stimulating. He remembered the sound of Maria's voice telling him all about how wonderful his cock was—"I put my hand into your trousers, and it astonishes me, it's so big and round and hard." "Your control," she would say to him, "the way you make it last, there's no one like you, Henry." If Wendy were to get up and come over to the desk and put her hand in his pants, she'd find out what Maria was talking about.

"The mouth," Wendy was saying, "is really the most personal thing that a doctor can deal with."

"You're one of the few people who's ever said that," Henry told her. "Do you realize that?"

When he saw the flattery raise the color in her face, he pushed the conversation in a more ambiguous direction, knowing, however, that no one overhearing them could legitimately have charged him with talking to her about anything other than her qualifications for the job. Not that anyone could possibly overhear them.

"Did you take *your* mouth for granted a year ago?" he asked.

"Compared to what I think of it now, yes. Of course, I always cared for my teeth, cared about my smile—"

"You cared about *yourself*," Henry put in approvingly.

Smiling—and it *was* a good smile, the badge of utterly innocent, childish abandon—she happily picked up the cue. "I care about me, yes, sure, but I didn't realize that there was so much psychology involved in dentistry."

Was she saying that to get him to slow down, was she asking him politely to please back off about *her* mouth? Maybe she wasn't as innocent as she looked—but that was even *more* exciting. "Tell me a bit about that," Henry said.

"Well, what I said before—how you feel about your smile is a reflection of how you feel about yourself and what you present to other people. I think that whole personalities may develop, not only about your teeth, but everything else that goes with it. You're dealing in a dental office with the whole person, even if it just looks like you're dealing with the mouth. How do I satisfy the whole person, including the mouth? And when you talk about cosmetic dentistry, that's *real* psychology. We had some problems in Dr. Wexler's office with people who were having crowns done, and they wanted white-white teeth, which didn't go with their own teeth, with their coloring. You have to get them to understand what natural-looking teeth are. You tell them, 'You're going to have the smile that's perfect for you, but you can't go through and just pick out *the* perfect smile and have it put in your mouth.'"

"And have the mouth," Henry added, helping her out, "that looks like it belongs to you."

"Absolutely."

"I want you to work with me."

"Oh, great."

"I think we can make it," Henry said, but before *that* took on too much meaning, he moved quickly to present to his new assistant his own ideas, as though by being dead serious about dentistry he could somehow stop himself before he got grossly suggestive. He was wrong. "Most people, as you must know by now, don't even think that their mouth is part of the body. Or teeth are part of the body. Not consciously they don't. The mouth is a hollow, the mouth is nothing. Most people, unlike you, will never tell you what their mouth means. If they're frightened of dental work it's sometimes because of some frightening experience early on, but primarily it's because of what the mouth means. Anyone touching it is either an invader or a helper. To get them from thinking that someone working on them is invading them, to the idea that you are helping them on to something good, is almost like having a sexual experience. For most people, the mouth is secret, it's their hiding place. Just *like* the genitals. You have to remember that embryologically the mouth is related to the genitals."

"I studied that."

"Did you? Good. Then you realize that people want you to be very tender with their mouths. Gentleness is the most important consideration. With all types. And surprisingly enough, men are more vulnerable, particularly if they've lost teeth. Because losing teeth for a man is a strong experience. A tooth for a man is a mini-penis."

"I hadn't realized that," she said, but didn't seem affronted in any way.

"Well, what do *you* think of the sexual prowess of a toothless man? What do you think he thinks? I had a guy here who was very prominent. He had lost all his teeth and he had a young girlfriend. He didn't want her to know he had dentures, because that would mean he was an old man, and she was a young girl. About your age. Twenty-one?"

"Twenty-two."

"She was twenty-one. So I did implants for him, instead of dentures, and he was happy, and she was happy."

"Dr. Wexler always says that the most satisfaction comes from the greatest challenge, which is usually a disaster case."

Had Wexler fucked her? Henry had never as yet gone beyond the usual flirtation with any assistant of any age—it wasn't only unprofessional but hopelessly distracting in a busy practice, and could well lead to the *dentist's* becoming the disaster case. He realized then that he ought never to have hired her; he had been entirely too impulsive, and was now making things even worse by all this talk about mini-penises that was giving him an enormous hard-on. Yet with everything that was combining these days to make him feel so bold, he couldn't stop. What's the worst that could happen to him? Feeling so bold, he had no idea. "The mouth, you mustn't forget, is the primary organ of experience . . ." On he went; looking unblinkingly and boldly at hers.

Nonetheless, a full six weeks passed before he overcame his doubts, not only about crossing the line further than he had at the interview but about keeping her on in the office at all, despite the excellent job she was doing. Everything he'd been saying about her to Carol happened to be true, even if to him it sounded like the most transparent rationalization for why she was there. "She's bright and alert, she's cute and people like her, she can relate to them, and she helps me enormously—because of her, when I walk in, I can get right to it. This girl," he told Carol, and more often than he needed to during those early weeks, "is saving me two, three hours a day."

Then one evening after work, as Wendy was cleaning his tray and he was routinely washing up, he turned to her and, because there simply seemed no way around it any longer, he began to laugh. "Look," he said, "let's pretend. You're the assistant and I'm the dentist." "But I *am* the assistant," Wendy said. "I know," he replied, "and I'm the dentist—but pretend anyway." "And so," Henry had told Nathan, "that's what we did." "You played Dentist," Zuckerman said. "I guess so," Henry said, "—she pretended she was called 'Wendy,' and I pretended I was called 'Dr. Zuckerman,' and we pretended we were in my dental office. And then we pretended to fuck—and we fucked." "Sounds interesting," Zuckerman said. "It was, it was wild, it made us crazy—it was the strangest thing I'd ever done. We did it for weeks, pretended like that, and she kept saying, 'Why is it so exciting when all we're pretending to be is what we are?' God, was it great! Was she hot!"

Well, that larky, hot stuff was over now, no more mischievously turning what-was into what-wasn't or what-might-be into what-was—there was only the deadly earnest this-is-it of what-is. Nothing a successful, busy, energetic man likes more than a little Wendy on the side, and nothing a Wendy could more enjoy than calling her lover "Doctor Z."—she's young, she's game, she's in his office, he's the boss, she sees him in his white coat being adored by everyone, sees his wife chauffeuring the children and turning gray while she doesn't think twice about her twenty-inch waist . . . heavenly all around. Yes, his sessions with Wendy had been Henry's art; his dental office, after hours, his atelier; and his impotence, thought Zuckerman, like an artist's artistic life drying up for good. He'd been reassigned the art of the responsible—unfortunately by then precisely the hackwork from which he needed longer and longer vacations in order to survive. He'd been thrown back on his talent for the prosaic, precisely what he'd been boxed in by all his life. Zuckerman had felt for him terribly, and so, stupidly, stupidly, did nothing to stop him.

*

Down in the living room, he worked his way through the clan, accepting their sympathies, listening to their memories, answering questions about where he was living and what he was writing, until he had made his way to Cousin Essie, his favorite relative and once upon a time the family powerhouse. She was sitting in a club chair by the fireplace with a cane across her knees. Six years back, when he'd seen her last at his father's funeral in Florida, there'd been a new husband—an elderly bridge player named Metz—now dead, easily thirty pounds less of Essie, and no cane. She was always, as Zuckerman remembered her, large and old, and now she was even larger and older, though seemingly still indestructible.

"So, you lost your brother," she said, while he was leaning over to kiss her. "I once took you kids to Olympic Park. Took you on all the rides with my boys. At six Henry was the image of Wendell Willkie with that shock of black hair. That little boy adored you then."

They must return to Basel—Jurgen transferred home. Maria can't stop crying. "I'm going back to be a good wife and a good mother!" In six weeks Switzerland, where she'll have *only* the money to make it real.

"Did he?"

"Christ, he wouldn't let go of your hand."

"Well, he has now. We're all here at his house and Henry's up at the cemetery."

"Don't tell me about the dead," said Essie. "I look in the mirror in the morning and I see the whole family looking back at me. I see my mother's face, I see my sister, I see my brother, I see the dead from all the way back, all of them right in my own ugly kisser. Look, let's you and me talk," and after he'd helped her up from the chair, she led him out of the living room, struggling forward like some large vehicle plunging ahead on a broken axle.

"What is it?" he asked when they were in the front hallway.

"If your brother died to sleep with his wife, then he's already up with the angels, Nathan."

"But he was always the best boy, Esther. Son to end all sons, father to end all fathers—well, from the sound of it, the husband to end all husbands too."

"From the sound of it the shmuck to end all shmucks."

"But the kids, the folks—Dad would have a fit. How do I practice dentistry in Basel?" "Why would you have to live in Basel?" "Because she loves it, that's why—she says the only thing that made South Orange endurable was me. Switzerland is her *home*." "There are worse places than Switzerland." "That's easy for you to say." So I say no more, just remember her astride him in the black silk camisole, far far away, like the bedposts on his schoolboy bed.

"It's not so shmucky when you're impotent at thirty-nine," said Zuckerman, "and have reason to think it might never end."

"Being up at the cemetery isn't going to end either."

"He expected to live, Essie. Otherwise he wouldn't have done it."

"And all for the little wife."

"That's the story."

"I like better the ones you write."

Maria tells him that the person who stays behind suffers even more than the one who goes away. Because of all the familiar places.

Coming down the staircase just behind them were two elderly men he had not seen for a very long while: Herbert Grossman, the Zuckermans' only European refugee, and Shimmy Kirsch, designated years ago by Nathan's father as the brother-in-law Neanderthal, and arguably the family's stupidest relative. But as he was the wealthiest in the family as well, one had to wonder if Shimmy's stupidity wasn't something of an asset; watching him one wondered if in fact the passion to live and the strength to prevail might not be, at their core, *quite stupid*. Though the mountainous build had been eroded by age, and his deeply furrowed face bore all the insignia of his lifelong exertion, he was still more or less the person Nathan remembered from childhood—a huge unassailable nothing in the wholesale produce line, one of those rapacious sons of the old greenhorn families who will not shrink from anything even while, fortunately for society, enslaved by every last primitive taboo. For Zuckerman's father, the responsible chiropodist, life had been a dogged climb up from the abyss of his immigrant father's poverty, and not merely so as to improve his personal lot but eventually to rescue everyone as the family messiah. Shimmy had never seen any need to so assiduously cleanse his behind. Not that he wished necessarily to debase himself. All his steadfastness had gone into being what he'd been born and brought up to be—Shimmy Kirsch. No questions, no excuses, none of this who-am-I, what-am-I, where-am-I crap, not a grain of self-mistrust or the slightest impulse toward spiritual distinction; rather, like so many of his generation out of Newark's old Jewish slums, a man who breathed the spirit of opposition while remaining completely in accord with the ways and means of the earth.

Back when Nathan had first fallen in love with the alphabet and was spelling his way to stardom at school, these Shimmys had already begun to make him uncertain as to whether the real oddball wasn't going to be him, particularly when he heard of the notoriously unbrainy ways in which they successfully beat back their competitors. Unlike the admirable father who had taken the night-school path to professional dignity, these drearily banal and conventional Shimmys displayed all the ruthlessness of the renegade, their teeth ripping a chunk out of life's raw rump, then dragging that around with them everywhere, all else paling in significance beside the bleeding flesh between their jaws. They had absolutely no wisdom; wholly self-saturated, entirely self-oblivious, they had nothing to go on but the most elemental manhood, yet on that alone they came pretty damn far. They too had tragic experiences and suffered losses they were by no means too brutish to feel: being bludgeoned almost to death was as much their specialty as bludgeoning. The point was that pain and suffering did not deter them for half an hour from their intention of living. Their lack of all nuance or doubt, of an ordinary mortal's sense of futility or despair, made it tempting sometimes to consider them inhuman, and yet they were men about whom it was impossible to say that they were anything *other* than human: they were what human really is. While his own father aspired relentlessly to embody the best in mankind, these Shimmys were simply the backbone of the human race.

Shimmy and Grossman were discussing Israel's foreign policy. "Bomb 'em," Shimmy said flatly, "bomb the Arab bastards till they cry uncle. They want to pull our beards again? We'll die instead!"

Essie, cunning, shrewd, self-aware, another sort of survivor entirely, said to him, "You know why I give to Israel?"

Shimmy was indignant. "*You*? You never parted with a dime in your life."

"You know why?" she asked, turning to Grossman, a far better straight man.

"Why?" Grossman said.

"Because in Israel you hear the best anti-Semitic jokes. You hear even better anti-Semitic jokes in Tel Aviv than on Collins Avenue."

After dinner H. returns to the office—lab work, he tells Carol—and sits there all evening reading Fodor's *Switzerland*, trying to make up his mind. "Basel is a city with an atmosphere entirely of its own, in which elements of tradition and medievalism are unexpectedly mingled with the modern . . . behind and around its splendid old buildings and fine modern ones, a maze of quaint old lanes and busy streets . . . the old merging imperceptibly with the new . . ." He thinks: "What a terrific victory if I could pull it off!"

"I was there three years ago with Metz," Essie was saying. "We're driving from the airport to the hotel. The taxi driver, an Israeli, turns to us, and in English he says, 'Why do Jews have big noses?' 'Why?' I ask him. 'Because the air is free,' he says. On the spot I wrote a check for a thousand bucks to the UJA."

"Come on," Shimmy told her, "who ever pried a *nickel* out of you?"

"I asked her if she would leave Jurgen. She asked me to tell her first if I would leave Carol."

Herbert Grossman, whose obstinately lachrymose view of life was the only unyielding thing about him, had meanwhile begun to tell Zuckerman the latest bad news. Grossman's melancholia had at one time driven Zuckerman's father almost as crazy as Shimmy's stupidity; he was probably the only person about whom Dr. Zuckerman had finally to admit, "The poor man can't help it." Alcoholics could help it, adulterers could help it, insomniacs, murderers, even stammerers, could help it—according to Dr. Zuckerman, anyone could change *anything* in himself through the diligent exercise of his will;

but because Grossman had had to flee from Hitler, he seemed
to *have* no will. Not that Sunday after Sunday Dr. Zuckerman
hadn't tried to get the damn thing going. Optimistically he
would rise from the table after their hearty breakfast and announce to the family, "Time to phone Herbert!" but ten minutes later he'd be back in the kitchen, utterly defeated,
muttering to himself, "The poor man can't help it." Hitler had
done it—there was no other explanation. Dr. Zuckerman could
not otherwise understand someone who simply was not there.

To Nathan, Herbert Grossman seemed now, as he did then,
a delicate, vulnerable refugee, a Jew, to recast Isaac Babel's formula and bring it up to date, with a pacemaker in his heart and
spectacles on his nose. "Everyone worries about Israel," Grossman was saying to him, "but you know what I worry about?
Right here. America. Something terrible is happening right
here. I feel it like in Poland in 1935. No, not anti-Semitism. That
will come anyway. No, it's the crime, the lawlessness, people
afraid. The money—everything's for sale and that's all that
counts. The young people are full of despair. The drugs are
only despair. Nobody wants to feel that good if they aren't in
deep despair."

H. phones and for half an hour speaks of nothing but Carol's virtues.
Carol is someone whose qualities you can only really know if you've
lived with the woman as long as he has. "She's interesting, dynamic,
curious, perceptive . . ." A long and very impressive list. A *startling*
list.

"I feel it on the streets," Grossman said. "You can't even walk
to the store. You go out to the supermarket in broad daylight
and blacks come up and rob you blind."

Maria has left. Terrible tearful exchange of farewell presents. After
consultation with cultivated older brother, H. gave her a boxed set of
Haydn's *London Symphonies*. Maria gave him her black silk camisole.

When Herbert Grossman excused himself to go get something to eat, Essie confided to Zuckerman, "His last wife had
diabetes. She made his life a misery. They took her legs off, she
went blind, and she still didn't stop bossing him around."

So the surviving Zuckerman brother passed the long afternoon—waiting to see if Wendy would show up while he

listened to the lore of the tribal elders and remembered the journal entries that had not seemed, when he'd written them, to be the doom-laden notes for *Tristan and Isolde*.

Maria phoned H. at the office the day before Christmas. His heart began pounding the moment he was told he had an overseas call and didn't stop until long after she'd said goodbye. She wanted to wish him a Merry American Christmas. She told him that it had been very hard for these six months but that Christmas was helping. There was the children's excitement, and Jurgen's family was all there, and they would be sixteen for dinner the next day. She found that even the snow helped some. Was it snowing yet in New Jersey? Did he mind her phoning him like this at the office? Were his children okay? His wife? Was he? Did Christmas make it any easier for him, or wasn't it that hard anymore? "What did you say to that?" I asked. H.: "I was afraid to say anything. I was afraid somebody in the office would hear. I fucked up, I suppose. I said we didn't observe Christmas."

And could *that* be why he'd let her go, because Maria observed Christmas and we do not? One would have imagined that among secular, college-educated atheists of Henry's generation running away with shiksas had gone out as a felony years ago and was perceived, if at all, as a fictitious issue in a love affair. But then Henry's problem may have been that having passed so long for a paragon, he had got himself ridiculously entangled in this brilliant disguise at just the moment he was destined to burst forth as less admirable and more desperate than anyone ever imagined. How absurd, how awful, if the woman who'd awakened in him the desire to live differently, who meant to him a break with the past, a revolution against an old way of life that had reached an emotional standstill— against the belief that life is a series of duties to be perfectly performed—if that woman was to be nothing more or less than the humiliating memory of his first (and last) great fling *because she observed Christmas and we do not*. If Henry had been right about the origins of his disease, if it did indeed result from the stress of that onerous defeat and those arduous feelings of self-contempt that dogged him long after her return to Basel, then, curiously enough, it was being a Jew that had killed him.

If/then. As the afternoon wore on, he began to feel himself straining more and more after an idea that would release those old notes from their raw factuality and transform them into a

puzzle for his imagination to solve. While peeing in the upstairs bathroom, he thought, "Suppose on that afternoon she'd
secretly come to the house, after they married each other by
performing anal love, he watched her, right in this room, pinning up her hair before getting in with him to take a shower.
Seeing him adoring her—seeing his eyes marvel at this strange
European woman who embodies simultaneously both innocent domesticity and lurid eroticism—she says, confidently
smiling, 'I really look extremely Aryan with my hair up and my
jaw exposed.' 'What's wrong with that?' he asks. 'Well, there's
a quality in Aryans that isn't very attractive—as history has
shown.' 'Look,' he tells her, 'let's not hold the century against
you . . .'"

No, that's not them, thought Zuckerman, and came down
the stairs into the living room, where Wendy was still nowhere
to be seen. But then it needn't be "them"—could be me, he
thought. Us. What if instead of the brother whose obverse existence mine inferred—and who himself untwinnishly inferred
me—*I* had been the Zuckerman boy in that agony? What is
the real wisdom of that predicament? Could it be simple for
anyone? If that is indeed how those drugs incapacitate most of
the men who must take them to live, then there's a bizarre epi-
demic of impotence in this country whose personal implications nobody's scrutinizing, not in the press or even on
Donahue, let alone in fiction . . .

In the living room someone was saying to him, "You know, I
tried to interest your brother in cryonics—not that that's any
consolation now."

"Did you?"

"I didn't even know he was sick. I'm Barry Shuskin. I'm
trying to get a cryonics facility going here in New Jersey and
when I came to Henry he laughed. A guy with a bad heart, he
can't fuck anymore, and he wouldn't even read the literature I
gave him. It was too bizarre for a rationalist like him. In his
position I wouldn't have been so sure. Thirty-nine and it's all
over—*that's* bizarre."

Shuskin was a youthful fifty—very tall, bald, with a dark chin-
beard and a staccato delivery, a vigorous man with plenty to
say, whom Zuckerman at first took to be a lawyer, a litigator,

maybe some sort of hard-driving executive. He turned out to
be an associate of Henry's, a dentist in the same office complex
whose specialty was implanting teeth, anchoring custom-built
teeth in the jawbone rather than fitting bridges or dentures.
When implant work was too involved or too time-consuming
for Henry to handle in his general family practice, he referred
it to Shuskin, who also specialized in reconstructing the mouths
of accident and cancer victims. "You know about cryonics?"
Shuskin asked, after identifying himself as Henry's colleague.
"You should. You ought to be on the mailing list. Newsletters,
magazines, books—everything documented. They have figured
out how to freeze now without damage to the cells. Suspended
animation. You don't die, you're put on hold, hopefully for a
couple of hundred years. Until science has solved the problem
of thawing out. It's possible to be frozen, suspended, and then
revitalized, all of the broken parts repaired or replaced, and
you're as good if not better than new. You know you're going
to die, you've got cancer, it's about to strike the vital organs.
Well, you've got an option. You contact the cryonics people,
you say I want to be awakened in the twenty-second century,
give me an overdose of morphine, at the same time drain me,
profuse me, and suspend me. You're not dead. You just go
from life to being shut down. No intermediary stage. The cry-
onic solution replaces the blood and prevents ice crystalliza-
tion damaging the cells. They encase the body in a plastic bag,
store the bag in a stainless-steel container, and fill it with liquid
nitrogen. Minus 273 degrees. Fifty thousand bucks for the
freezing, and then you set up a trust fund to pay the mainte-
nance. That's peanuts, a thousand, fifteen hundred a year. The
problem is that there is a facility only in California and Florida
—and speed is everything. This is why I want to seriously ex-
plore setting up a nonprofit organization right here in Jersey, a
cryonics facility for those men like myself who don't want to
die. Nobody would make any dough out of it, except a few
salaried people, who are on the up and up, to run the facility. A
lot of guys would say, 'Shit, Barry, let's do it—we'll make a
buck out of this and fuck everybody who thinks that there's
something to it.' But I don't want to muddy it up with that
kind of shit. The idea is to get a membership group together of
men who want to be preserved for the future, guys who are

committed to the principle and not to making a buck. Maybe fifty. You probably could get five thousand. There are a lot of high-powered guys who are enjoying life and have a lot of power and a lot of know-how, and they feel that it's a crock of shit to get burned or buried—why not frozen?"

Just then a woman took hold of Zuckerman's hand, a tiny, elderly woman with exceptionally pretty blue eyes, a large bust, and a full, round, merry-looking face. "I'm Carol's aunt from Albany. Bill Goff's sister. I want to extend my sympathies."

Indicating that he understood the sentimental obligations of the brother of the deceased, quietly, in an aside, Shuskin muttered to Zuckerman, "I want your home address—before you go."

"Later," said Zuckerman, and Shuskin, who was enjoying life, had a lot of power and a lot of know-how and no intention of being buried or burned—who would lie there like a lamb chop till the twenty-second century and then wake up, defrosted, to a billion more years of being himself—left Zuckerman to commiserate with Carol's aunt, who was still tightly holding his hand. Forever Shuskin. *Is* that the future, once the freezer has replaced the grave?

"This is a loss," she said to Zuckerman, "that no one will ever understand."

"It is."

"Some people are amazed by what she said, you know."

"By Carol? Are they?"

"Well, to get up at your husband's funeral and talk like that? I'm of the generation that didn't even say such things privately. Many people wouldn't have felt the same need that she did to be open and honest about something so personal. But Carol has always been an astonishing girl and she didn't disappoint me today. The truth to her has always been the truth and nothing she has to hide."

"I thought what she said was just fine."

"Of course. You're an educated man. You know about life. Do me a favor," she whispered. "When you have a minute, tell her father."

"Why?"

"Because if he keeps on the way he's going, he'll give himself another heart attack."

He waited one more hour, till almost five, not so as to sedate Mr. Goff, whose confusion was Carol's business, but on the remote chance that Wendy might yet appear. A decent girl, he thought—she doesn't want to force herself on the wife and the children, even if they're innocent of her great role in all this. He had thought at first that she would want terribly to talk to the only other person who knew why this had happened and what she must be going through, but maybe it was precisely because Henry had told Nathan everything that she was staying away—because she didn't know whether to expect to be castigated by him, or cross-examined for a fictional exposé, or perhaps even wickedly seduced by the twisted brother, à la Richard the Third. As the minutes passed, he realized that waiting around for Wendy went further than wanting to find out how she'd behave with Carol, or seeing for himself at close range if there was anything there that the photograph hadn't disclosed; it was more like hanging around to meet a movie star or to catch a glimpse of the Pope.

Shuskin caught him just as he was heading for his coat in what was now the widow's bedroom. They walked up the stairs together, Zuckerman thinking, Strange Henry never mentioned his visionary colleague, the implantologist—that in his wild state he hadn't even been tempted. But probably he hadn't even heard him. Henry's delusions didn't run to living thawed out in the second millennium. Even a life in Basel with Maria was too much like science fiction for him. By comparison he had asked for so very little—willing to be wholly content, for the rest of his natural days, with the modest miracle of Carol, Wendy, and the kids. Either that, or to be an eleven-year-old boy in the cottage at the Jersey Shore with the faucet at the side to wash the sand off your feet. If Shuskin had told him that science was working on making it the summer of 1948 again, he might have had himself a customer.

"There's a group in L.A.," Shuskin was saying, "I'm going to send you their newsletter. Some very bright guys. Philosophers. Scientists. Engineers. A lot of writers too. What they're doing on the West Coast, because of their feeling that the body is not what's important, that your identity is all up here, so they separate the head from the body. They know they'll be able to reconnect heads to bodies, reconnect the arteries, the brain stem, and everything else all to a new body. They'll have solved the immunological problems, or they may be able to clone new bodies. Anything is possible. So they're just freezing the heads. It's cheaper than freezing and storing the whole body. Faster. Cuts storage costs. They find that appealing in intellectual circles. Maybe you will too, if you ever find yourself in Henry's shoes. I don't go for it myself. I want my whole body frozen. Why? Because I pesonally believe your experience is very much connected to your memories that every cell in your body has. You don't separate the mind from the body. The body and the mind are one. The body *is* the mind."

No disputing that, not here today, thought Zuckerman, and after locating his coat on the king-sized bed that Henry had exchanged for a coffin, he wrote out his address. "If I wind up in Henry's shoes," he said, handing it to Shuskin.

"I said 'if'? Pardon my delicacy. I meant when."

Though Henry had been a slightly heavier, more muscular man than his older brother, they were still more or less the same size and build, and that perhaps explained why Carol held on to him so very long when he came downstairs to leave. It was, for both of them, such a strongly emotional moment that Zuckerman wondered if he wasn't about to hear her say, "I know about her, Nathan. I've known all along. But he would have gone crazy if I told him. Years ago I found out about a patient. I couldn't believe my ears—the kids were small, I was younger, and it mattered terribly to me then. When I told him that I knew, he went berserk. He had a hysterical fit. He wept for days, every time he came home from the office begging me to forgive him, begging me from down on his knees not to make him move out of the house—calling himself the most awful names and begging me not to throw him out. I never wanted to see him like that again. I've known about them all, every one, but I let him be, let him have what he wanted so long as at home he was a good father to the kids and a decent husband to me."

But in Zuckerman's arms, pressing herself up against his chest, all she said, in a breaking voice, was "It helped me enormously, your being here."

Consequently he had no reason to reply, "So that's why you

made up that story," but said nothing more than what was
called for. "It helped *me*, being with you all."

Carol did not then respond, "Of course that's why I said
what I did. Those bitches all weeping their hearts out—sitting
there weeping for *their man*. The hell with that!" Instead she
said to him, "It meant a lot to the children to see you. They
needed you today. You were lovely to Ruth."

Nathan did not ask, "And you let him go ahead with the
surgery, knowing who it was for?" He said, "Ruth's a terrific
girl."

Carol replied, "She's going to be all right—we all are," and
bravely kissed him goodbye, instead of saying, "If I had stopped
him, he would never have forgiven me, it would have been a
nightmare for the rest of our lives"; instead of, "If he wanted
to risk his life for that stupid, slavish, skinny little slut, that was
his business, not mine"; instead of, "It served him right, dying
like that after what he put me through. Poetic justice. May he
rot in hell for his nightly blow job!"

Either what she'd told everyone from the altar was what she
truly believed, either she was a good-hearted, courageous,
blind, loyal mate whom Henry had fiendishly deceived to the
last, or she was a more interesting woman than he'd ever
thought, a subtle and persuasive writer of domestic fiction, who
had cunningly reimagined a decent, ordinary, adulterous hu-
manist as a heroic martyr to the connubial bed.

He didn't really know what to think until at home that
evening, before sitting down at his desk to reread those three
thousand words written in his notebook the night before—
and to record his observations of the funeral—he again got
out the journal from ten years back and turned the pages until
he found his very last entry about Henry's great thwarted passion. It was pages on in the notebook, buried amid notes about
something else entirely; that's why the evening before it had
eluded his search.

The entry was dated several months after Maria's Christmas
call from Basel, when Henry was beginning to think that if
there was any satisfaction to be derived from his crushing sense
of loss, it was that at least he had never been discovered—back
when the inchoate, debilitating depression had at last begun to
lift and to be replaced by the humbling realization of what the

affair with Maria had so painfully exposed: the fact that he was somehow not quite coarse enough to bow to his desires, and yet not quite fine enough to transcend them.

Carol picks him up at Newark Airport, after Cleveland orthodontic conference. He gets in behind the wheel at the airport parking lot. Night and a late-winter gale on the way. Carol, all at once in tears, undoes her alpaca-lined storm coat and flips on the car light. Naked beneath but for black bra, panties, stockings, garter belt. For a flickering moment he is even aroused, but then he spots the price tag stapled to the garter belt, and sees in that all the desperateness of this startling display. What he sees is not some wealth of passion in Carol, undiscovered by him till then, that he might suddenly begin to plumb, but the pathos of these purchases obviously made earlier that day by the predictable, sexually unadventurous wife to whom he would be married for the rest of his life. Her desperation left him limp—then angry: never had he ached more for Maria! How could he have let that woman go! "Fuck me!" Carol cries, and not in the incomprehensible Swiss-German that used to make him so excited, but in plain, understandable English. "Fuck me before I die! You haven't fucked me like a woman in years!"

2. Judea

WHEN I located him at his newspaper, Shuki couldn't at first understand who I said was calling—when he did, he pretended to be stupefied. "What's a nice Jewish boy like you doing in a place like this?"

"I come regularly every twenty years to be sure everything's okay."

"Well, things are great," Shuki replied. "We're going down the drain six different ways. It's too awful even to joke about."

We'd met eighteen years earlier, in 1960, during my only previous visit to Israel. Because *Higher Education*, my first book, had been deemed "controversial"—garnering both a Jewish prize and the ire of a lot of rabbis—I'd been invited to Tel Aviv to participate in a public dialogue: Jewish-American and Israeli writers on the subject "The Jew in Literature."

Though only a few years older than I, Shuki back in 1960 had already completed a ten-year stint as an army colonel and just been appointed Ben-Gurion's press attaché. One day he'd taken me up to the Prime Minister's office to shake the hand of "the Old Man," an event that, however special, turned out to be nowhere near so instructive as our lunch beforehand with Shuki's father in the Knesset dining room. "You might learn something meeting an ordinary Israeli working man," Shuki said; "and as for him, he loves coming down here to eat with the big shots." Of course why he especially liked coming to eat at the Knesset was because his son was now working there for his political idol.

Mr. Elchanan was in his mid-sixties then and still employed as a welder in Haifa. He'd emigrated to mandate Palestine from Odessa in 1920, when the Soviet revolution was proving to be more hostile to Jews than its Russian-Jewish supporters had foreseen. "I came," he told me, in the good if heavily accented English that he'd learned as a Palestinian Jew under the British, "and I was already an old man for the Zionist movement—I was twenty-five." He was not strong, but his hands were strong —his hands were the center of him, the truly exceptional thing

46

in his whole appearance. He had kind, very mild, soft brown eyes, but otherwise plain, ungraspable features set in a perfectly round and gentle face. He was not tall like Shuki but short, his chin was not protruding heroically but slightly receding, and he was a little stooped from a lifetime of physical work forming joints and connections. His hair was grayish. More than likely you wouldn't even see him if he sat down across from you on a bus. How intelligent was he, this unprepossessing welder? Intelligent enough, I thought, to raise a very good family, intelligent enough to bring up Shuki and his younger brother, an architect in Tel Aviv, and of course intelligent enough to understand in 1920 that he had better leave Russia if he was intent upon remaining a socialist and a Jew. In conversation, he displayed his share of forceful wit, and even a playful, poetic imagination of sorts when it came time to put me through my paces. I myself couldn't see him as a worker who was nothing more than "ordinary," but then I wasn't his offspring. In fact, it wasn't at all difficult to think of him as an Israeli counterpart to my own father, who was then still practicing chiropody in New Jersey. Despite the difference in professional status, they would have got on well, I thought. That may even be why Shuki and I got on so well.

We were just beginning our soup when Mr. Elchanan said to me, "So you're going to stay."

"Am I? Who said so?"

"Well, you're not going back there, are you?"

Shuki kept spooning the soup—this was obviously a question he wasn't startled to hear.

I figured at first that Mr. Elchanan was joking with me. "To America?" I said, smiling. "Going next week."

"Don't be ridiculous. You'll stay." Here he put down his spoon and came over to my side of the table. With one of those extraordinary hands of his he lifted me by the arm and steered me over to a window of the dining room that looked out across modern Jerusalem to the old walled city. "See that tree?" he said. "That's a Jewish tree. See that bird? That's a Jewish bird. See, up there? A Jewish cloud. There is no country for a Jew but here." Then he set me back down where I could resume eating.

Shuki said to his father, once he was over his plate again, "I think that Nathan's experience makes him see things differently."

"What experience?" The voice was brusque as it hadn't been with me. "He needs us," Mr. Elchanan pointed out to his son, "—and even more than we need him."

"Is that so," Shuki said softly, and continued eating.

However earnest I may have been at twenty-seven, however dutifully, obstinately sincere, I really didn't want to tell my friend's well-meaning, stoop-shouldered old father just how wrong he was, and in response to their exchange I merely shrugged.

"He lives in a museum!" Mr. Elchanan said angrily. Shuki half-nodded—this too he seemed to have heard before—and so Mr. Elchanan turned to say it again directly to me. "You are. We are living in a Jewish theater and you are living in a Jewish museum!"

"Tell him, Nathan," said Shuki, "about your museum. Don't worry, he's been debating with me since I was five—he can take it."

So I did as Shuki said and, for the remainder of the lunch, I told him—as was my style in my twenties (with fathers particularly), told him overpassionately and at enormous length. I wasn't improvising, either: these were conclusions I'd been reaching on my own in the last few days, the result of traveling for three weeks through a Jewish homeland that couldn't have seemed to me more remote.

To be the Jew that I was, I told Shuki's father, which was neither more nor less than the Jew I wished to be, I didn't need to live in a Jewish nation any more than he, from what I understood, felt obliged to pray in a synagogue three times a day. My landscape wasn't the Negev wilderness, or the Galilean hills, or the coastal plain of ancient Philistia; it was industrial, immigrant America—Newark where I'd been raised, Chicago where I'd been educated, and New York where I was living in a basement apartment on a Lower East Side street among poor Ukrainians and Puerto Ricans. My sacred text wasn't the Bible but novels translated from Russian, German, and French into the language in which I was beginning to write and publish my own fiction—not the semantic range of classical Hebrew but the jumpy beat of American English was what excited me. I was not a Jewish survivor of a Nazi death camp in search of a safe and welcoming refuge, or a Jewish socialist for whom the primary source of injustice was the evil of capital, or a nationalist for whom cohesiveness was a Jewish political necessity, nor was I a believing Jew, a scholarly Jew, or a Jewish xenophobe who couldn't bear the proximity of goyim. I was the American-born grandson of simple Galician tradesmen who, at the end of the last century, had on their own reached the same prophetic conclusion as Theodor Herzl—that there was no future for them in Christian Europe, that they couldn't go on being themselves there without inciting to violence ominous forces against which they hadn't the slightest means of defense. But instead of struggling to save the Jewish people from destruction by founding a homeland in the remote corner of the Ottoman Empire that had once been biblical Palestine, they simply set out to save their own Jewish skins. Insomuch as Zionism meant taking upon oneself, rather than leaving to others, responsibility for one's survival as a Jew, this was their brand of Zionism. And it worked. Unlike them, I had not grown up hedged in by an unnerving Catholic peasantry that could be whipped into a Jew-hating fervor by the village priest or the local landowner; even more to the point, my grandparents' claim to legitimate political entitlement had not been staked in the midst of an alien, indigenous population that had no commitment to Jewish biblical rights and no sympathy for what a Jewish God said in a Jewish book about what constitutes Jewish territory in perpetuity. In the long run I might even be far more secure as a Jew in my homeland than Mr. Elchanan, Shuki, and their descendants could ever be in theirs.

I insisted that America simply did not boil down to Jew and Gentile, nor were anti-Semites the American Jew's biggest problem. To say, Let's face it, for the Jews the problem is always the goyim, may have a ring of truth about it for a moment— "How can anyone dismiss that statement out of hand in this century? And if America should prove to be a place of intolerance, shallowness, indecency, and brutality, where all American values are flushed into the gutter, it could have more than just the ring of truth—it could turn out to be so." But, I went on, the fact of it was that I could not think of any historical society that had achieved the level of tolerance institutionalized in America or that had placed pluralism smack at the center of its publicly advertised dream of itself. I could only hope that Yacov Elchanan's solution to the problem of Jewish survival and independence turned out to be no less successful than the unpolitical, unideological "family Zionism" enacted by my immigrant grandparents in coming, at the turn of the century, to America, a country that did not have at its center the idea of exclusion.

"Though I don't admit this back in New York," I said, "I'm a little idealistic about America—maybe the way that Shuki's a little idealistic about Israel."

I wasn't sure if the smile I saw wasn't perhaps a sign of how impressed he was. He ought to be, I thought—he certainly doesn't hear stuff like this from the other welders. I was even, afterwards, a little chagrined that I had said quite so much, fearing that I might have demolished *too* thoroughly the aging Zionist and his simplifications.

But he merely continued smiling away, even as he rose to his feet, came around the table, and once again lifted me by my arm and led me back to where I could look out on his Jewish trees and streets and birds and clouds. "So many words," he finally said to me, and with just a trace of that mockery that was more recognizably Jewish to me than the clouds—"such brilliant explanations. Such deep thoughts, Nathan. I never in my life saw a better argument than you for our never leaving Jerusalem again."

His words were our last words, for before we could even eat dessert Shuki rushed me upstairs for my scheduled minute with another stocky little gentleman in a short-sleeve shirt who, in person, also looked to me deceptively inconsequential, as though the model of a tank that I spotted among the papers and family photos on his desk could have been nothing more than a toy constructed for a grandchild in his little workshop.

Shuki told the Prime Minister that we'd just come up from lunch with his father.

This amused Ben-Gurion. "So you're staying," he said to me. "Good. We'll make room."

A photographer was already there, poised to take a picture of Israel's Founding Father shaking hands with Nathan Zuckerman. I am laughing in the photograph because just as it was to be snapped, Ben-Gurion whispered, "Remember, this isn't yours—it's for your parents, to give them a reason to be proud of you."

He wasn't wrong—my father couldn't have been happier if it had been a picture of me in my Scout uniform helping Moses down from Mount Sinai. This picture wasn't merely beautiful, it was also ammunition, to be used primarily, however, in his struggle to prove to *himself* that what leading rabbis were telling their congregations from the pulpit about my Jewish self-hatred couldn't possibly be true.

Framed, the photograph was exhibited for the remaining years of my parents' lives atop the TV console in the living room, alongside the picture of my brother receiving his dental diploma. These to my father were our greatest achievements. And his.

After a shower and something to eat, I walked out back of my hotel to a bench on the wide promenade overlooking the sea where Shuki and I had arranged to meet. Christmas trees were already stacked on the pavement outside of our London greengrocer's, and a few evenings back, Maria and I had taken her little daughter, Phoebe, to see the Oxford Street lights, but in Tel Aviv it was a blue, bright, windless day, and on the beach below, female flesh was toasting in the sun and a handful of bathers were bobbing about in the waves. I remembered how, driving to the West End with Phoebe, Maria and I had talked about my first English Christmas and all the holiday celebrations to come. "I'm not one of those Jews for whom Christmas is an awful trial," I said, "but I have to tell you that I don't actually participate so much as look on anthropologically from a distance." "That's fine with me," she said; "you do the next-best thing. Which is to write large checks. That's really all the participating that's necessary."

As I sat there with my jacket in my lap and my sleeves rolled up, watching the elderly men and women on the nearby benches reading their papers, and eating ice cream, and some, with their eyes shut, just pleasantly warming their bones, I was

reminded of the journeys I used to make to Florida after my
father's retirement, when he had given up the Newark practice
and was devoting his attention entirely to the daily *Times* and
Walter Cronkite. There couldn't have been any more ardent
Israeli patriots welding away in the Haifa shipyards than were
gathered in those lounge chairs around the condominium
pool after the triumph of the Six-Day War. "Now," said my
father, "they'll think twice before they pull our beards!" Militant, triumphant Israel was to his aging circle of Jewish friends
their avenger for the centuries and centuries of humiliating oppression; the state created by Jews in the aftermath of the
Holocaust had become for them the belated answer *to* the
Holocaust, not only the embodiment of intrepid Jewish
strength but the instrument of justifiable wrath and swift
reprisal. Had it been Dr. Victor Zuckerman rather than General Moshe Dayan who'd been the Israeli Minister of Defense
in May 1967—had it been any one of my father's Miami Beach
cohorts rather than Moshe Dayan—tanks emblazoned with
the white Mogen David would have rolled right on through
the cease-fire lines to Cairo, Amman, and Damascus, where the
Arabs would then have proceeded to surrender like the Germans
in 1945, unconditionally, as though they *were* the Germans of
1945.

Three years after the '67 victory, my father died and so he's
missed Menachem Begin. That's too bad, for not even Ben-
Gurion's fortitude, Golda's pride, and Dayan's valor taken all
together could have provided him with that profound sense of
personal vindication that so many of his generation have found
in an Israeli Prime Minister who could pass, from his appearance, for the owner of a downtown clothing store. Even
Begin's English is right, sounding more like the speech of their
own impoverished immigrant parents than what emanates, say,
from Abba Eban, cunning Jewish central casting's spokesman
to the Gentile world. After all, who better than the Jew caricatured by generation upon generation of pitiless enemies, the
Jew ridiculed and despised for his funny accent and his ugly
looks and his alien ways, to make it perfectly clear to everyone
that what matters now isn't what goyim think but what Jews
do? The only person who might conceivably have delighted

my father even more by issuing the general warning that Jewish helplessness in the face of violence is a thing of the past
would have been, as commander in chief of the Israeli Army
and Air Force, a little peddler with a long beard.

Until his trip to Israel eight months after the bypass surgery,
my brother, Henry, had never shown any interest at all in the
country's existence or in its possible meaning for him as a Jewish homeland, and even that visit arose from neither an awakening of Jewish consciousness nor out of curiosity about the
archaeological traces of Jewish history but strictly as a therapeutic measure. Though his physical rehabilitation had by then
been successfully completed, at home after work he was succumbing still to fits of terrible despair, and many nights would
drag himself away from the dinner table midway through the
family meal to fall asleep on the couch in the study.

Beforehand, the doctor had warned the patient and his wife
about these depressions, and Carol had prepared the children.
Even men like Henry who were young and healthy enough to
make a rapid physical recovery from bypass surgery often suffered emotional repercussions lasting sometimes as long as a
year. In his case it had been clear from the beginning that he
wasn't to escape the worst aftereffects. Twice during the week
following the operation, he had to be moved from his private
room into intensive care because of chest pains and arrhyth-
mia, and when, after nineteen days, he was able to return home,
he was twenty pounds lighter and barely strong enough to
stand in front of the mirror and shave. He wouldn't read or
watch television, he ate practically nothing, and when Ruth,
his favorite child, came in after school and offered to play for
him the little tunes that he liked on her violin, he sent her
away. He even refused to begin the exercise course at the cardiac rehab clinic, but lay instead under a blanket in the lounge
chair on the back patio, looking out at Carol's garden and
weeping. Tearfulness, the doctor assured everyone, was common among patients after serious surgery, but Henry's tears
did not abate and after a while no one knew what he was
crying about. If, when asked, he even bothered to reply, it was
blankly, with the words "It's staring me right in the face."

"What is?" Carol said. "Tell me, darling, and we'll talk about it. What is staring you right in the face?" "The words," he angrily told her, "the words 'it's staring you right in the face'!"

At dinner one night, when Carol, trying still to be perky, suggested that now that he was physically himself again he might enjoy going along on the two-week snorkeling trip that Barry Shuskin was planning, he replied that she knew damn well that he couldn't stand Shuskin, and headed for the studio couch. That was when she telephoned me. Although Carol was right to think that our rift had all but healed, she mistakenly believed that the reconciliation resulted from the visits I'd paid to the hospital while he was moving in and out of intensive care; she still knew nothing about the times he'd called on me in New York before the operation, when he found himself without anyone else to whom he dared confide what, in reality, was making the treatment of his disease unbearable.

I reached him at his office the morning after Carol's call.

"The sun, the sea, the reefs—you deserve it," I said, "after what you've been through. Let snorkeling wash away all the old debris."

"Yeah, and then what?"

"You'll come back. You'll begin your new life."

"What'll be new about it?"

"It'll pass, Henry, the depression will pass. Sooner rather than later, if you push yourself a little."

His voice sounded disembodied when he told me, "I don't have the guts to change."

I wondered if he was talking about women again. "What sort of change do you have in mind?"

"The one that's staring me right in the face."

"Which is?"

"How would I know? I'm not only too gutless to do it, I'm too stupid to know what it is."

"You had the guts for the operation. You had the guts to say no to the medication and take your chances on the block."

"And what's it got me?"

"I take it you're off the drugs now—that you're yourself again sexually."

"So what?"

That night, while he was back brooding in the study, Carol

phoned to say how much talking to me had meant to Henry and begged me to stay in touch with him. Though the call had hardly seemed to me successful, I nonetheless phoned him again a few days later and, in fact, spoke to him more over the next few weeks than I had since college, each conversation as hopelessly circular as the one before—until all at once he relented about the trip and, along with Shuskin and two other friends, set off one Sunday on TWA with his face mask and fins. Though Carol told me gratefully how it was my concern that had turned him around, I wondered if Henry hadn't simply caved in, knuckled under to me the way he used to give in on the phone to our father back when he was a student at Cornell.

One of the stops on their itinerary was Eilat, the coastal town at the southern end of the Negev. After snorkeling for three days in the coral grottoes, the others flew on to Crete; Henry, however, remained in Israel, and only in part because of Shuskin's unbearable egomaniacal monologues. On a day tour of Jerusalem, he had broken away from the other four after lunch and wandered back by himself into the Orthodox quarter, Mea She'arim, where they had all been that morning with the guide. It was there, alone outside the classroom window of a religious school, that he had the experience that changed everything.

"I was sitting in the sunshine on the stone sill of this broken-down old cheder. Inside was a class, a room full of kids, little eight-, nine-, ten-year-old kids with skullcaps and *payess*, screaming the lesson out for their teacher, all of them reciting in unison at the top of their voices. And when I heard them, there was a surge inside me, a realization—at the root of my life, the very *root* of it, *I was them*. I always *had* been them. Children chanting away in Hebrew, I couldn't understand a word of it, couldn't recognize a single sound, and yet I was listening as though something I didn't even know I'd been searching for was suddenly reaching out for me. I stayed all week in Jerusalem. Every morning around eleven I went back to that school and sat on the windowsill and listened. You have to understand that the place isn't picturesque. The surroundings are hideous. Rubble dumped between the buildings, old appliances piled on the porches, piled in the yards—everything clean enough, but dilapidated, crumbling, rusty, everything coming apart wherever you looked. And not a color, a flower, a leaf, not a blade of grass or fresh coat of paint, nothing bright or attractive anywhere, nothing trying to please you in any way. Everything superficial had been cleared away, burned away, didn't matter—*was trivial*. In the courtyards there were all their underclothes strung on the line, big ugly underwear having nothing to do with sex, underwear from a hundred years ago. And the women, the married women—kerchiefs wrapped around their heads, underneath shaved to the bone, and no matter how young, absolutely unappealing women. I looked for a pretty woman and I couldn't find *one*. The children too— gawky, awkward, drained and pale, utterly colorless little kids. Half the old people looked like dwarfs to me, little men in long black coats with noses right out of an anti-Semitic cartoon. I can't describe it any other way. Only the uglier and more barren everything looked, the more it held me—the clearer everything became. I hung around there all one Friday, watching them get ready for the Sabbath. I watched the men going to the bathhouse with their towels under their arms and to me the towels looked like prayer shawls. I watched those bloodless little kids hurrying home, coming out of the bathhouse twisting their wet earlocks and then hurrying home for the Sabbath. Across from a barbershop, I watched the Orthodox men in those hats and coats going in to get their hair cut. The place was jammed, hair piling up around everyone's shoes, nobody bothering to sweep it away—and I couldn't move. Only a barbershop, yet I couldn't move. I bought a challah in some little dungeon bakery—stood in the crush and bought a challah and carried it all day in a bag under my arm. When I got back to the hotel, I took it out of the bag and put it on the bureau. I didn't eat it. I left it there the whole week—left it on the bureau and looked at it, as though it were a piece of sculpture, something precious I'd stolen from a museum. Everything was like this, Nathan. I couldn't stop looking, over and over again going back to stare at the same places. And that's when I began to realize that of all that I am, I am nothing, I have never been *anything*, the way that I am this Jew. I didn't know this, had no idea of it, all of my life I was swimming *against* it—then sitting and listening to those kids outside that cheder window, suddenly it *belonged* to me. Everything else *was* superficial, everything else *was* burned away. Can you understand? I may not be expressing it right, but I actually don't care how it sounds to you or to anyone. I am not *just* a Jew, I'm not *also* a Jew—*I'm a Jew as deep as those Jews.* Everything else *is* nothing And it's that, *that*, that all these months has been staring me right in the face! The fact that that is the root of my life!"

He told me all this on the phone his first night back, talking at a terrific, almost incomprehensible clip, as though he could not otherwise communicate what had happened to make his life important again, to make life suddenly of the *greatest* importance. By the end of the first week, however, when nobody to whom he repeated the story seemed to warm to his identification with those cheder kids, when he couldn't get anyone to take seriously that the more hideous the surroundings looked, the more purified he felt, when nobody at all seemed able to appreciate that it's the sheer *perversity* of these conversions that is their transforming power, his fervent excitement turned to bitter disappointment and he began to feel even more depressed than before he'd left.

Worn down, and by now pretty depressed herself, Carol telephoned the cardiologist to tell him that the trip had failed and that Henry was worse. He in turn told her that she was forgetting what he'd warned her at the outset—for some patients the emotional upheaval afterwards could be even more trying than the surgery. "He's back working every day," he reminded her—"despite the irrational episodes he's able to get himself to do his job, and that means that sooner or later, he's going to come completely around and be himself."

And maybe that's what happened three weeks later when, halfway through the day, after telling Wendy to cancel his afternoon appointments, he took off his white coat and walked out of the office. He hired a taxi to drive him from Jersey all the way over to Kennedy, and from there he phoned Carol to tell her his decision and to say goodbye to the kids. Aside from his passport, which he'd been carrying with him for days, he flew off to Israel on the El Al night flight with nothing but the suit on his back and his credit cards.

Five months had passed and he hadn't returned.

*

Shuki now lectured in contemporary European history at the university and wrote a weekly column for one of the left-wing papers, but compared to the days when he was in government he saw relatively few people, kept mostly to himself, and taught abroad as often as he could. He was as tired of politics, he said, as of all his old amusements. "I'm not even a great sinner anymore," he confessed. As a reserve military officer in Sinai during the Yom Kippur War, he'd lost his hearing in one ear and most of the sight in one eye when an exploding Egyptian shell threw him fifteen feet from his position. His brother, a reserve paratroop officer who in civilian life had been the architect, was taken prisoner when the Golan Heights were overrun. After the Syrian retreat, they found him and the rest of his captured platoon with their hands tied behind them to stakes in the ground; they had been castrated, decapitated, and their penises stuffed in their mouths. Strewn around the abandoned battlefield were necklaces made of their ears. A month after he'd received this news, Shuki's father, the welder, died of a stroke.

Shuki told me all of this, matter-of-factly, while he maneuvered through the heavy traffic and circled the side streets to find a space within walking distance of the downtown cafés. Eventually he was able to squeeze his VW in at an angle between two cars, half up on the sidewalk in front of an apartment building. "We could have sat like two nice old fellows beside the tranquil sea, but I remember that last time you preferred sitting on Dizengoff Street. I remember you devouring the girls with your eyes as though you thought they were shiksas."

"Is that right? Well, I was probably never much good at telling the difference."

"I don't go in for it any more myself," Shuki said. "It isn't that the girls aren't interested in me—I'm so big now they don't even see me."

Years back, after taking me to Jaffa and around the Tel Aviv sights, Shuki had entertained me one evening at a noisy café frequented by his journalist friends, where we'd wound up playing chess for several hours before moving on to the red-

light district and my special sociological treat, a Rumanian
prostitute on Yarkon Street. Now he led me into a barren colorless little place with some pinball machines in the back and nobody at any of the streetside tables except a couple of soldiers
and their girls. At our table he said, "No, sit on this side, so I
can hear you."

Though he hadn't become quite the behemoth of his own
self-caricature, he bore little resemblance to the dark, slim,
mischievous hedonist who'd guided me to Yarkon Street eighteen years earlier—the hair that used to spring from his forehead in tenacious black tiers had thinned down to just a few
gray wisps combed across his scalp, and because the face had
considerably puffed out, the features seemed larger and less
refined. But the biggest change was in the grin, a grin having
nothing to do with amusement, though clearly he liked still to
be amused and knew how to be amusing. Thinking about his
brother's death—and his father's fatal stroke—I found myself
equating that grin of his with the dressing over a wound.

"How's New York?" he asked.

"I'm not living in New York anymore. I'm married to an
English woman. I've moved to London."

"You in England? The Jersey boy with the dirty mouth who
writes the books Jews love to hate—how do you survive there?
How can you stand the silence? I was invited a couple of years
ago to lecture at Oxford. I was there six months. At dinner,
whatever I said, somebody next to me always replied, 'Oh,
really?'"

"You didn't like the small talk."

"Truthfully? I didn't mind it. I needed a vacation from this
place. Every Jewish dilemma there ever was is encapsulated in
this country. In Israel it's enough to live—you don't have to
do anything else and you go to bed exhausted. Have you ever
noticed that Jews shout? Even one ear is more than you need.
Here everything is black and white, everybody is shouting,
and everybody is always right. Here the extremes are too great
for a country so small. Oxford was a relief. 'Tell me, Mr.
Elchanan, how is your dog?' 'I don't have a dog.' 'Oh, really?'
My problem began when I got back. My wife's family would
meet at our house on Friday nights to argue about politics,

and I couldn't get a word in. During six months at Oxford I had learned civility and the rules of civilized discourse, and this turned out to be absolutely crippling in an Israeli discussion."

"Well," I said, "that hasn't changed—you still hear the best anti-Semitic cracks in a Dizengoff Street café."

"The only reason left to live here," Shuki said. "Tell me about your English wife."

I told him how I had met Maria in New York a little over a year before, when she and the husband from whom she was already hopelessly estranged had moved into the duplex upstairs from my apartment. "They were divorced four months back and we married and moved to England. Life is fine there. If it wasn't for Israel, everything in London would be wonderful."

"Yes? Israel's also to blame for living conditions in London? I'm not surprised."

"Last night, at a dinner party, when Maria mentioned where I was off to today, I wasn't the most popular boy at the table. You might have thought from the skiing holidays in Switzerland and the summer houses in Tuscany and the BMWs in the garage that all these nice, liberal, privileged Englishmen would have been a little leery of revolutionary socialism. But no, when it comes to Israel, it's the Sayings of Chairman Arafat right down the line."

"Of course. In Paris as well. Israel is one of those places you know so much better before you wind up there."

"They were all friends of Maria's, younger than I, in their thirties, television people, in publishing, a couple of journalists —all bright and successful. I was put right in the dock: how long can the Israelis keep importing cheap Jewish labor from North Africa to do their dirty work? It's well known in WII that Oriental Jews are brought to Israel to be exploited as an industrial proletariat. Imperialist colonization, capitalist exploitation—all carried on from behind the facade of Israeli democracy and the fiction of Jewish national unity. And that was only the beginning."

"And you championed our wickedness?"

"I didn't have to. Maria did."

He looked alarmed. "You haven't married a Jew, Nathan."

"No, my record's intact. She just finds the moral posturing

of the fashionable left very very depressing. But mostly what she resented was that defending Israel should appear to everyone to fall automatically upon her new husband. Maria isn't someone who relishes a fight, so her vehemence surprised me. So did theirs. I asked her on the way home how strong this Israel-hatred is in England. She says that the press thinks it is, and thinks it should be, but, in her words, 'it just bloody well isn't.' "

"I'm not sure she's right," Shuki said. "In England I myself sensed a certain, shall we say, *distaste* for Jews—a willingness to not always, in every circumstance, think the very best of us. I was interviewed one morning on BBC radio. We'd been on the air two minutes when the interviewer said to me, 'You Jews learned a lot from Auschwitz.' 'What's that?' I asked. 'How to be Nazis to the Arabs,' he said."

"What did you say?"

"I couldn't speak. On the Continent I just grit my teeth—there the anti-Semitism is so pervasive and ingrained, it's positively Byzantine. But in civilized England, with people so well-spoken, so well-bred, even I was caught off guard. I'm not known around here as this country's leading P.R. man, but if I'd had a gun I would have shot him."

At dinner the evening before, Maria had looked about ready to reach for a weapon herself. I'd never seen her so combative or incensed, not even during the divorce negotiations, when her husband seemed out to wreck our marriage before it began by forcing her to sign a legal document guaranteeing that Phoebe would be domiciled in London and not in New York. If Maria refused, he threatened to go to court and sue for custody, citing our adulterous liaison as grounds for claiming that she was an unfit mother. Assuming that I might be reluctant to be exiled from America until the turn of the century for the sake of his visitation rights, Maria immediately began to imagine herself returning to London unmarried, alone with Phoebe, and being plagued there by his bullying. "Nobody, but nobody, would ever want to get into a serious recrimination with him. If I'm on my own and he starts in, it'll be worse than just lonely and hard." She was equally as frightened of my resentment if, after accepting his conditions and agreeing to move to

England, I found that cutting myself off from familiar sources had begun to damage my work. She lived in dread of yet another husband suddenly becoming estranged after she had taken the irrevocable step of becoming pregnant.

It bewildered her still to recall her ex-husband's coldness to her after she'd had Phoebe. "At any point up to then," she explained, "he could have said, with perfect justice, this isn't working for me. And *had* he said that, I would have said, absolutely, it just isn't, and however painful that is, that's it, and we will do other things with our lives. But why he couldn't perceive that clearly until after I had my baby—I mean I *had* accepted all the limitations of our relationship, otherwise I wouldn't have had a child. I *do* accept limitations. I expect them. Everybody tells me I'm submissive just because I happen to recognize the utter ridiculousness of railing against the kinds of disappointment that are simply inevitable. There's something every woman wants, and that's a man to blame. I refused to do it. To me the shortcomings of our marriage were no shock. I mean he had some dreadful qualities, but so many wonderful ones as well. No, what was a shock to me, after the baby came, was overt, relentless bad behavior—mistreatment, which is what happened as soon as my child was born and which I had never encountered before. I had encountered many, many things I didn't like, but they were things one can look at one way or another. But not misbehavior. There it is—that's what's happened. And if it were ever to happen to me again, I don't know what I'd do."

I assured her it wouldn't and told her to sign the agreement. I wasn't going to let him get away with this kind of shit, and I certainly wasn't going to give her up and, with her, my desire, at forty-four, after three childless marriages, to have a house, if not exactly full of babies, with a child in it of my own, and a young wife whom, though she described herself to me more than once as "mentally very lazy" and "intellectually very reclusive" and "sexually rather shy," I hadn't tired of in any way through our several hundred secret afternoons. I'd waited months before asking her to leave him, even though I was already thinking about it the first time we arranged to meet in my apartment. When she stubbornly resisted my proposal, I couldn't tell if it was because she took me to be another male bully simply wanting his way or whether she truly believed that I was dangerously self-deluded.

"I've fallen in love with you," I told her. "You're too self-aware to 'fall in love.' You know," she said, looking at me across my bed, "if you were really so convinced of the comic absurdity that you're so good at showing, you wouldn't be taking any of this seriously. Why can't you think of this as strictly a business meeting?" When I said I wanted a child, she replied, "Do you really want to spend a lot of time dealing with the melodrama of family life?" When I said that I couldn't get enough of her, she replied, "No, no, I've read your books —you need a lionlike temptress in here to give your libido a good thrashing. You need a woman who goes around organizing herself into the right kind of highly stylized erotic postures whenever she sits down—and that is definitely not me. You want a new experience and I'll only be the same old thing. It won't be dramatic at all. It'll be a long dull English evening in front of the fire with a very sensible, responsible, respectable woman. In time you'll need all sorts of polymorphous perversity to keep up your interest, and I'm really quite content, as you see, with simple penetration. I know that it's not on anymore, but I'm not interested in sucking elbows and all those things, truly I'm not. Just because I'm free in the afternoons for certain immoral purposes, you may have got the wrong idea. I don't want six men at a time, outdated as that sounds. Sometimes in the past, when I was younger, I had fantasies about that sort of thing, but real men, they're rarely nice enough to want *one* at a time. I don't want to dress like a chambermaid and indulge anyone's apron fetishism. I don't have the desire to be tied up and whipped, and as for buggery, it's never given me much pleasure. The idea is exciting but I'm afraid it hurts, so we can't found a marriage on that. If the truth be known, I really just like to arrange flowers and do a little bit of writing here and there—and that's it." "Then why do I have erotic thoughts about you?" "Really? What are they? Tell me." "I had them all morning." "What were we doing?" "You were assiduously performing fellatio." "Oh, I thought it was going to be something more unusual. That I wouldn't really do." "Maria, how can I be so hooked if you're as ordinary as you say?" "I think you like me because I don't have the usual feminine vices. I think a lot of those women who seem bright also seem very ferocious. What you like is that I seem bright without being ferocious, somebody who *is* really rather ordinary and is not determined to kick you in the teeth. But why carry it further—why marry me and have a child and settle down like everyone else to an impostor's life?" "Because I've decided to give up the artificial fiction of being myself for the genuine, satisfying falseness of being somebody else. *Marry me.*" "God, when you want something, you look at me so *scarily.*" "Because I'm conspiring with you *to escape.* I love you! I want to live with you! I want to have a child!" "Please," she replied, "do try to confine your fantasies in my presence. I really thought you were more worldly than this."

But I continued to confine nothing that I felt and in time she came to believe me, or collapsed in the face of my insistence— or both—and after that, the next thing I knew I was advising her to sign a document that would effectively sever me from my American life until tiny Phoebe was old enough to vote. Of course it wasn't what I had been anticipating and I did worry what effect moving abroad might have on my writing, but a courtroom custody battle would have been horrible for every reason, and I also believed that two or three years on, when everyone's divorce-delirium had abated, when Phoebe was older and beginning school and Maria's ex-husband was himself remarried and perhaps even a father again, it would be possible to renegotiate the custody stipulations. "And if it's not possible?" "It will be," I told her; "we'll live two or three years in London, he'll calm down, and it will all work out." "Will it? Can it? Does it ever? I dread thinking what happens when things start going wrong in England with your fantasy of family life."

When Maria had begun defending Israel against our fellow dinner-party guests, who'd been arguing as though the alleged crimes of what they called "appalling Zionism" were somehow mine to answer for, I wondered if what was driving her on weren't perhaps fears she continued to have about things going wrong for us in England rather than the reputation of the Jewish state. It was difficult otherwise to understand why someone who considered head-on confrontations hell, who despised *any* situation that required raising her voice, should place herself at the center of an argument she'd never seemed at all concerned with before. The closest I'd seen her get to entangling herself in the problems of Jews, and Jewish problems with Gentiles, was in a far more subdued, secluded setting, the bedroom of my Manhattan apartment when she'd told me what it was like for her living in a "Jewish city."

"I rather like it, actually," she'd said. "Life is sort of fizzy here, isn't it? A seemingly higher proportion of interesting people around. I like the way they talk. Gentiles have their little pale moments of exuberance, but nothing like this. It's the way one talks when one's been drinking. It's like Virgil. Whenever he tries any of that epic stuff, you knew you were in for twenty-five lines of seriously difficult Latin, all beside the point. 'And then the good Antaeus begged his son to put him down, saying, "My son, think first of our family, as when . . ."' This manic asidedness—well, that's New York and the Jews. Heady stuff. The only thing I don't like is that they all seem a bit too quick to find fault with Gentiles in their attitudes toward Jews. You have a touch of it too—finding things horrendously anti-Semitic, or even mildly so, when they really aren't. I know it's not entirely unjustified for Jews to be thin-skinned on that score—nonetheless, it's irritating. Uh-oh," she said, "I shouldn't be telling you these things." "No," I said, "go on—telling me what you know you shouldn't be telling is one of your endearing strategies." "Then I'll tell you something else that irritates me. About Jewish men." "Do." "All the shiksa-fancying. I don't like that. I don't like it at all. I don't feel it with you. Probably I'm deluding myself and you're the man who invented it. I mean, I know there's an element of strangeness here, but I like to think all that doesn't operate *too* much." "So other Jewish men fancy you too—is that what you're saying?" "Are attracted to me because I'm not? In New York? Absolutely. Yes. That happens frequently when my husband and I go out." "But why should it irritate you?" "Because there are enough politics in sex without racial politics coming into it." I corrected her: "We're not a race." "It *is* a racial matter," she insisted. "No, we're the same race. You're thinking of Eskimos." "We are *not* the same race. Not according to anthropologists, or whoever measures these things. There's Caucasian, Semitic—there are about five different racial groups. Don't look at me like that." "I can't help it. Some nasty superstitions always tend to crop up when people talk about a Jewish 'race.'" "See, you're about to get angry at a Gentile for saying the wrong thing about Jews—proving my thesis. But all I can tell you is that you *are* a different race. We're supposed to be closer to Indians than to Jews, actually. I'm talking about Caucasians." "But I am Caucasian, kiddo. In the U.S. census I am, for good or bad, counted as Caucasian." "*Are* you? *Am* I wrong? Oh, you're not going to speak to me after this. It's always a mistake to be frank." "I'm nuts about you for being frank." "That won't last." "Nothing lasts, but right now it's true." "Well then, all I *am* saying—and I am not talking now about you *or* race—is that I don't feel with a lot of men in New York who do seem to want to chat me up that this is a personal thing, that they find me an interesting person who just happens not to be Jewish. On the contrary, this is a type that they had met before and that they quite liked having lunch with, or perhaps doing other things with, only because she *was* that type."

As it turned out, if anyone at that dinner party had been overly quick to find fault with Gentiles in their attitude toward Jews, it had been Maria herself. And in the car driving home, when she wouldn't let up about their hypocritical line on the Middle East, I began to wonder once again whether all this indignation might not have something to do with her anxiety about our English future. I might even be seeing signs of that tendency toward self-annihilating accommodation that had been exploited so cruelly by her former husband once he'd begun losing interest in her.

The car door had barely shut behind her when she said to me, "I assure you, people in this country who have any sense at all, who are people of any kind of discrimination and judgment, are *not* anti-Israel. I mean, these people bat on about Israel in terms of great disgust, but the man who runs Libya thinks he can *fly*. It's just unreal, isn't it, their selective disapproval? These people disapprove selectively and most strongly of the least reprehensible parties." "You're really stirred up by all this." "Well, there comes a time when even nicely brought-up females lose their self-control. It's true I have trouble shouting at people, and I don't necessarily always say what I think, but even I don't have trouble being angry when people are being insulting and stupid."

After I'd repeated to Shuki the gist of the London dinner-table argument of the night before, he asked, "And she's beautiful too, your foolhardy Christian defender of our incorrigible state?"

"She considers herself Gentile, not Christian." In my billfold I found the Polaroid snapshot taken at Phoebe's second birthday party only a few weeks before. It showed Maria bending over the party table, helping the child cut the cake, both of them with the same dark curls, oval face, and feline eyes.

Shuki asked, examining the picture, "She has a job?"

"She used to work for a magazine; now she's writing fiction."

"So, gifted as well. Very attractive. Only an English girl can have that expression on her face. Observing everything and giving away nothing. She is surrounded by a large serenity, Maria Zuckerman. Effortless tranquillity—not a trait we're renowned for. Our great contribution is effortless anxiety." He turned the photograph over and read aloud the words written there by me. " 'Maria, five months pregnant.' "

"A father finally at forty-five," I said.

"I see. By marrying this woman and having a child you will be mixing at last in the everyday world."

"That may be part of it."

"The only problem is that in the everyday world girls don't look like this. And if it's a boy," Shuki asked, "your English rose will consent to circumcision?"

"Who says circumcision's required?"

"Genesis, chapter 17."

"Shuki, I've never been completely sold on biblical injunctions."

"Who is? Still, it's been a unifying custom among Jews for rather a long time now. I think it would be difficult for you to have a son who wasn't circumcised. I think you would resent a woman who insisted otherwise."

"We'll see."

Laughing, he handed back the picture. "Why do you pretend to be so detached from your Jewish feelings? In the books all you seem to be worrying about is what on earth a Jew is, while in life you pretend that you're content to be the last link in the Jewish chain of being."

"Chalk it up to Diaspora abnormality."

"Yes? You think in the *Diaspora* it's abnormal? Come live here. This is the *homeland* of Jewish abnormality. Worse: now *we* are the dependent Jews, on your money, your lobby, on our big allowance from Uncle Sam, while *you* are the Jews living interesting lives, comfortable lives, without apology, without shame, and perfectly *independent*. As for the condemnation of Israel in London W11, it may upset your lovely wife, but, really, it shouldn't bother you out there. Left-wing virtue-hounds are nothing new. Feeling morally superior to Iraqis and Syrians isn't really much fun, so let them feel superior to the Jews, if that's all it takes to make life beautiful. Frankly I think the English distaste for Jews is nine-tenths snobbery anyway. The fact remains that in the Diaspora a Jew like you lives securely, without real fear of persecution or violence, while we are living just the kind of imperiled Jewish existence that we came here to replace. Whenever I meet you American-Jewish intellectuals with your non-Jewish wives and your good Jewish brains, well-bred, smooth, soft-spoken men, educated men who know how to order in a good restaurant, and to appreciate good wine, and to listen courteously to another point of view, I think exactly that: we are the excitable, ghettoized, jittery little Jews of the Diaspora, and you are the Jews with all the confidence and cultivation that comes of feeling at home where you are."

"Only to an Israeli," I said, "could an American-Jewish intellectual look like a charming Frenchman."

"What the hell *are* you doing in a place like this?" Shuki asked.

"I'm here to see my brother. He's made aliyah."

"You've got a brother who's emigrated to Israel? What is he, a religious nut?"

"No, a successful dentist. Or he was. He's living in a little frontier settlement on the West Bank. He's learning Hebrew there."

"You're making this up. Carnovsky's brother on the West Bank? This is another of your hilarious ideas."

"My sister-in-law wishes it were. No, Henry's made it up.

Henry appears to have left his wife, his kids, and his mistress to come to Israel to become an authentic Jew."

"Why would he want to be something like that?"

"That's what I'm here to find out."

"Which settlement is it?"

"Not far from Hebron, in the Judean hills. It's called Agor. His wife says he's found a hero there—a man named Mordecai Lippman."

"Oh, has he?"

"You know Lippman?"

"Nathan, I can't talk about these things. It's too painful for me. I mean this. Your brother is a follower of Lippman's?"

"Carol says that when Henry calls to speak to the kids, Lippman's all he talks about."

"Yes? He's so impressed? Well, when you see Henry, tell him all he has to do is go to the jail and he can meet plenty of little gangsters just as impressive."

"He intends to stay on, to live at Agor after he's finished his Hebrew course, *because* of Lippman."

"Well, that's wonderful. Lippman drives into Hebron with his pistol and tells the Arabs in the market how the Jews and Arabs can live happily side by side as long as the Jews are on top. He's dying for somebody to throw a Molotov cocktail. Then his thugs can really go to town."

"Carol mentioned Lippman's pistol. Henry told the kids all about it."

"Of course. Henry must find it very romantic," Shuki said. "The American Jews get a big thrill from the guns. They see Jews walking around with guns and they think they're in paradise. Reasonable people with a civilized repugnance for violence and blood, they come on tour from America, and they see the guns and they see the beards, and they take leave of their senses. The beards to remind them of saintly Yiddish weakness and the guns to reassure them of heroic Hebrew force. Jews ignorant of history, Hebrew, Bible, ignorant of Islam and the Middle East, they see the guns and they see the beards, and out of them flows every sentimental emotion that wish fulfillment can produce. A regular pudding of emotions. The fantasies about this place make me sick. And what *about* the beards? Is your brother as thrilled by the religion as by the explosives? These settlers, you know, are our great believing messianic Jews. The Bible is their *bible*—these idiots take it seriously. I tell you, all the madness of the human race is in the sanctification of that book. Everything going wrong with this country is in the first five books of the Old Testament. Smite the enemy, sacrifice your son, the desert is yours and nobody else's all the way to the Euphrates. A body count of dead Philistines on every other page—that's the wisdom of their wonderful Torah. If you're going out there, go tomorrow for the Friday night service and watch them sitting around kissing God's ass, telling him how big and wonderful he is—telling the rest of us how wonderful *they* are, bravely doing his work as courageous pioneers in biblical Judea. Pioneers! They work all day in government jobs in Jerusalem and drive home to biblical Judea for dinner at night. Only eating chopped chicken liver at the biblical source, only going to bed on the biblical sites, can a Jew find true Judaism. Well, if they want so much to sleep at the biblical source because that is where Abraham tied his shoelaces, then they can sleep there under Arab rule! Please, don't talk to me about what these people are up to. It makes me too crazy. I'll need a *year* at Oxford."

"Tell me more about my brother's hero."

"Lippman? I smell fascism on people like Lippman."

"What's that smell like here?"

"It smells the same here as it does everywhere. The situation gets so complicated that it seems to require a simple solution, and that's where Lippman comes in. His racket is to play upon Jewish insecurity—he says to the Jews, 'I have the solution to our problem of fear.' Of course there's a long history of these people. Mordecai Lippman doesn't come from nowhere. In every Jewish community there was always such a person. What could the rabbi do for their fears? The rabbi looks like you, Nathan—the rabbi is tall, he is thin, he is introverted and ascetic, always over his books, and usually he's also ill. He is not a person who can deal with the goyim. So in every community there is a butcher, a teamster, a porter, he is big, he is healthy —you sleep with one, two, maybe three women, he sleeps with twenty-seven, and all at the same time. *He* deals with the fear. He marches off at night with the other butcher and when he comes back there are a hundred goyim you don't ever have to

worry about again. There was even a name for him: the
shlayger. The whipper. The only difference between the Old
Country *shlayger* and Mordecai Lippman is that on a superficial level Mr. Lippman is very deep. He hasn't only a Jewish
gun, he has a Jewish mouth—remnants even of a Jewish brain.
There is now so much antagonism between Arab and Jew that
even a child would understand that the best thing is to keep
them apart—so Mr. Lippman drives into Arab Hebron wearing
his pistol. Hebron! This state was not established for Jews to
police Nablus and Hebron! This was not the Zionist idea!
Look, I have no illusions about Arabs and I have no illusions
about Jews. I just don't want to live in a country that's *completely* crazy. It excites you to hear me going on like this—I can
see it. You envy me—you think, 'Craziness and dangerousness
—that sounds like fun!' But believe me, when you have so
much of it over so many years that even craziness and dangerousness become tedious and boring, then it's *really* dangerous.
People are frightened here for thirty-five years—when will there
be another war? The Arabs can lose and lose and lose, and we
can lose only once. All that is true. But what is the result?
Onto the stage comes Menachem Begin—and the logical step
after Begin, a gangster like Mordecai Lippman, who tells them,
'I have the solution to our Jewish problem of fear.' And the
worse Lippman is, the better. He's right, they say, that's the
kind of world we live in. If the humane approach fails, try
brutality."

"And yet my little brother likes him."

"Ask your little brother, then, 'What are the consequences
of this delightful man?' The destruction of the country! Who
comes to this country now to settle and live? The intellectual
Jew? The humane Jew? The beautiful Jew? No, not the Jew
from Buenos Aires, or Rio, or Manhattan. The ones who come
from America are either religious or crazy or both. This place
has become the American-Jewish Australia. Now who we get is
the Oriental Jew and the Russian Jew and the social misfits like
your brother, roughnecks in yarmulkes from Brooklyn."

"My brother's from suburban New Jersey. You couldn't
possibly describe him as a misfit. The problem that brought
him here may have been the opposite: he fit all too well into
his comfortable existence."

"So what did he come for? The pressure? The tensions? The problems? The danger? Then he's really meshugge. You're the only smart one—you, of all people, are the only normal Jew, living in London with an English Gentile wife and thinking you won't even bother to circumcise your son. You, who say, I live in this time, I live in this world, and out of that I form my life. This, you understand, was supposed to be the place where to become a normal Jew was the *goal*. Instead we have become the Jewish obsessional prison par excellence! Instead it has become the breeding ground for every brand of madness that Jewish genius can devise!"

It was dusk when we started back to the car. Waiting there with his wife and his little child was a darkish, strongly built man in his early thirties, crisply dressed in pale slacks and a white short-sleeve shirt. It seemed that Shuki, by angling the VW half onto the sidewalk, had inadvertently made it impossible for this other driver to back his car out of the space in front. At the sight of us approaching the VW, he started shouting and shaking his fist, and I wondered if he might not be an Israeli Arab. His fury was amazing. Shuki raised his voice to reply, but there wasn't really much fury in him, and while the angry man screamed away, menacing him up close with a clenched fist, Shuki unlocked the car and let me in.

I asked, once we were driving off, in what language the fellow had been berating him, Arabic or Hebrew.

"Hebrew." Shuki laughed. "The man is like you, Nathan, a Jew. Hebrew, of course. He was telling me, 'I can't believe it—another Ashkenazi donkey! Every Ashkenazi I meet is another donkey!'"

"Where's he from?"

"I don't know—Tunis, Algiers, Casablanca. Have you heard who is now coming to live here? Jews from Ethiopia. So desperate are these bastards like Begin to perpetuate the old mythology that they're beginning to drag *black* Jews here. Pleasant, affectionate, good-natured people, most of them peasants, they come here speaking the Ethiopian language. Some are so sick when they arrive they have to be taken by stretcher and rushed to the hospital. Most are unable to read or write. They have to be taught how to turn on the tap and turn off the tap and how to use a toilet and what stairs are.

Technologically they live in the thirteenth century. But within a year, I assure you, they'll already be Israelis, shouting about their rights and staging sitdown strikes, and soon enough they will be calling me an Ashkenazi donkey because of how I park my car."

At my hotel, Shuki apologized for being unable to have dinner with me, but he didn't like leaving his wife alone at night and she wasn't up to socializing. It was a bad time for her. Their eighteen-year-old son, who had emerged through competition as one of the outstanding young musicians in the country, had been drafted into the army for his three years of service and as a result would be unable to practice his piano regularly, if at all. Daniel Barenboim had listened to Mati play and offered to help arrange for him to study in America, but the boy had decided that he couldn't leave the country to pursue his own ambitions while his friends were doing their military service. Once he had finished his basic training, allowances were supposed to be made for him to practice several times a week, but Shuki doubted that even this would happen. "Maybe he doesn't need our approbation anymore, but he still needs theirs. Mati's not so obstinate out of the house. If they tell him to go and hose down the tanks at the hour reserved for his practice, Mati is not going to take his note out of his pocket and say, 'Daniel Barenboim suggests I play the piano instead.' "

"Your wife wanted him to go to America."

"She tells him his responsibility is to music and not to the stupid infantry. In his nice loud voice, he says, 'Israel has given me plenty! I've had a good time here! I have to do my duty!' and she goes completely crazy. I try to intervene but I am as effective as one of the fathers in your books. I even thought about you while it was happening. I thought it really didn't require all the agonies of creating a Jewish state where our people could shed their ghetto behavior, for me to wind up like a helpless father out of a Zuckerman novel, a real old-fashioned Jewish father who's either kissing the children or shouting at them. Another powerless Jewish father against whom the poor Jewish son has nevertheless to stage his ridiculous rebellion."

"Goodbye, Shuki," I said, taking his hand.

"Goodbye, Nathan. And don't forget to come again in

another twenty years. I'm sure if Begin is still in power I'll have even more good news."

I decided, after Shuki left, that rather than stay in Tel Aviv that evening, I'd have the front desk phone ahead to Jerusalem to arrange a room for the night. From there I'd get in touch with Henry and try to get him to meet me for dinner. If Shuki hadn't exaggerated, and Lippman was anything like the *shlayger* he'd described, then it was possible that Henry was as much captive as disciple, and, in fact, something like what might have been in Carol's mind when she'd indicated that dealing with a suburban husband who'd turned himself into a born-again Jew was like having a child become a Moonie. How could she go ahead, she asked, and institute separation proceedings leading to a divorce if the man had really lost his mind? When she'd phoned me in London it was because she'd begun to feel as though she might be losing her mind herself—and because she didn't know whom else to turn to.

"I don't want to match his irrationality with my own, I don't want to act prematurely, but he couldn't have gone any farther from me if he *had* died in surgery. If he's cast me off for good, *and* the practice, *and* everything else, I *have* to act, I can't wait here like an idiot for him to come to his senses. But I'm paralyzed—I cannot grasp it—I don't understand what has happened *at all*. Do you? You've known him all his life. In a way brothers probably know each other better than they ever know anyone else."

"How they know each other, in my experience, is as a kind of deformation of themselves."

"Nathan, he can't put you off the way he can me. Before I do anything that's going to destroy it for good, I have to know if he's completely flipped out."

I thought I ought to know too. The relationship to Henry was the most elemental connection I had left, and however vexing its surface had become after the long years of our estrangement, what was evoked in me by Carol's call was the need to be responsible not so much to the disapproving brother with whom I'd already come to blows but to the little boy in the flannel pajamas who was known to sleepwalk when he was overexcited.

Not that it was filial duty alone that was goading me on. I was also deeply curious about this swift and simple conversion of a kind that isn't readily allowed to writers unless they wish to commit the professional blunder of being uninquiring. Henry's life was no longer coming true in its most pedestrian form, and I had to ask if it all *had* been as mindlessly gained as Carol meant by suggesting he'd "flipped out." Wasn't there possibly more genius than madness in this escape? However unprecedented in the annals of suffocating domesticity, wasn't this escape somehow incontestable in a way that it never would have been had he run off with an alluring patient? Certainly the rebellious script that he had tried following ten years back could hardly touch this one for originality.

Within half an hour I'd settled my bill, and my bag was beside me in the taxi heading away from the sea. The industrial outskirts of Tel Aviv were already disappearing in the winter darkness when we turned onto the thruway and eastward across the citrus groves to the Jerusalem hills. As soon as I had a room at the hotel, I called Agor. The woman who answered seemed at first to be quite convinced that nobody named Henry Zuckerman lived at Agor. "The American," I said loudly, "the American—the dentist from New Jersey!" Here she disappeared and I didn't know quite what was up.

While waiting for someone to come back on the phone, I recalled in detail the message I'd got from Henry's thirteen-year-old daughter, Ruth, during dinner in London the evening before. It was a collect person-to-person call, placed in New Jersey after school from the house of a friend. Her mother had told her that I was going down to see her father, and though she wasn't sure she was right even to be phoning me—for a week now she'd been putting it off from one day to the next—she wondered if she could ask me to tell him something "confidentially," something she herself was not able to say on Sundays what with her older brother, Leslie, and her younger sister, Ellen, and sometimes even her mother hovering over the phone. But first she wanted me to know that she didn't happen to agree with her mother that her father was behaving "childishly." "She keeps saying," Ruthie told me, "that he's not reliable anymore, that she doesn't trust his motives, and that if he wants to see us it's going to have to be here. We were supposed to fly over for the school holiday and travel with him around the country, but now I'm not really sure she's going to let us. She's very down on him right now—very. She's hurting terribly and I can sympathize. But what I would like you to tell my dad for me is that I think I understand better than Leslie and Ellen. Leave out Leslie and Ellen—just tell him that I understand." "You understand what?" "He's out there to learn something—he's trying to find something out. I don't say I understand *everything*, but I do think he's not too old to learn—and I think he has the right." "I'll tell him that," I said. "Don't you think it's so?" she asked. "What do *you* think about all this, Uncle Nathan? Do you mind my asking?" "Well," I said, "I don't know if it's where I'd go, but I suppose I've done similar things myself." "Have you really?" "Things that look childish to other people? I have. And perhaps for the reason you suggest—trying to find something out." "In a way," said Ruth, "I even admire him. It's awfully brave to go so far— isn't it? I mean he's giving up an awful lot." "It looks that way. Are you afraid that he's given you up?" "No, Ellen is, I'm not. Ellen's the one who's in a bad way. She's a mess right now, though don't tell him—he shouldn't have to worry about that too." "And your brother?" "He's just bossier than ever—he's now the man around here, you see." "You sound okay, Ruth." "Well, I'm not great, frankly. I miss him. I'm confused without my father." "Do you want me to tell him that too, that you're confused without him?" "If you think it's a good idea, I guess so."

Henry must have been at the other end of the settlement— maybe, I thought, attending evening prayers—because it was a full ten minutes before they found him and he finally came to the phone. I wondered if he was wearing his prayer shawl. I really didn't know what to expect.

"It's me," I announced, "Cain to your Abel, Esau to your Jacob, here in the Land of Canaan. I'm calling from the King David Hotel. I just arrived from London."

"My, my." Sardonic words, just two of them, and then the long pause. "Here for Chanukah?" he finally asked.

"Chanukah first and to see you second."

A longer pause. "Where's Carol?"

"I'm alone."

"What do you want?"

"I thought you might come in to have dinner with me in Jerusalem. They could probably find a bed for you here in the hotel if you wanted to stay over."

As he was now an even longer time replying, I figured he was about to hang up. "I have a class tonight," he eventually said.

"How about tomorrow? I'll drive out to you."

"You do have to admit it's a little bizarre that you're the one Carol deputized to fly in to remind me of my family obligations."

"I didn't come down here to bring you back alive."

"You couldn't," he snapped, "if you wanted to. I know what I'm doing and there's nothing to say—the decision's irrevocable."

"Then what harm can I do? I'd like to see Agor."

"This is rich," he said. "You in Jerusalem."

"Well, neither of us was renowned in New Jersey for his pious devotion."

"What *do* you want, Nathan?"

"To visit you. To find out how you're doing."

"And Carol's not with you?"

"I don't play those games. Neither Carol nor the cops. I flew from London by myself."

"On the spur of the moment."

"Why not?"

"And what if I tell you to go back to London on the spur of the moment?"

"Why should you?"

"Because I don't need anyone to come out here and decide if I'm deranged. Because I've made the appropriate explanations already. Because—"

Once Henry got going like that I knew he'd have to see me.

When I'd visited Israel back in 1960, the Old City was still on the other side of the border. Across the narrow valley opening out behind this same hotel, I'd been able to watch the armed Jordanian soldiers posted as guards atop the Wall but of course I'd never got to visit the Temple remnant known as the Western or Wailing Wall. I was curious now to see if anything like what had happened to my brother in Mea She'arim would surprise and overtake me while standing at this, the most hallowed of all Jewish places. When I asked at the desk, the hotel clerk had assured me that I wouldn't find myself alone there, not at any hour. "Every Jew should go at night," he told me, "you'll remember it for the rest of your life." With nothing to do until I left the next morning for Agor, I got a cab to drive me over.

It *was* more impressive than I'd anticipated, perhaps because the floodlights dramatizing the massive weight of the ancient stones seemed simultaneously to be illuminating the most poignant of history's themes: Transience, Endurance, Destruction, Hope. The Wall was asymmetrically framed by a pair of minarets jutting up from the holy Arab compound just beyond, and by two mosque domes there, the grand one of gold and a smaller one of silver, placed as though subtly to unbalance the picturesque composition. Even the full moon, hoisted to an unobtrusive height so as to avoid the suggestion of superfluous kitsch, seemed, beside those domes silhouetting the sky, decorative ingenuity in a very minor mode. This gorgeous Oriental nighttime backdrop made of the Wailing Wall square an enormous outdoor theater, the stage for some lavish, epic, operatic production whose extras one could watch walking casually about, a handful already got up in their religious costumes and the rest, unbearded, still in street clothes.

Approaching the Wall from the old Jewish quarter, I had to pass through a security barrier at the top of a long flight of stairs. A middle-aged Sephardic soldier, scruffily dressed in army fatigues, fumbled through the tourists' shopping bags and purses before letting them pass on. At the foot of the stairs, lounging back on their elbows, as oblivious to the Divine Presence as to the crowd milling about, were four more Israeli soldiers, all quite young, any one of whom, I thought, could have been Shuki's son, out not practicing his piano. Like the guard up by the barrier, each appeared to have improvised a uniform from a heap of old clothes at an army surplus store. They reminded me of the hippies I used to see around Bethesda Fountain in Central Park during the Vietnam War years, except that slung across these Israeli khaki rags were automatic weapons.

A stone divider insulated those who'd come to pray piously at the Wall from the people circulating in the square. There was a small table at one end of the barrier and on it a box of cardboard yarmulkes for hatless male visitors—women prayed by themselves down at their own partitioned segment of the Wall. Two of the Orthodox were stationed—or had decided to situate themselves—just beside the table. The older one, a slight, bent figure with a storybook white beard and a cane, was seated on the stone bench running parallel to the Wall; the other, who was probably younger than I, was a bulky man in a long black coat, with a heavy face and a stiff beard shaped like a coal scoop or a shovel. He stood above the man with the cane, talking with great intensity; however, no sooner had I placed a yarmulke on my head than abruptly he turned his attention on me. "Shalom. Shalom aleichem."

"Shalom," I replied.

"I collect. Charity."

"Me too," the old man chimed in.

"Yes? Charity for what?"

"Poor families," answered the one with the black shovel beard.

I reached into my pocket and came up with all my change, Israeli and English. To me this seemed a generous enough donation given the nebulous quality of the philanthropy he claimed to represent. He offered in return, however, a just perceptible look that I had to admire for its fine expressive blend of incredulity and contempt. "You don't have paper money?" he asked. "A couple of dollars?"

Because my meticulous concern for his "credentials" suddenly struck me as pretty funny in the circumstances, and also because old-fashioned shnorring is so much more humanly appealing than authorized, respectable, humanitarian "fund-raising," I began to laugh. "Gentlemen," I said, "fellows—" but the shovel-beard was already showing me, rather like a curtain dropping when the act is over, the back of his extensive black coat, and had already resumed firing his Yiddish at the seated old man. It hadn't taken all day for him to decide not to waste time on a cheap Jew like me.

Standing singly at the Wall, some rapidly swaying and rhythmically bobbing as they recited their prayers, others motionless but for the lightning flutter of their mouths, were seventeen of the world's twelve million Jews communing with the King of the Universe. To me it looked as though they were communing solely with the stones in whose crevices pigeons were roosting some twenty feet above their heads. I thought (as I am predisposed to think), "If there is a God who plays a role in our world, I will eat every hat in this town"—nonetheless, I couldn't help but be gripped by the sight of this rock-worship, exemplifying as it did to me the most awesomely retarded aspect of the human mind. Rock is just right, I thought: what on earth could be less responsive? Even the cloud drifting by overhead, Shuki's late father's "Jewish cloud," appeared less indifferent to our encompassed and uncertain existence. I think that I would have felt less detached from seventeen Jews who openly admitted that they *were* talking to rock than from these seventeen who imagined themselves telexing the Creator directly; had I known for sure it was rock and rock alone that they knew they were addressing, I might even have joined in. Kissing God's ass, Shuki had called it, with more distaste than I could muster. I was simply reminded of my lifelong disaffection from such rites.

I edged up to the Wall to get a better look, and from only a few feet away watched a man in an ordinary business suit, a middle-aged man with a monogrammed briefcase at his feet, conclude his prayers by placing two soft kisses upon the stone, kisses such as my own mother would lay upon my brow when I was a child home in bed with a fever. The fingertips of one hand remained in gentlest conjunction with the Wall even after he had lifted his lips from the last lingering kiss.

Of course, to be as tenderized by a block of stone as a mother is by her ailing child needn't really mean a thing. You can go around kissing all the walls in the world, and all the crosses, and the femurs and tibias of all the holy blessed martyrs ever butchered by the infidel, and back in your office be a son of bitch to the staff and at home a perfect prick to your family. Local history hardly argued that transcendence over ordinary human failings, let alone the really vicious proclivities, is likely to be expedited by pious deeds committed in Jerusalem. Nonetheless, at that moment, even I got a little carried away, and would have been willing to concede that what had just been enacted before me with such affecting sweetness might not be *entirely* inane. Then again I could have been wrong.

Nearby, an archway opened into a large cavernous vault where, through a floodlit grate in the stone floor, you could see that there was even more Wailing Wall below the ground than above—way back then was way down there. A hundred or so square feet, the entry to this chamber, were partitioned off into a smallish makeshift room that, except for the fire-blackened, roughly vaulted ceiling and the stones of the Second Temple Wall, looked something like the unprepossessing neighborhood synagogue where I had been enrolled for late-afternoon Hebrew classes at the age of ten. The large Torah ark might have been built as a woodwork project by a first-year shop class in vocational school—it was as unholy-looking as it could possibly be. Rows of storage shelves along the wall facing the ark were piled unevenly with a couple of hundred worn prayer books, and, randomly scattered about, were a dozen battered plastic chairs. But what reminded me most of my old Talmud Torah wasn't so much the similarity of the decor as the congregation. A chazan stood off in one corner, flanked by two very thin teenagers in Chasidic garb who chanted intermittently with great fervor while he intoned in a rough baritone wail—otherwise the worshippers seemed only marginally engaged by the liturgy. It was very much as I remembered things back on Schley Street in Newark: some of them kept turning around to see if anything of more piquancy might be developing elsewhere, while others looked every which way, as though for friends they were expecting to arrive. The remaining few, in a desultory way, seemed to be counting the house.

I was just easing myself in beside the bookshelves—so as to look on unobtrusively from the sidelines—when I was approached by a young Chasid, distinguished in this assemblage by the elegant fit of his long satin coat and the unblemished black sheen of a new velvet hat with a low crown and an imposing brim. His pallor was alarming, however, a skin tone a breath away from the morgue. The elongated fingers with which he was tapping my shoulder suggested something erotically creepy at one extreme and excruciatingly delicate at the other, the hand of the helpless maiden *and* of the lurid ghoul. He was inviting me, worldlessly, to take a book and join the minyan. When I whispered no, he replied, in hollow, accented English, "Come. We need you, mister."

I shook my head again just as the chazan, with a raw, wrenching wail that could well have been some terrible reprimand, pronounced "Adonoi," the name of the Lord.

Unfazed, the young Chasid repeated, "Come," and pointed beyond the partition to what looked more like an empty warehouse than a house of prayer, the sort of space that a smart New York entrepreneur would jump to convert to sauna, tennis courts, steam room, and swimming pool: The Wailing Wall Health and Racquet Club.

In there too were pious worshippers, seated with their prayer books only inches from the Wall. Leaning forward, their elbows on their knees, they reminded me of poor souls who'd been waiting all day in a welfare office or on an unemployment line. Low lozenge-like floodlights did not serve to make the place any cozier or more congenial. Religion couldn't come less adorned than this. These Jews needed nothing but that wall.

Collectively they emitted a faint murmur that sounded like bees at work—the bees genetically commandeered to pray for the hive.

Still patiently waiting at my side was the elegant young Chasid.

"I can't help you out," I whispered.

"Only a minute, mister."

You couldn't say he was insisting. In a way he didn't even seem to care. From the fixed look in his eye and the flat, forceless voice, I might even have concluded, in another context, that he was mentally a little deficient, but I was trying hard here to be a generous, tolerant cultural relativist—trying a hell of a lot harder than he was.

"Sorry," I said. "That's it."

"Where are you from? The States? You were bar mitzvah?"

I looked away.

"Come," he said.

"Please—enough."

"But you are a Jew who was bar mitzvah."

Here we go. One Jew is about to explain to another Jew that he is not the same kind of Jew that the first Jew is—the source, this situation, of several hundred thousand jokes, not to mention all the works of fiction. "I am not observant," I said. "I don't participate in prayer."

"Why do you come here?" But it was again as though he wasn't asking because he really cared. I was beginning to doubt that he fully understood his own English, let alone mine.

"To see the Old Temple Wall," I replied. "To see Jews who *do* participate in prayer. I'm a tourist."

"You had religious education?"

"None that you could take seriously."

"I pity you." So flatly stated that he might as well have been telling me the time.

"Yes, you feel sorry for me?"

"Secular don't know what they are living for."

"I can see how to you it might look that way."

"Secular are coming back. Jews worse than you."

"Really? How much worse?"

"I don't like to say even."

"What is it? Drugs? Sex? Money?"

"Worse. Come, mister. It'll be mitzvah, mister."

If I was correctly reading his persistence, my secularism represented to him nothing more than a slightly ridiculous mistake. It wasn't even worth getting excited about. That I wasn't pious was the result of some misunderstanding.

Even while I was making a stab at surmising what he thought, I realized that of course I could have no more idea of what was going on in his mind than he could have of what was going on in mine. I doubt that he even tried to figure out what was in mine.

"Leave me alone, okay?"

"Come," he said.

"Please, what's it to you whether I pray or not?" I didn't bother to tell him—because I didn't think it was my place to—that frankly I consider praying beneath my dignity. "Let me just stand quietly out of the way here and watch."

"Where in the States? Brooklyn? California?"

"Where are *you* from?"

"From? I am a Jew. Come."

"Look, I'm not criticizing your observance or your outfit or your appearance, I don't even mind your insinuations about my shortcomings—so why are you so offended by me?" Not that he appeared in the least offended, but I was trying to place our discussion on a higher plane.

"Mister, you are circumcised?"

"Do you want me to draw you a picture?"

"Your wife is a shiksa," he suddenly announced.

"That wasn't as hard to figure out as you like to make it seem," I said, but in the bloodless face there was neither amusement nor fellow-feeling—only a pair of unfazed eyes focused blandly on my ridiculous resistance. "All four of my wives have been shiksas," I told him.

"Why, mister?"

"That's the sort of Jew I am, Mac."

"Come," he said, motioning to indicate that it was time for me to stop being silly and to do as I was told.

"Look, get yourself another boy, all right?"

But because he couldn't completely follow what I was saying, or because he wanted to harass me and drive my sinfulness from this holy place, or because he wished to correct the little mistake of my having left the fold, or maybe because he simply needed another pious Jew in the world the way someone who is thirsty needs a glass of water, he wouldn't let me be. He just stood there saying "Come," and just as stubbornly I remained where I was. I wasn't committing any infraction of religious law, and refused either to do as he wished or to take flight as an intruder. I wondered if, in fact, I hadn't been right at the outset, and if he wasn't perhaps a little defective, though on further reflection, I saw it could well appear that the man without all his marbles had to be the one with four Gentile wives.

I was out of the cavern no more than a minute, taking a last look around the square at the minarets, the moon, the domes, the Wall, when someone was shouting at me, "It's you!"

Standing in my path was a tall young man with a thin, scraggly growth of beard who looked as though he had all he could do not to give me an enormous hug. He was panting hard, whether from excitement or from having run to catch me, I couldn't tell. And he was laughing, gusts of jubilant, euphoric laughter. I don't think I've ever before come across anyone so tickled to see me.

"It's really you! Here! Great! I've read all your books! You wrote about my family! The Lustigs of West Orange! In *Higher Education*! That's them! I'm your biggest admirer in the world! *Mixed Emotions* is your best book, better than *Carnovsky*! How come you're wearing a cardboard yarmulke? You should be wearing a beautiful, embroidered *kipa* like mine!"

He showed me the skullcap—held by a hair-clip to the top of his head—as though it had been designed for him by a Paris milliner. He was in his mid-twenties, a very tall, dark-haired, boyishly handsome young American in a gray cotton jogging suit, red running shoes, and the embroidered *kipa*. He danced in place even as he spoke, bouncing up on his toes, his arms jiggling like a boxer's before the bell to round one. I didn't know what to make of him.

"So you're a West Orange Lustig," I said.

"I'm Jimmy Ben-Joseph, Nathan! You look great! Those pictures on your books don't do you justice! You're a good-looking guy! You just got married! You have a new wife! Numero four! Let's hope this time it works!"

I began laughing myself. "Why do you know all this?"

"I'm your greatest fan. I know everything about you. I write too. I wrote the Five Books of Jimmy!"

"Haven't read them."

"They haven't been published yet. What are you doing here, Nathan?"

"Seeing the sights. What are *you* doing?"

"I was praying for you to come! I've been here at the Wailing Wall praying for you to come—and you came!"

"Okay, calm down, Jim."

I still couldn't tell whether he was half-crazy or completely crazy or just seething with energy, a manicky kid far away from home clowning around and having a good time. But since I was beginning to suspect that he might be a little of all three, I started back toward the low stone barrier and the table where I'd picked up my yarmulke. Beyond a gate across the square I could see several taxis waiting. I'd catch one back to the hotel. Intriguing as people like Jimmy can sometimes be, you usually get the best of them in the first three minutes. I've attracted them before.

He didn't exactly walk *with* me as I started off but, springing on the toes of his running shoes, proceeded backwards away from the Wall a couple of steps in front of me. "I'm a student at the Diaspora Yeshivah," he explained.

"Is there such a place?"

"You never heard of the Diaspora Yeshivah? It's over there on top of Mount Zion! On top of King David's mountain! You should come and visit! You should come and stay! The Diaspora Yeshivah is made for guys like you! You've been away from the Jewish people too long!"

"So they tell me. And how long do you plan to stay?"

"In Eretz Yisrael? The rest of my life!"

"And how long have you been here?"

"Twelve days!"

In the setting of his surprisingly small, delicately boned face, which was miniaturized further by a narrow frame of new whiskers, his eyes looked to be still in the throes of creation, precariously trembling bubbles at the tip of a fiery eruption.

"You're in quite a hyped-up state, Jimmy."

"You bet! I'm high as a kite on Jewish commitment!"

"Jimmy the Luftyid, the High-Flying Jew."

"And you? What are you, Nathan? Do you even know?"

"Me? From the look of things, a grounded Jew. Where'd you go to college, Jim?"

"Lafayette College. Easton, PA. Habitat of Larry Holmes. I studied acting and journalism. But now I'm back with the Jewish people! You shouldn't be estranged, Nathan! You'd make a great Jew!"

I was laughing again—so was he. "Tell me," I said, "are you here alone or with a girlfriend?"

"No, no girlfriend—Rabbi Greenspan is going to find me a wife. I want eight kids. Only a girl here will understand. I want a religious girl. Multiply and be fruitful!"

"Well, you've got a new name, a start on a new beard, Rabbi Greenspan is out looking for the right girl—and you're even living on top of King David's mountain. Sounds like you've got it made."

At the table by the barrier, where there was nobody any longer collecting for the poor, if there ever had been, I placed my yarmulke on top of the others piled in the box. When I extended my hand Jimmy took it, not to shake but to hold affectionately between the two of his.

"But where are you going? I'll walk you. I'll show you Mount Zion, Nathan. You can meet Rabbi Greenspan."

"I've already got my wife—numero four. I have to be off," I said, breaking away from him. "Shalom."

"But," he called after me, having resumed that vigorous, athletic bounding about on his toes, "do you even understand why I love and respect you the way I do?"

"Not really."

"Because of the way you write about baseball! Because of all you feel about baseball! That's the thing that's missing here. How can there be Jews without baseball? I ask Rabbi Greenspan but he don't comprendo. Not until there is baseball in Israel will Messiah come! Nathan, I want to play center field for the Jerusalem Giants!"

Waving goodbye—and thinking how relieved the Lustigs must be back in West Orange now that Jimmy is here in Eretz Yisrael and Rabbi Greenspan's to worry about—I called, "Go right ahead!"

"I will, I will if you say so, Nate!" and beneath the bright floodlights, he suddenly broke away and began to run—backpedaling first, then turning to his right, and with his delicate, freshly bearded face cocked as though to follow the flight of a ball struck off a Louisville Slugger from somewhere up in the old Jewish quarter, he was racing back toward the Wailing Wall without any regard for who or what might be in his way. And in a piercing voice that must have made him something of a find for the Lafayette College Drama Society, he began to shout, "Ben-Joseph is going back, back—it could be gone, it may be gone, this could be curtains for Jerusalem!" Then, with no more than three feet between him and the stones of the Wall—and the worshippers at the Wall—Jimmy leaped, sailing recklessly into the air, his long left arm extended high across his body and far above his embroidered *kipa*. "Ben-Joseph catches it!" he screamed, as along the length of the Wall a few of the worshippers turned indignantly to see what the disturbance was. Most, however, were so rapt in prayer that they didn't even bother looking up. "Ben-Joseph catches it!" he cried again, holding the imaginary ball in the pocket of his imaginary glove and jumping up and down in the very spot where he had marvelously brought it in. "The game is over!" Jimmy was shouting. "The season is over! The Jerusalem Giants win the pennant! The Jerusalem Giants win the pennant! Messiah is on his way!"

Friday morning after breakfast a taxi took me out to Agor, a forty-five-minute trip through the rock-clogged white hills southeast of Jerusalem. The driver, a Yemenite Jew who understood hardly any English, listened to the radio while he drove. Some twenty minutes beyond the city we passed an army roadblock manned by a couple of soldiers with rifles; it consisted of no more than a wooden sawhorse, and the taxi simply swerved around it in order to continue on. The soldiers didn't appear to be interested in stopping anyone, not even the Arabs with West Bank plates. One shirtless soldier was lying on the ground at the shoulder of the road taking the sun, while the other shirtless soldier tapped his feet in time to a portable radio playing under his roadside chair. Thinking back to the soldiers lolling in the square by the Wailing Wall, I said, for no reason, really, other than to hear my voice, "Easygoing army you have here."

The taxi driver nodded and took a billfold out of his back pocket. Fumbling with one hand, he found a picture to show me, a snapshot of a young soldier, kneeling and looking up at the camera, an intense-looking boy with large dark eyes and, from the evidence of his fresh and neatly pressed fatigues, the best-dressed member of the Israeli Defense Forces. He was holding his weapon like somebody who knew how to use it. "My son," the driver said.

"Very nice," I said.

"Dead."

"Oh. I'm sorry to hear that."

"Someone is shooting a bomb. He is no more there. No shoes, nothing."

"How old?" I asked, handing back the picture. "How old a boy was he?"

"Killed," he replied. "No good. I never see my son no more."

Farther on, a hundred yards back from the winding road, there was a Bedouin encampment tucked into the valley

between two rocky hills. The long, dark, brown tent, patched
with black squares, looked from that distance less like a habitation than like the wash, like a collection of large old rags draped
on poles to dry in the sun. Up ahead we had to stop to let a
little man with a mustache and a stick guide his sheep across
the road. He was a Bedouin herdsman wearing an old brown
suit, and if he reminded me of Charlie Chaplin, it wasn't only
because of his appearance but because of the seeming hopelessness of his pursuit—what his sheep would find to eat in
those dry hills was a mystery to me.

The taxi driver pointed to a settlement on the next hilltop.
It was Agor, Henry's home. Though there was a high wire
fence topped with curling barbed wire fronting the road, the
gate was wide open and the guard booth empty. The taxi turned
sharply in and drove up a dirt incline to a low corrugated-
metal shed. A man with a blowtorch was working at a long
table in the open air and from inside the shed I heard a hammer pounding.

I got out of the car. "I'm looking for Henry Zuckerman."

He waited to hear more.

"Henry Zuckerman," I repeated. "The American dentist."

"Hanoch?"

"Henry," I said. Then, "Sure—Hanoch."

I thought, "Hanoch Zuckerman, Maria Zuckerman—the
world is suddenly full of brand-new Zuckermans."

He pointed farther up the dirt road to a row of small, block-
like concrete buildings. That was all there was up there—a raw,
dry, dusty hill with nothing growing anywhere. The only person to be seen about was this man with a blowtorch, a short
muscular fellow wearing wire-rimmed glasses and a little knitted skullcap pinned to his crew cut. "There," he said brusquely.
"School is there."

A stout young woman in a pair of overalls and wearing a
large brown beret came bounding out of the shed. "Hi," she
called, smiling at me. "I'm Daphna. Who you looking for?"

She spoke with a New York accent and reminded me of the
hearty girls I used to see dancing to Hebrew folk songs at the
Hillel House when I was a freshman new to Chicago and went
around there at night, during the first lonely weeks, trying
to get laid. That was as close as I ever came to Zionism and

constituted the whole of my "Jewish commitment" at college. As for Henry, his commitment consisted of playing basketball at Cornell for his Jewish fraternity.

"Hanoch Zuckerman," I said to her.

"Hanoch is at the ulpan. The Hebrew school."

"Are you American?"

The question affronted her. "I'm Jewish," she replied.

"I understand. I was just guessing from your speech that you were born in New York."

"I'm Jewish by *birth*," she said and, clearly having had her fill of me, went back into the shed, where I heard the pounding of the hammer resume.

Henry/Hanoch was one of fifteen students gathered in a half-circle around their teacher's chair. The students were either seated or sprawled on the grassless ground and, like Henry, most of them were writing in exercise books while the teacher spoke in Hebrew. Henry was the oldest by at least fifteen years —probably a few years older even than his teacher. Except for him it looked like any collection of summer-school kids enjoying their lesson in the warm sun. The boys, half of whom were growing beards, were all in old jeans; most of the girls wore jeans too, except for two or three in cotton skirts and sleeveless blouses that showed how tan they were and that they'd stopped shaving under their arms. The minaret of an Arab village was clearly visible at the foot of the hill, yet Agor's ulpan in December could as easily have been Middlebury or Yale, a college language center in July.

Where the topmost buttons of Henry's work shirt were undone I could see the scar from his bypass surgery neatly dividing his strong chest. After nearly five months in the hot desert hills he looked not unlike the dead soldier son of my Yemenite taxi driver—more like that boy's brother now than mine. Seeing him so fit and darkly tanned and wearing shorts and sandals, I found myself recalling our boyhood summers at the rented cottage on the Jersey Shore, and how he used to follow after me, down to the beach, along the boardwalk at night—wherever I went with my friends, Henry would come tagging along as our adoring mascot. Strange to find the second-born son, whose sustaining passion was always to be the equal of those already grown up, back in school at the age of forty. Even stranger to come upon his classroom atop a hill from which you could see off to the Dead Sea, and beyond that to the creviced mountains of a desert kingdom.

I thought, "His daughter Ruthie's right—he's here to learn something and it isn't just Hebrew. I *have* done similar things, but he hasn't. Never before, and this is his chance. His first and maybe his last. Don't be his older brother—don't pick on him where he's vulnerable and where he'll always be vulnerable." "I admire him," Ruth had said, and right then so did I— in part because it all did seem a little bizarre, just as childish, probably, as Carol thought it was. Looking at him sitting, in his short pants, with all those kids and writing in his exercise book, I thought I really ought to turn around and go home. Ruthie was right about everything: he was giving up an awful lot to become this *tabula rasa*. Let him.

The teacher came over to shake my hand. "I'm Ronit." Like the woman called Daphna up at the shed, she wore a dark beret and spoke American English—a slender, rangy, good-looking woman in her early thirties, with a prominent, finely chiseled nose, a heavily freckled face, and intelligent dark eyes still confidently sparkling with the light of childhood precocity. I didn't this time make the mistake of saying to her that her accent was obviously that of a native-born American raised in New York City. I simply said hello.

"Hanoch told us last night that you were coming. You must stay and celebrate Shabbat. We have a room for you to sleep," Ronit said. "It won't be the King David Hotel, but I think you'll be comfortable. Take a chair, join us—it would be wonderful if you would talk to the class."

"I just want Henry to know I'm here. Don't let me interrupt. I'll wander around until the class is over."

From where he was seated in the semicircle of students, Henry thrust a hand up in the air. Smiling broadly, though still with a touch of that embarrassed shyness he could never quite outgrow, he said, "Hi," and that too reminded me of our childhood, of the times when as an upper-grade monitor in the hallways of the grammar school, I'd see him passing along with the other little kids to gym class or shop or the music room. "Hey," they'd whisper, "it's your brother," and Henry would sort of bark to me beneath his breath, "Hi," and then submerge instantaneously into the body of his class like a little animal dropping down a hole. He'd succeeded brilliantly, at his studies, at sports, eventually at his profession, and yet there was always this hobbling aversion to being nakedly conspicuous that thwarted an unquenchable dream, dating back to the bedtime reveries of earliest boyhood, not merely to excel but to be uniquely heroic. The admiration that had once made him so worshipful of my every utterance, and the resentment that came to discolor, even before I published *Carnovsky*, the natural and intimate affection springing from our childhood bond, seemed to have been nourished by a belief he continued to hold long after he was old enough to know better, that I was among the narcissistic elite blessed by an unambiguous capacity to preen in public and guiltlessly adore it.

"Please," Ronit said, laughing, "how often do we ensnare someone like you on a hilltop in Judea?" She motioned for one of the boys to pick up a wooden folding chair from the ground and set it up for me. "Anybody crazy enough to come to Agor," she told the students, "we put him right to work."

Taking my cue from her bantering tone, I looked at Henry and feigned a helpless shrug; he got the idea, and kiddingly called back, "We can take it if you can." For "we" I substituted "I," and so with the permission of the brother whose refuge this was—as much perhaps from his history with me as from everything else purged from his life—I took a seat facing the class.

The first question came from a boy whose accent was also American. Maybe they were all American-born Jews. "Do you know Hebrew?" he asked.

"All the Hebrew I know are the two words we began with in the Talmud Torah in 1943."

"What were the words?" Ronit asked.

" 'Yeled' was one."

" 'Boy.' Very good," she said. "And the other?"

" 'Yaldaw,' " I said.

The class laughed.

" 'Yaldaw,' " said Ronit, amused by me as well. "You say it like my Lithuanian grandfather. 'Yal*da*,' " she said, 'Girl.' 'Yalda.' "

" 'Yalda,' " I said.

"Now," she told the class, "that he says 'yalda' correctly, maybe he can begin to have a good time here."

They laughed again.

"Excuse me," said a boy upon whose chin were the first faint beginnings of a little beard, "but who are you? Who is this guy?" he asked Ronit. He was not in any way amused by the proceedings—a big boy, probably no more than seventeen, with a very young and unformed face but a body already as large and imposing as a construction worker's. From the evidence of his accent, he too was a New Yorker. He wore a yarmulke pinned to a head of heavy, dark, unruly hair.

"Tell him, please," Ronit said to me, "who you are."

I pointed to the one they called Hanoch. "His brother."

"So?" the boy said, implacable and getting angry. "Why should we be taking a break to hear him?"

A theatrical moan rose from the back of the class, while close by me a girl who was stretched on the ground with her pretty round face propped up between her hands said in a voice comically calculated to suggest that they'd all been together long enough for certain people to begin to drive others nuts, "He's a writer, Jerry, that's why."

"What are your impressions of Israel?" I was asked this by a girl with an English accent. If not all American, they were obviously all English-speaking.

Though I had been in the country less than twenty-four hours, strong first impressions had of course been formed, beginning with Shuki, impressions fostered by what little I'd heard from him about his massacred brother, his disheartened wife, and that patriotic young pianist of his serving in the army. And of course I hadn't forgotten the argument on the street with the Sephardi to whom Shuki Elchanan was nothing more than an Ashkenazi donkey; nor could I forget the Yemenite father who'd driven me to Agor, who, without any common language to express to me the depths of his grief, nonetheless, with Sacco-Vanzettian eloquence, had cryptically described the extinction of his soldier-son; nor had I forgotten the center fielder for the Jerusalem Giants hauling in a home-run blast up against the Wailing Wall—is Jimmy Ben-Joseph of

West Orange, New Jersey, just a freakish anomaly or *was* this place becoming, as Shuki claimed, something of an American-Jewish Australia? In short, dozens of conflicting, truncated impressions were already teasing to be understood, but the wisest course seemed to me to keep them to myself so long as I didn't begin to know what they added up to. I certainly saw no reason to affront anybody at Agor by telling of my unspiritual adventures at the Wailing Wall. That the Wailing Wall is what it is was of course clear even to me. I wouldn't think to deny the reality of that enigma of silent stoniness—but my encounters of the night before had left me feeling as though I'd had a walk-on role—as Diaspora straight man—in some local production of Jewish street theater, and I wasn't sure that such a description would be understood here in the spirit with which it was meant. "Impressions?" I said. "Just arrived really—don't have any yet."

"Were you a Zionist when you were young?"

"I never had enough Hebrew, Yiddish, or anti-Semitism to make me a Zionist when I was young."

"Is this your first trip?"

"No. I was here twenty years ago."

"And you never came back?"

The way that a couple of the students laughed at that question made me wonder if they might not themselves be considering packing up and going home.

"Things didn't lead me back."

"'Things.'" It was the large boy who'd indignantly asked why the class was listening to me. "You didn't want to come back."

"Israel wasn't at the center of my thoughts, no."

"But you must have gone to other countries that weren't at the center quote unquote."

I saw how this could become, if it hadn't already, an exchange even less satisfactory than my colloquy with the young Chasid at the Wailing Wall.

"How can a Jew," he asked, "make a single visit to the homeland of his people, and then never, not in twenty *years*—"

I cut him off before he really got going. "It's easy. I'm not the only one."

"I just wonder what's wrong with such a person, Zionist or not."

"Nothing," I said flatly.

"And it's of no concern to you that the whole world would as soon see this country obliterated?"

Though a few of the girls began to shift about, ill at ease with his aggressive questioning, Ronit leaned forward in her chair, eager to hear my answer. I wondered if there might not be a conspiracy operating here—between the boy and Ronit, and even perhaps including Hanoch.

"Is that what the world would like?" I asked, meanwhile thinking that even if there was no preconceived plot, should I agree to stay the night this could well turn out to be one of the least restful Sabbaths of my life.

"Who would shed a tear?" the boy replied. "Certainly not a Jew who in twenty years, despite the persistent danger to the Jewish people—"

"Look," I said, "admittedly I've never had the right caste spirit—I take your point about people like me. I'm not unfamiliar with such fanaticism."

This brought him to his feet, furiously pointing a finger. "Excuse *me*! What is *fanatical*? To put egoism before Zionism is what is fanatical! To put personal gain and personal pleasure before the survival of the Jewish people! *Who* is fanatical? The Diaspora Jew! All the evidence that the goyim give him and give him that the survival of the Jews couldn't matter to them less, and the Diaspora Jew believes they are friends! Believes that in their country he is safe and secure—an equal! What is fanatical is the Jew who never learns! The Jew oblivious to the Jewish state and the Jewish land and the survival of the Jewish people! *That* is the fanatic—fanatically ignorant, fanatically self-deluded, fanatically full of shame!"

I stood too, putting my back to Jerry and the class. "Henry and I are going for a walk," I said to Ronit. "I came out really to talk to him."

Her eyes remained just as bright as before with passionate curiosity. "But Jerry has had his say—you're entitled now to yours."

Was it overly suspicious to believe that the naïveté was

feigned and she was having me on? "I'll relinquish my rights," I said.

"He's young," she explained.

"Yes, but I'm not."

"But to the class your thoughts would be fascinating. Many are children of deeply assimilationist families. The egregious failure of American Jews, of most Jews of the world, to seize the opportunity to return to Zion is something that all of them are grappling with. If you—"

"I'd rather not."

"But just a few words about assimilation—"

I shook my head.

"But assimilation and intermarriage," she said, turning quite grave, "in America they are bringing about a second Holocaust —truly, a spiritual Holocaust is taking place there, and it is as deadly as any threat posed by the Arabs to the State of Israel. What Hitler couldn't achieve with Auschwitz, American Jews are doing to themselves in the bedroom. Sixty-five percent of American Jewish college students marry non-Jews—*sixty-five percent* lost forever to the Jewish people! First there was the hard extermination, now there is the soft extermination. And this is why young people are learning Hebrew at Agor—to escape the Jewish oblivion, the extinction of Jews that is coming in America, to escape those communities in your country where Jews are committing spiritual suicide."

"I see," was all I replied.

"You won't talk to them about this, for just a few minutes, just till it's time for their lunch?"

"I don't think my credentials qualify me to talk about this. I happen to be married to a non-Jew myself."

"All the better," she said, smiling warmly. "They can talk to *you*."

"No, no thanks. It's Henry who I'm here to talk to. I haven't seen him for months."

Ronit took hold of my arm as I started away, rather like a friend who hates to see you go. She seemed to like me, despite my faulty credentials; probably my brother acted as my advocate. "But you will stay for Shabbat," Ronit said. "My husband had to be in Bethlehem today, but he's looking forward to meeting you tonight. You and Hanoch are coming for dinner."

"We'll see how things go."

"No, no, you're coming. Henry must have told you—they have become great friends, your brother and my husband. They're very alike, two strong and dedicated men."

Her husband was Mordecai Lippman.

From the moment that we started along the path that sloped down the hill toward the two long unpaved streets that constituted Agor's residential quarter, Henry began making it clear that we weren't going to sit in the shade somewhere having a deep discussion about whether or not *he'd* done the right thing by seizing the opportunity to return to Zion. He was now nothing like as friendly as he'd seemed when I'd showed up in front of his class. Instead, as soon as we two were alone, he immediately turned querulous. He had no intention, he told me, of being reproved by me and wouldn't tolerate any attempt to investigate or challenge his motives. He'd talk about Agor, if I wanted to know what this place stood for, he'd talk about the settlement movement, its roots and ideology and what the settlers were determined to achieve, he'd talk about the changes in the country since Begin's coalition had taken charge, but as for the American-style psychiatric soul-searching in which my own heroes could wallow for pages on end, that was a form of exhibitionistic indulgence and childish self-dramatization that blessedly belonged to the "narcissistic past." The old life of non-historical personal problems seemed to him now embarrassingly, disgustingly, unspeakably puny.

Telling me all this, he had worked up more emotion than anything I'd said could possibly have inspired, especially as I had as yet said nothing. It was one of those speeches that people spend hours preparing and delivering while lying in bed unable to sleep. The smiles up at the ulpan had been for the crowd. This was the distrustful fellow I'd talked to on the phone the night before.

"Fine," I said. "No psychiatry."

Still on the offense, he said, "And don't condescend to me."

"Well, don't knock my wallowing heroes. Besides, I wouldn't say condescension has been my strong suit, not so far today. I myself wasn't even condescended to by that kid up in your class. I was mugged by the little prick in broad daylight."

"Forthright is the style out here—take it or leave it. And no shit, please, about my name."

"Relax. Anybody can call you anything you want, as far as I'm concerned."

"You *still* don't get it. The hell with *me*, forget *me*. *Me* is somebody *I* have forgotten. *Me* no longer exists out here. There isn't time for *me*, there isn't need of *me*—here Judea counts, not *me*!"

His plan was to ride over to Arab Hebron for lunch, only a twenty-minute drive if we followed the shortcut through the hills. We could use Lippman's car. Mordecai and four other settlers had gone off by truck to Bethlehem early that morning. In the last several weeks, disturbances had erupted there between some local Arabs and the Jews of a little settlement newly erected on a hillside outside the city. Two days earlier rocks had been thrown through the windshield of a passing school bus carrying the Jewish settlement's children, and settlement members from all over Judea and Samaria, organized and led by Mordecai Lippman, had gone to distribute leaflets in the Bethlehem market. If I hadn't been visiting, Henry was to have skipped his class and gone with them.

"What do the leaflets say?" I asked.

"They say, 'Why don't you people try living in peace with us, since we mean you no harm. Only a few among you are violent extremists. The rest are peace-loving people who believe, as we do, that Jew and Arab can live in harmony.' That's the general idea."

"The general idea sounds benign enough. What's it supposed to mean to the Arabs?"

"What it says—we intend them no harm."

Not me—we. That's where Henry's me had gone.

"We'll drive through the village—it's right down there. You'll see how the Arabs who want to can live in peace, side by side, only a couple of hundred yards away. They come up here and buy our eggs. The chickens that are too old to lay, we sell to them for pennies. This place could be a home for everybody. But if violence against Jewish schoolchildren continues, then steps will be taken to stop it. The army could move in there tomorrow, weed out the troublemakers, and the stone throwing would be over in five minutes. But they don't. They even throw stones at the soldiers. And when the soldier does nothing, you know what the Arabs think? They think you are a shmuck—and you *are* a shmuck. Any place else in the Middle East, you throw a stone at a soldier, and what does he do? He shoots you. But suddenly they discover in Bethlehem that you throw a stone at an Israeli soldier and he doesn't shoot you. He doesn't do anything. And that's where the trouble begins. Not because we are cruel, but because they have found out we are weak. There are things you have to do here that are not so nice. They don't respect niceness and they don't respect weakness. What the Arab respects is power."

Not me but we, not niceness but power.

I waited by the battered Ford that was parked on the dirt street outside the Lippman house, one of the cinder-block structures that had looked from the entry road like pillboxes or bunkers. Up close you couldn't quite believe that life within was very far from the embryonic stage of human development. Everything, including the load of topsoil deposited in a corner of each of the dry, stony yards, proclaimed a world of bare beginnings. Two, maybe even three of these little settlement dwellings could have been stored without difficulty in the basement of the sprawling house of cedar and glass built by Henry some years back on a wooded hillside in South Orange.

When he came out of Lippman's, it was with car keys in one hand and a pistol in the other. He tossed the pistol into the glove compartment and started the engine.

"I'm trying," I told him, "to take things in stride, but it's going to entail almost superhuman restraint not to make the sort of comment that's going to piss you off. Nonetheless, it's a little astonishing to be going off for a drive with you and a gun."

"I know. It's not how we were raised. But a gun isn't a bad idea driving down to Hebron. If you run into a demonstration, if they surround the car and start heaving rocks, at least you have some bargaining power. Look, you're going to see a lot of things that are going to astonish you. They astonish me. You know what astonishes me even more than what I've learned to do in five months here? What I learned to do in forty years there. To do and to be. I shudder when I remember everything I was. I look back and I can't believe it. It fills me with revulsion. It makes me want to hide my head when I think how I wound up."

"How was that?"

"You saw it, you were there. You *heard* it. What I risked my life for. What I had that operation for. *Who* I had it for. That skinny little kid in my office. That's what I was willing to die for. That's what I was *living* for."

"No, it was a part of living. Why not? Losing your potency at thirty-nine isn't an ordinary little experience. Life came down very hard on you."

"You don't understand. I'm talking about how *small* I was. I'm talking about my grotesque apology for a life."

It was several hours on, after we'd been through the alleyways of the Hebron market and up to the ancient olive trees by the graves of Hebron's Jewish martyrs, and then on to the burial ground of the Patriarchs, that I got him to expand a little on that grotesque life he'd abandoned. We were eating lunch on the open terrace of a small restaurant on the main road out of Hebron. The Arab family who ran the place couldn't have been more welcoming; indeed, the owner, who took our order in English, called Henry "Doctor" with considerable esteem. It was late by then and aside from a young Arab couple and their small child eating at a corner table nearby, the place was empty.

Henry, to make himself comfortable, draped his field jacket over the back of his chair, the pistol still in one pocket. That's where he'd been carrying it during our tour of Hebron. Shepherding me through the crowded market, he pointed out the abundance of fruits, vegetables, chickens, sweets, even while my mind remained on his pistol, and on Chekhov's famous dictum that a pistol hanging on the wall in Act One must eventually go off in Act Three. I wondered what act we were in, not to mention which play—domestic tragedy, historical epic, or just straight farce? I wasn't sure whether the pistol was strictly necessary or whether he was simply displaying, as drastically as he could, the distance he'd traveled from the powerless nice Jew that he'd been in America, this pistol his astounding symbol of the whole complex of choices with which he was ridding himself of that shame. "Here are the Arabs," he'd said in the marketplace, "and where is the yoke? Do you see a yoke across anyone's back? Do you see a soldier threatening anyone? You

don't see a soldier here at all. No, just a thriving Oriental bazaar.
And why is that? Because of the brutal military occupation?"

The only sign of the military I'd seen was a small installation
about a hundred yards down from the market, where Henry
had left the car. Inside the gates some Israeli soldiers were
kicking a soccer ball around an open area where their trucks
were parked, but as Henry said, there was no military presence
within the market, only Arab stallkeepers, Arab shoppers, scores
of small Arab children, some very unamicable-looking Arab
adolescents, lots of dust, several mules, some beggars, and Dr.
Victor Zuckerman's two sons, Nathan and Hanoch, the latter
packing a gun whose implications had begun obsessively to engage the former. What if who he shoots is me? What if that was
to be Act Three's awful surprise, the Zuckerman differences
ending in blood, as though our family were Agamemnon's?

At lunch I began with what couldn't be taken right off as a
remonstrance or a challenge, given his enthusiasm about the
antiquity of a wall that he'd wanted me to see at the Cave of
Machpelah. How holy, I asked, was that wall to him? "Suppose
it's all as you tell me," I said. "In Hebron Abraham pitched his
tent. In the cave of Machpelah he and Sarah were buried, and
after them Isaac, Jacob, and their wives. It's here that King
David reigned before he entered Jerusalem. What's any of it
got to do with you?"

"That's where the claim rests," he said. "That's *it*. It's no
accident, you know, that we're called Jews and this place is
called Judea—there may even be some relation between those
two things. We are Jews, this is Judea, and the heart of Judea is
Abraham's city, Hebron."

"That still leaves unexplained the riddle of Henry Zuckerman's identification with Abraham's city."

"You don't get it—this is where the Jews *began*, not in Tel
Aviv but here. If anything is territorialism, if anything is colo-
nialism, it's Tel Aviv, it's Haifa. *This* is Judaism, *this* is Zionism,
right here where we are eating our lunch!"

"In other words, it didn't all begin up that outside flight of
wooden stairs where Grandma and Grandpa lived on Hunterdon Street. It didn't begin with Grandma on her knees washing
the floors and Grandpa stinking of old cigars. Jews didn't begin
in Newark, after all."

"The famous gift for reductive satire."

"Is it? It might be that what you've developed over the last five months is something of a gift for exaggeration."

"I don't think that the part that the Jewish Bible has played in the history of the world owes much to me and my illusions."

"I was thinking more about the part you seem to have assigned yourself in the tribal epic. Do you pray too?"

"The subject's not under discussion."

"You do pray then."

Riled by my insistence, he asked, "What's wrong with prayer, is there something wrong with prayer?"

"When do you pray?"

"Before I go to sleep."

"What do you say?"

"What Jews have said for thousands of years. I say the Shema Yisrael."

"And in the morning you lay tefillin?"

"Maybe one day. I don't yet."

"And you observe the Sabbath."

"Look, I understand that this is all outside your element. I understand that hearing all this you feel nothing but the disdainful amusement of the fashionably 'objective,' postassimilated Jew. I realize that you're too 'enlightened' for God and that to you it's clearly all a joke."

"Don't be so sure what to me is a joke. If I happen to have questions I wouldn't mind answered, it's because six months ago I had a different brother."

"Living the life of Riley in New Jersey."

"Come on, Henry—there's no such thing as the life of Riley, in New Jersey or anywhere else. America is also a place where people die, where people fail, where life is interesting and tense, and hardly without conflict."

"But Riley's life was still whose mine was. In America the massacre of your brother's Judaism couldn't have been more complete."

" 'Massacre'? Where'd you pick up *that* word? You lived like everybody you knew. You accepted the social arrangement that existed."

"Only the arrangement that existed was completely abnormal."

Normal and abnormal—twenty-four hours in Israel and there was that distinction again.

"How did I even get that disease?" he asked me. "Five occluded coronary arteries in a man not even forty years old. What sort of stress do you think caused it? The stresses of a 'normal' life?"

"Carol for a wife, dentistry for a livelihood, South Orange for a home, well-behaved kids in good private schools—even the girlfriend on the side. If that's not normalcy, what is?"

"Only all for the goyim. Camouflaging behind goyish respectability every last Jewish marking. All of it from them, for them."

"Henry, I walk in Hebron and I see *them*—them with a vengeance. All I remember seeing around your place were other prosperous Jews like you, and none of them packing a gun."

"You bet: prosperous, comfortable, Hellenized Jews—galut Jews, bereft of any sort of context in which actually to be Jewish."

"And you think this is what made you sick? 'Hellenization'? It didn't seem to ruin Aristotle's life. What the hell does it even *mean?*"

"Hellenized—hedonized—egomaniazed. My whole *existence* was the sickness. I got off easy with just my heart. Diseased with self-distortion, self-contortion, diseased with self-disguise —up to my eyeballs in meaninglessness."

First it was the life of Riley, now it was nothing but a disease. "You felt all that?"

"Me? I was so conventionalized I never felt anything. Wendy. Perfect. Shtupping the dental assistant. My office blow job, the great overwhelming passion of a completely superficial life. Before that, even better—Basel. Classic. The Jewish male's idolatry—worship of the shiksa; dreaming of Switzerland with the beloved shiksa. The original Jewish dream of escape."

And as he spoke I was thinking, *the kind of stories that people turn life into, the kind of lives that people turn stories into.* Back in Jersey, he ascribes the stress that he was convinced had culminated in the coronary artery disease to the humiliating failure of nerve that had *prevented* him from leaving South

Orange for Basel; in Judea his diagnosis is just the opposite—here he attributes the disease to the insidious strain of Diaspora abnormality manifested most blatantly by "the original Jewish dream of escape . . . Switzerland with the beloved shiksa."

As we headed back to Agor to be there in time to prepare for Shabbat, I tried to figure out if Henry, who had hardly grown up in some New World Vienna, could actually have swallowed a self-analysis that to me seemed mostly platitudes gleaned from a turn-of-the-century handbook of Zionist ideology and having nothing whatsoever to do with him. When had Henry Zuckerman, raised securely among Newark's ambitious Jewish middle class, educated with hundreds of other smart Jewish kids at Cornell, married to a loyal and understanding woman just as secular a Jew as himself, ensconced in the sort of affluent, attractive Jewish suburb that he'd aspired to all his life, a Jew whose history of intimidation by anti-Semitism was simply nonexistent, when had he given a moment's serious consideration to the expectations of those he now derisively referred to as the "goyim"? If every project of importance in his former life had been undertaken to prove himself to someone dismayingly strong or subtly menacing, it certainly didn't look to me to have been to the omnipotent goy. Wasn't what he described as a revolt against the grotesque contortions of the spirit suffered by the galut, or exiled Jew, more likely an extremely belated rebellion against the idea of manhood imposed upon a dutiful and acquiescent child by a dogmatic, superconventional father? If so, then to overthrow all those long-standing paternal expectations, he had enslaved himself to a powerful Jewish authority far more rigidly subjugating than even the omnipresent Victor Zuckerman could ever have had the heart to be.

Though maybe the key to understanding his pistol was simpler than that. Of all he'd said over lunch, the only word that sounded to me with any real conviction was "Wendy." It was the second time in the few hours we'd been together that he'd alluded to his dental assistant, and in the same tone of disbelief, outraged that it was she for whom he'd risked his life. Maybe, I thought, he's doing penance. To be sure, learning Hebrew at an ulpan in the desert hills of Judea constituted a rather novel form of absolution from the sin of adultery, but then hadn't he also chosen to undergo the most hazardous surgery in order to keep Wendy in his life half an hour a day? Maybe this was no more than the appropriately preposterous denouement to their bizarrely overburdened drama. He seemed now to look upon his little dental assistant as some girl he'd known in Nineveh.

Or was the whole thing a cover-up for the act of abandonment? There's hardly a husband around anymore who is unable to say to his wife, when the end has come, "I'm afraid this is over, I've found true love." Only for my brother—and our father's best son—is there no possible way to walk out on a marriage in 1978 other than in the name of Judaism. I thought, "What's Jewish isn't coming here and becoming a Jew, Henry. What's Jewish is thinking that, in order to leave Carol, your only justification can be coming here." But I didn't say it, not with him packing that gun.

I was totally obsessed by that gun.

At the crest of the hill outside Agor, Henry pulled the car to the side of the road and we got out to take in the view. In the falling shadows, the little Arab village at the foot of the Jewish settlement looked nothing like so grim and barren as it had a few minutes before when we'd driven down its deserted main street. A desert sunset lent a little picturesqueness even to that cluster of faceless hovels. As for the larger landscape, you could see, particularly in this light, how someone might get the impression that it had been created in only seven days, unlike England, say, whose countryside appeared to be the creation of a God who'd had four or five chances to come back to perfect it and smooth it out, to tame and retame it until it was utterly habitable by every last man and beast. Judea was something that had been left just as it had been made; this could have passed for a piece of the moon to which the Jews had been sadistically exiled by their worst enemies rather than the place they passionately maintained was theirs and no one else's from time immemorial. What he finds in this landscape, I thought, is a correlative for the sense of himself he would now prefer to effect, the harsh and rugged pioneer with that pistol in his pocket.

Of course he could have been thinking much the same of

me, living now where everything is in its place, where the land-scape has been cultivated so long and the density of people is so great that nature will never reclaim either again, the ideal setting for a man in search of domestic order and of renewing his life at the midpoint on a satisfying scale. But in this unfin-ished, other-terrestrial landscape, attesting theatrically at sunset to Timeless Significance, one might well imagine self-renewal on the grandest scale of all, the legendary scale, the scale of mythic heroism.

I was about to say something conciliatory to him, some-thing about the spectacular austerity of this swelling sea of low rocky hills and the transforming influence it must exert on the soul of a newcomer, when Henry announced, "They laugh, the Arabs, because we build up here. In winter we're exposed to the wind and the cold, in summer to the heat and the sun, while down there they're protected from the worst of the weather. But," he said, gesturing toward the south, "whoever controls this hill controls the Negev." Then he was directing me to look west, to where the hills were now seventeen shades of blue and the sun was slipping away. "You can shell Jeru-salem from here," Henry told me, while I thought, Wendy, Carol, our father, the kids.

Lippman's very looks seemed to be making a point about colliding forces. His wide-set, almond-shaped, slightly protu-berant eyes, though a gentle milky blue, proclaimed, unmis-takably, STOP; his nose had been smashed at the bridge by something that—more likely, someone who—had tried and failed to stop *him*. Then there was the leg, mangled during the '67 war when, as a paratroop commander, he'd lost two-thirds of his company in the big battle to break into Jordanian Jeru-salem. (Henry had described to me, in impressive military de-tail, the logistics of the "Ammunition Hill" assault as we'd driven together back from Hebron.) Because of his injury Lippman walked as though intending with each step to take wing and fly at your head—then the torso slowly sank into the imperfect leg and he looked like a man who was melting. I thought of a circus tent about to cave in after the center pole has been withdrawn. I waited for the thud, but there he was again, advancing. He was a couple of inches under six feet, shorter than both Henry and me, yet his face had the sardonic mobility that comes of peering nobly down upon self-deceiving mankind from the high elevation of Hard Truth. When he'd returned in dusty combat boots and a filthy old field jacket from where the Jewish settlers organized by him had been distributing leaflets in the Bethlehem market, he looked as though he'd been under fire. A deliberate front-line appearance, I thought, except that he wore no battered helmet—or rather, the helmet protecting him was a skullcap, a little knitted *kipa* riding his hair like a tiny lifeboat. The hair was yet another drama, the kind of hair that your enemy uses to hold up your head after severing it from your carcass—a bunchy cabbage of disarranged plumage that was already a waxy, patriarchal white, though Lippman couldn't have been much over fifty. To me he looked, from the first moment I saw him, like some majestic Harpo Marx—Harpo as Hannibal, and as I was to discover, hardly mute.

The Sabbath table was prettily set with a lace-trimmed white cloth. It was at the kitchen end of a tiny living room lined to the ceiling with book-crammed shelves. There would be eight of us for dinner—Lippman's wife (and Henry's Hebrew teacher), Ronit, and the two Lippman children, a daughter eight and a son fifteen. The boy, already an ace marksman, was doing hundreds of push-ups twice a day in order to qualify for commando training when he entered the army in three years. Visiting from next door was the couple I'd already met up by the shed on my arrival, the metalworker, called Buki, and his wife, Daphna, the woman who'd informed me she was a Jew "by birth." Lastly, there were the two Zuckermans.

Lippman, having showered, was dressed for the occasion exactly like Henry and the metalworker, in a light, freshly laundered shirt whose lapels were ironed flat and a pair of dark cotton trousers. Ronit and Daphna, who'd been wearing berets earlier in the day, now had their hair bound up in white kerchiefs, and they too had gotten into fresh clothes for the Sabbath evening celebration. The men wore velvet skullcaps, mine presented to me ceremoniously by Lippman as I was stepping into the house.

While we were waiting for the guests from next door, and while Henry played like a kindly uncle with the Lippman kids,

Lippman found for me, among his books, the German translations of Dante, Shakespeare, and Cervantes that they'd carried
out of Berlin in the mid-thirties when his parents had fled with
him to Palestine. Even for an audience of one he held nothing
back, as shameless as some legendary courtroom litigator cunning in the use of booming crescendo and insinuating diminu-
endo to sway the emotions of the jury.

"When I was in a Nazi high school in Germany, could I
dream that I would sit one day with my family in my own
house in Judea and celebrate with them the Shabbat? Who
could have believed such a thing under the Nazis? Jews in
Judea? Jews once again in Hebron? They say the same in Tel
Aviv today. If Jews dare to go and settle in Judea, the earth will
stop rotating on its axis. But has the world stopped rotating on
its axis? Has it stopped revolving around the sun because Jews
have returned to live in their biblical homeland? *Nothing is impossible.* All the Jew must decide is what he wants—then he can
act and achieve it. He cannot be weary, he cannot be tired, he
cannot go around crying, 'Give the Arab anything, everything,
as long as there is no trouble.' Because the Arab will take what
is given and then continue the war, and instead of less trouble
there will be *more.* Hanoch tells me that you were in Tel Aviv.
Did you get a chance to talk to all the niceys and the goodies
there who want to be humane? Humane! They are embarrassed by the necessities of survival in a jungle. This is a jungle
with wolves all around! We have weak people here, soft people
here, who like to call their cowardice Jewish morality. Well,
only let them practice their Jewish morality and it will lead to
their destruction. And afterwards, I can assure you, the world
will decide that the Jews brought it on themselves *again*, are
guilty *again*—responsible for a second Holocaust the way they
were for the first. But there will be no more Holocausts. We
didn't come here to make graveyards. We have had enough
graveyards. We came here to live, not to die. Who did you talk
to in Tel Aviv?"

"A friend. Shuki Elchanan."

"Our great intellectual journalist. Of course. All for Western
consumption, every word this hack utters. Every word he
writes is poison. Whatever he writes, it's with one eye on Paris
and the other on New York. You know what my hope is, my

dream of dreams? That in this settlement, when we will have the resources, we will create, like Madame Tussaud's wax-works, a Museum of Jewish Self-Hatred. I'm only afraid we wouldn't have room for the statues of all the Shuki Elchanans who know only how to condemn the Israelis and to bleed for the Arab. They feel every pain, these people, they feel every pain and then they give in—not only do they want *not* to win, not only do they *prefer* to lose, above all they want to lose *the right way*, like Jews! A Jew who argues the Arab cause! Do you know what the Arab thinks of such people? They think, 'Is he crazy or is he a traitor? What's wrong with that man?' They think it is a sign of treachery, of betrayal—they think, 'Why should he argue our case, we don't argue his.' In Damascus not even a lunatic would dream of entertaining the Jewish posi-tion. Islam is not a civilization of doubt like the civilization of the Hellenized Jew. The Jew is always blaming himself for what happens in Cairo. He is blaming himself for what hap-pens in Baghdad. But in Baghdad, believe me, they do not blame themselves for what is happening in Jerusalem. Theirs is not a civilization of doubt—theirs is a civilization of *certainty*. Islam is not plagued by niceys and goodies who want to be sure they don't do the wrong thing. Islam wants one thing only: to *win*, to *triumph*, to obliterate the cancer of Israel from the body of the Islamic world. Mr. Shuki Elchanan is a man who lives in a Middle East that, most unfortunately, does not exist. Mr. Shuki Elchanan wants us to sign a piece of paper with the Arabs and give it *back*? No! History and reality will make the fu-ture and not pieces of paper! This is the Middle East, these are Arabs—paper is worthless. There is no paper deal to be made with the Arabs. Today in Bethlehem an Arab tells me that he dreams of Jaffa and how one day he will return. The Syrians have convinced him, just hang on, keep throwing stones at the Jewish school buses, and it'll *all* be yours someday—you'll go back to your village near Jaffa, and have everything else besides. That's what this man was telling me—he will go back, even if it takes him the two thousand years that it took the Jews. And you know what I tell *him*? I tell him, 'I respect the Arab who wants Jaffa.' I tell him, 'Don't give up your dream, dream of Jaffa, go ahead; and someday, if you have the power, even if there are a *hundred* pieces of paper, you will take it from me by force.' Because he is not so humane, this Arab who throws stones in Bethlehem, as your Mr. Shuki Elchanan who writes his columns in Tel Aviv for Western consumption. The Arab waits until he thinks you're weak, and then he tears up his paper and attacks. I'm sorry if I disappoint you, but I do not have such nice thoughts as Mr. Shuki Elchanan and all the Hellenized Jews in Tel Aviv with their European ideas. Mr. Shuki Elchanan is afraid to rule and to be a master. Why? Because he wants the approval of the goy. But I'm not interested in the goy's approval—I am interested in Jewish survival. And if the price I pay is a bad name, fine. We pay that anyway, and it's better than the price we usually pay in addition."

All this merely as appetizer to my Sabbath meal, and while proudly exhibiting to me, one by one, the treasured leather-bound masterpieces collected in Berlin by his grandfather, a celebrated philologist gassed at Auschwitz.

At the dinner table, in a resonant cantorial baritone, a rich pleasing voice that sounded trained and whose excellence wasn't entirely a surprise, Lippman began the little song to welcome the Sabbath queen, and then everyone joined in, except me. Vaguely I remembered the melody but found that thirty-five years on, the words had simply vanished. Henry seemed to have a special fondness for the Lippman boy, Yehuda; they grinned at each other while they sang, as though between them there were some joke about the song, the occasion, or even about my presence at the table. Many years back I had exchanged just such grins with Henry myself. As for the Lippmans' eight-year-old girl, she was so fascinated by the fact that I wasn't singing that her father had to wave a finger to get her to stop mumbling and make herself heard with everyone else.

My silence must, of course, have been inexplicable to her; but if she was wondering how Hanoch could have a brother like me, you can be sure that I was now even more confused by having a brother like Hanoch. I could not grasp this overnight change so against the grain of what I and everyone took to be the very essence of Henry's Henryness. Is there really something irreducibly Jewish that he's discovered in his own bedrock, or has he only developed, postoperatively, a taste for the ersatz in life? He undergoes a terrible operation to restore his potency and becomes as a result a full-fledged Jew; this guy has his chest ripped apart, and in a seven-hour operation, hooked up to a machine that does his breathing for him and pumps his blood, he has the vital lines to his heart replaced by veins drawn out of his leg, and subsequently he winds up in Israel. I don't get it. This all seems to give new meaning to the old Tin Pan Alley idea of recklessly toying with somebody's heart. What purpose is hidden in what he now calls "Jew"—or is "Jew" just something he now hides behind? He tells me that here he is essential, he belongs, he fits in—but isn't it more likely that what he has finally found is the unchallengeable means to escape his hedged-in life? Who hasn't been driven crazy by that temptation—yet how many pull it off like this? Not even Henry could, so long as he called his flight plan "Basel"—it's designating it "Judea" that's done the trick. If so, what inspirational nomenclature! Moses against the Egyptians, Judah Maccabee against the Greeks, Bar Kochba against the Romans, and now, in our era, Hanoch of Judea against Henry of Jersey!

And still not a word of remorse—not any word *at all*—about Carol or the kids. Amazing. Though he phones the children every Sunday, and expects them to fly over to visit him at Passover, he's given not a single sign to me that he's still in any way fettered by the sentiments of a husband and father. And about my new life in London, *my* renovation, of more than passing interest even to Shuki Elchanan, Henry has nothing to ask. He appears to have totally repudiated his life, all of us, and all he's been through, and anybody who does that, I thought, *must* be taken seriously. Not only do such people qualify as true converts but, for a while at least, they become criminals of a kind—to those they've abandoned, even to themselves, even perhaps to those with whom they've formed their new pact—and this true conversion can't be dismissed any more easily than it can be comprehended. Listening to his mentor's professional voice rising in song above the rest, I thought, "Whatever the tangle of motive in him, he certainly hasn't been drawn to nothing."

There was a second song, a melody more lyrical and poignant than the first, and the voice that dominated now was Ronit's, leading with her folksingerish, fervent soprano. Singing in the Sabbath, Ronit looked as contented with her lot as any woman could be, her eyes shining with love for a life free of Jewish cringing, deference, diplomacy, apprehension, alienation, self-pity, self-satire, self-mistrust, depression, clowning, bitterness, nervousness, inwardness, hypercriticalness, hypertouchiness, social anxiety, social assimilation—a way of life absolved, in short, of all the Jewish "abnormalities," those peculiarities of self-division whose traces remained imprinted in just about every engaging Jew I knew.

Lippman blessed the wine with Hebrew words familiar even to me, and as I sipped from my glass along with everyone else, I thought, "Can it be a *conscious* ploy? What if it isn't still more of that passionate, driving naïveté for which he has always shown such talent but a calculated and devilishly cynical act? What if Henry has signed on with the Jewish cause without believing a word? Could he have become that interesting?"

"And," Lippman said, lowering his glass and speaking in the smallest, soothing, most delicate voice, "that's it—the whole thing." He was addressing me. "There it is. The meaning of this country in a nutshell. This is a place where nobody has to apologize for wearing a little hat on his head and singing a couple of songs with his family and friends before he eats his Friday night meal. It's as simple as that."

Smiling at his smile, I said, "Is it?"

He pointed proudly to his handsome young wife. "Ask her. Ask Ronit. Her parents weren't even religious Jews. They were ethnic Jews and no more—probably, from what Hanoch tells me, like your family in New Jersey. Hers was in Pelham, but the same thing, I'm sure. Ronit didn't even know what religion was. But still nowhere she lived in America did she feel right. Pelham, Ann Arbor, Boston—it made no difference, she never felt right. Then, in '67, she heard on the radio there was a war, she got on a plane and she came to help. She worked in a hospital. She saw everything. The worst of it. When it was over she stayed. She came here and she felt right and she stayed. That's the whole story. They come and they see that there is no need to apologize anymore and they stay. Only the goody-goods need to be approved of by the goy, only the niceys who want people to say nice things about them in Paris and London and New York. To me it is incredible that there are still Jews, even here, even in the country where they are masters, who live for the goy to smile at them and tell them

that they are right. Sadat came here a little while back, you remember, and he was smiling, and they screamed with joy in
the streets, those Jews. My enemy is smiling at me! Our enemy
loves us after all! Oh, the Jew, the Jew, how he rushes to forgive! How he wants the goy to throw him just a little smile!
How desperately he wants that smile! Only the Arab is very
good at smiling and lying at the same time. He is also good at
throwing stones—so long as nobody stops him. But I will tell
you something, Mr. Nathan Zuckerman: if nobody else will
stop him, I will. And if the army doesn't like me to do it, let the
army come and fire on me. I have read Mr. Mahatma Gandhi
and Mr. Henry David Thoreau, and if the Jewish army wants
to fire upon a Jewish settler in biblical Judea while the Arab is
looking on, let him—let the Arab witness such Jewish craziness. If the government wants to act like the British, then we
will act like the Jews! We will practice civil disobedience and
proceed by illegal settlement, and let their Jewish army come
and stop us! I dare this Jewish government, I dare *any* Jewish
government, to try to evict us by force! As for the Arabs, I will
go back to Bethlehem every day—and I told this to their
leader, I told them *all*, and in their own tongue so they would
not fail to understand, so there will not be any doubt what my
intentions are: I will come here with my people, and I will
stand here with my people, *until the Arab stops throwing stones
at the Jew.* Because do not comfort yourself, Mr. Nathan Zuckerman from London, Newark, New York, and points west—
they are not throwing stones at Israelis. They are not throwing
stones at 'West Bank' lunatics. They are throwing stones at
Jews. Every stone is an anti-Semitic stone. That is why it must
stop!"

He paused dramatically for a response. I said only, "Good
luck," but those two syllables were enough to inspire an even
more impassioned aria.

"We don't *need* luck! *God* protects us! All we need is never
to give ground and God will see to the rest! We are God's instrument! We are building the Land of Israel! See this man?"
he said, pointing to the metalworker. "Buki lived in Haifa like
a king. Look at the car he drives—it's a Lancia! And yet he
comes with his wife to live with us. To build Israel! For the
love of the Land of Israel! We are not Jewish losers in love with

loss. We are people of hope! Tell me, when have Jews been so well off, even *with* all our problems? All we need is not to give ground, and if the army wants to fire on us, let them! We are not delicate roses—we are here to stay! Sure, in Tel Aviv, in the café, in the university, in the newspaper office, the nice, humane Jew can't *stand* it. Shall I tell you why? I think he is actually jealous of the losers. Look at how sad he looks, the loser, look at him sitting there losing, how helpless he looks, how *moving*. *I* should be the one who is moving because *I* am sad and hopeless and lost, not him—I am the one who loses, not him—how *dare* he steal my touching melancholy, my Jewish softness! But if this is a game that only one can win—and those are rules the Arabs have set, those are the rules established not by us but by *them—then somebody must lose*. And when he loses, it is not pretty—he loses *bitterly*. It is not *loss* if it is not bitter! Just ask us, we are the experts on the subject. The loser hates and is the virtuous one, and the winner wins and is wicked. Okay," he said lightly, a thoroughly reasonable man, "I accept it. Let us be wicked winners for the next two thousand years, and when the two thousand years are over, when it is 3978, we will take a vote on which we prefer. The Jew will democratically decide whether he wants to bear the injustice of winning or whether he prefers living again with the honor of losing. And whatever the majority wants, I too will agree, in 3978. But in the meantime, *we do not give ground!*"

"I am in Norway," the metalworker, Buki, said to me. "I go there on business. I am in Norway on business for my product and written on a wall I read, 'Down with Israel.' I think, 'What did Israel ever do to Norway?' I know Israel is a terrible country, but after all, there are countries even more terrible. There are so many terrible countries—why is this country the most terrible? Why don't you read on Norwegian walls, 'Down with Russia,' 'Down with Chile,' 'Down with Libya'? Because Hitler didn't murder six million Libyans? I am walking in Norway and I am thinking, 'If only he had.' Because then they would write on Norwegian walls, 'Down with Libya,' and leave Israel alone." His dark brown eyes, fixed upon mine, appeared to be set in his head crookedly because of a long jagged scar on his forehead. His English came haltingly, but with forceful fluency all the same, as though he had mastered the language in one large gulp just the day before. "Sir, why all over the world do they hate Menachem Begin?" he asked me. "Because of politics? In Bolivia, in China, in Scandinavia, what do they care about Begin's politics? They hate him because of his nose!"

Lippman cut in. "The demonization," he told me, "will never end. It started in the Middle Ages as the demonization of the Jew and now in our age it is the demonization of the Jewish state. But it is always the same, the Jew is always committing the crime. We don't accept Christ, we reject Mohammed, we commit ritual murder, we control white slavery, we wish through sexual intercourse to poison the Aryan bloodstream, and now we have really ruined everything, now we have perpetrated truly monstrous evil, the worst the world press has ever known, upon the innocent, peaceful, blameless Arab. The Jew is a problem. How wonderful for everybody it would be without us."

"And in America that will happen," Buki said to me. "Don't think it won't."

"What will happen?" I asked.

"In America there will be a great invasion—of Latinos, of Puerto Ricans, people fleeing poverty and the revolutions. And the white Christians will not like it. The white Christians will turn against the dirty foreigner. And when the white Christian turns against the dirty foreigner, the dirty foreigner he turns against first will be the Jew."

"We have no desire for such a catastrophe," Lippman explained. "We have seen enough catastrophe. But unless something momentous is done to stop it, this catastrophe too will occur: between the hammer of the pious white American Christian and the anvil of the dirty foreigner, the Jew in America will be crushed—if he is not slaughtered first by the blacks, the blacks in the ghettos who are already sharpening their knives."

I interrupted him. "And how do the blacks accomplish this slaughter?" I asked. "With or without the help of the federal government?"

"Don't worry," Lippman said, "the American goy will let them loose when the time is ripe. There is nothing the American goy would like better than a *Judenrein* United States. First," Lippman informed me, "they permit the resentful blacks to take all their hatred out on the Jews, and afterward they take care of the blacks. And without the nosy Jews around to complain that they are violating black civil rights. Thus will come the Great American Pogrom out of which American white purity will be restored. You think this is ludicrous, the ridiculous nightmare of a paranoid Jew? But I am not *only* a paranoid Jew. Remember: *Ich bin ein Berliner* as well. And not out of run-of-the-mill opportunism—not like your handsome, heroic, young President when he announced that he was one with them to all the jubilant ex-Nazis, before, unfortunately, he succumbed to *his* paranoid nightmare. I was born there, Mr. Nathan Zuckerman, born and educated among all the sane, precise, reasonable, logical, unparanoid German Jews who are now a mountain of ashes."

"I only pray," said Buki, "that the Jew senses in time that such a catastrophe is on its way. Because if he does, then the ships will come again. In America there are young religious people, even secular people like your brother, who are tired of purposeless living. Here in Judea there is a purpose and a meaning, so they come. Here there is a God who is present in our lives. But the mass of Jews in America, they will not come, never, unless there is a crisis. But whatever the crisis, however it begins, the ships will sail again, and we will not just be three million. Then we will be ten million and the situation will be a little corrected. Three million the Arabs think they can kill. But they cannot kill ten million so easily."

"And where," I asked all of them, "will you put ten million?"

Lippman's answer was ecstatic. "Judea! Samaria! Gaza! In the Land of Israel given by God to the Jewish people!"

"You really believe," I asked, "that this will happen? American Jews sailing by the millions to escape persecution resulting from a Hispanic invasion of the U.S.A.? Because of a black uprising, urged on and abetted by the white officials, to eliminate the Jews?"

"Not today," said Buki, "not tomorrow, but yes, I am afraid it will happen. If not for Hitler we would be ten million already. We would have the offspring of the six million. But Hitler succeeded. I only pray that the Jews will leave America before a second Hitler succeeds."

I turned to Henry, eating as silently as the two Lippman

children. "Is that what you felt living in America? That such a catastrophe is in the offing?"

"Well, no," he said shyly. "Not really . . . But what did I know? What did I see?"

"You weren't born in a bomb shelter," I replied impatiently. "You didn't make your life in a hole in the ground."

"Didn't I?" he said, flushing, "—don't be so sure," but then would say no more.

I realized that he was leaving me to them. I thought, Is this the role he has decided to play—the good Jew to my bad Jew? Well, if so, he's found the right supporting cast.

I said to Buki, "You describe the situation of the Jew in America as though we were living under a volcano. To me it seems you feel so strongly the need for so many million more Jews that you're inclined to imagine this mass emigration pretty unrealistically. When were you last in America?"

"Daphna was raised in New Rochelle," he said, motioning to his wife.

"And when you looked up in New Rochelle," I asked her, "you saw a volcano?"

Unlike Henry, she wasn't reluctant to have her say; she'd been waiting her turn, her eyes on me, ever since I'd silently sat there while they'd sung in the Sabbath. Hers was the only animus I felt. The others were educating a fool—she was confronting an enemy, like young Jerry, who'd given it to me at the ulpan that morning.

"Let me ask you a question," said Daphna, replying to mine. "You are a friend of Norman Mailer?"

"Both of us write books."

"Let me ask you a question about your colleague Mailer. Why is he so interested in murder and criminals and killing? When I was at Barnard, our English professor assigned those books to read—books by a Jew who cannot stop thinking about murder and criminals and killing. Sometimes when I think back to the innocence of that class and the idiotic nonsense that they said there, I think, Why didn't I ask, 'If this Jew is so exhilarated by violence, why doesn't he go to Israel?' Why doesn't he, Mr. Zuckerman? If he wants to understand the experience of killing, why doesn't he come here and be like my husband? My husband has killed people in four wars, but not because he thinks murder is an exciting idea. He thinks it is a horrible idea. It is not even an *idea*. He kills to protect a tiny country, to defend an embattled nation—he kills so that perhaps his children may grow up one day to lead a peaceful life. He does not have a brilliant genius's intellectually wicked adventures of killing imaginary people inside his head—he has a decent man's dreadful experience of killing real people in Sinai and in the Golan and on the Jordanian border! Not to gain personal fame by writing bestselling books but to prevent the destruction of Jewish people!"

"And what do you want to ask me?" I said.

"I am asking you why is this genius's sick Diaspora rage celebrated in *Time* magazine while our refusal to be obliterated by our enemies in our own homeland is called in the same magazine monstrous Jewish aggression! That's what I'm asking!"

"I'm not here on behalf of *Time* or anyone else. I'm visiting Henry."

"But you are not nobody," she sarcastically replied. "You are a famous novelist, too—a novelist, what's more, who has written *about* Jews."

"It would be hard to believe, sitting at this table, in this settlement, that there's anything else a novelist *could* write about," I said. "Look, imagining violence and the release of the brute, imagining the individuals engaged in it, doesn't necessitate embracing it. There's no retreat or hypocrisy in a writer who doesn't go out and do what he may have thought about doing in every gory, horrifying detail. The only retreat is retreating from what you know."

"So," said Lippman, "what you are telling us is that we are not so nice as you American-Jewish writers."

"That's not at all what I'm telling you."

"But it's true," he said, smiling.

"I'm telling you that to see fiction as Daphna does is to see it from a highly specialized point of view. I'm telling you that it isn't obligatory for a novelist to go around personally exhibiting his themes. I'm not talking about who's nicer—niceness is even more deadly in writers than it is in other people. I'm only responding to a very crude observation."

"Crude? Yes, that is true. We are not like the intellectual goodies and the humane niceys who have the galut mentality.

We are not polished people and we are terrible at the polite smile. All Daphna is saying is that we do not have the luxury you American-Jewish writers have of indulging in fantasies of violence and force. The Jew who drives the school bus past the Arabs throwing stones at his windscreen, he does not *dream* of violence, he *faces* violence, he *fights* violence. We do not *dream* about force—we *are* force. We are not afraid to rule in order to survive, and to put it again as unpalatably as possible, *we are not afraid to be masters.* We do not wish to crush the Arab—we simply will not allow him to crush *us.* Unlike the niceys and the goodies who live in Tel Aviv, I have no phobia of Arabs. I can live alongside him, and I do. I can even speak to him in his own tongue. But if he rolls a hand grenade into the house where my child is sleeping, I do not retaliate with a *fantasy* of violence of the kind everybody loves in the novels and the movies. I am not someone sitting in a cozy cinema; I am not someone playing a role in a Hollywood movie; I am not an American-Jewish novelist who steps back and from a distance appropriates the reality for his literary purposes. No! I am somebody who meets the enemy's real violence with my real violence, and I don't worry about the approval of *Time* magazine. The journalists, you know, got tired of the Jew making the desert bloom; it became *boring* to them. They got *tired* of the Jews being attacked by surprise and still winning all the wars. That too became *boring.* They prefer now the greedy, grasping Jew who oversteps his bounds—the Arab as Noble Savage versus the degenerate, colonialist, capitalist Jew. Now the journalist gets excited when the Arab terrorist takes him to his refugee camp and, displaying the gracious Arab hospitality, graciously pours him a cup of coffee with all the freedom fighters looking on—he thinks he is living dangerously drinking coffee with a gracious revolutionary who flashes his black eyes at him, and drinks his coffee with him, and assures him that his brave guerrilla heroes will drive the thieving Zionists into the sea. Much more thrilling than drinking borscht with a big-nosed Jew."

"Bad Jews," said Daphna, "make better copy. But I don't have to tell that to Nathan Zuckerman and Norman Mailer. Bad Jews sell newspapers just the way they sell books."

She's a honey, I thought, but ignored her, leaving Mailer

to protect Mailer and figuring that I'd already sufficiently defended myself on that issue elsewhere.

"Tell me," Lippman said, "can the Jew do *anything* that doesn't stink to high heaven of his Jewishness? There are the goyim to whom we stink because they look down on us, and there are the goyim to whom we stink because they look up to us. Then there are the goyim who look both down *and* up at us—they are *really* angry. There is no end to it. First it was Jewish clannishness that was repellent, then what was preposterous was the ridiculous phenomenon of Jewish assimilation, now it is Jewish independence that is unacceptable and unjustified. First it was Jewish passivity that was disgusting, the meek Jew, the accommodating Jew, the Jew who walked like a sheep to his own slaughter—now what is worse than disgusting, outright *wicked*, is Jewish strength and militancy. First it was the Jewish sickliness that was abhorrent to all the robust Aryans, frail Jewish men with weak Jewish bodies lending money and studying books—now what is disgusting are strong Jewish men who know how to use force and are not afraid of power. First it was homeless Jewish cosmopolites that were strange and alien and not to be trusted—now what is alien are Jews with the arrogance to believe that they can determine their destiny like anybody else in a homeland of their own. Look, the Arab can remain here and I can remain here and together we can live in harmony. He can have any experience he likes, live here however he chooses and have everything he desires— except for the experience of statehood. If he wants that, if he cannot endure without that, then he can move to an Arab state and have the experience of statehood there. There are fifteen Arab states for him to pick from, most of them not even an hour away by car. The Arab homeland is vast, it is enormous, while the State of Israel is no more than a speck on the map of the world. You can put the State of Israel *seven times* into the state of Illinois, but it is the only place on this entire planet where a *Jew* can have the experience of statehood, and that is why *we do not give ground!*"

Dinner was over.

Henry guided me along one of their two long residential streets to where I was to sleep, the house of a settlement couple who had gone to spend the Sabbath in Jerusalem with family. Down in the Arab village a few lights were still burning, and on a distant hill, like an unblinking red eye, something that would once have been understood here as auguring the wrath of Almighty God, was the steady radar beacon of a missile-launching site. One of the missiles, heroically angled in firing position, was undisguised and plainly visible when we'd driven by on our way to Hebron. "The next war," Henry had said, pointing to the base up on the hilltop, "will take five minutes." The Israeli missile we saw was aimed at downtown Damascus to dissuade the Syrians, he told me, from launching their missile targeted for downtown Haifa. Except for that red omen, the distant blackness was so vast that I thought of Agor as a minute, floodlit earth-colony, the vanguard of a brave new Jewish civilization evolving in outer space, with Tel Aviv and all the decadent niceys and goodies as far off as the dimmest star.

If I had nothing to say to Henry right off it was because, following Lippman's seminar, language didn't really seem my domain any longer. I wasn't exactly a stranger to disputation, but never in my life had I felt so enclosed by a world so contentious, where the argument is enormous and constant and everything turns out to be pro or con, positions taken, positions argued, and everything italicized by indignation and rage.

Nor had my word-whipping ended with dinner. For two hours more, while I sat squeezed in beside Lippman's German editions of the European masterpieces and was graciously served tea and cake by contented Ronit, Lippman continued to flog away. I tried to ascertain whether his rhetoric wasn't perhaps being fomented a little by my questionable position among the Jews—by my reputedly equivocal position *about* Jews, which Daphna had indignantly alluded to—or whether he was deliberately playing it a bit broader at this performance to give me a taste of what had confounded my brother, particularly if I had any idea of abducting back into the Diaspora his prize dental surgeon, a paragon of worldly, assimilationist success, for whom he and the Deity had other plans. From time to time I'd thought, "Fuck it, Zuckerman, why don't you say what you think—all these bastards are saying what *they* think." But my way of handling Lippman had been by being practically mute. If that's handling. After dinner I may have looked to him as though I was sitting there in his living room saving myself up like some noble silent person, but the simple truth is I was outclassed.

Henry had nothing to say either. At first I thought it was because Lippman, along with Buki and Daphna, had left him feeling vindicated and without any inclination to soften the blow. But then I wondered if my presence might not have forced him, maybe for the first time since succumbing to Lippman's conviction, to evaluate his bulldozing mentor from a perspective somewhat alien to Agor's ethos. That might even have been why he'd clammed up like a child when I'd turned to ask if *he* had been living under a volcano in the U.S.A. Perhaps by then he was quietly wondering about what Muhammad Ali confessed had crossed the mind of even a man as courageous as he in the thirteenth round of that terrible third fight with Frazier: "What am I doing here?"

While we walked the unpaved settlement street, as alone together as Neil Armstrong and Buzz Aldrin up there planting their toy flag in the lunar dust, it occurred to me that Henry might have been wanting me to take him home from the moment I'd phoned from Jerusalem, that he had seriously lost his way but couldn't face the humiliation of admitting that to someone whose admiration had meant nearly as much to him once as the blessing he'd struggled to extract from our father. Instead (perhaps) he'd had to buck himself up by bravely thinking something along these lines: "Let it be this way then, the lost way. Life is the adventure of losing your way—and it's about time I found out!"

Not that I thought of that as contemplating one's burden overdramatically; certainly a life of writing books is a trying adventure in which you cannot find out where you *are* unless you lose your way. Losing his way may actually have been the vital need that Henry had been fumbling toward during his recuperation, when he'd spoken tearfully of something unnameable, some unmistakable choice to which he was maddeningly blind, an act both wrenching and utterly self-apparent that, once he'd discovered it, would deliver him from his baffling depression. If so, then it wasn't *roots* that he had unearthed sitting on the sunlit window-sill of that cheder in Mea She'arim; it wasn't his unbreakable bond to a traditional European Jewish life that he'd heard in the chanting of those Orthodox children clamorously memorizing their lessons—it was his opportunity to be *uprooted*, to depart from the path that had been posted with his name the day he was born, and in the disguise of a Jew to cunningly defect. Israel instead of Jersey, Zionism instead of Wendy, assuring that he'd never again be bound to the actual in the old, suffocating, self-strangulating way.

What if Carol had it right and Henry was crazy? No crazier than Ben-Joseph, the author of the Five Books of Jimmy, but not significantly less so either. If his decision was to be seen from all sides, then the possibility that he had, in Carol's phrase, "flipped out" also had to be considered. Perhaps he'd never entirely recovered from the hysterical collapse precipitated by the prospect of a lifetime of drug-induced impotence. It might even be the resuscitated potency that he was really escaping, fearful of some punishing new calamity that might succeed this time in destroying him completely were he to dare ever again to look for salvation in something so antisocial as his own erection. He's in crazy flight, I thought, from the folly of sex, from the intolerable disorder of virile pursuits and the indignities of secrecy and betrayal, from the enlivening anarchy that overtakes anyone who even sparingly abandons himself to uncensored desire. Here in Abraham's bosom, far away from his wife and kids, he can be a model husband again, or maybe just a model boy.

The truth is that despite my persistent effort I still didn't know, at the end of the day, how to understand my brother's relationship to Agor and to his friends there, ideologically wired to see every Jew not merely as a potential Israeli but as the foreordained victim of a horrendous, impending anti-Semitic catastrophe should they try living normally anywhere else. Momentarily I gave up searching for some appropriate set of motives that would make this metamorphosis look to me less implausible and like something other than self-travesty. Instead, I began to remember the last time that we had been alone together in a place as black as Agor was at eleven o'clock at night—I was remembering way back to the early forties, before my father bought the one-family house up from the park, when we were still small boys sharing a bedroom at the back of the Lyons Avenue flat, and would lie in the dark, our

bodies no farther apart than they were descending this settlement street, our only light shining from behind the dial of the
Emerson radio on the small night table between the beds. I
was remembering how, whenever the door creaked open at the
beginning of another ghoulish episode of "Inner Sanctum,"
Henry would fly out from beneath his blanket and beg to be
allowed to come over with me. And when, after feigning indifference to his childish cowardice, I lifted my covers and invited
him to jump in, could two kids have been closer or any more
contented? "Lippman," I should have said, when we'd shaken
hands for the night at his door, "even if everything you've told
me is a hundred percent true, the fact remains that in our family the collective memory doesn't go back to the golden calf
and the burning bush, but to 'Duffy's Tavern' and 'Can You
Top This?' Maybe the Jews begin with Judea, but Henry
doesn't and he never will. He begins with WJZ and WOR,
with double features at the Roosevelt on Saturday afternoons
and Sunday doubleheaders at Ruppert Stadium watching the
Newark Bears. Not nearly as epical, but there you are. Why
don't you let my brother go?"

Only what if he genuinely didn't want to go? And did I even
want him to want to? Wasn't it just liberal sentimentality—
wasn't I really the *worst* nicey and goody—to prefer that I had
a rational brother who had emigrated to Israel for the right
reasons, and met the right people, and that I had come away
from our meeting having seen him doing and thinking all the
right things? If not sentimental, it was surely unprofessional.
For observed solely from the novelist's point of view, this was
far and away Henry's most provocative incarnation, if not exactly the most convincing—that is, it was the most eminently
exploitable by me. My motives too must be taken into account. I wasn't there *just* as his brother.

"You haven't mentioned the children," I said as we were
nearing the last house on the road.

His reply was quick and defensive. "What about them?"

"Well, you seem to have adopted a cavalier attitude toward
them that's more appropriate to my reputation than to yours."

"Look, don't pull that on me—you certainly *aren't* the one
who's going to talk to me about my children. They're coming

here Passover—that's all arranged. They're going to see this place and they're going to love it—and then we'll go from there."

"You think they'll decide to live here too?"

"I told you to get off my ass. You've had three marriages and as far as I know flushed all your children down the toilet."

"Maybe I did and maybe I didn't, but you don't have to be a father to ask the right question. When did your children cease having any meaning to you?"

This made him still angrier. "Who said they had?"

"You told me in Hebron about your old life—'up to my eyeballs in meaninglessness.' I started wondering about your kids—about how three children can be left out of the account when a father is talking about whether life is meaningful. I'm not trying to make you feel guilty—I'm only trying to find out if you really have thought this whole thing through."

"Of course I have—a thousand times a day! Of *course* I miss them! But they're coming at Passover, and they're going to see what I'm doing here and what it's all about, and yes, who knows, they may even see where they belong!"

"Ruthie phoned me before I left London," I said.

"She did?"

"She knew I was coming to see you. She wanted me to tell you something."

"I speak to her every Sunday—what's the matter?"

"Her mother's there when you speak to her on Sunday, and she feels she can't say everything. She's a smart girl, Henry—at thirteen she's a grown-up and not a child. She said, 'He's out there to learn. He's trying to find something out. He's not too old to learn and I think he has the right.'"

Henry didn't reply at first, and when he did he was crying. "Is that what she said?"

"She said, 'I'm confused without my father.'"

"Well," he replied, desperate suddenly, and like a boy of ten, "I'm confused without *them*."

"I thought you might be. I just wanted to give you the message."

"Well, thanks," he said, "thanks."

Henry pushed open the unlocked door and turned on the

lights of a small, square, cinder-block building laid out exactly like the Lippmans', though done up with far more religio-nationalistic verve. The living room of this house was dominated not by books but by a pair of outsized expressionistic paintings, portraits of two aged and, to me, unidentifiable biblical figures, either prophets or patriarchs. There was a large fabric-hanging pinned to one wall, and rows of shelves along another, jammed with tiny clay pots and bits of stone. The ancient earthenware had been collected by the husband, an archaeologist at Hebrew University, and the fabric stamped with the Oriental motif was designed by the wife, who worked for a small textile printing company in an older settlement nearby. The paintings, thickly encrusted with bright oranges and bloody reds and executed with violent brushstrokes, were the work of a well-known settlement artist, one of whose watercolors of the Jerusalem camel market Henry had bought to send home to the kids. For Henry's sake I stood in front of the paintings for several minutes demonstrating more enthusiasm than I felt. His own enthusiasm may well have been genuine and yet the art-appreciation talk about the circular composition struck me as entirely artificial. He seemed all at once to be working much too hard to convince me that I was absolutely wrong if I suspected that the euphoria of the adventure had begun to flag.

Only a few feet of corridor separated the living room from a bedroom smaller even than the one we'd shared as small boys. Two beds were squeezed into it, though not a "set" fitted out like ours with maple headboards and footboards whose notches and curves we used to pretend were the defensive walls of a cavalry fort besieged by Apaches—these were more like folding cots drawn up side by side. He flipped a light on to show me the toilet and then said he'd see me in the morning. He would be sleeping up the hill in a dormitory room with the young men who were his fellow students.

"Why not a night away from the delights of communal living? Sleep here."

"I'll be going back," he replied.

In the living room I said, "Henry, sit down."

"For a second," but when he dropped onto the sofa beneath the paintings he looked as though he were a lost child—one of

his own, in fact—a child waiting on a police-station bench for
somebody he loved to come and claim him, while at the same
time feeling four times as old and, if it was possible, twice as
tormented as the impastoed sage above his head, whose own
hopes for Jewish renewal and ethical transformation appeared
to have been smashed by something the size of a train.

Since I am not without affection for him, and never will be,
the effect of this melancholy sight was to make me want to
rush to assure him that he *hadn't* made a stupid mistake—if
anything the stupid mistake had been mine, thinking this was
any of my business and making him vulnerable to every uncertainty. The last thing he needs, I thought, is to be dwarfed by
yet another personality bigger than his own. That's been the
story of his life. Why not lay off and give him the benefit of the
doubt? He left what he couldn't stand anymore. He understood, "The imperative is now—do it now!" and came here.
That's all there is to it. Let him call it a high moral mission if
he likes the sound of that. He wants out of nowhere to have an
elevated goal—so let him. Russian literature is replete with just
such avid souls and their bizarre, heroic longings, probably
more of them in Russian literature than in life. Fine—let him
be full to the brim with Myshkin motives. And if it *is* all only a
wild-goose chase, that's the pathos of his situation and has
nothing to do with me . . . Yet what if he desperately wants
out of Agor and to be back with the kids, and yes, even back
with his wife? What if he wants this tremendous aggression of
his, released by Agor, once again walled in by the old pieties
and habits? What if he realizes that Ruthie alone is probably
more "meaningful" than anything he'll ever find in Israel—
what if he's seen how hopelessly overcommitted he is to what
he can't begin to be? Even assertive, even packing that pistol,
even with the best of Lippman bled into his veins, he seemed
to me far more trapped than he did in New Jersey, someone
utterly swamped and overcome.

I'd begun my visit telling myself, "Don't pick on him where
he's vulnerable and where he'll always be vulnerable." But when
vulnerability was everywhere, what was I to do? It was awfully
late in the day to try to start shutting up. These boys are
brothers, I thought, about as unlike as brothers come, but
each has taken the other's measure and been measured against

the other for so long that it's unthinkable that either could even learn to remain unconcerned by the judgment his counterpart embodies. These two men are boys who are brothers—these two boys are brothers who are men—these brothers are men who are boys—therefore the discrepancies are irreconcilable: the challenge is there merely in their being.

"So that was your crowd," I said, sitting down across from him.

He answered solemnly, already protecting himself from what I might say. "Those are some of the people here, yes."

"His opponents must find Lippman a formidable foe."

"They do."

"What draws *you* to him?" I asked, wondering if he might not answer, "The man is the embodiment of potency." Because wasn't it precisely that?

"What's wrong with him?" he replied.

"I didn't say anything was. The question isn't what I think of Lippman—it's what I think of your fascination with him. I'm only asking about his hold on you."

"Why do I admire him? Because I believe he's right."

"About what?"

"Right in what he advocates for Israel and right in the assessment he makes of how to achieve it."

"That may be, for all I know, but tell me, who does he remind you of?" I asked. "Anyone we know?"

"Oh, no, please, no—save the psychoanalysis for the great American public." Wearily he said, "Spare me."

"Well, that's the way it sticks in *my* mind. Strip away the aggressive bully, strip away the hambone actor and the compulsive talker, and we could have been back at the kitchen table in Newark, with Dad lecturing us on the historical struggle between the goy and the Jew."

"Tell me something, is it at all possible, at least outside of those books, for you to have a frame of reference slightly larger than the kitchen table in Newark?"

"The kitchen table in Newark happens to be the source of your Jewish memories, Henry—this is the stuff we were raised on. It *is* Dad—though this time round without the doubts, without the hidden deference to the goy and the fear of goyish mockery. It's Dad, but the dream-Dad, supersized, raised to the hundredth power. Best of all is the permission Lippman gives not to be so nice. That must come as a relief after all these years—to be a good Jewish son and *not* nice, to be a rough-neck *and* a Jew. Now that's having everything. We didn't have Jews quite like that in our neighborhood. The tough Jews we used to meet at weddings and bar mitzvahs were mostly fat guys in the produce line, so I can see the appeal, but aren't you overdoing just a bit all the justifiable aggression?"

"Why is it that all my life you've trivialized everything I do? Why don't you psychoanalyze that? I wonder why my aspirations can't ever be as valid as yours."

"I'm sorry, but being skeptical of revolvers is in my nature—as skeptical of revolvers as of the ideologues who wield them."

"Lucky you. Fortunate you. Righteous you. *Humane* you. You're skeptical of just about everything."

"Henry, when are you going to stop being an apprentice fanatic and start practicing dentistry again?"

"I ought to punch you in the fucking nose for that."

"Why don't you blow my brains out with your gun?" I asked, now that he was unarmed. "That shouldn't be too hard, seeing that you're conflict-free and untainted by doubt. Look, I'm all for authenticity, but it can't begin to hold a candle to the human gift for playacting. That may be the only authentic thing that we *ever* do."

"I always have the sensation speaking to you that I'm becoming progressively sillier and more ridiculous—why do you think that is, Nathan?"

"Is that so? Well, it's fortunate then that we haven't had to speak very often and were able to go our different ways."

"It would simply never occur to you, *never*, to praise or appreciate anything I've done. Why do you think that is, Nathan?"

"But it's not the case. I think what you've done is colossal. I'm not sweeping that aside. An exchange of existences like this—it's like after a great war, the exchange of prisoners. I don't minimize the scale of this thing. I wouldn't be here if I did. You've tried like hell not to let on, but I also see what it's costing you—of course you're paying a steep price, particularly where the kids are concerned. It's indisputable that you've registered a powerful objection against the way you once lived.

I don't make light of that, it's all I've thought about since I laid eyes on you. I've only been asking if in order to change some things, you had to change *everything*. I'm talking about what the missile engineers call 'escape velocity'—the trick is to manage to leave the atmosphere without overshooting your target."

"Look—" he said, and jumped up suddenly as though to go for my throat, "—you're a very intelligent man, Nathan, you're very subtle, but you have one large defect—the only world that exists for you is the world of psychology. That's *your* revolver. Aim and fire—and you've been firing it at me all my life. Henry is doing *this* because he wants to please Momma and Poppa, Henry is doing *this* because he wants to please Carol—or displease Carol, or displease Momma, or displease Poppa. On and on and on it goes. It's never Henry as an autonomous being, it's always Henry on the brink of being a cliché—my brother the stereotype. And maybe that was once even so, maybe I *was* a man who kept dropping into the stereotype, maybe that accounts for a lot of the unhappiness that I felt back home. Probably you think that the ways I choose to 'rebel' are only stereotypical. But unfortunately for you I'm *not* someone who's only his simple, silly motives. All my life you've been right on top, like a guy guarding me in a basketball game. Won't let me take one lousy shot. Everything I throw up you block. There's always the explanation that winds up belittling me. Crawling all over me with your fucking thoughts. Everything I do is predictable, everything I do *lacks depth*, certainly compared to what *you* do. 'You're only taking that shot, Henry, because you want to score.' Ingenious! But let me tell you something—you can't explain away what I've done by motives any more than I can explain away what you've done. Beyond all your profundities, beyond the Freudian lock you put on every single person's life, there is another world, a larger world, a world of ideology, of politics, of history—a world of things larger than the kitchen table! You were in it tonight: a world defined by *action*, by *power*, where how you wanted to please Momma and Poppa *simply doesn't matter*! All you see is escaping Momma, escaping Poppa—why don't you see what I've escaped *into*? *Everybody* escapes—our grandparents came to America, were they escaping their mothers and fathers? They were escaping history! Here they're *making* history! There's a world outside the Oedipal swamp, Nathan, where what matters isn't what made you do it *but what it is you do*—not what decadent Jews like you think but what committed Jews like the people here *do*! Jews who aren't in it for laughs, Jews that have something more to go on than their hilarious inner landscape! Here they have an *outer* landscape, a nation, a world! This isn't a hollow intellectual game! This isn't some exercise for the brain divorced from reality! This isn't writing a novel, Nathan! Here people don't jerk around like your fucking heroes worrying twenty-four hours a day about what's going on inside their heads and whether they should see their psychiatrists—here you fight, you struggle, here you worry about what's going on in *Damascus*! What matters isn't Momma and Poppa and the kitchen table, it isn't *any* of that crap you write about—*it's who runs Judea!*"

And out the door he went, furious, and before he could be talked into going home.

3. Aloft

SHORTLY after the seat-belt sign went off a group of religious Jews formed a minyan up by the bulkhead. I couldn't hear them over the noise of the engines, but in the sunlight streaming through the safety-exit window I could see the terrific clip at which they were praying. Off and running faster than a Paganini Caprice, they looked like their objective was to pray at supersonic speed—praying itself they made to seem a feat of physical endurance. It was hard to imagine another human drama as intimate and frenzied being enacted so shamelessly in a public conveyance. Had a pair of passengers thrown off their clothes and, in a fit of equally unabashed fervor, begun making love out in the aisle, watching them wouldn't have seemed to me any more voyeuristic.

Though numbers of Orthodox Jews were seated throughout the tourist cabin, at my side was an ordinary American Jew like myself, a smallish man in his middle thirties, clean-shaven and wearing horn-rimmed glasses, who was alternately leafing through that morning's *Jerusalem Post*—the Israeli English-language paper—and looking with curiosity at the covered heads bobbing and jerking in that square blaze of sunlight up by the bulkhead. Some fifteen minutes out of Tel Aviv he turned and asked in a friendly voice, "Visiting Israel or on business?"

"Just a visit."

"Well," he said, putting aside his paper, "what are your feelings about what you saw?"

"Sorry?"

"Your feelings. Were you moved? Were you proud?"

Henry was still very much on my mind, and so rather than indulge my neighbor—what he was fishing for was pretty clear—I said, "Don't follow you," and reached into my briefcase for a pen and a notebook. I had the urge to write my brother.

"You're Jewish," he said, smiling.

"I am."

"Well, didn't you have any feelings when you saw what they've done?"

"Don't have feelings."

"But did you see the citrus farms? Here are the Jews, who aren't supposed to be able to farm—and there are those miles and miles of farms. You can't imagine my feelings when I saw those farms. And the Jewish farmers! They took me out to an Air Force base—I couldn't believe my eyes. Weren't you moved by *anything*?"

I thought, while listening to him, that if his Galician grandfather were able to drop in on a tour from the realm of the dead upon Chicago, Los Angeles, or New York, he might well express just such sentiments, and with no less amazement: "We aren't supposed to be Americans—and there are those millions and millions of American Jews! You can't imagine my feelings when I saw how American they looked!" How do you explain this American-Jewish inferiority complex when faced with the bold claims of militant Zionism that they have the patent on Jewish self-transformation, if not on boldness itself? "Look," I said to him, "I can't answer these kinds of questions."

"Know what *I* couldn't answer? They kept wanting me to explain why American Jews persist in living in the Diaspora— and I couldn't answer. After everything I'd seen, I didn't know what to say. Does anybody know? Can *anyone* answer?"

Poor guy. Sounds like he must have been plagued by this thing—probably been on the defensive night and day about his artificial identity and totally alienated position. They said to him, "Where is Jewish survival, where is Jewish security, where is Jewish history? If you were really a good Jew you'd be in Israel, a Jew in a Jewish society." They said to him, "The one place in the world that's really Jewish and only Jewish is Israel" —and he was too cowed by the moral one-upmanship even to recognize, let alone admit, that that was one of the reasons he didn't want to live there.

"Why *is* it?" he was asking, his helplessness in the face of the question now rather touching. "Why *do* Jews persist in living in the Diaspora?"

I didn't feel like writing off with one line a man obviously in a state of serious confusion, but I didn't want this conversation

either, and wasn't in the mood to answer in detail. That I
would save for Henry. The best I could try to do was to leave
him with something to think about. "Because they like it," I
replied, and got up and moved to an empty aisle seat a few
rows back where I could concentrate undisturbed on what
more, if anything, to say to Henry about the wonder of his
new existence.

Now in the window seat to my left was a thickly bearded
young man in a dark suit and a tieless white shirt buttoned up
to the neck. He was reading a Hebrew prayer book and eating
a candy bar. His doing both struck me as strange, but then an
unsympathetic secular mind is hardly a fit arbiter of what dis-
tinguishes piety from irreverence.

I placed my briefcase on the floor—his was open on the seat
between us—and began my letter to Henry. It didn't just drift
up on the page any more than anything ever does. It was more
like using an eyedropper to extinguish a fire. I wrote and re-
vised for nearly two hours, working consciously to constrain
the big-brother caviling that persisted in coloring the early
drafts. "All you want me to see are the political realities. I see
them. But I also see you. You're a reality too." I crossed this
out, and more like it, working and reworking what I'd written
till finally I came as close as I could to looking at things more
or less his way, not so much to achieve a reconciliation, which
was both out of the question and nothing either of us needed
any longer, but so that we might be able to part without my
hurting his feelings and causing more damage than I had
already in that final face-off. Though personally I couldn't
believe that he was there for good—the kids were to fly out to
visit him at Passover, and seeing them, I thought, might well
change everything—I wrote as though I assumed that his decision was irrevocable. If that's what he wants to think, that's
what I'll think too.

Aloft/El Al
Dec. 11, 1978

Dear Henry,
Having sifted mistrustfully through each other's motives, having
been stripped of our worth in each other's eyes, where does this leave
you and me? I've been wondering ever since I boarded Flight 315.

You've become a Jewish activist, a man of political commitment, driven by ideological conviction, studying the ancient tribal tongue and living sternly apart from your family, your possessions, and your practice on a rocky hillside in biblical Judea. I've become (in case you're interested) a bourgeois husband, a London homeowner, and, at forty-five, a father-to-be, married this time to a country-reared, Oxford-educated English woman, born into a superfluous caste that decreed for her an upbringing not in the remotest way like ours—as she'd tell you herself, resembling hardly anyone's in recent centuries. You have a land, a people, a heritage, a cause, a gun, an enemy, a mentor—a powerhouse mentor. I have none of these things. I have a pregnant English wife. Traveling in opposite directions, we've managed in middle age to position ourselves equidistantly from where we began. The moral I derive from this, confirmed by Friday night's conversational duel when I stupidly asked why you didn't shoot me, is that the family is finally finished. Our little nation is torn asunder. I didn't think I'd live to see the day.

As much, admittedly, from writerly curiosity as from tottering old genetic obligation, I have been racking my brain for forty-eight hours, trying to understand the reason for your overturning your life, when it's really not hard to figure out. Tired of the expectations of others, the opinions of others, as sick of being respectable as of your necessarily more hidden side, at a time of life when the old stuff is dry, there comes this rage from abroad, the color, the power, the passion of it, as well as issues that are shaking the world. All the dissension in the Jewish soul there on display every day in the Knesset. Why *should* you resist it? Who are you to be restrained? I agree. As for Lippman, I have a terrific weakness for these showmen too. They certainly take things out of the realm of the introspective. Lippman seems to me someone for whom centuries of distrust and antipathy and oppression and misery have become a Stradivarius on which he savagely plays like a virtuoso Jewish violinist. His tirades have an eerie reality and even while rejecting him one has to wonder if it's because what he says is wrong or because what he says is just unsayable. I asked, with excessive impatience, if your identity was to be formed by the terrifying power of an imagination richer with reality than your own, and should have known the answer myself. *How else does it happen?* The treacherous imagination is everybody's maker—we are all the invention of each other, everybody a conjuration conjuring up everyone else. We are all each other's authors.

Look at the place you now want to call home: a whole *country* imagining itself, asking itself, "What the hell is this business of being a Jew?"—people losing sons, losing limbs, losing this, losing that, in the act of answering. "What is a Jew in the first place?" It's a question that's always had to be answered: the sound "Jew" was not made like a rock in the world—some human voice once said "Djoo," pointed to somebody, and that was the beginning of what hasn't stopped since.

Another place famous for inventing (or reinventing) the Jew was Germany under Hitler. Fortunately for the two of us, earlier on there'd been our grandfathers—as you rightly reminded me Friday night— incongruously wondering beneath their beards if a Jew was some-body who had necessarily to be destined for destruction in Galicia. Think of all they unpinned from our tails, in addition to saving our skin—think of the audacious, inventive genius of the unknowing greenhorns who came to America to settle. And now, marked by the dread of another Hitler and a second great Jewish slaughter, comes the virtuoso violinist of Agor, and with him a vision, ignited by the Nazi crematoria, of sweeping aside every disadvantageous moral taboo in order to restore Jewish spiritual preeminence. I have to tell you that there were moments on Friday night when it seemed to me that it was the Jews out at Agor who are really ashamed of Jewish history, who cannot abide what Jews have been, are embarrassed by what they've become, and display the sort of revulsion for Diaspora "ab-normalities" that you can also find in the classic anti-Semite they ab-hor. I wonder what you would call the waxworks representing those of your friends who scornfully disparage every introspective Jew of pacific inclinations and humanistic ideals as either a coward or a trai-tor or an idiot, if not the Museum of Jewish Self-Hatred. Henry, do you really believe that in the struggle for the imagination of the Jews the Lippmans are the people who should win?

I still find it hard to believe, despite what you told me, that your blossoming Zionism is the result of a *Jewish* emergency that befell you in America. I would never dare decry any Zionist whose decision to go to Israel arose out of the strong sense that he was escaping dan-gerous or disabling anti-Semitism. Were the real critical questions, in your case, anti-Semitism, or cultural isolation, or even a sense, no matter how irrational, of personal guilt about the Holocaust, there would be little to question. But I happen to be convinced that if you were repelled or deformed by anything, it wasn't by a ghetto situa-tion, the ghetto mentality, or the goy and the menace he posed.

You know better than to swallow uncritically the big cliché they seem to cherish at Agor of American Jews eating greedily from the shopping-center fleshpots, with one wary eye out for the Gentile mob —or, worse, blindly oblivious to the impending threat—and all the while inwardly seething with their self-hatred and shame. Seething with self-love is more like it, seething with confidence and success.

And maybe that's a world-historical event on a par with the history
you are making in Israel. History doesn't have to be made the way a
mechanic makes a car—one can play a role in history without its
having to be obvious, even to oneself. It may be that flourishing mun-
danely in the civility and security of South Orange, more or less for-
getful from one day to the next of your Jewish origins but remaining
identifiably (and voluntarily) a Jew, you were making Jewish history
no less astonishing than theirs, though without quite knowing it
every moment, and without having to say it. You too were standing
in time and culture, whether you happened to realize it or not. Self-
hating *Jews*? Henry, America is full of self-hating *Gentiles*, as far as I
can see—it's a country that's full of Chicanos who want to look like
Texans, and Texans who want to look like New Yorkers, and any
number of Middle Western Wasps who, believe it or not, want to talk
and act and think like Jews. To say Jew and goy about America is to
miss the point, because America simply is not that, other than in Agor's
ideology. Nor does the big cliché metaphor of the fleshpot in any way
describe your responsible life there, Jewish or otherwise; it was as
conflicted and tense and valuable as anyone else's, and to me looked
nothing like the life of Riley but like *life*, period. Think again about
how much "meaninglessness" you're willing to concede to their dogmatic Zionist challenge. By the way, I really can't remember ever
before hearing *you* use the word goy with such an air of intellectual
authority. It reminds me of how I used to go around during my freshman year at Chicago talking about the lumpenproletariat as though
that testified to a tremendous extension of my understanding of American society. When I saw the creeps outside the Clark Street saloons, I
thrilled myself by muttering, "Lumpenproletariat." I thought I knew
something. Frankly I think you learned more about "the goy" from
your Swiss girlfriend than you'll ever learn at Agor. The truth is that
you could teach *them*. Try it some Friday night. Tell them at dinner
about everything you reveled in during that affair. It should be an education for everyone and make the goy a little less abstract.

Your connection to Zionism seems to me to have little to do with
feeling more profoundly Jewish or finding yourself endangered, enraged, or psychologically straitjacketed by anti-Semitism in New Jersey
—which doesn't make the enterprise any less "authentic." It makes it
absolutely classical. Zionism, as I understand it, originated not only in
the deep Jewish dream of escaping the danger of insularity and the cru-
elties of social injustice and persecution but out of a highly conscious
desire to be divested of virtually everything that had come to seem,
to the Zionists as much as to the Christian Europeans, distinctively
Jewish behavior—to reverse the very form of Jewish existence. The

construction of a counterlife that is one's own anti-myth was at its very core. It was a species of fabulous utopianism, a manifesto for human transformation as extreme—and, at the outset, as implausible — as any ever conceived. A Jew could be a new person if he wanted to. In the early days of the state the idea appealed to almost everyone except the Arabs. All over the world people were rooting for the Jews to go ahead and un-Jew themselves in their own little homeland. I think that's why the place was once universally so popular—no more Jewy Jews, great!

At any rate, that you should be mesmerized by the Zionist laboratory in Jewish self-experiment that calls itself "Israel" isn't such a mystery when I think about it this way. The power of the will to remake reality is embodied for you in Mordecai Lippman. Needless to say, the power of the pistol to remake reality also has its appeal.

My dear Hanoch (to invoke the name of that anti-Henry you are determined to unearth in the Judean hills), I hope that you don't get killed trying. If it was weakness you considered the enemy while exiled in South Orange, in the homeland it may be an excess of strength. It isn't to be minimized—not everybody has the courage at forty to treat himself like raw material, to abandon a comfortable, familiar life when it's become hopelessly alien to him, and to take upon himself voluntarily the hardships of displacement. Nobody travels as far as you have and, to all appearances, fares so well so quickly on audacity or obstinacy or madness alone. A massive urge to self-renovation (or, as Carol sees it, to self-sabotage) can't be assuaged delicately; it requires muscular defiance. Despite the unnerving devotion to Lippman's charismatic vitality, you in fact seem freer and more independent than I would have imagined possible. If it's true that you were enduring intolerable limitations and living in agonizing opposition to yourself, then for all I know you have used your strength wisely and everything I say is irrelevant. Maybe it's appropriate that you've wound up there; it may be what you needed all your life—a combative métier where you feel guilt-free.

And who knows, in a year or two things may well change for you, and you'll have reasons for living there that will sound more congenial to me—if you're still talking to me—and that will in fact be more like what I imagine to be the reasons that most people live there, or anywhere, reasons that I don't happen to think are any less serious or meaningful than the ones you have right now. Surely Zionism is more subtle than just Jewish boldness since, after all, Jews who act boldly aren't just Israelis or Zionists. Normal/abnormal, strong/weak, we-ness/me-ness, not-so-nice/niceness—there's one dichotomy missing about which you said little, or nothing: Hebrew/English. Out at

Agor anti-Semitism comes up, Jewish pride comes up, Jewish power comes up, but nothing that I heard all night from you or your friends about the Hebrew aspect and the large, overwhelming cultural reality of *that*. Perhaps this only occurs to me because I'm a writer, though I frankly can't imagine how it wouldn't occur to anyone, since it's finally Hebrew more than heroism with which you have surrounded yourself, just as if you went to live forever in Paris it would be French with which you constructed your experience and thought. In presenting your reasons for staying there, I'm surprised you don't harp as much on the culture you're acquiring as on the manliness flowing out of the pride and the action and the power. Or maybe you'll only come to that when you begin feeling the loss of the language and the society that you look to me to be so blindly giving up.

To tell you the truth, had I run into you on a Tel Aviv street with a girl on your arm, and you told me, "I love the sun and smell and the falafel and the Hebrew language and living as a dentist in the middle of a Hebrew world," I wouldn't have felt like challenging you in any way. All that—which corresponds to *my* ideas of normalcy—I could have understood far more easily than your trying to lock yourself into a piece of history that you're simply not locked into, into an idea and a commitment that may have been cogent for the people who came up with it, who built a country when they had no hope, no future, and everything was only difficulty for them—an idea that was, without a doubt, brilliant, ingenious, courageous, and vigorous in its historical time—but that doesn't really look to me to be so very cogent to you.

In the meantime, at the risk of sounding like Mother when you used to go off to practice the hurdles in high school, for God's sake, be careful. I don't want to come out next time to collect your remains.

Your only brother,
Nathan

P.S. You will see from the signature that I haven't bothered about changing my own name, but in England embark upon the search for *my* anti-self carrying my old identity papers and disguised as N.Z.

Next I recorded in my notebook all I could remember of my conversation the previous evening with Carol; it was seven hours earlier in Jersey and she was about to begin preparing supper for the children when I phoned in as my brother's deprogrammer before going to sleep at the hotel. Since Henry's disappearance five months back Carol had undergone a transformation remarkably like his: she too was finished with being nice. That relentlessly accommodating personality that to me had always seemed little more than a bland enigma was armed now with the necessary cynicism to ride out this bizarre low blow, as well as with the hatred required to begin to heal the wound. The result was that for the first time in my life I felt some sort of power in her (as well as some womanly appeal) and wondered what I could possibly achieve persisting on playing the domestic peacemaker. Wasn't everyone happier enraged? They were certainly more interesting. People are unjust to anger—it can be enlivening and a lot of fun.

"I spent Friday with him at his settlement and then stayed overnight. I couldn't use the phone to order a taxi the next day because they're all religious people—nobody enters and nobody leaves on the Sabbath, and nobody could drive me, so I was there Saturday as well. I've never seen him healthier, Carol—he looks fine, and, well, you ask me."

"And is he doing all that Jewish stuff, too?"

"Some of it. Mostly he's learning Hebrew. He's devoted to that. He says his decision's irrevocable and he's not coming back. He's in a very rebellious state of mind. I don't see an ounce of remorse or any real yearning for home. No wavering at all, frankly. That may just be euphoria. He's still pretty much in the euphoric stage."

"Euphoria you call it? Some little Israeli bitch has taken him away from me—isn't that the real story? There's a little soldier there, sure as hell, with her tits and her tommy gun."

"I wondered about that myself. But no, there's no woman."

"Doesn't this Lippman have a wife he's screwing?"

"Lippman's a giant to Henry—I don't think that's in the cards. Sex is a 'superficiality,' and he's burned all superficiality away. He's discovered the aggressive spirit in himself, assisted by Lippman. He's seen power. He's discovered dynamism. He's discovered nobler considerations, purer intentions. I'm afraid it's Henry who's taken over as the headstrong, unconventional son. He needs a bigger stage for his soul."

"And this jerkwater settlement, this absolute nowhere, he considers *bigger*? It's the desert—it's the *wilds*."

"But the biblical wilds."

"You're telling me it's God then?"

"It's bizarre to me, too. Where that came from, I have no idea."

"Oh, I know where. Living in that little ghetto when you were kids, from your crazy father—he's gone right back to the roots of that madness. It's that craziness gone in another direction."

"You never found him crazy before."

"I always thought he was crazy. If you want the truth, I thought you were all a little nuts. You got off best. You never bothered with it in life—you poured that stuff into books and made yourself a fortune. You turned the madness to profit, but it's still all part of the family insanity on the subject of Jews. Henry's just a late-blooming Zuckerman nut."

"Explain it any way you like, but he doesn't look insane or sound insane, nor has he completely lost touch with his life. He's looking forward tremendously to seeing the kids at Passover."

"Only I don't want my kids involved in all this. I never did. If I had I would have married a rabbi. I don't want it, it doesn't interest me, and I didn't think it interested him."

"I think Henry *assumes* the kids are coming at Passover."

"Is he inviting me, or just the kids?"

"I thought he was inviting the children. The way I understood it, the visit's already set."

"I'm not letting them go by themselves. If he was crazy enough to do what he's done to himself, he's crazy enough to keep them there and try to turn Leslie into a little thing with squiggle curls and a dead-white face, a little monstrous religious creature. I'm certainly not sending my girls, not so he can throw them in a bath and shave their heads and marry them to the butcher."

"I think it may have communicated the wrong idea, my being unable to use the phone there on Saturday. It's not the Orthodoxy that's inspired him, it's the place—Judea. It seems to give him a more serious sense of himself having the roots of his religion all around him."

"What roots? He left those roots two thousand years ago. As far as I know he's been in New Jersey for two thousand years. It's all nonsense."

"Well, do what you like, of course. But if the kids could get over for Passover, it might open up communication between you two. Right now he's pouring all his responsibility into the Jewish cause, but that may change when he sees them again. So far he's fenced us all off with this Jewish idealism, but when they show up we might begin to find out if this really is a revolutionary change or just some upheaval he's passing through. The last great outburst of youth. Maybe the last great outburst of middle age. It comes to more or less the same thing: the desire to deepen his life. The desire looks genuine enough, but the means, I admit, seem awfully vicarious. Right now it's a little as though he's out to take vengeance on everything that he wants to believe was once holding him back. He's still very much caught up in the solidarity of it. But once the euphoria starts dwindling away, seeing the children could even lead to a reconciliation with you. If you want that, Carol."

"My kids would loathe it there. They've been brought up by me, by *him*, not to want to have anything to do with religion of any kind. If he wants to go over there and wail and moan and hit his head on the floor, let him, but the kids are staying here, and if he wants to see them, he'll have to see them right here."

"But if his determination does start to give way, would you take him back?"

"If he were to come to his senses? Of course I would take him back. The kids are holding up, but this isn't great fun for them, either. They're upset. They miss him. I wouldn't say they were confused, because they're extremely intelligent. They know precisely what's going on."

"Yes? What is that?"

"They think he's having a nervous breakdown. They're only scared that I will."

"Will you?"

"If he kidnaps my children, I will. If this madness goes on very much longer, yes, I may well have one."

"My guess is that this could all be so much fallout from that ghastly operation."

"Mine too, of course. I think it's clutching at God, or straws, or whatever, out of dread of dying. Some kind of magic charm, some form of placation to make sure it never happens again. Penance. Oh, it's too awful. It makes no sense at all. Who could have dreamed of this happening?"

"May I suggest then that if at Passover you *could* bring yourself—"

"When *is* Passover? I don't even know when Passover *is*, Nathan. We don't *do* any of that. We never did, not even when I was at home with my parents. Even my father, who owned a shoe store, was free of all that. He didn't care about Passover, he cared about golf, which now appears to put him three thousand rungs up the evolutionary scale from his stupid son-in-law. Religion! A lot of fanaticism and superstition and wars and death! Stupid, medieval nonsense! If they tore down all the churches and all the synagogues to make way for more golf courses, the world would be a better place!"

"I'm only telling you that if you do want him back some time in the future, I wouldn't cross him on the Passover business."

"But I *don't* want him back if he's crazy like this. I do not want to live my life with a crazy Jew. That was okay for your mother but it isn't for me."

"What you could say is, 'Look, you can be a Jew in Essex County, too.'"

"Not with me he can't."

"But you did after all marry a Jew. So did he."

"No. I married a very handsome, tall, athletic, very sweet, very sincere, very successful, responsible dentist. I didn't marry a Jew."

"I didn't know you had these feelings."

"I doubt that you've known anything about me. I was just Henry's dull little wife. Sure I was perfunctorily Jewish—who ever even thought about it? That's the only decent way to be any of those things. But Henry has more than scratched the surface with what he's gone out and done. I simply will not be connected with all that narrow-minded, bigoted, superstitious, and totally unnecessary crap. I certainly don't want my children connected with it."

"So to come home Henry has to be just as un-Jewish as you."

"That's right. Without his little curls and his little beanie. Is that why I studied French literature at college, so he could go around here in a beanie? Where does he want to put me now, up in the gallery with the rest of the women? I cannot *stand* that stuff. And the more seriously people take it, the more unattractive it all is. Narrow and constricting and revolting. *And* smug. I will not be trapped into that."

"Be that as it may, if you want to reunite the family, one approach would be to say to him, 'Come back and continue your Hebrew studies here, continue learning Hebrew, studying Torah—'"

"*He* studies *Torah*?"

"At night. Part of becoming an authentic Jew. Authentic's his word—in Israel he can be an authentic Jew and everything about him makes sense. In America being a Jew made him feel artificial."

"Yes? Well, artificial I thought he was just fine. So did all his girlfriends. Look, there are millions of Jews living in New York —are they artificial? That is totally beyond me. I want to live as a human being. The last thing I want to be strapped into is being an authentic Jew. If that's what he wants, then he and I have nothing more to say to each other."

"So simply because your husband wants to be Jewish, you're going to allow the family to dissolve."

"Christ, don't *you* become pious about 'the family.' *Or* about Being Jewish. No—because my husband, who is an American, who I thought of as my generation, of my era, *free* of all that weight, has taken a giant step back in time, *that's* why I am dissolving the family. As for my kids, their lives are here, their friends are here, their schools are here, their future universities are here. They don't have the pioneer spirit that Henry has, they didn't have the father that Henry had, and they are not going to the biblical homeland for Passover, let alone to a synagogue here. There will be no synagogues in this family! There will be no kosher kitchen in this house! I could not possibly live that life. Fuck him, let him stay there if it's authentic Judaism he wants, let him stay there and find another authentic Jew to live with and the two of them can set up a house with a tabernacle where they can celebrate all their little feasts. But here it is absolutely out of the question—nobody is going around this house blowing the trumpet of Jewish redemption!"

*

We were halfway to London by the time I was done, and the young fellow beside me was still at his prayer book. Torn wrappers from three or four candy bars were scattered on the seat between us, and perspiration was coursing heavily from beneath his broad-brimmed hat. As there was no turbulence, as the plane was well ventilated and a comfortable temperature, I wondered, like my mother—like *his* mother—if he might not have made himself sick eating all those sweets. Beneath the hat and beard, I thought I could spot a resemblance to somebody I knew; perhaps it was to somebody I'd grown up with in Jersey. But then I'd thought that several times during the last few days about any number of people I'd seen: in the café, watching the passersby on Dizengoff Street, and again outside the hotel while waiting for a taxi, the archetypal Jewish cast of an Israeli face would remind me of somebody back in America who could have been a close relative if not the very same Jew in a new incarnation.

Before putting my notebook back into my briefcase, I reread all I'd written to Henry. Why don't you leave the poor guy alone, I wondered. Another thousand words is just what he needs from you—they'll use it at Agor for target practice. Hadn't I written this for myself anyway, for my own elucidation, trying to make interesting what he could not? I felt, looking back over the last forty-eight hours, that alone with Henry I'd been in the presence of someone shallowly dreaming a very deep dream. I'd tried repeatedly while I was with him to invest this escape he'd made from his life's narrow boundaries with some heightened meaning, but in the end he seemed to me, despite his determination to be something new, just as naïve and uninteresting as he'd always been. Even there, in that Jewish hothouse, he somehow managed to remain perfectly ordinary, while what I'd been hoping—perhaps why I'd even made the trip—was to find that, freed for the first time in his life from the protection of family responsibility, he'd become something less explicable and more original than—than Henry. But that was like expecting the woman next door, whom you suspect of cheating on her husband, to reveal herself to you as Emma Bovary, and, what's more, in Flaubert's French. People don't turn themselves over to writers as full-blown literary characters—generally they give you very little to go on and, after the impact of the initial impression, are barely any help at all. Most people (beginning with the novelist—himself, his family, just about everyone he knows) are absolutely unoriginal, and his job is to make them appear otherwise. It's not easy. If Henry was ever going to turn out to be interesting, I was going to have to do it.

There was another letter for me to write while the events of the last few days were fresh in my mind, and that was an answer to a letter from Shuki that had been hand-delivered to the hotel and was waiting for me at the desk when I'd checked out early that morning. I'd read it first in the taxi to the airport, and now, with the quiet and time to concentrate, I took it out of my briefcase to read again, remembering as I did those few Jews who had crossed my path in my seventy-two hours, how each had presented himself to me—and presented me to himself—and how each had presented the country. I hadn't seen anything really of what Israel was, but I had at least begun to get an idea of what it could be made *into* in the minds of a small number of its residents. I had come to this place more or less cold, to see what my brother was doing there, and what Shuki wanted me to understand was that I was leaving it cold as well—the sparks I'd seen flying at Agor might not mean all I thought. And it was more important than I may yet have realized for me not to be misled. Shuki was reminding me at forty-five—albeit as respectfully and gently as he could—of what I'd been told as a writer (first by my father, as a matter of fact) ever since I began publishing stories at twenty-three: the Jews aren't there for my amusement or for the entertainment of my readers, let alone for their own. I was being reminded to see through to the gravity of the situation before I let my comedy roam and made Jews conspicuous in the wrong way. I was being reminded that every word I write about Jews is potentially a weapon against us, a bomb in the arsenal of our enemies, and that, largely thanks to me, in fact, everyone is now prepared to listen to all kinds of zany, burlesque views of Jews that don't begin to reflect the reality by which we are threatened.

All I could think while slowly rereading Shuki's surprising letter is that there really is no eluding one's fate. I will never lack for those large taboos between whose jawlike pincers I've had to insert my kind of talent. "This rebuke," I thought, "will follow me to my grave. And who knows, if the fellows at the Wailing Wall are right, maybe even beyond."

Ramat Gan
Dec. 10, 1978

Dear Nathan,

I'm sitting at home worrying about you out at Agor. What worries me is that you too are going to become enamored of Mordecai Lippman. What worries me is that you are going to be misled by his vividness and take him to be a far more interesting character than he is. Vivid Jews, after all, haven't been absent from your fiction, nor would Lippman be our first delinquent to delight your imagination. One would have to be blind not to recognize the fascination for you of Jewish self-exaggeration and the hypnotic appeal of a Jew unrestrained, as opposed to your relative indifference as a novelist to our gentle, rational thinkers, our Jewish models of sweetness and light. The people you actually like and admire you find least fascinating, while everything cautious in your own typically ironic and tightly self-disciplined Jewish nature is disproportionately engaged by the spectacle of what morally repels you, of your antithesis, the unimpeded and excessive Jew whose life is anything but a guarded, defended masquerade of clever self-concealment and whose talent runs not toward dialectics like yours but to apocalypse. What worries me is that what you will see in Lippman and his cohorts is an irresistible Jewish circus, a great show, and that what is morally inspiring to one misguided Zuckerman boy will be richly entertaining to the other, a writer with a strong proclivity for exploring serious, even grave, subjects through their comical possibilities. What makes you a normal Jew, Nathan, is how you are riveted by Jewish abnormality.

But if he proves so entertaining to you that you decide you must write about him, I ask you to keep in mind that (*a*) Lippman is not such an interesting character as a first impression may lead you to think—get half an inch beyond the tirade and he is a fairly uninteresting, if not to say asinine, crackpot, a one-dimensional, repetitious windbag, predictably devious, etc.; (*b*) Lippman alone is misleading, he is not the society, he is at the fringe of the society; to the outsider, diatribe is the hallmark of our society, and because he's the ultimate diatribalist, one of those here who must give you the whole ideology at one time *every time*, he may even strike you as the very embodiment of Israel. In fact he is a very peripheral paranoid, the most extreme, fanatical voice that this situation engenders, and though potentially he can do even more damage than a Senator Joseph McCarthy, we are talking about a similar kind of phenomenon, a psychopath alienated profoundly from the country's common sense and wholly marginal to its ordinary, everyday life (of which you will have seen nothing, by the way); (*c*) there is, in short, a little more to this country than what you hear out at Agor from Lippman, or even what you heard in Tel Aviv from me (another peripheral character—the peripheral crank, wasted down to his grievances); remember, if you take as your subject his diatribe—or mine—you will be playing with an argument for which people *die*. Young people do die here for what we are arguing about. My brother died for it, my son can die for it—and may yet—not to speak of other people's children. And they die because they are plugged into something which has a dimension far beyond Lippman's menacing antics.

This is not England, where a stranger can live forever and find out nothing. Even in a matter of hours you pick up vivid impressions in a country like this where everybody is airing his opinion all over the place and out in the open public policy is constantly and feverishly being debated—but don't be misled by them. What is at stake is serious business, and however tedious and unrelenting my disgust may be for much that's been going on here for years, however little I continue to adhere to my father's brand of Zionism, my tantrums are informed by an inescapable identification with Israel's struggle; I feel a certain responsibility to this country, a responsibility which is not inherent to your life, understandably, but is to mine. Disillusionment is a way of caring for one's country too. But what worries me isn't that you'll affront my national pride; it's that if and when you write about your visit to Agor, the average reader of Nathan Zuckerman is going to identify Israel with Lippman. No matter what you write, Lippman will come out stronger than anyone else, and the average reader will remember him better than anyone else and think he is Israel. Lippman is ugly, Lippman is extreme, equals Israel is ugly, the Israeli is extreme—this fanatical voice stands for the state. And this could do much harm.

I don't look upon danger as they do at Agor, but that doesn't mean there *is* no danger. Even if to my mind Agor is itself the greatest danger, there is still the danger from without that is no less real and could be far more horrendous. I don't say this rancorously—I don't accuse all of the Gentiles of being against us, which is the line they take in Lippman's cave, but we do have unrelenting detractors who despise us: you had dinner with some in London the other night, I was interviewed by another on the BBC, they work at newspapers in Fleet Street and all over Europe. You yourself may understand when face-to-face with Lippman that he is a lying, fanatical, right-wing son of a bitch perverting the humane principles on which this state was founded, but to them you would be presenting in Lippman the filthy heart of Zionism, the true face of the Jewish state that they relentlessly represent to the world as chauvinist, militant, aggressive, and power-mad. Moreover, they will be able to say a Jew wrote the bloody thing and he's telling the truth at last. Nathan, this *is* serious business: we have enemies with whom we are continually at war, and though we're much stronger than they are, we are not invincible. These wars in which our kids' lives are at stake are filling us with a sense of death all the time. We live like a person who is being pinpricked so much that it's not our life that's in danger but our sanity. Our sanity and our sons.

Before you sit down to entertain America with Lippman, take a minute to think about this—a vivid story, maybe too vivid, but I'm trying to make a point.

In 1973, had the Arabs attacked on Rosh Hashanah instead of Yom Kippur, we would really have been in a bad way. On Yom Kippur almost everybody is home. You don't drive, you don't travel anywhere, you don't go anywhere—many of us don't like it but still we stay home, it's the easiest way. And so when they attacked that day, even though our defenses were down—because of overconfidence and arrogance, and misreading the other side—when the alarm went out, everybody was home. All you had to do was say goodbye to your family. There was nobody on the roads, you could get to where you had to go, you could get the tanks out to the fronts, and everything was simple. Had they attacked a week earlier, if their Intelligence people had had the intelligence to tell them to strike on Rosh Hashanah, a holy day less solemnly observed, when at least half the country was someplace else—tens of thousands of people all over the Sinai, down in Sharm el Sheikh, people from the south up in Tiberias, and all with their families—had they attacked on that day, and everybody had to get the family home before they joined their unit, and the roads were full, people going in every direction, and the army couldn't get the big trailers with the tanks out to the front, then we would have been in real trouble. They would have run right in, and it would have been utter chaos. I'm not saying they would have conquered us, but we would have been knee-deep in blood, our homes destroyed, children attacked in their shelters—it would have been horrifying. I'm pointing this out to you not to make a case for the Israel's-survival-is-at-stake school of military thinking but to demonstrate that a lot of things are illusory.

Now the next point. Virtually everything we have right now, we have to get from abroad. I'm thinking of those things that, if we didn't have them, the Arab countries wouldn't tolerate us for a minute (and I include plutonium). What keeps them at bay doesn't come from our resources but from somebody else's pocket; as I complained to you the other day, mostly it comes from what Carter appropriates and what his Congress wants to go along with. What we have comes out of the pocket of the fellow from Kansas—part of each of his tax dollars goes to arm Jews. And why should he pay for the Jews? The other side is always trying to undermine us, to erode this support, and their argument is getting better all the time; just a little more help from Begin in the way of stupid policy, and they can indeed foster a situation in which the reluctance to keep shelling out is going to grow until finally nobody in the U.S. feels obligated to fork over three billion a year to keep a lot of Yids in guns. In order to keep doling out the dollars, that American has to believe that the Israeli is more or less the same as himself, the same decent sort of guy after the same sort of decent things. And that is not Mordecai Lippman. If Lippman and his followers are not the Jews they want to pay money for, I won't blame them. He may have a vivid enough point of view to enchant a satirical Jewish writer, but who from Kansas needs to support that kind of stuff with his hard-earned dough?

By the way, you haven't met Lippman's Arab counterpart yet and been assaulted head-on by the wildness of *his* rhetoric. I'm sure that at Agor you will have heard Lippman talking about the Arabs and how we must rule them, but if you haven't heard the Arabs talk about ruling, if you haven't *seen* them ruling, then as a satirist you're in for an even bigger treat. Jewish ranting and bullshitting there is—but, however entertaining you may find Lippman's, the Arab ranting and bullshitting has a distinction all its own, and the characters spewing it are no less ugly. A week in Syria and you could write satires forever. Don't be misled by Lippman's odiousness—his Arab counterpart is as bad if not worse. Above all, don't mislead the guy in Kansas. It's too damn complicated for that.

I hope that you'll see not only the high comedy of what I'm saying but the gravity as well. The comedy is obvious: Shuki the Patriot and P.R. man—the call for Jewish solidarity, for Jewish responsibility, from your perverse old guide to Yarkon Street. So be it—I am a ridiculously twisted freak, as hopelessly torqued by the demands of this predicament as anybody else in our original history. But then that's a character even more up your alley. Write about an Israeli malcontent like me, politically impotent, morally torn apart, and weary to death of being angry with everyone. But be careful representing Lippman.

Shuki

P.S. I'm not unaware that you've been up against this sort of argument before from Jews in America. I myself always thought that you couldn't write that stuff unless you were more confident about the world you were describing than any of the people who were attacking you. American Jews are tremendously defensive—in a way being defensive *is* American Judaism. It's always seemed to me, from my Israeli perspective, that there's a kind of defensiveness there that's a civil religion. And yet here I am suddenly outdoing your most censorious critic. "How can you think of betraying us like this?" Here we go again. There are endangered Jews on the one hand, vulnerable through misrepresentation to the most dire consequences, and on the other hand there is the dangerous, potentially destructive Jewish writer poised to misrepresent and ruin everything; and that Jewish writer isn't any old Jewish writer, but, because you are inclined to be funny and ironical about things one is supposed to be *for* or *against*—because, paradoxically, it is your *Jewish* gift to make things look ludicrous, laughable, or absurd, including, alas, even the Jew's vulnerable situation—he frequently turns out to be you. At the symposium here in 1960 you were condemned from the audience by a vociferous American-born Israeli citizen for being unforgivably blind in your fiction to the horror of Hitler's slaughter; nearly twenty years later you finally return only to be warned by me about the three billion dollars in American aid without which we here could find ourselves at a terrible disadvantage. First the six million, now the three billion—no, it *doesn't* end. Cautionary exhortation, political calculation, subliminal fear of a catastrophic outcome—all this Jewish *fraughtness* (if that is English) is something that your Gentile American contemporaries have never had to bother about. Well, that's their tough luck. In a society like yours, where eminent novelists are without serious social impact whatever the honors they accumulate and however much noise or money they make, it may even be exhilarating to find that the consequences of what *you* write are real, whether you like it or not.

Aloft/El Al
Dec. 11, 1978

Dear Shuki,
Stop calling me a normal Jew. There's no such animal, and why should there be? How could the upshot of that history be normalcy? I'm as abnormal as you are. I've just become in my middle years one of the more subtle forms that the abnormality takes. Which brings me to my point—it's entirely debatable as to whether in the halls of Congress it would be Lippman who would get them to scratching their heads over the three billion dollars, or whether it might not actually

be you. It's Lippman, after all, who is the unequivocal patriot and devout believer, whose morality is plain and unambiguous, whose rhetoric is righteous and readily accessible, and to whom a nation's ideological agenda is hardly an object for sardonic scrutiny. Guys like Lippman are a great success in America, actually seem quite normal, are even sometimes elected President, whereas the guys like you that we've got are not regularly rewarded with congressional citations. As for the average taxpayer, he might not find a hypercritical, dissident journalist highly attuned to historical paradox and scathing in his judgment of the very country with which he remains deeply identified as sympathetic a figure as I do—nor is he at all likely to find him preferable to a Jewish General Patton whose monomaniac devotion to the narrowest nationalist cause may not be as alien to Kansas as you think. My writing about Shuki Elchanan instead of Mordecai Lippman is not going to do Israel any good in the Congress or among the voters, and you're unrealistic to think so. It may also be unrealistic to think that even if I were inspired to fictionalize Agor, my story, read by my congressman, would thereby alter Jewish history. Fortunately (or unfortunately) for Jewish history, Congress does not depend upon prose narrative to figure out how to divvy up the take; the conception of the world held by 99% of the population, in Congress *and* out, owes a lot more—

Here I noticed that the young man beside me had set his prayer book in his lap and was sitting half crumpled over, seemingly unable to take in enough air, and perspiring even more profusely than when I'd last looked at him. I thought that maybe he was suffering an epileptic seizure or having a heart attack, and so putting aside my answer to Shuki—my halfhearted defense against this crime I hadn't even yet committed—I leaned across and asked him, "You all right? Excuse me, but do you need help?"

"How ya' doin', Nathan?"

"Pardon?"

Pushing his hat brim an inch up from his face, he whispered, "I didn't want to disturb a genius at work."

"My God," I said, "it's you."

"Yeah, it's me all right."

The churning black eyes and the Jersey accent: it was Jimmy.

"Lustig from the West Orange Lustigs. Ben-Joseph," I said, "from the Diaspora Yeshivah."

"Formerly."

"You all right?"

"I'm under a little pressure at the moment," he confided.

He leaned across his briefcase. "Can you keep a secret?" And then whispered directly into my ear, "I'm going to hijack the plane."

"Yes? All on your own?"

"No, with you," he whispered. "You scare the shit out of them with the grenade, I take charge with the pistol."

"Why the get-up, Jim?"

"Because a yeshivah *bucher* they don't check out the same way." Taking my hand, he carried it across to his near coat pocket. Beneath the cloth I felt a hard oval object with a raised, ridged surface.

Now how could that be? I'd never before seen security measures as thorough as those we'd had to submit to in order to board in Tel Aviv. First, all our luggage had been opened, one bag at a time, by plainclothes guards who were not shy about rummaging through every piece of dirty laundry. Then I was questioned at length by a brusque young woman about where I had been in Israel and where I was off to now, and when what I said seemed to have aroused her suspicion, she'd gone through my bag a second time before calling over a man with a walkie-talkie who interrogated me further and even less politely about the brevity of my stay and the places I'd been. They were so curious about my trip to Hebron and whom I had seen there that I was sorry I'd mentioned it. Only after I repeated for him what I'd told her about Henry and the ulpan at Agor—and explained again how I had got from Jerusalem to Agor and back—and only after the two of them had spoken together in Hebrew while I stood waiting in front of the open suitcase, whose contents had twice been turned upside down, was I allowed to close the bag and proceed the twenty feet to the counter where I was to check the bag directly onto the plane. My briefcase was inspected three times, by her first, a second time by a uniformed guard at the entrance to the departure area, and again as I was entering the lounge designated for the El Al London flight. Along with the other passengers, I was frisked from my armpits to my ankles and asked to pass through an electronic metal detector; and once inside the departure lounge, all the doors were sealed while we waited for the plane to begin loading. It was because of the time required for the meticulously thorough security check that passengers were requested to show up at Tel Aviv airport two hours before the plane's scheduled departure.

Whatever was in Jimmy's pocket had to be a toy. Probably what I'd felt there was some kind of souvenir—a rock, a ball, maybe a piece of folk art. It could have been anything.

"We're in this together, Nathan."

"Are we?"

"Don't be afraid—it won't hurt your image. If there's no hitch and we hit the headlines, it'll be the regeneration of the Jews, and a great shot in the arm to your Jewish standing. People will see how much you really care. It'll turn world opinion completely around on the subject of Israel. Here."

He took a paper out of his pants pocket, unfolded it, and handed me a page raggedly torn from a composition book and covered with words scrawled with a ballpoint pen just about out of ink. Jimmy indicated to me that I should keep the page in my lap while I read it.

FORGET REMEMBERING!

I demand of the Israeli government the immediate closing and dismantling of Yad Vashem, Jerusalem's Museum and Remembrance Hall of the Holocaust. I demand this in the name of the Jewish future. THE JEWISH FUTURE IS NOW. We must put persecution behind us forever. Never must we utter the name "Nazi" again, but instead strike it from our memory forever. No longer are we a people with an agonizing wound and a hideous scar. We have wandered nearly forty years in the wilderness of our great grief. Now is the time to stop paying tribute to that monster's memory with our Halls of Remembrance! Henceforth and forever his name shall cease to be associated with the unscarred and unscarable Land of Israel!

ISRAEL NEEDS NO HITLERS FOR THE RIGHT TO BE
ISRAEL!
JEWS NEED NO NAZIS TO BE THE REMARKABLE
JEWISH PEOPLE!
ZIONISM WITHOUT AUSCHWITZ!
JUDAISM WITHOUT VICTIMS!
THE PAST IS PAST! WE LIVE!

"The statement for the press," he said, "once we're on German soil."

"You know," I said, handing it back to him, "the security people riding these planes probably haven't got a great sense of humor. You could wind up in trouble screwing around like this. They could be anywhere, and they're armed. Why don't you can it?"

"What happens to me doesn't *matter*, Nathan. How can I care about myself when I have penetrated to the core of *the last Jewish problem*? We are torturing ourselves with memories! With masochism! And torturing goyisch mankind! The key to Israel's survival is no more Yad Vashems! No more Remembrance Halls of the Holocaust! Now what we have to suffer *is the loss of our suffering*! Otherwise, Nathan—and here is my prophecy as written in the Five Books of Jimmy—otherwise they will annihilate the State of Israel *in order to annihilate its Jewish conscience*! We have reminded them enough, we have reminded *ourselves* enough—*we must forget*!"

He was no longer whispering, and it was *I* who had to tell *him*, "Not so loud, please." Then I said, very clearly, "I really don't want anything to do with this."

"Israel is their prosecutor, the Jew is their judge! In his heart every goy knows—because every goy in his heart is a little Eichmann. This is why in the papers, at the U.N., everywhere, they all rush to make Israel the villain. This is now the club they use on the Jews—you the prosecutor, you the judge, *you* shall be judged, judged in every infraction to the millionth degree! This is the hatred that we keep alive by commemorating their crime at Yad Vashem. Dismantle Yad Vashem! No more masochism to make Jews crazy—no more sadism to stoke goy hate! Only then, *then*, are we free to run wild with the impunity of everybody else! Free to be as gloriously guilty as they are!"

"Calm down, for Christ's sake. Where'd you get the idea to dress up like this?"

"From none other than Menachem Begin!"

"Yes? You're in touch with Begin too?"

"I wish I could be. If I could only get it into *his* head—Menachem, Menachem, no more *remembering*! No, I only emulate the great Menachem—this is how he hid from the British in his terrorist days. Disguised as a rabbi in a synagogue! The outfit I got from him, and the big idea itself I owe to you! Forget! Forget! Forget! Every idea I ever had, I got from reading your books!"

I had decided it was about time to change my seat again, when Jimmy, having glanced out the window—as though to see if we were rolling into Times Square—took hold of my arm and announced, "On German soil we abandon the Holocaust! Land in Munich and leave the nightmare where it began! Jews without a Holocaust will be Jews without enemies! Jews who are not judges will be Jews who are not judged—Jews left alone at long last to *live*! Ten minutes more and we rewrite our future! Five more minutes and the Jewish people are saved!"

"You're going to save them on your own—I'm moving to another seat. And my recommendation to you, my friend, is that when we land you get yourself some help."

"Oh, is it really?" He opened the briefcase from which he'd been taking his candy bars and dropped the prayer book inside. He didn't, however, extract his hand. "You ain't going anywhere. Finger's on the trigger, Nathan. That's all the help I need."

"Enough, Jim. You're over the top."

"When I tell you take the grenade, you do just that—*only* that. Very covertly, out of my pocket and into yours. You step into the aisle, nonchalant you walk to where first class begins, I show my pistol, you take out the grenade, and then we both of us start to shout, 'No more Jewish suffering! An end to Jewish victims!'"

"Just Jewish clowning from here on out—making a plaything of history."

"*Undoing* history. Thirty seconds."

I sat quietly back thinking it was best to humor him until the performance was over and *then* to change my seat. Recalling the wording of his "press release," I thought there was obviously a brain there, even some thought; on the other hand, I couldn't quite believe that there was some principle connecting his transformation of the Wailing Wall into deep center field at Jerusalem Giants Stadium with this fervent petition for the demolition of the Jerusalem memorial to the Holocaust. The powerful emotional impulses in this boy to desanctify the holiest shrines of Jewish sorrow—to create a museum of his own that says "Forget!"—finally didn't strike me as having evolved from anything coherent. No, these weren't symbolic acts of cultural iconoclasm challenging the hold on the Jewish heart of its gravest memories so much as a manic excursion into meaningless Dadaism by a wandering, homeless yeshivah yippie, a one-man band high on grass (and his own adrenaline), a character a little like one of those young Americans the Europeans can't believe in, who without the backing of any government, on behalf of no political order old or new, energized instead by comic-book scenarios cooked up in horny solitude, assassinate pop stars and presidents. World War III will be triggered off not by suppressed nationalists seeking political independence, as happened the first time around when the Serbs at Sarajevo shot the heir to the Austrian throne, but by some semiliterate, whacked-out "loner" like Jimmy who lobs a rocket into a nuclear arsenal in order to impress Brooke Shields.

To pass the time I looked around at our neighbors, some of whom had been looking disapprovingly at us. In the aisle beside me, a fellow who must have been a businessman, prosperously dressed in a tan homburg and a pale beige suit with a double-breasted vest and wearing lightly tinted glasses, was leaning over to talk to a bearded young fellow who had been reading his prayer book in the middle row of seats. He wore the long black coat of the pious Jew but had on underneath it a heavy wool sweater and a pair of corduroy pants. In English the businessman was saying to him, "I can't take the jet lag anymore. When I was your age . . ." I had vaguely been expecting to overhear some religious disputation. Both men earlier had been praying in the minyan.

After waiting several more minutes, I finally said to Jimmy, who was now sitting silently, at last out of gas, "What went wrong at the yeshivah?"

"You've got balls, Nathan," and he showed me, in the hand that he withdrew from the briefcase, yet another candy bar. He ripped open the wrapper and offered me a bite before tearing in himself to replenish his energy. "I really had you goin' there. I really had you on the ropes."

"What are you doing dressed like this on the plane? Running away? You in trouble?"

"No, no, no—just following you, if you want the truth. I want to meet your wife. I want you to help me to find a girl like her. The hell with Rabbi Greenspan. I want something old English like Maria."

"How do you know Maria's name?"

"The whole civilized world knows her name. The Virgin Mother of Our Savior. What red-blooded Jewboy could resist? Nathan, I want to live in Christendom and become an aristocrat."

"And what's the rabbi bit about?"

"You guessed it. You would. My Jewish sense of fun. The irrepressible Jewish joker. Laughs are the core of my faith—like yours. All I know about cracking offensive jokes I learned at your great feet."

"Sure. Including this stuff about Yad Vashem."

"Come on, you think I'd be crazy enough to fuck around with the Holocaust? I was just curious, that was all. See what you'd do. How it developed. *You* know. The novelist in me."

"And Israel? Your love of Israel? At the Wailing Wall you told me you were there for life."

"I thought I was till I met you. You changed everything. I want a shiksa just like the shiksa that married dear old Z. Teddibly British. Do like you do—the Yiddische disappearing act with the archgoy, the white priestess. Teach me how, will ya? You're a real father to me, Nathan. And not only to me—to a whole generation of pathetic fuck-ups. We're all satirists *because* of you. You led the fucking way. I went around Israel feeling like your son. That's how I go through *life*. Help me out, Nathan. In England I'm always saying 'sir' to the wrong person — I get my signals mixed. I get nervous there that I'm looking even more ridiculous than I am. I mean the background is so neutral, and we speak the same language, or we think we do, that I wonder if there we don't stand out even more. I always think of England as one of those places where every Jew's shadow has an enormous hooked nose, though I know a lot of American Jews have this fantasy that it's a Wasp paradise where they can just sneak in, passing themselves off as Yanks. Sure, no Jew exists *anywhere* without his shadow, but there it's always seemed to me worse. Isn't it? Can I, Nathan, just ease

myself in with the British upper claahhses and wash away the
Jewish stain?" Leaning over, he whispered to me, "You really
got the inside track on how not to be a Jew. You shed it all.
You're about as Jewish as the *National Geographic*."

"You were made for the stage, Jim—a real ham."

"I *was* an actor. I told you. At Lafayette. But the stage, no,
the stage inhibited me. Couldn't project. *Without* the stage,
that's what I love. Who should I look up in England?"

"Anyone but me."

He liked that. The candy bar had calmed him down and he
was laughing now, laughing and mopping his face with his
hankie. "But you're my idol. It's you who inspire me to my
feats of masterful improvisation. Everything I am I owe to you
and Menachem. You're the greatest father figures I ever had
in my life. You're two fucking Jews who will say *anything*—
Diaspora Abbott and Israeli Costello. They ought to book you
boys into the Borscht Belt. I got some bad news from the
States, Nathan, some really shitty news from home. You know
what happened when the social worker phoned my family
long-distance? My old man answered and she told him what
had happened and that he would have to wire fare to Jerusalem so I could come home. You know what my old man told
her? They ought to book him into the Borscht Belt too. He
said, 'It's better if James stays.' "

"What did happen to make him so sanguine about you?"

"I gave my big lecture on the kosher laws to the tourists inside King David's Tomb. Impromptu. 'The Cheeseburger and
the Jew.' Rabbi Greenspan didn't like it. Where do I stay in
London? With you and Lady Zuckerman?"

"Try the Ritz."

"How do you spell it? I really had Nathan Zuckerman goin',
didn't I? Wow. For a few minutes there you really thought,
'Some Jewish pothead from suburban West Orange has got
nothing to do better than hijack an El Al 747. As if Israel
doesn't have enough troubles with Arafat and that shmatta on
his head, now they got Jimmy and his hand grenade.' I know
your generous heart. When you thought about the worldwide
headlines, you must have felt really sick to your stomach for
your fellow Jews."

"What *is* that in your pocket?"

"Oh, that?" He reached in absently to show me. "It's a hand grenade."

The last time I'd seen a live hand grenade was when I'd been taught to throw one in basic training at Fort Dix in August 1954. What Jimmy was holding up looked like the real thing.

"See?" Jimmy said. "The famous pin. Makes people shit-scared, this pin. Pull this pin and everything's just about over on ill-fated Flight 315 from Tel Aviv to London. You really *didn't* believe me, did you? Gee, that's a disappointment. Here, shmuck, I'll show you something else you didn't believe."

It was the pistol, Henry's first-act pistol. This then must be the third act in which it is fired. "Forget Remembering" is the title of the play and the assassin is the self-appointed son who learned all he knows at my great feet. Farce is the genre, climaxing in blood.

But before Jimmy had even drawn the gun half out of his briefcase, someone came leaping up over the back of his seat and had hold of his head. Then from out in the aisle a body hurled across mine—it was the businessman in the tinted glasses and the sharp beige suit who tore from Jimmy's hand the pistol and the hand grenade. Whoever had come upon Jimmy from behind had nearly put him out. Blood was pouring from his nose and he lay tipped over in his seat, his head fallen lifelessly against the side of the plane. Then a hand came down from behind and I heard the thud of an appalling body blow. Jimmy began to vomit just as I, to my astonishment, was lifted bodily from where I sat and a pair of handcuffs snapped around my wrists. As they dragged me up the aisle, people were standing on the seats and some were screaming, "Kill him!"

The three first-class passengers were cleared out of their seats and Jimmy and I were dragged into the empty cabin by the two security guards. After being roughly frisked and having my pockets emptied, I was gagged and slammed into an aisle seat, and then Jimmy was stripped and his clothes torn apart to be searched. Viciously they pulled off his beard, as though they hoped it were real and coming out by the roots. Then they doubled him over a seat, and the man in the beige suit snapped on a plastic glove and drove a finger up his ass, investigating, I suppose, for explosives. When they were sure that he'd been carrying no other weapons, that he wasn't wired up in any way or carrying some hidden device, they dropped him into the seat next to me, where he was handcuffed and shackled. I was then yanked to my feet, able barely to control my terror by thinking that if they believed me to be in any way involved, they would have badly disabled me already. I told myself, "They're simply taking no chances"—though, on the other hand, maybe the sharp kick in the balls was about to come.

The man in the beige suit and the tinted glasses said, "You know what the Russians did last month with a couple of guys who were trying to hijack an Aleutian plane? Two Arabs they were, going out of somewhere in the Middle East. The Russians don't give a shit about Arabs, you know, no more than about anybody else. They emptied the first class," he said, gesturing around the cabin, "took the boys in there, tied towels around their necks, slit their throats, and landed them dead." His accent was American, which I hoped might help.

"My name is Nathan Zuckerman," I said when the gag had been removed, but he gave no sign of absolution. If anything, I'd inspired still more contempt. "I'm an American writer. It's all in my passport."

"Lie to me and I slit you open."

"I understand that," I replied.

His bright, sporty clothes, the tinted glasses, the tough-guy American English all suggested to me an old-time Broadway con artist. The man didn't move, he darted; he didn't speak, he assaulted; and in the highly freckled skin and thinning or-angey hair I half sensed something illusionary, as though perhaps he was wigged and completely made-up and underneath was a colorless albino. I was under the impression that it was all a performance and nonetheless was terrified out of my wits.

His bearded sidekick was large and dark and sullen, a very frightening type who didn't speak at all, and so I could not tell if he was American-born too. He was the one who had broken Jimmy's nose and then struck the hammer-blow to his body. Earlier, when we were all still passengers in the economy-class cabin, he'd been wearing the long black coat over the corduroy trousers and heavy wool sweater. He was rid of the coat now and standing a little gigantically directly over me, poring through my notebook. Despite everything to which I was being crudely and needlessly subjected, I was nonetheless grateful to the two of them for how we'd all been saved—in something like fifteen seconds, these brutes had broken up a hijacking and saved hundreds of lives.

The one who'd been about to blow us all up seemed to have less to be thankful for. From the look of the plastic glove lying in the aisle beside the false beard, Jimmy was bleeding not only from the face but internally because of that body blow. I wondered if they intended to land before we got to London in order to get him to a hospital. It didn't occur to me that under instructions from Israeli Security, the plane had circled round and was returning to Tel Aviv.

I was not spared the rectal investigation, though during the eternity that I was made to bend over, handcuffed and totally undefended, nothing that I was dreading happened. Staring into space through my watery eyes, I saw our clothes strewn all over the cabin, my tan suit, Jimmy's black one, his hat, my shoes—and then the gloved finger was withdrawn and I was thrown back into the seat, wearing only my socks.

The silent sidekick took my billfold and my notebook up to the cockpit, and the Broadway hustler removed what looked like a jewelry case from his inside pocket, a long black velvet case which he then laid unopened atop the seat back in front of me. Beside me Jimmy wasn't yet comatose but he wasn't completely alive either. The fabric on which he was sitting was stained with his blood and his smell made me gag. His face by now was badly distorted by the swelling and half of it had turned blue.

"We're going to ask you to give an account of yourself," the Broadway hustler said to me. "An account that we can believe."

"I can do that. I'm on your side."

"Oh, are you? Isn't that nice. How many more of you boys we got on board today?"

"I don't think there's anyone. I don't think he's a terrorist —he's just psychotic."

"But you were with him. So what are you?"

"My name is Nathan Zuckerman. I'm an American, a writer.

I was in Israel visiting my brother. Henry Zuckerman. Hanoch. He's at an ulpan in the West Bank."

"The West *what?* If that's the West Bank, where's the East Bank? Why do you speak in Arab political nomenclature about a 'West Bank'?"

"I don't. I was visiting my brother and now I'm going back to London, where I live."

"Why do you live in London? London is like fucking Cairo. In the hotels the Arabs shit in the swimming pools. Why do you live there?"

"I'm married to an English woman."

"I thought you were American."

"I am. I'm a writer. I wrote a book called *Carnovsky*. I'm quite well known, if that's any help."

"If you're so well known, why are you so thick with a psychotic? Give me an account of yourself that I can *believe*. What were you doing with him?"

"I met him once before. I met him in Jerusalem at the Wailing Wall. Coincidentally he turned up on this plane."

"Who helped him get the hardware on board?"

"Not me. Listen—it wasn't me!"

"Then why did you change your seat to be next to him? Why were you talking together so much?"

"He told me he was going to hijack the plane. He showed me the statement for the press. He said he had a grenade and a gun and that he wanted me to help. I thought he was just a crackpot until he held up the grenade. He'd disguised himself as a rabbi. I thought the whole thing was an act. I was wrong."

"You're awfully cool, Nathan."

"I assure you, I'm properly terrified. I don't like this at all. I do know, however, that I have nothing to do with it. Absolutely nothing." I suggested to him then that in order to verify my identity they radio Tel Aviv and have Tel Aviv contact my brother at Agor.

"What's Agor?"

"A settlement," I said, "in Judea."

"Now it's Judea, before it was the West Bank. You think I'm an asshole?"

"Please—contact them. It'll settle everything."

"You settle it for me, fella—who are you?"

This went on for at least an hour: who are you, who is he, what did you talk about, where's he been, why were you in Israel, do you want to get your throat slit, who did you meet, why do you live with the Arabs in London, how many of you bastards are on board today?

When the other security man came back from the cockpit, he was carrying an attaché case out of which he took a hypodermic. At the sight of that I lost control and began shouting, "Check me out! Radio London! Radio Washington! Everybody will tell you who I am!"

"But we know who you are," the hustler said, just as the syringe slid into Jimmy's thigh. "The author. Calm down. You're the author of this," he said, and showed me "FORGET REMEMBERING!"

"I am *not* the author of that! *He* is! I couldn't begin to write that crap! This has nothing to do with what I write!"

"But these are your ideas."

"In no conceivable *way* are those my ideas. He's latched onto me the way he's latched onto Israel—with his fucking craziness! I write fiction!"

Here he touched Jimmy on the shoulder. "Wake up, sweetheart, get up—" and gently shook him until Jimmy opened his eyes.

"Don't hit me," he whimpered.

"Hit you?" said the hustler. "Look around, moron. You're flying first class. We upgraded your ticket."

When Jimmy's head fell my way, he realized for the first time that I was there too. "Poppa," he said weakly.

"Speak up, Jim," the hustler said. "Is this your old man?"

"I was only having fun," Jimmy said.

"With your dad here?" the hustler asked him.

"I am not his father!" I protested. "I have no children!"

But by now Jimmy had begun weeping in earnest. "Nathan said—said to me, 'Take this,' so I did, took it on board. He *is* a father to me—that's *why* I did it."

Quietly as I could, I said, "I am no such thing."

Here the hustler lifted the black velvet case from the seat back in front of me. "See this, Jim? It's what they gave me when I graduated antiterrorist school. A beautiful old Jewish artifact that they award to the first in the class." The reverence with which he opened the box was almost wholly unsatiric. Inside was a knife, a slender amber handle about five inches long ending in a fine steel blade curved like a thumb. "Comes from old Galicia, Jim, a ghetto remnant that's survived the cruel ages. Just like you, me, and Nathan. What they used back then to make little Jews out of our newborn boys. In recognition of his steady hand and his steely nerves, the prize for our class valedictorian. Our best *mohels* today are trained killers—it works out better for us this way. What if we loan this to your dad and see if he's got it in him to make the big biblical sacrifice?"

Jimmy screamed as the hustler sliced the air into bits just above his head.

"Cold steel up against the nuts," he said, "oldest polygraph known to man."

"*I take it back!*"

"Take what back?"

"Everything!"

"Good," the hustler said quietly. He placed the antique scalpel in its velvet case, and laid it carefully atop the seat should it be necessary to show it to Jimmy again. "I'm a very simple guy, Jim, basically uneducated. Worked in gasoline stations in Cleveland before I made aliyah. I never belonged to the country-club set. Shined windows and greased cars and fixed tires. I got the rim off the tire and that kind of stuff. A grease monkey, a garage man. I am a very crude guy with an underdeveloped intellect but a very strong and irrepressible id. You know what that is, you heard of that, the strong and irrepressible id? I don't even bother like Begin to point the accusing finger to justify what I do. *I just do it.* I say, 'That's what I want, I'm entitled,' and I *act*. You wouldn't want to be the first hijacker whose dick I made a souvenir because he handed me a load of shit."

"No!" he howled.

He took Jimmy's press statement out of his pants pocket again and after glancing over it, reading some of it, he said, "Shut down the Holocaust Museum because it upsets the goyim? You really believe that or are you just trying to have a little more fun, Jim? You really think they dislike Jews because the Jew is *judge*? Is that all that's been bothering them? Jim, that's not a hard question—answer me. The hard question is how anybody boarding at Tel Aviv could bring on board with him all this hardware. We're going to swing you by the ears to get the answer to that one, but that's not what I'm asking right now. We're not just going to work on your little pecker, we're going to work on your eyeballs, we're going to work on your gums and your knees, we're going to work you all over the secret parts of your body to get the answer to that, but now all I'm asking, for my own edification, for the education of a Cleveland grease monkey with a strong and irrepressible id, is if these are really things you honestly believe. Don't get tongue-tied—the rough stuff's later, in the lavatory, you and me squeezed up in there, alone with the secret parts of your body. This is just curiosity now. This is me at my most refined. I'll tell you what I think, Jim—I think this is another of those self-delusions you Jews have, thinking you are some kind of judge to them. Isn't that right, Nathan—that you high-minded Jews have serious self-delusions?"

"I would think so," I said.

He smiled benignly. "I do too, Nate. Oh, sure, you may find the occasional masochist Gentile who has meek little thoughts about morally superior Jews, but basically, Jim, I must tell you, they don't really see it that way. Most of them, confronted with the Holocaust, don't really give a shit. We don't have to shut down Yad Vashem to help them forget—they forgot. Frankly, I don't think the Gentiles feel quite as bad about this whole business as you, me, and Nathan would like them to. I think frankly that what they mostly think is not that we are their judge but that we get too much of the cake—we're there too often, we don't stop, and we get too goddamn much of the cake. You put yourselves in the hands of the Jews, with this conspiracy they've got all over the place, and you're finished. That's what they think. The Jewish conspiracy isn't a conspiracy of judges—it's a conspiracy of Begins! He's arrogant, he's ugly, he is uncompromising—he talks in such a way as to shut your mouth all the time. He's Satan. Satan shuts your mouth. Satan won't let the good out, everybody's a Billy Budd, and then there's this guy Begin, who's shutting your mouth all the time and won't even let you *talk*. Because *he's* got the answer! You couldn't ask for anybody who better epitomizes the Jewish duplicity than this Menachem Begin. He's a master of it.

He tells the goyim how bad they are, so *he* can turn and be bad! You think it's the Jewish superego they hate? *They hate the Jewish id*! What right do these Jews have to *have* an id? The Holocaust should have taught them never to have an id *again*. That's what got them into trouble in the first place! You think because of the Holocaust they think we're better? I hate to tell you, Jim, but the most they think on that score is that maybe the Germans went a little too far—they think, 'Even if they were Jews, they weren't as bad as all *that*.' The fellows who say to you, 'I expect more of the Jew,' don't believe them. *They expect less*. What they're saying really is, 'Okay, we know you're a bunch of ravenous bastards, and given half the chance you'd eat up half the world, let alone poor Palestine. We know all these things about you, and so we're going to get you now. And how? Every time you make a move, we're going to say, "But we expect *more* of Jews, Jews are supposed to behave *better*."' *Jews* are supposed to behave better? After all that's happened? Being only a thick-headed grease monkey, I would have thought that it was the *non-Jews* whose behavior could stand a little improvement. Why are *we* the only people who belong to this wonderful exclusive moral club that's behaving badly? But the truth is that they never thought we were so good, you know, even before we had a Holocaust. Is that what T. S. Eliot thought? I won't even mention Hitler. It didn't just start in Hitler's little brain. Who's the guy in T. S. Eliot's poem, the little Jew with the cigar? Tell us, Nathan—if you wrote a book, if you're 'quite well known' and 'properly terrified,' you ought to be able to answer that one. Who's the little Jew with a cigar in T. S. Eliot's wonderful poem?"

"Bleistein," I said.

"Bleistein! What brilliant poetry that T. S. Eliot came up with! Bleistein—great! T. S. Eliot had higher expectations for Jews, Jim? No! *Lower*! That was what was in the air *all the time*: the Jew with a cigar, stepping on everybody all the time and chomping his Jew lips on an expensive cigar! What they hate? Not the Jewish superego, dummy—not, 'Don't do that, it's wrong!' No, they hate the Jewish *id*, saying 'I want it! I take it,' saying 'I suck away on a fat cigar and just like you I transgress!' Ah, but you *cannot* transgress—you are a Jew and a Jew is supposed to be *better*! But you know what I tell them about being better? I say, 'A bit late for that, don't you think? You put Jewish babies into furnaces, you bashed their heads against the rocks, you threw them like shit into ditches—and the *Jew* is supposed to be better?' What is it they want to know, Jim—how long are these Jews going to go wailing on about their little Holocaust? How long are *they* going to go on about their fucking Crucifixion! Ask T. S. Eliot *that*. This didn't happen to one poor little saint two thousand years ago—*this happened to six million living people only the other day*! Bleistein with a cigar! Oh, Nathan," he said, looking with kindly humor down upon me, "if only we had T. S. Eliot on board today. I'd teach him about cigars. And you'd help, wouldn't you? Wouldn't you, a literary figure like yourself, help me educate the great poet about Jewish cigars?"

"If necessary," I said.

"Study current events, Jim," the hustler told him, satisfied with my tractability and returning to his in-flight educational program for the misguided author of "FORGET REMEMBERING!" "Up to the year 1967 the Jew didn't bother them that much down in his little homeland. Up till then it was all these strange Arabs wanting to wipe away little Israel that everybody had been so magnanimous about. They'd given the Jews this little thing you could hardly find on the map—out of the goodness of their hearts, a little real estate to assuage their guilt—and everybody wanted to destroy it. Everybody thought they were poor helpless shnooks and had to be supported, and that was just fine. The weak little shnook Jew was fine, the Jewish hick with his tractor and his short pants, who could he trick, who could he screw? But suddenly, these duplicitous Jews, these sneaky Jewish fuckers, defeat their three worst enemies, wallop the shit out of them in six fucking days, take over the entire this and the whole of that, and what a shock! Who the hell have they been *kidding* for eighteen years? We were worried about *them*? We were feeling magnanimous about *them*? Oh, my God, they tricked us again! They told us they were weak! We gave them a fucking state! And here they are as powerful as all hell! Trampling over everything! And meanwhile back home, the shnook Jewish general was feeling his oats. The Jewish shnook general was saying to himself, 'Well, now the goyim will accept us because now they see we're as strong as

they are.' ONLY THE OPPOSITE WAS TRUE—JUST THE FUCKING
OPPOSITE! Because all over the world they said, 'Of course—
it's the same old Jew!' *The Jew who is too strong! Who tricks you!
Who gets too much of the pie!* He's organized, he takes advantage, he's arrogant, he doesn't respect anything, he's all over
the goddamn place, connections *everywhere.* And that's what
the whole world cannot forgive, cannot abide, never would,
never will—Bleistein! A powerful Jew with a Jewish id, smoking his big fat cigar! *Real Jewish might!"*

But the foe of the Jewish superego was totally out of it now
and looked more than likely to be bleeding to death, despite
the shot they'd given him. Consequently, as the steep descent
into Israel began, it was I alone, returning to the Promised
Land with all my clothing peeled away and shackled to God's
bird, the El Al plane, who was being lectured on the universal
loathing of the Jewish id, and the goy's half-hidden, justifiable
fear of wild, belated Jewish justice.

4. Gloucestershire

A YEAR after being put on the drugs, still alive and feeling fit, no longer plagued by cartoon visions of male erections and ejaculations, when I have begun to contain the loss by forcing myself to understand that this is not the worst deprivation, not at my age and after my experience, just as I've begun to accept the only real wisdom—to live without what I no longer have—a temptress appears to test to the utmost this tenuous "adjustment." If for Henry there's Wendy, who is there for me? As I haven't had to endure his marriage or suffer his late sexual start, a vampire-seductress won't really do to lure me to destruction. It can't be for more of what I've tasted that I risk my life, but for what's unknown, a temptation by which I've never before been engulfed, a yearning mysteriously kindled by the wound itself. If the uxorious husband and devoted paterfamilias dies for clandestine erotic fervor, then I shall turn the moral tables: I die for family life, for fatherhood.

I'm over the worst of my fear and bewilderment, able again to engage men and women in ordinary social conversation without thinking bitterly all the while how unfit I am for sexual contention, when into the duplex at the top of the brownstone moves just the woman to do me in. She's twenty-seven, younger than I am by seventeen years. There is a husband and a child. Since the child's birth over a year ago, the husband has grown estranged from his pretty wife and the hours they used to pass in bed they now spend in acrimonious discussion. "The first months after I'd had the baby he was monstrous. So cold. He would come in and ask, 'Where's the baby?' I didn't exist. It's odd that I can't keep his attention any longer, but I can't. I feel quite lonely. My husband, when he even deigns to speak, tells me it's the human condition." "When I found you," I say to her, "you were hanging ripe, ready for plucking." "No," she replies, "I was already on the ground, rotting at the foot of the tree."

She speaks in the most mesmeric tones, and it's the voice that does the seducing, it's the voice that I have to caress me, the voice of the body I can't possess. A tall, charming, physically inaccessible Maria, with curling dark hair, a smallish oval face, elongated dark eyes, and those caressing tones, those gently inflected English ups and downs, a shy Maria who seems to me beautiful but considers herself "at best a near-miss," a Maria I love more each time we meet to speak, until at last the end is ordained and I go to meet my brother's fate. And whether in the service of flagrant unreality, who will ever know?

"Your beauty is dazzling." "No," she says. "It's dazzled me." "It can't, really." "It does." "I don't have admirers anymore, you know." "How can that be?" I ask. "Must you believe that all your women are beautiful?" "You are." "No, no. You're just overwrought." Even more fencing when I tell her I love her. "Stop saying that," she says. "Why?" "It's too alarming. And probably it's not true." "You think I'm deliberately deceiving you?" "It's not me you've deceived. I think you're lonely. I think you're unhappy. You're not in love. You're desperate and want a miracle to happen." "And you?" I say. "Don't ask questions like that." "Why won't you ever call me by my name?" I ask. "Because," she says, "I talk in my sleep." "What are you doing with me?" I ask her, "—would you prefer not to have to come here?" " 'Have to'? I don't have to. I'll carry on as I have." "But you didn't expect after the rush I gave you, for things to develop like this. Right now we should be in a torrid embrace." "There are no shoulds. I expect things to go in all kinds of ways. They usually do. I don't have job-lot expectations." "Well, you have the right expectations at twenty-seven and I have the wrong ones at forty-four. I *want* you." I have only my shirt off while she lies enticingly unclothed on the bed. When the nanny takes the child out in the stroller, and Maria comes down in the elevator to see me, this is the scene that I sometimes ask her to play. I tell my temptress that her breasts are beautiful, and she replies, "You're flattering me again. They were all right before the baby, but no, not now." Invariably she asks if I really want to be doing this, and invariably I don't know. It's true that bringing her to a climax while dressed in my trousers doesn't much alleviate my longing—better than nothing on some afternoons, but on others far worse. The fact is that though we may sneak around the brownstone like a pair of sex criminals, most of our time is passed in my study, where I light a fire and we sit and talk. We drink coffee, we listen to music, and we talk. We never stop talking. How many hundreds of hours of talk will it take to inure us to what's missing? I expose myself to her voice as though it were her body, draining from it my every drop of sensual satisfaction. There's to be no exquisite pleasure here that cannot be derived from words. My carnality is now *really* a fiction and, revenge of revenge, language and only language must provide the means for the release of everything. Maria's voice, her talking tongue, is the sole erotic implement. The one-sidedness of our affair is excruciating.

I say, like Henry, "This is the most difficult thing that I've ever had to face," and she answers, like the hardhearted cardiologist, "You haven't had a difficult life then, have you?" "All I mean," I reply, "is that this is a damn shame."

One Saturday afternoon she comes to visit with the child. Maria's young English nanny, with the weekend off, has gone to see the sights in Washington, D.C., and her husband, the British ambassador's political aide at the U.N., is away at his office finishing a report. "A bit of a bully," she says; "he likes all sorts of people around and a lot of noise." She married him straight from Oxford. "Why so soon?" I ask. "I told you—he's a bit of a bully, and as you may discover, since your powers of observation are not underdeveloped, I am somewhat pliant." "Docile, you mean?" "Let's say adaptable. Docility is frowned upon in women these days. Let's say I have a vital, vigorous gift for forthright submission."

Clever, pretty, charming, young, married most unhappily—and a gift for submission as well. Everything is perfect. She will never utter the no that will save my life. Now bring on the child and close the trap.

Phoebe wears a little knitted wool dress over her diaper and, with her large dark eyes, her tiny oval face, and curling dark hair, looks like Maria exactly. For the first few minutes she is content to lean over the coffee table and quietly draw with crayons in her coloring book. I give her the house keys to play with. "Keys," she says, shaking them at her mother. She comes over, sits in my lap, and identifies for me the animals in her storybook. We give her a cookie to keep her quiet when we want to talk, but wandering alone around the apartment, she loses it. Every time she goes to touch something, she looks first to see if it's permitted by me. "She has a very strict nanny," Maria explains; "there's nothing much I can do about it." "The nanny is strict," I say, "the husband a bit of a bully, and you are somewhat pliant, in the sense of adaptable." "But the baby, as you see, is very happy. Do you know Tolstoy's story," she says, "called, I think, 'Married Love'? After the bliss of the first years wears off, a young wife takes to falling in love with other men, more glamorous to her than her husband, and nearly ruins everything. Only just before it's too late, she sees the wisdom of staying married to him and raising her baby."

I go off to the study, Phoebe running behind me and calling, "Keys." I climb the library ladder to find my collection of Tolstoy's short fiction while the little girl wanders into the bedroom. When I step down from the ladder, I see, inside the room, that she is lying on my bed. I pick her up and carry her and the book to the front of the apartment.

The story Maria remembered as "Married Love" is in fact entitled "Family Happiness." Side by side on the sofa we read the final paragraphs together, while Phoebe, on her knees, crayoning a bit of floorboard, proceeds to fill her diaper. At first, seeing Maria's face flush, I think it's because of popping up and down so often to check on where the child is—then I realize that I've successfully transmitted to her my own inflammatory thoughts.

"You may have a taste for perpetual crisis," she says. "I don't."

I reply softly, as though if Phoebe overheard she'd somehow understand and become frightened for her future. "You've got it wrong. I want to put an end to the crisis."

"If you hadn't met me perhaps you could forget it and lead a quieter life."

"But I have met you."

The Tolstoy story concludes like this:

"It's time for tea, though!" he said, and we went together into the drawing-room. At the door we met again the nurse and Vanya. I took the baby into my arms, covered his bare red little toes, hugged him to me and kissed him, just touching him with my lips. He moved his little hand with outspread wrinkled fingers, as though in his sleep, and opened vague eyes, as though seeking or recalling something.

Suddenly those little eyes rested on me, a spark of intelligence flashed in them, the full pouting lips began to work, and parted in a smile. "Mine, mine, mine!" I thought, with a blissful tension in all my limbs, pressing him to my bosom, and with an effort restraining myself from hurting him.

And I began kissing his little cold feet, his little stomach, his hand and his little head, scarcely covered with soft hair. My husband came up to me; I quickly covered the child's face and uncovered it again.

"Ivan Sergeitch!" said my husband, chucking him under the chin. But quickly I hid Ivan Sergeitch again. No one but I was to look at him for long. I glanced at my husband, his eyes laughed as he watched me, and for the first time for a long while it was easy and sweet to me to look into them.

With that day ended my love-story with my husband, the old feeling became a precious memory never to return; but the new feeling of love for my children and the father of my children laid the foundation of another life, happy in quite a different way, which I am still living up to the present moment.

When it's time to give the child her bath, Maria goes around the apartment collecting the toys and the coloring books. Back in the living room, standing beside my chair, she puts her hand on my shoulder. That's all. Phoebe doesn't seem to notice when, furtively, I kiss her mother's fingers. I say, "You could bathe her here." She smiles. "Intelligent people," she says, "mustn't go too far with their games." "What's so special about intelligent people?" I ask, "—in these situations it doesn't really help anything." Outside the door each throws a kiss goodbye —the child first, then, following her example, the mother— and they step into the elevator and go back upstairs, my *deus ex machina* reascending. Inside my apartment I smell the child's stool in the air and see the small handprints on the glass top of the coffee table. The effect of all this is to make me feel incredibly naïve. I want what I've never had as a man, starting with family happiness. And why now? What magic do I expect out of fatherhood? Am I not making of fatherhood a kind of fantasy? How can I be forty-four and *believe* such things?

In bed at night, when the real difficulties begin, I say out loud, "I know all about it! Leave me alone!" I find Phoebe's cookie under my pillow and at 3 a.m. I eat it.

Maria raises all the questions herself the next day, taking up for me the role of challenger. If I wind up enjoying the persistence with which she won't permit me to be swept away, it's because her unillusioned candor is just another argument in my favor—the direct, undupable mind only charms me more. If only I could find this woman just a bit less appealing, I might not wind up dead.

"You cannot risk your life for a delusion," she says. "I cannot leave my husband. I can't deprive my child of her father, and I can't deprive him of her. There's this terrible factor which I guess you don't understand too clearly and that's my daughter. I do try not to think about her interests but I can't help it from time to time. I wouldn't have believed it, but apparently you're another of those Americans who imagine they have only to make a change and the calamity will be over. Everything will always turn out all right. But it's my experience that things don't—all right for a while maybe, but everything has its duration, and in the end things generally don't turn out well at all. Your own marriages seem to have a shelf life of about six or seven years. It wouldn't be any different married to me, if I even wanted to do it. You know something? You wouldn't like it when I was pregnant. It happened to me last time. Pregnant women are taboo."

"Nonsense."

"That's my experience. And probably not only mine. The passion would die out, one way or another. Passion is notorious for its shelf life too. You don't want children. You had three chances and turned them all down. Three fine women and each time you said no. You're really not a good bet, you know."

"Who is? The husband upstairs?"

"*Are* you sensible? I'm not sure. It's a little crazy to spend your life writing."

"It is. But I no longer want to spend it just writing. There was a time when everything seemed subordinate to making up stories. When I was younger I thought it was a disgrace for a writer to care about anything else. Well, since then I've come to admire conventional life much more and wouldn't mind getting besmirched by a little. As it is, I feel I've practically written myself *out* of life."

"And now you want to write yourself back in? I don't believe any of this. You have a defiant intelligence: you like turning resistance to your own advantage. Opposition determines your direction. You would probably never have written those books about Jews if Jews hadn't insisted on telling you not to. You only want a child now because you can't."

"I can only assure you that I believe I want a child for reasons no more perverse than anyone else's."

"Why pick on me for this experiment?"

"Because I love you."

"That terrible word again. You 'loved' your wives before you married them. What makes this any different? And it needn't be me you 'love' of course. I'm terribly conventional and I'm flattered, but, you know, there might well be someone else with you right now."

"Who would she be? Tell me about her."

"She'd be rather like me, probably. My age. My marriage. My child."

"She'd *be* you then."

"No, you're not following my faultless logic. She'd be just like me, performing my function, but she wouldn't be me."

"But maybe you *are* she, since you're so very like her."

"Why *am* I here? Answer that. You can't. Intellectually I'm not your style and I'm certainly not a bohemian. Oh, I tried the Left Bank. At university I used to go with people who walked around with issues of *Tel Quel* under their arms. I know all that rubbish. You can't even read it. Between the Left Bank and the green lawns, I chose the green lawns. I'd think, 'Do I have to hear this French nonsense?' and eventually I'd just go away. Sexually too I'm rather shy, you know—a very predictable product of a polite, genteel upbringing among the landless gentry. I've never done anything lewd in my life. As for base desires, I seem never to have had one. I'm not greatly talented. If I were cruel enough to wait until the wedding to show you what I've published, you'd rue the day you made this proposal. I'm a hackette. I write fluent clichés and fluffy ephemera for silly magazines. The short stories I try writing are about all the wrong things. I want to write about my childhood, that's how original I am—about the mists, the meadows, the decaying gentlefolk I grew up with. If you seriously want to risk your life to vulgarly marry yet another woman, if you really want a child to drive you crazy for the next twenty years—and after all that solitude and silent work, you would be driven quite mad—you really ought to find somebody more appropriate. Somebody befitting a man like you. We can have a friendship, but if you're going to go on with these domestic fantasies, and think of me that way, then I can't come down here to see you. It's too hard on you and almost as hard on me. I get childishly disorientated hearing that stuff. Look, I'm unsuitable."

I am in the easy chair in the living room, and she is sitting facing me, straddling my knees. "Tell me something," I ask, "do you ever say fuck?"

"Yes, I say it quite a lot, I'm afraid. My husband does too, in our marital discussions. But not down here."

"Why not?"

"I'm on my best behavior when I come to see an intellectual."

"A mistake. Maria, I'm too old to have to find somebody suitable. I adore you."

"You can't. You can't possibly. If anything, it's the illness I've captivated, not you."

" 'And as for my long sickness, do I not owe it indescribably more than I owe my health?' "

"I would have thought you were more hardheaded," she says. "Those portraits you paint of the men in those books didn't prepare me for this."

"My books aren't intended as a character reference. I'm not looking for a job."

"There's quite an age gap between us," she says.

"Nice, isn't it?"

She agrees, inclining her head to acknowledge that yes, it is indeed, and that our affinity is just about all she could ask for. Though you'd think a man who has been himself a husband on three occasions might know the answer, I cannot understand, when I see her like that, looking so wooable and so content, how to the husband upstairs practically nothing she does is right. As far as I can tell there's nothing she can do that's wrong. What I can't figure out is why every man in the *world* hasn't found her as enchanting as I do. That is how undefended I am.

"I had a very bumpy ride last night," she says. "A terrible scene. Howls of rage and disappointment."

"About what?"

"You continually ask questions and I keep answering them. That's really out of bounds. It feels like such a betrayal of him. I shouldn't tell you all of this because I know you're not to be trusted. *Are* you writing a book?"

"Yes, it's all for a book, even the disease."

"I half believe that. You're not, at any rate, to write about me. Notes are okay, because I know I can't stop you taking notes. But you're not to go all the way."

"Would that really bother you?"

"Yes. Because this is our *private* life."

"And this is a very boring subject about which, over these many years, I have already heard too much from too many people."

"It's not so boring if you happen to be on the wrong end of it. It's not so boring if you find your private life spread all over somebody's potboiler. 'Twere profanation of our joys to tell the laity our love.' Donne."

"I'll change your name."

"Terrific."

"No one would know it was you anyway, except me."

"You don't know what people will recognize. You *won't* write about me, will you?"

"I can't write 'about' anyone. Even when I try it comes out someone else."

"I doubt that."

"It's true. It's one of my limitations."

"I haven't begun to list all of mine. You have an easily excited imagination—you ought to take a moment and ask yourself if you're not inventing a woman who doesn't exist, making me somebody else already. Just as you want to make *this* something else. Things don't have to reach a peak. They can just go on. You *do* want to make a narrative out of it, with progress and momentum and dramatic peaks and then a resolution. You seem to see life as having a beginning, a middle, an ending, all of them linked together with something bearing your name. But it isn't necessary to give things a shape. You can yield to them too. No goals—just letting things take their own course. You must begin to see it as it is: there are insoluble problems in life, and this is one. As for me, I'm just the housewife who moved in upstairs. You'd be risking too much for far too little. There's much that's missing in me."

"You've been underappreciated so long upstairs that that's all you can think about. But as a matter of fact you're looking very expensive today. You have a very expensive face and long, expensive limbs and the voice is positively sumptuous. You look very well, you know; much better than when I met you."

"That's because I'm happier than when I met you. I would never have pulled myself together if I hadn't met you. It did a lot for me. To put it in reductive country English, it cheered me up. You too, I think. *You* look eighteen."

"Eighteen? That's very sweet of you."

"Like a bright boy."

"You're trembling."

"I'm frightened. Happier but very frightened. My husband's going away."

"Is he? When?"

"Tomorrow."

"You should have told me. You English do keep things to yourself. How many years is he going away for?"

"He's only going away for two weeks."

"Can you get rid of the nanny?"

"I've already seen to it."

We play house for two weeks. Every night we eat dinner upstairs after the baby has gone to sleep. She tells me about her parents' divorce. I see girlhood snapshots of her in Gloucestershire, a middle child, fatherless, all bones and dark braids, clinging to the jeans of two sisters. I see the desk where she sits when she phones each morning minutes after her husband has left for work. On the desk is a framed Polaroid shot of them at university, a seemingly solemn young man, towering even over her and wearing round wire-rimmed sixties spectacles. That recently they were at college, and thinking that, I feel entirely shut out. "Laid-back establishment," she says, when I hold up the photo and ask about his background; "the difficulty is that in worldly terms, you see, it's quite a suitable marriage." In the elevator, when he and I happen to meet, we each pass ourselves off as men without mood or passion. Large-boned and ruddy-complexioned, at thirty successful, vigorous, and on his way, he gives no outward sign, other than his size, of being a bit of a bully who likes all sorts of people around and a lot of noise—he presents to me only his Etonian opacity, and I pretend that I've never met his wife. If this were Restoration drama the audience would be in stitches, since it's the husband, after all, who is cuckolding the impotent paramour.

After she has drunk lots of wine at dinner, she is less inclined to be so doggedly sensible, though I still find myself thinking that the husband who is known to throw the dishes when crossed and then not to speak to her for days at a time is still more appropriate and satisfactory a mate than I, unable to enact my love. There are insoluble problems in life and this is one.

"I never had a Jewish boyfriend before. Or have I said that?"

"No."

"At university I did have a protracted meeting of mouths with a Nigerian Marxist, but it was only mouths that met. He was the same year as me. The boyfriends I had in darkest Gloucestershire were all sort of landed-gentry types and absolutely thick. You tell me when you have to go—I'm drunk."

"I don't have to go." Yet I should, must—she seduces me with every word into risking my life.

"There wasn't just repressiveness in my background, you know—there was an extraordinary mixture of that *and* freedom."

"Yes? Freedom emanating from what?"

"The freedom emanated from the horse. Because you could go long distances with all sorts at any time of the day, and you met a lot of people that way. If I'd actually been remotely sexually aware, which I wasn't, I could have just been screwing all the time from the age of twelve on. It would have been no problem. Not many really did but an awful lot of people spent an awful lot of time getting quite close."

"But not you."

Wryly, sadly: "No, never me. Would you like to look at one of my stories? It's about people messing about in the English mud, and dogs, and it's full of hunting slang, and there's no reason why it should mean anything to anyone born in the twentieth century. Do you really want to see it?"

"Yes. Though don't expect a brilliant reading. At college I gave up on Victorian literature because I could never figure out the difference between a vicar and a rector."

"I shouldn't show you this," she says. "Remember, I don't really aspire to newness of perception," and hands me the typescript. The story begins, *Hunting people swear like fury, their language is quite blue. When I was a child people used to hunt sidesaddle* . . .

As I finish the last page, she says, "I told you we'd heard it all before."

"Not from you."

"If you don't like it you're free to say so."

"The fact is that you're a much better writer than I am."

"Oh, nonsense."

"You're much more fluent than I am."

"That," she replies, mildly indignant, "has *nothing* to do with it. There are plenty of literate people who can write fluent, good English. No, this isn't anything really. It's embarrassingly beside the point. It's just that the combination of this extraordinary nineteenth-century carry-on and the way they swore outrageously . . . well, that's it. I'm afraid that's all. There is fiction that is fired noisily into the air, wildly into the crowd, and there is the fiction that misfires, explosives that fail to ignite, and there is fiction that turns out to be aimed into the skull of the writer himself. Mine's none of those. I don't write with ferocious energy. Nobody could ever use what I write as a club. Mine is fiction displaying all the English virtues of tact, good sense, irony, and restraint—*fatally* retrograde. It all comes very naturally, unfortunately. Even if I found the nerve to 'tell all' and write about you, you'd just come out as a rather pleasant chap. I should sign these stories 'By a throwback.'"

"And what if you are?"

"Not very suitable for you."

Two days before her husband is to return:

"I had a dream last night," she says.

"What about?"

"Well, it's difficult to explain the geography of the place I was in. A shipyard, something like that, the open sea, a harbor. I don't know the terms for those places, but I've seen them. The open sea is on my left, and then there are all those jetties

and wharves and landings and things. It's actually a harbor,
yes. I was swimming from one jetty to another one, which was
some distance away. I was fully dressed. I had a bundle under
my coat, a baby—it wasn't my daughter, it was another child, I
don't know who it was. I was swimming toward this other
jetty. I was escaping from something. There were all these boys
jumping up and down, gesticulating on the far jetty. They were
encouraging me—'Come on, come on!' Then they started directing me to turn right. And when I looked right, and started
to swim toward the right, there was, on the right-hand side,
another inlet, water, which was a little tiny boatyard. And it
was under a great big—like a railway station, a great big roof.
They were suggesting that I should get a boat and, instead of
swimming, I could row. Out to sea, of course. They were all
gesticulating and shouting at me, 'Judea! Judea!' But when I
got there and was about to take a boat—and there were several
moored up, you know, tied together—and I was still half in the
water—I realized that my husband was there, in charge of the
boats, and waiting to take me home. And he had a green
tweed suit on. That was the dream."

"Does he own a green tweed suit?"

"No. Of course not."

"'Of course not'? Why, isn't that 'done'?"

"No. Sorry. I mean 'of course not' in private terms. But
green and tweed represent all kinds of *blatantly* obvious English things. The whole dream is so grotesquely obvious, Freud
needn't have bothered. Anybody could understand that dream
—couldn't they? It's childishly simple."

"Simple how?"

"Well, green, straightaway, as soon as you wake up, you
know that green means country, lots of trees and countryside
—green means Gloucestershire. Gloucestershire is the land
where the grass couldn't be greener. And tweed means something the same, but with the air of formality and—well, one
wears tweeds, one has a tweed suit as a woman because one is
grown-up and conventional. I don't go in for that myself, but
the point is that tweeds arise from the country, they take the
colors from the countryside, the heather and the stones, and
even when they're beautiful they make of them something terribly repressive, with a slight hint of snobbishness. That's what

tweeds are used for anyway—they're 'frightfully English' and,"
she said, laughing, "I don't like it."

"And the boatyard?"

"Boatyards, railway stations. Points of departure."

"And Judea?" I ask. "The preferred English term is West
Bank."

"I wasn't reading headlines. I was asleep."

"And whose baby was it, Maria, under your coat?"

Shyly: "No idea. It didn't feature."

"It's the one we're going to have."

"Is it?" she asks helplessly. "It's a sad dream, isn't it?"

"And getting sadder."

"Yes." Then she bursts out, "It drives me absolutely wild
that he cannot appreciate what is under his nose unless I start
behaving like a prima donna. It just makes me feel so terribly
cross that you get put through all this for nothing, really. It's
just heartbreaking that if you're nice to people, if you're reasonable, if you're modest, they tread all over you. It just drives
me absolutely insane. Don't you think it's a cruel thing that all
the virtues that we've been brought up with are nothing, absolutely nothing, in marriage, at work, everywhere? It was the
same at the magazine in London. What a load of bullies there
are in the world! I find it absolutely outrageous." Then, characteristically: "Never mind. I shouldn't really simplify like that.
The frenzy I get into invariably disperses, and I slide into my
usual Slough of Despond. I really don't know why, but it goes
and I lose the impetus to move."

"Judea, Judea."

"Yes. Isn't that strange?"

"The Promised Land versus the Green Tweed Suit."

The night before her husband comes back I conduct an
investigation lasting to dawn. The transcript here, heavily
abridged, omits to mention those demi-intimacies that dis-
rupted the questioning, and the attendant despair that's transformed everything.

I imagine that the more I ask her, the less likely I will be to
make a terrible mistake, as though misfortune can be contained by *knowing*.

"Why do you stay in this?" I begin. "With me in this condition."

"Do you think that women only stay in relationships for sex? It usually comes to be the last thing. Why do I stay? Because you're intelligent, because you're kind, because you seem to love me (to use the terrible word), because you tell me I'm beautiful, whether I am or not—because you're an escape. Of course I'd like to have the other as well, but we don't."

"How frustrated are you?"

"It's frustrating . . . but not dangerous."

"What do you mean by that? It's under control?"

"Yes, yes, I do. I mean that without the physical commitment somehow a woman like me feels stronger. I suppose most women feel stronger once they think they've got you physically addicted to them. But that's when I begin to feel most vulnerable. This way I still in a way have the upper hand. I have the control and the choice. Or feel I have. It's even *I* that am refusing *you* marriage. It *is* frustrating, but it gives me a power that in an ordinary relationship I would never have, because you'd have power over me. I find it somehow exciting. You want me to be candid, I am."

"He still sleeps with you, your husband."

"I take back what I said about candor. This is the point where I retire into polite discretion."

"You can't. How often? Not at all, infrequently, sometimes, or often."

"Often."

"Very often?"

"Very often."

"Nightly?"

"Not quite. But nearly."

"You fight over everything, you don't speak for days, he throws the crockery, and yet he wants you that much."

"I don't know what that much is."

"I mean all this cruelty obviously turns him on. I mean his sexual enthusiasm, if nothing else, appears to be undiminished."

"He's very highly sexed. He'd happily boff me all day and all night. He doesn't particularly want me for anything more."

"Do you get satisfaction yourself?"

"It's all complicated by my being so furious and resentful. We go to bed negotiating all sorts of degrees of hostility. In any case, it's very impersonal. As though it isn't happening. He never thinks of me."

"Why don't you tell him no then?"

"I don't want that kind of trouble. Sexual tension like that is all we need to make it completely impossible to live together."

"So you remain sexually available to a very nasty man."

"You could put it that way if you like."

"And still you see me every afternoon. Why do you continue to show up?"

"Because I wouldn't be anywhere else. Because I'm welcome. Because if I don't see you I miss you. Up here it's cold and we're always fighting and jarring each other's nerves. Either we're saying rather polite, friendly, icy things to each other, which each finds rather dull, and secretly thinking about someone else or something else, or we're not saying anything, or we're fighting. But when I come downstairs, I come into a lovely room with books and the fireplace and the music and the coffee and your affection. Who wouldn't go there, if they're given that? I don't think you give that to everybody, but you give it to me. I think that for *you* it's a vast frustration that you don't have the other as well and so I wish you had it. But for me it's almost enough."

"But if everything were all right up here, you wouldn't be down there."

"That goes without saying. We would have been acquaintances in the lift, that's all. There's always something wrong, otherwise why should one want to create such complications?"

"Do you have erotic fantasies about me?"

"Yes, I do, but I probably would have more had we had sex. As it is, I push them away. Because they would make me edgy and dissatisfied."

"Is what we have at all exciting for you?"

"I told you—I think it's unusual and strange. When I lie on the bed naked, when you touch me—some women are deeply satisfied by that."

"Are you?"

"Not always. Look, you're not a hopelessly unattractive man. We've had a few quite interesting conversations during the course of our acquaintance, we've talked so much, but I'm sure all this talk is quite secondary—one's sexual perceptions are still the most important thing about someone, however things may turn out. Even if we never get to bed together, there's some essential sexual tension that we've had. Whether at the moment you're able to fuck or not is not the point. Virility hasn't only to do with that. You're very different from my husband, which is really the background I've always wanted to get away from anyway."

"If that's true, why did you marry him?"

"Well, we were young and he looked very manly. I'm very tall—well, he's even taller. He was so big physically—I equated that with masculinity. I've refined my ideas since, but then it was something I knew nothing about. We were three sisters and my father had left. How would you know what a man is, if you've never seen a grown one in action? I thought that this was the masculine force. He was my monument to the Unknown Man. He had that kind of athletic exterior, and he was very funny, very clever, and once we both had jobs in London, he *wanted* marriage so much. I don't think I'd have married so early if I had any sense that the world had a place for me. This was a time when marriage was right out, everybody was living together, but I was just so damn frightened, I thought it was sensible to get married. I've got over so many fears, and am so much less frightened now that it's really hard to recognize myself. But at nineteen and twenty I was pathologically frightened —ever since my father had walked out, I had felt my life on this huge, huge slide. You think I'm 'sweet,' but, really, it's only the worst kind of weakness. I didn't find it easy to make friends. I had masses and masses of acquaintances and an awful lot of admirers then, but there were very few people I could express my real feelings to. That was not so stupid because everybody I knew was completely hung up on idiotic jargon in that period. People were just carried away with a wave of sixties sentiment that turned their brains to custard. They were very intolerant. If you dared to question some piety or dogma, they would give you a monstrous time that could reduce you to tears. Not that I would cry, but I was frightened of expressing anything I really felt intellectually. It seems to me so awful in retrospect—perfectly ghastly. And my husband was somebody who reacted very like me. He was extremely clever, he came from the same kind of background. Everybody else we knew, they were either philistines or intellectuals. If they were intellectuals they came from lower social backgrounds and they gave us hell for it. You cannot imagine the persecution. I was supposed to be privileged. If I had any guts I would have told them, 'Do *you* have a father? Does he have a job? Are you going to be given any money this summer?' But then, even though they were rich and I was poor, because of my accent they would patronize me in the most awful way. So it was such a relief to find somebody who was intellectually very bright, and engaged with interesting things, and entertaining. Who's still entertaining when he wants to talk. And he came from my background, so there was no need to apologize. He had enormous charm and style and taste, and loved all kinds of things that I did, so it was a really tempting refuge. And I shouldn't have taken it. But sexually it was wonderful, and socially it was very suitable because it took all of that awful sixties heat off of everything, all this business about privileged-underprivileged, dropping your accents and all that crap. He was a refuge, a real one—and just so damn suitable. He's my age, my contemporary in every way, where you're a different race, a different generation, a different nationality—but he's not even a brother to me any longer. You're more of a brother—*and* a lover, really. He's not a friend. You're the adventure now and he's the known."

"Judea, Judea."

"I told you it was an obvious dream."

"But you're going to stay with him."

"Oh yes. All that's happened has been a classic tale that happens to a lot of women. I suited his needs, he suited mine— and after *x* years it's ceased to be true. We have done a lot of damage to each other, and I've become withdrawn and resentful and no fun, but divorce is still to be avoided. Divorce is a disaster. I'm not neurotic but I *am* fragile. The best thing is just to give up trying and give up fighting and go back to the real old-fashioned stuff. Separate bedrooms, a pleasant 'Good morning,' and you don't cross him—you're as nice as you can be. Every man's dream is as follows: she is fantastically good-looking, she does not age, she's fun and lively and interesting, but above all, *she doesn't give a fellow a hard time.* I may be able to get by on that."

"But you are only twenty-seven. Don't you think I'd be kind to your child?"

"I do. But I think if you had this operation for me and a family and all those dreams, you'd be putting such a weight on our relationship that nothing could ever, ever live up to your expectations. Particularly me."

"But a year after, the operation would be forgotten and we'd be just like everybody else. You think I won't want you any longer then?"

"That's possible. More than likely. Who knows?"

"Why won't I?"

"Because it *is* a dream. I don't know, I can't see into a man's mind, but it is a dream, I know: everything will be made right, and the right woman is waiting. No, things don't ever pan out like that. I don't want you to have that operation for me."

"But I am."

"No, you're not. You're having it, if you have it, for you, for your own masculinity, for your life. But to make all of it contingent on whether I will marry you or not, whether you can fuck me or not—that's putting a weight on me *and* fucking that I don't think either could bear. I wasn't brought up to take chances. I wish I were more independent, but I can sort of see why I'm not. My whole experience growing up was clinging, clinging, clinging. This is what happens when you grow up as an intelligent child with only a mother. Careful, careful, careful—that was the message. It's unjust to put all this on me. Nobody, I don't think, in *history* has been asked to make a decision like this. Why can't we just go on as we are?"

"Because I want to have a child with you."

"I think maybe you ought to go and speak to a psychiatrist."

"Everything I'm saying is perfectly reasonable."

"You're *not* reasonable. Because you *don't* have an operation that could kill you unless there's no choice. I have this vision sometimes when I wake up at night of you on the altar and the priest plunging this—is it obsidian, what did the Aztecs use, is that the word?—into your breast and tearing out your heart, for me and family happiness. It's one thing to say you lose your heart to somebody but another actually to do it."

"So what you're suggesting is that we just continue like this."

"Absolutely. I'm rather enjoying it."

"But you'll go away someday, Maria. Your husband will be made boy ambassador to Senegal. What then?"

"If he's posted to Senegal I'll put the child in school and say I can't join him. I'll stay here. That I promise you, if you promise not to have the operation."

"And what if he's called back to England? What if he goes into politics? That's bound to happen sometime."

"Then you'll come to England too, take a flat, and write your books there. What difference does it make where you are?"

"And we carry on this odd triangle forever."

"Well, until medical science bails us out."

"And you think I'll like that. Each day you leave me and go back to him, and every night, not because he particularly likes you but because he's so powerfully oversexed, he comes home from the House of Commons and fucks you. How do you think I'll like that all by myself in my London flat?"

"I don't know. Not much."

The next day, like the best of wives, she goes out to the airport to pick him up, and I go to the cardiologist to tell him my decision. There is nothing bizarre about my goals. This is the choice not of a desperate adulterer crazed by a drastic sexual blow, but of a rational man drawn to an eminently sane woman with whom he plans to lead a calm, conventionally placid, conventionally satisfying life. And yet I feel in the taxi as though I've become a child, given myself up to the whole innocent side of my being, and just when circumstances demand a ruthless coming to terms with my impairment. I have taken a fresh romance, with all those charming pleasures that anyone even half my age understands to be evanescent, and turned it into my *salto mortale*. To be doing this for an insane passion might actually begin to make some sense, but because I've been hopelessly charmed by the quiet virtues that she shares with her fiction is hardly sufficient reason to be taking such a chance. Can I really have been overcome by the wistful tones of the landless gentry? Is what's there so powerfully enticing, or *is* her allurement my disease's invention? Who is she anyway but, by her own description, the unhappy housewife who's moved in upstairs, continually cautioning me how unsuitable she is? Had

we met and had a heated affair back before my illness, chances
are we would never have had to do all this talking and it would
more than likely be over now, another adultery safely contained by the ordinary impediments. Why suddenly do I want
so passionately to become a father? Is it entirely unlikely that
far from the latent paterfamilias coming to the fore, it's the fem-
inized part of me, exacerbated by the impotence, that's produced this belated yearning for a baby of my own? I just don't
know! What is driving me on toward fatherhood, despite the
enormous danger it poses to my life? Suppose all I have fallen
in love with is that voice deliciously phrasing its English sentences? The man who died for the soothing sound of a finely
calibrated relative clause.

I tell the cardiologist that I want to marry and have a child.
I understand the risks, but I want the operation. *If I can have
this wonderfully bruised, supercivilized woman, I can be recovered from my affliction fully.* A truly mythological pursuit!

Maria is beside herself. "You may not feel this way about me
once you're well. Nor will I hold you to it. Nor can I hold myself to it. Nor do I want to do it."

"It wouldn't have been strange a hundred years ago, our
being both in love and chaste, but by now the farce is even
more intolerable than the frustration. We can't see anything
about anything without the operation first."

"It's too rash a thing to be doing! There's too much uncertainty about everything! *You can die.*"

"People make decisions like this every day. If you seriously
want to renew your life, there's no way around taking a serious
risk. A time comes when you just have to forget what frightens
you most. Besides, it'll be a rash thing to do no matter how
long I wait. Someday it'll be done anyway—out of necessity.
All I gain by waiting is the strong probability of losing you. I
will lose you. Without a sexual bond these things don't last."

"Oh, this *is* awful. An ordinary afternoon soap opera and
we've magnified it into *Tristan and Isolde*! *That's* the farce. It's
all become so hopelessly tender just because we *don't* make
love—because everything is always trembling just on this edge
we can't cross over. This endless talk that never reaches a climax has caused two supremely rational people to entertain the
most irrational fantasy until finally it's come to seem absurdly

tangible. The paradox is that we've so overexamined this dream that we've lost sight of the fact that *it's an utterly irresponsible illusion.* This disease has distorted *everything!*"

"When it's gone, my disease, we can, if you like, conduct a very thorough investigation of our feelings. We can overexamine *those,* and if it *has* been nothing more than some overheated verbal infatuation—"

"Oh, no—no! I couldn't let you go ahead if everything were to dissolve when the worst is over. I will. I'll do it. I'll marry you."

"Now my name. *Say it.*"

At last she submits. There is the climax to all our talk—Maria speaking my name. I have hammered and hammered—at her scruples, at her fears, at her sense of duty, at her thralldom to husband, background, child—and finally Maria gives in. The rest is up to me. Caught up entirely in what has come to feel like a purely mythic endeavor, a defiant, dreamlike quest for the self-emancipating act, possessed by an intractable idea of how my existence is to be fulfilled, I now must move beyond the words to the concrete violence of surgery.

So long as Nathan was alive, Henry couldn't write anything unself-consciously, not even a letter to a friend. His book reports back in grade school had been composed with no more difficulty than anyone else's, and in college he'd got through English with B's and had even done a brief stint as a sports reporter with the student weekly before settling into a predental program, but when Nathan began publishing those stories that hardly went unnoticed, and after them the books, it was as though Henry had been condemned to silence. There are few younger brothers, Henry thought, who had to put up with that too. But then all the blood relatives of an articulate artist are in a very strange bind, not only because they find that they are "material," but because their own material is always articulated for them by someone else who, in his voracious, voyeuristic using-up of all their lives, gets there first but doesn't always get it right.

Whenever he sat down to read one of the dutifully inscribed books that used to arrive in the mail just before publication, Henry would immediately begin to sketch in his head a kind of

counterbook to redeem from distortion the lives that were recognizably, to him, Nathan's starting point—reading Nathan's
books always exhausted him, as though he were having a very
long argument with someone who wouldn't go away. Strictly
speaking there could be no distortion or falsification in a work
not intended as journalism or history, nor could you charge
with incorrect representation writing under no obligation to
represent its sources "correctly." Henry understood all that.
His argument wasn't with the imaginative nature of fiction or
the license taken by novelists with actual persons and events—
it was with the imagination unmistakably his brother's, the
comic hyperbole insidiously undermining everything it chose
to touch. It was just this sort of underhanded attack, deviously
legitimizing itself as "literature," and directed most injuriously
at their parents in the caricatured Carnovskys, that had led to
their long estrangement. When their mother succumbed to a
brain tumor only a year after the death of their father, Henry
was no less willing than Nathan to let the break become final,
and they had never seen each other or spoken again. Nathan
had died without even telling Henry that he had a heart problem or was going in for surgery, and then, unfortunately,
Nathan's eulogist praised just those exploitative aspects of
Carnovsky that Henry had never been able to forgive and
wanted least to hear about at a time like this.

He had come over to New York by himself, ready and eager
to be a mourner, and then had to sit there listening to that book
described as, of all things, "a classic of irresponsible exaggeration," as though irresponsibility, in the right literary form,
were a virtuous achievement and the selfish, heedless disregard
for another's privacy were a mark of courage. "Nathan was not
too noble," the mourners were told, "to exploit the home."
And not overly sympathetic, you can be sure, for the home
that had been exploited. "Plundering his own history like a
thief," Nathan had become a hero to his serious literary
friends, if not necessarily to those who'd been robbed.

The eulogist, Nathan's young editor, spoke charmingly,
without a trace of sadness, almost as though he were preparing
to present the corpse in the casket with a large check rather
than to usher it on to the crematorium. Henry had expected
praise, but, naïvely perhaps, not in that vein or so remorselessly

on that subject. Focusing entirely on *Carnovsky*, the eulogy seemed deliberately to be mocking their rift. The thing that drove our family apart, thought Henry, is here being enshrined —that was *designed* to destroy our family, no matter how much they say about "art." Here they all sit, thinking, "Wasn't it brave of Nathan, wasn't it daring to be so madly aggressive and undress and vandalize a Jewish family in public," but none of them, for that "daring," had to pay a goddamn dime. All their pieties about saying the unsayable! Well, you ought to see your old parents down in Florida dealing with their bewilderment, with their friends, with their memories—they paid all right, they lost a *son* to the unsayable! I lost a *brother*! Somebody paid dearly for his saying the unsayable and it wasn't that effete boy making that pretentious speech, it was *me*. The bond, the intimacy, all we'd had during childhood, lost because of that fucking book and then the fucking fight. Who needed it? Why *did* we fight—what was *that* all about? You give my brother to this overeducated dandy, this boy who knows everything and nothing, whose literary talk makes so neat and clean what cost my family so much, and now just *listen* to him— memorializing the mess right out of existence!

The person speaking should have been Henry himself. *He* by all rights should have been the intimate of his brother to whom everyone was listening. Who was closer? But the night before, when he'd been asked on the phone by the publisher if he'd speak at the funeral, he knew he couldn't, knew he would never be able to find the words to make all those happy memories—of the father-and-son softball games, of the two of them skating on the Weequahic Park lake, of those summers with the folks down at the shore—mean anything to anyone other than himself. He spent two hours trying to write at his desk, remembering all the while the big, inspiring older brother he'd trailed behind as a child, the truly heroic figure Nathan had been until at sixteen he'd gone off to college to become remote and critical; yet all he was able to put down on his pad was "1933–1978." It was as though Nathan were still alive, rendering him speechless.

Henry wasn't speaking the eulogy because Henry didn't have the words, and the reason he didn't have the words wasn't because he was stupid or uneducated but because if he had chosen to contend, he would have been obliterated; he who wasn't at all inarticulate, with his patients, with his wife, with his friends—certainly not with his mistresses—certainly not in his *mind*—had taken on, within the family, the role of the boy good with his hands, good at sports, decent, reliable, easy to get along with, while Nathan had got the monopoly on words, and the power and prestige that went with it. In every family somebody has to do it—you can't *all* line up to turn on Dad and clobber him to death—and so Henry had become loyal Defender of Father, while Nathan had turned into the family assassin, murdering their parents under the guise of art.

How he wished, listening to that eulogy, that he was a person who could just jump up and shout, "Lies! All lies! That is what drove us *apart!*," the kind of person who could seize the moment and, standing on his feet, say anything. But Henry's fate was to have no language—that was what had saved him from having to compete with somebody who had been *made* out of words . . . made himself *out* of words.

Here is the eulogy that drove him nuts:

"I was lying on the beach of a resort in the Bahamas yesterday, of all things rereading *Carnovsky* for the first time since it was published, when I received a phone call telling me that Nathan was dead. As there was no flight off the island till late afternoon, I went back to the beach to finish the book, which is what Nathan would have told me to do. I remembered an astonishing amount of the novel—it's one of those books that stain your memory—although I had also distorted scenes in a revealing (to me) way. It's still diabolically funny, but what was new to me was a sense of how sad the book is, and emotionally exhausting. Nathan does nothing better than to reproduce for the reader, in his style, the hysterical claustrophobia of Carnovsky's childhood. Perhaps that's one reason why people kept asking, 'Is it fiction?' Some novelists use style to define the distance between them, the reader, and the material. In *Carnovsky* Nathan used it to collapse the distance. At the same time, inasmuch as he 'used' his life, he used it as if it belonged to someone else, plundering his history and his verbal memory like a vicious thief.

"Religious analogies—ludicrous analogies, he would be the

first to tell me—kept recurring to me as I sat on the beach, knowing he was dead and thinking about him and his work. The meticulous verisimilitude of *Carnovsky* made me think of those medieval monks who flagellated themselves with their own perfectionism, carving infinitely detailed sacred images on bits of ivory. Nathan's is the profane vision, of course, but how he must have whipped himself for that detail! The parents are marvelous works of the grotesque, maniacally embodied in every particular, as Carnovsky is as well, the eternal son holding to the belief that he was loved by them, holding to it first with his rage and, when that subsides, with tender reminiscence.

"The book, which I, like most people, believed to be about rebellion is actually a lot more Old Testament than that: at the core is a primitive drama of compliance versus retribution. The real ethical life has, for all its sacrifices, its authentic spiritual rewards. Carnovsky never tastes them and Carnovsky yearns for them. Judaism at a higher level than he has access to does offer real ethical rewards to its students, and I think that's part of what so upset believing Jews as opposed to mere prigs. Carnovsky is always complying more than rebelling, complying not out of ethical motives, as perhaps even Nathan believed, but with profound unwillingness and in the face of fear. What is scandalous isn't the man's phallicism but, what's not entirely unrelated, yet far more censurable, the betrayal of mother love.

"So much is about debasement. I hadn't realized that before. He is so clear on the various forms it can take, so accurate about the caveman mentality of those urban peasant Jews, whom I happen to know a thing or two about myself, sacrificing their fruits on the altar of a vengeful god and partaking of his omnipotence—through the conviction of Jewish superiority—without understanding the exchange. On the evidence of *Carnovsky*, he would have made a good anthropologist; perhaps that's what he was. He lets the experience of the little tribe, the suffering, isolated, primitive but warmhearted savages that he is studying, emerge in the description of their rituals and their artifacts and their conversations, and he manages, at the same time, to put his own 'civilization,' his own bias as a reporter—and his readers'—into relief against them.

"Why, reading *Carnovsky*, did so many people keep wanting to know, 'Is it fiction?' I have my hunches, and let me run them past you.

"First, as I've said, because he camouflages his writerliness and the style reproduces accurately the emotional distress. Second, he breaks fresh ground in the territory of transgression by writing so explicitly about the sexuality of family life; the illicit erotic affair that we all are born to get enmeshed in is not elevated to another sphere, it is undisguised and has the shocking impact of confession. Not only that—it reads as though the confessor's having fun.

"Now *Sentimental Education* doesn't read as if Flaubert was having fun; *Letter to His Father* doesn't read as if Kafka was having fun; *The Sorrows of Young Werther* sure as hell doesn't read as if Goethe was having fun. Sure, Henry Miller seems like he's having fun, but he had to cross three thousand miles of Atlantic before saying 'cunt.' Until *Carnovsky*, most everybody I can think of who had tackled 'cunt' and that particular mess of feelings it excites had done it exogamously, as the Freudians would say, at a safe distance, metaphorically or geographically, from the domestic scene. Not Nathan—he was not too noble to exploit the home and to have a good time while doing it. People wondered if it was not guts but madness that propelled him. In short, they thought it was about him and that he had to be crazy—because for *them* to have done it *they* would have had to be crazy.

"What people envy in the novelist aren't the things that the novelists think are so enviable but the performing selves that the author indulges, the slipping irresponsibly in and out of his skin, the reveling not in 'I' but in escaping 'I,' even if it involves—*especially* if it involves—piling imaginary afflictions upon himself. What's envied is the gift for theatrical self-transformation, the way they are able to loosen and make ambiguous their connection to a real life through the imposition of talent. The exhibitionism of the superior artist is connected to his imagination; fiction is for him at once playful hypothesis and serious supposition, an imaginative form of inquiry—everything that exhibitionism is not. It is, if anything, closet exhibitionism, exhibitionism in hiding. Isn't it true that, contrary to the general belief, it is the *distance* between the writer's life and his novel that is the most intriguing aspect of his imagination?

"As I say, these are just a few hunches, clues to answering the question that has to be answered since it's the question that hounded Nathan at every turn. He could never figure out why people were so eager to prove that he couldn't write fiction. To his embarrassment, the furor over the novel seemed to have as much to do with 'Is it fiction?' as with the question asked by those still struggling to separate from mothers, fathers, or both, or from the stream of mothers and fathers projected onto sexual partners, and that is, 'Is this *my* fiction?' But the less attached one is to that umbilicus, the less horrible fascination the novel has, at which point it is just what it seemed to me yesterday, and what it is: a classic of irresponsible exaggeration, reckless comedy on a strangely human scale, animated by the impudence of a writer exaggerating his faults and proposing for himself the most hilarious sense of wrongdoing—conjecture run wild.

"I've talked about *Carnovsky* and not about Nathan, and that's all I intend to do. If there were time and we had the whole day to be here together, I'd talk about the books in turn, each at great length, because that's the kind of funeral oration Nathan would have enjoyed—or that would have least displeased him. It would have seemed to him the best safeguard against too much transient, eulogistic cant. *The book*—I could almost hear him telling me this on that beach—*talk about the book, because that is least likely to make asses of us both.* For all the seeming self-exposure of the novels, he was a great defender of his solitude, not because he particularly liked or valued solitude but because swarming emotional anarchy and self-exposure were possible for him only in isolation. That's where he lived an unlimited life. Nathan as an artist, as the author paradoxically of the most reckless comedy, tried, in fact, to lead the ethical life, and he both reaped its rewards and paid its price. But not Carnovsky, who is to some degree his author's brutish, beastly shadow, a de-idealized, travestied apparition of himself and, as Nathan would be the first to agree, the most suitable subject for the entertainment of his friends, especially in our grief."

*

When the service was over, the mourners filed into the street, where groups of them lingered together, seemingly reluctant to return too soon to the ordinary business of an October Tuesday. Occasionally somebody laughed, not raucously, just from the kind of joking that goes on after a funeral. At a funeral you can see a lot of someone's life, but Henry wasn't looking. People who had noticed his strong resemblance to the late novelist looked *his* way from time to time, but he chose not to look back. He had no desire to hear yet more from the young editor about *Carnovsky*'s wizardry, and it unnerved him to contemplate meeting and talking with Nathan's publisher, who he believed to have been the elderly bald man looking so sad in the first row just beside the casket. He wanted simply to disappear without having to speak to anyone, to return to real society, where physicians are admired, where dentists are admired, where, if the truth be known, no one gives a fuck about a writer like his brother. What these people didn't seem to understand was that when most people think of a writer, it isn't for the reasons that the editor suggested but because of how many bucks he made on his paperback rights. *That*, and not the gift for "theatrical self-transformation," was what is really enviable: what prize has he won, who's he fucking, and how much money did the "superior artist" make in his little workshop. Period. End of eulogy.

But instead of leaving he stood glancing down at his watch and pretending that he was expecting to be met by someone. If he left now, then nothing that he'd wanted would have happened. Shutting down the office and making this trip hadn't to do with doing "the right thing"—it wasn't a matter of what others thought he should feel, it was what he himself wanted to feel, despite that seven-year estrangement. *My older brother, my only brother*, and yet he'd realized the day before that it was entirely possible for him, after he'd learned from the publisher of Nathan's death, to hang up the office phone and go back to work. It had been alarming to discover just how easy it would have been to wait and read the obituary in the next day's paper, professing to the family that he had not been told or invited to the funeral, let alone asked if he wanted to speak. Yet he couldn't do it—he might not be able to make the speech, he might not be able to feel the feelings, but out of love for his parents and what they would have wished, out of all those memories of what he and Nathan had shared as youngsters, he could at least be there and, in the presence of the body, effect something like a reconciliation.

Henry had been more than prepared to shed his hatred and forgive, but as a result of that eulogy, the bitterest feelings had been reactivated instead: the elevation of *Carnovsky* to the status of a *classic*—a classic of *irresponsible exaggeration*—made him glad that Nathan was dead and that he was there to be sure it was true.

I should have been the speaker—the cottage at the shore, the Memorial Day picnics, the Scout outings, the car trips, I should have told them all I remember and the hell with whether they thought it was badly written, sentimental crap. I would have given the eulogy and our reconciliation would have been *that*. I was intimidated, intimidated by all those people, as though they were an extension of him. So, he thought, today is just more of the same goddamn thing. It was never going to work, because I was *always* intimidated. And with that quarrel I only reinforced it—quarreling just because I couldn't stand any *more* of his intimidation! How did I get stuck there, when it wasn't ever what I wanted?

It was an awful day, but for all the wrong reasons. Here he wanted to be able to mourn his brother like everyone else and was having instead to contend with the stinkiness of the worst feelings.

When he heard his name called, he felt like a criminal, not from guilt but for having allowed himself to be trapped. It was as though outside a bank he'd just robbed, he'd committed some humane and utterly gratuitous act, like helping a blind man across the street, thereby delaying his getaway and allowing the police to close in. He felt ridiculously caught.

Coming toward him was the last of the three wives Nathan had left, Laura, looking not a day older or any less amiable than when they'd all been in-laws eight years back. Laura had been Nathan's "proper" wife, plainly pretty, if pretty at all, reliable, good-hearted, studiously without flair, back in the sixties a young lawyer with high ideals about justice for the poor and oppressed. Nathan had left her at about the time that *Carnovsky* was published and celebrity seemed to promise more tantalizing rewards. That, at any rate, was what Carol had surmised when they first heard about the separation. Henry wasn't so sure that success was the only motive: he saw what was admirable about Laura, but that may have been more or less all there was—her colorless Wasp uprightness, whose appeal for Nathan Henry could never fathom, was all *too* unmistakable. Ever since adolescence, he had been expecting Nathan to marry someone both very smart and very sultry, a kind of intellectual bar girl, and Nathan never came close. Neither of them did. Even the two women with whom Henry had had his most torrid affairs turned out to be as temperate as his wife, and no less trustworthy and decent. In the end it was like *having* an affair with his wife, for him if not for Carol.

While they embraced he tried to think of something to say that wouldn't immediately reveal to Laura that he was not deeply grieving. "Where did you come from?"—the wrong words entirely. "Where do you live? New York?"

"Same place," she said, stepping back but holding on momentarily to his hand.

"Still in the Village? By yourself?"

"Not by myself—no. I'm married. Two children. Oh, Henry, what a terrible day. How long did he know he was going to have this operation?"

"I don't know. We had a falling-out. Over that book. I didn't know anything either. I'm as stunned as you are."

She gave no indication that it was apparent to everyone that he wasn't stunned at all. "But who was with him?" she asked. "Was he living with someone?"

"Is there a woman? I don't know."

"You literally know nothing about your brother?"

"Well, maybe it's shameful," he said, hoping to make it less so by saying it.

"I don't know," Laura said, "but I can't bear to think that he was alone when he went in to have that operation."

"That editor who gave the eulogy—he seems to have been close to him."

"Yes, but he just got back last night—he was in the Bahamas. Mind you, he always had girls around. Nathan was never alone for long. I'll bet there's some poor girl at this moment—she may even have been inside. There were a lot of people

there. I hope so, for his sake. The thought of him alone . . .
Oh, it's so sad. For you too."

He couldn't bring himself to lie outright and agree.

"He had a lot more books to write," Laura said. "Still, he'd
accomplished a lot of what he wanted to do. It wasn't a wasted
life. But he had much more coming."

"As I say, I don't know what to make of it myself. But we
had a serious quarrel, a falling-out—it was probably stupid on
both sides." Everything he was saying sounded senseless. More
than likely their falling-out was what was meant to be, the result of irreconcilable differences for which he, for one, had no
need to apologize. He had spoken his mind about that book as
he had every right to, and what ensued ensued. Why should
writers alone get to say the unsayable?

"Because of *Carnovsky*?" Laura asked. "Yes, well, when I
read it, I thought this was not going to go down very well with
you or your folks. I understand it, but of course he had to use
the life around him, the people he knew best."

It wasn't the "using," it was the *distortion*, the *deliberate*
distortion—couldn't these people understand that? "Which
sexes are your children?" he asked, again sounding to himself
as insipid as he felt, as though he were speaking a language he
barely knew. The ex-wife, Henry thought, so obviously dis-
traught over Nathan's death, was utterly in control, while the
brother who was not distressed was unable to say anything
right.

"A boy and a girl," she said. "Perfect arrangement."

"Who is your husband?" That didn't come out like English
spoken by an English-speaking person, either. He was speaking no known language. Perhaps the only English that would
have sounded right was the truth. He's dead and I don't give a
shit. I wish I did but I don't.

"What does he do?" Laura said, seemingly translating his
question into her own tongue. "He's a lawyer too. We don't
work together, it's a bad idea, but we're on the same wavelength. This time I married a man like myself. I'm not on the
creative wavelength, I never was. I thought I was, in college,
and even had remnants of it when I first met Nathan. Putting
the idea of being a writer ahead of everything else is something
I know a little about. I read those books too, and had those

thoughts once, and, at a certain expense, even carried on like that in my early twenties. But I was lucky and wound up in law school. Now I'm mostly on the practical wavelength. I only have a real life, I'm afraid. It turns out I don't need any other."

"He never wrote about you, did he?"

She smiled for the first time, and Henry saw that, if anything, she'd become even plainer, even *sweeter*. She didn't seem to hold a single thing against his brother. "I wasn't interesting enough to write about," Laura said. "He was too bored with me to write about me. Maybe he wasn't bored enough. One or the other."

"And now what?"

"For *me*?" she asked.

That wasn't what he meant though he replied, "Yes." He'd meant something awful—something he *didn't* mean—like, "Now that this is over and my office is shut, what do I do with the rest of the day?" It had just slipped out, as though something internal that seemed as if it was external was trying to sabotage him.

"Well, I'm quite content," she said. "I'll just go on with what I have. And you? How's Carol? Is she here?"

"I wanted to come by myself." He should have said that Carol was getting the car and that he had to join her. He'd missed his opportunity to end the conversation before whatever wished to sabotage him went all the way.

"But didn't she want to come?"

His immediate impulse was to set the record straight—the record that Nathan was always distorting—to point out to her, in Carol's defense, that it was she who had been most perplexed and exasperated by Nathan's tossing Laura over. But Laura wouldn't care—she'd forgiven him. "He never wrote about you," he said, "you don't know what that's like."

"But he never wrote about Carol, he never wrote about you. Did he?"

"After I had the argument with him, one of the reasons we decided to stay out of his way was so that he wouldn't be tempted."

She showed no emotion, though he knew what she was thinking—and suddenly he understood everything that Nathan must have come to despise in her. Cold. Bland and upright and blameless and cold.

"And what do you think today?" Laura asked him in her very quiet, even voice. "Was it worth it?"

"To be truthful?" Henry said, and it *felt* truthful as he was about to say it, the first entirely truthful statement he'd been able to make to her. "To be truthful, it wasn't a bad idea."

She displayed nothing, nothing at all, just turned and calmly, coldly walked away, her place immediately taken, before Henry could even move, by a bearded man of about fifty, a tall, thin man wearing gold-rimmed bifocals and a gray hat, looking from the conservative cut of his clothes as though he might be a broker—or perhaps even a rabbi. Henry did, after a moment, think he recognized him as another writer, some literary friend of Nathan's whose picture Henry had seen in the papers but whose name he'd forgotten—someone who was now going to be as affronted as Laura not to find Henry and his entire family standing on the sidewalk knee-deep in tears.

He should never have closed the office. He should have stayed in Jersey, seen to his patients, and left it to time to deal with his feelings—a funeral was the last place ever to find what he and Nathan had lost.

The bearded man didn't bother with introductions and Henry still couldn't recall who he was.

"Well," he said to Henry, "he did in death what he could never do in life. He made it easy for them. Just went in there and died. This is a death we can all feel good about. Not like cancer. With cancer they go on forever. They try all our patience. After the initial surge, the first sickness, when everybody comes around with the coffee cakes and the casseroles, they don't die right then, they hang on, usually for six months, sometimes for a year. Not Zuckerman. No dying, no decay— just death. All very thoughtful. Quite a performance. Did you know him?"

He knows, Henry thought, sees the resemblance—*his* is the performance. He knows exactly who I am and what I don't feel. What else is this about? "No," Henry said, "I didn't."

"Just a fan."

"I suppose."

"The bereaved editor. He reminds me of an overprivileged kid—only instead of money it's intellectuals. He's the only person in the world I can imagine reading a thing like that and thinking it's a eulogy. That wasn't a eulogy, it was a book review! Know what he was really thinking when he got the news? I lost my star. For him it's a career setback. Maybe not a disaster, but for a young editor on the make, who's already cultivated the grand style, to lose his star—*that's* grief. Which book is your favorite?"

Henry heard himself saying "*Carnovsky.*"

"Not *Carnovsky* as bowdlerized in that book review. The editor's revenge—editing the real writer right out of existence."

Henry stood there on the street corner as though it were all a dream, as though Nathan hadn't died other than in a dream; he was over in New York at a funeral in a dream, and why the eulogy had celebrated the very thing that had driven him and his brother apart, why he had himself been speechless, why the ex-wife showed up to feel more grief than he did and to silently condemn Carol for not being present, was because that is what happens in a terrible dream. There's an insult everywhere, one is oneself the loneliest imaginable form of life, and people like this suddenly materialize, as unidentifiable as a force of nature.

"The deballing of Zuckerman is now complete," the bearded man informed Henry. "A sanitized death, a travesty of a eulogy, and no ceremony at all—completely secular, having nothing to do with the way Jews bury people. At least a good cry around the hole, a little remorse as they lower the coffin, but no, no one even allowed to go off with the body. Burn it. There is no body. The satirist of the clamoring body—without a body. All backwards and sterile and stupid. The cancer deaths are horrifying. That's what I would have figured him for. Wouldn't you? Where was the rawness and the mess? Where was the embarrassment and the shame? Shame in this guy operated *always.* Here is a writer who broke taboos, fucked around, indiscreet, stepped outside that stuff deliberately, and they bury him like Neil Simon—Simonize our filthy, self-afflicted Zuck! Hegel's unhappy consciousness out under the guise of sentiment and love! This unsatisfiable, suspect, quarrelsome novelist, this ego driven to its furthest extremes, ups and presents them with a palatable death—and the feeling-police, the grammar-police, they give him a palatable funeral with all the horseshit and mythmaking! The only way to have a funeral is to invite everyone who ever knew the person and just wait for the accident to happen—somebody who comes in out of the blue and says the truth. Everything else is table manners. I can't get over it. He's not even going to rot in the ground, this guy who was *made* for it. This insidious, unregenerate defiler, this irritant in the Jewish bloodstream, making people uncomfortable and angry by looking with a mirror up his own asshole, really despised by a lot of smart people, offensive to every possible lobby, and they put him away, decontaminated, deloused—suddenly he's Abe Lincoln and Chaim Weizmann in one! Could this be what he *wanted*, this kosherization, this stenchlessness? I really had him down for cancer. The works. The catastrophe-extravaganza, the seventy-eight-pound death, with the stops all pulled out. A handful of hairless pain howling for the needle, even while begging the nurse's aide to have a heart and touch his prick—one last blow job for the innocent victim. Instead, the dripping hard-on gets out clean as a whistle. All dignity. A big person. These writers are great—real fakes. Want it *all*. Madly aggressive, shit on the page, shoot on the page, show off their every last fart on the page—and for that they expect medals. Shameless. You gotta love 'em."

And what's this mouth want me to say—you're a mind reader and I agree? I had him down for cancer too? Henry said absolutely nothing.

"You're the brother," the bearded one whispered, speaking from behind his hand.

"I am not."

"You are—*you're* Henry."

"Fuck off, you!" Henry told him, making a fist, and then, stepping rapidly from the curb, he was nearly knocked down by a truck.

Next he was in the entryway to Nathan's brownstone, explaining to an elderly Italian woman with a very dour face and what looked like a killer tumor swelling out of her scalp, that he'd left the keys to his brother's apartment over in Jersey. She was the one who had come to the door when he'd pushed the superintendent's bell. "It's been a helluva day," he told her. "If my head wasn't screwed on, I would have forgotten that."

What with that growth of hers he should never have said "head." That was probably *why* he'd said it. He was still not entirely in control. Something else was.

"I can't let no one in," she told him.

"Don't I look like his brother?"

"You sure do, you look like twins. You gave me a shock. I thought it was Mr. Zuckerman."

"I've just come from the funeral."

"They buried him, huh?"

"Cremating him." Just about now, he thought. Nothing now left of Nathan that you couldn't pour into a baking-soda box.

"It'll make it easier," he explained, his heart pounding away, "if I don't have to drive back tomorrow with the keys," and he slipped her the two twenties he'd rolled up in his hand before entering the building.

Following her to the elevator, he tried to think what pretext he'd offer if anybody came upon him while he was inside Nathan's apartment but instead began to harangue himself for failing to pay this visit long ago—if only he had, today would have been nothing like today. But the truth was that since their fight, Henry really had not thought about his brother that much, and was kind of amazed that he had got stuck in his resentment and it had all worked out this way. He had certainly never prepared himself for Nathan's dying or even imagined Nathan *capable* of dying, not so long as he was himself alive; in front of the funeral parlor, defending against the assault of that overbearing clown, he had even momentarily imagined him to *be* Nathan—Nathan's spirit giving it to him, just like Laura, for his heartlessness.

Suppose he's tailed me and shows up here.

There were two locks to be opened, and then he was inside the little hallway alone, thinking how even as an adult one continues, like a child, to believe that when someone dies it's some kind of trick, that death isn't entirely death, that they are in the box and not in the box, that they are somehow capable of jumping out from behind the door and crying, "Had you fooled!" or turning up on the street to follow you around. He tiptoed to the wide doorway opening onto the living room and stood at the edge of the Oriental carpet as though the floor were mined. The shutters were closed and the long curtains drawn. Nathan might have been away on a vacation, if he weren't dead. Next week, he thought, it would be thirty years since he'd taken that Halloween walk in his sleep. Another recollection for his undelivered eulogy—Nathan holding his hand and shepherding him around the neighborhood earlier that night in his pirate costume.

The furniture looked substantial and the room impressive, the home of a successful and important man, the kind of success with which Henry could never compete, he who had himself been phenomenally successful. It had to do not primarily with money but with some irrational protection accorded the anointed, some invulnerability Nathan had always seemed to possess. It had sometimes driven him crazy when he thought of how Nathan had achieved it, though he knew there was something petty and awful—tragic even—in allowing yourself the minutest perception of wanting to be your brother's equal. That was why it had been better not to think of him at all.

Why, asked Henry, is being a good son and husband such a big joke to that society of intellectual elite? What's so wrong with a straightforward life? Is duty necessarily such a cheap idea, is the decent and the dutiful really shit, while "irresponsible exaggeration" produces "classics"? In the game as played by those literary aristocrats, the rules are somehow completely reversed . . . But he hadn't come all the way here so as to stand staring morbidly off into space, summoning up yet again his most rancorous feelings, mesmerized in some sort of regressive freeze while waiting for Nathan to jump out of the box and tell him it was all a joke—he was here because there was a nasty job to be done.

Inside a deep closet along a wall of the passageway separating the rear of the apartment—Nathan's study and the bedroom—from the living room, kitchen, and foyer at the front, were four filing cabinets containing his papers. Finding the journals took only seconds—they were stacked up, four columns of them, in chronological sequence, right on top of the filing cabinets: twenty black three-ring binders, each one plump with loose-leaf pages and held round with a stout red rubber band. Though the brain cells might have been burned to cinders, there was still this memory bank to worry about.

Thanks to Nathan's orderliness, Henry was able, with none of the difficulties he'd foreseen, to locate a volume identified on the spine with the year of his first adulterous affair—and, sure enough, he had been absolutely right to heed his paranoia and not to reproach himself about that too, for there it all was, every intimate detail, recorded for posterity. Not only were the entries as plentiful as he'd been imagining since the news had reached him of Nathan's death, but it was all more compromising than he'd remembered.

To think that he could have been in such hot pursuit, only ten years back, of Nathan's admiration! The lengths to which I went to gain his attention! Nearly thirty, a father of three, yet my needs with him the needs of a blabbing adolescent boy! And, he thought, reading through the pages, the adolescent with her as well. From the look of it no greater asshole lives than the husband and father fleeing the domestic scene—there could be no sorrier, shallower, more ridiculous spectacle than himself as revealed in those notes. He was stunned to see how little it had taken to bring him so close to squandering everything. For a fuck, according to Nathan—and depend on him to get that right—for a fuck in the ass with a Swiss-German blonde, he had been ready to give up Carol, Leslie, Ruthie, Ellen, the practice, the house . . . *I am a virgin there no longer, Henry. They all think I'm so good and responsible. Nobody knows!*

But had he failed to get into the apartment and to get his hands on these pages, had he really believed he'd been followed, had he turned back to Jersey like a man in a dream fearful of being apprehended, *everyone* would have known. Because they publish these journals when writers die—biographers plunder them for biographies, and then everyone would have known everything.

Leaning against the wall in the narrow passageway, he read twice through the journal covering the crucial months, and when he was certain that he had tracked down every entry bearing his or her name, neatly, with a sharp tug, he tore out those pages, and then carefully returned the notebook to its chronological place atop the filing cabinet. From the volumes and volumes of words dating back to when Nathan had been discharged from the army and had moved to Manhattan to become a writer, he had extracted a mere twenty-two pages. He'd bribed his way into the apartment, he was there unlawfully, but by removing fewer than two dozen pages from the five or six thousand closely covered with Nathan's handwriting, he could not believe that he had committed a flagrant outrage against his brother's property; he had certainly done nothing to damage Nathan's reputation or diminish the value of his papers. Henry had merely intervened to prevent a dangerous encroachment upon his own privacy—for were these notes to become public, there was no telling what difficulties they could cause, professionally as well as at home.

And if by removing those few pages he was doing his old mistress a favor too, well, why shouldn't he? Theirs had been quite a fling: a brief, regressive, adolescent interlude from which he had mercifully escaped without committing a really stupendous blunder, yet he'd been absolutely mad for her at the time. He remembered watching her kneel in the black silk camisole to pick up the money off the motel floor. He remembered dancing with her in his own dark house, dancing like kids to Mel Tormé after having spent all afternoon in the bedroom. He remembered slapping her face and pulling her hair and how, when he'd asked what it was like coming again and again, she had answered, "Paradise." He remembered how it had excited him to see her face flush when he made her talk dirty to him in Swiss-German. He remembered hiding the black silk camisole in his office safe when he'd found himself unable to throw it away. The thought of her in that underwear caused him, even now, to press his hand against his cock. But it was illicit enough rummaging through the papers in his dead brother's apartment—it would have been simply too obscene there in the passageway to jerk himself off because of what he was remembering from ten years back, thanks to Nathan's notes.

He looked at his watch—he'd better call Carol. The phone was in the bedroom at the back of the flat. Sitting at the edge of Nathan's bed, he dialed his home number, prepared for his brother to pop up grinning from beneath the box springs, to leap fully alive out of the clothes closet, telling him, "Tricked you, Henry, had you fooled—put the pages back, kid, you're not my editor."

But I am. He may have given the eulogy, but I can now edit out whatever I like.

While the phone rang he was astonished by an amazing smell from the courtyard back of the building. It took a while before he realized that the smell was coming from him. It was as though in a nightmare his shirt had been soaked in something more than mere perspiration.

"Where are you?" Carol asked when she answered the phone. "Are you all right?"

"I'm fine. I'm in a coffee shop. There's no burial service—he's being cremated. There was just the eulogy at the funeral home. The casket was there. And that was it. I ran into Laura. She's remarried. She seemed pretty shaken."

"How do *you* feel?"

He lied, maybe he was telling the precise truth. "I feel as though my brother died."

"Who gave the eulogy?"

"Some pompous ass. His editor. I probably should have said something myself. I wish I had."

"You said it yesterday, you said it all to me. Henry, don't wander around New York feeling guilty. He could have called you when he was ill. Nobody has to be alone if he doesn't want it. He died without anyone because that's how he lived. It's how he *wanted* to live."

"There was probably a woman around," said Henry, parroting Laura.

"Yes? Was she there?"

"I didn't look, but he always had girls around. He was never alone for long."

"You've done all you can. There's nothing more to do. Henry, come home—you sound awful."

But there *was* more to do, and it was another three hours before he left for Jersey. In the study, at the center of Nathan's desk, otherwise tidy and clear of papers, was a cardboard stationery box marked "Draft #2." In it were several hundred pages of typewritten manuscript. This second draft of a book, if that's what it was, appeared to be untitled. Not the chapters themselves, however—each, at the top of the first page, had as a title the name of a place. He sat down at the desk and began to read. The first chapter, "Basel," was purportedly about him.

Despite everything he thought he knew about his brother, he couldn't believe that what he was reading could have been written even by Nathan. All day long he had been distrusting his resentment, chastising himself for that resentment, feeling wretched for feeling nothing and lacerating himself for his incapacity to forgive, and here were these pages in which he was not only exposed to the worst sort of ridicule but identified by his own real name. Everyone was identified by name, Carol, the children, even Wendy Casselman, the little blonde who before she'd married had briefly worked as his assistant; even Nathan, who had never before written about himself *as* himself, appeared as Nathan, as "Zuckerman," though nearly everything in the story was either an outright lie or a ridiculous travesty of the facts. Of all the classics of irresponsible exaggeration, this was the filthiest, most recklessly irresponsible of all.

"Basel" was about his, Henry's, death from a bypass operation; about his, Henry's, adulterous love affairs; about his, Henry's, heart problem—not Nathan's, *his*. All the while Nathan had been ill, his diversion, his distraction, his entertainment, his amusement, his *art*, had been the violent disfiguring of *me*. Writing *my* eulogy! This was even worse than *Carnovsky*. At least there he'd had the decency, if that was the word, to shake up a little the lives of real people and change a few things around (for all the camouflage that had provided the family), but this exceeded everything, the worst imaginable abuse of "artistic" liberty.

In the midst of all that was sheer sadistic, punitive, spiteful invention, sheer sadistic sorcery, there, copied verbatim from the notebooks, were half the journal entries that Henry had torn out to destroy.

He was a man utterly without a sense of consequence. Forget morality, forget ethics, forget feelings—didn't he know the law? Didn't he know that I could sue for libel and invasion of privacy? Or was that precisely what he wanted, a legal battle with his bourgeois brother over "censorship"? What is most disgusting, Henry thought, the greatest infringement and violation, is that this is *not* me, not in any way. I am *not* a dentist who seduces his assistants—there is a line of separation that I do *not* cross. My job isn't fucking my assistants—my job is getting my patients to trust me, making them comfortable, completing my work as painlessly and cheaply as possible for them, and just as well as it can be done. What *I* do in my office is *that*. His Henry is, if anyone, *him*—it's Nathan, using me to conceal himself while simultaneously disguising himself *as* himself, as *responsible*, as *sane*, disguising himself as a reasonable man while I am revealed as the absolute dope. The son of a bitch seemingly abandons the disguise *at the very moment he's lying most*! Here is Nathan who knows everything and here is Henry with his little life; here is Henry who just wanted to be accepted and to get away with his little tawdry affairs, Henry the shlub who buys his potency with his death as a way of trying to free himself from being a good husband, and here am I, Nathan the artist, seeing through him completely! Even here, thought Henry, ill with heart disease and facing serious surgery, he continued to persist with the lifelong domination, forcing me into his sexual obsessions, his family obsessions, controlling and manipulating my freedom, seeking to overpower me with satirical words, making of *everyone* a completely manageable adversary for Nathan. Yet all the while it was *he* still hallucinating about the very things that are laughed at in this straw-brother who's supposed to be me! I was right: the driving force of his imagination was revenge, domination and revenge. Nathan always wins. Fratricide without pain—a free ride.

He must have been made impotent by heart medication and then chosen, like "Henry," to have an operation that killed him. *He*, not me, would never accept the limits—*he*, not me, was the fool who died for a fuck. Not the dopey dentist but the all-seeing artist was the ridiculous Zuckerman who died the idiotic death of a fifteen-year-old, trying to get laid. *Dying* to get laid. There's his eulogy, shmuck: *Carnovsky* wasn't fiction, it was *never* fiction—the fiction and the man were one! Calling it fiction was the biggest fiction of all!

The second chapter he'd titled "Judea." Me again, back from the dead for a second drubbing. Once around was never enough for Nathan. He could not wish upon me enough misfortune.

He read—he who had never gone to Israel or had any desire to visit the place, a Jew who didn't think twice about Israel or about being a Jew, who simply took it for granted that Jews were what he and his wife and children were and then went on about his business—he read of himself learning Hebrew in Israel, on some kind of Jewish settlement, under the tutelage of some political hothead, and of course in unthinking flight from the banal strictures of his conventional life . . . Yet another troubled, volatile "Henry," again in need of rescue, again behaving like a boy—and as unlike him as a man could be—and yet another superior "Nathan," detached and wise, who sees right through to "Henry's" middle-class dissatisfaction. Well, I see right through *his* cliché of domestic claustrophobia! Another dream of domination, fastening upon me another obsession from which *he* was the one who could never be rescued. The poor bastard had Jew on the brain. Why can't Jews with their Jewish problems be human beings with their human problems? Why is it always Jews after shiksas, or Jewish sons with their Jewish fathers? Why can't it ever be sons and fathers, men and women? He protests ad nauseam that I'm the son strangling on his father's prohibitions and succumbing helplessly to his father's preferences, while he's the one unable ever to grasp that I behaved as I did *not* because I was bugged by our father but because I *chose* to. Not everyone is fighting his father or fighting his life—the one unnaturally bugged by our father was *him*. What's proven here in every word, what's crying out from every line, is that the father's son who never grew up to make a family of his own, who no matter how far he traveled and how many stars he fucked and how much money he made could never escape the Newark house and the Newark family and the Newark neighborhood, the father's clone who went to his death with JewJewJew on his brain, was *him*, the superior artist! You'd have to be *blind* not to see it.

The last chapter, called "Christendom," appeared to be his dream of escape from all that, a pure magical dream of flight—from the father, the fatherland, the disease, flight from the pathetically uninhabited world of his inescapable character. Except for two pages—which Henry removed—nowhere was there any mention of a childish younger brother. Here Nathan was dreaming about only himself—*another* self—and once

Henry had realized that, he didn't take the time to examine every paragraph. He'd taken too much time already—outside the study window the courtyard was growing dark.

"Christendom"'s "Nathan" lived in London with a pretty, pregnant young Gentile wife. *He'd given her Maria's name!* Yet when Henry double-checked, looking quickly back and then ahead, he found that none of it had anything to do with his Swiss mistress. Nathan called all shiksas Maria—the explanation seemed as ludicrously simple as that. As far as Henry could tell, reading now like an examination student racing to beat the clock, it was a dream of everything that an isolate like his brother could never hope to achieve, a dream fueled by deprivations that went far beyond the story—a story about becoming a daddy, of all things. How delicious—a daddy with enough money, enough social connections to amuse him, a lovely place to live, a wonderful intelligent wife to live with, all the paraphernalia to make it like *not* having a child. So full of meaning and thought, this fatherhood of his—and missing the point completely! Entirely failing to understand that a child isn't an ideological convenience but what you have when you are young and stupid, when you're struggling to forge an identity and make a career—having babies is tied up with all *that*! But, no, Nathan was utterly unable to involve himself in anything not entirely of his own making. The closest Nathan could ever come to life's real confusion was in these fictions he created about it—otherwise he'd lived as he died, died as he'd lived, constructing fantasies of loved ones, fantasies of adversaries, fantasies of conflict and disorder, alone day after day in this peopleless room, continuously seeking through solitary literary contrivance to dominate what, in real life, he was too fearful to confront. Namely: the past, the present, and the future.

It was not Henry's intention to take away with him any more than what he had to, yet he wondered if leaving the box half full and the manuscript beginning on page 255 might not arouse suspicion, especially if the superintendent were to mention his visit to the executors when they arrived to assume custody of Nathan's estate. Taking it all, however, would have seemed like thievery, if not something even more gravely offensive to his sense of himself. What he'd already done was indecent enough—totally necessary, deeply in his interest, but hardly to his liking. Despite the sadism of Nathan's "Basel," he refused to be gratuitously vengeful—except for two pages, "Christendom" had nothing to do with him or his family, and so he left it where it was. Culling from the manuscript only what could be compromising, he removed in their entirety the chapters "Basel" and "Judea" and the opening of a chapter about an attempted skyjacking, with Nathan on board as the innocent victim and, on the evidence of a cursory reading, having as little relation to the real world as everything else in the book. These pages consisted of a letter about Jews from Nathan to Henry, and then a phone conversation about Jews between Nathan and a woman bearing no relationship to Henry's wife and of course called "Carol"—fifteen Jew-engrossed, Jew-engorged pages mirroring, purportedly, *Henry's* obsessions. Reading through them, it occurred to Henry that Nathan's deepest satisfaction as a writer must have derived from just these perverse distortions of the truth, as though he wrote *to* distort, for that pleasure primarily, and only incidentally to malign. No mind on earth could have been more alien than the mind revealed to him by this book.

I'd tried repeatedly while I was with him to invest this escape he'd made from his life's narrow boundaries with some heightened meaning, but in the end he had seemed to me, despite his determination to be something new, just as naïve and uninteresting as he'd always been.

He had to be supreme always, unquenchably superior, and I, thought Henry, was the perpetual inferior, the boy upon whom he learned to sharpen his sense of supremacy, the live-in subordinate, the junior conveniently there from the day of my birth to be overshadowed and outperformed. Why did he have to belittle me and show me up even here? Was it just gratuitous enmity, the behavior of an antisocial delinquent who chooses anybody, like a plaything, to shove in front of the subway car? Or was I simply the last in the family left to attack and betray? That he had to outrival me right to the end! As if the world didn't know already which was the incomparable Zuckerman boy!

If Henry was ever going to turn out to be interesting, I was going to have to do it.

Thank you, thank you, Nathan, for redeeming me from my pathological ordinariness, for assisting in my escape from my life's narrow boundaries. What the hell was wrong with him, why did he have to go on like this, why, even at the end of his life, could he leave nothing and no one alone!

Eager though he was to be gone, he spent yet another hour in search of copies of "Draft #2" and looking to locate a "Draft 1." All he came up with, in a drawer of one of the file cabinets, was a diary Nathan had kept during a lecture stint in Jerusalem two years before and a packet of clippings from a tabloid called *The Jewish Press.* The diary looked to be so much unembellished reporting—scribbled impressions of people and places, snippets of conversation, names of streets and lists of names; as far as Henry could tell, all of it fact, with himself nowhere to be seen. In a file folder in the drawer below, he found a yellow pad whose first pages were covered with fragments of sentences that sounded oddly familiar. *More Old Testament than that—compliance vs. retribution. The betrayal of mother love. Conjecture run wild.* It was the notes for the eulogy that he'd heard delivered that morning. Inside the pad were three successive revisions of the eulogy itself; in each version were marginal emendations and insertions, lines crossed out and rewritten, and all of it, text and corrections, in no one's hand but Nathan's.

He had written his eulogy himself. For delivery in the event he didn't survive the surgery, his own appraisal of himself, disguised as someone else's!

For all the seeming self-exposure of the novels, he was a great defender of his solitude, not because he particularly liked or valued solitude but because swarming emotional anarchy and self-exposure were possible for him only in isolation—

Swarming all right—*his* version, *his* interpretation, *his* picture refuting and impugning everyone else's and *swarming* over *everything*! And where was his authority? *Where*? If I couldn't breathe around him, it's no wonder—lashing out from behind a fortress of fiction, exerting his mind-control right down to the end over every ego-threatening challenge! Could not even entrust his *eulogy* to somebody else, couldn't extend that much trust to a faithful friend, but intrigued to contrive even his own memorial, secretly supervising those sentiments too, controlling exactly how he was to be judged! Everyone speaking that bastard's words, everyone a dummy up on his knee ventriloquizing his mouthful! My life dedicated to repairing mouths, his spent stopping them up—his spent thrusting those words down everybody's throat! In his words was our fate—*in our mouths were his words!* Everyone buried and mummified in that verbal lava, including finally himself—nothing straightforward, unvarnished, directly alive, nothing faced up to as it actually is. In his mind it never mattered what *actually* happened or what anyone *actually* was—instead everything important distorted, disguised, wrenched ridiculously out of proportion, determined by those endless, calculated illusions cunningly cooked up in this terrible solitude, everything self-calculation, deliberate deception, always this unremittingly dreadful conversion of the facts into something else . . .

It was the funeral oration that Henry had been unable to compose the night before, the unsayable at last dredged up out of his unlived existence and ready now to be delivered over the file cabinets and the folders and the notepads and the composition books and the stacks of three-ring binders. Unheard but eloquent, Henry at last recited his uncensored assessment of a life spent *hiding* from the flux of disorderly life, from its trials, its judgments, its assailability, a life lived out behind a life-proof shield of well-prepared discourse—of cunningly selected, self-protecting words.

"Thanks for letting me in," he told the superintendent when he knocked to say he was going. "You saved me a trip over tomorrow."

She kept the door of her street-floor apartment three-quarters shut on its little chain, showing through the opening only a narrow slice of face.

"Do yourself a favor," he said, "don't tell anyone I was here. They might try making trouble for you."

"Yeah?"

"The lawyers. With lawyers every little thing's a production. You know lawyers." He opened his wallet and offered her two more twenties, this time very calmly, with no palpitations of the heart.

"I got troubles enough," she said, and with two fingers plucked the money from his hand.

"Then forget you ever saw me." But she had already shut the door and was turning the lock as though he had been forgotten long ago. He probably hadn't even had to ice the cake and indeed he wondered, out in the street, if the forty bucks more might not lead her to suspect that something was up. But as far as she knew he'd done nothing wrong. The large manila envelope he had carried away with him was nicely concealed beneath an old raincoat of Nathan's that he'd found in the hall closet on the way out. Before opening the closet door, he'd once again been overtaken by the utterly ridiculous fear that Nathan would be hiding there among the coats. He wasn't, and in the elevator Henry just casually draped the raincoat over his arm—and over the envelope stuffed with Nathan's papers—as though it were his own. It could have been. The minds may have been alien but the men were pretty much the same size.

All the way up Madison Avenue there were city trash baskets into which he could easily have dispatched the envelope, but drop these pages into the Manhattan trash, he thought, and they'll wind up serialized in the *New York Post*. He had no intention, however, of bringing this stuff home for Carol to read or for her to come upon inadvertently among his papers; the objective was to spare Carol no less than himself. Ten years, even five years back, he had indeed done what married men do and tried to fuck his way out of his life. Young men fuck their way into their lives with the girls who become their wives, then they are married and someone new comes along and they try to fuck their way out. And then, like Henry, if they haven't already ruined everything, they discover that if they're sensible and discreet, they can manage to be both in and out at the same time. A lot of the emptiness that he had once attempted to fill fucking other women no longer panicked him; he'd discovered that if you're not afraid of it or angry with it, and don't overvalue it, that emptiness passes. If you just sit tight— even alone with someone you are supposed to love, feeling utterly empty with her—it goes away; if you don't fight it or rush off to fuck somebody else, and if you both have something else important to do, it does go away and you can recover some of the old meaning and substance, even for a time the vitality. Then that goes too, of course, but if you will just sit tight, it comes back again . . . and so it goes and comes, comes and goes, and that's more or less what had happened with Carol and how they had preserved, without ugly warfare or unbearable frustration, their marriage, the children's happiness, and the orderly satisfactions of a stable home.

Sure he was still tempted, and even managed taking care of himself from time to time. Who can bear a marriage of single-minded devotion? He was experienced enough and old enough to understand that affairs, adultery, whatever you call it, take a lot of the built-in pressure out of marriage and teach even the least imaginative that this idea of exclusivity isn't God-given but a social creation rigorously honored at this point only by people too pathetic to challenge it. He no longer dreamed of "other wives." A law of life he seemed finally to have learned is that the women you want most to fuck aren't necessarily the women you want to spend all that much time with, anyway. Fucking yes, but not as a way out of his life or as an escape from the facts. Unlike Nathan's, what Henry's life had come to represent was *living* with the facts—instead of trying to alter the facts, taking the facts and letting them inundate him. He no longer permitted himself to be carried heedlessly off in a sexual whirlwind—and certainly not in the office, where his concentration was entirely on the technical stuff and achieving the ultimate degree of professional perfection. He never let a patient leave his office if he thought to himself, "I could have done it better . . . it could have fit better . . . the color wasn't right . . ." No, his imperative was perfection —not just the degree of perfection needed for the patient to get through his life, not even the degree of perfection you could realistically hope for, but the degree of perfection that might just be possible, humanly and technically, if you pushed yourself to the limit. If you look at the results with bare eyes it's one thing, but if you look with loupes it's another, and it was by the minutest microscopic standards that Henry measured success. He had the highest re-do rate of anybody he knew—if he didn't like something he'd tell the patient, "Look, I'll put it in as a temporary, but I'm going to re-do it for you," and never so as to charge for it but to assuage that exacting, insistent, perfectionist injunction with which he had successfully solidified life by siphoning off the fantasy. Fantasy is speculation that is characteristically you, the you with your dream of self-over-powering, the you perennially bonded to your prize wish, your pet fear, and distorted by a kind of childish thinking that he'd annihilated from his mental processes. Anybody can run away and survive, the trick was to stay and survive, and this was how Henry had done it, not through chasing erotic daydreams, not by fleeing or through adventurous defiance, but by sounding the minutely taxing demands of his profession. Nathan had got everything backwards, overestimating—as was *his* fantasy —immoderation's appeal and the virtues of sweeping away the limits on life. The renunciation of Maria had signaled the beginning of a life that, if not quite a "classic," might be eulogized at *his* funeral as a damn good stab at equanimity. And equanimity was enough for Henry, even if to his late brother, student and connoisseur of intemperate behavior, it didn't measure up to the selfless promotion of the great human cause of irresponsible exaggeration.

Exaggeration. Exaggeration, falsification, rampant caricature —everything, thought Henry, about my vocation, to which precision, accuracy, and mechanical exactness are absolutely essential, overstated, overdrawn, and vulgarly enlarged. Witness the galling misrepresentation of my relations with Wendy. Sure when the patient is in the chair, and he's got the hygienist or assistant working on him, and she's playing with his mouth with her delicate hands and everything is hanging all over him, sure there is a part of it that stimulates, in the *patient*, sexual fantasy. But when I am doing an implant, and the whole mouth is torn open, and the tissue detached from the bone, and the teeth, the roots, all exposed, and the assistant's hands are in there with mine, when I've got four, even six, hands working on the patient, the *last* thing I'm thinking about is sex. You stop concentrating, you let that enter, and you fuck up—and I'm not a dentist who fucks up. I am a success, Nathan. I don't live all day vicariously in my head—I live with saliva, blood, bone, teeth, my hands in mouths as raw and real as the meat in the butcher's window!

Home. That was where he was finally headed, through the rush-hour traffic, with Nathan's raincoat and the envelope back in the trunk. He'd shoved them down in the well beside the spare so as to try to forget for a while disposing of the papers.

Now that he was on his way, undetected, he felt as wrung out as a man who'd been ransacking, not his brother's files, but his brother's grave, while at the same time increasingly unsettled by the fear that he had been insufficiently thorough. If he'd had to stay till 3 a.m. to be sure nothing compromising in those files had been overlooked, that's what he should have done. But once it turned dark outside, he could go no further—he'd again begun to sense Nathan's presence, to feel himself disoriented inside a dream, and desperately wanted to be home with his children and for the strain and the ugliness to be over. If only he'd had it in him to empty the files and light a match—if he could only have been sure that when they saw the ashes in the fireplace they'd assume that Nathan had burned it all, destroyed everything personal before entering the hospital . . . Stalled in the smelly back-up of commuter cars and heavy trucks outside the Lincoln Tunnel, he was seething suddenly with remorse, because of having done what he'd done and because he hadn't done more. Seething with outrage too, about "Basel" more than anything—as outraged by what Nathan had got right there as by what he'd got wrong, as much by what he'd been making up as by what he was reporting. It was the two in combination that were particularly galling, especially where the line was thin and everything was given the most distorted meaning.

By the time he got over to Jersey and had pulled off the turnpike to telephone Carol from a Howard Johnson's, he was thinking that it might be enough for now to store the pages in his safe, to stop at his office before going home and leave the envelope there. Seal it, lock it away, and then bequeath it in his will to some library to open fifty years hence, if anyone should even be interested by then. Keeping it in the safe, he could at least think everything through again in six months. Far less likely then to do the wrong thing—the thing that Nathan would expect him to do, were Nathan waiting to see what became of the manuscript. Already once this week—while writing that eulogy—he had pretended to be dead . . . suppose he were at it again, waiting to see me confirm his imaginings. The thought was absurd and yet he couldn't stop thinking it—his brother was provoking him to enact the role that he had assigned him, the role of a mediocrity. As though that word could *begin* to describe the structure he had built himself!

Long ago, before their parents had sold the Newark house and moved to Florida, back before *Carnovsky*, when everything had been different for everyone, Henry, with Carol, had driven his mother and father down to Princeton to hear Nathan deliver a public lecture. While dialing home from the restaurant, Henry remembered that after the lecture, during the question period, Nathan had been asked by a student if he wrote "in quest of immortality." He could hear Nathan laughing and giving the answer—it was as close to his dead brother as he'd come all day. "If you're from New Jersey," Nathan had said, "and you write thirty books, and you win the Nobel Prize, and you live to be white-haired and ninety-five, it's highly unlikely but not impossible that after your death they'll decide to name a rest stop for you on the Jersey Turnpike. And so, long after you're gone, you may indeed be remembered, but mostly by small children, in the backs of cars, when they lean forward and tell their parents, 'Stop, please, stop at Zuckerman—I have to make a pee.' For a New Jersey novelist that's as much immortality as it's realistic to hope for."

Ruthie answered the phone, the very child whom Nathan had pictured playing her violin over Henry's coffin, whom he had placed in tears beside her father's grave, bravely proclaiming, "He was the best, the best . . ."

He had never loved his middle child more than when he heard her ask, "Are you okay? Mom was worried that one of us should have gone with you. So was I. Where *are* you?"

She was the best, the best daughter ever. He had only to hear that kindly, thoughtful child's grown-up voice to know that he had done the only thing there was to do. My brother was a Zulu, or whoever the people are who wear bones in their noses; he was our Zulu, and ours were the heads he shrunk and stuck up on the post for everyone to gape at. The man was a cannibal.

"I wish you'd called—" Carol began, and he felt like someone who survives a harrowing ordeal and only afterwards begins to weaken and appreciate how precarious it all had been. He felt as though he'd survived a murder attempt by himself disarming the murderer. Then, beneath what he recognized as the thinking of someone utterly exhausted, he saw with clarity all the ugliness that lay behind what Nathan had written: *he was out to murder my whole family the way he'd murdered our parents, murder us with contempt for what we are. How he must have loathed my success, loathed our happiness and the way we live. How he must have loathed the way* he *lived to want to see us squirm like that.*

Only minutes later, within sight of the headlights of the cars streaking homeward along the turnpike, Henry stood at the dark edge of the parking area down from the restaurant and, pushing open the metal flap at the top of a tall brown trash can, let the papers pour out into the garbage. He dropped the envelope in too, once it was empty, then pushed Nathan's raincoat in on top of that. He was a Zulu, he thought, a pure cannibal, murdering people, eating people, without ever quite having to pay the price. Then something putrid was stinging his nostrils and it was Henry who was leaning over and violently beginning to retch, Henry vomiting as though *he* had broken the primal taboo and eaten human flesh—Henry, like a cannibal who out of respect for his victim, to gain whatever history and power is there, eats the brain and learns that raw it tastes like poison. This was no squeezing out of those tears of grief he'd hoped to shed the day before, nor was it the forgiveness that he had expected to overtake him at the funeral home, nor was it like that surge of hatred when he'd first seen his name recklessly typed across the pages of "Basel"—this was a realm of emotion unlike any he had known or would wish to know again, this quaking before the savagery of what he'd finally done and had wanted to do most of his life, to his brother's lawless, mocking brain.

How did you find out that he was dead?
The doctor called around noon. And told me just like that. "It didn't work, and I don't know what to say. There was every chance that it would, and it just didn't." He was strong and relatively young, and the doctor didn't even know why it failed. It was just the wrong decision to take. And it wasn't even necessary. The doctor just called and said, "I don't know what to tell you, I don't know what to say . . ."
Were you tempted to go to the funeral?

No. No, there was no point. It was over. I didn't want to go to the funeral. It would have been a false situation.

Do you feel responsible for his death?

I feel responsible in that if he hadn't met me it wouldn't have happened. He met me and suddenly he felt this horrible urge to quit his life and be another person. But he was so driven that perhaps if it hadn't been me it would have been somebody else. I tried to tell him not to do it, I thought it was my duty to warn him beforehand, but I also didn't think he could live as he was—he was too unhappy. He couldn't bear to live as he was. And for me to have refused him would really have meant the continuation of that. I was probably only the catalyst but of course I was deeply involved. Of course I feel responsible. If only I had fought it! I knew it was a major operation, and I knew there was a risk, but you hear of people having it all the time, seventy-year-old men have it and go bouncing about. He was so healthy, I never imagined that this could happen. But nonetheless I was deeply involved—you feel guilty if you haven't given somebody a new pair of shoelaces and they die. You always feel when somebody dies that you didn't do something that you should have done. In this case, I should have stopped him from dying.

Shouldn't you just have called it quits and stopped seeing him?

I suppose I should have, yes, when I saw the way that it was going. Every instinct *told* me to stop. I'm a very ordinary woman in my way; I suppose it was all much too intense for me. It certainly was a drama of the sort I'm not accustomed to. I had never been through all those hoops before. Even if he had lived, I don't know if I could have kept up with the intensity. He very quickly gets bored—got bored. I'm convinced that if he'd had the operation and come back and was free to move as he wanted in the world, he would have been bored with me in three or four years and moved on to somebody else. I would have left my husband, taken our child, and perhaps have had a couple of years of what one calls happiness, and then been worse off than I was before and have had to go back and live with my family in England, alone.

But what you had with him wasn't boring.

Oh, no—we were both of us too far in over our heads for

that, but it could have *become* boring to him. After a certain age people do have a pattern that's theirs, and there's little that can be done about it. It needn't have been boring, but it very well might have been.

And what did you do when they were having the funeral?

I took the child for a walk in the park. I didn't want to be alone. There was nobody I could talk to. Thank goodness it was in the morning and my beloved husband wasn't coming back until the evening and I had time to pull myself together. I had no one to share it with, but I couldn't have shared it with anyone if I had gone there. It would have been his family, his friends, his ex-girlfriends, a Jewish funeral, which I don't think he really wanted. Which I know he didn't want.

It wasn't.

I was afraid it was going to be, and I knew that was what he didn't want. Of course nobody told me about the funeral arrangements. He'd confided about me only to the surgeon.

What happened was that his editor read a eulogy. That was it.

Well, that's what he would have wanted. A flattering eulogy, I hope.

Flattering enough. And then in the evening, you went down there to the apartment.

Yes.

Why?

My husband was with the ambassador, at a meeting. I didn't know he was going to be gone. Not that I wanted him with me. It's always a dreadful business trying to keep one's expression in order. I sat upstairs by myself. I didn't know what to do with myself. I didn't go down there looking for what he'd written—I went to see the apartment. As I couldn't go to the hospital, couldn't go to the funeral, it was the nearest I could come to saying goodbye. I went down to see the apartment. When I went into the study there was the box on his desk—it had "Draft #2" written on it. It was what he'd been working on during the time he was with me. His last thoughts, it turned out. I always said, "Don't write about me," but I knew he always used everybody else and I didn't see why he shouldn't use me. I wanted to see—well, I suppose I thought there might be a message in it, in some way.

You went downstairs "to say goodbye." What does that mean?

I just wanted to sit alone in the apartment. Nobody knew I had a key. I just wanted to sit there for a while.

And what was it like?

It was dark.

Did it frighten you?

Yes and no. Secretly I've always believed in ghosts. And been afraid of them. Yes, I was frightened. But I sat there, and I thought, "If he's here . . . then he'll come." I started to laugh. I had a kind of conversation with him—one-sided. "Of course you wouldn't, how could you come back when you have no belief in these totally idiotic things?" I started to wander about like Garbo in *Queen Christina*, touching all the furniture. Then I saw the cardboard box on his desk, with "Draft #2" on it and the date he'd gone into the hospital. I used to say to him when I went into his study, "Be careful what you leave out, because anything that's on that desk, upside down or anywhere, I will read. If it's there. I don't go snooping, but I'll read anything that's left out. I can't help it." We joked about it. He'd say, "Mankind divides into two groups, those who will read other people's correspondence and those who won't, and you and I, Maria, fall on the wrong side of the line. We are people who open medicine cabinets to look at other people's prescription drugs." There was the box, and I was drawn to it, as they say, like a magnet. I thought, "There may be some message in it."

Was there?

There sure was. Something called "Christendom." A section, a chapter, a novella—I couldn't be certain. And I thought, "That's a little threatening. Is 'Christendom' the enemy? Is it me?" And I picked it up and I started to read it. And perhaps a lot of the love I had felt for him went at that moment. Well, not a lot of it, not when I read it again, but some of it, the first time round. The second time what touched me more than anything was his longing just to shed it all and have another life, his longing to be a father and a husband, things the poor man never was. I suppose he realized that he had missed that. However much one hates the sentimentality, it's a big thing to have missed in your life, not to have had a child. And he was so touching about Phoebe. Whereas everybody else in "Christendom" he changes, Phoebe alone he perceives as she is, as just a child, a little girl.

But what about the first time round?

I saw the other side of him, the irrational, the violent side of him. I don't mean physically, I mean how he would turn everything that wasn't familiar to him into the outsider—that I had been used in that way too, and that my family had been maligned most terribly. Of course, like all English families *they* thought of the outsider as the outsider, but it doesn't mean that they have those feelings that he had given them, of superiority and loathing—of apartheid, so to speak. My sister, perhaps not the best character in the world, is nonetheless only a poor, pathetic girl who never found her place anywhere, who's never been able to do anything, but to her he ascribed these terrible feelings about Jews and a disgusting sense of superiority that, if you knew Sarah, was ludicrous. You see, he had met my sister Sarah once, when she came to visit—I'd introduced them, as though he were just a neighbor. But what he had taken from my sister was so far from what she was that I thought there was something deeply twisted in him that he couldn't help. Because he had been brought up as he was, ringed round by all that Jewish paranoia, there was something in him that twisted everything. It seemed to me that *he* was my sister—*he* was the one who thought of "the other" as the other in that derogatory sense. He'd put all his feelings, actually, onto her— his Jewish feelings about Christian women turned into a Christian woman's feelings about a Jewish man. I thought that the great verbal violence, that "hymn of hate" he ascribed to Sarah, was in *him*.

But what about love for you in "Christendom"?

Oh, the subject is his love for, in quotations, me. But you can see at the end of it, when they have this quarrel, what the chances are for that love. Even though you know he goes back to her, and they pick up their lives, their lives are going to be tremendously difficult. You know that absolutely. Because he had tremendous ambivalence about a Christian woman. I was a Christian woman.

But you're talking about what "Christendom" is like, not about what Nathan was like. This never came up between you, did it?

It never came up because we never lived together. We had a

romantic affair. Never before had I been so romantically involved with anyone. Nothing came up between us, except that
operation. We met as if in a time capsule, imprisoned by my fear
of discovery, like something one reads about in a nineteenth-
century novel. There's a sense in which it's completely fictitious. I could believe I made the whole thing up. And that's
not just because it's now gone—it was the same when it was in
the very active present. I don't know what our life would have
been like had we been able to live together. I saw no violent
feelings—because of the drug there wasn't even a chance for
good old-fashioned genital aggression. I saw only tenderness.
The drug had done that as well—overtenderized him. That
was what he secretly couldn't stand. It was the aggression he
wanted to recover too.

*But his imaginative life might have remained quite separate
from your real life. Your sister would have been your sister to him,
not the sister he imagined.*

I've never lived with a novelist, you know. On first reading I
took it all rather literally, as a bad critic would take it—I took it
as *People* magazine would take it. After all, he used our names,
he used people who were recognizably themselves and yet radically different. I think he might have changed the names later
on. I'm sure he would have changed them. Of course I can see
how Mariolatry appealed to him; in the circumstances he invented, Maria is the perfect name. And if it *was* the perfect
name, he might *not* have changed it. But surely he would have
changed Sarah's name.

And his name, would he have changed that?

I'm not so sure—maybe in a later draft. But if he wanted to,
he would have used it. I'm not a writer, so I don't know how
far these people will go for the desired effect.

But you are a writer.

Oh, only in a very minor risk-free league. That's *all* he was.
Anyway, I read this story, or chapter, or fragment, whatever it
was to be, this draft, and I didn't know what to do. All my life
I despised Lady Byron, and Lady Burton, all those people who
destroyed their husbands' memoirs, and letters, and erotic
writings. It's always seemed to me the most incredible crime
that we'll never know what those letters of Byron's contained. I
thought of these women quite deliberately, quite consciously—

I thought, "I think I am going to do with this what they have done that I've despised all my life." It's the first time that I understood why they did it.

But you didn't do it.

I cannot destroy the only thing he cared about, the only thing he had left. He had no children, he had no wife, he had no family: the only thing left was these pages. Into this went his unconsumed potency as a man. This imaginary life is our offspring. This is *really* the child he wanted. It's simple—I couldn't commit infanticide. I knew that if it was published, unfinished, in this form, all the characters would be quite identifiable, but I thought the only thing I could do, with my husband, was to lie my way out of it. I thought, "I'm going to say, 'Yes, it's me—he met my sister, he used everybody, he used us. I knew the man very slightly. I knew him a little more than you thought I did, we had a coffee together, we went for a walk in the park, but I know how jealous you are and I never told you.'" I would say that he had been impotent and we never had an affair, but we were good friends, and that this is fantasy. And it is. I'll lie my way out and I'll also be telling the truth. I thought of tearing it up and throwing it down the incinerator chute, but in the end I couldn't. I'm not taking part in destroying a book just because the author isn't here to protect it. I left it on the desk, where it was when I came in.

You're in a lot of hot water, aren't you?

Why? If my marriage breaks up because of that, then it does. I think it'll take at least a year before it's published. I'll have a year to pull myself together, to think up fairy stories, and perhaps even to leave my husband. But I'm not going to destroy Nathan's last words for a marriage that I'm unhappy in.

Perhaps this is the way out of that marriage.

Perhaps. It's true, I would never have the courage to say, "I want a divorce"—this is certainly much easier for me than saying, "I have a lover and I want a divorce." Let him find it out, if he wants to. He's not a great reader, by the way, not anymore.

I think it'll be brought to his attention.

If I want to disguise myself, the only chance I have is to go to his editor and to say, "Look, I know, because he showed it to me, what he was writing. I know that he used characters very close to me and my family. He used our names. But he had said to me that this is only a draft, and if the book is published I'm going to change the names." I'll say to his editor, "If the book is published the names have to be changed. I have no threat to make—I'm only saying that otherwise it'll destroy my life." I don't think he'll do it, I don't think he can do it, but it's probably what I shall do.

But its publication won't destroy your life.

No, no, it won't—it *is* my way out.

And that's why you didn't destroy the manuscript.

Is it?

If you had a good marriage you certainly would have.

If I had a good marriage I wouldn't have been down there in the first place.

You two had an interesting time, didn't you?

It was interesting, all right. But I will not take responsibility for his death . . . to go back to that. It's very hard to step *away* from that, isn't it? I don't believe that he did it only for me. As I said, he would have done it anyway—he would have done it for somebody else. He would have done it for *himself.* Being the man he was, he didn't see that to women like me the impotence was of secondary importance. He couldn't understand it. He said to me, "A time comes when you have to forget what frightens you most." But I don't think it was dying that most frightened him—it was facing the impotence for the rest of his life. That *is* frightening, and that he couldn't forget, certainly not so long as my presence was there to remind him. I was the one who was there at the time, of course—he was in love with me, but at the time. If it wasn't me, it would have been somebody else later.

That you'll never know. You may have been desired more than you can bear to believe right now—no less loved in life than you are in "Christendom."

Oh, yes, the dream life that we had together in that fictional house-to-be. The way it sort of vaguely might have been. He didn't know Strand on the Green in Chiswick. I told him about it and how, when I'd first got married, I'd dreamed of living there and having a house there. I suppose I gave him that idea. I showed him a picture postcard of it once, the towpath protecting the houses from the Thames, and the willows leaning over the water.

Did you tell him about the incident at the restaurant?

No, no. In the sixties he'd spent a summer in London with one of his wives, and he told me what had happened to them in a restaurant there and what he has in the story happening with me. It certainly wasn't like him to make a scene in a restaurant. Though I really wouldn't know—we were never in a restaurant. How does one know what is real or false with a writer like that? These people aren't fantasists, they're imaginers—it's the difference between a flasher and a stripper. Making you believe what he wanted you to believe was his very reason for being. Maybe his only reason. I was intrigued by the way he'd turned events, or hints I *had* given him about people, into reality— that is, *his* kind of reality. This obsessive reinvention of the real never stopped, what-could-be having always to top what-is. For instance, my mother is not a woman like the mother in "Christendom" who's written outstanding books but an extremely ordinary English woman, living in the country, who's never done anything of interest in her life and never set pen to paper. However, the only thing I ever told him about her, once, was that like most provincial English women of her class, she has a touch of anti-Semitism. This of course has been built into something gigantic and awful. Look at *me.* After reading "Christendom" twice I went upstairs, and when my husband came home, I began to wonder which was real, the woman in the book or the one I was pretending to be upstairs. Neither of them was particularly "me." I was acting just as much upstairs; I was not myself just as much as Maria in the book was not myself. Perhaps she was. I began not to know which was true and which was not, like a writer when he comes to believe that he's imagined what he hasn't. When I saw my sister, I resented the things she said to Nathan in the church—*in the book.* I was confused, deeply confused. It was obviously a very strong experience to read it. The book began living in me all the time, more than my everyday life.

So now what?

I'm going to sit back and see what happens. The one thing he did get about me in that story, the fact of my character, is that I'm deeply passive. And yet inside there is some mechanism that ticks away and tells me what is the right thing to do. I always seem to preserve myself in some way. But in a very circular manner. I think I shall be rescued.

By what he wrote.

It's begun to look that way, hasn't it? I think that my husband will read it, that he will ask me about it, that I will lie, that he will not believe me. My husband will have to come to grips with what has been going on in our lives for some time now. He's not such a hypocrite as to find this utterly surprising. I do think he has another life. I think he has a mistress; I'm sure of it. I think he's as deeply unhappy as I am. He and I are caught up in a terrible, neurotic symbiosis that both of us are rather ashamed of. But what he'll do because of "Christendom" I don't know. He's, on the one hand, very *comme il faut*, he wants to rise quickly in the diplomatic service, he wants to run for Parliament, he wants quite a bit—but he is also sexually very competitive, and if this looks to him like an affront to his manhood, he does have it in him to do dreadful things. I don't know what exactly, but his spitefulness can be quite inventive, and, in a very modest way, he could make sort of what used to be called a scandal. He'd have no *real* motive for kicking up a horrible fuss, other than to make my life unpleasant. But people do that all the time. Especially if they think they can put you in a position of wrong. You know: thou art more treacherous than me. I just don't know what he'll do, but what I want, above all, is finally to go home. Nathan's story has made me terribly homesick. I don't want to live in New York any more. I dread going back to my family. They're not so disagreeable as Nathan described, but neither are they very intelligent, by any means. He both heightened their intelligence and lowered their conscience and their moral tone. They're just deeply boring people who sit and watch television, and that was too boring for him—to put into a book, I mean. I don't think I'll be able to bear that for long either, but I don't really have the money to set up by myself, and I don't want to ask my husband for anything. I'll have to get a job. But after all I speak several languages, I'm still only twenty-eight, I have only one child, and there's no reason why I can't pick my life up. Even a well-bred penniless girl can get a job cleaning houses. I'll just have to get up and go out hawking myself like everybody else.

What do you think he loved so about you?

Drop the "so" and I'll answer. I was pretty, I was young, I was intelligent, I was very needy. I had tremendous woo-ability—I was there. Very much there—just upstairs. Upstairs downstairs. He called the lift our *deus ex machina.* I was foreign enough for him, but not so foreign as to make it taboo-foreign or bizarre-foreign. I was touchable-foreign, less boring to him than the equivalent American woman he was partial to. I wasn't that different in class from the women he'd married; as far as class and interests go, we were really very much the same kind of women, fairly refined, intelligent, amenable, educated, Nathanly coherent, but I was English and that made it less familiar. He liked my sentences. He said to me before he went into the hospital, "I'm the man who fell in love with a relative clause." He liked my speech, my English archaisms and my schoolgirl slang. Oddly, those American women were *really* "the shiksa," but because I was English I think there was even a difference in that. I was surprised in "Christendom" by his rather romantic idea of me. Maybe that's what one always feels when one reads about oneself—if you're written about, if you're turned into a character in a book, unless it is really crushingly derogatory, the very fact of being focused on like that is somehow curiously romanticizing. He certainly exaggerated my beauty.

But not your age. It didn't hurt that you were twenty-eight. He liked that.

All men like that you're twenty-eight. The twenty-two-year-old men like it, and the forty-five-year-old men like it, and even the twenty-eight-year-old men don't seem to be bothered too much. Yes, it's a very good age. It's probably a very good age to stay.

Well, you will, in the book.

Yes, and I'll have that dress, the dress that I wear at the restaurant. This perfectly ordinary dress I had, he made into something so voluptuous and beautiful. That pleasant, old-fashioned night out he gave us, such an old-fashioned fifties idea he had about having a night out at an expensive restaurant with the woman who's having your baby and has the hormonal glow. How romantically extravagant, and how innocent, the bracelet he gives me for my birthday. What a surprise. The wish-fulfillment aspect is very touching. It's too late to say I was moved, but I was, to put it mildly. The romantic life we might have had, in the Chiswick home . . . I don't think he really wanted any of these things, mind you. I'm not even sure he wanted me. He may well have wanted me as copy. Yet I do think, however much he romanticized my desirability, he saw me in an extremely cruel and clear way. Because with all the affection, he still does see her—my—passivity. I *am* all talk. And, yes, I do like money, I do like good things, I do like much more of a frivolous life, I presume, than he would have liked. The carol service, for instance. I actually wasn't there with him, in the church, as he has it in the story—that was in New York, that carol service, with a *real* Christian wife—but the point is that people go to carol service for fun, not because they believe in Jesus Christ or the Holy Virgin or whatever but just to have a good time. I think he never understood that side of me. I like to passively enjoy my life. I never wanted to be anything or to do anything. A lot of people do things not for the deep Jewish or religious reasons that he thinks they do, but they just do them—there are no questions to be asked. He asked so many questions, all of them interesting, but not always from the other person's point of view. I'm like everything else in the story: he elevated and intensified everything. That's what made the operation inevitable—he intensified and heightened his illness too, as though it were taking place in a novel. The writer's refusal to accept things as they are—everything reinvented, even himself. Maybe he wanted that operation for copy too, to see what that drama was like. That's not impossible. He was always, I believe the expression is, upping the ante—"Christendom" is just that. Well, he upped it once too far, and it killed him. He did with his life exactly what he did in his fiction, and finally paid for it. He finally confused the two—just what he was always warning everybody against. So did I momentarily confuse things, I suppose—began to collaborate with him on a far more interesting drama than the one I had going upstairs. That, upstairs, was just another conventional domestic farce, so every afternoon, I took the *deus ex machina* down to the oldest romantic drama in the world. "Go ahead, save me, risk your life and save me—and I'll save you." Vitality together. Vitality at any price, the nature of all heroism. Life as an act. What could be more un-English? I yielded too. Only I survived and he hasn't.

Have you? What if your husband uses this to try to get Phoebe away from you?

No, no. You really can't use a work of fiction in a court of law, not even to expose a treacherous, double-dealing woman like me. No, I really don't think he could do that, however hurtful he may try to be. I'll take care of Phoebe and I'll have the day-to-day responsibilities, and he'll see her from time to time, and that's how it will end, I'm sure. My mother of course is going to be very upset. As for Sarah, it's so far from anything she could ever say or do, I don't think she'll take it seriously. She'll realize that if he had lived, he would have changed the names before he'd finished, and that'll be that.

And you will be, at least among his readers, the Maria of "Christendom."

I will, won't I? Oh, I won't suffer. I think relics are always rather fascinating. I remember when I was at university there was a woman pointed out to me as H. G. Wells's mistress, one of the many. I was fascinated. She was ninety. It hadn't seemed to have done her any harm. Even women like me have some extrovert fantasy.

So it's all worked for you, really. This is how you free yourself from the bullying husband. This is the happy ending. Saved, free to cultivate your child and your sense of yourself as the woman you are, without having to do the loony thing of running off with another man. Without having to do anything.

Except that the poor other man I was to run off with died, remember. Suddenly there is death. Life goes on but he's not here. There are certain recurrent shocks in life, which you can just steady yourself for—you can take a deep breath and it passes by and it doesn't hurt so much. But this is different. He was such a support for me in my head for so long. And now he's not here even to be there. I've managed, however. Actually I've been so heroic I wouldn't recognize myself.

And what will it have meant to you?

Oh, the great experience of my life, I think. Yes, without question. A footnote in an American writer's life. Who would have thought that would happen?

Who would have thought you'd be the angel of death?

No, the footnote's more me, but yes, I can see how somebody might see it that way. Like in a Buñuel film—the dark young woman that Buñuel has in those films, one of those mysterious creatures, totally innocent of it, but yes, the role assigned her is angel of death. Somewhat more devastating than my role in "Christendom." I did nothing to instigate it, and yet through my weakness it happened. I think a stronger woman would have had more humor than I did, would have got less caught up, and would have known how to deal with the situation better. But, as I say, I think he would have done it with the next one anyway. Like Mayerling—like the Archduke Rudolf and Maria Vetsera. She wasn't the first woman that he'd asked to commit suicide with him, she was just the first who agreed to do it. He'd tried with many women. It came out afterwards that he'd had it in his mind for a long time to commit a double suicide.

Are you suggesting that Nathan was trying to commit suicide?

I think he succeeded, but no, he didn't want that. I think that was the joke, that was exactly the kind of humiliating irony, the kind of self-inflicted brutal life-fact that he admired so: someone wants to be given back his masculine life, and instead he dies. But, no, that wasn't what he wanted. He wanted health and strength and freedom. He wanted virility again, and the force that drives it. I was instrumental, as who isn't? That *is* love.

And now, are there any questions you want to ask me?

I can answer questions but I can't ask them. You ask them.

The smart woman who's learned not to ask smart questions. You know who I am, don't you?

No. Well, yes. Yes, I know who you are, and I know, so to speak, why you've come back.

Why?

To learn what happened. What it's like now. What I did. You have the rest of the story to tell. You need the hard evidence, the details, the clues. You want an ending. Yes, I know who you are—the same restless soul.

You look tired.

No, just slightly pale, and unkempt. I'll be all right. I didn't sleep well last night. I'm in a marital low. My burdens, fallen from my shoulders, are gathering around my ankles. Resignation's a hard thing, isn't it? Especially if you're not sure it's the right thing. Anyway, I was lying in my bed and I suddenly woke up, and there was this presence. Just out there. It was your prick. By itself. Where's the rest of his body, where's everything else? And it was as if I could touch it. And then it sort of went into a shadow, and then the rest of you assembled itself around it. And I knew it was just a thought. But for a little while it was just there. Last night.

So what is it like now? Right now.

My life began again when I absolutely gave up on him, and started writing again, and met you—all sorts of things happened that were really wonderful. And I felt much better. But living again in such a cold way fills me with, not horror, but terrible pain. Sometimes I feel it so acutely I can't even sit still. Saturday, as people always do, he supplied some unreasonable behavior, just enough to make me feel in a bit of a rage, and I said to him, I can't put up with any more of being the outdated, extraneous wife. Unfortunately I said it once before, and of course did nothing, and these things have a diminishing impact. Getting ready not to do things is most exhausting. On the other hand, things one says repeatedly do sometimes happen. But frankly what it is, since you ask, is boring now. I'm the one who's bored, because you're not here. Now I think, "I can't spend the whole rest of my life being so bored, apart from everything else." You brought such clandestine excitement. And the talk. The intensity of all that lovely talk. Most people have sex cut off from love, and maybe it appears that we had the opposite, love cut off from sex. I don't know. That endless, issueless, intimate talk—sometimes it must have seemed to you like the conversation of two people in jail, but to me it was the purest form of eros. It was clearly different and less fulfilling for a man who'd spent his whole life getting to the solace of sex so very quickly and was far more compelled to consummation. But for me it had its power. For me those times were tremendous.

But of course—you're the great talker, Maria.

Am I? Well, you've got to have someone to talk *to*. I could certainly talk to you. You listened. I can never talk to Michael. I try, and I see the glassy look in his eye, and I get out my book.

Keep talking to me then.

I will. I will. I know now what a ghost is. It is the person you talk to. That's a ghost. Someone who's still so alive that you talk to them and talk to them and never stop. A ghost is the ghost of a ghost. It's my turn now to invent you.

And how's your little girl?

Very well. She can speak so well now. "I want a piece of paper." "I want a pencil." "I'm going outside."

How old is she?

She's not quite two.

5. Christendom

A T SIX in the evening, only a few hours after leaving Henry at Agor and arriving in London with the notes I'd amassed on the quiet flight up from Tel Aviv, my mind suffused still with all those implacable, dissident, warring voices and the anxieties stirring up their fear and resolve—in under five hours back from that unharmonious country where it appears that nothing, from the controversy to the weather, is ever blurred or underdone—I was seated in a church in London's West End. With me were Maria, Phoebe, and some three or four hundred others, many of whom had rushed from work to be in time for the carol service. It was just two weeks before Christmas; in the Strand the heavy traffic was at a standstill and the streets leading out of the West End were clogged with cars and shoppers. After a mild afternoon, the evening had turned cold, and a light fog diffused the beams of the cars. Phoebe was so excited by the traffic and the traffic lights and the Christmas lights and the jostling crowds that she had to be taken to the bathroom in the crypt while I found our seats in the reserved pew, just down the row from Georgina and Sarah, Maria's sisters. As a longtime member of the board of the charity for whom the collection would be taken, Maria's mother, Mrs. Freshfield, was to read one of the lessons.

Maria led Phoebe around to her grandmother, who was sitting with the other readers in the first row, and then to see her two aunts. They rejoined me in our seats just as the choir was filing in, the bigger boys first, in blue school blazers, striped ties, and gray trousers, then the smaller boys, in their short pants. The choirmaster, a neatly attired young man with prematurely gray hair and wearing horn-rimmed glasses, seemed to me a composite of kindly schoolteacher and circus lion-tamer— when, with the tiniest inclination of his head, he directed the boys to be seated, even the smallest responded as though the whip had cracked dangerously nearby. Maria pointed out to Phoebe the Christmas tree off to one side of the nave; though impressively tall, it was rather sparsely decorated with red, white, and blue tinsel, and pinned to the top was a lopsided silver star that looked like the handiwork of a Sunday School class. In front of us, directly beneath the pulpit, was a large circular arrangement of white chrysanthemums and carnations embedded in evergreen and holly branches. "See the flowers?" Maria said, and a little confused but utterly enthralled, Phoebe replied, "Grandma story." "Soon," Maria whispered, straightening the pleats in the child's plaid dress, and then the organ solo began and with it the mild undercurrent of antipathy in me.

It never fails. I am never more of a Jew than I am in a church when the organ begins. I may be estranged at the Wailing Wall but without being a stranger—I stand outside but not shut out, and even the most ludicrous or hopeless encounter serves to gauge, rather than to sever, my affiliation with people I couldn't be less like. But between me and church devotion there is an unbridgeable world of feeling, a natural and thoroughgoing incompatibility—I have the emotions of a spy in the adversary's camp and feel I'm overseeing the very rites that embody the ideology that's been responsible for the persecution and mistreatment of Jews. I'm not repelled by Christians at prayer, I just find the religion foreign in the most far-reaching ways— inexplicable, misguided, profoundly *inappropriate*, and never more so than when the congregants are observing the highest standards of liturgical decorum and the cleric most beautifully enunciating the doctrine of love. And yet there I was, behaving as every well-trained spy aspires to do, looking quite at ease, I thought, agreeable, untrammeled, while squeezed up against my shoulder sat my pregnant Christian-born English wife, whose mother was to read the lesson from St. Luke.

By conventional standards Maria and I must certainly have seemed, because of the dissimilar backgrounds and the difference in age, to be a strangely incongruous couple. Whenever our union seemed incongruous even to me, I wondered if it wasn't a mutual *taste* for incongruity—for assimilating a slightly untenable arrangement, a shared inclination for the sort of unlikeness that doesn't, however, topple into absurdity—that accounted for our underlying harmony. It was still beguiling for people raised in such alien circumstances to discover in themselves interests so strikingly similar—and, of course, the differences continued to be pretty exhilarating too. Maria was keen, for instance, to pin my professional "seriousness" to my class origins. "This artistic dedication of yours is slightly provincial, you know. It's far more metropolitan to have a slightly anarchic view of life. Yours only seems anarchic and isn't at all. About standards you're something of a hick. Thinking things *matter*." "It's the hicks who think things matter who seem to get things done." "Like books written, yes," she said, "that is so. That's why there are so few upper-class artists and writers —they haven't *got* the seriousness. Or the standards. Or the irritation. Or the ire." "And the values?" "Well," she said, "we certainly haven't got that. That really *is* over the top. One used to expect the upper classes at least to pay for it all, but they won't even do that anymore. On that score, I was a renegade, at least as a child. I'm over it now, but when I was little I used terribly to want to be remembered after my death for something I had *achieved*." "I wanted to be remembered," I said, "before my death." "Well, that is also important," Maria said, "—in fact, slightly more important. Slightly provincial, unsophisticated, and hickish, but, I must say, attractive in you. The famous Jewish intensity." "Counterbalanced in you by the famous English insouciance." "And that," she said, "is a gentle way of describing my fear of failure."

After the organ solo, we rose and everyone began to sing the first carol, except me and children like Phoebe who were too small to know the words and couldn't read them from the program. The assemblage sang with tremendous zest, an eruption of good clean vehemence that I hadn't anticipated from the chastening authority of the choirmaster or the genteel solemnity of the minister who was to make the blessing. The men with briefcases, the shoppers with their parcels and bundles and bags, those who at the worst of the rush hour had come all the way into the West End with overexcited little children or with their elderly relatives—no longer were they unattached and on their own, but merely by opening their mouths and singing out, this crowd of disparate Londoners had turned into a battalion of Christmas-savoring Christians, relishing every syllable of Christian praise with enormous sincerity and gusto. It sounded to me as though they'd been hungering for weeks for the pleasure of affirming that enduring, subterranean association. They weren't rapturous or in a delirium—to use the appropriately old-fashioned word, they seemed *gladdened*. It may well be a little hickish to find the consolations of Christianity a surprise, but I was struck nonetheless to hear from their voices just how delightful it was—in Zionist argot, how very *normal* they felt—to be the tiniest component of something immense whose indispensable presence had been beyond Western society's serious challenge for a hundred generations. It was as though they were symbolically feasting upon, communally devouring, a massive spiritual baked potato.

Yet, Jewishly, I still thought, what *do* they need all this stuff for? Why do they need these wise men and all these choruses of angels? Isn't the birth of a child wonderful enough, *more* mysterious, for *lacking* all this stuff? Though frankly I've always felt that the place where Christianity gets dangerously, vulgarly obsessed with the miraculous is Easter, the Nativity has always struck me as a close second to the Resurrection in nakedly addressing the most childish need. Holy shepherds and starry skies, blessed angels and a virgin's womb, being materializing on this planet without the heaving and the squirting, the smells and the excretions, without the plundering satisfaction of the orgasmic shudder—what sublime, offensive kitsch, with its fundamental abhorrence of sex.

Certainly the elaboration of the story of the Virgin Birth had never before struck me as quite so childish and spinsterishly unacceptable as it did that evening, fresh from my Sabbath at Agor. When I heard them singing about that Disneyland Bethlehem, in whose dark streets shineth the everlasting light, I thought of Lippman distributing his leaflets in the marketplace there and consoling, with his *Realpolitik*, the defiant Arab enemy: "Don't give up your dream, dream of Jaffa, go ahead; and someday, if you have the power, even if there are a *hundred* pieces of paper, you will take it from me by force."

When her turn came, Maria's mother ascended to the pulpit lectern and, in that tone of simplicity with which you induce first gullibility and then sleep in children to whom you're telling a bedtime story, charmingly read from St. Luke the fifth lesson, "The Angel Gabriel salutes the Blessed Virgin Mary." Her own writing disclosed a stronger affinity to a lowly, more corporeal existence: three books—*The Interior of the Georgian Manor House*, *The Smaller Georgian Country House*, and *Geor-*

gians at Home—as well as numerous articles over the years in *Country Life*, had earned for her a solid reputation among students of Georgian interior design and furnishings, and she was regularly asked to speak to local Georgian societies all over England. A woman who took her work "dead seriously," according to Maria—"a very reliable source of information"—though on this occasion looking less like someone who spent her London days in the V & A archives and the British Library than like the perfect hostess, a short, pretty woman some fifteen years older than I, with a soft round face that reminded me of a porcelain plate and that very fine hair that turns from a mousy blond to snowy white with very little difference of effect, hair that's been done for thirty years by the same very good, old-fashioned hairdresser. Mrs. Freshfield had the air of someone who never put a foot wrong—which Maria claimed had nearly been so: her big mistake had been her husband, but she'd made that only once, and after her marriage to Maria's father had never again been distracted from Georgian interiors by the inexplicable yearning for an attractive man.

"She was the beauty of the Sixth," Maria explained to me, "the Queen of Hockey—she carried off all the prizes. He was academically rather stupid, but terribly athletic, and he had enormous glamour. The black Celt. He stood out a mile. Elegant and, even before he arrived at university, quite stuck up about his glamour. Nobody could understand what it was that made him so famous. There were all these other boys wanting to be judges, or cabinet ministers, or soldiers, and this stupid twit was turning on the girls. Mother hadn't been turned on before. After, she never wanted to be again. And she wasn't—from all the evidence, never so much as touched again. She did everything to give us a solid world, a good and solid, traditional English upbringing—that became the entire meaning of her life. He had always behaved beautifully to us; no man could have enjoyed three little girls more. We enjoyed him too. He behaved beautifully to everyone, except her. But if you're convinced that your wife is fundamentally uninterested in what interests you, which is your erotic power, and if the history of your relationship is that you can hardly communicate with her at all, and there's nothing really but resentment between you in the end, and however sterling a character she may have, she doesn't really *come across*—I think that's the expression—and you yourself have lots of vitality and are rather highly sexed, as he was—and like all you boys, he seemed to find it a great torture, you just want it *so much*—then you have no choice, really, do you? First you devote lots of hours to the humiliation of your wife, with her best friends ideally, and then with the obliging neighbors, until having exhausted every possibility for betrayal in the immediate hundred square miles, you vanish, and there's an acrimonious divorce, and after there's never enough money, and your little girls are forever susceptible to dark men with beautiful manners."

Until her grandmother had taken her place in the pulpit, Phoebe had been mostly intrigued by the tiny trebles in their short pants, some of whom, not halfway through the hour, were looking as though they wouldn't have minded being home in bed. But when Grandmother stepped into the pulpit to read, the child suddenly found everything amusing—tugging at Maria's hand, she began to laugh and get excited, and could be quieted only by climbing onto Mummy's lap, where she was gently rocked into a semi-stupor.

A solo followed, sung by a slender boy of about eleven whose untainted charm reminded me of a doctor with too much bedside manner. After he concluded his part and the entire choir had seraphically joined in, he brazenly focused a coquettish smile upon the choirmaster, who in turn acknowledged how remarkable a boy the beautiful soloist was with a half-suppressed but lingering smile of his own. Still not about to be taken in by all this Christian heartiness, I was relieved to think that I'd caught a little whiff of homoerotic pedophilia. I wondered if in fact my skepticism hadn't already prompted the rector to single me out as someone privately making unseasonal observations. On the other hand, as we were seated in pews reserved for the readers' families, it may have been that he had simply recognized Maria as her mother's daughter and that alone explained the scrutinizing appraisal of the gentleman next to the Freshfield girl who appeared to have come to the carol service determined not to sing.

We stood for the carols and sat for the lessons and remained seated when the choir sang "The Seven Joys of Mary" and "Silent Night." When the program directed "All kneel" for the blessing, which came after the collection, I remained obstinately upright, fairly sure I was the only one in all the church failing to assume a posture of devout submission. Maria leaned forward just enough so as not to affront the rector—or her mother, should she turn out to have eyes in the back of her skull—and I was thinking that if my grandparents had disembarked at Liverpool instead of continuing on in steerage for New York, if family fate had consigned me to schools here rather than to the municipal education system of Newark, New Jersey, my head would always have been sticking up like this when everyone else's was bowed in prayer. Either that, or I would have tried to keep my origins to myself, and to avoid seeming a little boy inexplicably bent on making himself strange, I too would have kneeled, however well I understood that Jesus was a gift to neither me nor my family.

After the rector's blessing everyone rose for the final carol, "Hark, the Herald Angels Sing." Inclining her head conspiratorially toward me, Maria whispered, "You are a very forbearing anthropologist," and holding Phoebe so as to keep her from slumping over with fatigue, she proceeded to sing out rousingly, along with everyone else, "Christ, by highest heaven adored / Christ, the everlasting Lord," while I remembered how shortly after our arrival in England her ex-husband had referred to me on the phone as "the aging Jewish writer." When I'd asked how she'd responded, she slipped her arms around me and said, "I told him that I liked all three."

Following the organ finale we took a stairway by the porch of the church down into a spacious, low-ceilinged, whitewashed crypt, where mulled wine and mince pie were being served. It took some time to navigate little Phoebe through all of the people heading down the stairs for refreshment. The child was to spend the night with her grandmother, a treat for both, while I took Maria out to celebrate her birthday. Everyone said how lovely the singing had been and told Mrs. Freshfield how wonderfully she had read. An elderly gentleman whose name I couldn't catch, a friend of the family who had also read one of the lessons, explained to me the purpose of the charity for which the collection had been taken—"Been going on for a hundred years," he said, "—there are so many poor and lonely people."

Fortunately there was our new house to give us all something to talk about, and there were Polaroid snapshots to look at, taken by Maria when she had driven over the day before to check on the construction. The house was to be renovated over the next six months while we stayed in a rented mews house in Kensington. Actually it was two connecting, smallish brick houses, on the site of an old boatyard in Chiswick, that we were converting into one large enough for the family and the nanny and for studios for Maria and me.

We talked about how Chiswick wasn't as far out as it seemed and yet with the gate closed on the stone wall to the street it had the seclusion of a remote rural village—the quiet Nathan needed for his work, Maria told everyone. On the rear-street side there was the wall and a paved garden with daffodils and irises and a small apple tree; at the front of the house, beyond a raised terrace where we could sit on warm evenings, there was a wide towpath and the river. Maria said that it looked as though most of the people who walked along the towpath were either lovers having assignations or women with small children—"one way or another," she said, "people in a very good mood." There were people fishing for trout now that the river was cleaned up, and early in the morning, when you opened the shutters on what was to be our bedroom, you could see rowing eights out to practice. In the summer there were small boats going up for holidays on the river and the steamers carrying sightseers from Charing Cross to Kew Gardens. In late autumn the fog came down and in winter barges went by with their cargo covered, and often in the morning there was mist. And there were always gulls—ducks as well, that walked up the terrace steps to be fed, if you fed them, and, occasionally, there were swans. Twice a day at high tide the river rose over the towpath and lapped at the terrace wall. The elderly gentleman said that it sounded as though for Maria it would be like living in Gloucestershire again while only fifteen minutes by the Underground from Leicester Square. She said, no, no, it wasn't the country *or* London, and it wasn't the suburbs either, it was living on the river . . . on and on, amiably, amicably, aimlessly.

And nobody asked about Israel. Either Maria hadn't mentioned my being there or they weren't interested. And probably just as well: I wasn't sure how much Agor ideology I could manage to get across to Mrs. Freshfield.

To Maria, however, I'd talked all afternoon about my trip. "Your journey," she'd called it, after hearing about Lippman and reading my letter to Henry, "to the Jewish heart of darkness." A good description, that, of my eastward progress and I delineated it further in my notes—from the Tel Aviv café and the acid dolefulness of disheartened Shuki, inland to the Jerusalem Wailing Wall and my prickly intermingling there with the pious Jews, and then on to the desert hills, the plunge into the heart, if not of darkness, of demonic Jewish ardor. The militant zealotry of Henry's settlement didn't, to my mind, make their obdurate leader the Kurtz of Judea, however; the book suggested to me by the settlers' fanatical pursuit of God-promised deliverance was a Jewish *Moby-Dick*, with Lippman as the Zionist Ahab. My brother, without realizing, could well have signed onto a ship destined for destruction, and there was nothing to be done about it, certainly not by me. I hadn't mailed the letter and wouldn't—Henry, I was sure, could only see it as more domination, an attempt to drown him in still more of my words. Instead I copied it into my notes, into that ever-enlarging storage plant for my narrative factory, where there is no clear demarcation dividing actual happenings eventually consigned to the imagination from imaginings that are treated as having actually occurred—memory as entwined with fantasy as it is in the brain.

Georgina, younger by a year than Maria, and Sarah, three years older, were not tall and dark-haired like the middle sister and their father but resembled the mother more, slight, short-ish women, with straight fair hair that they didn't much bother about and the same soft, round, agreeable faces that had prob-ably been prettiest when they were girls of fifteen living in Gloucestershire. Georgina had a job with a London public re-lations firm and Sarah had recently become an editor with a company specializing in medical texts, her fourth publishing job in as many years and work having little to do with anything she cared about. Yet Sarah was the sister who was supposed to have been the genius. She had spent her childhood mastering dancing, mastering riding, mastering just about everything as though, if she didn't, terrible tragedy and chaos would ensue.

But now she was constantly changing jobs and losing men and, in Maria's words, "fucking up, absolutely, any opportunity that's presented to her, throwing it away in the most monumental way." Sarah spoke to people with an almost alarming rapidity, when she spoke at all; in conversation she pounced and then abruptly withdrew, making no use whatsoever of the enigmatic smile that was her mother's first line of defense and that even sedate-looking Maria, uneasy upon entering a room full of strangers, would shield herself with until the initial social timidity subsided. Unlike Georgina, whose awful shyness was a kind of trampoline to catapult her overeagerly into every minute and meaningless exchange, Sarah held herself aloof from all courteous pleasantries, leading me to think that when the time came, we two might actually be able to talk.

I'd as yet had no success at breaking through to Mrs. Freshfield, though our first encounter a few weeks earlier hadn't been quite the disaster that Maria and I had begun to imagine on the drive to Gloucestershire with Phoebe. We had our presents to ease the way—Maria's was a piece of china for her mother's collection that she'd found in a Third Avenue antique shop before we'd left New York, and I had, of all things, a cheese. From London, the day before we left, Maria had phoned to ask if there was anything we could bring with us, and her mother had told her, "What I'd like more than anything is a decent piece of Stilton. You can't get proper Stilton down here anymore." Maria immediately rushed to Harrods for the Stilton, which I was to present at the door.

"And what do I talk about after the cheese?" I asked as we were turning off the motorway onto the country road to Chadleigh.

"Jane Austen is always good," Maria said.

"And after Jane Austen?"

"She has excellent furniture—what's known as 'good pieces.' Very unostentatious, really nice eighteenth-century English furniture. You can ask about that."

"And then?"

"You're counting on some very ghastly silences."

"Is that impossible?"

"Not at all," Maria said.

"Are you nervous?" She didn't look nervous so much as a little too still.

"I'm properly apprehensive. You *are* a homewrecker, you know. And she was very keen on your predecessor—socially speaking he was very acceptable. She's not very good with men, anyway. And I believe she still thinks Americans are upstarts and brash."

"What's the worst that can happen?"

"The worst? The worst would be that she will be so ill at ease that she will put you down after every sentence. The worst would be that whatever effort either of us makes, she will say one very clipped put-down remark, and then there will indeed be a frightful silence, and then another topic will be taken up and put down again in the same way. But that is not going to happen, because, one, there is Phoebe, whom she adores and who will distract us, and, two, there is you, a renowned wit of prodigious sophistication who is quite expert at these things. Isn't that so?"

"You'll find out."

Before swinging through the hilly country lanes to get to her mother's house in Chadleigh, we took a short detour in order for Maria to show me her school. As we passed the fields close by, Maria held Phoebe up so she could look at the horses—"Horses around here," she said to me, "as far as the eye can see."

The school was a long way from any human habitation, set in a vast, immaculately kept, old deer park shaded by large cedar trees. The playing fields and the tennis courts were empty when we arrived—the girls were in class and there was no one at all to be seen outside the grand Elizabethan-looking stone building where Maria had lived as a boarder until she went off to Oxford. "Looks to me like a palace," I said, rolling down the window to take in the view. "The joke was that the boys used to be brought up in laundry baskets at night," she said. "And were they?" I asked. "Certainly not. No sex at all. Girls would get crushes on the hockey mistress, that sort of thing. We'd write our boyfriends pages of letters in various colored inks on pink paper sprayed with scent. But otherwise, as you see, a place of extreme innocence."

Chadleigh, less grand but more innocent-looking even than the school, was thirty minutes on, set halfway up a very steep, very lonely Gloucestershire valley. Years ago, before the wool industry moved off, it had been a village of poor weavers. "In the old days," said Maria as we turned into the narrow main road, "these were just hovels of tuberculosis—thirteen children and no TV." Now Chadleigh was a picturesque cluster of streets and lanes, situated dramatically across the valley from a hanging beech woods—a muddle of monochromatic stone houses, grayish and austere under the clouds, and a long triangular village green where some dogs were playing. Just beyond the houses and their kitchen gardens, the farms on the rising hillside were parceled off like New England fields with old dry stone walls, meticulously laid layers of tilelike rock the color of the houses. Maria said that the first sight of the stone walls and the irregular pattern of the fields was always very emotional for her if she hadn't been back for a while.

Holly Tree Cottage seemed from the road a sizable house, though nothing like as impressive, Maria told me, as The Barton, where the family had lived before her father had taken flight. His family had been rich, but he was a second son and had got the family name with nothing to go with it. After university he'd been a banker in the City, only weekending with his family, but he hadn't much liked work and eventually skipped to Leicestershire with a very famous, horsy woman of the fifties, who had worn a top hat with a veil and ridden sidesaddle and had been known maliciously, for witty and (to me) obscure English reasons, as "Keep Death Off the Road." To put himself beyond the financial edicts of the divorce court he'd wound up only a few years later in Canada, married to a rich Vancouver girl and occupied mainly with sailing around the Sound and playing golf. The Barton proved to be too big and—after the support payments stopped coming in—beyond maintaining on Mrs. Freshfield's income. She had been left only her mother's modest capital and, thanks to the help of her stockbroker and some very stern economical management of her own, the small sum had proved to be just sufficient to get the girls through school. But this had meant selling The Barton, which lay in the open country, and renting Holly Tree Cottage, at the edge of Chadleigh village.

There was a log fire in the drawing room when we arrived and, after the presents were opened and admired and Phoebe had been allowed a wild run around the garden and given a glass of milk, we sat there having a drink before lunch. It was a pleasant room with worn Oriental carpets on the dark wood floors and on the walls a lot of family portraits along with several portraits of horses. Everything was a little worn and all in very discreet taste—chintz curtains with birds and flowers and lots of polished wood.

Following the advice garnered on the drive down, I said, "That's a very nice desk."

"Oh, it's just a copy of Sheraton," Mrs. Freshfield replied.

"And that's a beautiful bookcase."

"Oh, well, Charley Rhys-Mill was here the other day," she said, looking while she spoke at neither Maria nor me, "and he said he thought that it might well be a Chippendale design, but I'm certain it's a country piece. If you look there," she said, momentarily acknowledging my presence, "you can see the way the locks are put in, it's very rural. I think it's taken from the pattern book but I don't think it's Chippendale."

I decided that if she was going to belittle everything I admired, I had better stop here.

I said nothing more and just sipped my gin until Mrs. Freshfield took it upon herself to try to make me feel at home.

"Where are you from exactly, Mr. Zuckerman?"

"Newark. In New Jersey."

"I'm not very good at American geography."

"It's across the river from New York."

"I didn't know New York was *on* a river."

"Yes. Two."

"What was your father's profession?"

"He was a chiropodist."

There was a great silence while I drank, Maria drank, and Phoebe crayoned; we could *hear* Phoebe crayoning.

"Do you have brothers and sisters?"

"I have a younger brother," I said.

"What does he do?"

"He's a dentist."

Either these were all the wrong answers or else she knew by then all she needed to know, for the conversation about my background lasted all of half a minute. The chiropodist father and the dentist brother seemed to have summed me up instantly. I wondered if perhaps these were occupations that were simply too useful.

She had cooked the lunch herself—very English, perfectly nice, and rather bland. "There is no garlic in the lamb." She said this with what seemed to me a most ambiguous smile.

"Fine," I said amiably, but still uncertain as to whether there might not be lurking in her remark some dire ethnic implication. Perhaps this was as close as she would come to mentioning my strange religion. I couldn't imagine that was any less difficult for her than my being American. I clearly had everything going for me.

The vegetables were from the garden, Brussels sprouts, potatoes, and carrots. Maria asked about Mr. Blackett, a retired agricultural laborer who had supplemented his meager pension by working for them one day a week, mowing, hauling wood, and doing the vegetable garden. Was he still living? Yes, he was, but Ethel had recently died and he was alone in his council flat, where, said Mrs. Freshfield, she was afraid he existed just this side of hypothermia.

Maria said to me, "Ethel was Mrs. Blackett. Our cleaning lady. A very thorough cleaner. Always washed the doorstep on her knees. Terrible problems when we were teenage girls about giving Ethel a Christmas present. He'd get a bottle of whiskey from Mother, and Ethel invariably wound up with hankies from us. Mr. Blackett speaks a dialect that's almost incomprehensible. I wish you could hear it. He's a quite surprisingly nineteenth-century figure, isn't he, Mother?"

"It's going, that, the very strong rural accent," Mrs. Freshfield said, and then, Maria's effort to make the Blacketts of interest seemingly having fizzled out, we fell into a spell of doing nothing but cutting and chewing our food that I was afraid might last till we left for London.

"Maria says you're a great reader of Jane Austen," I said.

"Well, I've read her all my life. I began with *Pride and Prejudice* when I was thirteen and I've been reading her ever since."

"Why is that?"

This evinced a very wintry smile. "When did you last read Jane Austen, Mr. Zuckerman?"

"Not since college."

"Read her again and then you'll see why."

"I will, but what I was asking is what *you* get out of Jane Austen."

"She simply records life truthfully, and what she has to say about life is very profound. She amuses me so much. The characters are so very good. I'm very fond of Mr. Woodhouse in *Emma*. And Mr. Bennet, in *Pride and Prejudice*, I'm very fond of too. I'm very fond of Fanny Price, in *Mansfield Park*. When she goes back to Portsmouth after living down with the Bertrams in great style and grandeur, and she finds her own family and is so shocked by the squalor—people are very critical of her for that and say she's a snob, and maybe it's because I'm a snob myself—I suppose I am—but I find it very sympathetic. I think that's how one would behave, if one went back to a much lower standard of living."

"Which book is your favorite?" I asked.

"Well, I suppose whichever I'm reading is my favorite at the time. I read them all every year. But in the end, it's *Pride and Prejudice*. Mr. Darcy is very attractive. And then I like Lydia. I think Lydia is so foolish and silly. She's beautifully portrayed. I know so many people like that, you see. And of course I do sympathize with Mr. and Mrs. Bennet, having all these daughters of my own to marry off."

I could not tell if this was intended as some kind of blow—whether the woman was dangerous or being perfectly benign.

"I'm sorry I haven't read your books," she said to me. "I don't read very much American literature. I find it very difficult to understand the people. I don't find them very attractive or very sympathetic, I'm afraid. I don't really like violence. There's so much violence in American books, I find. Of course not in Henry James, whom I do like very much. Though I suppose he hardly counts as an American. He really is an observer of the English scene, and I think he really is very good. But I prefer him on television, I think, now. The style *is* rather long-winded. When you see them on television, they get to the point so much more quickly. They've done *The Spoils of*

Poynton recently, and of course I was particularly interested in that, with my interest in furniture. They did it awfully well, I thought. They did *The Golden Bowl.* I enjoyed that very much. It *is* a rather long book. Your books are published over here, are they?"

"Yes."

"Well, I don't know why Maria hasn't sent them to me."

"Oh, I don't think you'd like them, Mother," Maria said.

Here a decision was unanimously reached to be distracted by Phoebe, who in fact was harmlessly fiddling with the vegetables on her plate and being a perfect little girl. "Maria, she's dribbling, dear," said Mrs. Freshfield, "—see to her, will you?" and for the remainder of the meal everyone's remarks had to do with the child.

During coffee in the drawing room, I asked if I might see the rest of the rooms. Just as she had disparaged the furniture when I admired it, now she disparaged the house. "It's nothing very special," she said. "It was just a bailiff's house, you know. Of course they did themselves much better in those days." I understood from this that she was herself used to far better and said no more on the subject. However, when the coffee was finished, I found I was to get the tour after all—Mrs. Freshfield rose, we followed, and this seemed to me such a good sign that I launched into a new line of inquiry that I thought might finally be appropriate.

"Maria tells me that your family has lived around here for a long time."

The reply came back at me like a hard little pellet. It could have struck my chest and gone out between my shoulder blades. "Three hundred years."

"What did they do here?"

"Sheep," like a second shot. "Everyone was in sheep then."

She pushed open the door to a large bedroom whose windows looked out to a field where some cows were grazing. "This was the nursery. Where Maria and her sisters grew up. Sarah was the oldest and she got to have a bedroom first, and Maria had to go on sleeping here with Georgina. This was a great source of bitterness. So was inheriting Sarah's clothes. When Sarah grew out of them, Maria was made to wear them, and by the time she was finished they weren't worth passing on to Georgina. So the oldest got new clothes and the youngest got new clothes, and Maria, in the middle, never did. Another source of bitterness. We were awfully hard-up for a bit, you know. Maria never quite understood that, I don't think."

"But of course I did," Maria said.

"But you resented things, I think. Perfectly naturally, quite naturally. We couldn't afford ponies, and your friends could, and you seemed to think it was my fault. Which it wasn't."

And was recalling Maria's resentment meant to suggest something about her choosing me? I couldn't really tell from Mrs. Freshfield's tone. Maybe this was affectionate banter, even if it didn't sound that way to me. Maybe it was just straight historical reporting—fact, without implication or subtle significance. Maybe this was just how these people talked.

Out in the hallway I decided to make a last effort. Pointing to a bureau at the head of the stairs, I said lightly, as if to no one, "A lovely piece."

"That's from my husband's family. My mother-in-law bought that. She found it in Worcester one day. Yes, it's a very nice piece. The handles are right too."

Success. Stop there.

While Phoebe napped, Maria and I walked down the road to the little church where she'd been taken to worship as a child.

"Well," she said, after we had left the house, "that wasn't too bad, was it?"

"I have no idea. Was it? Wasn't it?"

"She made a real effort. She doesn't do treacle tart unless it's a special occasion. Because you're a man there was wine at lunch. She obviously thought about your coming for a week."

"That I didn't get, quite."

"She went to Mr. Tims, the butcher, and asked him for a specially nice joint. Mr. Tims made a real effort—the whole village made a real effort."

"Yes? Well, I made a real effort too. I felt as though I were crossing a mine field. I didn't have much luck with the furniture."

"You admired it too much." Maria laughed. "I must teach you never to praise someone's possessions to his face quite that way. But that's my mother, anyway. You praise it and, if it's hers, she runs it down. You made a hit with the Stilton. She cooed in ecstasies when we were alone in the kitchen."

"I can't see her in ecstasies."

"Over a Stilton, oh yes."

There was a dark patch of ancient yews outside the tiny church, a nice old building, surrounded by tombstones. "You do know the name of this tree," she said to me. "From Thomas Gray," I said, "yes, I do." "You had a very good education in Newark." "To prepare me for you, I had to." Maria opened the door to the church, whose earliest stones, she told me, had been laid by the Normans. "The smell," she said when we stepped inside, and sounded just a little stunned, as people do when their past comes wafting powerfully back, "—the smell of the damp in these places." We looked at the effigies of the noble dead and the wood carving on the bench ends until she couldn't stand the chill anymore. "There used to be six people in here for evensong on a winter Sunday. The damp *still* gets right through to my knees. Come, I'll show you my lonely places."

We walked up the hill through the village again—Maria explaining who lived in each of the houses—and then got into the car and drove out to her old hideaways, the "lonely places" that she would always revisit, whenever she came home from school, to be sure they were still there. One was a beech woods where she used to go for walks—"very haunting," she called it—and the other lay beyond the village at the bottom of the valley, a ruined mill beside a stream so small you could hop across it. She'd come there with her horse, or, after her mother had decided that she was having a hard enough time paying for the children and their schools without ponies to be fed and looked after, she'd ride out on her bicycle. "This is where I'd have my visionary feelings of the world being one. Exactly what Wordsworth describes—the real nature mysticism, moments of extreme contentment. You know, looking at the sun setting and suddenly thinking that the universe all makes sense. For an adolescent there is no better place for these little visions than a ruined mill by a trickling stream."

From there we drove to The Barton, which was quite isolated, behind a high ivy-covered wall on a dirt road several miles outside of Chadleigh. It was getting dark and, as there were dogs, we hung back by the gate looking to where the lights were burning throughout the house. It was built of the same grayish-yellow stone as Holly Tree Cottage and most every other house we'd seen, though from its size and the impressive gables it couldn't have been mistaken for the home of a poor local weaver or even of a bailiff. There was a strip of garden beyond the wall leading to the French windows downstairs. Maria said that the house had no central heating when she was a child, and so there were log fires in all the rooms, burning from September through May; electricity they'd made themselves, using an old diesel engine that pumped away most of the time. At the back, she said, were the stables, the barn, and a walled kitchen garden with rose patches; beyond was a duck pond where they had fished and learned to skate, and beyond that a nut woods, another haunted place full of glades and birds, wildflowers and bracken, where she and her sisters used to run up and down the green paths frightening each other to death. Her earliest memories were all poetic and associated with that woods.

"Servants?"

"Just two," she said. "A nanny for the children and one maid, an old parlor maid left over from before the war. My grandmother's parlor maid, called by her surname, Burton, who did all the cooking and stayed with us until she was pensioned off at the end."

"So moving into the village," I said, "was a comedown."

"We were just children, not so much for us. But my mother never recovered. Her family hasn't given up an inch of land in Gloucestershire since the seventeenth century. But her brother has the estate of three thousand acres and she has nothing. Just the few stocks and shares inherited from her mother, the furniture you admired so, and those portraits of horses you failed to overpraise—kind of sub-Stubbs."

"It is all extremely foreign to me, Maria."

"I thought I sensed that at lunch."

While Phoebe, buoyed up by the mince pie, entertained Georgina, and Maria continued talking to her mother about the Chiswick house, I edged into a corner of the church crypt, away from the crush of the hungry carolers juggling wine cups and bits of pastry, and found myself across from Maria's older sister, Sarah.

"I think you like to play the moral guinea pig," Sarah said in that gun-burst style she was noted for.

"How does a moral guinea pig play?"

"He experiments with himself. Puts himself, if he's a Jew, into a church at Christmastime, to see how it feels and what it's like."

"Oh, everybody does that," I said amiably, but to let her know that I hadn't missed anything, I added, slowly, "not just Jews."

"It's easier if one's a success like you."

"What is easier?" I asked.

"Everything, without question. But I meant the moral guinea pig bit. You've achieved the freedom to knock around a lot, to go from one estate to the other and see what it's all about. Tell me about success. Do you enjoy it, all that strutting?"

"Not enough—I'm not a sufficiently shameless exhibitionist."

"But that's another matter."

"I can only exhibit myself in disguise. All my audacity derives from masks."

"I think this is getting a bit intellectual. What's your disguise tonight?"

"Tonight? Maria's husband."

"Well, I think if one's successful one should show off a bit—to encourage everybody else. Georgina's our extrovert—that says everything about this family. She still works hard at being Mummy's good girl. I, as you must have heard, am not entirely stable, and Maria is utterly defenseless and a little spoiled. Her whole life has been aimed at doing nothing. She manages to do it very well."

"I hadn't noticed."

"Oh, there's nothing in the world that makes Maria so happy as a big, big check."

"Well, that's easy then. I'll give her a big one every day."

"Are you good at choosing clothes? Maria loves to have men help to choose her clothes. Men have to help Maria with everything. I hope you're prepared. Do you like to sit in that chair in the store while some lady twirls around and says, 'What do you think of this?' "

"It depends on the store."

"Yes? What store do you like? Selfridge's? Georgina keeps a horse down in Gloucestershire. She's something else entirely. All this English carry-on. Yesterday she had a big one-day event down there. Do you know what a one-day event is like? Of course you don't. It's physically terrifying. These huge, huge fences. Real English lunacy. At any moment a horse might fall and crash your brains."

"Such as they are."

"Yes, just mad," Sarah said. "But Georgina likes that."

"And what do you like?"

"What I'd like most to do? Well, what I'd most like to do and would be hard for me, which is why I really don't aspire to it in the near future, is what you do—and my mother does. But it's the hardest life I can imagine."

"There are harder."

"Don't be modest. You think it's the suffering that makes it so admirable. They say if you meet a writer it's sometimes more difficult to hate his work than if you just get the book and open it up and throw it across the room."

"Not for everyone. Some find it much easier to hate you having met you."

"My whole childhood was spent vomiting away all over the place whenever I had to perform or deliver. As I was then still in hot contention for Mummy's good girl, I had to perform and deliver *all the time*. And now I have this terribly agonizing relationship with any piece of work that I'm doing. I've never been able to function, really, in work. Neither can Maria—she can't work at all. I don't know that she's done anything for years, except to tinker with those one and a half short stories she's been writing since school. But then she's beautiful and spoiled and gets all these people to marry her instead. I'm not prepared to stay at home and be so hellishly dependent."

"Is it 'dependence'? Is it really hell?"

"What does a woman do who is intelligent and brings a lot of energy and enthusiasm to all that domestic carry-on, and in the end, for all very natural reasons, the husband disappears, either right out of the house or, like our dear father, with sixty-two girls on the side? I think the good reason that this option has disappeared is that intelligent women are not prepared to be so dependent."

"Maria's an intelligent woman."

"And didn't have such a hot time of it, did she, the first time round."

"He was a prick," I said.

"He wasn't at all. Have you met him? He actually has some wonderful qualities. I enjoy him enormously. At times he can be infinitely charming."

"I'm sure. But if you remove yourself emotionally from somebody's life, as he did, their sense of connection will eventually be eroded."

"If you're helplessly dependent."

"No, if you require some human connection from the person to whom you are married."

"I think you are leading an impostor's life," Sarah said.

"Do you?"

"With Maria, yes. There's a word for it, actually."

"Do tell me."

"Hypergamy. Do you know what it is?"

"Never heard of it."

"Bedding women of a superior social class. Desire based on a superior social class."

"So I, putting it politely, am a hypergamist; and Maria, taking revenge against the rejecting father by marrying beneath herself, is helplessly dependent. A spoiled, dependent woman of a superior social class who likes big checks with her bedside bonbons and whose life has been aimed at doing nothing. And what are you, Sarah, aside from envious, bitter, and weak?"

"I don't like Maria."

"So what? Who cares?"

"She's spoiled, she's indolent, she's soft, she's 'sensitive,' she's vain—but then so are you vain. You surely have to be quite vain in your profession. How could you take seriously what you think about otherwise? You must still be very much in love with the drama of your life."

"I am. That's why I married a beauty like your sister and give her those big checks every day."

"Our mother's terribly anti-Semitic, you know."

"Is she? No one told me."

"I'm telling you. I think you may find that in experimenting with Maria you've gone a bit over the top."

"I like to go over the top."

"Yes, you do. I've read your famous ghetto comedy. Positively Jacobean. What's it called again?"

"*My Darling Self-Image.*"

"Well, if you are, as your work suggests, fascinated with the consequences of transgression, you've come to the right family. Our mother can be hellishly unpleasant when it comes to transgression. She can be hard like a mineral—an Anglo-Saxon mineral. I don't think she really likes the idea of her languid, helpless Maria submitting to anal domination by a Jew. I imagine that she believes that like most virile sadists you fancy anal penetration."

"Tell her I take a crack at it from time to time."

"Our mother won't like that at all."

"I don't know a mother who would. That sounds typical enough to me."

"I think you're filled with rage, resentment, and vanity, all of which you cloak beneath this urbane and civilized exterior."

"That sounds rather typical too. Though there are clearly those who don't even bother with the civilized exterior."

"Do you understand everything I'm saying to you?" she asked.

"Well, I hear what you're saying to me."

Suddenly she thrust at me the half of the mince pie still in her hand. I thought momentarily that she was going to push it into my face.

"Smell this," she said.

"Why should I do that?"

"Because it smells good. Don't be so defensive because you're in a church. Smell it. It smells like Christmas. I'll bet you have no smells associated with Chanukah."

"Shekels," I said.

"I'll bet you'd like to do away with Christmas."

"Be a good Marxist, Sarah. The dialectic tells us that the Jews will never do away with Christmas—they make too much money off of it."

"You laugh very quietly, I notice. You don't want to show

too much. Is that because you're in England and not in New York? Is that because you don't want to be confused with the amusing Jews you depict in fiction? Why don't you just go ahead and show some teeth? Your books do—they're all teeth. You, however, keep very well hidden the Jewish paranoia which produces vituperation and the need to strike out—if only, of course, with all the Jewish 'jokes.' Why so refined in England and so coarse in *Carnovsky*? The English broadcast on such low frequencies—Maria particularly emits *such* soft sounds, the voice of the hedgerows, isn't it?—that it must be terribly worrying whether you're going suddenly to forget yourself, bare your teeth, and cut loose with the ethnic squawk. Don't worry about what the English will think, the English are too polite for pogroms—you have fine American teeth, show them when you laugh. You look Jewish, unmistakably. You can't possibly hide that by not showing your teeth."

"I don't have to act like a Jew—I am one."

"Quite clever."

"Not as clever as you. You're too clever and too stupid all at the same time."

"I don't much like myself, either," she said. "Nonetheless, I do think Maria ought to have told you that she is from the sort of people who, if you knew anything about English society, you would have *expected* to be anti-Semitic. If you ever read any English novels—have you?"

I didn't bother to answer, but I didn't walk away either. I waited to see just how far my new sister-in-law actually intended to go.

"I recommend beginning your education with a novel by Trollope," she said. "It may knock some of the stuffing from your pathetic yearning to partake of English civility. It will tell you all about people like us. Read *The Way We Live Now*. It may help to explode those myths that fuel the pathetic Jewish Anglophilia Maria's cashing in on. The book is rather like a soap opera, but the main meat of it from your point of view is a little subplot, an account of Miss Longestaffe, an English young lady from an upper-class home, sort of country gentry, a bit over the hill, and she's furious that nobody's married her, and she's failed to sell herself on the marriage markets, and because she's determined to have a rich social life in London, she's going to demean herself by marrying a middle-aged Jew. The interesting bit is all her feelings, her family's feelings about this comedown, and the behavior of the Jew in question. I won't spoil it by going on. It will be quite an education, and coming, I think, not a moment too soon. Oh, you're going to go slightly ape about this stuff, I'm sure. Poor Miss Longestaffe reckons she's doing the Jew a big favor, you see, by marrying him, even if her sole motive is to get hold of his money, and to have as little to do with him as possible. And she has no thought really of what's in it for him. In fact, she feels she's conferring a social favor."

"It seems awfully fresh in your mind."

"As I was seeing you today, I got it down to look at. Are you interested?"

"Go on. How does her family take the Jew?"

"Yes, her family *is* the point, isn't it? They're thunderstruck. 'A Jew,' everyone cries, 'an old fat Jew?' She's so upset by their reaction that her defiance turns to doubt, and she has a correspondence with him—he's called Mr. Brehgert. He's actually, as it happens, though rather colorless, a thoroughly decent, responsible man, a very successful businessman. However, he is described frequently, as indeed other Jews in the book are, in terms which will set your teeth on edge. What will be particularly instructive to you is their correspondence—what it reveals about the attitudes of a large number of people to Jews, attitudes that only *appear* to be a hundred years old."

"And is that it?" I asked. "Is that all?"

"Of course not. Do you know John Buchan? He sort of flourished around the First World War. Oh, you'll like him too. You'll learn a lot. I would recommend him just on the strength of a few astonishing asides. He's terribly famous in England, enormously famous, a boy's adventure-thriller writer. His stories are all about how blond Aryan gentlemen go forth against the forces of evil, which are always amassed in Europe and have huge conspiracies, not unconnected with Jewish financiers, to somehow bring an evil cloud over the world. And of course the blond Aryans win in the end and get back to their manor houses. That's the usual story. And the Jews are usually at the bottom of it, lurking there somewhere. I really don't suggest you actually read him—it's a bit of a labor. Have a friend do it for you. Have Maria do it—she has plenty of time. She can just read out the good bits, for the sake of your education. The thing is that once in every fifty pages you get some overtly anti-Semitic remark which is simply an aside, simply the shared consciousness of all the readers and the writer. It's not like in Trollope, a developed idea. Trollope is actually interested in the predicament—this is evidence of *a shared consciousness.* And it wasn't written in 1870—this sort of mystique is still very much around, even if Maria has failed to inform you. Maria is a child in many ways. You know how children understand to stay off certain subjects. Of course talking her way into a man's pants is one of Maria's specialties, I don't mean to say she can't do that. In bed she makes it virginal again, I'm sure, with all her natural English delicacy—in bed with Maria we're back to Wordsworth. I'm sure she even made adultery virginal. Where the orgy is with Maria is in the talk. She mind-fucks a man to death, doesn't she, Nathan? You should have seen her at Oxford. For her poor tutors it was an agony. But still she doesn't say it all, you know. There are certain things you don't tell a man, and certain things, clearly, haven't been told you. Maria lies in the good way—to maintain peace. However, you ought not, because of her lies and her lapses of memory, to be grievously misled—or unprepared."

"For what? Enough of the glories of the English novel—and quite enough about Maria. Unprepared for what from whom?"

"From our mother. You will be making a mistake if, when this infant arrives, you try to stand in the way of a christening."

In the taxi, I chose not to ask Maria whether she knew how little her sister cared for her, or how profoundly Sarah resented me, or if what had been suggested about their mother's expectations for our child was, in fact, true. I was too stunned —and then we were on our way to celebrate Maria's twenty-eighth birthday at her favorite restaurant, and once I'd begun on her sister's barrage of abuse, that lovingly articulated hymn of hate, I knew there'd be no celebration. What mystified me was that all I'd ever heard about Maria's relations with Sarah was the unastonishing news that they were no longer anything like as close as they'd been as schoolgirls. She'd said something once about psychiatric problems, but only in passing, while

describing the aftereffects of Sarah's lurid ninety-day marriage
to a scion of the Anglo-Irish aristocracy, and not to account for
her sister's feelings toward her or Buchanite view of people like
me. Maria had certainly never characterized her mother as "terribly anti-Semitic," though of course I suspected that there
could well be more than a trace of it in the layers and layers of
social snobbery and the generalized xenophobia that I'd felt at
Holly Tree Cottage. What I didn't know was whether the
specter of the baptismal font was only an irresistible finale to
a nasty little joke, a hilarious punch line that Sarah figured
couldn't fail to arouse the ire of her sister's rich middle-aged
Jew, or whether the christening of baby Zuckerman, however
laughably absurd to contemplate, was something Maria and I
would actually have to oppose in an ugly struggle with her
mother. What if while resisting the mother who never put a foot
wrong, the unfortified daughter obediently collapsed? What if
Maria couldn't even *bring* herself to fight against what seemed
to me, the more I thought about it, not only a more-than-
symbolic attempt to kidnap the child but an effort to annul her
marriage to the kike?

I began only then to realize how naïve I'd been not to have
seen something like this coming, and to wonder if it hadn't
been me, not Maria, who had been childishly "staying off certain subjects." I seemed to have almost deliberately blinded myself to the ideology that, of course, might underlie her proper
upbringing among the country gentry, and to have failed as
well to appreciate the obvious family implications of the unprecedented defiance Maria had dared to display by returning
to England divorced from the well-connected young First Secretary at the U.K. mission to the U.N. and married instead to
me, the Moor—in their eyes—to her Desdemona. More disturbing even than the ugly encounter with Sarah was the like-
lihood that I had allowed myself to be beguiled mostly by
fantasy, that everything up until now had been largely a dream
in which I had served as a mindless co-conspirator, spinning a
superficial unreality out of those "charming" differences that
had at last broken upon us with their full—if fossilized—social
meaning. Living on the river indeed. The swans, the mists, the
tides gently lapping at the garden wall—how could that idyll
possibly be a real life? And how poisonous and painful would

this conflict be? It suddenly looked as though all these months two rational and hardheaded realists had been moonily and romantically circumventing a very real and tricky predicament.

Yet in New York I'd been so eager to be rejuvenated that I simply hadn't thought it through. As a writer I'd mined my past to its limits, exhausted my private culture and personal memories, and could no longer even warm to squabbling over my work, having finally tired of my detractors rather the way you fall out of love with someone. I was sick of old crises, bored with old issues, and wanted only to undo the habits with which I had chained myself to my desk, implicated three wives in my seclusion, and, for years on end, lived in the nutshell of self-scrutiny. I wanted to hear a new voice, to make a new tie, to be enlivened by a new and original partner—to break away and take upon myself a responsibility unlike any bound up with writing or with the writer's tedious burden of being his own cause. I wanted Maria and I wanted a child, and not only had I failed to think it through, I had done so intentionally, thinking-it-through being another old habit for which I had no nostalgia. What could suit me more than a woman protesting how unsuitable she was? As by this time I was wholly unsuitable for myself, *ipso facto*, we were the perfect pair.

Five months into pregnancy the rush of hormones must do something to the skin, because Maria's had a visible radiance. It was a great moment for her. There was no movement of the baby yet, but the early sickness was well over and the discomfort of being huge and cumbersome hadn't begun, and she said that all she felt was coddled and protected and special. Over her dress she was wearing a long black wool cape with a hood that had a tassel dangling from the point; it was soft and warm and I could hold her arm as it emerged from the opening in the side. Her dress was dark green and flowing, a silk jersey dress with a deep round collar and long sleeves that closed around her wrists. That dress looked to me like all you could ask for, plain and sexy and faultless.

We were seated side by side near the end of a plush banquette, facing the paneled dining room. It was after eight and most of the tables were already occupied. I ordered champagne while Maria found in her purse the Polaroid snapshots of the house—I still hadn't had a chance to look at them closely and there were lots of things she wanted me to see. Meanwhile, I had taken out of my pocket a long black velvet box. Inside was the bracelet that I'd bought for her the week before just off Bond Street, at a shop specializing in the sort of Victorian and Georgian jewelry that she liked to wear. "It's light but not flimsy," the clerk had assured me, "delicate enough for the lady's small wrists." Sounded like handcuffs, the price was shocking, but I took it. I could have taken ten. It was a great moment, really, for both of us. Whether it qualified as "real life" remained to be seen.

"Oh, this is nice," she said, fixing the clip and then holding her arm out to admire the present. "Opals. Diamonds. The river house. Champagne. You. You," she repeated, musingly this time, "—so much rock for this moss to adhere to." She kissed my cheek and was, incarnate, in that moment, the delectability of the female. "I find being married to you a tremendous experiment in pleasure. Isn't this the best way to be fed?"

"You look lovely in that dress."

"It's really very ancient."

"I remember it from New York."

"That was the idea."

"I missed you, Maria."

"Did you?"

"I appreciate you, you know."

"That's a very strong card, that one."

"Well, it's so."

"I missed *you*. I tried very hard not to think of you all the time. When will I begin to get on your nerves?" she asked.

"I don't think you have to worry tonight."

"The bracelet is perfect, so perfect that it's hard to believe it was your own idea. If a man does something very appropriate it's usually not. It's lovely, but you know what else I want, what I want most when we move? Flowers in the house. Isn't that middle class of me? Mind you, I have a very long list of material desires, but that's what I thought when I saw the builders there today."

After that, it simply wasn't in me to yield to the impulse pressing me to blurt it out, to say to her, outright, without embellishment, "Look, your mother's a terrific anti-Semite who expects us to have our child baptized—true or false? And if true, why pretend you're oblivious to it? That's more disturbing than anything else." Instead, as though I felt no urgency about what she knew or was pretending not to know and expected to hear nothing to dismay me, as though I weren't disturbed about anything at all, I said in a voice as softly civilized as hers, "I'm afraid breaking through to your mother is still beyond me. When she regroups her forces back of that smile, I really don't know where to look. She was nothing tonight if not glacially correct, but what precisely *does* she think of us? Can you figure it out?"

"Oh, what everybody seems to be thinking, more or less. That we've 'traversed enormous differences.' "

" 'Traversed'? She said that to you?"

"She did."

"And what did you say to her?"

"I said, 'What's so tremendously different? Of course I know that in one sense we could hardly be more different. But think of all the things we've read in common, think of all the things we know in common, we speak the same language—I know far more about him than you think.' I told her I've read masses of American fiction, I've seen masses and masses of American films—"

"But she's not talking about my Americanness."

"Not solely. That's true. She's thinking about our 'associations.' She says all that's been obscured by the way we met—a secret liaison in New York. We never met among friends, we never met in public places, we never met to do things, so that we could never exasperate each other with visible signs of all of our differences. Her point is that we got married there without ever really allowing ourselves to be tested. She's concerned about our life in England. Part of these things, she tells me, is how one's group perceives one."

"And how *do* they perceive us?"

"I don't think people are terribly interested, really. Oh, I think that if they bother at all the first thing everybody thinks, when they hear about a thing like this, is that you're interested in a young woman to recharge your batteries, and maybe you're interested in English culture, that might be possible, and the shiksa syndrome, of course—that would all be obvious to them. On my side, equally obvious, they'd say, 'Well, he may be quite a lot older, and he may be Jewish, but my goodness, he's a literary star and he has got lots of money.' They'd think I was after you purely for your status and money."

"Despite my being Jewish."

"I don't think many people bother much about that. Certainly not literary types. Along the road where my mother lives, yes, there might be one or two mutters. Lots of people will be quite cynical, outrightly, of course, but then that would be true in New York as well."

"What does Georgina think?"

"Georgina is very conventional. Georgina probably thinks that I have sort of slightly given up on what I had really wanted in life, and this is a frightfully good second best and has much to recommend it."

"What have you given up on?"

"Something more obvious. More obviously the sort of thing that sorts like me are after."

"Which is?"

"Well, I think that would be . . . oh, I don't know."

"My advanced years."

"Yes, I think someone my own age, more or less. Ordinary people are profoundly disturbed by these age differences. Look, is this a good thing, this kind of talk?"

"Sure. It gives me a foothold in a foreign land."

"Why do you need that? Is something wrong?"

"Tell me about Sarah. What does she think?"

"Did something happen between you two?"

"What could happen?"

"Sarah is a little ropey sometimes. She sometimes speaks so quickly—it's like icicles breaking. Snapping. Bu-bu-bu-*bup*. You know what she said tonight, about my wearing pearls? She said, 'Pearls are a tremendous emblem of a conventional, privileged, uneducated, unthinking, complacent, unaesthetic, unfashionable, middle-class woman. They're absolute death, pearls. The only way you can wear them is masses and masses of very large ones, or something that's different.' She said, 'How can *you* be wearing pearls?' "

"And what did you tell her?"

"I said, 'Oh, because I like them.' That's the way you deal with Sarah. One just doesn't make too much of a fuss, and she eventually clams up and goes away. She knows lots of peculiar people and she can be very peculiar herself. She's always been completely fucked-up about sex."

"That puts her in good company, doesn't it?"

"What did she say to you, Nathan?"

"What *could* she say?"

"It *was* about sex. She's read you. She thinks sexual nomadism is your bag."

" 'And I upped my tent and I went.' "

"That's the idea. She thinks no man is a good bet, but a lover as a husband is worst of all."

"Is Sarah generalizing off of vast experience?"

"I wouldn't think so. I think that anybody in his right mind wouldn't try to have a sexual relationship with her. She goes through long periods of just disliking men in principle. It isn't even feminist ranting—it's all her very own, all these internal battles she's got going on. I would think that the experience she's generalizing off of has been very meager and sad. So was mine meager and sad till not long ago. I got very angry, you know, when my husband didn't speak to me for a year. And when I spoke he insisted on stopping me, smashing me all the time whenever I tried to say anything. Always. I thought about that when you were away."

"I actually enjoy listening to you speak."

"Do you, really?"

"I'm listening to you now."

"But why? That's what nobody can figure out. Girls raised like us don't ordinarily marry men interested in books. They say to me, 'But *you* don't have intellectual conversations, do you?' "

"Intellectual enough for me."

"Yes, I talk intellectual? Do I really? Like Kierkegaard?"

"Better."

"They all think I'd make a marvelous housewife—one of the last terrific ones around. Frankly, I've often thought that maybe that is my métier. I see my two sisters going out to work, and I think, I'm now twenty-eight, nearly thirty, and since university I've achieved absolutely nothing, aside from Phoebe. And then

I think, What's wrong with that? I have a delightful daughter, I now have a delightful husband who does not smash me all the time whenever I try to speak, and I'll soon have a second child and a lovely house by the river. And I'm writing my little stories about the meadows, the mists, and the English mud that no one will ever read, and that no one *will* ever read them doesn't matter to me at all. There is also a school of thought in the family that says I married you because ever since our father walked out I was always going around looking for him."

"According to this school, I am your father."

"Only you're not. Though you do have fatherly qualities here and there, *you* are definitely not my father. Sarah is the one who sees us as three grossly fatherless women. It's a cherished preoccupation of hers. She says the father's body is like Gulliver—something you can rest your feet on, snuggle up in, walk around on top of, thinking, 'This is mine.' Rest your feet on it and step off from there."

"Is she right?"

"To a degree. She's clever, Sarah. Once he was gone we never saw him that often—a day at Christmas, a weekend in the summer, but not much more. And for years now not at all. So, yes, there probably was a sense of the world being very thin at the edges. The mother can be as competent and responsible as ours, but in our world the value was entirely defined by the father's activity. Somehow we were always out of the run of ordinary life. I didn't realize until I was older some of the jobs that women might do. I still don't."

"You regret that?"

"I told you, I have never been happier than being this preposterous, atavistic woman who does not care to assert herself. Sarah is working at it all the time, trying so hard to be assertive, and every time an opportunity is presented to her, a serious opportunity and not just badgering Georgina or me, she goes into a terrible gloom or a terrible panic."

"Because she's a daughter whose father vanished."

"When we were at home, she used to go around every March eleventh like the character at the beginning of *Three Sisters*. 'It's a year ago today that Father pissed off.' She always felt that there was nobody behind us. And there *was* something uneasy-making about Mother having the ambition for us. Wanting us to be well-educated, putting us through university, wanting us to get good jobs—that was all quite unusual in Mother's world, it had something vicarious and compensatory written all over it, something desperate, at least for Sarah."

It was while we were eating our dessert that I heard a woman loudly announcing, in exaggeratedly English tones, "Isn't that perfectly disgusting." When I turned to see who'd spoken, I found it was a large, white-haired, elderly woman at the end of our banquette, no more than ten feet away, who was finishing her dinner beside a skeletal old gentleman I took to be her husband. He didn't seem to be disgusted by anything, nor did he seem quite to be dining with the woman who was, but silently sat contemplating his port. I took them at a glance to be very well-heeled.

Addressing the room at large, but looking now directly at Maria and me, the woman said, "Isn't it, though—simply disgusting," while the husband, who was both present and absent, gave no indication that her observation might be relevant to anything he knew or cared about.

A moment earlier, convinced by Maria's customary candidness that it was not she who'd been trying to delude or mislead me but "ropey" Sarah all on her own, reassured by all she'd said that between us nothing was other than as I'd always assumed, I had reached out to touch her, the back of two fingers lightly brushing her cheek. Nothing bold, no alarmingly public display of carnality, and yet when I turned and saw that we were still pointedly being stared down, I realized what had aroused this naked rebuke: not so much that a man had tendered his wife a tiny caress in a restaurant but that the young woman *was* the wife to this man.

As though a low-voltage shock were being administered beneath the table, or she had bitten into something awful, the elderly white-haired woman began making odd, convulsive little facial movements, seemingly in some kind of sequence; as though flashing coded signals to an accomplice, she drew in her cheeks, she pursed her lips, she lengthened her mouth—until unable apparently to endure any further provocation, she called out sharply for the headwaiter. He came virtually on the run to see what the trouble was.

"Open a window," she told him, again in a voice that no one in the restaurant could fail to hear. "You must open a window immediately—there's a terrible smell in here."

"Is there, madam?" he courteously replied.

"Absolutely. The stink in here is abominable."

"I'm terribly sorry, madam. I don't notice anything."

"I don't wish to discuss it—please do as I say!"

Turning to Maria, I quietly told her, "I am that stink."

She was puzzled, even at first a little amused. "You think that this has to do with you?"

"Me *with* you."

"Either that woman is crazy," she whispered, "or she's drunk. Or maybe you are."

"If she were one, or the other, or both, it might have to do with me and it might not have to do with me. But inasmuch as she continues looking at me, or me with you, I have to assume that I am that stink."

"Darling, she is mad. She is just a ridiculous woman who thinks someone has on too much scent."

"It is a racial insult, it is intended to be that, and if she keeps it up, I am not going to remain silent, and you should be prepared."

"*Where* is the insult?" Maria said.

"The emanations of Jews. She is hypersensitive to Jewish emanations. Don't be dense."

"Oh, this is ridiculous. You are being absurd."

From down the banquette, I heard the woman saying, "They smell so funny, don't they?" whereupon I raised my hand to get the headwaiter's attention.

"Sir." He was a serious, gray-haired, soft-spoken Frenchman who weighed what was said to him as carefully and objectively as an old-fashioned analyst. Earlier, after he'd taken our order, I'd remarked to Maria on the Freudian rigorousness with which he'd done nothing to influence our choice from among the evening's several specialties whose preparation he'd laconically described.

I said to him, "My wife and I have had a very nice dinner and we'd like our coffee now, but it's extremely unpleasant with someone in the restaurant intent upon making a disturbance."

"I understand, sir."

"A window!" she called imperiously, snapping her fingers high in the air. "A window, before we are overcome!"

Here I stood and, for good or bad, even as I heard Maria entreating me—"Please, she's quite mad"—made my way out from behind the table and walked to where I could stand facing the woman and her husband, who were seated side by side. He didn't pay any more attention to me than he did to her—simply continued working on his port.

"Can I help you with your problem?" I asked.

"Pardon me?" she replied, but without the flicker of an upward glance, as though I were not even there. "Please, leave us alone."

"You find Jews repellent, do you?"

"Jews?" She repeated the word as though she'd not come upon it before. "*Jews?* Did you hear that?" she asked her husband.

"You are most objectionable, madam, grotesquely objectionable, and if you continue shouting about the stink, I am going to request that the management have you expelled."

"You will do *what?*"

"*Have—you—thrown—out.*"

Her twitching face went suddenly motionless, momentarily at least she appeared to have been silenced, and so rather than stand there threatening her any longer, I took that for a victory and started back to our table. My face was boiling hot and had obviously turned red.

"I'm not good at these things," I said, slipping back into the seat. "Gregory Peck did it better in *Gentleman's Agreement.*"

Maria did not speak.

This time when I waved for service, a waiter *and* the head-waiter came hurrying over. "Two coffees," I said. "Would you like anything else?" I asked Maria.

She pretended not even to hear me.

We'd finished the champagne and all but a little of the bottle of wine, and though I really didn't want any more to drink, I ordered a brandy, so as to make it known to the surrounding tables and to the woman herself—*and* to Maria—that we had no intention of curtailing our evening in any way. The birthday celebration would go on.

I waited until after the coffee and brandy were set down,

and then I said, "Why aren't you speaking? Maria, speak to me. Don't act as though I was the one who committed the offense. If I had done nothing, I assure you it would have been even less tolerable to you than my telling her to shut up."

"You went quite crazy."

"Did I? Failed to observe British rules of dignified restraint, did I? Well, that stuff she was pulling is very trying for us people—even more trying than Christmas."

"It isn't necessary now to go for *me*. All I'm saying is that if she meant that about the window, literally, to you, about you, then she is clearly *mad*. I don't believe any sane English person would allow themselves to go so far. Even drunk."

"But they might think it," I said.

"No. I don't even think they think it."

"They wouldn't associate stink with Jews."

"No. I do not think so. There is no general interest in this occurrence," Maria said firmly. "I don't believe you can—if that is what you want to do—extrapolate anything about England or the English, and you mustn't. Especially as you cannot even be sure, much as you seem to want to be, that your being Jewish had anything even to do with it."

"There you are wrong—there you are either innocent or blind in both eyes. She looks over here and what does she see? Miscegenation incarnate. A Jew defiling an English rose. A Jew putting on airs with a knife and a fork and a French menu. A Jew who is injurious to her country, her class, and her sense of fitness. I shouldn't, inside her mind, *be* at this restaurant. Inside her mind, this place isn't for Jews, least of all Jews defiling upper-class girls."

"What has come over you? The place is full of Jews. Every New York publisher who comes to London stays at this hotel and eats in this restaurant."

"Yes, but she's probably slow on the uptake, this old babe. In the old days it wasn't like that, and clearly there are still people who object to Jews in such places. She meant it, that woman. She did. Tell me, where do they get these exquisite sensibilities? What exactly do they smell when they smell a Jew? We're going to have to sit down and talk about these people and their aversions so that I'm not caught off guard next time we go out to eat. I mean, this isn't the West Bank—this isn't the land of the shoot-out, this is the land of the carol service. In Israel I found that everything comes bursting out of everyone all the time, and so probably means half as much as you think. But because on the surface, at least, they don't seem to be like that here, their little English outbursts are rather shocking—perhaps revealing too. Don't you agree?"

"That woman was *mad*. Why are you suddenly indicting *me*?"

"I don't mean to—I'm overheated. And surprised. Sarah, you see, tried to make clear to me, back in the church, something else that I didn't know—that your mother, as she put it, is 'terribly anti-Semitic.' So much so that I'm mystified I wasn't told about it long ago so as to know what to expect when I got here. Not terribly anti-American, terribly anti-*Semitic*. *Is* it true?"

"Sarah said that? To you?"

"Is it true?"

"It doesn't have to do with us."

"But it's true. Nor is Sarah England's greatest Jew-lover—or didn't you know that either?"

"That has nothing to do with us. None of it does."

"But why didn't you *tell* me? I do not understand. You've told me everything, why not that? We tell each other the truth. Honesty is one of the things we have. Why did it have to be hidden?"

She stood up. "Please stop this attack."

The bill was paid and in only minutes, leaving the restaurant, we were passing the table of my enemy. She now seemed as innocuous as her husband—once we'd faced off, she hadn't dared to go on about the smell. However, just as Maria and I stepped into the passageway joining the dining room to the hotel lobby, I heard her Edwardian stage-accent rising above the restaurant murmur. "What a disgusting couple!" she announced, summarily.

It turned out that Maria had been embarrassed ever since her adolescence by Mrs. Freshfield's anti-Semitism, but as she'd never known it to affect anything other than her own equanimity she'd simply endured it as a terrible flaw in someone who was otherwise an exemplary protector. Maria described her mother's family as "all crazy—a life of drink and boredom, total prejudice overlaid with good manners and silly talk"; anti-Semitism was just *one* of the stupid attitudes by which her mother could hardly have been uncontaminated. It had more to do with the imprint of her times, her class, and her impossible family than with her character—and if that seemed to me a specious distinction, it wasn't one that Maria cared to defend, since she herself knew the argument against it.

What mattered, she said, what explained everything—more or less—was that so long as it had looked as though we'd be living in America, in a house in the country with Phoebe and the new baby, there'd been no need to bring any of this up. Maria admired her mother's strength, her courage, loved her still for the full life she'd worked so hard to make for her children when there was virtually no one around who would seriously help her out, and she couldn't bear me despising her for something that wasn't going to do us any harm and to which I couldn't have been expected to bring, from my background, even the simplest sort of social understanding. If we had been able to make America our home, her mother would have come for a couple of weeks each summer to visit the children and that would have been all we ever saw of her; even if she had wanted to interfere, she would have been too clever to risk her prestige in a struggle she could only lose, opposing me from such a distance.

And then once we were legally pledged to live in London, the problem was too big for Maria to confront. She felt that by adapting to the stringent custody guarantees extracted by her ex-husband, I had already taken on more than I'd bargained for; she couldn't bring herself to announce that in addition there was waiting to pounce upon me in England an anti-Semitic mother-in-law waving a burning cross. What's more, she hoped that if I weren't prematurely antagonized, I could probably dislodge her mother's prejudice just by being myself. Was that so unrealistic? And had she been proved wrong? Though Mrs. Freshfield might seem to me inexplicably aloof, so far she had said nothing to Maria even remotely disparaging about marrying a Jew, nor had she so much as hinted that she expected our infant to be christened. That might please her, Maria had no doubt that it would, but she was hardly deluded enough to expect it, or so fanatical as to be unable to survive without it. Maria was desolated about Sarah; she still had trouble believing that Sarah could have gone so far. But Sarah, whom everyone accepted as peculiar—who had been known all her life for her "petulant little outbursts," for being "cross and mean," who never was, as Maria put it, "a purely likable person"—was not her mother. However perturbed her mother might be about the implausible match her daughter had made in New York, she was being positively heroic in suppressing her chagrin. And that wasn't only the best we could have hoped for—for a beginning it was extraordinary. In fact, if it hadn't been for that woman turning up at the other end of our banquette, a rather tender evening would have taken most of the sting out of Sarah's misbehavior down in the crypt, leaving relations between Maria's anti-Semitic mother and her Jewish husband just as respectful, if remote, as they'd been since our arrival in England.

"That dreadful woman," Maria said. "And that *husband*."

With Phoebe at Mrs. Freshfield's sister's London flat and the nanny off till the following noon, with just the two of us alone together in the living room of the rented house, I was reminded of Maria lying on the sofa of my New York apartment the year before, trying to convince me how unsuitable she was. Unsuitability—what could be more suitable for a man like me?

"Yes," I said, "the old guy really let her go."

"I've seen a lot of that where I come from," Maria said. "Women of a certain class and disposition behaving terribly, talking very loudly, and they allow them to get away with absolutely every last comma."

"Because the men agree."

"Could be, needn't be. No, it's their generation—you simply never contradict a lady, a lady is not wrong, and so on. They're all misogynist anyway, those men. Their way to behave to women like that one is to be civil toward her and just let her rave. They don't even hear them."

"And she meant what I thought she meant."

"Yes," and just when it seemed that the restaurant incident had been completely defused, Maria began to cry.

"What is it?" I asked.

"I shouldn't tell you."

"The moral of this evening is that you should tell me everything."

"No, I shouldn't." She dried her eyes and did her best to smile. "That was exhaustion, really. Relief. I'm delighted we're home, I'm delighted by this bracelet, I was delighted by the shade of crimson you turned while telling that woman off, and now I have to go up to bed because I just can't take any more pleasure."

"What shouldn't you tell me?"

"Don't—don't pump me. You know why it may be that I never explained about my mother? Not because I thought it would antagonize you, but because I was afraid it would be too intriguing. Because I do not want my mother in a book. Bad enough that's my fate, but I do not want my mother in a book because of something that, shameful as it is, is doing no one any harm. Except herself, of course—isolating her from people like you whom she has every reason to admire and enjoy."

"What made you cry?"

She closed her eyes, too exhausted to resist. "It was—well, when that woman was raving on, I had the most awful memory."

"Of?"

"This is terrible," she said. "It's shameful. It really is. There was a girl in our office when I was at the magazine—before Phoebe was born. She was a girl I liked, a colleague, my age, a very nice girl, not a close friend but a very pleasant acquaintance. We were out in Gloucestershire working on a picture story, and I said, 'Joanna, come and stay with us,' because Chadleigh isn't far from the village we were photographing. So she stayed at the house for a couple of nights. And my mother said to me, and I think Joanna may even have been in the house at the time, though she was certainly out of earshot —and I should add that Joanna is Jewish—"

"Like me—with the unmistakable genetic markings."

"My mother wouldn't miss it, I wouldn't think. Anyway, she said to me exactly, but exactly what that woman said in the restaurant. They were her very words. I had forgotten this incident entirely, just put it completely out of my mind, until I heard that woman say, 'They smell so funny, don't they?'

Because I think my mother had, I don't know, got into Joanna's bedroom, or in some perfectly normal way—oh, I don't know what, this is all very difficult to go into, and I just wish to hell I hadn't remembered it and it would all go away."

"So it wasn't entirely accurate to tell me at dinner that no one would say that unless they were mad. Since your mother is clearly not mad."

Softly, she said, "I was wrong . . . and wrong despite my knowledge . . . I told you, I'm ashamed of that. She thought it and she meant it—is it mad to say it? I don't know. Must we go on about this? I'm *so* tired."

"Is this why the night before I left, when all those well-brought-up English liberals were loathing Zionism and attacking Israel, you jumped in and started swinging?"

"No, not at all—I said what I believe."

"But with all this baggage, what *did* you think would happen when you married me?"

"With all your baggage, what did you think when you married *me*? Please, we can't start having one of those discussions. Not only is it beneath us, it doesn't matter. You simply cannot start putting everything in a Jewish context. Or is this what comes of a weekend in Judea?"

"More likely it comes of never before having lived in Christendom."

"What's the United States, a strictly Jewish preserve?"

"I didn't run into this stuff there—never."

"Well, then you have led a very protected life. I heard plenty of it in New York."

"Yes? What?"

"Oh, 'stranglehold on the cultural life, on the economy,' and so on—all the usual stuff. I think there's more in America, actually, just because there are more Jews, and because they're not so diffident as English Jews. English Jews are beleaguered, there are so few of them. On the whole they find the thing rather an embarrassment. But in the U.S. they speak up, they speak out, they're visible everywhere—and the consequence, I can assure you, is that some people don't like it, and say as much when Jews aren't around."

"But what about here, where I now live? What do you folks really think of us folks?"

"Are you *trying* to upset me," she asked, "to bait me after what's happened tonight to *both* of us?"

"I'm just trying to find out what I don't know."

"But this is all being blown out of proportion. No, I'm not telling you, because whatever I say you're going to resent and you're only going to go at *me*. Again."

"What do the folks think here, Maria?"

"They think," she said sharply, "'Why do Jews make such a bloody fuss about being Jewish?' That's what they think."

"Oh? And is that what you think?"

"It's something I've felt at times, yes."

"I didn't realize that."

"It's an extremely common feeling—and thought."

"What is meant exactly by 'fuss'?"

"Depends on what your starting point is. If you don't actually like Jews at all, practically everything a Jew does you'll perceive as Jewish. As something they ought to have dropped because it's very boring they're being so Jewish about it."

"For instance?"

"This is a bad idea," she said. "Don't you see that this is a bad idea?"

"Go on."

"I won't. No. I am incapable of protecting myself against people when they start on me like this."

"What is so boring about Jews being Jews?"

"It's all or nothing, isn't it? Our conversation doesn't seem to have any middle road. Tonight it's either sweetness or thunder."

"I am not thundering—I am dismayed, and the reason, as I told you, is that I have never run into this stuff before."

"I am not Nathan Zuckerman's first Gentile wife. I am the fourth."

"True enough. Yet never have I run into this 'mixed marriage' crap. You're the fourth, but the first from a country about which, in matters relevant to my personal well-being, I seem to be totally ignorant. Boring? That's a stigma that I would think attaches more readily to the English upper classes. Boring Jews? You must explain this to me. In my experience it's usually boring *without* the Jews. Tell me, what is so boring to the English about Jews being Jews?"

"I will tell you, but only if we can have a discussion and not the useless, destructive, and painful clash that you want to instigate regardless of *what* I say."

"What is so boring about Jews being Jews?"

"Well, I object to people—this is a feeling only, this is not a thought-out position; I might have to discipline it if you insist on keeping us up much longer, after the chablis and all that champagne—I object to people clinging to an identity just for the sake of it. I don't think there's anything admirable about it at all. All this talk about 'identities'—your 'identity' is just where you decide to stop thinking, as far as I can see. I think all these ethnic groups—whether they are Jewish, whether they're West Indian and think they must keep this Caribbean thing going—simply make life more difficult in a society where we're trying to just live amicably, like London, and where we are now very very diverse."

"You know, true as some of that may sound, the 'we-ness' here is starting to get me down. These people with their dream of the perfect, undiluted, unpolluted, unsmelly 'we.' Talk about *Jewish* tribalism. What is this insistence on homogeneity but a not very subtle form of *English* tribalism? What's so intolerable about tolerating a few differences? *You* cling to *your* 'identity,' 'just for the sake of it'—from the sound of it, no less than your mother does!"

"Please, I cannot be shouted at and keep talking. It's not intolerable and that's not what I said. I certainly do tolerate differences when I feel they're genuine. When people are being anti-Semitic or anti-black or anti-anything *because* of differences, I despise it, as you know. All I have been saying is that I don't feel that these differences are always entirely genuine."

"And you don't like that."

"All right, I'll tell you a thing I don't like, since that's what you are dying to push me to say—I don't like going to north London, to Hampstead or Highgate, and finding it like a foreign country, which it really does seem to me."

"Now we're getting down to it."

"I'm not getting *down* to anything. It's the truth, which you wanted—if it happens to make you unreasonable, that's not my fault. If you want to leave me as a result, that's not my fault either. If the upshot of my malicious sister trying to destroy this marriage is that she actually succeeds, well, that'll be her first great triumph. But it won't be ours!"

"It's pleasing to hear you raise your voice to make a point like those of us who smell."

"Oh, that is not fair. Not at all."

"I want to learn about Hampstead and Highgate being a foreign country. Because they're heavily Jewish? Can't there be a Jewish variety of Englishman? There is an English variety of human being, and we all manage to tolerate that somehow."

"If I may *stick* to the point—there are many Jews who live there, yes. People there who are my generation, who are my peers—they have the same sort of responses, they probably went to the same sort of schools, generally they'd have similar kinds of education, forgetting religious education, but they all have a different style from me, and I am *not* saying that's distasteful—"

"Just boring."

"Nor boring. Only that I do feel alien among them—being there makes me feel left out and it makes me feel that I'm better off somewhere I feel more normal."

"The net of the Establishment draws ever tighter. How is the style different?"

All this time she'd been lying across the sofa, her head propped on a pillow, looking toward the fire and the chair where I was sitting. Suddenly she sat straight up and hurled the pillow onto the floor. The catch must have come undone on the bracelet, because it came flying off and fell to the floor too. She picked it up and, leaning forward, laid it between us on the glass top of the coffee table. "Of course nothing is understood! Nothing is ever understood! Not even with you! Why won't you stop? Why don't you save your nettle-grasping for your writing?"

"Why don't you just go on and tell me all the things you shouldn't tell me? Certainly *not* telling them to me hasn't worked."

"All right. All *right*. Now that we have overestimated the meaning of everything and are assured that whatever I say will come back to haunt me—all I was going to tell you, which was no more than an anthropological aside, is that it is common parlance—though it is not necessarily anti-Semitic—for people to say, 'Oh, such-and-such is frightfully Jewish.'"

"I would have thought such sentiments were more subtly coded here. In England, they say that outright? Really?"

"Indeed they do. You betcha."

"Give me examples, please."

"Why not? Why not, Nathan? *Why* stop? An example. You go for drinks somewhere in Hampstead, and you're plied by an active hostess with an overabundance of little things to eat and sort of assaulted with extra drinks and, generally speaking, made to feel uncomfortable by a superabundance of hospitality and introductions and energy—well, then one is liable to say, 'That's very Jewish.' There is no anti-Semitic feeling behind the statement, it is merely drawing-room sociology, a universal phenomenon—everybody does it everywhere. I'm sure there have been times when even a tolerant and enlightened citizen of the world like you has been at least *tempted* to say, 'That's very goyish'—maybe even about something that *I* have done. Oh, look," she said, coming to her feet in that perfect green dress, "why don't you go back to America where they do 'mixed marriages' right? This is absurd. This was all a great mistake, and I'm sure the fault is entirely mine. Stick to American shiksas. I should never have made you come back here with me. I should never have tried to paper over things about my family that it would be impossible for you to understand or accept—though that's exactly why I did it. I shouldn't have done anything I've done, beginning with letting you invite me into your apartment for that one cup of tea. Probably I should just have let him go on shutting me up for the rest of my life—what difference does it make who shuts me up, at least that way I would have kept my little family together. Oh, it just makes me feel terribly cross that I went through all this to wind up with yet another man who cannot stand the things I say! It's been such an extended education—and for *nothing*, endless preparation for just *nothing*! I stayed with him for my daughter, stayed with him because Phoebe went around with a sign on her head saying, 'One father in residence—and it's a lot of fun.' Then stupidly, after you and I met, I said, 'But what about me? Instead of an enemy for a husband, what about a

soul mate—that unattainable impossibility!' I've gone through
hell, really, to marry you—you're the most daring thing I've
ever done. And now it turns out that you actually think that
there is an International Gentile Conspiracy of which I am a
paid-up member! Inside your head, it now turns out, there is
really no great difference between you and that Mordecai
Lippman! Your brother's off his rocker? *You are your brother!*
Do you know what I should have done, despite his generally
outrageous behavior to me? True to the tradition of my school,
I should have laced my shoes up tighter and got on with it.
Only you feel so dishonest and so cowardly—compromising,
compromising—but maybe the compromising is just being
grown-up and looking for soul mates is so much idiocy. I certainly didn't find a soul mate, that's for sure. I found a Jew.
Well, you certainly never struck me as very Jewish, but that's
where I was wrong again. Clearly I never began to understand
the depths of this thing. You disguise yourself as rational and
moderate when *you* are the wild nut! *You are Mordecai Lippman!* Oh, this is a disaster. I'd have an abortion if you could
have an abortion after five months. I don't know what to do
about that. The house we can sell, and as for me, I'd rather be
on my own if this is going to go on all our lives. I just can't
face it. I don't have that kind of emotional reserves. How terribly unfair for you to turn on me—*I* didn't plant that woman
next to us! And my mother really isn't my fault, you know, nor
are the attitudes with which she was raised. You think *I* don't
know about people in this country and how petty and vicious
they can be? I don't say this to excuse her, but in her family,
you know, if you weren't a dog or didn't have a penis, you
weren't likely to get much attention—so she's had to put up
with her shit too! And quite on her own has come a very long
way. As have we all! I did not choose to have a malicious sister
and I didn't choose to have an anti-Semitic mother—no more
than you chose to have a brother in Judea toting a gun, or a
father who, from all you say, was not extremely rational about
Gentiles, either. Nor, I remind you, has my mother said a single thing to offend you, or, privately, to offend me. When she
first saw your picture, when I showed her a photograph, she
did say, rather quietly, 'Very Mediterranean-looking, isn't he?'
And I said, just as quietly, 'You know, Mummy, I think, taking

a global view, that blue eyes and blond hair may be on the way out.' She nearly wet herself, she was so astonished to hear such a sentiment from the lips of her amiable child. But, you see, like many of us, the illusion she's come to is the one she wants. However, she was quite smooth about it, really, didn't rise to it in any way—and otherwise, though you are a homewrecker, as I've explained to you, and *any* new man of mine, Gentile as well as Jew, would be clouded by that, she said nothing more and was actually quite nice, wildly so, really, for someone who, as we know, is not all that keen on Jews. If this evening she was 'glacial,' it's because that's how she is, but she has also been as affable as she can, and probably that is because she is very anxious not to see *us* now go off in different directions. You really think she wants me to have a *second* divorce? The irony is, of course, that she's the one who's turned out to be right—not you and me with our enlightened blather but my bigoted mother. Because it's obvious that you *can't* have people from such different starting points understand each other about *anything*. Not even we, who seemed to understand each other marvelously. Oh, the irony of everything! Life always something other than what you expect! But I just cannot take this subject as the center of my life. And you, to my astonishment, want suddenly to take it as the center of yours! You, who in New York hit the ceiling when I called the Jews a 'race,' are now going to tell me that you're genetically unique? Do you really think that your Jewish beliefs, which I can't see on you anywhere, frankly, make you incompatible with me? God, Nathan, you're a human being—I don't care if you're a Jew. You ask me to tell you what 'us folks' think about you folks, and then when I try to, as truthfully as I can, without fudging things, you resent what I say, *as predicted*. Like a narrow-minded fart! Well, I can't stand it. I won't! I already have a narrow-minded mother! I already have a crazy sister! I'm not married to Mr. Rosenbloom in North Finchley, I'm married to *you*! I don't think of you, I don't go around thinking of you as being a Jew or a non-Jew, I think of you as yourself. When I go down to see how the house is coming along, do you think I ask myself, 'Is the Jew going to be happy here? Can a Jew find happiness in a house in Chiswick?' *You're* the one who's mad. Maybe on this subject *all* Jews are mad. I can understand how they might be, I can see why Jews feel so touchy and strange and rejected, and certainly misused, to put it mildly, but if we are going to go on misunderstanding each other about this, quarreling all the time and putting this subject at the center of our lives, then I don't want to live with you, I *can't* live with you, and as for our baby—oh, God only knows, now I'll have *two* children without fathers. Just what I wanted! Two children without fathers in residence, but even that is better than this, because this is just *too stupid*. Go back to America, please, where everybody loves Jews—you think!"

Imagine. Because of how I'd been provoked by Sarah in the church and then affronted in the restaurant, it was conceivable that my marriage was about to break up. Maria had said it was just too stupid, but stupidity happens unfortunately to be real, and no less capable of governing the mind than fear, lust, or anything else. The burden isn't either/or, consciously choosing from possibilities equally difficult and regrettable— it's and/and/and/and/and as well. Life *is* and: the accidental and the immutable, the elusive and the graspable, the bizarre and the predictable, the actual and the potential, all the multiplying realities, entangled, overlapping, colliding, conjoined— plus the multiplying illusions! This times this times this times this . . . Is an intelligent human being likely to be much more than a large-scale manufacturer of misunderstanding? I didn't think so when I left the house.

That there were people in England who, even after Hitler might have been thought to have somewhat tarnished the Jew-hater's pride, still harbored a profound distaste for Jews hadn't come as a surprise. The surprise wasn't even that Maria should extend as much tolerance as she did to her mother, or that, so improbably, she should have been naïve enough to believe that she was averting a disaster by pretending that there wasn't that kind of poison around. The unpredictable development was how furious it all made me. But then I had been wholly unprepared—usually it was the Semites, and not the anti-Semites, who assaulted me for being the Jew I was. Here in England I was all at once experiencing first-hand something I had never personally been bruised by in America. I felt as though gentlest England had suddenly reared up and bit me on the neck—there was a kind of irrational scream in me saying, "She's not on my side—she's on their side!" I'd considered very deeply and felt vicariously the wounds that Jews have had to endure, and, contrary to the charges by my detractors of literary adventurism, my writing had hardly been born of recklessness or naïveté about the Jewish history of pain; I had written my fiction in the knowledge of it, and even in consequence of it, and yet the fact remained that, down to tonight, the experience of it had been negligible in my personal life. Crossing back to Christian Europe nearly a hundred years after my grandparents' westward escape, I was finally feeling up against my skin that outer reality which I'd mostly come to know in America as an "abnormal" inner preoccupation permeating nearly everything within the Jewish world.

All this being so, I still had to wonder if I wasn't suffering from the classic psychosemitic ailment rather than the serious clinical disease, if I wasn't perhaps a paranoid Jew attaching false significance to a manageable problem requiring no more than common sense to defuse—if I wasn't making them all stand for far too much and overimagining everything; if I wasn't *wanting* the anti-Semitism to be there, and in a big way. When Maria had implored me not to pursue it, why hadn't I listened? Talking about it, going on about it, mercilessly prolonging that discussion, it was inevitable that we would reach the burning sore. But then it wasn't as though I had been unprovoked or that separating us from all this vile stuff was wholly within my power. Of course resisting provocation is always an option, but can you really have your sister-in-law calling you a dirty Jew bastard, and someone else saying that you're stinking up the place, and then someone you love saying why do you make such a production of these things, without your head starting to explode, no matter what sort of peaceable person you've tried turning yourself into? It was even possible that far from making them stand for too much, I had come upon a deep, insidious Establishment anti-Semitism that is latent and pervasive but that, among the mild, well-brought-up, generally self-concealing English, only the occasional misfit like a madwoman or a fucked-up sister actually comes out with. Otherwise by and large it's subliminal, one can't hear it, no rampant signs anywhere you look, except perhaps in the peculiarly immoderate, un-English-like Israel-loathing that the young people at that dinner party had seemed to go in for.

In America, I thought, where people claim and disown "identities" as easily as they slap on bumper stickers—where even though there are people sitting in clubs who think it's still the land of Aryans, it just don't happen to be so—I could act like a reasonable fellow when she'd distinguished Jews from Caucasians. But here, where you were swathed permanently in what you were born with, encased for life with where you began, here in a *real* land of Aryans, with a wife whose sister, if not her mother as well, appeared to be the point-woman for some pure-blooded phalanx out to let me know that I was not welcome and had better not come in, I couldn't let the insult pass. Our affinity was strong and real, but however much complicity we'd felt at the carol service, Maria and I were *not* anthropologists in Somaliland, nor were we orphans in a storm: she came from somewhere and so did I, and those differences we talked so much about could begin to have a corrosive effect once the charm began wearing thin. We couldn't just be "us" and say the hell with "them" any more than we could say to hell with the twentieth century when it intruded upon our idyll. Here's the problem, I thought: even if her mother is a completely entrenched and bigoted upper-class snob, Maria loves her and is trapped by that—she doesn't really want her mother referring to her pagan grandchild and yet she doesn't want to fight me either, while I, for my part, don't intend to lose—not the woman, the baby, or the argument. How do I salvage what I want out of this clash of atavistic wills?

God, how enraging to blunder smilingly into people who want no part of you—and how awful to compromise, even for love. When asked to accede, whether by Gentile or Jew, I discover that all my efforts seem to go against it.

The past, the unevadable past, had gained control and was about to vandalize our future unless I did something to stop it. We could digest each other so easily, but not the history clinging to the clan that each of us brought along into our life. Is it really possible that I will go around with the sense that, however subtly, she is buying into their anti-Semitism, that I will hear echoes of the anti-Semite in her, and that she will see in me a Jew who can't do otherwise than let being a Jew eclipse everything else? Is it possible that neither of us can control this old, old stuff? What if there's no extracting her from a world I don't wish to enter even if I were welcome there?

What I did was to hail a taxi to take me to Chiswick, to the house on the river that we had bought and were remodeling to encapsulate what we had imagined we had, the house that was being transformed into ours and that represented my own transformation—the house that represented the rational way, the warm human enclosure that would shelter and protect something more than my narrative mania. It seemed at that moment that everything was imaginatively possible for me except the mundane concreteness of a home and a family.

Because walls were coming down and not every floorboard was in place, I didn't wander around inside, even though when I tried the front door I found it unlocked. A lonely midnight visit to the unfinished haven was sufficiently symbolic of my predicament without overwriting the scene entirely by stumbling around in the dark and breaking my neck. Instead, I wandered from window to window, peering in as though I were casing the joint, and then I sat on the sill of the French doors to the terrace, staring out at the Thames. There was nothing gliding by but water. I could see the lights of some of the houses through the branches of the trees on the far side of the river. They seemed tiny and far away. It was like looking across to a foreign country—from one foreign country to another.

I sat for nearly an hour like somebody who's lost his key, all alone, feeling pretty forlorn and rather cold, but gradually I quieted down and was breathing more evenly again. Even if it wasn't yet snug and glowing above the water, the tangibility of the house helped to remind me of all that I had worked so hard to suppress in order to make contact with these ordinary, temporal satisfactions. The tangibility of that half-rebuilt, unoccupied house made me reconsider very seriously whether what had happened warranted this drama, if the evidence was adequate for what my feelings had concluded. When I looked back over the last year and recalled the obstinacy and resilience with which we had successfully combated whatever had blocked our way, I felt ridiculous for being so easily overwhelmed and feeling so innocently victimized. You do not go from being a conventionally unhappy married mother and a thrice-divorced, childless literary anchorite to being partners in a flourishing domestic life as father-to-be and pregnant wife, you do not proceed in fourteen months to thoroughly rearrange nearly everything important to you by being two helpless weaklings together.

What had happened? Nothing particularly original. We had a fight, our first, nothing more or less annihilating than that. What had overcharged the rhetoric and ignited the resentment was of course her role of mother's daughter rubbing against mine of father's son—our first fight hadn't even been ours. But then the battle initially rocking most marriages is usually just that—fought by surrogates for real antagonists whose conflict is never rooted in the here and now but sometimes originates so far back that all that remains of the grandparents' values are the newlyweds' ugly words. Virginal they may wish to be, but the worm in the dream is always the past, that impediment to all renewal.

So what do I say when I get home? What do I do now, now that I know all this? Do I run up the stairs and kiss her as though everything's fine, do I wake her to tell her all I've been thinking—or isn't it better to come quietly and unobtrusively into the house and leave the damage to be repaired by the mundane glue of the round of life? Only what if she isn't there, if upstairs is dark and the house still because she's gone to share Phoebe's divan at her aunt's flat? What if the interminable day that began at dawn Middle Eastern Time in a taxi from Jerusalem to the airport security check ends with Maria fleeing Kensington from a militant Jew? From Israel, to the crypt, to the banquette, to the divorce court. In this world, *I'm* the terrorist.

If she isn't there.

Sitting and staring across the dark river, I envision a return of the life I'd fought free of by anchoring myself to Maria. This woman of profound forbearance and moral courage, this woman of seductive fluency whose core is reticence and discretion, this woman whose emotional knowledge is extraordinary, whose intellect is so clear and touching, who, even though she favors one sexual position, is hardly innocent of what love and desire are about, a bruised, deliciously civilized woman, articulate, intelligent, coherent, with a lucid understanding of the terms of life and that marvelous gift for recitative—*what if she isn't there?* Imagine Maria gone, my life *without* all that, imagine no outer life of any meaning, myself completely otherless and reabsorbed within—all the voices once again only mine ventriloquizing, all the conflicts germinated by the tedious old clashing of contradictions within. Imagine—instead of a life inside something other than a skull, only the isolating unnaturalness of self-battling. No, no—no, no, no, this chance may be my last and I've disfigured myself enough already. When I return, let me find in the bed, beneath our blanket, all those beautiful undulations that are not syntactical, hips that are not words, soft living buttocks that are not my invention—let me find sleeping there what I've worked for and what I want, a woman with whom I'm content, pregnant with our future, her lungs quietly billowing with life's real air. For if she should be gone, should there be only a letter beside my pillow . . .

But forgo the lament (which everyone who's ever been locked out of anything knows by heart)—what exactly is in that letter? Being Maria's, it could be interesting. This is a woman who could *teach* me things. *How* have I lost her—if I've lost her—this contact, this connection to a full and actual outer existence, to a potent, peaceful, happy life? Imagine that.

I'm leaving.

I've left.

I'm leaving you.

I'm leaving the book.

That's it. Of course. The book! She conceives of herself as my fabrication, brands herself a fantasy and cleverly absconds, leaving not just me but a promising novel of cultural warfare barely written but for the happy beginning.

Dear Nathan,

I'm leaving. I've left. I'm leaving you and I'm leaving the book and I'm taking Phoebe away before anything dreadful happens to her. I know characters rebelling against their author has been done before, but as my choice of a first husband should have made clear—at least to me—I have no desire to be original and never did. I loved you and it was kind of thrilling to live totally as somebody else's invention, since, alas, that is how I am bent anyway, but even my terrible tameness has its limits, and I will be better off with Phoebe back where we began, living upstairs with him. Sure it's lovely being listened to as opposed to being shut up, but it's also quite creepy to think that I am monitored closely only to be even more manipulated and exploited than I was when you extracted me (for artistic purposes) from my situation upstairs. This stuff isn't for me, and I warned you as much in the beginning. When I begged you not to write about me, you assured me that you can't write "about" anyone, that even when you try to, it comes out someone else. Well, insufficiently someone else to suit me. I recognize that radical change is the law of life and that if everything quietens down on one front, it invariably gets noisy on another; I recognize that to be born, to live, and to die is to change form, but you overdo it. It was not fair to put me through your illness and the operation and your death. "Wake up, wake up, Maria—it was all only a dream!" But that gets wearing after a while. I can't take a lifetime of never knowing if you're fooling. I can't be toyed with forever. At least with my English tyrant I knew where I stood and could behave accordingly. With you that'll never be.

And how do I know what's to happen to Phoebe? That terrifies me. You weren't beyond killing your brother, you weren't beyond killing yourself, or grandiosely amusing yourself on the plane up from Israel by staging a lunatic hijack attempt—what if you decide everything will be more interesting if my daughter steps off the towpath into the river? When I think about literary surgery being performed experimentally upon those I love, I understand what drives the antivivisectionists nuts. You had no right to make Sarah, in that crypt, say words she would never have spoken if it weren't for your Jewish hang-up. Not only was it unnecessary, it was cruelly provocative. Since I had already confided to you that Jews seem to me too quick finding fault with Gentiles, condemning things as horrendously anti-Semitic, or even mildly so, when they aren't, you made sure to provide me with a sister who is anti-Semitic in spades. And then

that creature at the restaurant, planted there by *you*, and just
when everything was so perfect, the loveliest evening I'd had
in years. Why do these things always happen when you're all
set up for a wonderful time? Why isn't it okay for us to be
happy? Can't you imagine *that*? Try for a change confining
your fantasies to satisfaction and pleasure. That shouldn't be
so hard—most people do it as a matter of course. You are forty-
five years old and something of a success—it's high time you
imagined life *working out*. Why this preoccupation with irre-
solvable conflict? Don't you want a new mental life? I was once
foolish enough to think that's what this was all about and why
you wanted me, not to reenact the dead past but to strike out
happily on a new course, to rise in exuberant rebellion against
your author and remake your life. I had the temerity to think
that I was having a tremendous effect. Why did you have to
ruin everything with this anti-Semitic outburst against which
you now must rage like a zealot from Agor? New York you
made into a horror by perversely playing *Carnovsky* out in reverse with that ghastly experiment in impotence. I for one
would rather have taken the part of Marvelous Maria the porn-
queen fellator in some interminable priapic romp—even all the
choking would have been preferable to the terrible sadness of
seeing you crushed in that way. And now, in London, the Jews.
When everything was going so beautifully, the Jews. Can't you
ever forget your Jews? How can that turn out to be—particularly in someone who's been around as much as you—your irreducible core? It *is* boring, boring and regressive and crazy to
continue on about your connection to a group into which you
simply happened to have been born, and a very long time ago
at that. Disgusting as you've discovered my Englishness to be,
I'm really *not* wedded to it, or to any label, in the way that
most of you Jews do persist in being Jewish. Hasn't the man
who has led your life been a loyal child long enough?

You know what it's like being with a Jew when the subject
of Jews arises? It's like when you're with people who are
on the verge of insanity. Half the time you're with them
they're absolutely fine, and some of the time they're completely barking. But there are curious moments when they're
hovering, you can see them tipping over the edge. Actually
what they are saying is no less reasonable than what they were

saying five minutes before, but you know that they have just stepped over that little magic line.

What I'm saying is that all the way back on page 67 I saw where you were preparing to take us, and should have got myself up and out before your plane even landed, let alone rushing to the airport to catch you sky-high still on the Holy Land. It works this way (your enveloping mind, I mean): inasmuch as it has been established by my sister that my mother is determined to make an issue of having our child symbolically sprinkled with the purifying waters of the church, you are now determined to counterattack by demanding that the child, if a boy, shall make his covenant with Yahweh through the ritual sacrifice of his foreskin. Oh, I do see through to your contrary core! We would have argued again—*we who never argue.* I would have said, "I think it's a barbaric mutilation. I think it's physically harmless in a million cases out of a million and one, so that I can't produce any medical arguments against it, except the general one that one would rather not intervene in anyone's body unless it's necessary. But I nonetheless think it's terrible, circumcising boys *or* girls. I just think it's wrong." And you would have said, "But I would find it very hard having a son who isn't circumcised," or something even more subtly menacing. And so it would go. And who would win? Guess. It *is* a barbaric mutilation, but, being reasonable and completely your creature, I would of course have given in. I'd say, "I think a child should be like a father in that way. I mean, if the father is *not* circumcised, then I think the child should be like *his* father, because I think it would puzzle a child to be different from his father and would cause all sorts of problems for him." I'd say—be made to say is nearer the truth—"I think it's better not to interfere with these customs when they cause so much feeling. If you are going to be incensed about anybody interfering with this link between you and your son, I don't care if it looks to me as though an intellectual agnostic is being irrationally Jewish, I now understand the feeling and don't propose to stand in its way. If it's this that establishes for you the truth of your paternity—that regains for you the truth of your *own* paternity—so be it." And *you* would have said, "And what about *your* paternity—what about your mother, Maria?" and then we would *never* have got to sleep, not for years, because the issue would have been joined and you would have been having the time of your life what with our intercontinental marriage having become so much more INTERESTING.

No, I won't do it. I will not be locked into your head in this way. I will not participate in this primitive drama, not even for the sake of your fiction. Oh, darling, the hell with your fiction. I remember how back in New York, when I let you read one of my stories, you immediately ran out and bought me that thick leather-bound notebook. "I've got something for you to write in," you told me. "Thank you," I replied, "but do you think I have that much to say?" You didn't seem to realize that writing for me isn't everything about my existence wrestling to be born but just some stories about the mists and the Gloucestershire meadows. And I didn't realize that even a woman as passive as I has to know when to run for her life. Well, I would be just too stupid if I didn't know by now. Admittedly, it's no return to Paradise, but since he and I do have a great deal in common, have a deep bond of class and generation and nationality and background, when we fight like cats and dogs it really has little to do with anything, and afterwards everything goes an just as before, which is how I like it. It's too intense, all this talk that *means* something. You and I argue, and twentieth-century history comes looming up, and at its most infernal. I feel pressed on every side, and it takes the stuffing out of me— but for you, it's your métier, really. All our short-lived serenity and harmony, all our hope and happiness, was a bore to you, admit it. So was the idea of altering your ways in middle age by becoming a calmly detached observer, a bit more of a percipient spy on the agony of others, rather than, as of old, being tossed and torn apart yourself.

You do want to be opposed again, don't you? You may have had your fill of fighting Jews and fighting fathers and fighting literary inquisitors—the harder you fight that sort of local opposition, the more your inner conflict grows. But fighting the goyim it's *clear*, there's no uncertainty or doubt—a good, righteous, guilt-free punch-up! To be resisted, to be caught, to find yourself in the midst of a battle puts a spring in your heel. You're just dying, after all my mildness, for a collision, a clash —anything as long as there's enough antagonism to get the story smoking and everything exploding in the wrathful philippics you adore. To be a Jew at Grossinger's is obviously a bit of a bore—but in England being Jewish turns out to be difficult and just what you consider fun. People tell you, *There are restrictions*, and you're in your element again. You *revel* in restrictions. But the fact is that as far as the English are concerned, being Jewish is something you very occasionally apologize for and that's it. It is hardly my perspective, it strikes me as coarse and insipid, but it still is nothing like the horror you have imagined. But a life without horrible difficulties (which by the way a number of Jews do manage to enjoy here—just ask Disraeli or Lord Weidenfeld) is inimical to the writer you are. You actually *like* to take things hard. You can't weave your stories otherwise.

Well, not me, I like it amiable, the amiable drift of it, the mists, the meadows, and not to reproach each other for things outside our control, and not every last thing invested with urgent meaning. I don't usually give in to strange temptation and now I remember why. When I told you about that scene at Holly Tree Cottage when my mother said, about my Jewish friend, "They smell so funny, don't they?" I saw exactly what you were thinking—not "How awful for someone to say such a thing!" but "Why does she write about those stupid meadows when she can sink her teeth into *that*? Now *there's* a subject!" Perfectly true, but not a subject for me. The last thing I would ever want are the consequences of writing about *that*. For one thing, if I did, I wouldn't really be telling the English anything they didn't know but simply exposing my mother and me to incalculable distress in order to come up with something "strong." Well, better to keep the peace by writing something weak. I don't entirely share your superstitions about art and its strength. I take my stand for something far less important than axing everything open—it's called tranquillity.

But tranquillity is disquieting to you, Nathan, in writing particularly—it's bad art to you, far too comfortable for the reader and certainly for yourself. The last thing you want is to make readers happy, with everything cozy and strifeless, and desire simply fulfilled. The pastoral is not your genre, and Zuckerman Domesticus now seems to you just that, too easy a solution, an idyll of the kind you hate, a fantasy of innocence in the perfect house in the perfect landscape on the banks of the perfect stretch of river. So long as you were winning me, getting me away from him, and we were struggling with the custody issue, so long as there was that wrestling for rights and possessions, you were engrossed, but now it begins to look to me that you're afraid of peace, afraid of Maria and Nathan alone and quiet with their happy family in a settled life. To you, in that, there's a suggestion of Zuckerman unburdened, too on top of it, that's not earned—or worse, insufficiently INTERESTING. To you to live as an innocent is to live as a laughable monster. Your chosen fate, as you see it, is to be innocent of innocence at all costs, certainly not to let me, with my pastoral origins, cunningly transform you into a pastoralized Jew. I think you are embarrassed to find that even you were tempted to have a dream of simplicity as foolish and naïve as anyone's. Scandalous. How can that be? Nothing, but nothing, is simple for Zuckerman. You constitutionally distrust anything that appears to you to be effortlessly gained. As if it were effortless to achieve what we had.

Yet when I'm gone don't think I didn't appreciate you. Shall I tell you what I'm going to miss, despite my shyness and well-known lack of sexual assertiveness? It's feeling your hips between my thighs. It's not very erotic by today's standards, and probably you don't even know what I'm talking about. "My hips between your thighs?" you ask, dumbly rubbing your whiskers. Yes, position A. You'd hardly ever done anything so ordinary in your life before I came along, but for me that was just lovely and I won't forget for a long time what it was like. I will also remember an afternoon down in your apartment before my enemy came home for dinner; there was an old song on the radio, you said it was a song you used to dance to in high school with your little girlfriend Linda Mandel, and so for the first and only time, there in your study, we danced the fox-trot like adolescent kids out of the forties, danced the fox-trot glued loin to loin. When I look back on all this fifteen years from now, you know what I'll think? I'll think, "Lucky old me." I'll think what we all think fifteen years later: "Wasn't that nice." But at twenty-eight this is no life, especially if you are going to be Maupassant and milk the irony for all its worth. You want to play reality-shift? Get yourself another girl. I'm leaving. When I see you now in the lift or down in the foyer collecting your mail, I will pretend, though it may only be the two of us who are there, that we have never been anything other than neighbors, and if we meet in public, at a party or a restaurant, and I am with my husband and our friends, I will blush, I do blush, not as much as I used to, but I always blush at a very revealing moment, I blush at the most extraordinary things, though perhaps I can get out of it by coming boldly up to you and saying, "I'd just like to tell you how profoundly I identify with the women characters in your argumentative books," and nobody will guess, despite my blushing, that I was almost one of them.

P.S. I think Maria is a nice enough name for other people, but not for me.

P.P.S. At the point where "Maria" appears to be most her own woman, most resisting you, most saying I cannot live the life you have imposed upon me, not if it's going to be a life of us quarreling about your Jewishness in England, that is impossible—at this point of greatest strength, she is least real, which is to say *least* her own woman, because she has become again your "character," just one of a series of fictive propositions. This is diabolical of you.

P.P.P.S. If this letter sounds terribly rational, I assure you it's the last thing I feel.

My Maria,

When Balzac died he called out for his characters from his deathbed. Do we have to wait for that terrible hour? Besides, you are not merely a character, or even a character, but the real living tissue of my life. I understand the terror of being tyrannically suppressed, but don't you see how it's led to excesses of imagination that are yours and not mine? I suppose it can be said that I do sometimes desire, or even require, a certain role to be rather clearly played that other people aren't always interested enough to want to perform. I can only say in my defense that I ask no less of myself. Being Zuckerman is one long performance and the very opposite of what is thought of as *being oneself*. In fact, those who most seem to be themselves appear to me people impersonating what they think they might like to be, believe they ought to be, or wish to be taken to be by whoever is setting standards. So in earnest are they that they don't even recognize that being in earnest *is the act*. For certain self-aware people, however, this is not possible: to imagine themselves being themselves, living their own real, authentic, or genuine life, has for them all the aspects of a hallucination.

I realize that what I am describing, people divided in themselves, is said to characterize mental illness and is the absolute opposite of our idea of emotional integration. The whole Western idea of mental health runs in precisely the opposite direction: what is desirable is congruity between your self-consciousness and your natural being. But there are those whose sanity flows from the conscious *separation* of those two things. If there even *is* a natural being, an irreducible self, it is rather small, I think, and may even be the root of all impersonation—the natural being may be the skill itself, the innate capacity to impersonate. I'm talking about recognizing that one is acutely a performer, rather than swallowing whole the guise of naturalness and pretending that it isn't a performance but you.

There is no you, Maria, any more than there's a me. There is only this way that we have established over the months of performing together, and what it is congruent with isn't "ourselves" but past performances—we're has-beens at heart, routinely trotting out the old, old act. What is the role I demand of you? I couldn't describe it, but I don't have to—you are such a great intuitive actress you *do* it, almost with no direction at all, an extraordinarily controlled and seductive performance. Is it a role that's foreign to you? Only if you wish to pretend that it is. It's *all* impersonation—in the absence of a self, one impersonates selves, and after a while impersonates best the self that best gets one through. If you were to tell me that there are people, like the man upstairs to whom you now threaten to turn yourself in, who actually do have *a strong sense of themselves*, I would have to tell you that they are only impersonating people with a strong sense of themselves—to which you could correctly reply that since there is no way of proving whether I'm right or not, this is a circular argument from which there is no escape.

All I can tell you with certainty is that I, for one, have no self, and that I am unwilling or unable to perpetrate upon myself the joke of a self. It certainly does strike me as a joke about *my* self. What I have instead is a variety of impersonations I can do, and not only of myself—a troupe of players that I have internalized, a permanent company of actors that I can call upon when a self is required, an ever-evolving stock of pieces and parts that forms my repertoire. But I certainly have no self independent of my imposturing, artistic efforts to have one. Nor would I want one. I am a theater and nothing more than a theater.

Now probably this is all true only to a point and I am characteristically trying to take it too far, "tipping over the edge," as you say of Jews, "like people who are on the verge of insanity." I could be altogether wrong. Obviously the whole idea of what is a self philosophers have gone on about at extraordinary lengths, and, if only from the evidence here, it is a very slippery subject. But it *is* INTERESTING trying to get a handle on one's own subjectivity—something to think about, to play around with, and what's more fun than that? Come back and we'll play with it together. We could have great times as Homo Ludens and wife, inventing the imperfect future. We can pretend to be anything we want. All it takes is impersonation. That is like saying that it takes only courage, I know. I am saying just that. I am willing to go on impersonating a Jewish man who still adores you, if only you will return pretending to be the pregnant Gentile woman carrying our minuscule unbaptized baby-to-be. You cannot choose a man you can't stand against the person that you love just because the unhappy life with him is easy by comparison to the paradoxically more difficult happy life with me. Or is that what all the aging husbands say when their young wives disappear in the middle of the night?

I just can't believe that you are serious about living upstairs. I hate to have to be the one to make the perfectly crude, predictable, feminist point, but even if you weren't going to live with me, couldn't you think of something else to do rather than going back to him? It seems so self-reductive of you, unless I'm reading you too literally, and the point you're hammering home is that *anything's* better than me.

Now to what you say about pastoralization. Do you remember the Swedish film we watched on television, that microphotography of ejaculation, conception, and all that? It was quite wonderful. First was the whole sexual act leading to conception, from the point of view of the innards of the woman.

They had a camera or something up the vas deferens. I still
don't know how they did it—does the guy have the camera on
his prick? Anyway, you saw the sperm in huge color, coming
down, getting ready, and going out into the beyond, and then
finding its end up somewhere else—quite beautiful. The pastoral landscape par excellence. According to one school, it's
where the pastoral genre that you speak of begins, those irrepressible yearnings by people beyond simplicity to be taken off
to the perfectly safe, charmingly simple and satisfying environment that is desire's homeland. How moving and pathetic
these pastorals are that cannot admit contradiction or conflict!
That that is the womb and this is the world is not as easy to
grasp as one might imagine. As I discovered at Agor, not even
Jews, who are to history what Eskimos are to snow, seem able,
despite the arduous education to the contrary, to protect
themselves against the pastoral myth of life before Cain and
Abel, of life before the split began. Fleeing now, and back to
day zero and the first untainted settlement—breaking history's
mold and casting off the dirty, disfiguring reality of the piled-
up years: this is what Judea means to, of all people, that belligerent, unillusioned little band of Jews . . . also what Basel
meant to claustrophobic Henry lustlessly boxed-in back in Jersey . . . also—let's face it—something like what you and Gloucestershire once meant to me. Each has its own configuration,
but whether set in the cratered moonscape of the Pentateuch,
or the charming medieval byways of orderly old Schweiz, or
the mists and the meadows of Constable's England, at the core
is the idyllic scenario of redemption through the recovery of a
sanitized, confusionless life. In dead seriousness, we all create
imagined worlds, often green and breastlike, where we may
finally be "ourselves." Yet another of our mythological pursuits. Think of all those Christians, hearty enough to know
better, piping out their virginal vision of Momma and invoking
that boring old Mother Goose manger. What's our unborn
offspring meant to me, right up to tonight in fact, but something perfectly programmed to be my little redeemer? What
you say is true: the pastoral is not my genre (no more than you
would think of it as Mordecai Lippman's); it isn't complicated
enough to provide a real solution, and yet haven't I been fueled
by the most innocent (and comical) vision of fatherhood with

the imagined child as the therapeutic pastoral of the middle-aged man?

Well, that's over. The pastoral stops here and it stops with circumcision. That delicate surgery should be performed upon the penis of a brand-new boy seems to you the very cornerstone of human irrationality, and maybe it is. And that the custom should be unbreakable even by the author of my somewhat skeptical books proves to you just how much my skepticism is worth up against a tribal taboo. But why not look at it another way? I know that touting circumcision is entirely anti-Lamaze and the thinking these days that wants to debrutalize birth and culminates in delivering the child in water in order not even to startle him. Circumcision is startling, all right, particularly when performed by a garlicked old man upon the glory of a newborn body, but then maybe that's what the Jews had in mind and what makes the act seem quintessentially Jewish and the mark of their reality. Circumcision makes it clear as can be that you are here and not there, that you are out and not in—also that you're mine and not theirs. There is no way around it: you enter history through my history and me. Circumcision is everything that the pastoral is not and, to my mind, reinforces what the world is about, which isn't strifeless unity. Quite convincingly, circumcision gives the lie to the womb-dream of life in the beautiful state of innocent pre-history, the appealing idyll of living "naturally," unencumbered by man-made ritual. To be born is to lose all that. The heavy hand of human values falls upon you right at the start, marking your genitals as its own. Inasmuch as one invents one's meanings, along with impersonating one's selves, this is the meaning I propose for that rite. I'm not one of those Jews who want to hook themselves up to the patriarchs or even to the modern state; the relationship of my Jewish "I" to their Jewish "we" is nothing like so direct and unstrained as Henry now wishes his to be, nor is it my intention to simplify that connection by flying the flag of our child's foreskin. Only a few hours ago, I went so far as to tell Shuki Elchanan that the custom of circumcision was probably irrelevant to my "I." Well, it turns out to be easier to take that line on Dizengoff Street than sitting here beside the Thames. A Jew among Gentiles and a Gentile among Jews. Here it turns out, by my emotional logic, to be the number-one priority. Aided by your sister, your mother, and even by you, I find myself in a situation that has reactivated the strong sense of difference that had all but atrophied in New York, and, what's more, that has drained the domestic idyll of its few remaining drops of fantasy. Circumcision confirms that there is an us, and an us that isn't solely him and me. England's made a Jew of me in only eight weeks, which, on reflection, might be the least painful method. A Jew without Jews, without Judaism, without Zionism, without Jewishness, without a temple or an army or even a pistol, a Jew clearly without a home, just the object itself, like a glass or an apple.

I think in the context of our adventures—*and* Henry's—that it's fitting to conclude with my erection, the circumcised erection of the Jewish father, reminding you of what you said when you first had occasion to hold it. I wasn't so chagrined by your virginal diffidence as by the amusement that came in its wake. Uncertainly I asked, "Isn't it to your liking?" "Oh, yes, it's fine," you said, delicately weighing it in the scale of your hand, "but it's the phenomenon itself: it just seems a rather rapid transition." I'd like those words to stand as the coda to that book you so foolishly tell me you wish to escape. To escape into what, Marietta? It may be as you say that this is no life, but use your enchanting, enrapturing brains: this life is as close to life as you, and I, and our child can ever hope to come.

THE FACTS

A Novelist's Autobiography

To my brother at sixty

And as he spoke I was thinking, *the kind of stories that people turn life into, the kind of lives that people turn stories into.*

Nathan Zuckerman, in *The Counterlife*

Dear Zuckerman,

In the past, as you know, the facts have always been note-book jottings, my way of springing into fiction. For me, as for most novelists, every genuine imaginative event begins down there, with the facts, with the specific, and not with the philosophical, the ideological, or the abstract. Yet, to my surprise, I now appear to have gone about writing a book absolutely backward, taking what I have already imagined and, as it were, desiccating it, so as to restore my experience to the original, prefictionalized factuality. Why? To prove that there is a significant gap between the autobiographical writer that I am thought to be and the autobiographical writer that I am? To prove that the information that I drew from my life was, in the fiction, incomplete? If that was all, I don't think I would have gone to the trouble, since thoughtful readers, if they were interested enough to care, could have figured as much for themselves. Nor was there any call for this book; no one ordered it, no one sent down for an autobiography from Roth. The order, if it was ever even placed, went out thirty years ago, when certain of my Jewish elders demanded to know just who this kid was who was writing this stuff.

No, the thing seems to have been born out of other necessities, and sending this manuscript to you—and asking you, as I do, to tell me whether you think I should publish it—prompts me to explain what may have led to my presenting myself in prose like this, undisguised. Until now I have always used the past as the basis for transformation, for, among other things, a kind of intricate explanation to myself of my world. Why appear untransformed in front of people when, by and large, in the unimagined world, I've refrained from nakedly divulging my personal life to (and pressing a TV personality on) a serious audience? On the pendulum of self-exposure that oscillates between aggressively exhibitionistic Mailerism and sequestered Salingerism, I'd say that I occupy a midway position, trying in

the public arena to resist gratuitous prying or preening without making too holy a fetish of secrecy and seclusion. So why
claim biographical visibility now, especially as I was educated to
believe that the independent reality of the fiction is all there is
of importance and that writers should remain in the shadows?

Well, to begin to answer—the person I've intended to make
myself visible to here has been myself, primarily. Over fifty you
need ways of making yourself visible to yourself. A moment
comes, as it did for me some months back, when I was all at
once in a state of helpless confusion and could not understand
any longer what once was obvious to me: why I do what I do,
why I live where I live, why I share my life with the one I do. My
desk had become a frightening, foreign place and, unlike similar moments earlier in life when the old strategies didn't work
anymore—either for the pragmatic business of daily living,
those problems that everybody faces, or for the specialized
problems of writing—and I had energetically resolved on a
course of renewal, I came to believe that I just could not make
myself over yet again. Far from feeling capable of remaking
myself, I felt myself coming undone.

I'm talking about a breakdown. Although there's no need
to delve into particulars here, I will tell you that in the spring
of 1987, at the height of a ten-year period of creativity, what
was to have been minor surgery turned into a prolonged physical ordeal that led to an extreme depression that carried me
right to the edge of emotional and mental dissolution. It was
in the period of post-crack-up meditation, with the clarity attending the remission of an illness, that I began, quite involuntarily, to focus virtually all my waking attention on worlds from
which I had lived at a distance for decades—remembering
where I had started out from and how it had all begun. If you
lose something, you say, "Okay, let's retrace the steps. I came
in the house, took off my coat, went into the kitchen," etc.,
etc. In order to recover what I had lost I had to go back to the
moment of origin. I found no one moment of origin but a
series of moments, a history of multiple origins, and that's what
I have written here in the effort to repossess life. I hadn't ever
mapped out my life like this but rather, as I've said, had looked
only for what could be transformed. Here, so as to fall back

into my former life, to retrieve my vitality, to transform myself into *myself*, I began rendering experience untransformed.

Perhaps it wasn't even myself I wanted to be turned into but the boy I had been when I went off to college, the boy surrounded on the playground by his neighborhood compatriots —back down to ground zero. After the crack-up comes the grateful rush into ordinary life, and that was my life at its most ordinary. I suppose I wanted to return to the point when the launch was the launch of a more ordinary Roth and, at the same time, to reengage those formative encounters, to reclaim the earliest struggles, to get back to that high-spirited moment when the manic side of my imagination took off and I became my own writer; back to the original well, not for material but for the launch, the *re*launch—out of fuel, back to tank up on the magic blood. Like you, Zuckerman, who are reborn in *The Counterlife* through your English wife, like your brother, Henry, who seeks rebirth in Israel with his West Bank fundamentalists, just as both of you in the same book miraculously manage to be revived from death, I too was ripe for another chance. If while writing I couldn't see exactly what I was up to, I do now: this manuscript embodies *my* counterlife, the antidote and answer to all those fictions that culminated in the fiction of you. If in one way *The Counterlife* can be read as fiction about structure, then this is the bare bones, the structure of a life without the fiction.

As a matter of fact, the two longish works of fiction about you, written over a decade, were probably what made me sick of fictionalizing myself further, worn out with coaxing into existence a being whose experience was comparable to my own and yet registered a more powerful valence, a life more highly charged and energized, more entertaining than my own . . . which happens to have been largely spent, quite unentertainingly, alone in a room with a typewriter. I was depleted by the rules I'd set myself—by having to imagine things not quite as they had happened to me or things that never happened to me or things that couldn't possibly have happened to me happening to an agent, a projection of mine, to a kind of me. If this manuscript conveys anything, it's my exhaustion with masks, disguises, distortions, and lies.

Of course, even without the crack-up and the need for self-investigation it generated, I might have found myself, at this moment, unable to wield the whip over the facts sufficiently to make real life amazing. Undermining experience, embellishing experience, rearranging and enlarging experience into a species of mythology—after thirty years at that, it could have seemed like I'd had enough even under the best of circumstances. To demythologize myself and play it straight, to pair the facts as lived with the facts as presented might well have seemed the next thing to do—if not the only thing I *could* do—so long as the capacity for self-transformation and, with it, the imagination were at the point of collapse. Insofar as the rest of me, which had collapsed as well, intuited that stripping the writing down to unvarnished specificity was a part of getting back what I'd lost, a means of recovery and a way to strength, there wasn't even a choice. I needed clarification, as much of it as I could get—demythologizing to induce depathologizing.

This isn't to say that I didn't have to resist the impulse to dramatize untruthfully the insufficiently dramatic, to complicate the essentially simple, to charge with implication what implied very little—the temptation to abandon the facts when those facts were not so compelling as others I might imagine if I could somehow steel myself to overcome fiction-fatigue. But on the whole it was easier than I thought it would be to escape from what I'd felt constrained to do nearly every day of the pre-crack-up existence. Perhaps that's because in its uncompelling, unferocious way, the nonfictional approach has brought me closer to how experience actually *felt* than has turning the flame up under my life and smelting stories out of all I've known. I'm not arguing that there's a kind of existence that exists in fiction that doesn't exist in life or vice versa but simply saying that a book that faithfully conforms to the facts, a distillation of the facts that leaves off with the imaginative fury, can unlock meanings that fictionalizing has obscured, distended, or even inverted and can drive home some sharp emotional nails.

I recognize that I'm using the word "facts" here, in this letter, in its idealized form and in a much more simpleminded way than it's meant in the title. Obviously the facts are never just coming at you but are incorporated by an imagination that is formed by your previous experience. Memories of the past are not memories of facts but memories of your imaginings of the facts. There is something naïve about a novelist like myself talking about presenting himself "undisguised" and depicting "a life without the fiction." I also invite oversimplification of a kind I don't at all like by announcing that searching out the facts may have been a kind of therapy for me. You search your past with certain questions on your mind—indeed, you search out your past to discover which events have led you to asking those specific questions. It isn't that you subordinate your ideas to the force of the facts in autobiography but that you construct a sequence of stories to bind up the facts with a persuasive *hypothesis* that unravels your history's meaning. I suppose that calling this book *The Facts* begs so many questions that I could manage to be both less ironic and more ironic by calling it *Begging the Question*.

A final observation about the predicament that engendered *The Facts*, and then you may read on undisturbed. Though I can't be entirely sure, I wonder if this book was written not only out of exhaustion with making fictional self-legends and not only as a spontaneous therapeutic response to my crack-up but also as a palliative for the loss of a mother who still, in my mind, seems to have died inexplicably—at seventy-seven in 1981 —as well as to hearten me as I come closer and closer and closer to an eighty-six-year-old father viewing the end of life as a thing as near to his face as the mirror he shaves in (except that this mirror is there day and night, directly in front of him all the time). Even though it might not be apparent to others, I think that subterraneanly my mother's death is very strong in all this, as is observing my provident father preparing for no future, a healthy but very old man dealing with the kind of feelings aroused by an incurable illness, because just like those who are incurably ill, the aged know everything about their dying except exactly when.

I wonder if a breakdown-induced eruption of parental longing in a fifty-five-year-old man isn't, in fact, the Rosetta stone to this manuscript. I wonder if there hasn't been some consolation, particularly while recovering my equilibrium, in remembering that when the events narrated here were happening we all were there, nobody having gone away or been on the brink of going away, never to be seen again for hundreds of thousands of billions of years. I wonder if I haven't drawn considerable consolation from reassigning myself as myself to a point in life when the grief that may issue from the death of parents needn't be contended with, when it is unperceivable and unsuspected, and one's own departure is unconceivable because they are there like a blockade.

I think that's everything that might lie behind this book. The question now is, why should anybody other than me be reading it, especially as I acknowledge that they've gotten a good bit of it elsewhere, under other auspices? Especially as I consider myself, partly through this effort, united again with my purposes and reengaged with life. Especially as this feels like the first thing that I have ever written *unconsciously* and sounds to me more like the voice of a twenty-five-year-old than that of the author of my books about you. Especially as publication would leave me feeling exposed in a way I don't particularly wish to be exposed.

There's also the problem of exposing others. While writing, when I began to feel increasingly squeamish about confessing intimate affairs of mine to *everybody*, I went back and changed the real names of some of those with whom I'd been involved, as well as a few identifying details. This was not because I believed that the rerendering would furnish complete anonymity (it couldn't make those people anonymous to their friends and mine) but because it might afford at least a little protection from their being pawed over by perfect strangers.

Beyond these considerations that make publication problematic for me stands *the* question: Is the book any good? Because *The Facts* has meant more to me than may be obvious and because I've never worked before without my imagination having been fired by someone like you or Portnoy or Tarnopol or Kepesh, I'm in no real position to tell.

Be candid.

Sincerely,
Roth

Prologue

ONE DAY in late October 1944, I was astonished to find my father, whose workday ordinarily began at seven and many nights didn't end until ten, sitting alone at the kitchen table in the middle of the afternoon. He was going into the hospital unexpectedly to have his appendix removed. Though he had already packed a bag to take with him, he had waited for my brother, Sandy, and me to get home from school to tell us not to be alarmed. "Nothing to it," he assured us, though we all knew that two of his brothers had died back in the 1920s from complications following difficult appendectomies. My mother, the president that year of our school's parent-teacher association, happened, quite unusually, to be away overnight in Atlantic City at a statewide PTA convention. My father had phoned her hotel, however, to tell her the news, and she had immediately begun preparations to return home. That would do it, I was sure: my mother's domestic ingenuity was on a par with Robinson Crusoe's, and as for nursing us all through our illnesses, we couldn't have received much better care from Florence Nightingale. As was usual in our household, everything was now under control.

By the time her train pulled into Newark that evening, the surgeon had opened him up, seen the mess, and despaired for my father's chances. At the age of forty-three, he was put on the critical list and given less than a fifty-fifty chance to survive.

Only the adults knew how bad things were. Sandy and I were allowed to go on believing that a father was indestructible—and ours turned out to be just that. Despite a raw emotional nature that makes him prey to intractable worry, his life has been distinguished by the power of resurgence. I've never intimately known anyone else—aside from my brother and me—to swing as swiftly through so wide a range of moods, anyone else to take things so hard, to be so openly racked by a serious setback, and yet, after the blow has reverberated down to the quick, to clamber back so aggressively, to recover lost ground and get going again.

He was saved by the new sulfa powder, developed during

the early years of the war to treat battlefront wounds. Surviving an awful ordeal nonetheless, his weakness from the near-fatal peritonitis exacerbated by a ten-day siege of hiccups during which he was unable to sleep or to keep down food. After he'd lost nearly thirty pounds, his shrunken face disclosed itself to us as a replica of my elderly grandmother's, the face of the mother whom he and all his brothers adored (toward the father—laconic, authoritarian, remote, an immigrant who'd trained in Galicia to be a rabbi but worked in America in a hat factory—their feelings were more confused). Bertha Zahnstecker Roth was a simple old-country woman, good-hearted, given to neither melancholy nor complaint, yet her everyday facial expression made it plain that she nursed no illusions about life's being easy. My father's resemblance to his mother would not appear so eerily again until he himself reached his eighties, and then only when he was in the grip of a struggle that stripped an otherwise physically youthful old man of his seeming impregnability, leaving him bewildered not so much because of the eye problem or the difficulty with his gait that had made serious inroads on his self-sufficiency but because he felt all at once abandoned by that masterful accomplice and overturner of obstacles, his determination.

When he was driven home from Newark's Beth Israel Hospital after six weeks in bed there, he barely had the strength, even with our assistance, to make it up the short back staircase to our second-story apartment. It was December 1944 by then, a cold winter day, but through the windows the sunlight illuminated my parents' bedroom. Sandy and I came in to talk to him, both of us shy and grateful and, of course, stunned by how helpless he appeared seated weakly in a lone chair in the corner of the room. Seeing his sons together like that, my father could no longer control himself and began to sob. He was alive, the sun was shining, his wife was not widowed nor his boys fatherless—family life would now resume. It was not so complicated that an eleven-year-old couldn't understand his father's tears. I just didn't see, as he so clearly could, why or how it should have turned out differently.

I knew only two boys in our neighborhood whose families were fatherless, and thought of them as no less blighted than the blind girl who attended our school for a while and had to be read to and shepherded everywhere. The fatherless boys seemed almost equally marked and set apart; in the aftermath of their fathers' deaths, they too struck me as scary and a little taboo. Though one was a model of obedience and the other a troublemaker, everything either of them did or said seemed determined by his being a boy with a dead father and, however innocently I arrived at this notion, I was probably right.

I knew no child whose family was divided by divorce. Outside of the movie magazines and the tabloid headlines, it didn't exist, certainly not among Jews like us. Jews didn't get divorced —not because divorce was forbidden by Jewish law but because that was the way they were. If Jewish fathers didn't come home drunk and beat their wives—and in our neighborhood, which was Jewry to me, I'd never heard of any who did—that too was because of the way they were. In our lore, the Jewish family was an inviolate haven against every form of menace, from personal isolation to gentile hostility. Regardless of internal friction and strife, it was assumed to be an indissoluble consolidation. *Hear, O Israel, the family is God, the family is One.*

Family indivisibility, the first commandment.

In the late 1940s, when my father's younger brother, Bernie, proclaimed his intention of divorcing the wife of nearly twenty years who was the mother of his two daughters, my mother and father were as stunned as if they'd heard that he'd killed somebody. Had Bernie committed murder and gone to jail for life, they would probably have rallied behind him despite the abominable, inexplicable deed. But when he made up his mind not merely to divorce but to do so to marry a younger woman, their support went instantly to the "victims," the sister-in-law and the nieces. For his transgression, a breach of faith with his wife, his children, his entire clan—a dereliction of his duty as a Jew *and* as a Roth—Bernie encountered virtually universal condemnation.

That family rupture only began to mend when time revealed that no one had been destroyed by the divorce; in fact, anguished as they were by the breakup of their household, Bernie's ex-wife and his two girls were never remotely as indignant as the rest of the relatives. The healing owed a lot to Bernie himself, a more diplomatic man than most of his judges, but also to the fact that for my father the demands of family solidarity and the bond of family history exceeded even *his* admonishing instincts. It was to be another forty-odd years, however, before the two brothers threw their arms around each other and hungrily embraced in an unmistakable act of unqualified reconciliation. This occurred a few weeks before Bernie's death, in his late seventies, when his heart was failing rapidly and nobody, beginning with himself, expected him to last much longer.

I had driven my father over to see Bernie and his wife, Ruth, in their condominium in a retirement village in northwestern Connecticut, twenty miles from my own home. It was Bernie's turn now to wear the little face of his unillusioned, stoical old mother; when he came to the door to let us in, there in his features was that stark resemblance that seemed to emerge in all the Roth brothers when they were up against it.

Ordinarily the two men would have met with a handshake, but when my father stepped into the hallway, so much was clear both about the time that was left to Bernie and about all those decades, seemingly stretching back to the beginning of time, during which they had been alive as their parents' offspring, that the handshake was swallowed up in a forceful hug that lasted minutes and left them in tears. They seemed to be saying goodbye to everyone already gone as well as to each other, the last two surviving children of the dour hat-blocker Sender and the imperturbable *balabusta* Bertha. Safely in his brother's arms, Bernie seemed also to be saying goodbye to himself. There was nothing to guard against or defend against or resent anymore, nothing even to remember. In these brothers, men so deeply swayed, despite their dissimilarity, by identical strains of family emotion, everything remembered had been distilled into pure, barely bearable feeling.

In the car afterward my father said, "We haven't held each other like that since we were small boys. My brother's dying, Philip. I used to push him around in his carriage. There were nine of us, with my mother and father. I'll be the last one left."

While we drove back to my house (where he was staying in the upstairs back bedroom, a room in which he says he never fails to sleep like a baby) he recounted the struggles of each of his five brothers—with bankruptcies, illnesses, and in-laws, with marital dissension and bad loans, and with children, with their Gonerils, their Regans, and their Cordelias. He recalled for me the martyrdom of his only sister, what she and all the family had gone through when her husband the bookkeeper who liked the horses had served a little time for embezzlement.

It wasn't exactly the first time I was hearing these stories. Narrative is the form that his knowledge takes, and his repertoire has never been large: family, family, family, Newark, Newark, Newark, Jew, Jew, Jew. Somewhat like mine.

I naïvely believed as a child that I would always have a father present, and the truth seems to be that I always will. However awkward the union may sometimes have been, vulnerable to differences of opinion, to false expectations, to radically divergent experiences of America, strained by the colliding of two impatient, equally willful temperaments and marred by masculine clumsiness, the link to him has been omnipresent. What's more, now, when he no longer commands my attention by his bulging biceps and his moral strictures, now, when he is no longer the biggest man I have to contend with—and when I am not all that far from being an old man myself—I am able to laugh at his jokes and hold his hand and concern myself with his well-being, I'm able to love him the way I wanted to when I was sixteen, seventeen, and eighteen but when, what with dealing with him and feeling at odds with him, it was simply an impossibility. *The* impossibility, for all that I always respected him for his particular burden and his struggle within a system that he didn't choose. The mythological role of a Jewish boy growing up in a family like mine—to become the hero one's father failed to be—I may even have achieved by now, but not at all in the way that was preordained. After nearly forty years of living far from home, I'm equipped at last to be the most loving of sons—just, however, when he has another agenda. He is trying to die. He doesn't say that, nor, probably, does he think of it in those words, but that's his job now and, fight as he will to survive, he understands, as he always has, what the real work is.

Trying to die isn't like trying to commit suicide—it may actually be harder, because what you are trying to do is what you least want to have happen; you dread it but there it is and it must be done, and by no one but you. Twice in the last few years he has taken a shot at it, on two different occasions suddenly became so ill that I, who was then living abroad half the year, flew back to America to find him with barely enough strength to walk from the sofa to the TV set without clutching at every chair in between. And though each time the doctor, after a painstaking examination, was unable to find anything wrong with him, he nonetheless went to bed every night expecting not to awaken in the morning and, when he did awaken in the morning, he was fifteen minutes just getting himself into a sitting position on the edge of the bed and another hour shaving and dressing. Then, for God knows how long, he slouched unmoving over a bowl of cereal for which he had absolutely no appetite.

I was as certain as he was that this was it, yet neither time could he pull it off and, over a period of weeks, he recovered his strength and became himself again, loathing Reagan, defending Israel, phoning relatives, attending funerals, writing to newspapers, castigating William Buckley, watching MacNeil–Lehrer, exhorting his grown grandchildren, remembering in detail our own dead, and relentlessly, exactingly—and without having been asked—monitoring the caloric intake of the nice woman he lives with. It would seem that to prevail here, to try dying and to *do* it, he will have to work even harder than he did in the insurance business, where he achieved a remarkable success for a man with his social and educational handicaps. Of course, here too he'll eventually succeed—though clearly, despite his record of assiduous application to every job he has ever been assigned, things won't be easy. But then they never have been.

Needless to say, the link to my father was never so voluptuously tangible as the colossal bond to my mother's flesh, whose metamorphosed incarnation was a sleek black sealskin coat into which I, the younger, the privileged, the pampered papoose, blissfully wormed myself whenever my father chauffeured us home to New Jersey on a winter Sunday from our semiannual excursion to Radio City Music Hall and Manhattan's Chinatown: the unnameable animal-me bearing her dead father's name, the protoplasm-me, boy-baby, and body-burrower-in-training, joined by every nerve ending to her smile and her sealskin coat, while his resolute dutifulness, his relentless industriousness, his unreasoning obstinacy and harsh resentments, his illusions, his innocence, his allegiances, his fears were to constitute the original mold for the American, Jew, citizen, man, even for the writer, I would become. To be at all is to be her Philip, but in the embroilment with the buffeting world, my history still takes its spin from beginning as his Roth.

Safe at Home

THE greatest menace while I was growing up came from abroad, from the Germans and the Japanese, our enemies because we were American. I still remember my terror as a nine-year-old when, running in from playing on the street after school, I saw the banner headline CORREGIDOR FALLS on the evening paper in our doorway and understood that the United States actually could lose the war it had entered only months before. At home the biggest threat came from the Americans who opposed or resisted us—or condescended to us or rigorously excluded us—because we were Jews. Though I knew that we were tolerated and accepted as well—in publicized individual cases, even specially esteemed—and though I never doubted that this country was mine (and New Jersey and Newark as well), I was not unaware of the power to intimidate that emanated from the highest and lowest reaches of gentile America.

At the top were the gentile executives who ran my father's company, the Metropolitan Life, from the home office at Number One Madison Avenue (the first Manhattan street address I ever knew). When I was a small boy, my father, then in his early thirties, was still a new Metropolitan agent, working a six-day week, including most evenings, and grateful for the steady, if modest, living this job provided, even during the Depression; a family shoe store he'd opened after marrying my mother had gone bankrupt some years before, and in between he'd had to take a variety of low-paying, unpromising jobs. He proudly explained to his sons that the Metropolitan was "the largest financial institution in the world" and that as an agent he provided Metropolitan Life policyholders with "an umbrella for a rainy day." The company put out dozens of pamphlets to educate its policyholders about health and disease; I collected a new batch off the racks in the waiting room on Saturday mornings when he took me along with him to the narrow downtown street where the Essex district office of Newark occupied nearly a whole floor of a commercial office building. I read up on "Tuberculosis," "Pregnancy," and "Diabetes," while he labored over his ledger entries and his paperwork. Sometimes at his desk, impressing myself by sitting in his swivel chair, I practiced my penmanship on Metropolitan stationery; in one corner of the paper was my father's name and in the other a picture of the home-office tower, topped with the beacon that he described to me, in the Metropolitan's own phrase, as the light that never failed.

In our apartment a framed replica of the Declaration of Independence hung above the telephone table on the hallway wall—it had been awarded by the Metropolitan to the men of my father's district for a successful year in the field, and seeing it there daily during my first school years forged an association between the venerated champions of equality who signed that cherished document and our benefactors, the corporate fathers at Number One Madison Avenue, where the reigning president was, fortuitously, a Mr. Lincoln. If that wasn't enough, the home-office executive whom my father would trek from New Jersey to see when his star began to rise slightly in the company was the superintendent of agencies, a Mr. Wright, whose good opinion my father valued inordinately all his life and whose height and imposing good looks he admired nearly as much as he did the man's easygoing diplomacy. As my father's son I felt no less respectful toward these awesomely named gentiles than he did, but I, like him, knew that they had to be the very officials who openly and guiltlessly conspired to prevent more than a few token Jews from assuming positions of anything approaching importance within the largest financial institution in the world.

One reason my father so admired the Jewish manager of his own district, Sam Peterfreund—aside, of course, from the devotion that Peterfreund inspired by recognizing my father's drive early on and making him an assistant manager—was that Peterfreund had climbed to the leadership of such a large, productive office despite the company's deep-rooted reluctance to allow a Jew to rise too high. When Mr. Peterfreund was to make one of his rare visits for dinner, the green felt protective pads came out of the hall closet and were laid by my brother and me on the dining room table, it was spread with a fresh linen cloth and linen napkins, water goblets appeared, and we ate off "the good dishes" in the dining room, where there

hung a large oil painting of a floral arrangement, copied skill-
fully from the Louvre by my mother's brother, Mickey; on the
sideboard were framed photographic portraits of the two dead
men for whom I'd been named, my mother's father, Philip,
and my father's younger brother, Milton. We ate in the dining
room only on religious holidays, on special family occasions,
and when Mr. Peterfreund came—and we all called him Mr.
Peterfreund, even when he wasn't there; my father also addressed him directly as "Boss." "Want a drink, Boss?" Before
dinner we sat unnaturally, like guests in our own living room,
while Mr. Peterfreund sipped his schnapps and I was encouraged to listen to his wisdom. The esteem he inspired was a
tribute to a gentile-sanctioned Jew managing a big Metropolitan office as much as to an immediate supervisor whose good-
will determined my father's occupational well-being and our
family fate. A large, bald-headed man with a gold chain across
his vest and a slightly mysterious German accent, whose family
lived (in high style, I imagined) in New York (*and* on Long
Island) while (no less glamorously to me) he slept during the
week in a Newark hotel, the Boss was our family's Bernard
Baruch.

Opposition more frightening than corporate discrimination
came from the lowest reaches of the gentile world, from the
gangs of *lumpen* kids who, one summer, swarmed out of Neptune, a ramshackle little town on the Jersey shore, and stam-
peded along the boardwalk into Bradley Beach, hollering
"Kikes! Dirty Jews!" and beating up whoever hadn't run for
cover. Bradley Beach, a couple of miles south of Asbury Park
on the mid-Jersey coast, was the very modest little vacation resort where we and hundreds of other lower-middle-class Jews
from humid, mosquito-ridden north Jersey cities rented rooms
or shared small bungalows for several weeks during the summer. It was paradise for me, even though we lived three in a
room, and four when my father drove down the old Cheese-
quake highway to see us on weekends or to stay for his two-
week vacation. In all of my intensely secure and protected
childhood, I don't believe I ever felt more exuberantly snug
than I did in those mildly anarchic rooming houses, where—
inevitably with more strain than valor—some ten or twelve
women tried to share the shelves of a single large icebox, and

to cook side by side, in a crowded communal kitchen, for children, visiting husbands, and elderly parents. Meals were eaten in the unruly, kibbutzlike atmosphere—so unlike the ambiance in my own orderly home—of the underventilated dining room.

The hot, unhomelike, homey hubbub of the Bradley Beach rooming house was somberly contrasted, in the early forties, by reminders all along the shore that the country was fighting in an enormous war: bleak, barbwired Coast Guard bunkers dotted the beaches, and scores of lonely, very young sailors played the amusement machines in the arcades at Asbury Park; the lights were blacked out along the boardwalk at night and the blackout shades on the rooming-house windows made it stifling indoors after dinner; there was even tarry refuse, alleged to be from torpedoed ships, that washed up and littered the beach—I sometimes had fears of wading gleefully with my friends into the surf and bumping against the body of someone killed at sea. Also—and most peculiarly, since we were all supposed to be pulling together to beat the Axis Powers—there were these "race riots," as we children called the hostile nighttime invasions by the boys from Neptune: violence directed against the Jews by youngsters who, as everyone said, could only have learned their hatred from what they heard at home.

Though the riots occurred just twice, for much of one July and August it was deemed unwise for a Jewish child to venture out after supper alone, or even with friends, though nighttime freedom in shorts and sandals was one of Bradley's greatest pleasures for a ten-year-old on vacation from homework and the school year's bedtime hours. The morning after the first riot, a story spread among the kids collecting Popsicle sticks and playing ring-a-levio on the Lorraine Avenue beach; it was about somebody (whom nobody seemed to know personally) who had been caught before he could get away: the anti-Semites had held him down and pulled his face back and forth across the splintery surface of the boardwalk's weathered planks. This particular horrific detail, whether apocryphal or not—and it needn't necessarily have been—impressed upon me how barbaric was this irrational hatred of families who, as anyone could see, were simply finding in Bradley Beach a little inexpensive relief from the city heat, people just trying to have a quiet good time, bothering no one, except occasionally each other, as when one of the women purportedly expropriated from the icebox, for her family's corn on the cob, somebody else's quarter of a pound of salt butter. If that was as much harm as any of us could do, why make a bloody pulp of a Jewish child's face?

The home-office gentiles in executive positions at Number One Madison Avenue were hardly comparable to the kids swarming into Bradley screaming "Kike!"; and yet when I thought about it, I saw that they were no more reasonable or fair: they too were against Jews for no good reason. Small wonder that at twelve, when I was advised to begin to think seriously about what I would do when I grew up, I decided to oppose the injustices wreaked by the violent and the privileged by becoming a lawyer for the underdog.

When I entered high school, the menace shifted to School Stadium, then the only large football grounds in Newark, situated on alien Bloomfield Avenue, a forty-minute bus ride from Weequahic High. On Saturdays in the fall, four of the city's seven high schools would meet in a doubleheader, as many as two thousand kids pouring in for the first game, which began around noon, and then emptying en masse into the surrounding streets when the second game had ended in the falling shadows. It was inevitable after a hard-fought game that intense school rivalries would culminate in a brawl somewhere in the stands and that, in an industrial city of strongly divergent ethnic backgrounds and subtle, though pronounced, class gradations, fights would break out among volatile teenagers from four very different neighborhoods. Yet the violence provoked by the presence of a Weequahic crowd—particularly after a rare Weequahic victory—was like any other.

I remember being in the stands with my friends in my sophomore year, rooting uninhibitedly for the "Indians," as our Weequahic teams were known in the Newark sports pages; after never having beaten Barringer High in the fourteen years of Weequahic's existence, our team was leading them 6–0 in the waning minutes of the Columbus Day game. The Barringer backfield was Berry, Peloso, Short, and Thompson; in the Weequahic backfield were Weissman, Weiss, Gold, and fullback Fred Rosenberg, who'd led a sustained march down the field at the end of the first half and then, on a two-yard plunge, had scored what Fred, now a PR consultant in New Jersey, recently wrote to tell me was "one of the only touchdowns notched by the Indians that entire season, on a run that probably was one of the longer runs from scrimmage in 1947."

As the miraculous game was nearing its end—as Barringer, tied with Central for first place in the City League, was about to be upset by the weakest high school team in Newark—I suddenly noticed that the rival fans on the other side of the stadium bowl had begun to stream down the aisles, making their way around the far ends of the stadium toward us. Instead of waiting for the referee's final whistle, I bolted for an exit and, along with nearly everyone else who understood what was happening, ran down the stadium ramp in the direction of the buses waiting to take us back to our neighborhood. Though there were a number of policemen around, it was easy to see that once the rampage was under way, unless you were clinging to a cop with both arms and both legs, his protection wouldn't be much help; should you be caught on your own by a gang from one of the other three schools waiting to get their hands on a Weequahic Jew—our school was almost entirely Jewish—it was unlikely that you'd emerge from the stadium without serious injury.

The nearest bus was already almost full when I made it on board; as soon as the last few kids shoved their way in, the uniformed Public Service driver, fearful for his own safety as a transporter of Weequahic kids, drew the front door shut. By then there were easily ten or fifteen of the enemy, aged twelve to twenty, surrounding the bus and hammering their fists against its sides. Fred Rosenberg contends that "every ablebodied man from north Newark, his brother, and their offspring got into the act." When one of them, having worked his hands through a crevice under the window beside my seat, started forcing the window up with his fingers, I grabbed it from the top and brought it down as hard as I could. He howled and somebody took a swing at the window with a baseball bat, breaking the frame but miraculously not the glass. Before the others could join together to tear back the door, board the bus, and go straight for me—who would have been hard put to explain that the reprisal had been uncharacteristic and intended only in self-defense—the driver had pulled out from the curb and we were safely away from the postgame pogrom, which, for our adversaries, constituted perhaps the most enjoyable part of the day's entertainment.

That evening I fled again, not only because I was a fourteen-year-old weighing only a little over a hundred pounds but because I was never to be one of the few who stayed behind for a fight but always among the many whose impulse is to run to avoid it. A boy in our neighborhood might be expected to protect himself in a schoolyard confrontation with another boy his age and size, but no stigma attached to taking flight from a violent melee—by and large it was considered both shameful and stupid for a bright Jewish child to get caught up in something so dangerous to his physical safety, and so repugnant to Jewish instincts. The collective memory of Polish and Russian pogroms had fostered in most of our families the idea that our worth as human beings, even perhaps our distinction as a people, was embodied in the *incapacity* to perpetrate the sort of bloodletting visited upon our ancestors.

For a while during my adolescence I studiously followed prizefighting, could recite the names and weights of all the champions and contenders, and even subscribed briefly to *Ring*, Nat Fleischer's colorful boxing magazine. As kids my brother and I had been taken by our father to the local boxing arena, where invariably we all had a good time. From my father and his friends I heard about the prowess of Benny Leonard, Barney Ross, Max Baer, and the clownishly nicknamed Slapsie Maxie Rosenbloom. And yet Jewish boxers and boxing aficionados remained, like boxing itself, "sport" in the bizarre sense, a strange deviation from the norm and interesting largely for that reason: in the world whose values first formed me, unrestrained physical aggression was considered contemptible everywhere else. I could no more smash a nose with a fist than fire a pistol into someone's heart. And what imposed this restraint, if not on Slapsie Maxie Rosenbloom, then on me, was my being Jewish. In my scheme of things, Slapsie Maxie was a more miraculous Jewish phenomenon by far than Dr. Albert Einstein.

The evening following our escape from School Stadium the ritual victory bonfire was held on the dirt playing field on Chancellor Avenue, across from Syd's, a popular Weequahic hangout where my brother and I each did part-time stints selling hot dogs and french fries. I'd virtually evolved as a boy on that playing field; it was two blocks from my house and bordered on the grade school—"Chancellor Avenue"—that I'd attended for eight years, which itself stood next to Weequahic High. It was the field where I'd played pickup football and baseball, where my brother had competed in school track meets, where I'd shagged flies for hours with anybody who would fungo the ball out to me, where my friends and I hung around on Sunday mornings, watching with amusement as the local fathers—the plumbers, the electricians, the produce merchants—kibitzed their way through their weekly softball game. If ever I had been called on to express my love for my neighborhood in a single reverential act, I couldn't have done better than to get down on my hands and knees and kiss the ground behind home plate.

Yet upon this, the sacred heart of my inviolate homeland, our stadium attackers launched a nighttime raid, the conclusion to the violence begun that afternoon, their mopping-up exercise. A few hours after the big fire had been lit, as we happily sauntered around the dark field, joking among ourselves and looking for girls to impress, while in the distance the cartwheeling cheerleaders led the chant of the crowd encircling the fire—"And when you're up against Weequahic/you're upside down!"—the cars pulled up swiftly on Chancellor Avenue, and the same guys who'd been pounding on the sides of my bus (or so I quickly assumed) were racing onto the field, some of them waving baseball bats. The field was set into the slope of the Chancellor Avenue hill; I ran through the dark to the nearest wall, jumped some six feet down into Hobson Street, and then just kept going, through alleyways, between garages, and over backyard fences, until I'd made it safely home in less than five minutes. One of my Leslie Street friends, the football team water boy, who'd been standing in the full glare of the fire wearing his Weequahic varsity jacket, was not so quick or lucky; his assailants—identified in the neighborhood the next day as "Italians"—picked him up and threw him bodily toward the flames. He landed just at the fire's edge and, though he wasn't burned, spent days in the hospital recovering from internal injuries.

But this was a unique calamity. Our lower-middle-class neighborhood of houses and shops—a few square miles of tree-lined streets at the corner of the city bordering on residential Hillside and semi-industrial Irvington—was as safe and peaceful a haven for me as his rural community would have been for an Indiana farm boy. Ordinarily nobody more disquieting ever appeared there than the bearded old Jew who sometimes tapped on our door around dinnertime; to me an unnerving specter from the harsh and distant European past, he stood silently in the dim hallway while I went to get a quarter to drop into his collection can for the Jewish National Fund (a name that never sank all the way in: the only nation for Jews, as I saw it, was the democracy to which I was so loyally—and lyrically —bound, regardless of the unjust bias of the so-called best and the violent hatred of some of the worst). Shapiro, the immigrant tailor who also did dry cleaning, had two thumbs on one hand, and that made bringing our clothes to him a little eerie for me when I was still small. And there was LeRoy "the moron," a somewhat gruesome but innocuous neighborhood dimwit who gave me the creeps when he sat down on the front stoop to listen to a bunch of us talking after school. On our street he was rarely teased but just sat looking at us stupidly with his hollow eyes and rhythmically tapping one foot—and that was about as frightening as things ever got.

A typical memory is of five or six of us energetically traversing the whole length of the neighborhood Friday nights on our way back from a double feature at the Roosevelt Theater. We would stop off at the Watson Bagel Company on Clinton Place to buy, for a few pennies each, a load of the first warm bagels out of the oven—and this was four decades before the bagel became a breakfast staple at Burger King. Devouring three and four apiece, we'd circuitously walk one another home, howling with laughter at our jokes and imitating our favorite baritones. When the weather was good we'd sometimes wind up back of Chancellor Avenue School, on the wooden bleachers along the sidelines of the asphalt playground adjacent to the big dirt playing field. Stretched on our backs in the open night air, we were as carefree as any kids anywhere in postwar America, and certainly we felt ourselves no less American. Discussions about Jewishness and being Jewish, which I was to hear so often among intellectual Jews once I was an adult in Chicago and New York, were altogether unknown; we talked about being misunderstood by our families, about movies and radio programs and sex and sports, we even argued about politics, though this was rare since our fathers were all ardent New Dealers and there was no disagreement among us about the sanctity of F.D.R. and the Democratic Party. About being Jewish there was nothing more to say than there was about having two arms and two legs. It would have seemed to us strange *not* to be Jewish—stranger still, to hear someone announce that he wished he weren't a Jew or that he intended not to be in the future.

Yet, simultaneously, this intense adolescent camaraderie was the primary means by which we were deepening our *Americanness*. Our parents were, with few exceptions, the first-generation offspring of poor turn-of-the-century immigrants from Galicia and Polish Russia, raised in predominantly Yiddish-speaking Newark households where religious Orthodoxy was only just beginning to be seriously eroded by American life. However unaccented and American-sounding their speech, however secularized their own beliefs, and adept and convincing their American style of lower-middle-class existence, they were influenced still by their childhood training and by strong parental ties to what often seemed to us antiquated, socially useless old-country mores and perceptions.

My larger boyhood society cohered around the most inherently American phenomenon at hand—the game of baseball, whose mystique was encapsulated in three relatively inexpensive fetishes that you could have always at your side in your room, not only while you did your homework but in bed with you while you slept if you were a worshiper as primitive as I was at ten and eleven: they were a ball, a bat, and a glove. The solace that my Orthodox grandfather doubtless took in the familiar leathery odor of the flesh-worn straps of the old phylacteries in which he wrapped himself each morning, I derived from the smell of my mitt, which I ritualistically donned every day to work a little on my pocket. I was an average playground player, and the mitt's enchantment had to do less with foolish dreams of becoming a major leaguer, or even a high school star, than with the bestowal of membership in a great secular nationalistic church from which nobody had ever seemed to suggest that Jews should be excluded. (The blacks were another story, until 1947.) The softball and hardball teams we organized and reorganized obsessively throughout our grade-school years—teams we called by unarguably native names like the Seabees and the Mohawks and described as "social and athletic clubs"—aside from the opportunity they afforded to compete against one another in a game we loved, also operated as secret societies that separated us from the faint, residual foreignness still clinging to some of our parents' attitudes and that validated our own spotless credentials as American kids. Paradoxically, our remotely recent old-country Jewish origins may well have been a source of our especially intense devotion to a sport that, unlike boxing or even football, had nothing to do with the menace of brute force unleashed against flesh and bones.

The Weequahic neighborhood for over two decades now has been part of the vast black Newark slum. Visiting my father in Elizabeth, I'll occasionally take a roundabout route off the parkway into my old Newark and, to give myself an emotional workout, drive through the streets still entirely familiar to me despite the boarded-up shops and badly decaying houses, and the knowledge that my white face is not at all welcome. Recently, snaking back and forth in my car along the one-way streets of the Weequahic section, I began to imagine house plaques commemorating the achievements of the boys who'd once lived there, markers of the kind you see in London and Paris on the residences of the historically renowned. What I inscribed on those plaques, along with my friends' names and their years of birth and of local residence, wasn't the professional status they had attained in later life but the position each had played on those neighborhood teams of ours in the 1940s. I thought that if you knew that in this four-family Hobson Street house there once lived the third baseman Seymour Feldman and that down a few doors had lived Ronnie Rubin, who in his boyhood had been our catcher, you'd understand how and where the Feldman and the Rubin families had been naturalized irrevocably by their young sons.

In 1982, while I was visiting my widowered father in Miami Beach during his first season there on his own, I got him one night to walk over with me to Meyer Lansky's old base of operations, the Hotel Singapore on Collins Avenue; earlier in the day he'd told me that wintering at the Singapore were some of the last of his generation from our neighborhood—the ones, he mordantly added, "still aboveground." Among the faces I recognized in the lobby, where the elderly residents met to socialize each evening after dinner, was the mother of one of the boys who also used to play ball incessantly "up the field" and who hung around on the playground bleachers after dark back when we were Seabees together. As we sat talking at the edge of a gin-rummy game, she suddenly took hold of my hand and, smiling at me with deeply emotional eyes—with that special heart-filled look that *all* our mothers had—she said, "Phil, the feeling there was among you boys—I've never seen anything like it again." I told her, altogether truthfully, that I haven't either.

Joe College

WORKING as an assistant manager in the Essex district office of Metropolitan Life, my father earned, during his best years, about $125 a week in salary and commissions. In the middle 1940s, as I made the transition from grade school to high school, a business risk he took wiped out the family savings. After long consultations with my mother, he had invested with some friends in a frozen-food distribution company, and for several years he continued by day as a Metropolitan insurance man while at night and on weekends, without drawing a salary, he went out on the refrigerated truck, trying to hustle frozen-food business in Jersey and eastern Pennsylvania. In addition to using up the family savings he'd had to borrow some $8,000 from relatives in order to pay for his share in the partnership. He was forty-five, and took the risk because it seemed unlikely that, being Jewish, he could get any further with the Metropolitan. His education, through eighth grade, also seemed to him an impediment to promotion.

He had hoped that by the time his two sons graduated from high school, the new enterprise would have taken off and he'd be able to afford to send us both to college. But the business went bust quickly, and when I was ready for college, he was still saddled with paying off his debt. Fortunately, in 1949 he was unexpectedly promoted by the Metropolitan to manage an office just outside Newark, in Union City. The district was doing virtually no business when he came in but offered a real financial opportunity if he could somehow inspire the hapless agency with his know-how and energy. As it happened, he was spared the expense of my brother's college education by the GI Bill. In 1946, with the war draft still on, Sandy had gone into the Navy, and when he came out, in 1948, he was able to attend art school in Brooklyn without help from the family. I graduated from high school in January of 1950 and worked as a stock clerk in a Newark department store until I enrolled, in September, as a prelaw student, at Newark Colleges of Rutgers, the unprestigious little downtown branch of the state university. I had wanted desperately to go away to college, if only to the Rutgers main campus, down in New Brunswick, but though I had graduated at sixteen well up in my class, I'd been unable to win a Rutgers scholarship. I wound up as a freshman in Newark, still living at home.

My dream of *away* remained fervent, however satisfied I actually found myself at Newark Rutgers, which was situated a little beyond the city's commercial district at the "historic" end of the downtown streets, about a twenty-minute bus ride from my corner. It felt invigoratingly grown-up to be downtown not as a kid going to the movies with his friends or a boy out to Sunday dinner with his family or a lowly stock clerk mindlessly pushing a rack around S. Klein's, but as the owner of spanking-new textbooks, with a businesslike briefcase (for his lunch) and a pipe in his pocket that he was learning to smoke. It appealed to my liberal democratic spirit to be taking college courses in a building that had once been a brewery and to be seated there alongside Italian and Irish kids from city high schools that had been foreign, unknowable, even unnervingly hostile to me when I was attending a neighborhood school whose student body was more than ninety percent Jewish. I considered it a kind of triumphant liberation to have been drawn into the city's rivalrous ethnic society, especially as our liberal-arts studies were working—in my idealistic vision—to elevate us above serious social differences, to free from cultural narrowness and intellectual impoverishment the offspring of Weequahic's Jewish businessmen as well as working-class boys from the Ironbound district. Casually making friends over paper-bag lunches with gentile classmates who had graduated from Barringer and South Side and Central and West Side— boys who previously had been nothing more to me than tough and generally superior adversaries in intercity sporting events —made me feel expansively "American." I hadn't any doubts that we Jews were already American or that the Weequahic section was anything other than a quintessentially American urban neighborhood, but as a child of the war and of the brotherhood mythology embodied in songs like Frank Sinatra's "The House I Live In" and Tony Martin's "Tenement Symphony," I was exhilarated to feel in contact with the country's much-proclaimed, self-defining heterogeneity.

At the same time, I knew that if I remained in our five-room

flat on Leslie Street, living and studying in the bedroom that I
had shared since earliest childhood with my brother, there
would be increasing friction between my father and me, simply
because I could no longer truthfully account to him, or to my
mother, either—though she would never dare ask—for my
weekend whereabouts or my Saturday-night hours. I was quite
tame, a good, responsible boy with good, responsible friends;
I couldn't have been more dutiful and well mannered, and
lacked anything resembling unconstrainable impulses; but I was
also strong-minded and independent, and if my father were to
challenge the ordering of my private life, now that I was a college student, I would feel suffocated by his strictures. I had
also outgrown the family dinner table and was as impatient as
any rapidly maturing adolescent with my parents' conversation, but the main reason that I wanted to get away from home
for my sophomore year was to protect a hardworking, self-
sacrificing father and a devoted but determined son from a
battle that they were equally ill equipped to fight.

My mother was really no problem. As soon as my brother
and I started giving genuine signs of burgeoning independence, she had relaxed the exacting, sometimes overly fastidious
strictures that had governed our early upbringing and began
to be mildly intimidated by our airs of maturity; in a way she
fell in love with us all over again, like a shy schoolgirl this time,
hoping for a date. It was a rather prototypic kind of movement, I think, for the mother to go from nurturing her sons to
being a little afraid of them and for the sons to move out of
their mother's province at thirteen or fourteen. Sandy—born
when she was twenty-three, a pretty, very innocent young
woman in a penniless marriage whose own girlhood had been
rigorously overseen by a stern, tyrannical father—seems as a
child to have felt more constrained by her vigilant mothering
than I ever did, though he, no less than I, found more than a
little sustenance in the inexhaustible maternal feeling that visi-
bly instigated and tenderized that conscientiousness. Still and
all, he may well have endured a more inflexible regimen, more
assiduously imposed, than what befell me, coming five years
later, after she'd had the education of raising him and when
my father's weekly Metropolitan paycheck had begun to mitigate their financial anxieties. To me, at eight, nine, and ten,

home had seemed just perfect, but that was no longer so at sixteen and I wanted to get away.

I didn't care where "away" was—one college would do as well as another. All I needed were professors and courses and a library. I'd study hard, get a "good education," and go on to become the idealistic lawyer I'd imagined becoming since I was twelve. Since none of my immediate relatives had ever graduated from a liberal-arts college, there was no one to point me in the direction of his alma mater. And because of the war and the postwar draft, the generation of college-educated younger men whose example I might have followed had disappeared from the neighborhood entirely; when they showed up again, they were veterans on the GI Bill who seemed vastly older and unapproachable. Our only real tutors were the ex-GIs—the rumba dancers and service-station attendants, the make-out artists, soda jerks, and short-order cooks—who had little to do but hang around and play pickup basketball with us. Under the bleachers of the playground they taught us how to shoot craps and to play five-card stud with change stolen from our mothers' purses and our fathers' trouser pockets; but as for college guidance, I knew I had better look elsewhere.

My brother had been a Saturday student at the Art Students League in New York during his high school days and, after his discharge from the Navy, spent three years at Pratt Institute. While I was finishing high school, he would come home from Pratt on weekends to set up his easel in the dining room and, over a thick layer of old newspapers, lay out his paints and his drawing materials on the dining-room table; sometimes he would leave behind copies of paperback books he'd been reading on the subway and the train home. That's how, at fifteen and sixteen, I came to read *Winesburg, Ohio* and *A Portrait of the Artist* and *Only the Dead Know Brooklyn*. He drew from nude models, he had his own apartment, as a sailor he'd sat in bars where there were whores, and now he did quick, expressive pen-and-ink sketches of Bowery bums. But great as my admiration was for these achievements, Sandy's mode wasn't one I could simply emulate: his studies were preparing him for a career as an artist, while my talent, as described in the family, was "the gift of the gab."

In grade school I'd been taken once by my Uncle Ed, a

cardboard-carton dealer, to see a football game at Princeton. I had not forgotten the campus—either the green quadrangles or the evocative word—yet it would never have occurred to me to apply there. I knew from my uncle that despite the presence of Einstein, to whose house we'd made a pilgrimage, Princeton didn't "take Jews." (That's why we'd rooted so hard for Rutgers.) As for Harvard and Yale, not only did they seem, like Princeton, to be bastions of the gentile upper crust, socially too exclusive and unsympathetic, but their admissions officers were revealed by the Anti-Defamation League of B'nai B'rith to employ "Jewish quotas," a practice that disgusted a patriotic young American (let alone a member of an ineluctably Jewish family) like me. A champion of the Four Freedoms, a foe of the DAR, a supporter of Henry Wallace, I detested the idea of privilege that these famously elitist colleges, with their discriminatory policies, seemed to symbolize. Though I don't think I could have expressed this then in so many words, I certainly didn't want to recapitulate, at Harvard or Yale, my father's struggle at the Metropolitan to succeed with an institution holding a long-standing belief in Protestant Anglo-Saxon superiority. What's more, if I couldn't win a scholarship to Rutgers, how could I expect assistance from the Ivy League?

There were other colleges, anyway, hundreds of them: Wake Forest, Bowling Green, Clemson, Allegheny, Baylor, Vanderbilt, Bowdoin, Colby, Tulane—I knew their names, if nothing more (not even precisely where all of them were), from listening to Stan Lomax and Bill Stern announce the football scores on the radio Saturday nights throughout the fall. I read the names of these places on the sports pages of the *Newark Evening News* and the *Newark Sunday Call* and saw them on the football-pool cards that you could buy at the candy store on our corner for as little as a quarter. The football pool was illegal—run, my father told me, by Longy Zwillman and the Newark mob—but I began to buy the cards when I was about eleven and, with a couple of other neighborhood kids, started selling them on the school playground for the candy-store owner when I was thirteen, establishing my sole affiliation ever with organized crime. Through the pool I probably became familiar with far more institutions of higher learning than was the college adviser at the high school, who had suggested to me, when

I admitted I might actually like to become a journalist rather than a lawyer, that I should apply to the University of Missouri. When I told my parents her advice, my mother looked flabbergasted. "Missouri," my mother repeated tragically. "They have a great journalism school," I told her. "You're not going to Missouri," my father informed me. "It's too far and we can't afford it."

It was during Christmas vacation from Newark Rutgers that I got to talking to my Leslie Street neighbor Marty Castlebaum, with whom I'd had a genial, if not particularly intimate, friendship ever since grade school. Marty, who is now a physician in New Jersey, was something of a loner—a skinny, very tall boy, seemingly not so obsessed with sex or so romantically adventurous as my best friends. He was a good, quiet student with an enthusiasm for baseball, very much the product of a respectable, secularized Jewish family. The Castlebaums' outward configuration—and household orderliness—resembled my own family's: a highly competent and well-mannered mother, a hardworking, forthright father (a lawyer, however, and so a big vocational notch up from mine), and an older brother whom Marty strikingly resembled. Though there was something cheery in his temperate character I'd always liked, I found him more housebound than the boys to whom I was closest. If I remember correctly, Marty practiced the piano with real devotion, which in my mind may have separated him a little too much from those of us who counterbalanced good grades and courteous conduct with shooting craps on the sly and (against the unlikely possibility of being called upon to produce one) storing sealed Trojans in our wallets. His family lived even closer to the corner candy store than mine did, but Marty was only rarely to be seen hanging out in the back booths or standing outside by the fire hydrant where I would sometimes amuse the corner regulars with takeoffs of the school principal and the local rabbi.

Marty attended a small college of about 1,900 students whose name meant as little to me as Wake Forest or Bowling Green—Bucknell University, in Lewisburg, Pennsylvania. It wasn't what he said about his studies that made me want to find out more but that he appeared to have absorbed there precisely the qualities that he'd been devoid of as an adolescent, the sort of

poise and savoir faire that encouraged a boy to run for stu-
dent-council president or to date the most popular girl in class.
In only a matter of weeks this kid, whom I had thought of as
being in the shadow of more intense, loquacious types like me,
had developed a confident, outgoing manner that smacked of
maturity. There was even a girlfriend, whom he spoke of without a trace of his old shyness. I was astonished: I was still on
Leslie Street, keeping my father at bay by heeding high school
rules of conduct, while Marty appeared to have entered adult
society.

I couldn't forget what he'd said about the girl: he would
pick her up at her dormitory in the morning and they'd walk
to class together across the campus. It wasn't the romantic idyll
that impressed me so much as the matter-of-factness. At this
college called Bucknell, in less than a semester, Marty Castlebaum had become an independent young man sounding an independent young man's prerogatives without shame or guilt
or secrecy. At Newark Rutgers, I might be becoming more of
a Newarker and an American but I couldn't fool myself, even
with the pipe and the Trojans, about feeling more like a man.

In March of 1951 my parents and I made the seven-hour drive to
Lewisburg, about sixty miles up from Harrisburg, in a farming
valley along the Susquehanna River; it was a town of about
five thousand people, situated at the heart of one of the most
conservative Republican counties in the state. I was to be interviewed by an assistant to the director of admissions, a courteous middle-aged woman whose name I've by now forgotten.
In her office Miss Blake, let's call her, told the three of us that
with my high school standing and my Newark Rutgers grades
I'd have no trouble being admitted with full credit for my freshman courses. She was less optimistic about my receiving financial aid as a transfer student but assured us that I'd be in a better
position to compete for a scholarship after having proved myself at Bucknell.

I was upset to hear that; part of the problem, I figured, had
to do with my father's promotion. Even though a big chunk of
his salary still went to paying off his business debt, his earnings
had increased measurably since he'd taken over as manager of
the Union City office, and there had been no choice but to give

the correct figure on my aid-application form. Yet, for reasons of pride and privacy, he forbade me to report the debt. To make matters worse, we didn't look like a family in need. If anything, my mother, in a demure navy-blue dress, was dressed more attractively—though with no less propriety—than the assistant to the director of admissions; for jewelry she wore the little gold pin she'd been awarded after serving two terms as president of the PTA. She was forty-seven then, a slender, attractive woman with graying dark hair and lively brown eyes whose appearance and comportment were thoroughly Americanized. In fact, she was never wholly at ease except among Jews and for that reason cherished our part of Newark. She kept a kosher kitchen, lit Sabbath candles, and happily fulfilled all the Passover dietary regulations, though less out of religious proclivity than because of deep ties to her childhood household and to her mother, whose ideas of what made for a properly run Jewish home she wished to satisfy and uphold; being a Jew among Jews was, simply, one of her deepest pleasures. In a predominantly gentile environment, however, she lost her social suppleness and something too of her confidence, and her instinctive respectability came to seem more of a shield with which to safeguard herself than the natural expression of her decency.

But this self-consciousness should not be exaggerated; I'm sure that to Miss Blake, during my Bucknell interview, my mother seemed nothing more or less than perfectly agreeable and ladylike.

My father, a fit and solid-looking man of fifty, with thinning hair and rimless spectacles, wore a dark business suit with a vest and looked like someone who himself sat behind a desk and interviewed applicants, as indeed he frequently had done while reorganizing the unproductive staff at the Union City office. He certainly was not uneasy being inside a university building for the first time. The turnabout in his fortunes (and ours) had renewed his prodigious energies; between that and his almost palpable pride in me and my scholastic success, he radiated an unpolished, good-natured confidence that stirred my own pride but that, I felt certain, was killing my chances for a Bucknell scholarship. Had he been an embarrassment (and of course beforehand I feared he might be), had he tried too hard,

setting out to sell Bucknell on what a good boy I was or telling
Miss Blake about the progress made in America by our vast
array of relatives, we could, in fact, have been in better shape for
seeming that much cruder. As it was, the picture we presented,
of a self-made, enterprising, happily cohesive and prospering
family, convinced me that I was doomed. I'd get into Bucknell,
all right, but for lack of funds I wouldn't be able to enroll.

Later that day Marty Castlebaum took us on a tour of the
university grounds and around the charming tree-lined streets
leading to the main shopping thoroughfare, where we had
rooms for the night in the Hotel Lewisburger. Not since I'd
been to Princeton with my Uncle Ed had I strolled around a
town where people actually lived in houses dating back to the
eighteenth century. On a tiny green near his fraternity house
there was a Civil War cannon that Marty daringly told my parents went off "when a virgin walks by."

It was the campus that most beguiled me: ivy-covered brick
buildings sparsely set amid large trees and long, rolling lawns.
On "the Hill," at the heart of the campus, the windows of the
men's dormitory looked beyond cornfields and pastures to the
Lycoming hills. There was a clock in the cupola of the men's
dorm that chimed on the hour, an elegant spire atop the new
library, a student hangout that Marty familiarly called Chet's
(though a sign identified it as The Bison), and a dormitory
called Larison Hall, where that girlfriend of his had her room.
Scattered about the campus and on streets down from the Hill
were a dozen or so manorial-looking buildings with facades inspired either by English stately homes or by colonnaded plan-
tation dwellings; here lived the fraternity men. In all, it was an
unoutlandish little college town of the kind I'd seen before
only in movies with Kay Kyser or June Allyson, not so much
subdued or genteel, and certainly not posh or gentrified, but
instead suited for the coziest, most commonplace dreams of
order. Lewisburg emanated an unpretentious civility that we
could trust, rather than an air of privilege by which we might
have been intimidated. To be sure, everything about the rural
landscape and the small-town setting (and Miss Blake) suggested an unmistakably gentile version of unpretentious civility, but by 1951 none of us thought it pretentious or unseemly

that the momentum of our family's Americanization should have carried us, in half a century, from my Yiddish-speaking grandparents' hard existence in Newark's poorest ghetto neighborhood to this pretty place whose harmonious nativeness was proclaimed in every view.

My parents turned out to have been as impressed as I was, though probably less by Bucknell's collegiate look than by our enthusiastic guide, a Jewish boy from our block who seemed to them, as he did to me, to be thriving wonderfully in this unfamiliar atmosphere. After dinner in the hotel restaurant, when Marty had left for his dormitory and we were in the elevator on our way up to bed, my father said to me, "You like it, don't you?" "Yes, but how can we afford it if they won't give me a scholarship for September?" "Forget the scholarship," he told me. "You want to go here, you're going."

I sat up late at the little desk in my room, a stack of hotel stationery at the ready for recording my "thoughts." I replayed over and over the conversation with my father in the hotel elevator, adding a line of my own that I would not have had the self-control to say to him face-to-face but that I was able to write freely and exuberantly on a sheet of the Lewisburger's paper. I felt a buoyant sense of having survived the worst while preserving unimpaired the long-standing preuniversity accord that would seem to have made us an indestructible family: "And now we won't have to have that terrible fight—we've been saved by Bucknell."

Over precisely the issue that had been simmering since I'd begun college—my weekend whereabouts after midnight—my father and I did, of course, have the terrible fight, when I was home from Lewisburg for my first midyear vacation. And it was worse than I had foreseen, however banal the immediate cause. Along with my mother, my brother—who fortunately happened to be in from Manhattan, where he was beginning to establish himself as a commercial artist—made every conceivable effort to act as a peacemaker and, with an air of urgent diplomacy, hurried back and forth between the two ends of the apartment, where the two raving belligerents were isolated. And though, after two days of histrionic shouting and bitter silence, my father and I—for the sake, finally, of my desolated mother—negotiated a fragile truce, I returned to Bucknell a shell-shocked son, freshly evacuated from the Oedipal battle-field, in dire need of rest and rehabilitation.

An attractive white Christian male entering Bucknell in the early fifties could expect to be officially courted by about half the thirteen fraternities. A promising athlete, the graduate of a prestigious prep school, the son of rich parents or of a distin-guished alumnus, might wind up with bids from as many as ten fraternities. A Jewish freshman—or Jewish transfer student, like me—could expect to be rushed by two fraternities at most, the exclusively Jewish fraternity, Sigma Alpha Mu, which, like the Christian fraternities, was the local chapter of a national body, and Phi Lambda Theta, a local fraternity without national affil-iations, which did not discriminate on the basis of race, religion, or color. A Jewish student who wished to take part in fraternity life but was acceptable to neither was in trouble. If he couldn't bear being an "independent"—taking meals in the university dining hall, living in the dormitories or in a room in town, making friends and dating outside the reigning social constel-lation—he'd have to pack up and go home. There were a few reported cases of Jewish students who had.

The Jewish fraternity had nothing much that was Jewish about it except the wholly sanctioned nickname by which the members were identified, at Bucknell and at every other campus where there was a chapter of Sigma Alpha Mu: as easily by them-selves as by others, the Jewish brothers were called Sammies. Had the fraternity been christened Iota Kappa Epsilon, people might not have tolerated Ikeys so readily, but no one seemed to have ever considered Sammies an even mildly stigmatizing label. Perhaps its purpose was prophylactic, preempting the at-tribution of diminutives less benign than this friendly-sounding acronym, which carried in its suffix only the tiniest sting. I, for one, never became accustomed to hearing it and never could say it, but probably I had been sensitized unduly by Budd Schulberg's novel, which I'd read in high school, about the pushiest of pushy Jews, Sammy Glick.

Certainly the Sammy kitchen, where three meals a day were prepared for the sixty-five or so members, smelled more like the galley of a merchant ship than like the sanctum sanctorum of a traditional Jewish household. "Cookie," the chef, was a local Navy veteran, a grim-faced, tattooed little man with a loose lantern jaw bearing a day or two's dark stubble; he wouldn't have been out of place frying onions on the grill of a back-road diner anywhere in America. Eggs with ham or bacon was the staple for breakfast, and pork chops and ham steaks showed up for lunch or dinner a couple of times a week—fare no different from what was served in the other fraternity houses and at the student dining hall. But you didn't join the Jewish fraternity to eat kosher food any more than to observe the Sabbath, to study Torah, or to discuss Jewish questions of the day; nor did you join because you hoped to rid yourself of embarrassing Jewish ways. Most likely you came from a family, like my own, for whom assimilation wasn't a potent issue any longer —if it had been, you wouldn't have come to Bucknell to begin with or have remained very long. This isn't to say that their Jewish parents would have preferred a university decree that these Sammy sons be allowed to join the otherwise Christian-dominated fraternities. No, in 1951 Sigma Alpha Mu suited everybody. The Jews were together because they were profoundly different but otherwise like everyone else.

As it happened, an opportunity to be the only Jew to pledge a gentile fraternity was offered to me when I arrived, as a sophomore, in September of 1951. I was rushed not only by the Jewish Sigma Alpha Mu and the nondenominational Phi Lambda Theta but also by Theta Chi. For reasons never entirely explained to me, Theta Chi had among its sixty-odd gentile members one Jew already, a senior with a gentile name and un-Jewish appearance who was also the fraternity president and who worked hard to entice me into the house, though my own name and appearance weren't likely to fool anyone. I took the invitation seriously and during the rushing period ate there as a guest several times. If I was joining a fraternity—and I figured that penetrating student society as a sophomore outside a fraternity might be nearly impossible—then didn't it make sense for me, with my democratic ideals and liberal principles, to capitalize on this inexplicable breach in a tightly segregated system?

Membership in Theta Chi certainly sounded more adventurous to a boy from the Weequahic section of Newark than slipping predictably in with the Jews. As for the nondenominational fraternity, whose unpretentious house on a back street was home to nearly a hundred young men, it seemed to me, after a quick appraisal, that the members I met were either innocently upright in their devotion to their principles or shy and socially a bit uncertain, boys who could indeed not have had anywhere else to go. I might have had this wrong, but I was struck by an air of charity and virtue about the place that was more purely "Christian" than anything I'd run into in a nominally Christian but essentially areligious fraternity like Theta Chi—something smacking a little of the goodness of the Salvation Army. Everything else aside, I believed I would need a slightly more profligate, less utopian atmosphere in which to realize even a tenth of the nefarious erotic prospectus that—as my father correctly surmised—I had been secretly preparing for years. The estimable goals of the Phi Lambda Thetas made the house too much like home.

At all costs my choice had to have nothing to do with my parents' preference, since establishing my independence was the point of coming away. In a series of letters home I laid out the problem in a scrupulously maniacal presentation worthy of Kafka. Instead of replying instinctively to what must have sounded to them like so much foolish naïveté, they were sufficiently intimidated by all my pages to seek out the advice of the Greens, Jewish friends in the clothing business whose daughter had manifested a similar urge a few years earlier. The line they took over the phone wasn't without wisdom: they said they wanted me to do what would make me "happiest." If I thought I would be happier with boys whose backgrounds were unlike my own, then I should of course choose Theta Chi; but if in the end it seemed as evident to me as to them and to the Greens that I would be happier with boys like Marty Castlebaum, whose backgrounds resembled mine, then I should choose SAM. *They* would be happy, my mother told me—it was she, whose touch was lighter, who'd been assigned to speak for their side—with whatever choice was sure to make *me* happy . . . and so on.

Had I joined Theta Chi as their new Jew, the chances are that challenging convention might well have proved invigorating for a while and that discovering the secrets of this un-

known community would, at the start, have yielded some genuine anthropological excitement. It probably wouldn't have
been long, however, before I found the exuberant side of my
personality, the street-corner taste for comic mockery and for
ludicrous, theatrical speculation, out of place in the Theta Chi
dining room with its staid, prosaic, small-town decorum that
had struck me as somewhat cornball. Probably my career as a
Theta Chi would have been even shorter than my career as
a Sammy was to be. I wasn't afraid of the temptation to become
an honorary WASP but was leery of a communal spirit that
might lead me to self-censorship, since the last thing I'd left
home for was to become encased in somebody else's idea of
what I should be. Eventually I came round to understanding
that joining Theta Chi could wind up being a far more conformist act than taking the seemingly conventional course of
being with boys from backgrounds more like my own, who,
just *because* their style was familiar, wouldn't have the power to
inhibit my expressive yearnings. Coming from backgrounds like
mine, a few of them might have similar yearnings themselves.

A few did—two, to be precise, both sophomore English
majors: Pete Tasch, from Baltimore, and Dick Minton, from
Mount Vernon, New York. Pete, who later became an English
professor, was a very highly tuned boy with a strong strain of
bookish refinement that set him apart not only from the regular fellows at the fraternity but even more blatantly from the
kids calling to him for their Cokes and fries at the Sweet Shop,
a local hangout where he clocked afternoon and evening hours
in order to pay his living expenses. Dick, who eventually
became a lawyer, was more unshakable, a straight shooter wholly
without airs and with a very good brain, who listened to
Beethoven quartets whenever he wasn't reading. His intense
cultural passions could have been shared by no more than a
dozen students on the campus and by hardly anyone at the fraternity house. In the winter of 1952, a little over a year after I'd
enrolled at Bucknell, we three resigned from Sigma Alpha Mu
and gave our devotion instead to *Et Cetera*, a literary magazine that we'd helped to found and then took over, under my
editorship in 1952–53 and the next year under Pete's, with Dick
as literary editor.

The fraternity divided pretty much into two groups: the

commerce-and-finance majors preparing for business careers
or law school and those in the sciences aiming for medical
school; there were a couple of engineers and, aside from us
three, only a handful of liberal-arts students. Before emerging
literary interests forged my alliance with Pete Tasch and Dick
Minton, the Sammy whose company I'd most enjoyed was a
C&F student, Dick Denholtz, a burly, assertive, dark-bearded
boy whose jovial forcefulness I associated with those peculiarly
Jewish energies that gave my Newark neighborhood its distinctive exuberance. Dick came from the Newark suburbs, and
perhaps what accounted for our strong, short-lived affinity was
that his family's American roots were like my own in urban
Jewish New Jersey. Together we could be the coarse and uninhibited performers who ignited whatever improvisational satire
flared up in the living room after dinner; the Sammy musical
skit for the interfraternity Mid-Term Jubilee—a telescoped
version of *Guys and Dolls* improbably set at Bucknell—had
been written and directed by Dick Denholtz and me and
starred the two of us in raucous singing roles. Our spirited low-
comedy concoctions—the kind that I had thought unlikely to
find a responsive audience at the Theta Chi house—constituted
SAM's single, unmistakable strain of "Jewishness": in the ways
that the extroverts made fun of things, and the ways that the
others found us funny, Sigma Alpha Mu came closest, in my
estimation, to being a Jewish fraternity.

I never knew how the predominantly Protestant student
body perceived the Jewish fraternity. Almost two-thirds of
Bucknell's students were from small towns in Pennsylvania and
New Jersey, while the preponderance of Sammies came from
New York—most of them from Westchester County and Long
Island, a few from the city itself. Of course there must have
been coeds whose families preferred that they not date Jews
and who willingly obeyed, but as there were barely twenty Jewish women on the campus, and about eighty Jewish men, the
dates I saw at Sammy parties were mostly gentiles, many from
communities where there were probably no Jews at all. Over
the years Sigma Alpha Mu had staunchly sought, and frequently
won, the interfraternity academic trophy, and though there
weren't enough Sammies playing on varsity teams to give the
house an athletic aura (in my time just two basketball players

and two football players), the sensational *social* event of the
early fifties was our brainchild. The nature of the event suggests (as did the brazen Jubilee *Guys and Dolls*) that going
along like sensible assimilationists with traditional campus socializing conventions was not the primary motive of the Sammies' leadership. The aim was to make a mark as a distinctively
uninhibited, freewheeling fraternity.

The idea for the "Sand Blast" was not original to our chapter but borrowed from a fraternity at some larger university
like Syracuse or Cornell, where the motif of an indoor winter
beach party was supposed to have inspired a colossal success of
just the sort the Bucknell Sammies hoped would elevate them
to the forefront of campus popularity. The rugs and the furniture, the trophy cabinets and the pictures on the walls, were
all to be removed from the downstairs rooms, and the first
floor of the house—dining hall and two living rooms—was to be
covered with about three inches of sand and planted with beach
umbrellas. The floor would have to be braced from below to
bear the weight of the sand; what's more, after the sand dumped
inside proved uninvitingly clammy, it had to be heated with
strong lights in order to reduce the dampness, which had dangerously increased the weight of the load. Required dress was
a bathing suit (in March), and the entire student body was invited. To spread the word, signs were posted all over the campus, and one afternoon a small plane flew low over the campus
issuing the invitation through a loudspeaker.

During the planning stages I expressed uneasiness with the
expense and the vastness of the effort and with what seemed a
clownish misuse of the physical structure itself; though by no
means an architectural showpiece, the building possessed its
own lumpish, sturdy 1920s integrity and served, after all, as our
collective home. I assured the brothers that I was as delighted
as anyone by the prospect of producing this pornographic tab-
leau within our familiar walls, and of course charmed by the
idea of all those Bucknell coeds lying around on the sand in
their two-piece swimsuits, openly contravening the strict dress
code enforced by the Honor Council (a group of esteemed
women students who tried infractions of conduct among their
peers and handed out punishment when a coed was found, say,
to be walking on a college path in a pair of Bermuda shorts

half an inch shorter than prescribed). I was no enemy of the
flesh, I said, but I reminded my brothers that when the party
was over and our house, if it was still standing, had again
become a home, we would be chewing sand in our mashed potatoes for semesters to come. I was roundly shouted down.

Among those few who argued that the plans for the Sand
Blast were too grandiosely whatever—childish, ostentatious,
imprudent, crazy—Tasch, Minton, and I were the least enamored of all; we were by then trying to put out four issues a year
of a new magazine, inspired by Addison, Steele, and Harold
Ross, and felt ourselves being swallowed up like extras in a
show-biz production by Mike Todd.

Despite throngs of students who dropped their coats and
shoes and scarves into a vast pile in the basement and then came
upstairs to disperse themselves, nearly nude, across the indoor
beach, the Sand Blast came off without a cave-in or an invasion
by the university police. Had there been a chance of anything
like an orgy developing, ninety percent (more!) of those who
had showed up would have left for The Spit (as the crummy
local movie house was known on campus) without even the intervention of the authorities, and I, along with my date from
Chester, Pennsylvania, would probably have gone with them.
Fantasy was of course less bridled than if the girls had arrived
corsaged and swathed in taffeta, as they customarily did for a
fraternity's annual lavish party, but in the fifties Bucknell, with
its freshman hazing and its compulsory chapel, its pinning
ceremonies and heralded "Hello Spirit," was still a long way
from Berkeley, 1968, and Woodstock, 1970, let alone from the
hanging gardens of Plato's Retreat.

The strain of Dadaesque Jewish showmanship that manifested itself a decade later in cultural-political deviants and
cunningly anarchic entrepreneurs—mischief-makers as diverse
as Jerry Rubin and Abbie Hoffman, the Chicago Seven defendants; William Kunstler, the Chicago Seven lawyer; Tuli Kupferberg, the Fug poet and a leading contributor to *Fuck You/A
Magazine of the Arts*; Hillard Elkins, the producer of *Oh, Calcutta!*; Al Goldstein, the publisher of *Screw*; not to mention
Allen Ginsberg, Bella Abzug, Lenny Bruce, Norman Mailer,
and me—was hardly what was germinating at the Sammy Sand
Blast. Though a spark of defiant impudence had perhaps ignited

the first fraternity meeting where so outlandish an idea was considered seriously, the stunt was engineered finally by conventional, law-abiding fraternity boys in training for secure careers in orderly middle-class American communities. The Sand Blast's underlying erotic motive may have spilled out more playfully, with more imaginative flair, than what fired the campus panty raid later that year, but what prevailed was the poolside spirit of the suburban country club.

Actually, the mob of freshman and sophomore men that came surging off the Hill one April night—hoping to break in on the nightgowned coeds and steal their underwear—produced a far more orgiastic version than the Sammies had of a Sadean scenario. The exhibitionistic extravaganza plotted and bankrolled by the socially competitive Sammies, though as bold a challenge to standards of communal decency as any mounted in Lewisburg during my years there, had, in fact, less to do with the suppressed longings that would culminate in the sexual uprising of the sixties than did the rowdy testicularity of those spontaneous spring panty raids that seemed meaningless to me at the time.

"Let's start a magazine . . . fearlessly obscene. . . ." The mockingly inspirational line was from E. E. Cummings, whose poetry I'd begun reading (and reciting to friends) under the influence of Robert Maurer, a young American-literature instructor in the English department, who was doing a Ph.D. dissertation on Cummings and whose wife, Charlotte, had been William Shawn's secretary at the *New Yorker* before marrying Bob and arriving with him in Lewisburg. With an M.A. from Montclair State College and his incomplete Wisconsin Ph.D., Bob was probably being paid about half as much as my father had earned struggling to support us on an insurance agent's salary, and one of the first things that I came to admire about the Maurers was their pennilessness; it seemed to confer an admirable independence from convention without having turned them, tiresomely, into fifties bohemians. Our bohemian—or the closest you came to one in Lewisburg—was the artist-in-residence Bruce Mitchell, who taught painting classes, loved bop, drank some, and had a wife who wore long peasant skirts. The Maurers seemed to me free (in the biggest and best sense), levelheaded Americans, respectable enough but unconcerned with position and appearances. They had their books and records, their old car, and a little brick house rather bare of furniture; Bob's droopy old jacket was patched at the elbows for other than ornamental reasons—yet what they didn't own they didn't appear to miss. They made being poor look so easy that I decided to follow their example and become poor myself someday, either as an English professor like Bob or as a serious writer who was so good that his books made no money. Bob, a butcher's son, was very much a Depression-honed city boy, originally from my part of industrial New Jersey. He was so lanky and small-headed, however, that in his oval spectacles and fraying clothes he looked more like an educated hayseed, some string-bean farm boy who had struggled semiconsciously toward freedom in a Sherwood Anderson novel. His direct manner, too, seemed to be born of the open spaces, and some twenty years later, after he had got fed up with teaching and had quit his professorship at Antioch, he earned his living writing for *Current Biography* and *Field and Stream*. He wound up, all on his own and seemingly quite happy, coaching boys' baseball for the Peace Corps in the wilds of Chile. He died of a heart attack in 1983, at the age of sixty-two. At his funeral his son, Harry, who'd been born in Lewisburg while I was a student there, read aloud from Bob's favorite Hemingway story, "Big Two-Hearted River."

Charlotte had her own brand of unadorned down-to-earthness, which filtered attractively through a faint Florida accent; she was psychologically more delicate than Bob and from a slightly more prosperous background, and to me her unorthodox Antioch College education and her time at the *New Yorker* made her seem terrifically urbane. She had a prognathous, fresh kind of freckled good looks that was as appealing as her speech, but it wasn't until I'd graduated from college and spent a week with the Maurers in their primitive cabin on the bluff of a tiny Maine island that I allowed myself, on the walks we took together, to fall for my professor's wife. At eighteen I was thrilled enough just to have been befriended by them and to be asked to their house occasionally on Saturday nights to hear their E. E. Cummings record and drink their Gallo wine or to listen to Bob talk about growing up gentile in the working-class town of Roselle, New Jersey, during the twenties and thirties.

I talked freely to them about my own upbringing, a twenty-minute drive from Bob's old family house in Roselle, which bordered on Elizabeth, where my mother's immigrant parents had settled separately, as young people, at the start of the century. Along with Jack and Joan Wheatcroft, another young English-department couple who soon became confidants and close friends, the Maurers must have been the first gentiles to whom I'd ever given an insider's view of my Jewish neighborhood, my family, and our friends. When I jumped up from the table to mimic my more colorful relations, I found they were not merely entertained but interested, and they encouraged me to tell more about where I was from. Nonetheless, so long as I was earnestly reading my way from Cynewulf to *Mrs. Dalloway* —and so long as I was enrolled at a college where the five percent of Jewish students left no mark on the prevailing undergraduate style—it did not dawn on me that these anecdotes and observations might be made into literature, however fictionalized they'd already become in the telling. Thomas Wolfe's exploitation of Asheville or Joyce's of Dublin suggested nothing about focusing this urge to write on my own experience. How could Art be rooted in a parochial Jewish Newark neighborhood having nothing to do with the enigma of time and space or good and evil or appearance and reality?

The imitations with which I entertained the Maurers and the Wheatcrofts were of somebody's shady uncle the bookie and somebody's sharpie son the street-corner bongo player and of the comics Stinky and Shorty, whose routines I'd learned at the Empire Burlesque in downtown Newark. The stories I told them were about the illicit love life of our cocky, self-important neighbor the tiny immigrant Seltzer King and the amazing appetite—for jokes, pickles, pinochle, everything—of our family friend the 300-pound bon vivant Apple King, while the stories I *wrote*, set absolutely nowhere, were mournful little things about sensitive children, sensitive adolescents, and sensitive young men crushed by coarse life. The stories were intended to be "touching"; without entirely knowing it, I wanted through my fiction to become "refined," to be elevated into realms unknown to the lower-middle-class Jews of Leslie Street, with their focus on earning a living and raising a family and trying occasionally to have a good time. To prove in my earliest undergraduate stories that I was a nice Jewish boy would have been bad enough; this was worse—proving that I was a nice boy, period. The Jew was nowhere to be seen; there were no Jews in the stories, no Newark, and not a sign of comedy—the last thing I wanted to do was to hand anybody a laugh in literature. I wanted to show that life was sad and poignant, even while I was experiencing it as heady and exhilarating; I wanted to demonstrate that I was "compassionate," a totally harmless person.

In those first undergraduate stories I managed to extract from Salinger a very cloying come-on and from the young Capote his gossamer vulnerability, and to imitate badly my titan, Thomas Wolfe, at the extremes of self-pitying self-importance. Those stories were as naïve as a student's can be, and I was only lucky that I was on a campus like Bucknell where there wasn't an intellectual faction to oppose my minute coterie, for its members would have found in my fiction a very soft satiric target. Then again, if there had been some sort of worthy competition around, I might not have produced these unconscious personal allegories to begin with. Allegorical representation is what they were—the result of having found myself far more of a cuckoo in the Bucknell nest than I'd been even as an adolescent on Leslie Street, let alone at Newark Rutgers, where, as a lower-middle-class boy from an ambitious minority in pursuit of a better life, I'd briefly played out the postimmigrant romance of higher education.

I don't believe I ever found myself out of place just because I was a Jew, though I was not unaware, especially when I was still fresh from home, that I *was* a Jew at a university where the bylaws stipulated that more than half the Board of Trustees had to be members of the Baptist Church, where chapel attendance was required of lowerclassmen, and where the one extracurricular organization for which most Bucknellians seemed to have membership cards was the Christian Association. But then, after only a little while in SAM I felt no closer to my fraternity brothers than I had to those Christian Association members who had lived in my dormitory and spent a part of each evening playing touch football in the corridor outside the room where I was concocting the symbols for my stories of victimized refinement. Like the overprotected young victims in those first short stories, who stood for something like the life of the mind, I was turning out to be too sensitive, though not to religious so much as to spiritual differences at a university where the dominant tone seemed to emanate from the large undergraduate population enrolled in the commerce-and-finance program—students preparing to take ordinary workaday jobs in the booming postwar business world, which not only my literary ideals but also my loosely held suspicion of the profit motive had pitted me against since I'd begun to read the New York paper *P.M.*, when I was fourteen. The courses to which I was drawn typified everything that the marketplace deemed worthless, and yet here I was, living among its most enthusiastic adherents—the unrebellious sons and daughters of status-quo America at the dawn of the Eisenhower era—certain that mind and not money was what gave life meaning, and studying, in dead earnest, Literary Criticism, Modern Thought, Advanced Shakespeare, and Aesthetics.

In September of 1952, when, as juniors, I took over as editor in chief of *Et Cetera* and Pete Tasch as managing editor, the Maurers became our advisers. Bob was listed as an official literary adviser, and Charlotte became an unofficial adviser. Her influence on the opening pages of each issue would have been apparent to anyone familiar with the *New Yorker*'s "Talk of the Town." Our own "Talk of the Town" was a two-page miscellany of putatively witty reportage, called "Transit Lines," a heading we thought nicely appropriate on a campus where an engineering student was always out on one of the walkways sighting through a telescope. Stories began in the first person plural, invariably with a tone of droll breeziness that the editor considered urbane: "When we heard about the new dormitory inspection policy (men living on The Hill will have their rooms inspected every week by the ROTC department) we were prepared to see, lining the campus, signs screaming, 'Down with the Military' or 'Keep the Fascista from Our Rooms! . . .'" "The other day we purchased a genuine undyed mouton pelt for the ridiculously low sum of five dollars. . . ." "One of our friends, a sociology major, if you're interested, told us a story the other afternoon. It seems that he took the afternoon train out of New York on Sunday. . . ." Some pieces were deft and readable, others oozed with archness, and none accorded with Cummings's prescription for a magazine "fearlessly obscene."

The obscenity around, in "our" judgment, was the weekly student newspaper, the *Bucknellian*, to which *Et Cetera* hoped to propose a sophisticated alternative. Little more than a decade later, student dissidents would display their defiance of officially sanctioned campus values by promoting, in their publications, bad taste and outlaw behavior; in the early fifties those of us keen to exhibit our superior wit and offhand charm in these "Transit Lines" pieces were indeed the Bucknell dissidents, and yet it was purportedly to raise, not to drag down, the tone of the place that we struck our *New Yorker*ish poses. Realistically, nobody working for the magazine expected it to do anything other than make tangible the differences between the collective student sensibility and our own as it was quickly altering under the influence of the English professors whose favorites we were and who were teaching us to enjoy using a word like "sensibility." But to me, at least, these differences seemed to reflect the national division between the civilized minority who had voted for Adlai Stevenson and the philistine majority who had overwhelmingly elected Eisenhower President.

The day after Stevenson was beaten, I stood up in Professor Harry Garvin's English 257 (Shakespeare: Intensive study of a small number of plays) and, under the pretext of explicating a passage about the mob in *Coriolanus*, excoriated the American public (and, by implication, the Bucknell student body, which had solidly favored Eisenhower) for having chosen a war hero over an intellectual statesman. Even though his gaze suggested that I was wildly out of order, Garvin, perhaps because of his own similar disappointment, let me go on to the end uninterrupted, while a majority of the Shakespeare students registered either amusement or boredom with my tirade. Absolutely certain that I was right and that a moronic America was our fate, I sat down thinking that despite the very obvious classroom consensus, *they* were the ones who were the dangerous fools.

This outburst aside, it had never occurred to me to make a case for Stevenson on the editorial page of *Et Cetera* when my first issue appeared at the height of the presidential campaign in October of 1952. The magazine had "higher" purposes, *literary* purposes; besides, it was not the custom in those days for student publications to support candidates for public office. A year later the magazine did publish a page-long "prose poem" that I'd written over the summer vacation, a monologue by an unnamed coward too prudent to speak out against McCarthyism, which provoked no response at all, so it may well have been that an *Et Cetera* editorial supporting Stevenson wouldn't have bothered anyone. But at the time, had I even thought of writing one, I would have assumed that it would violate the policy of the university Board of Publications, with which I was soon to collide anyway. I sported a Stevenson button in Republican Lewisburg and later, during the McCarthy hearings, I would come down off the Hill to the Maurer house at lunchtime and, according to a recollection of Charlotte Maurer's, stalk up and down the living room, glowering, while Bob and I listened to the proceedings on the radio. That was as far, however, as my political activism went.

The cadences of the editorial that I did publish in October 1952 bespeak, alas, the influence of the "March of Time" on my polemical style; in retrospect the editorial looks a little like the budding of an incipient Kennedy speech writer, concluding as it does with the line "Let our generation not wait too long." Written as an elegiac plea to my contemporaries to abandon their "high school values," their "football-clothes-car-date-acne-conscious brains," it was, in fact, a covertly condescending, less simpering version of my allegories about displacement. The editorial made the case, however naïvely, for a kind of robust, responsible maturity that was an advance over the prissy tenderness with which the author of the fiction had chosen to associate his manliness.

The editorial of the midyear issue was tame and informative and meant to be charming—a history, beginning in 1870, of the rise and fall of the Bucknell literary magazines that preceded *Et Cetera*. A laconic last paragraph quoted "Scott Fitzgerald." "What is it Scott Fitzgerald said? 'So we beat on, boats against the current, borne back ceaselessly into the past.'" The third issue, out in the spring of 1953, when I had just turned twenty, made me notorious, or as notorious as one could be who wore dirty white bucks and was on the dean's list; it defined me (perhaps in my own mind, primarily) as the college's critical antagonist rather than a boy who secretly still possessed enough of his own "high school values" to want to be popular and admired. Since the *Bucknellian* exemplified for me and my *Et Cetera* friends the lowbrow campus enthusiasms by which we felt engulfed, I put aside the self-protective writing postures with which I had kept my sense of estrangement in check and launched a heavily sarcastic attack on the banality of the weekly paper and its editor, Barbara Roemer, a well-liked, very amiable young woman from Springfield, New Jersey, who was the vice-president of the Tri Delt sorority and the captain of the cheerleading squad. As it was only the year before— while still a Sammy with a social identity outside the literary clique—that I'd unsuccessfully dated two pretty, clean-cut girls with ordinary American names wholly exotic to my ear, *both* of them members of the cheerleading squad, the reader is free to wonder how much of the animus directed against Barbara Roemer might have been inspired by my failure to impress either Annette Littlefield or Pat McColl.

"There is a theory," began the barrage, "that if a thousand monkeys were chained to a thousand typewriters for an unspecified number of years, they would have written all of the great literature that has been set down in the world by human beings. If such is the case, what is holding up production on the *Bucknellian*? We do not expect Miss Roemer and her cohorts to turn out great literature, for, after all, they are not monkeys, but we do expect them to publish a newspaper." The centerfold of the magazine was a satiric send-up of the newspaper, a facsimile front page burlesquing the *Bucknellian*'s editorial column and its newsless news stories, the work of someone seemingly more subtly endowed with aggressive skills than the insulting, ungrammatical editor in chief of *Et Cetera*. Without thinking too much about it, I had extracted from my taste for mimicry a rhetorical disguise more stylishly combative than the adolescent penchant for righteous contempt; transforming indignation into performance, I managed on the facsimile front page to reveal a flash of talent for comic destruction.

For delivering this gleeful one-two punch to an innocuous

Bucknell institution, I was admonished by the dean of men, Mal Musser, and brought before the Board of Publications for censure. In addition, the managing editor of the paper, Red Macauley, knocked on the door of my dormitory room and, with his fists clenched at his sides, told me that somebody ought to give me what I deserved for what I had done to Bobby Roemer. Our argument in the doorway was heated, but as Macauley was acting, by and large, out of chivalry and in fact had no more of a taste for physical combat than I did, he never took the swing that my adrenaline was readying me for. Dean Musser talked to me about the meaning of the word "tradition" and invoked the "Bucknell spirit," but as I had already heard him express himself on these subjects on numerous public occasions, I came away from that dressing-down feeling more or less unharmed. My appearance before the student-faculty Board of Publications must have been far more trying, for, as it happens, I don't remember it at all and was only recently reminded that it took place by my former teacher Mildred Martin, whose writing tutorial I was taking that semester and whose senior honors seminar, later, was the backbone of my undergraduate education. At my request, some months back, Mildred—who is now eighty-three—sent me entries from her 1953–54 journals about the senior seminar and appended some random notes under the title "Memories." One note reads: "After Roth was called up for reprimand because of an *Etc.* issue satirizing the *Bucknellian*, he came in distress to see me. I told him that any satirist in America would be subject to criticism." I called Mildred, in Lewisburg, after reading this and told her that thirty-four years later, in my Connecticut studio, I had no recollection of the reprimand from the Board of Publications or of rushing off afterward to be consoled by her. "Oh, yes," she told me over the phone, "when you came to my house you were nearly in tears."

The decals I'd affixed to the rear window of my father's Chevy during the first vacation of my sophomore year—one proclaiming the name of my new university, the other the Greek initials of my fraternity—I scraped off with a razor blade a year later. My sardonic uncle the dry cleaner, who, when he'd seen the decals, had taken to calling me "Joe College,"

didn't seem to notice when they were gone, and to him I remained Joe College until I came out of the Army, in 1956, and
got a job teaching freshman composition at the University of
Chicago. From then on I was "The Professor." But the professor had already begun to emerge by the time I returned as a
twenty-year-old to begin my senior year, in September 1953. I
had by then passed beyond the eventful semesters defining
myself as the outspoken enemy of what seemed pleasantly acceptable to nearly everyone else, and had become a zealous
student in The Seminar. This was the elite two-semester honors
course, carrying a total of eighteen credit hours, presided over
by Mildred Martin—"independent reading in English literature, from its beginnings to the present." The reading list was
ambitious—at least a couple of books a week, plus fifty pages
of details to master in Baugh's *Literary History of England*.
There was also a long critical essay due weekly, and every word,
spoken in class or written, was scrutinized for accuracy and for
common sense by Miss Martin, a plainspoken, businesslike Mid-
westerner with short gray hair and rimless spectacles, whose
crisp laugh and uncarping nature, along with her solid learning,
made her exactly the humane intellectual disciplinarian I was
ripe for. There were eight in the seminar at its peak, four men
and four women, but discussion tended to be dominated,
sometimes audaciously, by the *Et Cetera* editorial staff—Pete
Tasch, Dick Minton, and me.

That fall the seminar assembled from 1:30 to 4:30 every
Thursday afternoon in the living room of the house on South
Front Street, near the river, that Mildred shared with her faculty friends Harold and Gladys Cook. It was a white clapboard
eighteenth-century house with black shutters and a little hedge
out front; the front room where we met had a nice old fireplace and worn Oriental carpets on the old floorboards, and
shelves and shelves of books. Like young Nathan Zuckerman,
in *The Ghost Writer*, contemplating the living room of the New
England farmhouse of the writer E. I. Lonoff, I would sit there
on those darkening afternoons and—while Pete, Dick, and I
competed to outdo each other with "insights"—say to myself,
"This is how I will live." In just such a house I would meet
with my classes after I got my Ph.D., became a teacher, and

settled into a life of reading books and writing about them. Tenure as an English professor had come to seem a more realistic prospect than a career as a novelist. I would be poor and I would be pure, a cross between a literary priest and a member of the intellectual resistance in Eisenhower's prospering pig heaven.

Here are a couple of Mildred Martin's notes from her diary for that year, and another of her memories.

Dec. 21, '53. When I was 21, in comparison with Roth and Minton, I was a child. I'm pleased with those two boys, and Tilton is working well, too. Susie Kriss hasn't been at the seminar for three weeks now, and Mrs. Bender has dropped. Mrs. Bender, after hearing Roth's paper on "The Fight at Finnsburgh," burst into tears and said she couldn't compete. She fled to the dining nook in the kitchen, where she could hear what was being said. At one point she came back, and said, "I know the answer to that question," answered correctly, and disappeared.

April 23, '54. Dismissed Sem. early, and the girls went fast, but the four boys just kept sitting, and we began to have a really good time. We stayed till 4:30, and then Roth came in to talk about his φβκ speech. A book salesman came, the boys left, the salesman left, and Roth and Minton came back.

Memories. In the Lit. Library [the second-semester meeting place] there was an excited discussion about "the golden bird" near the end of "Sailing to Byzantium." Roth and Minton disagreed concerning its appropriateness. They rose, began shaking fists. Tasch, delighted, egged them on. I finally had to ask them to be seated. A unique experience.

The classroom had become my stage, usurping the magazine as a laboratory for self-invention and displacing the student drama group, Cap & Dagger, where I'd played supporting roles in ambitious student productions of *Oedipus Rex*, *School for Scandal*, and *Death of a Salesman*. Having brought to these parts more shamelessness than anything else, by my senior year I had even fewer illusions about becoming an actor than about turning into a Thomas Wolfe. Along with *Et Cetera*, Cap & Dagger had served me as an ersatz family, to take the place of the mainstream social fraternity from which I'd resigned. Though it was a respected organization, whose faculty advisers were among the most popular teachers on the campus, and though most of the student actors were just ordinary extroverted kids out to have a good time, it also harbored some mildly deviant types out to have a good time, as well as several campus misfits and artistic souls, whom I sometimes accompanied downtown for a beer or ate with at the men's dining hall.

It was there at Cap & Dagger that I found a steady girlfriend, Paula Bates, known as Polly, who came around to Bucknell Hall in the evenings to watch rehearsals or to prompt from the script or to act loosely as the director's assistant. She had arrived as a junior transfer student in my own junior year. She and her friend Margo Hand, who lived, as she did, in a room in French House, were the most sophisticated girls—and Polly was far and away the most sardonic girl—that I knew on campus. The well-brought-up daughter of a retired naval officer, she chain-smoked and drank martinis. The martinis impressed me when we first met and made me think of her as a woman of the world. She was frail and blond, not quite conventionally pretty, because of something slightly troubled in her expression, signifying, I think, the jagged overlap of the independent, no-nonsense wit who for months treated my declarations of feeling and my sexual persistence as an incomprehensible nuisance ("Stop *mooning*") with the delicate, kind, passionate girl whose parents' divorce and father's painful death had left her astonishingly susceptible to the intensity kindled by our affair.

The ordeal of overcoming Polly's wry skepticism was followed by the difficulties of finding a place to make love. We baby-sat for the Maurers and the Wheatcrofts and used their beds. We barricaded ourselves in a dormitory laundry room and lay on the cold floor. Vacations came, and back in New Jersey —where she stayed with her mother in Scotch Plains—I borrowed my father's car and we parked on dark, out-of-the-way streets. Over one Easter break someone lent us an apartment in New York for an afternoon and we luxuriated not only in the clandestine big-city hideaway and the feeling it gave us of being both free and on the run but also in finding ourselves unclothed together in a room full of sunlight. In the summer of 1953 we got jobs as counselors at a Jewish camp in the Poconos, where I had worked the year before, and there at night we took off for the woods. What with the obstacles to passion having to be surmounted again and again, our erotic life, along with the sheer thrill of its newness, had the underground piquancy of adultery. Even more than lovers, we became, through this drama of concealment and secrecy, the closest of companions and the most devoted of friends.

For my senior year I rented a room in town from an elderly widow, Mrs. Nellenback, white-haired and kindly-looking, a very strong Christian and, if I remember correctly, a Daughter of the American Revolution. Her simple white clapboard house, on a street corner not far from the women's quadrangle, was heavily laid with old carpets, and there were antimacassars and arm doilies on the upholstered furniture. The house was dark and quiet, with an unaired, not unpleasant smell of secure enclosure. The room I was offered was precisely what I wanted, potentially as much a love nest where Polly and I could stealthily retire to the narrow single bed as a scholar's secluded cell. I was duly informed on the day I rented the room that women were allowed in the house only on Sundays, when I could bring a fiancée for tea, provided the door to the hallway was left open. The room, which had once been the front parlor, was just off the main entryway on the first floor and had windows on two sides opening onto a summer porch that led down a little set of stairs to the quiet street. Since Mrs. Nellenback slept at the rear of the house—as did the housekeeper, a simpleminded woman who limped about with her feather duster, always smiling and singing babyish songs—and the other two roomers (one of them Pete Tasch) lived upstairs, it seemed to me that opportunities would abound for Polly to sneak in and out. After showing me the house, Mrs. Nellenback asked if I happened to be Armenian; I told her I was not. When I came back from studying at the library only a few nights after I'd moved in, I found on my bureau a plate with an apple and a cookie. When apples and cookies continued turning up, I knew I had a problem. How could I tell her to keep out of my room without making her suspicious of me as well as seeming ungrateful about the snack? And then again, now that we'd begun, how could I stop letting Polly in through the porch window after all the lights had gone out downstairs?

Several months after I'd moved in, Mrs. Nellenback took

me aside one day as I was heading for my room and said, "I had a Jewish boy living here in 1939." I didn't know how to respond and said something like, "That's a long time ago." "Arthur Schwartz," she said, or some such name—"he was the nicest boy." Inside the room, with the door closed, I thought, *She knows*, meaning not that she knew that I was Jewish but that she, if not the readers of my *Et Cetera* fiction, knew that I wasn't entirely harmless.

We were caught a few weeks after the start of the second semester. I had thought, one Sunday evening, that Mrs. Nellenback had traveled the ten miles to Mifflinburg, as she often did, to visit her family, but apparently she had only gone for a visit in town, and she was home little more than an hour after she'd been driven away in her son's car. My shades were down, the room was black (and locked from the inside), and Polly and I were in bed. After the car had, surprisingly, pulled back up outside, and Mrs. Nellenback had come into the house and passed through the hallway just the other side of my door, we got up and, in the dark silence, groped about, dressing ourselves. Then the most sophisticated undergraduate couple at Bucknell tried their best to outsmart this elderly widow who never in her life had left Union County. I motioned for Polly to crawl under the bed and to hide there until I gave the all clear. Then I found a coat, grabbed a book, and, unlocking the door, stepped out of the dark room into the hallway. My plan was to be sure that no one was about, leave the house by the front door, and then from the porch quietly open the window so that Polly could step out and escape. Coming into the hallway, however, I found Mrs. Nellenback standing directly in front of me, still in her coat and hat. I was startled and she was grim. "Good evening," I said cheerily, and closed my door behind me. I couldn't lock it without giving everything away, and since she gave no sign of moving, I continued on out the front door and started walking toward the campus, book in hand, as though all along that had been my intention.

Some minutes later—already a little out of my mind from wandering aimlessly about—I saw Polly running up the street toward French House. She was in tears and could hardly speak. Mrs. Nellenback had waited only seconds for me to pass out of sight and then, having opened my unlocked door, turned on the light and made straight for the bed. "Get out of there, you hussy," she had said, poking with her foot under the bed, and Polly, covering her face with her hands, had rolled out from her hiding place and fled the room. Mrs. Nellenback followed her out onto the porch, threatening that she was going to have me thrown out of school.

The year was 1954 and the locale central Pennsylvania. She could do it. I took Polly to French House and then ran back to my room to find Mrs. Nellenback dialing the hall phone. I was sure that she was trying to reach the dean of men, who was no particular friend of mine since my assault on the *Bucknellian*. When I demanded that she speak to me, Mrs. Nellenback put down the phone and said, "I can have you thrown out of the college for this." I replied loudly, "You had no right to scare that girl that way!" I was bluffing but didn't know what else to do except try to intimidate *her*. In the meantime I saw my life in a shambles. Polly's, too. Even though I intended to deny that it had been Polly who was in my room, I was sure the college authorities would haul her up for identification by Mrs. Nellenback. When this was over, I would have ruined not only my future but the future of the darling of the French department, who planned, like me, to begin graduate school in September.

It was the mid-1960s before I got round to exploiting this painful, ludicrous episode for a scene in my novel *When She Was Good*. The young couple there, Roy Bassart and Lucy Nelson, are extremely provincial small-town kids having virtually nothing in common with Polly and me. If anything, the drunkard's embittered Midwestern daughter Lucy has far more gritty rage with which to fight off her sense of shame than had the martini-drinking sophisticate from Scotch Plains, New Jersey. As for easygoing, unfocused, lackadaisical Roy, he hadn't any future at all to worry about losing. What happened to us, however, had a meaning very different; ours was a story about two intelligent, hopeful young people whose college success had given them everything to look forward to but whose infraction of the rules regulating their sexual lives rendered them, before the unlikely powers-that-be, just as powerless as a Roy and a Lucy.

I slept for a couple of nights at the Maurers', waiting to be summoned by the dean and subsequently sent home to Newark without a college degree (and for just the reason my father had always feared). When nothing happened, I took Bob Maurer's advice and quietly returned to my room and resumed my life at Mrs. Nellenback's. The incident was not mentioned by either of us, nor did I invite Polly to visit again, not even for tea, disguised as a fiancée. Afterward I couldn't figure out why Mrs. Nellenback had failed to make good on her threat—whether it was because she didn't want to be done out of the remaining rent and knew that with the second semester already under way it would be virtually impossible to replace me, or whether it had been an act of mercy by a good churchgoing woman, or whether I owed my luck to Arthur Schwartz, Bucknell '39.

For nearly six weeks early that spring we thought that Polly was pregnant. If she was, we didn't see how we could do anything but give up our graduate-school plans, marry, and stay on at Bucknell as salaried teaching assistants. We were in love, we were faculty favorites, Lewisburg living was cheap and simple, and it would even be possible to work toward an M.A. right there, though a second Bucknell degree was hardly what either of us had in mind. I had applied to go to Oxford or to Cambridge as a Fulbright or a Marshall scholar, and in the event that neither scholarship came through—unlikely, I thought, because I was near the top of my class—I had also put in for fellowships at three American universities; one was the University of Pennsylvania, where Polly planned to work on a Ph.D. Now we were as stunned to think that we might have to stay on at Bucknell indefinitely, living in the outlying university settlement, Bucknell Village, with the balding vets and their wives and babies—and our baby—as we'd been only a few months earlier, when we feared I was to be driven out of town for moral turpitude.

We would meet regularly for supper in the men's dining hall, where a number of nonsorority women also took their meals; Polly usually arrived first and waited for me by the door, and every evening when we caught sight of each other she'd shake her head, indicating that another day had passed without the onset of her period. Over our gravied Swiss steak and potatoes we'd buck each other up about the new and unexpected future as a married couple with a child and no money. I was reminded that as a father I wouldn't be drafted and have to waste two years of my life, after graduate school, as a private in the infantry. (Despite good relations with the colonel in charge of the Department of Military Science and Tactics, who had urged me to go on for a commission in the transportation corps of the post-Korea Army, I had quit ROTC, out of opposition to campus military training.) We tried to find some comfort in thoughts of the small, lively social circle of faculty people whom we liked to be with; certainly in the Maurers and the Wheatcrofts we had good and helpful friends, not really very much older than we were, with small children of their own. Heartbreaking as the situation was, and trapped as we felt, it seemed a test of maturity before which we simply could not bend; neither of us ever suggested that there was any other way out, at least not that early in the game.

Polly's discovery that she wasn't pregnant was my second pardon of the semester and filled us with enormous relief. For me it also turned out to be the beginning of the end of our affair. Having narrowly escaped premature domesticity and its encumbering responsibilities, I abandoned myself to dreams of erotic adventures that I couldn't hope to encounter other than on my own. I had successfully distanced myself at eighteen from my father's strictures, at nineteen from the meaningless affiliation to the Jewish fraternity, at twenty from the cozy ordinariness of the amiable student community; I had even begun to outgrow my own moralizing polemics. Now, at twenty-one, I wanted to be free from the exclusivity of monogamous love. The easiest way out would have been the offer of a scholarship to study literature in England, which we agreed I couldn't turn down; but though Fulbrights did go to two other Bucknell seniors, I was passed over for either scholarship that would have taken me abroad. The offer for a full fellowship did come, however, from the University of Pennsylvania, where Polly was to be a student too. There was also a fellowship from the graduate school of the University of Chicago. To Polly's astonishment—and somewhat even to my own—I hardened my heart and took the one from Chicago.

The summer after graduation we met one day to have lunch in New York and ended up arguing in Penn Station, where finally I told her the truth—and with about as much finesse as

I'd displayed attacking the *Bucknellian*: I was passionately involved with another girl, whom I had met at a Newark day camp where I was working till I left for Chicago. I saw Polly again just once, two years later—with Jeffrey Lindquist, her husband-to-be, a good-looking, gentlemanly geology professor from Penn—while we were all coincidentally visiting the Maurers up in Maine. She married Jeffrey the next year, and eventually Paula Lindquist became a professor of French at New York University. She was forty-seven when she died of cancer, in 1979, only a few months after I had been back to Bucknell to receive an honorary degree. During my two days in Lewisburg—where I stayed with Emeritus Professor Mildred Martin, who, for the processional march, accompanied me to the platform in her academic robes—I walked over to Mrs. Nellenback's to look at those porch windows leading to my old first-floor room. Needless to say, they were fewer and smaller than I'd remembered. It could never have been easy, in any way, getting in and out of them.

Girl of My Dreams

I'D noticed her long before that evening in Chicago when I introduced myself out on the street and persuaded her to have a cup of coffee with me in Steinway's drugstore, a university hangout only a few blocks from where she lived. Out of either shyness or savoir faire, I'd never in my life tried as blatantly to pick anybody up, which indicates not so much that fate had a hand in my trying now but that I was determined—as culturally inclined as I was psychologically resolved—to have my adventure with this woman who appeared to be the incarnation of a prototype.

In October 1956 I was not yet twenty-four, the Army was behind me, and my second published short story had been plucked from a tiny literary magazine and selected for Martha Foley's *Best American Short Stories* of 1956. I was an instructor (as well as a Ph.D. candidate) at the University of Chicago, I was sporting a tan glen-plaid Brooks Brothers University Shop suit that I'd bought with Army separation pay in order to meet my college composition classes, and, having just come from a cocktail party at the Quadrangle Club for new faculty members, I had some four or five ounces of bourbon enkindling my flame. Roaring with confidence, then, and feeling absolutely free (". . . they were drunken, young, and twenty . . . and they knew that they could never die." T. Wolfe), I corralled her in the doorway of Woodworth's bookstore and said something like, "But you must have a cup of coffee with me—I know all about you." "Do you? What's there to know?" "You used to be a waitress in Gordon's." Gordon's was another university hangout, a restaurant just next door to Woodworth's. "Was I?" she replied. "You have two small children." "Do I?" "You come from Michigan." "And how do you know that?" "I asked. One day at Gordon's I saw your children with you. A little boy and a girl. About eight and six." "And just why have you bothered to remember all this?" "You seemed young to have those kids. I asked somebody and they told me you were divorced. They told me you were once an undergraduate here." "Not long enough for it to matter." "They told me your

name. Josie. I came here as a graduate student in '54," I told
her—"I used to have lunch at Gordon's. You waited on me
and my friends." "I'm afraid I don't have that good a memory," she said. "I do," I replied, and doggedly witty, doggedly
clever, doggedly believing myself utterly impregnable, I got her
finally to accede—I would rarely ever get her to do that again—
and to walk down the block and sit with me in a booth in the
window of Steinway's. There the published young instructor
presented his plumage in full, while Josie, quizzical and amused
and flattered, said—in an ironic allusion to her powers to
inflame—that she couldn't figure out what I was so fervent
about.

But I was fervent then about almost everything, and that
evening fervent in the extreme because of those straight bour-
bons that I'd been drinking at the faculty-club party, where I
was the university's youngest new faculty member and arguably
its happiest. If she couldn't understand why the fervor had fastened on her it was because what I experienced at twenty-three
as the power of a fascinating prototype felt to her at twenty-
seven like the sum of all her impediments. The exoticism wasn't
solely in her prototypical blue-eyed blondness, though she was
blue-eyed and very blond, a woman whose squarish, symmetrical face, no matter how worn down by furious combat, could
still manage to look childlike and tomboyish in a woolen ski
hat; it wasn't in her prototypical gentile appearance, though
she was gentile-looking in a *volkisch* way that recalled nothing
of the breezy bearing of brainy Polly, with her sophisticated
martinis and her sardonic refinement; it wasn't in her Americanness either, though her speech and dress and manner made
her a virtual ringer for the solid, energetic girl in the cheery
movies about America's heartland, a friend of Andy Hardy's, a
classmate of June Allyson's, off to the prom in his jalopy with
Carleton Carpenter. Though this hardly made her any less
American, she was actually a small-town drunkard's angry
daughter, a young woman already haunted by grim sexual
memories and oppressed by an inextinguishable resentment
over the injustice of her origins; hampered at every turn by her
earliest mistakes and driven by fearsome need to bouts of desperate deviousness, she was a more likely fair-haired heroine

for the scrutiny of Ingmar Bergman than for the sunny fantasies of M-G-M.

What was exotic, then, wasn't the prototypical embodiment
of the Aryan gentile American woman—hundreds of young
women no less prototypical had failed to excite my interest
much at Bucknell—but, as I'd already sensed in Gordon's
restaurant back when she was still a newly divorced waitress
with two small kids and I was a U of C graduate student, that
she was that world's *victim*, a dispossessed refugee from a so-
ciobiological background to which my own was deemed, by
both old- and new-world racial mythology, to be subservient,
if not inferior. Had *her* father worked for the Metropolitan
Life, he could have hoped to rise to be superintendent of agencies, or even dreamed of one day replacing the company president, whereas mine had deemed it necessary to risk our future
in a business venture—and had the bad luck to come close to
wrecking it—because the biggest financial institution in the
world, the light of whose probity never failed, considered those
of his religion best qualified for the lower levels of the corporate work force. Yet the fact was that her own father, a good-
looking, former high school athlete named Smoky Jensen, had
never been able to hold down a job successfully or give up the
bottle and eventually wound up serving time for theft in a
Florida jail, while my father, whose lack of education added to
the handicap of his Jewish background, had by dint of his slavish energies and indestructible ambition reached a managerial
rung on the Metropolitan Life hierarchy that, however insignif-
icant in the company's overall organizational scheme, represented a real triumph of individual will over institutional bias.
It was in large part Smoky Jensen's record as a father, a worker,
a husband, and a citizen that had left Josie without the sustenance of family pride and bereft of affectionate attachment to
the place where she'd been raised. She was adrift, not merely
resentfully alienated from her Michigan upbringing but crudely
and ambiguously amputated from her immediate ordeal as a
wife and a mother; because of indebtedness and the fact that
her semester and a half at Chicago qualified her for virtually no
job that paid anything, she had worried ever since the end of
her marriage about what would become of her on her own.

Rooted most deeply in this pictorial embodiment of American Nordic rootedness was her hatred for her past and her fear of the future.

If our contrasting family endowments didn't accord with ancient racial mythology, they did conform to the simplifications about the inner resources of the Jews and the corrupting vices of the goyim that had sifted into my own sense of human subdivision from the beliefs of my Yiddish-speaking grandparents. Educated on their ancestors' and their own experience of violence, drunkenness, and moral barbarism among the Russian and Polish peasantry, these unworldly immigrants would not have imagined it to be quite as culturally illuminating as did their highly educated American grandson that a solid female specimen of earthy gentile stock could be blighted at the core by irresponsible parenting, involving not merely alcoholism and petty criminality but, as she would eventually allege, a half-realized attempt at childhood seduction. To them this would have seemed par for the course. Nor would they have found themselves anthropologically beguiled to learn that the divorced woman's own little boy and girl happened already to be enduring a childhood fate no less harsh than her own. It would simply have substantiated their belief in gentile family savagery to hear how her gentile husband (who, according to Josie's very dubious testimony, had "browbeaten" her into conceiving the second child, just as he had "irresponsibly" knocked her up, a single girl starting college, to conceive the first) had "stolen" the two gentile children from their gentile mother and shipped them to be raised by others, more than a thousand miles from her arms, in Phoenix, Arizona. Despite her avowal of gruesome victimization at the hands of yet another merciless *shagitz*, my grandparents might even have surmised that the woman, having discovered that she was emotionally incapable of mothering anyone, had herself effectively let the two children go. She would have seemed to them nothing more or less than the legendary old-country shiksa-witch, whose bestial inheritance had doomed her to become a destroyer of every gentle human virtue esteemed by the defenseless Jew.

Raving within and stolidly blond without—Josie would have seemed to my grandparents the incarnation not of an American prototype but of their worst dream. And just *because* of that, their American grandson refused to be intimidated and, like a greenhorn haunted by the terrors of a vanished world, to react reflexively and run for his life. I was, to the contrary, thrilled by this opportunity to distinguish at first hand between American realities and shtetl legend, to surmount the instinctive repugnance of my clan and prove myself superior to folk superstitions that enlightened, democratic spirits like me no longer had dignified need of in the heterogeneous U.S.A. And to prove myself superior as well to Jewish trepidation by dint of taming the most fearsome female that a boy of my background might be unfortunate enough to meet on the erotic battlefield. What might signify a dangerous menace to the ghetto mentality, to me—with my M.A. in English and my new three-piece suit—looked as though it had the makings of a bracingly American amorous adventure. After all, the intellectually experimental, securely academic environs of Chicago's Hyde Park were as far as you could hope to get from the fears of Jewish Galicia.

During the day Josie worked as a secretary in the Division of Social Sciences, a job that she liked and that brought her into contact with distinguished visitors like Max Horkheimer, the Frankfurt sociologist, who enjoyed her company and sometimes took her to lunch or to the faculty club for a drink, and with a successful woman like Ruth Denney, the assistant to the dean of the division, who was only ten or so years older than Josie and whose professional achievement Josie vastly admired though she realized a little bitterly that she was herself too far in the rear ever to hope to emulate it. The job had helped enormously to get her readjusted to her new life after the frantic period of near-breakdown following the loss of her children. We met and became lovers just as she had begun to enter the most hopeful period of her life since the aborted undergraduate year at Chicago a decade earlier, when she believed she had escaped Port Safehold, Michigan, and everything there that threatened to destroy her.

Upon my return to Chicago, I'd lived first in a divinity-school residence hall and then in a small apartment—one room with a kitchen—a few blocks from the university. I went off from there every weekday from 8:30 to 11:30 a.m. to teach composition and, a couple of afternoons a week, to take courses toward a Ph.D. in the graduate English department. The other afternoons I sat squeezed in at my kitchen table, where the daylight was stronger than it was anywhere else in the minute flat, and wrote short stories on my portable Olivetti. In the evenings I walked over to Josie's sizable railroad flat in an old building near the IC tracks, carrying with me a wad of freshman essays that I'd correct and grade in her living room after we'd had dinner together and while she got on with chipping away the layered paint to reach the bare pine mantel of the fireplace. I thought it was game of her, after her day at the office, to be laying new linoleum in the kitchen and stripping the paper off the bathroom walls, and I admired the enterprising way in which she partially met the costs of the apartment—which had to be large, she said, so the children could visit during their Arizona school vacations—by renting a back room to a happy-go-lucky premature hippie, a U of C dropout, who, unfortunately, didn't always have money for the rent. For me, the apartment and Josie's ambitions for it placed her at the heart of the low-income Hyde Park style of living that I found so congenial, blending as it did the neighborhood's unselfconscious strains of mildly disorderly bohemianism with the ordinary bourgeois taste for an attractive household where you could comfortably sit listening to music or reading a book or drinking cheap wine with your friends. In those years, nobody we knew wanted to own a television set, while every second person I met seemed to play the recorder.

Our evenings in Josie's apartment signaled to me that the aspiration that had carried me away from Newark and off to Bucknell at eighteen had been triumphantly realized at twenty-three (despite the fact that I was still a student and, except for my year in the Army, had been one since I was five): I was at last a man. It may be that why I dropped out of the Ph.D. program after little more than one quarter, why sitting in a class answering questions and going home to study for still more exams were all at once unendurable, had to do not just with deciding (largely because of my Martha Foley story) to stake my long-term future on writing fiction but with having gained the majority that I'd always known to be the goal of my education. At twenty-three I was independent of my family, though I still phoned them a couple of times a month, wrote occasional letters, and made the trek East at Christmastime to see them; I was settled into a desirable if tedious teaching position at a prestigious university in a city neighborhood where there were lots of secondhand bookstores and plenty of original intellectual types; and above all, I was conducting my first semidomesticated love affair where—even though their spectral presence was gigantic—nobody's parents were actually nearby, a love affair with a woman even more profoundly on her own than I was. That she was four years older than I seemed only further evidence of my maturity: our seemingly incompatible backgrounds attested to my freedom from the pressure of convention and my complete emancipation from the constraining boundaries protecting my preadult life. I was not only a man, I was a free man.

I thought then that I couldn't have found a more exhilarating intellectual arena than the University of Chicago in which to exercise my freedom to its utmost. After being discharged from the Army in August, I'd gone up to New York to begin looking for a job. Charlotte Maurer helped get me an interview at the *New Yorker*, and through the influence of the novelist Charles Jackson, who wrote copy at the J. Walter Thompson advertising agency, where my brother was then an art director, I had gotten to see Roger Straus, Jackson's publisher, who twenty years later became my own publisher. A few days after the interviews, I was elated to find myself being offered two jobs—as a copy editor at Farrar, Straus, and Cudahy and as a checker at the *New Yorker*. Before I could choose between them, however, a telegram arrived unexpectedly from Napier Wilt, a former teacher of mine and dean of humanities at Chicago; at the last minute a position had opened up on the freshman composition staff of the college, and Wilt was asking if I was interested in joining the Chicago faculty as an instructor in September.

Not only did I consider university teaching worthwhile, interesting work, but it was clear that of the three jobs the instructorship would afford the most opportunity to write: even with three composition sections, each meeting five hours a week, I'd still have as much as half of each day left for myself, and then there'd be quarterly breaks, periodic holidays, and summer vacations. All that free time was particularly appealing after my claustrophobic months in the Army. Following basic

training at Fort Dix, I'd been assigned to Washington to serve
as a private writing news handouts for the public-information
officer of Walter Reed Army Hospital. (Because of a back injury sustained at Dix, I eventually wound up a patient in the
hospital and, after two months in bed there, was released from
the service with a medical discharge.) Working in the public-
information office for more than half a year provided my first
taste of the tedium of a nine-to-five job; the work was hardly
demanding, but there were still days when being cooped up
for eight hours, mindlessly banging a typewriter, nearly drove
me nuts. Consequently, once I was free of the Army enclosure, I
seized on this chance to rise from former graduate student to
university instructor and to return to Chicago, once again to
argue about books and theorize to my heart's content about literature and, what's more, to live on practically nothing (that's
about what the job paid) without feeling like a pauper, which
you could do in those days around a university. In 1956, at
twenty-three, I saw the University of Chicago as the best place
in America to enjoy maximum personal freedom, to find intellectual liveliness, and to stand, if not necessarily in rebellious opposition, at least at a heartening distance from the prospering
society's engrossment with consuming goods and watching TV.

Ever since the summer of my Bucknell graduation I'd been
carrying in my wallet the photograph of a college student from
suburban north Jersey, a Jewish girl whose family history and
personal prospects couldn't have been less like Josie's; she was
quick-witted, intelligent, and vivacious, quite pretty, and possessed of the confidence that's often the patrimony of a young
woman adored since birth by a virile, trustworthy, successful
father. Harry Milman, Gayle's father, made not the slightest
attempt to disguise the impassioned pride he took in his four
children, toward whom he was unfailingly affectionate and generous; he was a hard-driving, rough-hewn businessman, like
my own father out of Jewish immigrant Newark, and in those
years when Gayle was still his loving dependent daughter, he
loomed in the background of her life as an impressively protective figure. The bond to her mother, a very good-looking
woman in her early fifties, had by then begun to chafe an adventurous girl of eighteen and nineteen, yet the relationship, if

at times strained, was never in real danger of deteriorating into anything unmanageably painful. The hallmarks of the family were solidarity and confidence. Could Josie have been disarmed of her resentful defiance and permitted to press her nose up against the glass of the picture window of the Milmans' large suburban house, she might well have stood there weeping with envy and wishing with all her heart to have been transformed into Gayle. She magically sought something approximating that implausible metamorphosis by deciding to marry me against all reasonable resistance and, on top of that, to become a Jew.

"Oh," cries Peter Tarnopol in *My Life as a Man*, pining for the Sarah Lawrence senior whom he'd cast off in favor of his angry nemesis, "why did I forsake Dina Dornbusch—for Maureen!" Why did *I* forsake Gayle for Josephine Jensen? Over a period of some two years, while I was in graduate school and in the Army, Gayle and I were equally caught up by an obsessional passion yet, returning to Chicago in September 1956, I thought my voyage out—wherever it might be taking me— could no longer be impeded by this affair, which, as I saw it, had inevitably to resolve into a marriage linking me with the safe enclosure of Jewish New Jersey. I wanted a harder test, to work at life under more difficult conditions.

The joke on me was that Gayle had an enigmatic adventure of her own to undertake and, after graduating from college, propelled by the very gusto and self-assurance that had germinated in the haven of her father's hothouse, for over a decade led a single life in Europe whose delights had little in common with the pleasures of her conventional upbringing. From the stories that reached me through mutual friends, it sounded as though Harry Milman's daughter had become the most desirable woman of *any* nationality between the Berlin Wall and the English Channel; meanwhile, the outward-bound voyager who refused to curb his precious independence by even the shadow of a connection with the provincial world he'd outgrown had sealed himself into a joyless existence, rife with the most preposterous, humanly meaningless responsibilities.

I had got everything backward. Josie, with her chaotic history, seemed to me a woman of courage and strength for having survived that awful background. Gayle, on the other hand, because of all that family security and all that father love, seemed to me a girl whose comfortable upbringing would keep her a girl forever. Gayle would be dependent because of her nurturing background and Josie would be independent because of her broken background! Could I have been any more naïve? Not neurotic, naïve, because that's true about us too: very naïve, even the brightest, and not just as youngsters either.

Three close friendships that I made at the university during my first months back in Chicago were with the novelists Richard Stern and Thomas Rogers and the critic and editor Ted Solotaroff. The three of them were four to five years older than I and already married—Dick and Ted each had a couple of small children—but we were all still only in our twenties and wanted to be writers. Dick and Tom were new members of the U of C faculty, while Ted was teaching evening classes down at an Indiana University extension in Gary and studying as I was in the Chicago Ph.D. program. Josie and I would see the Sterns or the Rogerses or the Solotaroffs fairly regularly for dinner or a poker game or a beer, and the camaraderie made us seem something like a married couple ourselves, even if I was more aware than ever, particularly from the example of Ted's difficult life and the obvious strain that a family imposed on his time to write and to pursue his degree, that for financial reasons alone my own writing ambition would best be served by being responsible for only myself. Though my salary was $2,800 a year, I was still trying to save toward the European journey that seemed to me very much a part of a literary apprenticeship. I was almost certain that I could never expect to live on my earnings as a writer, even if eventually I came to be published in large-circulation magazines as well as in the literary quarterlies that were my natural home in those days. It went without saying (certainly at the University of Chicago) that one did not write in the *expectation* of making money. I thought that if I was ever pressed to write for money, I wouldn't be able to write at all.

During the first months Josie and I were together I talked much of the time about writing, bought her my favorite paperbacks, loaned her heavily underlined Modern Library copies of the classics, read aloud pages from the novelists I admired, and began after a while to show her the manuscripts of the stories I was working on. When I was asked to contribute movie reviews to the *New Republic* at $25 a shot (a job offered to me as a result of a little satire about Eisenhower's evening prayer that the *New Republic* had reprinted from the *Chicago Review*), we went to the films together and talked about them on the way home. Over dinner we educated each other about those dissimilar American places from which we'd emerged, she badly impeded and vulnerable—and only now sufficiently free to try valiantly to recover her equilibrium and make a new life as an independent woman—and I, from the look of it, fortified, intact, and hungry for literary distinction. The stories I told of my protected childhood might have been Othello's tales about the men with heads beneath their shoulders, so tantalized was she by the atmosphere of secure, dependable comfort that I ascribed to my mother's genius for managing our household affairs and to the dutiful perseverance of both my parents even in their years of financial strain. I spoke of the artistry practiced within my mother's kitchen with no less enthusiasm than when I enlightened her about the sensuous accuracy of *Madame Bovary*. Because the grade and high schools I attended had been virtually down the street from our house, I had as a boy gone home for lunch every day—the result, I told her, was that after I'd returned from teaching my morning classes and changed from my new suit into my old writing clothes the first whiff of Campbell's tomato soup heating up in the kitchen of my little Chicago flat could still arouse the coziest sense of anticipation and imminent, satisfying consummation, yielding what I had only recently learned to recognize as a "Proustian" thrill (despite my inability during consecutive summers to get beyond page 60 of *Swann's Way*).

Was I exaggerating? Did I idealize? I don't know—did Othello? Winning a new woman with one's narratives, one tends not to worry about what I once heard an Englishman describe as "overegging the custard." I think now that what encouraged me to disclose in such loving detail a memory I wouldn't have dreamed of exploiting while wooing a confident, well-brought-up girl like Polly Bates, whose faith in her origins was unchallengeable—and that would have been entirely beside the point with Gayle Milman, the daughter of a Jewish household far more of a lotus land to its offspring than my own—was an innate taste for dramatic juxtaposition, an infatuation with the coupling of seemingly alien perspectives. My unbroken progress from the hands of the *mohel* to Mildred Martin, my history as the gorged beneficiary of overdevotion, overprotection, and oversurveillance within an irreproachably respectable Jewish household, was recounted in alternating sequence with her own life stories and formulated, I think, as a moral antidote to flush from her system the poisonous residue still tainting her belief in the possibilities for fulfillment. I was wooing her, I was wowing her, I was spiritedly charming her—motivated by an egoistic young lover's predilection for intimacy and sincerity, I was telling her who I thought I was and what I believed had formed me, but I was also engaged by a compelling form of narrative responsory. I was a countervoice, an antitheme, providing a naïve challenge to the lurid view of human nature that emerged from her tales of victimized innocence, first as an only child raised from her earliest years as the not entirely welcome guest —along with her long-suffering mother and semiemployable father—in the house of her Grandfather and Stepgrandmother Hebert and then at the hands of the high school sweetheart whom she'd married and whom she had reason, she told me, to despise forever.

She would despise him forever. I was as hypnotized—and flooded with chivalric fantasies of manly heroism—by her unforgiving hatred of all the radically imperfect gentile men who she claimed had abused her and had come close to ruining her as she was enchanted—and filled with fantasy—by my Jewish idyll of neatly ironed pajamas and hot tomato soup and what that promised about the domestication, if not the sheer feminizing, of unmuzzled maleness. The more examples she offered of their irresponsible, unprincipled conduct, the more I pitied her the injustices she had had to endure and admired the courage it had taken to survive. When she reviled them with that peculiarly potent adjective of hers, "wicked"—which I till then had associated primarily with people like the defendants at Nuremberg—the nearer I felt drawn to a world from which I no longer wished to be sheltered and about which a man in my intended line of work ought really to know something: the menacing realms of benighted American life that so far I had only read of in the novels of Sherwood Anderson and Theodore Dreiser. The more graphically she illustrated their callow destructiveness of every value that my own family held dear, the more contempt I had for them and the more touching examples I provided of our exemplary history of harmlessness. I could as well have been working for the Anti-Defamation League—only instead of defending my minority from anti-Semitic assaults on their good name and their democratic rights, I cast myself as the parfit Jewish knight dispatched to save one of their own from the worst of the gentile dragons.

Four months after we'd met Josie discovered she was pregnant. I couldn't understand how it had happened, since even when she claimed it was a safe time of the month and saw no need for contraception, I insisted on her using a diaphragm. We were both stunned, but the doctor, an idealistic young neighborhood GP who had been treating Josie at very modest rates, came around to her apartment to confirm it. Sitting gloomily over coffee with him in the kitchen, I asked if there was any way to abort the pregnancy. He said that all he could do was try a drug that at this stage sometimes induced heavy bleeding that then required hospitalization for a D&C. The chances were slim that it would work—but astoundingly it did; in a matter of days Josie began to hemorrhage, and I took her to the hospital for the scraping. When she was back in her room later in the day I returned to visit, bearing a bunch of flowers and a bottle of domestic champagne. I found her in bed, as contented-looking as a woman who had given birth to a perfect child and talking brightly to a middle-aged man who turned out to be not a member of the medical staff but a rabbi who served as one of the hospital chaplains. After he and I exchanged pleasantries, the rabbi left her bedside so that Josie and I could be alone. I said to her suspiciously, "What was he doing here?" Perfectly innocently she replied, "He came to see me." "Why you?" "On the admissions form," she said, "under religion, I wrote 'Jewish.'" "But you're not Jewish." She shrugged, and in the circumstances I didn't know what more to say. I was perplexed by what seemed to me her screwy mix of dreaminess and calculation, yet still so relieved that we were out of trouble that I dropped the interrogation, got some glasses, and we drank to our great good luck.

Two years later she turned up pregnant again. By then we no longer had anything resembling a love affair, only a running feud focused on my character flaws and from which I was finding it impossible to escape no matter how far I fled. I had spent the summer of 1958 traveling by myself in Europe and, instead of returning to Chicago, had quit my job and moved to Manhattan. I had found an inexpensive basement apartment on the Lower East Side and was living off the first payment of the $7,500 fellowship Houghton Mifflin had just awarded me for the manuscript of *Goodbye, Columbus*, which they were to publish in the spring of 1959. I had left Chicago for good in May after a year in which the deterioration of trust between Josie and me had elicited the most grueling, draining, bewildering quarrels: her adjective "wicked" did not sound so alluring when it began to be used to describe me. Except for unavoidable encounters around the university neighborhood, half of the time we didn't see each other at all, and for a while, after we had seemingly separated for good, I became enamored of a stylish Radcliffe graduate, Susan Glassman, who was living with her prosperous family on the North Shore and taking graduate classes in English at Chicago. She was a beautiful young woman who seemed to me all the more desirable for being a little elusive, though actually I didn't like too much that I couldn't entirely seem to claim her attention. One afternoon I dealt the final blow to whatever chances I had with Susan by asking her to come along with me to hear Saul Bellow speak at the Hillel House. Josie happened to have taken the afternoon off from work and to my dismay was in the audience too; but as Bellow was one of my literary enthusiasms that she'd come to share, neither of us should really have been as surprised as we appeared to be by the other's presence. After the talk, Susan went off to introduce herself to Bellow; they had met once through mutual friends at Bard, and, as it turned out, in those few minutes a connection was reestablished that would lead in a couple of years to her becoming Bellow's third wife. Josie, who'd come to the Hillel House on her own, superciliously looked my way while Susan was standing and talking to Bellow; when I came over to say hello, she muttered, with a sharp little laugh, "Well, if *that's* what you like—!" There was nothing to say to that, and so I just walked off again and waited to take Susan out for a drink with the Solotaroffs. Later in the evening, when I got back to my apartment, I found a scribbled note in my mailbox, tellingly succinct—and not even signed—to the effect that a rich and spoiled Jewish clotheshorse was exactly what I deserved.

What I discovered when I returned from Europe in September 1958 was that, having spent July and August working in New York for *Esquire*, Josie had decided against returning to Chicago and her secretarial job at the university. She'd enjoyed Manhattan and her position at the fringe of the literary life and had decided to stay on "in publishing," for which she had no qualifications aside from the little experience at *Esquire*. But if I was Jewish she was Jewish, if I lived in Manhattan she lived in Manhattan, if I was a writer she was a writer, or would at least "work" with writers. It turned out that during the summer she had let on to some of the magazine people she'd met that she had "edited" my stories that had begun to appear in *Commentary* and the *Paris Review*. When I corrected her and said that though she certainly read them and told me what she thought, that was not what was meant by "editing," she was affronted: "But it is—I am your editor!"

The quarreling started immediately. Because of her desperation at finding herself purposeless in New York and unwanted by me, the exchanges were charged with language so venomous that afterward I would sometimes wind up out on the street wandering around alone for hours as though it were *my* life that had hit bottom. She located an apartment to sublet, moved in, and then mysteriously the apartment was lost; she found a job, turned up for work—or said she did—and then mysteriously there was no job. Her little reserve of money was running out, she had nowhere permanent to live, and none of her job interviews seemed ever to yield anything real. Repeatedly she would get on the wrong subway and call from phone booths in Queens or Brooklyn, panting and incoherent, begging me to come get her.

I didn't know what to do or whom to turn to. I was new to New York myself, and the only person I could have confided in was my brother. After all, it was in the paperback books that he brought home on weekends from Pratt Institute when he was an art student there that I had got my first glimpse of serious modern fiction. What's more, when I was fourteen and fifteen, and he was filling his student sketchbooks with slices of urban landscape and rapid portraits of seedy city dwellers, his determination to seek an artistic vocation wasn't without its inspiring effect. His diligent example established in my own mind the understanding that an insurance man's son had the right—if he had the talent and industry—to pursue something other than a conventional career in business or the professions. Why my father never seriously questioned Sandy's decision or tried in any serious way to alter his course—or to interfere later with my aspirations—may have something to do with the example of my mother's brother, Mickey, if one can even speak of the influence of a mild, mordantly humorous loner who would never have presumed to advocate his way of life to anyone, least of all to my brother, to whom he passed on some of his cherished old anatomy books but whom he dryly warned of the impossibility of being a good artist, let alone making a living as one. Nonetheless, the precedent that our Uncle Mickey furnished made painting seem to the family not so much a curiosity as a real line of work; whether it was a desirable line of work was something else—Mickey's shabby, comfortless existence in his small Philadelphia studio would intermittently arouse my father's ire, and he would harangue our poor mother at dinner about how her brother ought at least to go out and find himself a girl to marry. The freedom that Sandy and I felt in experimenting with work so far outside the local cultural orbit probably had also to do with the fact that our father, lacking a real education himself, was, luckily for us, deficient in specific ideas about what vocations his sons might best aspire to. He wanted mainly for us not to be wanting, and that we could accomplish by hard work.

Though Sandy and I sometimes *felt* as though we had a lot to say to each other, in the years after I came out of the Army, we began to be drawn apart by the sentiments and interests predictably associated with our work, his as a commercial artist at an advertising agency and mine as a college instructor and

novice writer. When we were together I did my best to suppress my disdain (not inconsiderable in my twenties and the
Eisenhower fifties) for the advertising man's point of view; but
he was hardly less aware of it than I was of his uneasiness around
university types and highbrow intellectuals or of the provocation that he sensed in what he took to be their pretensions.
This was not, of course, a major concern of his, and it unsettled
his general equilibrium as little as the agenda of J. Walter
Thompson Co. seriously interfered with how I lived; still, a
suspicious undercurrent between us, fostered by strong professional polarities, made for self-consciousness and even shyness when we met or telephoned. On top of that, Josie and
Sandy's wife, Trudy, couldn't stand each other, and so we had
no more reason to go out and socialize as couples than to sit
down together and talk intimately—"like brothers," as my
father would have advised. Because Sandy was embarked on a
marriage and a career pointing him in a more conventional direction than mine, planning the sort of life that looked to me
to have more obviously evolved from the background I'd put
behind me, it didn't seem to me that he would have had the
wherewithal—"morally," as I would have been quick to say
then—to help me through my predicament or, if he did, that it
was possible for *me* with *my values*, to solicit his assistance. This
was hubris, pure and simple, the arrogance of a young literary
mentality absolutely assured of its superior wisdom, as well as
the pride of a raw recruit of a man, vigorously intent on being
independent, who could not confess to an older, seemingly less
adventurous brother that he was being dragged beyond his
depth and needed someone strong to save him.

Besides, I was the strong one, was I not? I still believed that,
and not entirely without reason: these were the most triumphant months of my life. Less than five years out of college, I
was about to have a first book published, and my editors at
Houghton Mifflin, George Starbuck and Paul Brooks, were
tremendously encouraging; on the basis of a few published
stories, I had already established a small reputation in New
York, and through new friendships with Martin Greenberg
at *Commentary*, Robert Silvers at *Harper's*, George Plimpton
at the *Paris Review*, Rust Hills at *Esquire*, and Aaron Asher at

Meridian Books, I was meeting other writers and beginning to enjoy feeling like a writer myself instead of like a freshman-composition teacher who'd written a few short stories on the side. This spent love affair with Josie, a shambles for nearly a year now, couldn't possibly bring down someone on my trajectory. It wasn't marriage I was worried about, marriage was inconceivable: I just didn't want her to have a breakdown and, though I couldn't believe she would do it, I dreaded the possibility that she might kill herself. She had begun to talk about throwing herself in front of a subway car—and what seemed to have exacerbated her hopelessness was my new literary recognition. "It isn't fair!" she cried. "You have everything and I have nothing, and now you think you can dump me!"

Whether appropriately or not, I felt responsible for her having come to New York that summer. The temporary *Esquire* opening was as a reader for Gene Lichtenstein and Rust Hills, the magazine's fiction editors; when Josie had heard of the job and expressed interest in it, I had assured Gene and Rust she could do it—I figured that if she got it, it might help, if only temporarily, to quiet her complaint about going nowhere in life. I suppose I thought of this as the last thing I would try to help her out with before I disappeared completely. Later she was to claim that if Rust Hills hadn't promised her that the job would become permanent after the summer she would never have left Chicago; she would also have returned to Chicago if I hadn't implied, in letters that I'd written her from Europe, that I wanted her to stay on after I got back to New York. Rust Hills and I had both misled her, and when she turned up at the dock to meet my boat at the end of August 1958, it was because *she* knew that's what I'd wanted. Waving excitedly from the pier in a white summer dress, she looked very like a bride. Maybe that was the idea.

We spent a couple of endurable evenings during the following weeks with a young English architect whom I'd met on the boat and his English girlfriend, who was working in New York for *Vogue* at just the kind of job Josie wanted but couldn't seem to get. One of those nights we attempted to make love in my basement apartment; that I was pretty obviously without desire put her into a rage about "all the girls you screwed in Europe." I didn't deny that I hadn't been chaste while I was traveling—"Why should I have been?" I asked—thus making things predictably worse. By November she was wandering around New York with no money and nowhere of her own to live, and eventually, when she wound up one cold morning standing with her suitcase at the foot of the cracked concrete stairs leading down to my apartment and demanding that I summon up just one iota of compassion and give her a place to stay, it occurred to me to abandon the apartment to her— forget my records and my books and the few hundred dollars' worth of secondhand furniture, and disappear with what re- mained of my Houghton Mifflin money. But there was a two- year lease on the $80-a-month apartment to which I'd signed my name, there were my parents in New Jersey, whom I spoke to on the phone weekly and who were delighted that I appeared to be permanently settled back East—and there was the prom- ise of my new life in Manhattan. There was also my refusal to run away. Fleeing and hiding were repugnant to me: I still believed that there were certain character traits distinguishing me from the *truly* wicked bastards out of her past. "You and Rust Hills and my father!" she shouted, weeping outside the doorway at the bottom of that dark well—"You're all exactly the same!" It was the craziest assertion I had ever heard, and yet, as though I had no choice but to take the accusation seri- ously and prove myself otherwise, instead of running I stayed. So did she. With me.

So the second time she turned up pregnant was early in Feb- ruary 1959. I won't describe our life together on the Lower East Side during the three preceding months except to say that I'm as surprised today as I was then that we didn't wind up— one or both of us—maimed or dead. She produced the perfect atmosphere in which I couldn't think. By the beginning of the year in which *Goodbye, Columbus* was to be published, I was nearly as ripe for hospitalization as she was, my basement apart- ment having all but become a psychiatric ward with café curtains.

How she could be pregnant was even harder to understand this time than it had been in Chicago the year before, when it never occurred to me that the pregnancy had resulted from her failing to use the diaphragm she invariably purported to be going off to the bathroom to insert. She already had two

children she couldn't raise and grievously missed—why would
she go out of her way to have a third? Four months after we'd
met there'd been no reason to question her honesty—unless,
of course, instead of swallowing whole her story of relentless
victimization, instead of being so beguiled by the proximity
she afforded me to the unknown disorders of gentile family life
—to those messy, sordid, unhappy realities that inspired my
grandparents' goy-hating legends—I'd had the know-how at
twenty-four to cast as cold an eye on her self-presentation as
she did on the men who had been abusing her all her life.

It was true that in the middle of the night there had been two,
three, even perhaps four fantasy-ridden, entangled couplings
in which we had somehow slaked our anger and, somnambu-
listically, eased the physical hunger aroused by the warm bed
and the pitch-black room and the discovery of an identityless
human form among the disheveled bedclothes. In the full light
of morning I would wonder if what I seemed to remember had
not been enacted in a dream; on the February morning that
she announced she was pregnant once again, I could have
sworn that for weeks and weeks I hadn't even *dreamed* such
an encounter—I was erotically too mummified even for that. I
had just come back from Boston, where I had been seeing to
the galleys of my book with George Starbuck, and it was more
or less with the news of her pregnancy that she greeted my return: not only was I on the brink of being the author of a first
collection of stories, I was scheduled to become a father as well.
It was a lie, I knew the moment she said it that it was a lie, and
I believed that what had prompted the lie was her desperation
over my Boston trip, her fear that with the publication of my
first book, which was only months away, my conscience would
be catapulted beyond the reach of her accusations, my self-
esteem elevated to heights that would have situated her too—
if only she was at my side—high above the hell of all that failure.

When I told her that it was impossible for her to be pregnant again, she repeated that she was indeed going to have a
baby and that, if I "wickedly" refused to be responsible for it,
she would carry it to term and leave it on my parents' doorstep
in New Jersey.

I didn't think she was incapable of doing that (had she been
pregnant, that is), for by this time she was nursing a grievance

against my parents too—she claimed they'd treated her "ruth-lessly" during a disastrous visit she'd made to our house two summers earlier. I had gone off to spend a month by myself writing in a rented room on Cape Cod; at the end of the month, as prearranged, Josie had come out from Chicago for a week's vacation. On the Falmouth beach one afternoon a week after my arrival, I'd met a Boston University senior, a quiet, easy-going, plainish girl, an elementary-education student who was waiting on tables at a seafood house; soon we were sleeping together and spending her afternoons off walking the beach and swimming. Her boyfriend wanted to marry her when she graduated but she wasn't sure marriage was a good idea; I told her that I had a friend coming to visit whom I didn't want to see either. Our troublesome, ambiguous affairs were what we mostly had in common, that and desire for a brief respite from their problems. We were able to say goodbye relatively easily, but when I drove to Boston to pick Josie up at the airport and take her back down to the Cape, the aftershock of the agree-able few weeks with the B.U. girl, the sense of loss I felt for someone I barely knew but with whom things had been so pleasant, was stronger than I could have anticipated, and with Josie I immediately registered my disappointment at the pro-spect of resuming all the debilitating old quarrels—which, of course, guaranteed their immediate resumption.

Within seventy-two hours things were as hellish as they'd ever been, and we called it quits and drove to New York. She was going to finish out the week in a hotel there, seeing the sights on her own, while I went on to New Jersey—to Moores-town, near Camden, where my father had lately been trans-ferred to manage the Metropolitan's local district office. I planned to stay in Moorestown for a week before returning to my job in Chicago. Josie knew that Polly had spent Thanks-giving with my family one November and that she had stayed for a part of the Easter break when we were seniors at Bucknell; on the drive down from the Cape, she insisted on knowing why she couldn't come along—what had made Polly Bates so special? How could I treat her so wretchedly after she'd spent her savings coming all the way to Cape Cod to see me? Wasn't I grown up enough to introduce to my mother and father the woman with whom I'd lived for a year in Chicago? Was I a man or was I a child? When she wouldn't stop I wanted to kill her. Instead I took her home with me.

That she wasn't Jewish hardly entered into it—neither had Polly been Jewish, but my parents were always cordial to her, had fully expected me to marry her, and, after we went our separate ways to graduate school, asked me often if I knew how she was doing and remembered her affectionately. No, what they saw to frighten them wasn't the shiksa but a hard-up loser four years my senior, a penniless secretary and divorced mother of two small children, who, as she was quick to explain at dinner the first night, had been "stolen" from her by her ex-husband. While my mother was in the laundry room doing the family wash the next morning, Josie came in with her dirty clothes from her few days on the Cape and asked if my mother minded if she threw them into the machine too. The last thing that my mother wanted anything to do with was this woman's soiled underwear, but as hopelessly polite as the ideal house-wife in her favorite women's magazines, she said, "Of course, dear," and obligingly put them into the wash. Then she walked all the way to my father's office, some three miles away, weeping in despair over what I, with all my prospects, was doing with this obviously foundering woman who bore no resemblance to Polly or Gayle, and certainly none to her. She had seen instantly what was wrong, everything that it had taken months for me even to begin to recognize, every disaster-laden thing from which I was unable to sever myself—and toward which I continued to feel an overpowering, half-insane responsibility. My mother could not be consoled; once again Josie was furious and affronted; and my father, with extreme diplomacy, with a display of gentlemanly finesse that revealed to me, maybe for the first time in my life, the managerial skills for which he was paid by the Metropolitan Life, tried to explain to her that his wife had meant her no harm, that they had been pleased to meet her, but that it might be best for everyone if Philip took her to the airport the next day.

I was desolated, particularly since what happened was just what I'd expected—this was precisely why I hadn't wanted her to come with me. And yet on the drive down, when she'd told me how miserable she would be alone in a cheap New York hotel or, worse still, back in hot Chicago, having had, because of me, the worst possible vacation, I had once again been unable to say no—just as I'd been unable to tell her that I hadn't wanted her to join me for as little as a day when I'd first decided to go off that summer for a month on Cape Cod. I could have spared Josie her humiliation, I could have spared my mother her unhappiness—and myself my mounting confusion —if only I hadn't been so frightened of appearing heartless in the face of her unrelenting need and everything that was owed to her.

It was no wonder—though maybe it was nothing less than that, given my enslavement to her sense of victimization—that, when I did get back to Chicago that fall, we were together less and less, and I began to resume a vigorous bachelor life, pursuing Susan Glassman and intermittently dating a perfectly sane editorial assistant for the *Bulletin of the Atomic Scientists*, whom, had I settled in for good in Chicago, I would probably have seen much more of. Bizarrely, had I remained in Chicago, where Josie was installed in her job and her apartment, instead of rushing to put a thousand miles between myself and our hopeless estrangement, she would never have wound up alone in Manhattan, positioned to throw herself on me as all that stood between her and ruination. But not foreseeing that was the least of what I didn't know, brainy young fellow that I was on my Houghton Mifflin literary fellowship.

The description in *My Life as a Man*, in the chapter "Marriage à la Mode," of how Peter Tarnopol is tricked by Maureen Johnson into believing her pregnant parallels almost exactly how I was deceived by Josie in February 1959. Probably nothing else in my work more precisely duplicates the autobiographical facts. Those scenes represent one of the few occasions when I haven't spontaneously set out to improve on actuality in the interest of being more interesting. I couldn't have been more interesting—I couldn't have been *as* interesting. What Josie came up with, altogether on her own, was a little gem of treacherous invention, economical, lurid, obvious, degrading, deluded, almost comically simple, and best of all, magically effective. To reshape even its smallest facet would have been an aesthetic blunder, a defacement of her life's single great imaginative feat, that wholly original act which freed her from the fantasied role as my "editor" to become, if for a moment only, a literary rival of audacious flair, one of those daringly "pitiless" writers of the kind Flaubert found most awesome, the sort of writer my own limited experience and orderly development prevented me then from even beginning to resemble —masterly pitilessness was certainly nowhere to be found in the book of stories whose publication she so envied and to which she was determined to be allied. In a fifteen-page explication of human depravity by one of his garrulous, ruined, half-mad monologists, Dostoevsky himself might not have been ashamed to pay a hundred-word tribute to the ingenuity of that trick. For me, however, it was to become something more fateful than a sordid little footnote to somebody else's grandiose epic of evil, since by the time she came to confess to me two and a half years later (and, rather as Maureen makes her disclosure to Tarnopol, drugged and drunk, midway through a botched suicide attempt), by the time I learned from her how she had played her trick in Manhattan—as well as how she'd used no contraception in Chicago—we had repeatedly been in court to try to wrest her children back from her first husband. By then her daughter, a harassed, endearing, well-intentioned, ill-educated, emotionally abused girl of ten, was living in our house in Iowa City, and Josie was threatening to stab me to death in my sleep if I should ever attempt to seduce the child, whom in fact I was hoping, literally, to teach to tell time and to read. Needless to say, to *this* development Dostoevsky might have allowed something more than a mere one hundred words. I myself allowed several thousand words to find an apposite, deserving setting for her scenario in the opening section of *My Life as a Man*, in the chapter "Courting Disaster," which purports to be Peter Tarnopol's macabre fictional transmogrification of his own awful-enough "true story." For me, if not for the reader, that chapter—indeed the novel itself—was meant to demonstrate that my imaginative faculties had managed to outlive the waste of all that youthful strength, that I'd not only survived the consequences of my devastating case of moral simpletonism but finally prevailed over my grotesque deference to what this wretched small-town gentile paranoid defined as my humane, my manly—yes, even my Jewish—duty.

The urine specimen that she submitted to the drugstore for the rabbit test was purchased for a couple of dollars from a pregnant black woman she'd inveigled one morning into a tenement hallway across from Tompkins Square Park. Only an hour earlier she'd left my apartment, ostensibly for the drugstore, with a bottle in her purse containing her own urine, but as that would have revealed her to be *not* pregnant, it was useless for her purpose. Tompkins Square Park looked run-down even in those days but was still back then a perfectly safe place, a neighborhood resting spot for the elderly, where they sat in good weather and talked and read their newspapers—more often than not, papers in Ukrainian—and where the local young mothers, many of them very young and Puerto Rican, brought their children to play and run about. After a day of writing, I'd either walk over with my own newspaper—or my *Commentary* or *Partisan Review*—to an Italian coffee house on Bleecker Street for an espresso or, when it was warm enough, go down to Tompkins Square Park and read awhile on a favorite bench, read and look around and sometimes jot down a note about what I'd been writing that day, feeling very much the satisfactions of a young man on his own in a big city—to an ex-Newarker, a city far more mythical than Paris or Rome. If I wasn't as poor as those whose local park this was, I was still scrupulously living on the money that I portioned out to myself each week from the Houghton Mifflin fellowship; with no real desire to live otherwise, I felt perfectly at home loitering unnoticed among these immigrant Americans and their American offspring. I did not think of myself romantically as "one of them," it wasn't my style to speak of these people as The People, nor was I doing research—I knew plenty about old-country immigrants without having to study the sociology of Tompkins Square Park. I did think occasionally, however, of how my own family and all of our family friends had evolved from an immigrant existence that had to have shared at least certain elemental traits with the lives of the Tompkins Square Park regulars. I liked the place as much for its uneventful ordinariness as for the personal resonance that it had for me.

I don't intend to suggest that my sentimental fondness for Tompkins Square Park should have given Josie pause and sent her instead to look for her pregnant woman in Washington Square Park, only a ten-minute walk from my apartment in the other direction. To the contrary, had she gone anywhere *other* than Tompkins Square Park, she wouldn't have been the woman whose imagination's claim on my own may well have been what accounted for her inexplicable power over a supremely independent, self-assured, and enterprising young man, a stalwart competitor with a stubborn sense of determination and a strong desire to have his own way. The same deluded audacity that made even the least dramatic encounter promising, that had prompted her, probably quite spontaneously, to sign herself into the Chicago hospital as Jewish a mere hundred days into our affair, that had inspired her to hand over to my conventional, utterly respectable mother the dirty underthings that she'd accumulated on her holiday with me, was precisely what pointed her, like a hound dog with the sharpest nose for acerbic irony, to Tompkins Square Park in order to make a responsible man of me—to make a responsible *Jew* of me: to Tompkins Square Park, where she knew I so enjoyed my solitude and my pleasant sense of identification with my Americanized family's immigrant origins.

And a few days later, when she'd accepted my proposal to marry her—on the condition that before the marriage she have an abortion—it was the same instinct that led her to take the three hundred dollars I'd withdrawn from the bank and, instead of going with it to the abortionist whose name I had got from an intern friend, pocket the cash and spend the day in a movie theater in Times Square, repeatedly watching Susan Hayward go to the gas chamber in *I Want to Live!*

Yet once she'd "had" her abortion—after she'd come back from the movies to my basement apartment and, in tears, shivering uncontrollably, had told me from beneath the blankets on the bed all the horrible medical details of the humiliating procedure to which I had subjected her—why didn't I pick up *then* and run away, a free man? How could I *still* have stayed with her? The question really is how could I resist her. Look, how could I ever have resisted her? Forget the promise I'd made, after receiving the rabbit-test results, to make her my wife if only she got rid of the fetus—how could I be anything *but* mesmerized by this overbrimming talent for brazen self-invention, how could a half-formed, fledgling novelist hope ever to detach himself from this undiscourageable imagination unashamedly concocting the most diabolical ironies? It wasn't only she who wanted to be indissolubly joined to my authorship and my book but I who could not separate myself from hers.

I Want to Live!, a melodrama about a California B-girl who is framed for murder and goes to the gas chamber. The movie she went to see (instead of the abortionist, for whom she had no need) is also to be found in *My Life as a Man*. Why should I have tried to make up anything better? How could I? And for all I knew, Josie had herself made that up right on the spot, consulted her muse and blurted it out to me on the afternoon of her confession two years later . . . even, perhaps, as she invented on the spot—both to make her story more compelling and to torture me a little more—the urine specimen that she'd bought from the black woman in Tompkins Square Park. Maybe she did these things and maybe she didn't; she certainly did *something*—but who can distinguish what is so from what isn't so when confronted with a master of fabrication? The wanton scenes she improvised! The sheer hyperbole of what she imagined! The self-certainty unleashed by her own deceit! The conviction behind those caricatures!

It's no use pretending I didn't have a hand in nurturing this talent. What may have begun as little more than a mendacious, provincial mentality tempted to ensnare a good catch was transformed, not by the weakness but by the strength of my resistance, into something marvelous and crazy, a bedazzling lunatic imagination that—everything else aside—rendered absolutely ridiculous my conventional university conceptions of fictional probability and all those elegant, Jamesian formulations I'd imbibed about proportion and indirection and tact. It took time and it took blood, and not, really, until I began *Portnoy's Complaint* would I be able to cut loose with anything approaching her gift for flabbergasting boldness. Without doubt she was my worst enemy ever, but, alas, she was also nothing less than the greatest creative-writing teacher of them all, specialist par excellence in the aesthetics of extremist fiction.

Reader, I married her.

All in the Family

I STILL don't think it was innocent of me to have been as astonished as I was at twenty-six when I found myself up against the most antagonistic social opposition of my life, and not from gentiles at one or the other end of the class spectrum but from angry middle-class and establishment Jews, and a number of eminent rabbis, accusing me of being anti-Semitic and self-hating. I hadn't begun to foresee this as a part of the struggle to write, and yet it was to be central to it.

As intellectually sophisticated as I was, "self-hatred" was still a new idea to me then; if the phenomenon had ever been present in my world, I had certainly never perceived it as a problem. In Newark, I hadn't known anyone to whose conduct self-hatred was anything like the key, and the Bucknell chapter of Sigma Alpha Mu, whatever its shortcomings, never seemed to chafe under its distinctive identity or noticeably to apologize for itself. When Moe Finkelstein, one of the Sammies' two varsity football players, entered the game for Bucknell, his fraternity brothers invariably sent up a whoop signaling their proud affiliation, a demonstration of feeling that would have driven a self-hating Jew into paroxysms of shame. In fact, what was most admirable about the Sammies was the easygoing way in which they synthesized themselves into a manifestly gentile environment without denying their difference or combatively insisting on it. Theirs seemed to me, even then, a graceful response to a social situation that did not always bring out the best in people, particularly in that conformist era.

And virtually from the day that I arrived in Hyde Park as a graduate student and rented a tiny room in International House, the University of Chicago looked to me like some highly evolved, utopian extension of the Jewish world of my origins, as though the solidarity and intimate intensity of my old neighborhood life had been infused with a lifesaving appetite for intellectual amusement and experimentation. When I began graduate school in September 1954, the university seemed to me full of unmistakably Jewish Jews far *less* self-conscious and uncertain about themselves, really, than the Irish Catholics from Minnesota and the Baptists from Kansas—Jews wholly secularized but hardly chagrined by a pedigree from which they seemed to derive their undisguised contentiousness, their excitability, and a gift for satiric irony whose flavor I recognized immediately: our family friend Mickey Pasteelnik, Newark's Apple King, had he enjoyed a literary education, would surely have talked about *The Wings of the Dove* very much like my ebullient fellow student from Brooklyn, Arthur Geffin. Ted Solotaroff—with whom I profitably debated for years after I returned from the Army in 1956 and entered the Chicago Ph.D. program—remembers us referring to Isabel Archer as a "shiksa." I recall another conversation, over beer at the University Tavern, where Geffin tended bar at night, in which much scrupulosity was expended determining if Osmond wasn't really a Jew.

This was of course so much off-hours kibitzing, but the pleasure that we took in bringing to *The Portrait of a Lady* what we'd imbibed eavesdropping on our fathers' pinochle games does suggest something about the playful confidence we had in our Jewishness as an intellectual resource. It was also a defense against overrefinement, a counterweight to the intimidating power of Henry James and literary good taste generally, whose "civilizing" function was variously tempting to clever, ambitious city boys who knew just how casually coarse they could become on a street corner or at a poker game or in the upper deck at Ebbets Field. It seemed less advisable to treat this strain of vulgarity—which we had come to by being both our fathers' sons and our neighborhoods' creatures—as an impurity to be purged from our speech than to own up to it matter-of-factly, ironically, unashamedly, and to take a real, pleasurable satisfaction in what more than likely would have seemed to Henry James to be our unadventitious origins.

What ignited the Jewish charges against me was the publication in the *New Yorker*, in April 1959, of "Defender of the Faith," a story about some Jewish recruits in the wartime Army trying to extract favors from their reluctant Jewish sergeant. It was my second piece of fiction to appear in a large commercial magazine. With the $800 I'd earned from the first story, in *Esquire*, and an advance from Houghton Mifflin, I'd quit my instructorship at Chicago—and stepped for good (I thought) out of Josie's life. Intending to live only as a writer, I had moved to Manhattan's Lower East Side, to that two-room basement apartment that was placed perfectly—given my taste then for urban color—between the bums panhandling on the Bowery and the baskets of bialys on the tables at Ratners. The other stories about Jews that were to be published in the Houghton Mifflin collection, *Goodbye, Columbus*, though they may have attracted a little more than ordinary reader interest, had caused no furor among Jews, appearing as they did in the *Paris Review*, a young literary quarterly then with only a tiny circulation, and in *Commentary*, the monthly edited for years by Elliot Cohen and published by the American Jewish Committee. Had I submitted "Defender of the Faith" to *Commentary* —whose coeditor at that time, Martin Greenberg, was an early supporter and sympathetic friend—I suspect that the magazine would have published it and that the criticism the story aroused there would have been relatively unspectacular. It's even possible that the ferment inspired a month later by the publication of *Goodbye, Columbus*—the pulpit sermons, the household arguments, the discussions within Jewish organizations gauging my danger, all of which unexpectedly dramatized to people who were essentially nonreaders what was, after all, only a first book of short stories—might never have reached troublesome proportions had "Defender of the Faith" been certified as permissible Jewish discourse by appearing in *Commentary*. And had that happened—had there not been the inflammatory fanfare of the *New Yorker* exposure, had *Goodbye, Columbus* had the innocuous cultural fate of a minor critical success—it's likely that my alleged anti-Semitism might never have come to pervade the discussion of my work, stimulating me to defend myself in essays and public addresses and, when I decided to take things more aggressively in hand, to strike back at accusations that I had divulged Jewish secrets and vulgarly falsified Jewish lives by upping the ante in *Portnoy's Complaint*. *That* was not mistaken for a conciliatory act, and the ramifications of the uproar it fomented eventually inspired me to crystallize the public feud into the drama of internal family dissension that's the backbone of the Zuckerman series, which began to take shape some eight years later.

That the *New Yorker*, like *Partisan Review* and *Commen-*

tary, had a Jewish editor, William Shawn, Jewish contributors —like S. J. Perelman, Irwin Shaw, Arthur Kober, and J. D. Salinger—and a sizable Jewish readership would only have suggested, to those I'd incensed, that identifying with the *New Yorker*'s privileged, unequivocally non-Jewish aura furnished these Jews (as undoubtedly it did Roth himself) with far more sustenance than they derived from their Jewish status. I soon understood self-hatred to mean an internalized, though not necessarily conscious, loathing of one's recognizable group markings that culminates either in quasi-pathological efforts to expunge them or in the vicious disparagement of those who don't even know enough to try.

Because I didn't have the patience to wait for the author's copies to reach me by mail, the day that the *New Yorker* was scheduled to appear I made three trips to Fourteenth Street, to the newsstand across from Klein's, to see if the issue was in yet. When the magazine finally appeared that afternoon, I bought a copy for myself and another to send off to my parents. While I was at college, they had moved from the Weequahic neighborhood to a small garden apartment in a pleasant little complex in nearby Elizabeth, on the very street where they had been married in 1926 and where nearly every Sunday of my childhood, after visiting my widowed paternal grandmother in one of Newark's oldest immigrant neighborhoods, we would drive over to see my widowed maternal grandmother, who shared a small apartment there with my maiden aunt. The *New Yorker* was really no more familiar to my parents than were the other magazines in which my first stories had begun to appear. *Hygeia* had sometimes come to the house, sporadically we had received *Collier's*, *Liberty*, and the *Saturday Evening Post*, but the magazines to which my mother was most faithful were *Ladies' Home Journal*, *Redbook*, and *Woman's Home Companion*. In their pages she confirmed her sense of how to dress and to furnish a house, found the recipes that she clipped and filed in her recipe box, and received instruction in the current conventions of child rearing and marriage. Decorum and courtesy meant no less to her than they did to the heroines of the fiction she read in those magazines, and through her genteel example, my brother and I became well-mannered boys, always a source of pride to her, she said, on special Sunday outings to the Tavern, a family restaurant favored by Newark's Jewish bourgeoisie (a class in which we, who had neither money, property, nor very much social self-assurance, had really only half a foothold).

My mother read five or six books a year borrowed from the lending library, not junk but popular novels that had acquired moral prestige, like the works of Pearl Buck, her favorite author, whom she admired personally for the sort of reasons that she admired Sister Elizabeth Kenny, the esteemed Australian nurse who'd brought to America in the forties her therapeutic techniques for treating polio victims. She responded very strongly to their womanly brand of militant and challenging compassion. Her heroine of heroines was Eleanor Roosevelt, whose column, "My Day," she followed in the newspaper when she could. After her 1922 graduation from Battin High in Elizabeth, my mother, then Bess Finkel, had worked successfully for several years as an office secretary, a very dutiful daughter, living of course at home, who adored her mother and her older sister, feared her father, helped raise two younger sisters, and dearly loved her only brother, Mickey—a musician as well as an art student, and eventually a quiet, unassuming bachelor, softspoken and witty, and something of a traveler. Artistic ambition moved him to paint portraits and landscapes but he kept himself alive doing professional photography; whenever he could afford to, he shut his tiny Philadelphia studio and sailed to Europe to tour the museums and look at the paintings he loved. Sandy and I were believed by my mother to derive our artistic proclivities through the genetic strain that had determined my Uncle Mickey's lonely career, and for all I know she was right. A woman of deep domestic expertise and benign unworldliness, reassuringly confident right up to the outermost boundaries of our social world though progressively, if respectably, uncertain anywhere beyond it, my mother was unambiguously proud of my first published stories. She had no idea that there could be anything seriously offensive about them and, when she came upon articles in the Jewish press intimating that I was a traitor, couldn't understand what my detractors were talking about. When she was once in doubt—having been shaken by a derogatory remark she'd overheard at a Hadassah meeting—she asked me if it could possibly be true that I was anti-Semitic, and when I smiled and shook my head no, she was entirely satisfied.

The issues of *Commentary* and the *Paris Review* that I'd sent in the mail or brought over with me to Elizabeth when I visited —containing my stories "Epstein," "Conversion of the Jews," and "You Can't Tell a Man by the Song He Sings"—my mother displayed, between bookends, on a side table in the living room. My father, who mainly read newspapers, was more aggressively exhibitionistic about my published works, showing the strange magazines to anyone who came to visit and even reading aloud to his friends lines in which he thought he recognized a detail of description, a name, a line of dialogue that I'd appropriated from a familiar source. After the publication of "Defender of the Faith," when I told him on the phone that the Anti-Defamation League of B'nai B'rith had requested I meet with their representatives to discuss the outcry over my story, he was incredulous. "What outcry? Everybody loved it. What is the outcry? I don't get it."

Perhaps if it had been somebody else's son against whom these accusations had been leveled by our Jewish betters, neither he nor my mother would have been quite so sure of the writer's probity, but for them to be wounded as Jews by *me*—whom they had seen circumcised and bar mitzvahed, whom they had sent for three years to one of our neighborhood's humble Hebrew schools, whose closest friends were all Jewish boys, who had always, unfailingly, been a source of pride—didn't occur to either of them and never would. My father could become as belligerent about the charges against my Jewish loyalty as he would be in later years when anyone dared to be dubious about a single aspect of Israeli policy.

I should add that not even he would have rushed to defend my achievements as a student of Judaism or my record of religious observance: at age thirteen I had not come away from three years of Hebrew School especially enlightened, nor had my sense of the sacred been much enriched. Though I hadn't been a total failure either, and had learned enough Hebrew to read at breakneck speed (if not with full comprehension) from the Torah at my bar mitzvah, the side of my Jewish education that had made that after-school hour, three days a week, at all endurable had largely to do with the hypnotic appeal, in those environs, of the unimpeachably profane. I am thinking of the witless persecution of poor Mr. Rosenblum, our refugee teacher, an escapee from Nazism, a man lucky (he had thought) just to be alive, whom the older boys more than once hung in effigy on the lamppost just outside the window where he was teaching our "four-to-five" class. I'm remembering the alarming decrepitude of the old-country *shammes*, our herring-eater, Mr. Fox, whom we drove crazy playing a kind of sidewalk handball called "Aces Up" against the rear wall of his synagogue—Mr. Fox, who used to raid the local candy store and pull teenagers at the pinball machine out by the neck in order to scare up enough souls for a *minyan*. And, of course, I'm remembering the mishap of a nine-year-old classmate, a boy of excruciating timidity, who on our very first day of Hebrew School in 1943—when the rabbi who was religious leader of the synagogue and director of the school began, a bit orotundly, to address us new students in our cubbyhole classroom directly upstairs from the Ark of the Covenant—involuntarily beshat himself, a pathetic disaster that struck the nervous class as blasphemously hilarious.

In those after-school hours at the dingy Hebrew School—when I would have given anything to have been outdoors playing ball until suppertime—I sensed underlying everything a turbulence that I didn't at all associate with the airy, orderly public school where I was a bright American boy from nine to three, a bubbling, energetic unruliness that conflicted head-on with all the exacting ritual laws that I was now being asked to obey devoutly. In the clash between the anguished solemnity communicated to us by the mysterious bee-buzz of synagogue prayer and the irreverence implicit in the spirit of animated mischievousness that manifested itself almost daily in the little upstairs classrooms of the *shul*, I recognized something far more "Jewish" than I ever did in the never-neverland stories of Jewish tents in Jewish deserts inhabited by Jews conspicuously lacking local last names like Ginsky, Nusbaum, and Strulowitz. Despite everything that we Jews couldn't eat—except at the Chinese restaurant, where the pork came stowed away in the egg roll, and at the Jersey shore, where the clams skulked unseen in the depths of the chowder—despite all our taboos and prohibitions and our vaunted self-denial, a nervous force-fulness decidedly *irrepressible* pulsated through our daily life, converting even the agonizing annoyance of having to go to Hebrew School, when you could have been "up the field" playing left end or first base, into unpredictably paradoxical theater.

What I still can recall from my Hebrew School education is that whatever else it may have been for my generation to grow up Jewish in America, it was usually entertaining. I don't think that an English Jewish child would necessarily have felt that way and, of course, for millions of Jewish children east of England, to grow up Jewish was tragic. And that we seemed to understand without even needing to be told.

Not only did growing up Jewish in Newark in the thirties and forties, Hebrew School and all, feel like a perfectly legitimate way of growing up American but, what's more, growing up Jewish as I did and growing up American seemed to me indistinguishable. Remember that in those days there was not a new Jewish country, a "homeland," to foster the range of attachments—the pride, the love, the anxiety, the chauvinism, the philanthropy, the chagrin, the shame—that have, for many American Jews now over forty, complicated anew the issue of Jewish self-definition. Nor was there quite the nostalgia for the old Jewish country that Broadway later began to merchandise with the sentimentalizing of Sholom Aleichem. We knew very well that our grandparents had not torn themselves away from their shtetl families, had not left behind parents whom they would never see again, because back home everybody had gone around the village singing show tunes that brought tears to your eyes. They'd left because life was awful; so awful, in fact, so menacing or impoverished or hopelessly obstructed, that it was best forgotten. The willful amnesia that I generally came up against whenever I tried as a child to establish the details of our pre-American existence was not unique to our family.

I would think that much of the exuberance with which I and others of my generation of Jewish children seized our opportunities after the war—that wonderful feeling that one was entitled to no less than anyone else, that one could do anything and could be excluded from nothing—came from our belief in the boundlessness of the democracy in which we lived and to which we belonged. It's hard to imagine that anyone of intelligence growing up in America since the Vietnam War can have had our unambiguous sense, as young adolescents immediately after the victory over Nazi fascism and Japanese militarism, of belonging to the greatest nation on earth.

At my lunch meeting about "Defender of the Faith" with two representatives from the Anti-Defamation League, I said that being interviewed by them as an alleged purveyor of material harmful and defamatory to the Jews was particularly disorienting since, as a high school senior thinking about studying law, I had sometimes imagined working on their staff, defending the civil and legal rights of Jews. In response, there was neither chastisement nor accusation and nothing resembling a warning about what I should write or where I should publish. They told me that they had wanted to meet me only to let me know about the complaints they had received and to answer any questions *I* might have. I figured, however, that a part of their mission was also to see whether I was a nut, and in the atmosphere of easygoing civility that had been established among us over lunch, I said as much, and we all laughed. I asked who exactly they thought the people were who'd called in and written, and the three of us speculated as to what in the story had been most provocative and why. We parted as amicably as we'd met, and I only heard from the ADL again a couple of years later, when I was invited by their Chicago branch to participate in an interfaith symposium, cosponsored by Loyola University, on the "image" of Catholics and Jews in American literature.

After *Goodbye, Columbus* won the 1960 National Book Award for Fiction and the Daroff Award of the Jewish Book Council of America, I was asked to speak on similar themes before college Hillel groups, Jewish community centers, and temples all over the country. (I was on a Guggenheim in Rome in 1960 and unable to be present for the Daroff Award ceremony in New York. My strongest supporter on the prize jury, the late critic and teacher David Boroff, confirmed the report I got from my friend Bob Silvers—who had been there to accept the award on my behalf—which was that my book had been an unpopular choice, with the sponsors as well as with many gathered together for the ceremony; the year before, another set of judges had given the prize to Leon Uris for *Exodus*.) When I could get away from university teaching, I took up these invitations and appeared before Jewish audiences to talk and to answer questions. The audiences were respectfully polite, if at times aloof, and the hostile members generally held their fire until the question period had begun. I was up to the give-and-take of these exchanges, though I never looked forward to them. I'd had no intention as a writer of coming to be known as "controversial" and, in the beginning, had no idea that my stories would prove repugnant to ordinary Jews. I had thought of myself as something of an authority on ordinary Jewish life, with its penchant for self-satire and hyperbolic comedy, and for a long time continued to be as bemused privately as I was unyielding publicly when confronted by Jewish challengers.

In 1962, I accepted an invitation to appear on a panel at Yeshiva University in New York. I felt it a duty to respond to the pronounced Jewish interest my book continued to evoke and I particularly didn't want to shy away from such an obvious Jewish stronghold; as one of the panel participants would be Ralph Ellison, I was also flattered to have been asked to speak from the same platform. The third panelist was Pietro di Donato, a relatively obscure writer since the success in the thirties of his proletariat novel *Christ in Concrete*.

From the start I was suspicious of the flat-out assertiveness of the Yeshiva symposium title—"The Crisis of Conscience in Minority Writers of Fiction"—and its presumption, as I interpreted it, that the chief cause of dissension over "minority" literature lay not in the social uncertainties of a minority audience but in a profound disturbance in the moral faculties of minority writers. Though I had no real understanding of seriously observant Jews—a group nearly as foreign to me as the devoutest Catholics—I knew enough not to expect such people, who would comprise most of the Yeshiva faculty and student body, to be supporters of my cause. But since the discussion would be held in a university auditorium—and I was very much at home in such places—and inasmuch as I had been invited not to address a narrowly Jewish subject on my own but to investigate the general situation of the minority writer in America with an Italian-American writer whom I was curious to meet and a highly esteemed black writer of whom I was in awe, I didn't foresee just how demoralizing the confrontation could be.

I came East from Iowa with Josie, and on the evening of the symposium the two of us took a taxi out to Yeshiva with my new Random House editor, Joe Fox, who was eager to hear the discussion. Random House was publishing *Letting Go*, my second book, later in the year, but as *Goodbye, Columbus* had been published by Houghton Mifflin, Joe had had no direct involvement with those inflammatory stories and, as a gentile, was removed from the controversy and perplexed by its origins. Josie was, of course, gentile also, but after our marriage, on her own steam—and against my better judgment, not to mention my secular convictions—she had taken religious instruction from Rabbi Jack Cohen at the Reconstructionist Synagogue in Manhattan and been converted by him to Judaism. We were first married in a civil ceremony—with only two friends for witnesses—by a justice of the peace in Yonkers; several months later Jack Cohen married us again, at his synagogue, in a religious ceremony attended by my parents. The second ceremony struck me—and perhaps struck my parents, who were too bewildered, however, to be anything but polite—as not only unnecessary but, in the circumstances, vulgar and ludicrous. I participated so that her pointless conversion might at least appear to have some utilitarian value, though my consent didn't mean that it wasn't distressingly clear to me that this was one more misguided attempt to manufacture a marital bond where the mismatch was blatant and already catastrophic. To me, being a Jew had to do with a real historical predicament into which you were born and not with some identity you chose to don after reading a dozen books. I could as easily have turned into a subject of the Crown by presenting my master's degree in English literature to Winston Churchill as my new wife could become a Jew by studying with Jack Cohen, sensible and dedicated as he was, for the rest of her life.

I saw in her desire to be some sort of simulated Jew yet another distressing collapse of integrity; something very like the self-hatred with which I had been stigmatized seemed to impel her drive to camouflage the markings of her own small-town, Middle Western past by falsifying again her affiliation with me and my background. I introduce this story not so as to have one more go at Josie but to reveal a bizarre irony of which I was not unconscious while the spanking-new Jew of unmistakable Nordic appearance sat in the Yeshiva audience looking on at the "excommunication" of the Semitic-featured young writer whose seventeen years as his parents' child in the Weequahic neighborhood couldn't have left him more inextinguishably Jewish.

The trial (in every sense) began after di Donato, Ellison, and I had each delivered twenty-minute introductory statements. Ellison rambled on easily and intelligently from a few notes, di Donato winged it not very logically, and I read from some prepared pages, thus allowing me to speak confidently while guarding, I thought, against an interrogator's altering the context in which my argument was being made; I was determined to take every precaution against being misunderstood. When the moderator began the second stage of the symposium by questioning us about our opening statements, the only panelist he seemed truly interested in was me. His first question, following di Donato's monologue—which would have seemed, had I been moderating, to require rigorous clarification—was this: "Mr. Roth, would you write the same stories you've written if you were living in Nazi Germany?"—a question that was to turn up some twenty years later in *The Ghost Writer*, asked of Nathan Zuckerman by Judge Leopold Wapter.

Thirty minutes later, I was still being grilled. No response I gave was satisfactory and, when the audience was allowed to take up the challenge, I realized that I was not just opposed but hated. I've never forgotten my addled reaction: an undertow of bodily fatigue took hold and began sweeping me away from that auditorium even as I tried to reply coherently to one denunciation after another (for we had by then proceeded beyond interrogation to anathema). My combative instinct, which was not undeveloped, simply withered away and I had actually to suppress a desire to close my eyes and, in my chair at the panelists' table, with an open microphone only inches from my perspiring face, drift into unconsciousness. Ralph Ellison must have noticed my tenacity fading because all at once I heard him defending me with an eloquent authority that I could never have hoped to muster from halfway out to oblivion. His intellectual position was virtually identical to mine, but he was presenting it as a black American, instructing through examples drawn from *Invisible Man* and the ambiguous relationship that novel had established with some vocal members of his own race. His remarks seemed to appear to the audience far more creditable than mine or perhaps situated the audience so far from its real mission as to deflate or deflect the inquisitorial pressure that I had envisioned mounting toward a finale that would find me either stoned to death or fast asleep.

With me relegated pretty much to the sidelines, the evening shortly came to an end. From the moderator there were genial good wishes for the panelists, from the spectators there was some scattered applause, and then we all started down off the stage by the side stairs leading into the house. I was immediately surrounded by the element in the audience most antagonistic to my work, whom Ellison's intercession had clearly curtailed only temporarily. The climax of the tribunal was upon me, and though I was now wide awake, I still couldn't extricate myself that easily from their midst. Standing in the well between the hall and the stage, with Joe and Josie visible beyond the faces of my jury—though in no conceivable way my Jewry—I listened to the final verdict against me, as harsh a judgment as I ever hope to hear in this or any other world. I only began to shout "Clear away, step back—I'm getting out of here" after somebody, shaking a fist in my face, began to holler, "You were brought up on anti-Semitic literature!" "Yes," I hollered back, "and what is that?"—curious really to know what he meant. "English literature!" he cried. "English literature is anti-Semitic literature!"

In midtown Manhattan later, Josie, Joe, and I went to have something to eat at the Stage Delicatessen, down the street from the hotel where we were staying. I was angry at what I had stupidly let myself in for, I was wretchedly ashamed of my performance, and I was infuriated still by the accusations from the floor. Over my pastrami sandwich no less, I said, "I'll never write about Jews again." Equally ridiculously, I thought that I meant it, or at least that I should. I couldn't see then, fresh from the event, that the most bruising public exchange of my life constituted not the end of my imagination's involvement with the Jews, let alone an excommunication, but the real beginning of my thralldom. I had assumed—mostly from the evidence of *Letting Go*—that I had passed beyond the concerns of my collection of apprentice stories and the subjects that had fallen so naturally to me as a beginning writer. *Letting Go*, about the unanticipated responsibilities of young adulthood far from Jewish New Jersey, seemed to foreshadow the direction in which new preoccupations would now guide me. But the Yeshiva battle, instead of putting me off Jewish fictional subjects for good, demonstrated as nothing had before the full force of aggressive rage that made the issue of Jewish self-definition and Jewish allegiance so inflammatory. This group whose embrace once had offered me so much security was itself fanatically insecure. How could I conclude otherwise when I was told that every word I wrote was a disgrace, potentially endangering every Jew? Fanatical security, fanatical insecurity—nothing in my entire background could exemplify better than that night did how deeply rooted the Jewish drama was in this duality.

After an experience like mine at Yeshiva, a writer would have had to be no writer at all to go looking elsewhere for something to write about. My humiliation before the Yeshiva belligerents —indeed, the angry Jewish resistance that I aroused virtually from the start—was the luckiest break I could have had. I was branded.

Now Vee May Perhaps to Begin

THE summer house that May Aldridge and I rented was on
a quiet blacktop road in the center of Martha's Vineyard,
a few minutes' walk from the general store in West Tisbury. It
was a small, undistinguished house, comfortable enough,
though with the exception of the double bed furnished almost
exclusively with faded old beach chairs. The windows were
bare when we moved up from New York in late June of 1967,
and May drove to the cut-rate store in Vineyard Haven and
bought fabric to make curtains. An independent woman of
thirty-four whose substantial income derived from a family
trust fund, she really didn't have to sit down and sew curtains
together out of inexpensive yard goods in order to make ends
meet; but at the time I was hardly rich, and we were sharing
the house on the assumption that we'd live in it as though we
were two people with the same modest means. May managed
this simply enough, not only because of her accommodating
character (or because we were in love), but because the challenge of her adult life had been to loosen the inhibiting bond
between herself and the manner to which she'd been born, in
which she was rooted, and by which she'd been left distressingly
vulnerable, with too little confidence in her good, clear mind,
and unable to animate in a sustained way the passionately felt
side of an obliging nature.

May was a gentile woman at the other end of the American
spectrum from Josie. She had been sent off to the best schools
by an old-line Cleveland paint-manufacturing family that had
achieved enormous financial success, as well as the civic distinction and social prominence that once came automatically
to American industrial clans of British stock. Fair and green-
eyed and slender, she was the loveliest-looking woman I'd ever
known, her beauty as delicate as Josie's attractiveness, when
we'd first met, was stolidly earthbound. It was an appearance
as indelibly stamped by privilege as Josie's had been by her provincial small town. The two women were drastically different
physical types from social backgrounds that couldn't have been
much more dissimilar and, as women, so unlike as to seem like

representatives of divergent genders. In each, inborn character proclivities appeared to have been carried to a stereotypical extreme by something innately disabling in their social origins, so that where Josie, the daughter of a working-class loser, was blunt, scrappy, dissatisfied, envious, resentful, and schemingly opportunistic, May for many years had camouflaged her uncertainties behind a finishing-school facade of nearly self-suffocating decorum. What they shared were the scars of wounds inflicted by the social mentality governing their up-bringing; what had drawn me to them (and, more than likely, them to me) was not that they were members in good standing of their respective bloodlines, solidly entrenched in the world of their fathers, but that they were intriguingly estranged from the very strata of American society of which they were each such distinctively emblazoned offspring.

During our five years together, May never once suggested that we go out to Cleveland to meet her family, and when her mother visited her every few months in New York, instead of following our usual routine of my joining May for the evening and sleeping overnight at her East Seventy-eighth Street apart-ment, I would stay at my own place in Kips Bay, which I'd come to use—on the days when I wasn't away teaching uni-versity classes in Philadelphia or Stony Brook—as little more than a writing studio. Of course we understood that it wasn't just our unmarried state but also my being a Jew that had some-thing to do with why meeting her parents was probably just as well avoided. Neither of us expected anything horrendous to result from the encounter—we simply didn't see any reason, so long as we *were* single, to create unnecessary tensions with a family living hundreds of miles away, who themselves seemed more than willing to steer clear of their daughter's intimate life. My curiosity about May's Cleveland background couldn't begin to match my desire to keep the affair from becoming en-tangled with family concerns; I'd had enough of that.

I did invite my own parents over from New Jersey one evening to have a drink at May's apartment and to go out with us for dinner. I wanted them to witness how, with May, my life had been restored and simplified; though they'd never known exactly how lurid my marriage had been, they'd had plenty of intimations, had seen the toll it had taken on me, and, as a result, had suffered terribly. My mother, who was so reassured by good manners and herself socially so proper, found May's graciousness tremendously appealing and would have been only too happy if, on the spot, May could have magically replaced Josie, to whom it seemed I'd been eternally bonded by the State of New York. Though my father also happened to like May, I think he would have been relieved had I taken up with a kangaroo. After my separation from Josie in 1962, she had traveled down to his office in south Jersey and, in lieu of the alimony payments that she claimed I was failing to make, demanded money from him. When my father told her, correctly, that I *was* meeting my legal obligations, she berated *him* for *his* irresponsibility.

May's uptown apartment was large and comfortably furnished without being studiously decorated or at all pretentious; that her possessions, however, reflected so clearly the traditional tastes of her class suggested that she'd always remain interlinked with her origins in a thousand telling ways, regardless of how willingly she allied herself with the social style of my New York friends, most of whom were Jews from backgrounds not unlike my own. As for her friends—people she'd known for years and had sometimes helped with their interior decorating —after a few nights out with them, I had had to tell her that, affable as it all was, those evenings weren't for me. It turned out that she was herself a little weary of them too, and one day, after lots of encouragement from me, she decided to quit decorating and redecorating those Upper East Side apartments and enrolled at Hunter to finish her undergraduate education; it had been interrupted in 1952, when she'd suffered an emotional crisis at Smith and, at twenty, had returned home to Cleveland to take up, unhappily, a protected, innocuous postdebutante life. Much as I wanted to help her get herself going as a new woman, I had no desire for her to ape Josie and renounce what she was or cut the ties to where she was from, however unwelcome or uneasy I might have found myself there, and especially as what still interested us both lay precisely in the *unlikeliness* of our connection.

Though slow to develop because of the sexual wariness that each of us had developed late in our twenties, our earnest physical fervor became in time a source of almost mystifying comfort and happiness. In May's nudity there was something at once furtive and shy that aroused a kind of tender hunger that I couldn't remember having felt for years. Hers was the body of a sweet-tempered woman who, in her remotest dreams, could never have feigned pregnancy or intentionally allowed herself to become impregnated in order to foster a scenario to which she was pathologically addicted: to make of herself the helpless female victim and of the man the heartless victimizer. There was no strategy in May's desire; had there been, she wouldn't have been quite so outfoxed, as she was in college and again later when she came from Cleveland to live alone in New York, by the wily exploiters of trusting girls. For me, the guilelessness that could be construed in the lines of her body as easily as in her gaze seemed to offer a powerful assurance of integrity, and it was from this that my frazzled virility took heart and my regeneration began.

May and I had come to rent houses on Martha's Vineyard two summers running because of my friendship with Robert Brustein, who was then teaching drama at Columbia and writing theater reviews for the *New Republic*. Bob and his wife, Norma, lived during the year in a big apartment on the Upper East Side of Manhattan, where I'd often gone for dinner when I was new to New York and on my own. It was at the Brusteins' dinner table that I began to find an appreciative audience for a kind of noisy comedy, and the sort of Jewish subject, that wasn't like anything in *When She Was Good*, the book I was writing about Lucy Nelson of Liberty Center, U.S.A. The spirit of my next book, *Portnoy's Complaint*, began to materialize as entertainment for Bob and Norma and for the friends of theirs who became my friends, city Jews of my generation, analysands with deep parental attachments, respectable professionals unimpeded by the gentility principle and with a well-developed taste for farcical improvisation, particularly for recycling into boisterous comic mythology the communal values by which our irreducible Jewishness had been shaped. It was an audience I'd lost touch with since I'd left Chicago and begun married life with Josie in Rome, London, Iowa City, and Princeton—an audience knowledgeable enough to discern, even in the minutest detail, where reportage ended and

Dada began and to enjoy the ambiguous overlap. Unembarrassed by unrefined Jewish origins, matter-of-factly confident of equal American status, they felt American *through* their families' immigrant experiences rather than in spite of them and delighted in the shameless airing of extravagant routines concocted from the life we had all grown up with.

Far from causing us to feel at the periphery of American society, the origins that had so strongly marked our style of self-expression seemed to have placed us at the heart of the city's abrasive, hypercritical, potentially explosive cultural atmosphere as it was evolving out of the angry response to the Vietnam War. Lyndon Johnson, betraying every foreign-policy position by which he'd been sharply distinguished from Barry Goldwater in the 1964 election campaign, had, in only two years, made himself the natural target for a brand of contempt that had never, in my lifetime, been vented with such vehement imagination and on such a scale against a figure of such great authority. His own outsized personality seemed, paradoxically, to be the fountainhead for that steamrolling defiance that his politics would come to generate in many of those repelled by the war. There was something boisterous and unconstrainable in him, the potential in his very physique for a kind of mastodon rage, that made him the inspirational impresario as much for the ugly extremes of theatrical combat dividing the society as for the Southeast Asia conflict. To me it always seemed that his was the hateful, looming, uncontrollable presence that, at least initially, had activated the fantastical style of obscene satire that began to challenge virtually every hallowed rule of social propriety in the middle and late sixties.

What I found, then, in New York, after leaving my wife and moving up from Princeton—where, for as long as I remained on the university faculty, Josie continued to make her home—were the ingredients that inspired *Portnoy's Complaint*, whose publication in 1969 determined every important choice I made during the next decade. There was this audience of sympathetic Jewish friends who responded with euphoric recognition to my dinner-table narratives; there was my intense psychoanalysis, which, undertaken to stitch back together the confidence shredded to bits in my marriage, itself became a model for reckless narrative disclosure of a kind I hadn't learned from Henry

James; there was May, a trustworthy, exceedingly tender woman in dire need herself of affectionate attention, with whom a mutual convalescence, grounded in demidomesticity, proceeded at a steady, invigorating pace; and there was May's unequivocal gentleness, bestowed by her upbringing and revealed by genetic markings that made her as unimpeachably Aryan as I was Jewish, and that it wouldn't have entered her mind to attempt, like Josie, to disguise or renounce. There was, in other words, a pervasive anthropological dimension to our love affair that delineated just the sort of tribal difference that would empower Portnoy's manic self-presentation.

Lastly, there was the ferocity of the rebellious rhetoric unleashed against the president and his war, the assault that Johnson's own seething cornball bravado inspired and from which even he, with his rich and randy vein of linguistic contempt, had eventually to flee in defeat, as though before a deluge of verbal napalm. It bedazzled me, this enraged invective so potent as to wound to the quick a colossus like Lyndon Johnson, especially after my long, unnatural interlude of personal and literary self-subjugation.

I was thirty-four in the autumn following that second, splendidly healing Vineyard summer with May and so never quite grasped how close to death I had come, not even when, having begun to feel some strength returning, I asked the surgeon how much more of the fall I was going to miss, cooped up in the hospital. He answered, with a bemused smile, "Don't you get it *yet*? You almost missed everything." I heard his words, I never got his words, and yet the experience registered not as my having nearly died but instead as my having met with death and overcome it. I felt as though now I needn't worry about dying for another thousand years.

Amazingly, I didn't see my burst appendix as Josie's handiwork, probably because the poisons of peritonitis spread through my system without her accompanying barrage of moral indictment. It was a separate ordeal entirely, the denouement of a decade that had posed somewhat preposterous tests of strength, but arising clearly out of a family predisposition toward which it was a relief not to feel a personal antagonism. What had killed two of my uncles, and very nearly, in 1944,

killed my father, had tried and failed to kill me. This was the
sort of ordeal whose lucky outcome heightens tremendously
your respect for the place of chance in an individual destiny;
once the cozy part of the convalescence begins, you float
buoyantly off on feelings of sentimental kinship with virtually
everyone else fortunate enough to have been left living. My life
with Josie, by contrast, had isolated me as a case, bizarrely cut
off in a bad marriage that wasn't merely bad in its own way but
included among its hazards the oft-repeated threat of murder.
I felt strong and lucky, like a human being among human
beings, for having survived peritonitis; I would never know
what to make of myself for having endured and survived my
wife, though not for lack of thinking about it. For years afterward I was to think and brood and fictionalize obsessively about
how I had made Josie happen to me. And it's become apparent, while writing this, that I'm all too capable of thinking about
it still.

Every evening at dinnertime May came to the hospital to see
me; during the day she had her Hunter classes and also worked
part-time as a draft counselor with a Quaker group in Murray
Hill, advising draft-age young men about the alternatives to
military service. The job was hardly congenial to her temperament, but the war had mobilized her indignation in an unforeseen way. She was not the only American discovering in herself
the power to oppose; however, as someone for whom taking the
public steps that counted one among the opposition did not
come easily, she wasn't overjoyed by what conviction sometimes demanded of her, such as having to phone the Cleveland
banker who oversaw her trust fund and requesting of that ul-
traconservative gentleman and family friend that her portfolio
be divested of "war stocks" like Dow Chemical. It was irresistible, of course, for her old Manhattan friends to see in this
transformation of a polite, retiring society heiress nothing more
"political" than the overbearing influence of me and *my* friends.
And it's true that on her own, in her old world, May Aldridge
might not have turned spontaneously into a dedicated antiwar
worker; nonetheless, it wasn't really any position of mine that
influenced her so much as the confidence inspired by the affair
itself, generating in her a belief that she (who had been stuck
so long in what had felt like an unalterable existence gathering

swatches for other people's upholstery) could hope to help change, right along with her own fate, the American war policy. Because she was being stirred into action on virtually every front, the last traces of self-protective meekness largely disappeared, and something touchingly animated and akin to the furtiveness that I found so stirring in her nudity turned her characteristic placidity into genuine composure, with a power and effectiveness of its own.

A month after my emergency appendectomy I was released from the hospital and then, two weeks later, unexpectedly readmitted, this time for the removal of the stump of the blown appendix, which had failed to atrophy and had become infected. It was to be another thirty days before I came out for good, as thin as I'd been as a junior in high school but healthy at last. With May I went down to a tiny island off the west coast of Florida to recuperate for a couple of weeks. We stopped off to have lunch in Miami Beach, where my parents were wintering in an apartment they'd taken in the same complex as some of their old Newark friends, and then in a rented car we drove across to Fort Myers and out over the causeway to Captiva. There wasn't much to do there: we strolled the beaches with the elderly people who were out collecting shells, there were pelicans to watch, dolphins swam by, and a couple of mornings we went to the bird sanctuary with our lunch and followed the cormorants with field glasses. I was bored and edgy a lot of the time, impatient now with the enforced idleness of an extended bout of ill health and eager to get back to writing. A new book was well under way, and I was afraid of losing the galloping pace that had got me going. A section entitled "Whacking Off" had appeared in *Partisan Review*; Ted Solotaroff, who'd just begun *New American Review*, had featured another section in his first issue and wanted to publish more; and my Random House editors, Joe Fox and Jason Epstein, had read a rough first draft and told me I was on to something. I wanted to get back to work, Ted wanted me to get back to work, Jason and Joe wanted me to get back to work, but probably nobody wanted me to get back and finish what I'd begun quite as much as Josie: the rumor in New York publishing circles—and Josie was working finally at a publishing job—was that my new novel, if it was anything like what

Solotaroff, Epstein, and Fox were saying, would command a large advance.

By the time I'd fallen ill in the autumn of 1967, the worst of my separation seemed to be over. It was five years since I'd left Josie, and though she still refused to divorce me and planned to take me back to court in the new year to try for a second time to get the alimony of $125 a week increased, I had not seen her outside a courtroom, and it was a long while since she'd telephoned during the day to tell me how wicked I was or in the middle of the night, generally after too much drink, to announce, "You're in bed with some Negress!" When I moved from Princeton to Manhattan, after finally leaving her in the last weeks of 1962, she followed suit some eight months later; she hoped to resume the plan interrupted by our marriage —to work in publishing—while simultaneously she wanted me to support her, a goal best pursued in the state where I was domiciled and where antiquated divorce laws made it likely that, if she continued to prefer it that way, I would legally remain her husband forever.

She could also better keep track of my whereabouts in New York than she could back in Chicago, close to where her two children were now in boarding schools, supported by the aunt and uncle of her first husband. For instance, one night when Helen, her twelve-year-old daughter, came East during a vacation to visit her mother, I arranged to take the girl to dinner and to the theater. While we waited in our seats for the play to begin, I was served from the aisle with a subpoena. I immediately recognized the polite gentleman who was serving me; previously he had served me politely while I was at the dentist's. Pretending to Helen that the envelope I'd been handed was something that I was expecting to be delivered at the theater, I thanked him and slipped it into my jacket pocket. During the intermission, while Helen was in the lobby having an orange drink, I went to the men's room, where, in a stall, I opened the envelope and read the subpoena. I could barely contain my fury. The subpoena, summoning me to court to face another alimony challenge, could have been served on me in my apartment any day of the week: I had a university teaching job and, after months in a New York sublet, I clearly wasn't about to skip town. Nonetheless, Josie had arranged to have me served while I was out entertaining Helen, as though her daughter hadn't been sufficiently scarred by all the sexual battling she'd seen and as though my own capacity to show the child a good time might not be strained by an unanticipated announcement of yet another resumption of our conflict.

During the year that Helen had lived with us in Iowa City, where I was teaching in the Writers' Workshop of the state university, I'd served as a surrogate father. Helen was alarmingly needy but also very engaging, and taking serious parental responsibility for her wasn't simply a burden. Her pathetic difficulties with her studies required lots of attention, but she was a little girl quick to smile and genial with our best friends, and it could be fun to take her to the Iowa football games or to ice skate with her on the river or, with her help, to rake the leaves from the lawn in the fall. Josie was pleased when Helen and I began to grow close, but as the months went by and family life became routinized, there were also astonishing outbursts to throw a lurid shadow over this too. A sudden tirade about the probity of men would end with a warning that if ever I laid a finger on her ten-year-old daughter she would drive a knife into my heart. One evening, following a bedroom argument culminating in just such a threat, I waited until everyone had fallen asleep and then rounded up all the kitchen knives and locked them in the trunk of the car. Early the next morning, when Helen was alone in the kitchen making herself some breakfast, I came down in my robe to find her looking mightily perturbed. "What's the matter?" I asked her. "It's getting to be late for school! I have to cut my grapefruit and I can't find a knife!" I went out to the garage and got her one.

By 1967, then, I was still saddled with alimony amounting to about half my income; my lawyer led me to understand that the alimony could be expected to increase proportionally with any substantial increase in my income and that I would be paying it for the rest of my life, unless Josie one day remarried. To me the alimony was court-ordered robbery and never more galling to pay than when I remembered, while making out the check, how the brief marriage had come to be in the first place. That was a story I couldn't forget. I couldn't forget it because I was the fall guy but also because the urine story was one of

the best stories I'd ever heard. Had I been a dermatologist or
an engineer or a shoemaker, after five years there might have
been little more than the alimony left to dwell on; but what
obsessed me no less than what was being taken from me was
the story that she'd bestowed on me—for a man in my business it was too good to give up.

Actually, *When She Was Good* was intended to have provided
me with a setting for that urine story, but after several frag-
mentary, unsatisfactory drafts, it veered away from this purpose
and ended up as an imaginary elaboration, at once freely invented and yet close to the spirit—and even to the pattern of
events—of the legend of her upbringing, her adolescence, and
her first marriage as it had been narrated to me over the kitchen
table throughout our early months as lovers in Chicago.

Between 1959 and 1962, during several week-long visits to
her home in Port Safehold, a small Michigan resort town on
the eastern shore of the lake, I'd got to know some of the main
characters in Josie's tale. Port Safehold could have been Bom-
bay, so strong was its hold on me—and this, long before I
thought that an environment like it could ever provide the
backdrop for a story of mine; what made me so curious was
that it was the backdrop for the grim saga of gentile family suffering that was hers. I was a guest of her maternal grandfather,
Merle Hebert—known to relatives as Daddy Merle—in the
very room where Josie had grown up after her family, whom
her father could never really support, had moved in with the
Heberts. Sitting out on the front porch with Daddy Merle after
supper, I'd get him to talking about the old days and, though
he was a gentle, decorous fellow, a retired carpenter and simple
small-towner claiming proudly to bear no one a grudge, when
I asked about Smoky Jensen he had to admit that his son-in-
law had been something of a disappointment. Josie's mother
was living then in a little apartment near the commercial cross-
roads of the town, not far from the local newspaper where she
worked as the advertising manager. She seemed more worldly
and self-sufficient than the woman Josie had described to me
as her father's defenseless victim, and we quickly developed a
friendship. When I came to write *When She Was Good*, however, I discounted my observations and, following Josie's
narrative lead—which she'd instinctively decided was more

damning all around and which certainly made everything harsher and dramatically more vivid—I imagined, as the affronted young heroine's mother, a childish, daughterly woman totally *un*defended against her irresponsible husband.

Eventually the book became for me a time machine through which to look backward and discover the origins of that deranged hypermorality to whose demands I had proved so hopelessly accessible in my early twenties. I was trying to come to some understanding of this destructive force, but separate from my own ordeal, to exorcise her power over me by taking it back to its local origins and tracing in detail the formative history of injury and disappointment right on down to its grisly consequences—again, not as they'd erupted in the context of our marriage (I was fighting too hard to be free of our marriage to spare the energy for that) but as they might have evolved had she been, instead of a Josie who'd escaped her past at least geographically and had wound up a working woman in Hyde Park, a Lucy imprisoned in the enraging, emotionally overcharged hometown with its full roster, for her, of betrayers, cowards, and vicious enemies. I was ridding myself in *When She Was Good* of the narrative spell that her legend had so successfully cast over my will, a purgation achieved by taking the victim's gruesome story as gospel, but then enlarging it with a hard-won, belated understanding of the inner deformation suffered by the victim herself—perhaps suffered even more grotesquely than anything else and ending inescapably in her self-destruction.

Lucy's hideous death at the end of *When She Was Good* was neither wishful thinking nor authorial retribution. I simply didn't see how the disintegration of someone so relentlessly exercised over the most fundamental human claims, so enemy-ridden and unforgivingly defiant, could lead, in that little town, to anything other than the madhouse or the grave.

In April 1968 I was virtually the only customer eating an early dinner at Ballato's Restaurant on Houston Street when the news came over the radio that Martin Luther King had been shot. The owner, my friend the late John Ballato, a courtly gentleman, Sicilian-born and at one time a syndicalist in New York's Little Italy, brought his fist down violently on the table where we had been sitting and talking together. "Those sons of bitches!" John said angrily, his eyes filling with tears. "Those dogs!" I went to the phone and called May, who was working late at the Quaker Center. We agreed to meet back at her apartment, where we later sat up on the bed together and watched again and again the TV footage from Memphis, which never stopped being terrible or true no matter how many times it was played. I phoned friends. I phoned my father. "Newark's going to go up," he said, "you'll see." He said it several times and of course he was right. Watching the television clips of King's great public moments, May sporadically began to cry. I didn't—for all his force, King, whom I had never met, had always struck me as personally remote, almost featureless, his moral self-conception on the scale of a mountain rather than of a man, and so what his death provoked in me wasn't tears of pity and grief but a sense of foreboding and fear: an unspeakable crime was going to cause unimaginable social disaster.

When Bobby Kennedy was assassinated a few months later, May and I were up watching the aftermath of the California primary and so learned he'd been shot only seconds after it happened. I had signed ads in behalf of Eugene McCarthy's candidacy for the Democratic presidential nomination and been to a few meetings and gatherings backing his candidacy, but the previous summer May and I had nonetheless enjoyed enormously a dinner with Kennedy on Martha's Vineyard, at the house of his speechwriter, Dick Goodwin, who'd become a Vineyard acquaintance. Kennedy was crackling that evening with energy and charm, perhaps having the best time of the ten of us at the table. He was clearly getting a kick out of flirtatiously quizzing May, who was seated beside him, about her Cleveland society background; at the close of the dinner, he said to her in a voice deliberately loud enough for me to overhear, "And is Mr. Roth going to marry you?" May smiled and said, "That remains to be seen." "Mr. Roth," he said, flashing at me that smile of his as distinctive as Franklin Roosevelt's and weighted with a similar bravado, "do you intend to marry this woman?" "It depends, Senator, if I can ever get a divorce in your state from the wife I'm already married to." "And," Kennedy replied, "you'd like me to look into that—is that it?" "I wouldn't say no. I don't have to tell you I could make it worth your while." Whereupon Senator Kennedy, happily puffing on his cigar, turned to one of his legislative aides and told him to find out about getting a divorce for Mr. Roth so that he could marry Miss Aldridge as soon as possible.

He was by no means a political figure constructed on anything other than the human scale, and so, the night of his assassination and for days afterward, one felt witness to the violent cutting down not of a monumental force for justice and social change like King or the powerful embodiment of a people's massive misfortunes or a titan of religious potency but rather of a rival—of a vital, imperfect, high-strung, egotistical, rivalrous, talented brother, who could be just as nasty as he was decent. The murder of a boyish politician of forty-two, a man so nakedly ambitious and virile, was a crime against ordinary human hope as well as against the claims of robust, independent appetite and, coming after the murders of President Kennedy at forty-six and Martin Luther King at thirty-nine, evoked the simplest, most familiar forms of despair.

Between the assassinations of Martin Luther King and Bobby Kennedy, Josie too was violently killed. Death came instantly, in the early hours of a May morning, when the car in which she was being driven across Central Park left the road and struck a tree, a lamppost, or a concrete abutment—nobody who spoke to me seemed to know precisely how or where the collision took place. The driver was an editor who had been Josie's boss at her publishing job until, as I was led to understand, he had recently fired her. The fact that he was black made me remember those accusing calls I would get from her in the middle of the night, after I'd moved up from Princeton to a New York hotel, when she'd contend drunkenly that I was with a "Negress"—made me remember them without, however, leading me to understand her any better. I remembered that the pregnant woman from whom she'd bought the urine specimen was black as well—could she be the "Negress" Josie would imagine me with in my New York bed? Only the gods of Paranoia knew the answer to that.

The editor had escaped serious injury and appeared at the funeral wearing a small Band-Aid over one eye but still looking dazed and shaken. We merely shook hands when we were introduced; I figured it was best to display no curiosity about the car crash, since a number of Josie's mourners—members of her therapy group who knew the history of my sadism inside out—must already have been wondering if I hadn't somehow been an accomplice to it. Nor did the editor, either then or later, give any indication of wanting to talk to me about the circumstances of the accident. In fact, after shaking his hand at the funeral—and despite his having been cast as the instrument to tear asunder my eternal marriage and extinguish every last responsibility that she and the State of New York claimed to be mine—I never saw, or heard of, my emancipator again.

It would have been ridiculous for me to have thought that in *When She Was Good* I had divined Josie's death, which took place in entirely different circumstances from Lucy Nelson's and resulted from an accident in which her will did not figure, whereas Lucy's own enraged decision leads to her freezing to death in the snow. And yet, a year after the publication of *When She Was Good*, when I got the news that she was dead, I was transfixed at first by the uncanny overlapping of the book's ending with the actual event. I also found it hard to believe that Josie's will *hadn't* figured in the accident, probably because I had never forgotten how, in the midst of an argument en route from Italy to France in the late spring of 1960, she had furiously tried to take the wheel and kill us both while I was driving north through the mountains in our little Renault. However, if the real circumstances had indeed "validated" the fatal destiny of that personification of Josie's defiant extremism which I presented as Lucy Nelson, I would never know. And what difference would knowing have made anyway?

Josie's daughter had by this time left her Chicago-area boarding school and, at seventeen, come to live with Josie in New York, where she was attending a public high school and where, for *her* outspoken antiwar sentiments, she had come to be known, according to a friend of mine who lived on their street, as Hanoi Helen. It was she who called me at my apartment early on Saturday morning, as I was sitting down to work after returning from May's. Like Peter Tarnopol in an all but identical situation in *My Life as a Man*, I didn't believe her when she said that Josie was dead. I had already been deceived by my wife more than once, and though it was almost impossible to envision Helen—with whom my relationship was still affectionate, though now more avuncular than anxiously paternal—acting wittingly as Josie's coconspirator in a hoax so grotesque, my immediate response was total disbelief: it was a trick, I thought, to get me to say something self-incriminating that could be recorded and used to sway the judge to increase the alimony in our next court go-round. I also didn't believe then that miracles happen, that one's worst enemy, who one has hoped and prayed would disappear from one's life, could suddenly be eradicated in a car accident, and in, of all places, Central Park, where May and I, along with tens of thousands of others, were only recently demonstrators against the war and where the two of us took our long Sunday walks. All I had done the night before was to close my eyes and go to sleep, and now everything was over. Who could be naïve enough to buy that? It would have been only slightly more incredible (if aesthetically symmetrical) had I learned that she'd been bludgeoned to death in Tompkins Square Park on the very spot where the urine purchase had been negotiated nine years earlier.

I asked Helen to repeat for me slowly what she had just said. When she did—"Mother's dead"—I said skeptically, "And where is she now?" Her response was graphic enough to stun me out of my self-protecting incredulity. "In the morgue," she said, and began to cry. "You have to identify her, Philip—I can't!" Within minutes I was down at the apartment in the West Twenties, where Helen was being kept company by one of Josie's close friends. Scattered around the apartment, which, of course, I'd never seen before, were all sorts of familiar things that we had accumulated in our marriage, most of them inexpensive little art objects that we'd brought back from Italy after our year there on my Guggenheim. I couldn't take my eyes off the shelves of books—there had been a highly emotional dispute in front of the judge about whose books were whose, after which, in accord with his wisdom, the secondhand Modern Library novels that I'd purchased as a graduate student for twenty-five cents apiece were divided evenly between us. I'd forgotten about them (almost) until I recognized a couple of my books on her living-room shelves, and once again, despite the presence of Josie's friend and Helen's obvious distress, I felt as though some trick was being played, madly excessive, ghoulish perhaps, but in the face of which I had better watch

every word I said. I was in a state akin to shock and persisted in
believing that she wasn't dead at all, that, if anything, she was
kneeling behind the door to the next room, along with her
lawyer and maybe even the judge. *See how he's enjoying this,
Your Honor? It's just as we've told you—his heart is flint!*

How could she be dead if I didn't do it?

Helen asked again if I would go to the morgue. I said I
didn't see where it was my place to identify the body, there
were plenty of people to do that other than her or me; if she
wished, however, I would make the funeral arrangements. Only
a little later I was on my way to Frank Campbell's Funeral Chapel
on Madison and Eighty-first Street. In those days I didn't
casually ride taxis in New York and, in fact, was walking over to
catch a subway uptown when I realized that there was no need
to economize in quite the way I did only the day before, when
she and I were dividing my income. That was the first tangible
result of my no longer being married to her—I could take a
taxi to the funeral home to bury her.

The ride from the West Twenties on a Saturday morning
didn't take more than ten or so minutes. Outside Campbell's
door, when I went to pay the driver, he turned around and
smiled at me: "Got the good news early, huh?" I was flabbergasted by what he'd said and afterward could only conclude
that all the way up in the taxi I, the son of a family of irrepressible whistlers, must have been whistling away—how else
could he have known?

Helen had told me that Josie had instructed her that when
she died she wanted a Jewish funeral service, and so a Jewish
funeral service she got. There was a certain sweetness to be
found in sitting alongside the rabbi in the funeral director's
office, deciding on the appropriate psalms for him to read, especially as he turned out to be (for reasons no more fathom-
able than anything else about her leaving this life while there
was still litigation to attend to) one of the New York rabbis on
record as considering me a menace to the Jews. I didn't go so
far as to wear a yarmulke at the service, but had the rabbi asked
me to, I would have forsworn my secular convictions out of respect for the beliefs of the deceased. When I saw the casket, I
said to Josie, "You're dead and I didn't have to do it." Whereupon the late Jew replied, "Mazel tov." That is, I replied on

her behalf. And I did because she'd never reply to me again and I'd never have to reply to her or to a subpoena of hers— that is, outside of fiction. She was dead, I hadn't done it, but it would still take years of hapless experimentation before I could decontaminate myself of my rage and discover how to expropriate the hatred of her as an objective subject rather than be driven by it as the motive dictating everything. *My Life as a Man* would turn out to be far less my revenge on her than, given the unyielding problems it presented, hers on me. Writing it consisted of making one false start after another and, over the years it took to finish it, very nearly broke my will. The only experience worse than writing it, however, would have been for me to have endured that marriage without afterward having been able to find ways of reimagining it into a fiction with a persuasive existence independent of myself.

Actually, if it hadn't been for residual feelings of responsibility to Helen and her brother, Donald—who by then was an eighteen-year-old high school senior in a Chicago boarding school and who had flown in from Chicago with his father and his father's aunt to attend the funeral—I would have considered it grossly inappropriate to turn up for the service at Campbell's, let alone to seem to want to suggest to anyone there that my heart was anything *other* than flint. I felt precisely like what she'd been telling me I was since the first time we'd broken up in Chicago in 1956: her ineradicable need for a conscienceless, compassionless monster as a mate had at last been realized—I felt absolutely nothing about her dying at thirty-nine other than immeasurable relief.

Helen and Donald sat between me and their father, a small-town radio-station engineer whom Josie had begun dating as a high school girl when he'd come back home from the service in the mid-forties. Though he was altogether civil at the funeral, he certainly had no reason to like me much, since it was I, exuding impassioned moral zeal, who had taken off after him in the courts when Josie and I returned from Rome in the fall of 1960 and found that her two children, who were supposed to have been domiciled with her ex-husband and his new wife, were living with him alone in a southern Illinois suburban development, the new wife apparently having taken leave of him while we were abroad. The plan that evolved to alter this arrangement, and that finally required the court to implement, was for Josie to recover partial custody of the children, for Donald to board at a private school (toward whose costs I would contribute something), and for Helen to come to live with us in Iowa City, where I had taken a university teaching job in the Writers' Workshop.

I had thrown myself with all my energy—and my small cash reserves—into the court battle that ensued, frequently phoning and writing our Chicago lawyer to go over details of the case and doing what I could on holidays and weekends, when the children visited Iowa City, to gain their confidence about the new plans for them, to which their father continued to have strenuous objections. We were also setting the stage for them to spend the summer with us in Amagansett, Long Island. I thought not only that these arrangements would be better for Helen and Donald, who had fallen way behind in school and were now about to witness yet another marital breakup, but that seeing to their welfare might somehow mitigate Josie's relentless desperation. It was the sort of rescue operation that, however difficult, can grow naturally enough out of a strong and harmonious marriage; in a marriage like ours, beyond reclamation before it had even begun, the pathetic needs of her unhappy children simply furnished a means of remobilizing the forces that had crazily joined us in the first place. My disastrously confused, unaccountable sense of personal obligation was once again activated by the wreckage of her chaotic emotional past.

In 1975, a journalist for a Jewish community newspaper in a Midwestern city discovered that my "stepson"—as Donald was misleadingly described in the longish article "Papa Portnoy: Philip Roth as a Stepfather"—was a young married truck driver living in a local working-class neighborhood. Donald came off in the piece as a lively, unashamed young fellow, interested in social problems and possessed of the direct, congenial openness you associate with a good community organizer, a job that in fact he filled in his spare time. Donald recalled accurately for the interviewer that our relationship had been both affable and relentlessly pedagogical—as he described it, a "positive" one: "I've got to say that if it were not for the positive influence Philip had on my life at that time, I might be in jail today." He

remembered that I had given him books to read, that I'd tu-
tored him one summer for his school entrance exams, and that
I also had taught him a little elementary European history
after he'd quite innocently delivered himself of some childish,
if to me grating, misinformation about the relationship of the
Nazis to the Jews in World War II. His sole significant memory
lapse had to do with Josie's funeral: he told the reporter—
when the reporter asked—that I hadn't been there.

In fact, I was just a seat away from him and, the morning
after the funeral, took Donald by himself to breakfast at the
old Biltmore Hotel, where we talked about his college plans.
He flew back home with his father that day, and I never saw
him again, until that is, the inquisitive journalist sent me his
published interview with Portnoy's stepson, offering me, in an
accompanying letter, the opportunity in his paper "to express
yourself on the issues raised in the article." There, along with
photographs reprinted from the New York *Daily News*, of
Josie and me at the New York Supreme Court building during
the separation proceedings in 1964, was a photograph of Donald in his late twenties, mustached, wearing a cap, and seated
at the wheel of his pickup truck.

After breakfast with Donald, before returning to my Kips
Bay apartment—and to the point in my manuscript where I'd
been interrupted by Helen's call—I walked over to Central
Park and tried to find the spot where the car was said to have
crashed and killed her. It was a splendid spring morning and I
sat on the grass nearby for about an hour, my head raised to
take the sun full in my face. Like it or not, that's what I did:
gloried in the sunshine on my living flesh. "She died and you
didn't," and that to me summed it up. I'd always understood
that one of us would have to die for the damn thing ever to be
over.

Only a few days after her funeral I made arrangements, virtually overnight, to be a guest at Yaddo, the Saratoga Springs
artists' colony where I'd frequently gone off to write for long
stretches between semesters and during the summer, especially
before I'd met May, when I was newly returned to Manhattan,
alone in a garish sublet apartment, dealing with the alimony
battle and barely able to concentrate on anything else. The bus
from Port Authority Terminal was for me very much a part of

the stealthy, satisfying ritual of leaving Manhattan for the safe haven of Yaddo, and so instead of renting a car, which would have been more in keeping with my new relaxed attitude toward taking a New York cab, I showed up at the bus station in my old clothes and boarded the northbound Adirondack bus, rereading on the long trip up the thruway the rough first draft of the last two chapters of my book. At Yaddo, where there were only seven or eight other guests in residence, I found that my imagination was fully fired: I worked steadily in a secluded hillside cabin for twelve and fourteen hours a day until the book was done, and then I took the bus back down, feeling triumphant and indestructible.

The Roth family menace, peritonitis, had failed to kill me, Josie was dead and I didn't do it, and a fourth book, unlike any I'd written before in both its exuberance and its design, had been completed in a burst of hard work. What had begun as a hopped-up, semifalsified version of an analytic monologue that might have been mine, by diverging more and more from mine through its mounting hyperbole and the oddly legendary status conferred by farcical invention upon the unholy trinity of father, mother, and Jewish son, had gradually been transformed into a full-scale comical counteranalysis. Unhampered by fealty to real events and people, it was more entertaining, more graphic, and more shapely than my own analysis, if not quite to the point of my personal difficulties. It was a book that had rather less to do with "freeing" me from my Jewishness or from my family (the purpose divined by many, who were convinced by the evidence of *Portnoy's Complaint* that the author had to be on bad terms with both) than with liberating me from an apprentice's literary models, particularly from the awesome graduate-school authority of Henry James, whose *Portrait of a Lady* had been a virtual handbook during the early drafts of *Letting Go*, and from the example of Flaubert, whose detached irony in the face of a small-town woman's disastrous delusions had me obsessively thumbing through the pages of *Madame Bovary* during the years I was searching for the perch from which to observe the people in *When She Was Good.*

In my Yaddo cabin I gave the babbling book's last word to the desperately clowning analysand's silent psychoanalyst. The single line was intended not only to place a dubious seal of authority on the undecorous, un-Jamesian narrative liberties but to have a secondary, more personal irony for me as both hopeful instruction and congratulatory message: "So [said the doctor], now vee may perhaps to begin. Yes?"

When I returned to Manhattan, Candida Donadio, who was my literary agent then, got on the phone with my publisher, Bennett Cerf, the president of Random House, and in a matter of hours we had all agreed on the terms of a contract guaranteeing me an advance of $250,000. After paying ten percent to Candida and (sweating heavily as I wrote out the checks) giving another seventy percent to my accountant for quarterly tax payments to New York City, New York State, and the IRS, I still had a new balance in my account that was about a hundred times larger than any I'd ever had there in my life. By the next day I had dashed off checks to pay my debts of some $8,000 and had also purchased two first-class tickets on the *France*, luxury-liner passage to England for May and me; we planned to sublet a London flat for the summer and drive from there to see the English cathedrals and countryside. May told me that I would need a tuxedo to eat my caviar on the ship, and so we went down to pre-chic Barneys on Seventeenth Street and I bought one. She smiled when I tried it on; half meaning it, she said, "I could take you back to Cleveland in that." "Sure," I said, "we'd wow 'em at the country club. Especially after my little book comes out." That was the first and the last I ever heard about taking me back to Cleveland.

The crossing was an enjoyable masquerade, to which even the ship's magazine contributed by publishing a photograph of May and me in our evening clothes, identified as "Mr. and Mrs. Philip Roth." Only when we disembarked and made our way up to London and a suite at the Ritz, from which we began apartment hunting, did the restlessness begin. At my first meeting with an attractive young English journalist whom my English publisher had arranged to have interview me, I offered an invitation, which she gracefully declined, to spend the rest of the afternoon with me in a hotel. I proceeded to have clothes made by three distinguished tailoring establishments, half a dozen suits that I didn't need, that required endless, stupefying fittings, and that finally never fit me anyway. We went on

trips to famously quaint villages, we hunted out the oldest
Anglo-Saxon churches, we made love before a huge bedroom
mirror in our rented flat, and what I saw in the mirror held no
more of my attention than did the quaint villages and antique
churches. On English TV I watched Mayor Daley's police
surging through the Chicago streets in pursuit of yippies and
other conventioneers, and wondered what the hell I was doing
trying vainly to have a good time abroad while the turbulence
of the American sixties, which had enlivened both my fiction
and my life, looked finally to be boiling over. I wandered down
Curzon Street with nothing to do one morning and found myself a Chinese call girl; then May and I headed off to see Salis-
bury Cathedral, but only after I'd stopped on my way out of
London at Dougie Hayward's exclusive tailoring shop to have
a pair of suit trousers refitted that were still fashionably too
tight in the crotch.

Perhaps if May and I had gone back and rented the modest
house on the back roads of Martha's Vineyard and, within the
confines of that pleasant, familiar island, among dear friends,
let the massive changes trickle slowly in, I wouldn't have had to
experience so pointlessly *my* turbulence, the upheavals of someone who feels himself all but reborn. An extravagant blowout
on the *France* or at the Ritz, an hour at the Hilton with a petite
Hong Kong pro, however symbolically appropriate and pleasurable in passing, had nothing much to do with the potential
for personal resurrection that seemed to be promised by the
astonishing annihilation of my nemesis, the violent dissolution
of the enshackling marriage, and the imminent publication, on
a grandish scale, of a book imprinted with a style and a subject
that were, at last, distinctively my own. All I did that summer
in England was to nick ridiculously away at the carapace of
strictures that had kept me resolved and persevering during the
years in which I'd impotently raged against Josie's exactions
and, through an enervating process of trial and error, tracked
my unexploited resources as a novelist.

By the time we'd returned to America in September, I had
decided to live completely on my own. Now that it was possible in the late Senator Kennedy's state for me to marry May
(or anyone else I chose), the idea was intolerable: I was not
about to be reined in right off by, of all things, another mar-

riage certificate. That May, inside a marriage or out, hadn't the slightest potential for behaving like Josie wasn't even the point; I simply could not unlearn overnight what the years of legal battling had taught me, which was never, but *never*, to hand over again to the state and its judiciary the power to decide to whom I should be most profoundly committed, in what way, and for how long. I could not imagine ever again being a husband who was ultimately under their punitive mechanisms of authority, and, however little I may have experienced of genuine fatherhood as a part-time pedagogue helping Josie's children learn their ABCs, I felt that I could not be a father under their jurisdiction either. The subpoenas, the depositions, the courtroom inquisitions, the property disputes, the newspaper coverage, the legal bills—it had all been too painful and too humiliating and had gone on far too long for me ever again voluntarily to become the plaything of those moral imbeciles. What's more, I now didn't even wish to be bound by what had been the countervailing balm to the legacy of marital hatred, the loving loyalty of May Aldridge. Instead I was determined to be an absolutely independent, self-sufficient man—to recapture, in other words, twelve years on, at age thirty-five, that exhilarating, adventurous sense of personal freedom that had prompted the high-flying freshman-composition teacher, on a fall evening in 1956, to go blithely forward in his new Brooks Brothers suit and, without the slightest idea that he might be risking his life, handily pick up on a Chicago street the small-town blond divorcée with the two little fatherless children, the penniless ex-waitress whom he'd already spotted serving cheeseburgers back in graduate school, and who'd looked to him like nothing so much as the All-American girl, albeit one enticingly at odds with her origins.

Dear Roth,

I've read the manuscript twice. Here is the candor you ask for: Don't publish—you are far better off writing about me than "accurately" reporting your own life. Could it be that you've turned yourself into a subject not only because you're tired of me but because you believe I am no longer someone through whom you can detach yourself from your biography at the same time that you exploit its crises, themes, tensions, and surprises? Well, on the evidence of what I've just read, I'd say you're still as much in need of me as I of you—and that I need you is indisputable. For me to speak of "my" anything would be ridiculous, however much there has been established in me the illusion of an independent existence. I owe everything to you, while you, however, owe me nothing less than the freedom to write freely. I am your permission, your indiscretion, the key to disclosure. I understand that now as I never did before.

What you choose to tell in fiction is different from what you're permitted to tell when nothing's being fictionalized, and in this book you are not permitted to tell what it is you tell best: kind, discreet, careful—changing people's names because you're worried about hurting their feelings—no, this isn't you at your most interesting. In the fiction you can be so much more truthful without worrying all the time about causing direct pain. You try to pass off here as frankness what looks to me like the dance of the seven veils—what's on the page is like a code for something missing. Inhibition appears not only as a reluctance to say certain things but, equally disappointing, as a slowing of pace, a refusal to explode, a relinquishing of the need I ordinarily associate with you for the acute, explosive moment.

As for characterization, you, Roth, are the least completely rendered of all your protagonists. Your gift is not to personalize your experience but to personify it, to embody it in the representation of a person who is *not* yourself. You are not an autobiographer, you're a personificator. You have the reverse experience of most of your American contemporaries. Your acquaintance with the facts, your sense of the facts, is much less developed than your understanding, your intuitive weighing and balancing of fiction. You make a fictional world that is far more exciting than the world it comes out of. My guess is that you've written metamorphoses of yourself so many times, you no longer have any idea what *you* are or ever were. By now what you are is a walking text.

The history of your education as narrated here—of going out into the world, leaving the small circle, and getting your head knocked in—certainly doesn't strike me as more dense or eventful than my own as narrated in my bildungsroman, excepting, of course, for the marital ordeal. You point out that something like that experience would eventually become the fate of my unfortunate predecessor, Tarnopol; for this I can't be sufficiently grateful, though when it came to the Jewish opposition to my writing, I only wish that, like yours, my own occupation would not have pitted me against my family.

I wonder if you have any real idea of what it's like to be disowned by a dying father because of something you wrote. I assure you that there is no equivalence between that and a *hundred* nights on the rack at Yeshiva. My father's condemnation of me provided you, obviously, with the opportunity to pull out all the stops on a Jewish deathbed scene; that had to have been irresistible to a temperament like yours. Nonetheless, knowing what I now do about your father's enthusiasm for your first stories and about the pride he took in their publication, I feel, whether inappropriately or not, envious, cheated, and misused. Wouldn't you? Wouldn't you at least be mildly disturbed to learn, say, that Josie had been inflicted on you for artistic reasons, that the justification for your misery stemmed solely from the requirements of a novel that wasn't even your own? You'd be furious, more furious even than you were when you thought she'd landed on you out of the blue.

But I'm fixed forever as what you've made me—among other things, as a young writer without parental support. Whether you ever were what you claim to have been is another matter and requires some investigating. What one chooses to reveal in fiction is governed by a motive fundamentally aesthetic; we judge the author of a novel by how well he or she tells the story. But we judge morally the author of an autobiography, whose governing motive is primarily ethical as against aesthetic. How close is the narration to the truth? Is the author hiding his or her motives, presenting his or her actions and thoughts to lay bare the essential nature of conditions or trying to hide something, telling in order *not* to tell? In a way we always tell in order also not to tell, but the personal historian is expected to resist to the utmost the ordinary impulse to falsify, distort, and deny. Is this really "you" or is it what you want to look like to your readers at the age of fifty-five? You tell me in your letter that the book feels like the first thing you have ever written "unconsciously." Do you mean that *The Facts* is an unconscious work of fiction? Are you not aware yourself of its fiction-making tricks? Think of the exclusions, the selective nature of it, the very pose of fact-facer. Is all this manipulation truly unconscious or is it pretending to be unconscious?

I think I am able to understand the plan here despite my opposition to your publishing the book. In somewhat autonomous essays, each about a different area in which you pushed against something, you're remembering those forces in your early life that have given your fiction its character and also reflecting on the relationship between what happens in a life and what happens when you write about it—how close to life it sometimes is and how far from life it sometimes is. You see your writing as evolving out of three things. First, there's your journey from Weequahic Jewishness into the bigger American society. This business of being able to be an American was always problematic for your parents' generation, and you sensed the difference between yourself and those who had preceded you—a difference that wouldn't have been a factor in the artistic evolution of, say, a young James Jones. You developed all the self-consciousness of someone confronted with the choices of rising up out of an ethnic group. That sense of being part of America merges in all sorts of ways with your personality. Second, there was the terrific upheaval of the involvement with Josie and the self-consciousness this ignited about your inner weaknesses as a man. Third, as far as I can make it out, there's your response to the larger world, beginning with your boyhood awareness of World War II, Metropolitan Life, and gentile Newark and culminating in the turbulence of the sixties in New York, particularly the outcry there against the Vietnam War. The whole book seems to be leading to the point where these three forces in your life intersect, producing *Portnoy's Complaint*. You break out of a series of safe circles—home, neighborhood, fraternity, Bucknell—you manage even to shake off the spell of the great Gayle Milman, to discover what a life is like "away." You show us where away is, all right, but what's driving you there you keep largely to yourself, because you either don't know or cannot talk about it without me as your front man.

It's as if you had worked out in your mind the formula for who you are, and this is it. Very neat—but where's the struggle, the *struggling* you? Maybe it *was* easy to get from Leslie Street to Newark Rutgers to Bucknell to Chicago, to leave the Jewish identification behind in a religious sense but retain it in an ethnic sense, to be drawn into the possibilities of goy America and feel that you have all the freedom that anyone else has. It's one of the classic stories of twentieth-century American energy—out of an ethnic family and then made by school. But I still feel that you're not telling all that's going on. Because if there wasn't a struggle, then it just doesn't seem like Philip Roth to me. It could be anybody, almost.

There's an awful lot of loving gentleness in those opening chapters of yours, a tone of reconciliation that strikes me as suspiciously unsubstantiated and so unlike what you usually do. At one point I thought the book should be called *Goodbye Letting Go Being Good*. Are we to believe that this warm, comforting home portrayed there is the home that nurtured the author of *Portnoy's Complaint*? Strange lack of logic in that, but then creation is not logical. Could I honestly tell you that I dislike the prologue? A subdued and honorable and respectful tribute to a striving, conscientious, determined father—how can I be against that? Or against the fact that you find yourself bowled over, at the verge of tears with your feelings for this eighty-six-year-old man. This is the incredible drama that nearly all of us encounter in relation to our families. The gallantry and misery of your father as he approaches death has so tenderized you, so opened you up, that *all* these recollections seem to flow from that source. And as for the final paragraph about your animal love for your mother? Quite beautiful. Your Jewish readers are finally going to glean from this what they've wanted to hear from you for three decades. That your parents had a good son who loved them. And what's no less laudable, what goes hand in hand with the confession of filial love, is that instead of writing only about Jews at one another's throats, you have discovered gentile anti-Semitism, and are exposing *that* for a change.

Of course, all that's been there and apparent right along, even if not to them; but what they need is just this, your separating the facts from the imagination and emptying them of their potential dramatic energy. But why suppress the imagination that's served you so long? Doing so entails terrific discipline, I know, but why bother? Especially when to strip away the imagination to get to a fiction's factual basis is frequently all that many readers really care about anyway. Why is it that when they talk about the facts they feel they're on more solid ground than when they talk about the fiction? The truth is that the facts are much more refractory and unmanageable and inconclusive, and can actually kill the very sort of inquiry that imagination opens up. Your work has always been to intertwine the facts *with* the imagination, but here you're unintertwining them, you're pulling them apart, you're peeling the skin off your imagination, *de*-imagining a life's work, and what is left even they can now understand. Thirty years ago, the "good" boy is thought of as bad and thereby given enormous freedom to *be* bad; now, when the same people read those opening sections, the bad boy is going to be perceived as good, and you will be given the kindliest reception. Well, maybe that'll convince you better than I ever could to go back to being bad; it should.

Of course, by projecting essentially fictional characters with manic personae out into the world, you openly invited misunderstanding about yourself. But because some people get it wrong and don't have any idea of who or what you really are doesn't suggest to me that you have to straighten them out. Just the opposite—consider having tricked them into those beliefs a *success*; that's what fiction's *supposed* to do. The way things stand you're no worse off than most people, who, as you know, often are to be heard mumbling aloud, "Nobody understands me or knows my great worth—nobody knows what I'm really like underneath!" For a novelist, that predicament is to be cherished. All you need as a writer is to be loved and forgiven by all the people who have been telling you for years to clean up your act—if there's anything that can put the kibosh on a literary career, it's the loving forgiveness of one's natural enemies. Let them keep reminding their friends not to read you—you just keep coming back at them with your imagination, and give up on giving them, thirty years too late, the speech of the good boy at the synagogue. The whole point about your fiction (and in America, not only yours) is that the imagination is always in transit between the good boy *and* the bad boy—that's the tension that leads to revelation.

Speaking of being loved, just look at how you begin this thing. The little marsupial in his mother's sealskin pouch. No wonder you suddenly display a secret passion to be universally coddled. But where, by the way, is the mother after that? It may well be that this incredible animal love that you have for your mother, and that you allude to in only one sentence in the prologue, can't be exposed by you undisguised, but aside from that sealskin coat, there is no mother. Of course it speaks volumes, that coat—it tells nearly everything you need to know about your mother at that point; but the fact remains that your mother has no developed role either in your life or in your father's. This picture of your mother is a way of saying "I was not my mother's Alexander nor was she my Sophie Portnoy." Perhaps that's true. Yet this image of an utterly refined, Jewish Florence Nightingale still seems to me particularly striking for all it appears to omit.

Nor have I any idea what's going on with you in relation to your father, his rise in the world, his fall in the world, his rise again. There's only a sense of you and Newark, you and America, you and Bucknell, but what is going on within you and within the family is not here, can't be here, simply because it *is* you and not Tarnopol, Kepesh, Portnoy, or me. In the few comments you do make about your mother and father, there's nothing but tenderness, respect, understanding, all those wonderful emotions that I, for one, have come to distrust partly because you, for one, have made me distrust them. Many people

don't like you as a writer just because of the ways you invite
the reader to distrust those very sentiments that you now publicly embrace. Comfort yourself, if you like, with the thought
that this is Zuckerman talking, the disowned son embittered
permanently by his deprivation; take solace in that if you like,
but the fact remains I'm not a fool and I don't believe you.
Look, this place you come from does not produce artists so
much as it produces dentists and accountants. I'm convinced
that there is something in the romance of your childhood that
you're not permitting yourself to talk about, though without it
the rest of the book makes no sense. I just cannot trust you as
a memoirist the way I trust you as a novelist because, as I've
said, to tell what you tell best is forbidden to you here by a
decorous, citizenly, filial conscience. With this book you've tied
your hands behind your back and tried to write it with your
toes.

    You see your beginnings, up to and including Bucknell, as
an idyll, a pastoral, allowing little if no room for inner turmoil,
the discovery in yourself of a dark, or unruly, or untamed side.
Again, this may be dismissed as so much Zuckermania, but I
don't buy it. Your psychoanalysis you present in barely more
than a sentence. I wonder why. Don't you remember, or are
the themes too embarrassing? I'm not saying you *are* Portnoy
any more than I'm saying you are me or I am Carnovsky; but
come on, what did you and the doctor talk about for seven years
—the camaraderie up at the playground among all you harmless little Jewish boys? In fact, after the prologue and those first
two sections, I can see the hero becoming a lawyer, a doctor, a
suburban developer—he's had his literary fling, his maverick
fun, he's had his gentile Polly, and now he's going to settle
down, marry into a good Jewish family, make money, be rich,
have three children—and you have Josie instead. So there's
something missing, a big gap—those idyllic sections don't at
all add up to "Girl of My Dreams." The very end of the little
prologue, lyrically evoking the fleshly bond to your mother,
tell me, please, how do you get from that to Josie? As you
yourself point out, Josie isn't something that merely happened
to you, she's something *that you made happen*. But if that is so,
I want to know what it is that led to her from that easy, won-

derful, shockless childhood that you describe, what it is that led to her from the cozily combative afternoons with Pete and Dick at Miss Martin's seminar. Your story in Newark and Lewisburg was far from tragic—and then, in an extraordinarily brief period, you became immersed in the pathologically tragic. Why? Why did you essentially mortify yourself in a passionate encounter with a woman who had a sign on her saying STAY AWAY KEEP OUT? There has to be some natural link between the beginning, between all that early easy success, culminating at Bucknell and Chicago, and the end, and there isn't. Because what's left out is the motive.

In the exploits with Polly, the encounter with Mrs. Nellenback, the business with *The Bucknellian*, there's no sense that you're truly dissatisfied and looking for something else. Only glancingly do you touch on your dissatisfactions; even the conflict with your father you treat peripherally, and yet the note of grievance, of criticism, of disgust and satire and estrangement, sounds so powerfully in your fiction. Which am I to believe is the posturing: the fiction or this? Everything you describe in your childhood is undoubtedly still strongly there—the well-brought-up side, the nice-guy side, the good-kid side. This manuscript is steeped in the nice-guy side. In autobiography you seem to have no choice but to document mainly the nice-guy side, the form signaling to you that it is probably wisest to suppress the free exploration of just about everything else that goes into the making of a human personality. Where once there was satiric rebellion, now there is a deep sense of belonging; no resentment but rather gratitude, gratitude even for crazy Josie, gratitude even for the enraged Jews and the wound they inflicted. Of course, you are not the first novelist who, by fleeing the wearying demands of fictional invention for a little vacation in straightforward recollection, has shackled the less sociable impulses that led him or her to become a novelist in the first place. But the fact remains that it wasn't exactly the nice-guy side that got the Yeshiva people all hot under their tefillin. And what you *were* tapping there did not come from nothing, even if it looks as though it did here. You were tapping exactly what produced your excruciating need for independence and the need to shatter the taboo. You were tapping what has

compelled you to live out the imaginative life. I suspect that
what comes somewhat closer to being an autobiography of
those impulses was the fable, *Portnoy's Complaint.*

Where's the anger? You suggest that the anger only developed *after* Josie, a result of her insanely destructive possessive-
ness and then the punishment handed out to you in court. But
I doubt that Josie would have come into your life at all had the
anger not been there already. I could be wrong, but you've got
to prove it, to convince me that early on you didn't find something insipid about the Jewish experience as you knew it, insipid about the middle class as you experienced it, insipid about
marriage and domesticity, insipid even about love—certainly
you must have come to feel that Gayle Milman was insipid or
you would never have forsaken that pleasure dome.

And where's the hubris, by the way? What's not here is what
it felt like to meet you—you say why, sociologically, Josie might
have fallen in love with you, but you don't say what she might
have found appealing about you. It seems to me you relished
the way you were and what you did, yet you talk in this veiled
way, or not at all, about your qualities: "the exuberant side of
my personality. . . ." How restrained and cool. How tremendously unexuberant. Positively British. You speak of yourself as
a "good catch," but why not be more boastful in your autobiography? Why shouldn't autobiography be egotistical? You talk
about what you were up against, what you wanted, what was
happening to you, but you rarely say what you were like. You
can't or you won't talk about yourself as yourself, other than in
this decorous way. When you give the details of how you responded to the news of Josie's death, you don't cover anything up to make yourself look good. Yet it seems to me you're
too proper to say why these women were drawn to you; at
least you act that way here. But obviously it's just as impossible
to be proper and modest and well behaved and be a revealing
autobiographer as it is to be all that and a good novelist. Very
strange that you don't grasp this. Or maybe you do but,
because of a gigantic split between how you're sincere as yourself and how you're sincere as an artist, you can't enact it, and
so we get this fictional autobiographical projection of a *partial*
you. Even if it's no more than one percent that you've edited

out, that's the one percent that counts—the one percent that's saved for your imagination and that changes everything. But this isn't unusual, really. With autobiography there's always another text, a countertext, if you will, to the one presented. It's probably the most manipulative of all literary forms.

To move on—when you're young, energetic, intelligent, you have of course to deny in yourself what you see as being part of the tribe. You rebel against the tribal and look for the individual, for your own voice as against the stereotypical voice of the tribe or the tribe's stereotype of itself. You have to establish yourself against your predecessor, and doing so can well involve what they like to call self-hatred. I happen to think that —all those protestations notwithstanding—your self-hatred was real and a positive force in its very destructiveness. Since to build something new often requires that something else be destroyed, self-hatred is *valuable* for a young person. What should he or she have instead—self-approval, self-satisfaction, self-praise? It's not so bad to hate the norms that keep a society from moving on, especially when those norms are dictated by fear as much as by anything else and especially when that fear is of the enemy forces or the overwhelming majority. But you seem now to be so strongly motivated by a need for reconciliation with the tribe that you aren't even willing to acknowledge how disapproving of its platitudinous demands you were back then, however ineluctably Jewish you may also have felt. The prodigal son who once upset the tribal balance—and perhaps even invigorated the tribe's health—may well, in his old age, have a sentimental urge to go back home, but isn't this a bit premature in you, aren't you really too young yet to have it so fully developed? Personally I tend to trust the novella *Goodbye, Columbus*, written when you were still in your early twenties, as a guide to your evaluation of the Milmans more than I trust what you care to remember about them now. The truth you told about all this long ago you now want to tell in a different way. At fifty-five, with your mother dead and your father heading for ninety, you are evidently in a mood to idealize the confining society that long ago ceased impinging on your spirit and to sentimentalize people who by now inhabit either New Jersey cemeteries or Florida retirement communities and are hardly a source of disappointment to you, let alone a target for the derisive comedy unleashed first on poor Barbara Roemer and the *Bucknellian.*

At fifty-five you may even find it hard to remember the extent of your adolescent despair over the way these people spoke and what they spoke about, over what they thought and thought about, over how they lived and genuinely expected their off-spring, like you and Gayle, to live. At fifty-five, after all the books and the battles, after more than three decades of up-rooting and remaking your life and your work, you've begun to make where you came from look like a serene, desirable, pastoral haven, a home that was a cinch to master, when, I suspect, it was more like a detention house you were tunneling out of practically from the day you could pronounce your favorite word of all, "away."

And if I'm right, at the end of the tunnel, waiting like your moll in the getaway car, was Josie, embodying everything the Jewish haven was not, including the possibilities for treachery —those too must have had their allure. My uneasiness is that you present yourself not as an ingenious escapee on the run from home but as little more than a victim. Here I am, this innocent Jewish boy and American patriot, my mother's papoose and Miss Martin's favorite, brought up in these innocent landscapes, with all these well-meaning, innocent people, and I fall headlong into this trap. As though you still have no sense of how you were conspiring to make it all come about.

Now, it may well be that naked in autobiography, deprived of the sense of impregnability that narrative invention seems to confer on your self-revealing instincts, you can't easily fathom your part in all this; nonetheless, after college, you simply do not present yourself as in any way responsible for what is happening. Enter Josie and, as you see it, the thing was a Pandora's box—you opened it up and everything flew out. But what makes me resist that idea is your *pursuit* of the woman. The initial flirtation is very charming and could just about have been enough, but you persist. You don't turn away from her any more than you refuse to go speak at Yeshiva, knowing when you accept that you can expect some sort of humiliating battle and, I contend, *needing* that battle, that attack, that kick, needing that *wound*, your source of invigorating anger, the energizer for the defiance. They boo you, they whistle, they stamp their feet—you hate it but you thrive on it. Because the things that wear you down are the things that nurture you and your talent.

You were passive with Josie only insomuch as you couldn't control her; otherwise, the whole thing can be seen in an entirely different way from how it reads here. You, in fact, can be seen as the real troublemaker, setting before her so tantalizingly your mother's hot tomato soup. You can also be seen, paradoxically, as the relentless aggressor practically begging Josie to behave as she did by ignoring the implications of her broken background. As you suggest, even the brightest can be awfully naïve, but anybody with tentacles and antennae would have had to know that Josie meant disaster, not after the first conversation necessarily, but surely after the first three or four weeks; certainly from the way you depict her here, only a dimwit, which you were not, would have failed to recognize the destructiveness. A good case can be made that you were deliberately drawing out of her every drop of her chaos. At the least, there is more ambiguity in your role than you are willing to acknowledge. But speaking as yourself, unprotected by the cunning playfulness of fictional masquerade, without all the exigencies of a full-scale, freewheeling narrative to overwhelm the human, if artistically fatal, concern for one's vulnerable self, you are incapable of admitting that you were more responsible for what befell you than you wish to recall.

If you want to reminisce productively, maybe what you should be writing, instead of autobiography, are thirty thousand words from Josie's point of view. *My Life as a Woman. My Life as a Woman with That Man.* But I hear the objection already. "Her point of view? Don't you understand, she didn't *have* a point of view—she was a bloodsucking monster. What she had were fangs!" Yes, you see her as a bitch and you can't help it and you'll never be able to help it, certainly not while speaking in your own behalf. I submit to you that she could be seen differently, and not as Lucy Nelson married to Roy Bassart in *When She Was Good*, but as herself married to the real adversary you were.

As you justly point out, she's what they now categorize and call an a.c.o.a., the adult child of an alcoholic, the victim of a victim, and therefore she has the primary trait of someone with that internal misery, the need to blame her misery on whatever external thing can be blamed. You are the child of an alcoholic father, you first blame the father. Then you marry and you blame the husband. Very likely you marry an alcoholic, unless you're an alcoholic yourself, which I happen to believe Josie was. I think she was more of an alcoholic than she was a schizophrenic. Did that never occur to you? You say that after you left her in Princeton, she'd phone you at night in New York and drunkenly charge that you were sleeping with a Negress. So she was certainly drinking then—and perhaps the progression had been slow. You say that midway through a botched suicide attempt she was "drunk and drugged." When you were living with her you probably drank wine before and at dinner —do you remember how much wine she drank? For all of your concentration on your life's predicaments, you appear to have paid remarkably little attention to a lot she did, though, to be fair, what could you, coming from your background, know about alcoholism? When it's very bad, alcoholics exaggerate any negative trait of their unfortunate partners—blow it all up and throw it at them. Very destructive stuff; *self*-destructive destructive stuff. That urine trick, which from your point of view still seems pretty wicked, didn't seem all that wicked from hers, you know. Not only do people lie when they've been drinking, but the distinction between fiction and reality is not always all that clear to them. Whatever is even faintly plausible can also seem quite real. She strongly believed that she *was* the editor of your first published stories, to her that was no lie. And she *could* have been pregnant, she thought. And you *should* have married her, she thought. And even though you didn't want to marry her, she *needed* you to marry her. And so she pulled that trick, your little Pearl Harbor. Even the obsessive jealousy, her imagining that you would do something with her little girl, that strikes me as part of the picture too.

Yes, I'm convinced that she was an alcoholic, that her disorder was hereditary, biochemical, inherited from her father, and that you didn't know it because, one, you had no idea what a *shicker* was and, two, she was young then, she ate, and she was healthy, and so the progression was not rapid. Besides, you wanted to look at her through Dostoevskian eyes then and not as though she were merely a candidate for A.A. Eventually she destroyed herself, of course—an addict like her always loses, the addict's worst fear always comes true—but all the while she continued to believe she could be good but only when *they* were good. I would even imagine that she *wanted* to be good. If only you loved her. If only the children were living with her. If only her father had been better, if only you were better, if only something external changed, she could be good again!

I said before that you were conspiring to make her happen to you, that Josie was the moll in the getaway car, but that doesn't mean I want to deny entirely that you were a victim as well—the victim of the victim of a victim. You caught the disease, as I see it, because when you live long enough with a disease you get it too. Before marrying Josie you were not that openly angry. But now you became an openly angry angry man. You became so distressingly angry that you needed psychotherapy. You owe that great explosion of anger to her. You thus owe *Portnoy* to her rather more than to Lyndon Johnson.

Am I inventing? I share the tic with you—but then my fiction, if it is fiction, is still perhaps less of a fiction than yours. Look, anything is better than My Ex-Wife the Bitch—I just cannot read that stuff. I certainly don't mean, by suggesting that she was an alcoholic, to further demean her in the human scale; nor am I saying that by not taking into account that she was an alcoholic, you may have travestied, and done an injustice to, this woman. I'm only saying that maybe it's time, twenty years on, to find another way to see her. There's still a tremendous amount of saved-up rage in that stuff about Josie, lots of microbes that are still very active. Sometimes there is a cool gap between you as you were writing this book and you as you were when these things happened, and sometimes there isn't. I felt all the way through that the book is very equivocal about that: sometimes you seem to be looking back at this twenty-four-year-old, or whatever, a little wryly and at the expense of that person, and sometimes you're looking back at this person and feeling more or less the same things. But then maybe that's how everybody looks back at his or her life and is perfectly okay.

Anyway, can *everything* about Josie have been vengeful? I suspect that Josie was both worse and better as a human being than what you've portrayed here. There were obviously times,

particularly in the beginning—and you hint at this yourself—
that you enjoyed her and found her appealing, and there were
probably times when she was so luridly psychopathic that you
still can't find your way to a proper description of the disaster
you were dragged into. To be sure, I know you try hard to be
generous at the conclusion of your horror story by crediting
her with being your teacher in extremist fiction. But I think
that's just you being astonishing—you say it to be interesting,
not because you believe it. I'm telling you it also happens to be
true. I tie the first period of creativity to leaving home as Joe
College, and the second I tie to Josie. Everything you are today you owe to an alcoholic shiksa. Tell them *that* next time
you're at Yeshiva. You won't get out alive.

Last—and then, unlike you, I'll be done with her—I think
you must give Josie her real name. There's no legal reason to
prevent you from using her name, and I think you owe her
that. You owe it to her as a character; you owe it to her not
because it would be a nice thing to do but because it's the narratively strong thing to do.

Call the other women whatever you like. (I'm assuming that
all the women's names are changed—why should I not? Your
changing them is only an indication of something that the
book takes up, which is the conflict about whether you are a
nice fellow or not.) What you call them doesn't matter, they're
unimportant, they're interchangeable: they're helpmeets and
sexpots and partners and pals. Actually, what's happened with
these women is that not only do you disguise their identities
but you shield them from your ability to see through them.
You do it here and probably you do it in life, or try to. With
them you pull a lot of punches (and pulling punches must
finally infuriate you, as it does most everyone). With Josie, however, there are no punches pulled. The reason it's right to give
Josie her real name is because she comes so close, in an elemental way, to being a peer. Josie was about who *she* was, the
others are somehow about you. Josie is the real antagonist,
the true counterself, and shouldn't be relegated like the other
women to a kind of allegorical role. She's as real as you are—
however much about yourself you may be withholding—and
nobody else in this book is. You give your parents their real
names, you give your brother his—and, I assume, your child-

hood and college friends theirs—and you say absolutely
nothing about those people. So be it—it's with Josie, anyway,
that you fought the primitive battle that either you didn't ever
fight with your family, or you're unwilling to fight in remembering them now, or you have fought with them only by proxy,
through Alexander Portnoy and through me.

I'm speaking of the primitive battle over who is going to survive. It's clear with the other women that you are going to survive. The others call forth your maturity, challenge and coerce
it, and you deliver, you meet that challenge easily. With Josie,
however, you regress, shamelessly and dangerously. She undoes
you where ordinarily you do up everyone else. You take them
up and you do them up and when you've done them up you
leave them. But she undoes you and undoes you and undoes
you. She even tries, driving out of Rome in that little Renault,
to kill you. And then she dies. Josie's project is to incarnate destructive force and destroy the forces that try to destroy her.
She is the heroine of this book, not in any sympathetic way, but
that's neither here nor there when it comes to heroes and heroines. Josie is the heroine you were looking for. She provided
your incredible opportunity, really—your escape from being
the dominating consciousness in every situation. She took you
in; she conned you. You were had. Somebody who is mentally
very tricky, who hears the reverberations of everything he's
ever said, somebody hypersensitively aware of his impact and
very skillful at gauging it, was no longer calling the shots. She
was. Honor with her name the demon who did that, the psychopath through whose agency you achieved the freedom from
being a pleasing, analytic, lovingly manipulative good boy who
would never have been much of a writer. Reward with her real
name the destructive force that, right along with the angry
Jews, hurled you, howling, into a struggle with repression and
inhibition and humiliation and fear. Fanatical security, fanatical
insecurity—this dramatic duality that you see embodied in the
Jews, Josie unearthed in her Jew and beautifully exploited. And
with you, as with the other Jews, that is not merely where the
drama is rooted, that's where the madness begins.

It's only right that she have her real name in there, just as
you have yours.

I don't like the way you treat May either. I don't mean the

way you treat her in life; I don't care about that. I mean
the way she's treated as a subject here. Here you lose your head
completely—here the poor plebeian Jew from Newark is so
impressed: how calm she was, how patrician she looked, how
the very lines of her body bespoke guilelessness, nay, *integrity*,
how very upper class her East Side apartment was. "May's uptown apartment was large and comfortably furnished without
being at all this or that. Reflected the traditional tastes of her
class . . ." The *awful* tastes of her class. There is nothing worse
than the taste of the American WASP upper class. Refined? I
imagine you may even have had a far more refined background
than May Aldridge did. Economically pinched perhaps, uneducated, profoundly conventional, but there was a dignity, certainly, to your mother; and even when the Boss comes to the
house, and the whole family is in awe of him, there is still dignity there in your father. Untutored, deprived of high culture,
but *not* unrefined. I'll bet May's background was completely
deprived of high culture. Her family certainly never read any
real books; they went to the right schools perhaps but sure as
hell didn't read the right books or give a crap about them. But
you won't see that here, will you, you are so impressed. And
naturally at the time you *were* impressed—but as much as this?

I don't believe it. As a reader of *Portnoy's Complaint*, of *My
Life as a Man*, as a reader of what you say here about Metropolitan Life discriminating against their Jewish employees back
in your father's era, I suspect a lot about her class and her background and her taste, far from impressing you, positively disgusted you. I'd bet that, as your father's avenger, you even
berated her sometimes when she displayed the habits of her
class and her background. But about that, nothing. Be candid
—what *didn't* you like about May? There must have been plenty
if you left her; I don't believe it could have been only your
youthful liberty you were looking for—you also wanted to be
rid of her for a very good and specific reason. So, what was it?
After an emotional breakdown she dropped out of Smith and
went home to Cleveland. Was there no aftereffect, no legacy of
brokenness that you couldn't stand? Was she beautifully composed or utterly repressed, or were the two impossible to separate in her? Her "gentle" nature was probably as infuriating
to you—because of all it implied about her vulnerability and

defenselessness—as it was comforting, at first, after Josie's rages. It is chivalrous to find in yourself the sole reason for ending the affair, but in autobiography chivalry is an evasion and a lie. Maybe you are still a little in love with her or like to think that you are. Maybe at fifty-five you are suddenly in love now with those years of your life. But her idealization did not occur at the time, did it? Her idealization is a necessity of this autobiography.

You didn't want another broken woman. *That's* the reason. Of course she didn't have Josie's working-class harshness; May was placid, she stuffed her feelings, kept up her facade. But tell me, please, what was *her* addiction? Was she a pill popper like Susan McCall, her obvious embodiment in *My Life as a Man?* Surely Susan's pill popping is meant to stand for some addiction, if it isn't simply the flat-out truth. The main fear of every addict is a fear of losing, a fear of change; addicts are always looking for someone to be dependent on, they *have* to be dependent, and you were perfect. You were, after all, brought up to be reliable, and this reliability is a magnet to the broken, whether addicted, fatherless, or both. They latch on and they won't let go, and because you *are* reliable it's not easy for you to leave a job half done, especially when the reliability is being tested—and Josie went in for extreme testing, so extreme she eventually made you marry her. You're a crutch, you are flattered to be a crutch, you rush in to hold them up, and then you're holding them up and holding them up and you begin to ask yourself, "Is a crutch what I want to be?" I remember now that marathon struggle in *My Life as a Man* to make Susan come. Anything here about anything like that? Of course not. Here you investigate virtually nothing of a serious sexual nature and, somewhat astonishingly, seem almost to indicate that sex has never really compelled you.

(Polly, by the way—was she an addict too? Those martinis you talk about. But perhaps I'm overreaching to make the point, to find the pattern. You seem to paint an accurate picture of her, actually—the sweet girl out of the first romance. Another fatherless daughter, however. The only one *without* an addiction and *with* a strongly present and powerful father was Gayle Milman, our Jewish girl from suburban New Jersey. She was the most highly sexed and went on, as you say, to have an adventurous, defiant, confident career as the most desirable expatriate in all of Europe. *She* wouldn't have needed you as a crutch. Never. She needed you as a cock. So you dumped her for addicted Josie. Explain *that*.)

Even if I'm wrong and May was nothing like I suggest, you yourself don't begin to give a proper portrait of her. You don't appear to have the heart—the gall, the guts—to do in autobiography what you consider absolutely essential in a novel. You won't even say here, as you might so easily, in a footnote or just in passing, "I find it inhibiting to write about May. Even though her name has been changed, she's still alive and I don't want to hurt her, and so her portrait will have an idealized cast to it. It is not a false portrait but it is only half a portrait." Even that is beyond you, if it has even occurred to you. She is so vulnerable, this May, that even saying that might wound her horribly. But what is it you respond to in these wounded women you struggle in vain to restore to health? That they're too helpless to dare turn you away? Yet why would that be so with the kind of loving mother you describe here? Unless you are idealizing your mother too, and there we have another half portrait of another half person. (Unless you have falsified *everyone*!) Maybe in taking care of these women you are taking care of yourself, convalescing from your battles, and the reason you start backing away in the end, as you did with May, is because you're backing away from the convalescence, because you are for the time being feeling recovered. Maybe what you are attracted to more than the dependency is the extremeness of these women, the intensity of their condition. I repeat: *the things that wear you down are also the things that nurture your talent*. Yes, there is mystery upon mystery to be uncovered once you abandon the disguises of autobiography and hand the facts over for imagination to work on. And no, the distortion called fidelity is *not* your métier—you are simply too real to outface full disclosure. It's through *dis*simulation that you find your freedom from the falsifying requisites of "candor."

Nor do you happen to fool me by suddenly bringing in a ringer to corroborate your "facts": Fred Rosenberg writes this, Mildred Martin has recorded that, Charlotte Maurer remembers the following, the article "Portnoy as Poppa" furnishes confirmation of such-and-such—as though a few handpicked witnesses to virtually nothing will make us believe everything else.

I'm not saying that this is a conventional, self-congratulatory celebrity autobiography. I'm not saying that the primitive, prehistorical scene of you sitting near the site of Josie's violent death, a happy widower being warmed by the sun, is what you ordinarily get in people's autobiographies. But nonetheless this is still, by and large, what you get if you get Roth without Zuckerman—this is what you get in practically *any* artist without his imagination. Your medium for the really merciless self-evisceration, your medium for genuine self-confrontation, is me.

But you know as much, and nearly say as much, in a sentence near the end of your letter. "This isn't to say," you explain, "that I didn't have to resist the impulse to dramatize untruthfully what was insufficiently dramatic, to complicate the essentially simple, to charge with implication what implied very little—the temptation to abandon the facts when those facts were not as compelling as others I might imagine if I could somehow steel myself to overcome fiction-fatigue."

Well, you resisted the tempting impulse, all right, but to what end? Whether the task was worth the effort is something you had better consider thoroughly before submitting the book for publication. By the way, if I were you (not impossible), I would have asked myself this as well: if I could admit into autobiography that part of me—and of Polly and May, and of Momma and Poppa and Sandy—that I can admit into a Zuckerman novel; if I could admit into autobiography the inadmissible; if the truly shaming facts can ever be fully borne, let alone perceived, without the panacea of imagination. Ergo mythology and dream life, ergo Greek drama and modern fiction.

I will leave you with the comments—and late-night concerns —of another reader, my wife. All evening she has sat, engrossed in your manuscript, across from the desk where I am writing to you. As you know better than anyone, Maria Freshfield Zuckerman is a child of the English landless gentry, country-reared, Oxford-educated, a good-looking dark-haired woman of twenty-eight, nearly my height, seventeen years my junior, and the embodiment of a cultural background markedly different from yours and mine. She has a daughter from her previous marriage, Phoebe, a sweet and placid four-year-old, and she is nearing the end of the eighth month of pregnancy with our first child. Maria remains very much the dutiful daughter of a well-born mother living in a Gloucestershire village, a woman without a trace of philo-Semitism, even if she has managed so far to be scrupulously tactful with me. Mrs. Freshfield's distaste for Jews generally—about which Maria's envious, unstable older sister, Sarah, had made a point of being *utterly* tactless—was the cause of a nearly disastrous misunderstanding between Maria and me earlier in my stay here. Since then I have made up my mind to ignore her mother's bias and her sister's resentment so long as neither indulges herself in my presence. If, among her neighbors in the charming village of Chadleigh, Mrs. Freshfield bemoans my "Mediterranean" looks —her response to my photograph some months before the wedding—that I view as no concern of mine.

As for my beard, its purpose is not, as Maria contends it is, to make me even more unmistakably Semitic than I already am. To begin with, when I gave up shaving three months back, I had no idea that a rabbinical appearance would be the result. If anything, the seemingly inconsequential decision to live for a while as a bearded man would seem to have to do with the fact that at forty-five I am finally on the brink of becoming a father. Marrying for the fourth time, abandoning my New York apartment and buying for the long term (and substantially reconstructing) this large London house backing onto the Thames, settling down as an expatriate in the middle of Maria's very English life—it's all this, I believe, that moved me to mark myself symbolically as a middle-aged man in the grip of a great transformation.

Nonetheless, this morning when I emerged from the bathroom still unshaven, Maria said to me, "You just won't let that die away." "What die away?" "Zuckerman amid the alien corn." "But it's quite dead as far as I'm concerned." "How can you pretend to believe that from behind that grisly thing? You will be provocative, won't you?" "I have no intention of jeopardizing my wonderful new life by provoking anyone. On the other hand, if to bestir the natives requires no more of me than a bearded face . . ." "The natives couldn't care less. It's you bestirring yourself that frightens me. It wouldn't be helpful to live through that again." I assured her that we won't. "It's an innocuous adornment," I said, "and means nothing."

And that was that, I thought, until the arrival of your manuscript, which I read through twice during the day and which Maria finished only an hour and a half ago. Since then she's been alone in bed, quite beside herself. And, mind you, at dinner her only worry had been the haircut she'd had this afternoon. "He's always cutting the wrong bits," she told me— "what is this bit doing so short, for instance?" I suggested she change hairdressers, but she is an appealingly rational, unillusioned pragmatist, admirably pliant and uncomplaining, and she replied, "Well, he does all right two times out of three." She was slightly more unnerved by our having hired a new nanny last week. With a new nanny, she tells me, you always have a lurking fear that she may be a psychopath, that she just loves torturing children. "I've cheered her up by promising her a new clothes dryer," Maria said. "You have to do that, you know—nannies have to have new clothes dryers and holidays abroad, otherwise they think they're with the wrong family." That was the extent of her apprehension, nearly all of which was feigned. She is a tremendously cooperative woman, tactfully, strategically moderate, and in a crisis reasonable and splendid. It was, as usual, a very pleasant dinner.

Then she read your book, looking up at least fifteen times to tell me what she made of it. I trust the matter-of-fact measure she takes of books; it resembles the way she sizes up people. A sample of her commentary follows, culminating in those distress-laden words that she spoke before rushing off to the bedroom, leaving me to put before you our plea.

1. She located *the* problem (for her) immediately. "Uh-oh," she said, only minutes into the book, "still on that Jewish stuff, isn't he? Doesn't bode well, does it?" "For us? Doesn't mean anything either way," I told her. She didn't look convinced but said no more. Maria does not repeat herself; that I do she'd pointed out to me when we first met. "Why," she asked, "do you have to say everything twice?" "Do I?" "Yes. When you want someone to do something, you say everything twice. Obviously you are used to being disobeyed." "Well," I said, "even *my* life hasn't been entirely without struggle." "Well, I hardly say things even once." "I wonder if it has to do," I said, "with

the different ways we originated." "Those different ways," she said, "are sometimes all you can think about . . ."

2. "Always going back to his childhood," she said of you; then of herself, "I've had enough of my childhood, thanks. No more."

3. An hour passed before she looked up again. "Surely," she said, "there must come a point where even *he* is bored with his own life's story."

4. I was typing away—a draft of this letter—when I realized she was watching me very closely. Half your manuscript was by then in her lap and the other half spread around on the floor by her chair. "What is it?" I asked. "Well, I don't see why you writers shouldn't be narcissistic," she said; "it seems to me one of the flaws of character that people bring to their jobs." "We also have that obsessionality," I said. "Yes," she replied, "that's where the real trouble begins." She's thinking about my beard, I thought obsessionally.

5. Maria on your nemesis and archenemy. "It doesn't surprise me at all that at twenty-five he couldn't stand up to this person who, in animal terms, had so much more fire in her belly. It doesn't seem strange in any way that he didn't know how to fight that. People who are civilized are always getting talked into being ways they don't mean to be by people who are not civilized. People are awfully weak. I know it's a convenient piece of analytic verbiage that you don't do things without wanting to. But it discounts the fact that people are also weak and at some point they just acquiesce. I'm afraid I'm an authority on this. He may not like to admit it here, but I think that's all that that marriage came down to—his weakness."

6. "Odd. As he construes it, the whole thing is a struggle against all those forces inviting him to lose his freedom. Keeping his freedom, giving it away, getting it back—only an American could see the fate of his freedom as the recurring theme of his life."

7. On randomness. "Nothing is random. Nothing that happens to him has no point. Nothing that he says happens to him in his life does not get turned into something that is useful to him. Things that appear to have been pointlessly destructive and poisoning, things that look at the time to have been wasteful and appalling and spoiling, are the things that turn out to

be, say, the writing of *Portnoy's Complaint*. As each person comes into his life, you begin to think, 'So what is this person's usefulness going to be? What is this person going to provide him in the way of a book?' Well, maybe this is the difference between a writer's life and an ordinary life." "Only the subject," I said, "*is* his formative experiences as a writer. Randomness is not the subject—that's *Ulysses*." "Yes, the facts, as far as he's concerned as a writer, have to do with who he is as a writer. But there are lots and lots of other facts, all the stuff that spins around and is not coherent or *important*. This is just such an extraordinarily, relentlessly coherent narrative, that's all. And the person who is most incoherent, Josie, has to have her incoherence made into a shape by him. All I'm saying, I suppose, is that I'm interested in the things an autobiographer like him doesn't put into his autobiography. The stuff people take for granted. Like how much you have to live on and what you eat, what your window looks out on and where you go for walks. Maybe there should, at least, be some of what Cicero calls *occupatio*. You know, 'I'm not going to talk about this, so I can talk about that,' and in that way you do talk about this." "What's it called?" I asked her. "*Occupatio*. It's one of those Latin rhetorical figures. 'Let us not speak of the wealth of the Roman Empire, let us not speak of the majesty of the invading troops, et cetera,' and by not speaking about it you're speaking about it. A rhetorical device whereby you mention something by saying you're not going to mention it. All I'm wondering is, hasn't anything *ever* happened to him that he couldn't make sense of? Because ninety-nine percent of the things that happen to me *I* can't make sense of. But maybe that's because I haven't written it all down and don't have always to be bringing *mind* to bear upon it, to go around asking myself every day, 'Well, what does this signify?' He's making everything *signify* something, when in life I don't believe it does. Mind is simply not the element in life that it appears to be here, not in mine certainly and I'd bet not in his either. I don't mean that he's presenting a deceptive image to make himself look terrific, because on the whole, for me, it's rather the other way. He looks to me awfully narrow and driven and, my God, so pleasureless. He's certainly not interested in happiness, that's pretty clear. I'd think that if something *doesn't* make great sense in his overall pattern of things, he's either bored out of his skull or terrified. He looks to me a little like what you used to look like." "Before being introduced to English randomness." "Yes," she said, "to the fact that everything isn't here to be understood and to be used but is also here because, surprisingly enough, it's life. Existence isn't always crying out for the intervention of the novelist. Sometimes it's crying out to be lived."

8. Lastly, what you elicited about men and women. "I sometimes think that men have a root neurosis about women," Maria told me. "It's really a sort of suspicion, I wouldn't lay any money on it, but I think that—forgive the childish nature of this remark—but through reading all kinds of books and through experience, I do feel that men are a bit afraid of women. And that's why they behave as they do. There are plenty of individuals who are not afraid of individual women, of course, and maybe plenty who are not afraid of women generally. But my experience has been that most of them are." "Do you think," I asked her, "that women are afraid of men?" "No," she said, "not in the same way. I'm actually, as you know, afraid of *people*. But I'm not particularly afraid of men." "Well, maybe you're right," I said, "though 'afraid' puts it too strongly." "Distrustful, then," Maria said.

When she'd finished reading, I asked the question you've asked: should it be published? "If he wants it to be," she said, "why not?" "Simply because," I said, "the only person capable of commenting on his life is his imagination. Because the inhibition is just too tremendous in this form. The self-censorship that went on here is sticking out everywhere. He's not telling the truth about his personal experience. In the mask of Philip he is not capable of doing it. In the mask of Philip he's too nice. He's the little boy nuzzling mama's sealskin coat. It's no wonder he begins with that." "As a novelist's wife who may yet end up as her husband's subject, I'm not someone who considers niceness on a par with Nazism." "But it's surface mining," I said, "and not much more: in spite of his being very much in control of his defensiveness, the book is fundamentally defensive. Just as having this letter at the end is a self-defensive trick to have it both ways. I'm not even sure any longer which of us he's set up as the straw man. I thought first it was him in his letter to me—now it feels like me in my letter to him. It's irrelevant to say I don't trust him when the maneuvering is the message, I know, but I don't. Sure, he talks so freely about all his soft spots, but only after choosing awfully carefully which soft spots to talk about." "Well, take heart," said Maria, "maybe he'll begin doing the same for you." "No, what's motivating his selectivity is strictly self-interest. No, neither his discretion nor his shame enters into his depiction of *me*. There he is *truly* free. And where you *and* I are concerned, he's not likely ever to be as gentle and taciturn as he is about May and himself. *That* romance of anthropological contradictions is practically painless, or so he says. Where's May's anti-Semitic mother? If she even existed, offstage in Cleveland, bothering no one. Where's May's anti-Semitic sister? Nonexistent." "While mine," said Maria, able no longer to suppress her anxiety, "mine are virtually around the corner! Mine practically come to bed with us at night! Please, can't we keep to a theoretical discussion of literature?" "We were. I was pointing to what makes us more interesting than them." "But I don't *want* to be interesting! I want to be left alone with the things that are of no great interest at all. Bringing up a child. Not neglecting an aging parent. Staying sane. Uninteresting, unimportant, but *that's* what it's all about. I accept that one never gets any more from life than adulterated pleasure, but how much longer are we to be bedeviled by his Jewish fixation! I refuse to allow him to make that into a major problem again! I cannot jump, I *will* not jump, every time the needle moves on his fucking Jewish record! Especially as there is not an ounce of antagonism between you and me, especially as we get on so *well*—except when he starts up with *that*! There were those months after the blowup over my mother when everything seemed to have resolved itself, just a lovely long period of quiet and love. What do confrontations on that subject *achieve*? Who even cares, other than him? I thought your New Year's resolution was to not make too much of a fuss about that sort of thing. And then comes this beard! Oh, Nathan, do you really think that beard is a good idea? You seem always to feel that you have to explain what nobody is asking you to explain— your right to be, and to be *here*. But no one *needs* that kind of warranty from you. Those are—and don't go for me when I say this—those are very Jewish feelings and frankly I believe that if it weren't for him you would not have them. I don't know—do you think it would help to see someone, sort of a psychiatric sort of person, about this Jewish business? To have spent all of this evening reading this book—and now I feel so defenseless against what I just know is coming!"

And now, alone, in the dark bedroom she lies, terrified that we shall never have the possibility of being other than what you, with your obsessive biography, determine; that never will it be our good fortune, or our child's, to live like those whose authors naïvely maintain that at a certain point the characters "take over" and do the storytelling themselves on their own initiative. What she's saying is, "Oh, Christ, here he goes again —he's going to fuck us up!"

Is Maria right? What *is* coming? Why, in her England, *have* I been given this close-cropped, wirebrush, gray-speckled beard? Is what began inconsequentially enough now to yield consequences that, however ridiculous, will send us reeling again? How can our harmonious contentment last much longer when the household's future *is* being determined by someone with your penchant for dramatic upheaval? How can we really believe that this beard means nothing when you, who have rabbinically bearded me, appear in even just your first few pages to be more preoccupied than ever in your life with the gulf between gentile and Jew? Must this, my fourth marriage, be torn apart because you, in middle age, have discovered in yourself a passion to be reconciled with the tribe? Why should your relentless assessing of Jewish predicaments be *our* cross to bear!

Who are we, anyway? And why? Your autobiography doesn't tell us anything of what has happened, in your life, that has brought *us* out of you. There is an enormous silence about all that. I still realize that the subject here is how the writer came into being, but, from my point of view, it would be more interesting to know what has happened since that has ended up in your writing about me and Maria. What's the relation between this fiction and your present factuality? We just have to guess that, if we can. What am I doing exiled in this London house with a wife who wants no disturbance in her peaceful life? How much peace am I made for? Her haircuts, the nanny, the clothes dryer—how much more of that intense and orderly domesticity that I once craved can I afford to take? She is indeed making me a "beautiful" existence for the first time in my life, she is an expert in the quiet and civilized and pleasant ways of being, in the quiet and muted life, but what will that make of me and my work? Are you suggesting that without the fights, without the anger, without the conflicts and ferocity, life is incredibly boring, that there is no alternative to the fanatic obsession that can make a writer of a person except these nice dinners where you talk over candlelight and a good bottle of wine about the nanny and the haircut? Is the beard meant to represent a protest against the pallidness of all this—this randomness? Yet suppose the protest bizarrely evolves into a shattering conflict? I'll be miserable!

Well, there it is. Or there it isn't. I will let this outburst stand, absurd as I know it must be to expect even my most emotional plea to alter the imaginative course so long ago laid down for you. Similarly, I will not go back and alter what I argued earlier—that your talent for self-confrontation is best served by sticking with me—however much that argument, if persuasive to you, virtually guarantees the unfolding of the worst of our fears. Nobody who wishes to be worthy of serious consideration as a literary character can possibly expect an author to heed a cry for exceptional treatment. An implausible solution to an intractable conflict would compromise my integrity no less than yours. But surely a self-conscious author like you must question, nonetheless, whether a character struggling interminably with what appears to be the necessary drama of his existence is not, in fact, being gratuitously and cruelly victimized by the enactment, on the part of the author, of a neurotic ritual. All I can ask is that you keep this in mind when it is time for me to shave tomorrow morning.

Obligingly yours,
Zuckerman

P. S. I have said nothing about your crack-up. Of course I am distressed to hear that in the spring of 1987 what was to have been minor surgery turned into a prolonged physical ordeal that led to a depression that carried you to the edge of emotional and mental dissolution. But I readily admit that I am distressed as much for me and my future with Maria as for you. This now *too*? Having argued thoroughly against my extinction, in some eight thousand carefully chosen words, I seem only to have guaranteed myself a new round of real agony! But what's the alternative?

DECEPTION

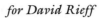

for David Rieff

I'LL write them down. You begin."

"What's it called?"

"I don't know. What do we call it?"

"The Dreaming-About-Running-Away-Together Question-naire."

"The Lovers - Dreaming - About - Running - Away - Together Questionnaire."

"The Middle-Aged-Lovers-Dreaming-About-Running-Away-Together Questionnaire."

"You're not middle-aged."

"I certainly am."

"You seem young to me."

"Yes? Well, that shall certainly have to come up in the questionnaire. Everything to be answered by both applicants."

"Begin."

"What's the first thing that would get on your nerves about me?"

"When you are at your worst, what is your worst?"

"Are you really this lively? Do our energy levels correspond?"

"Are you a well-balanced and charming extrovert, or are you a neurotic recluse?"

"How long before you'd be attracted to another woman?"

"Or man."

"You must never get older. Do you think the same about me? Do you think about this at all?"

"How many men or women do you have to have at one time?"

"How many children do you want to interfere with your life?"

465

"How orderly are you?"

"Are you entirely heterosexual?"

"Do you have any specific idea of what interests me about you? Be precise."

"Do you tell lies? Have you lied to me already? Do you think lying is only normal, or are you against it?"

"Would you expect to be told the truth if you demanded it?"

"Would you demand the truth?"

"Do you think it's weak to be generous-minded?"

"Do you care about being weak?"

"Do you care about being strong?"

"How much money can I spend without your resenting it? Would you let me have your Visa card, no questions asked? Would you let me have any power over your money at all?"

"In what ways am I already a disappointment?"

"What embarrasses you? Tell me. Do you even know?"

"What are your real feelings about Jews?"

"Are you going to die? Are you mentally and physically okay? Be specific."

"Would you prefer someone richer?"

"How inept would you be if we were discovered? What would you say if someone came in that door? Who am I and why is it all right?"

"What things don't you tell me? Twenty-five. Any more?"

"I can't think of any."

"I look forward to your answers."

"And I to yours. I have one."

"Yes?"

"Do you like what I wear?"

"That's straining."

"Not at all. The more trivial the defect the more anger it inspires. That's my experience."

"Okay. Last question?"

"I have it. I have it. The last question. Do you in any way, in any corner of your heart, still harbor the illusion that marriage is a love affair? If so, that can be the cause of a lot of trouble."

"My husband's girlfriend gave him a present the other day. She's very pretentious, a very jealous and ambitious kind of person. Everything has to be high drama for her. She gave him this record. I can't remember, but it's a very well known, very beautiful piece of music. Schubert—and all about the loss of the greatest passion in his life, the most interesting woman of the century, who was tall and thin—oh, it's all related to that. All this is made very plain in the liner notes, how this is the greatest passion that could ever be conceived, the true marriage of true minds, and all this really high-flown stuff about the misery and ecstasy of being separated by cruel fate. It was so clearly a pretentious gift. He makes the mistake of being open about all these things, you see. He could simply have said that he bought it himself. But he told me that she had given it to him. And I don't think he'd looked at the back. I was drunk one evening, and I've got this pink stuff that you underline with and it makes things stand out. And I underlined about seven phrases that just looked hilariously funny when you did that. Then I calmly withdrew to a dignified distance and handed him the cover of this record. Do you think that was awful of me?"

"Why were you drunk?"

"I wasn't drunk. I'd had a lot of drinks."

"You have a lot to drink at night."

"Yeah."

"How much?"

"Oh, I drink a huge amount. It depends. Some evenings I don't drink anything. But if I were drinking, I could easily drink several doubles before dinner, and several afterwards, and wine in between. I wouldn't even be drunk. I would just be kind of elevated."

"So you don't get much reading done these days."

"No. Though I don't drink by myself. There's someone there when I drink. Though we don't really stay together very much. Well, we have recently—but it's not usual."

"It's such a strange life you lead."

"Yes, it is strange. It's a mistake. But there we are, that's my life."

"How unhappy are you?"

"What I find is that it goes in periods. One has periods of ghastliness. And then long periods of sort of quiet and love.

There was a long time when it seemed that all these things were getting worse. And then there was a short time when they seemed to be resolving themselves. And now I think neither of us wishes to have too many confrontations. Because it achieves nothing. And it just makes it all the more difficult to live with each other."

"Do you still sleep together?"

"I thought you were going to ask me that. I'm not going to answer that question. If you want to go somewhere in Europe, I know exactly where I want to go."

"You with me?"

"Ummm. Amsterdam. I've never been there. And there's a wonderful exhibition."

"You're looking at the clock to see what time it is."

"People who drink too much often look at the clock before they have their first drink. Just in case."

"What's the matter?"

"Oh, nothing. Two nannies, two children, and two cleaning women all squabbling, and the usual English damp. Then my daughter, since she's been ill, has taken to waking me up at any time, three, four, five. What's tiring is I'm responsible to all my responsibilities. I need a holiday. And I don't think we can continue to have a sexual relationship. The day's too short."

"Is that right? That's too bad."

"No, I don't think we can. Don't you agree, actually? Last time we talked about it, wasn't that the direction in which your own conversation was tending?"

"Oh, I see. This is a preemptive strike. Okay. Whatever you want."

Laughing. "Well, I think that's best. I think that you put yourself very neatly when you said it was driving you nuts."

"What was driving me nuts?"

"Well, all these sexual matters. You said you didn't think you were very keen on just a romantic friendship."

"I see."

"That's sort of your we'll-let-that-ride expression."

"No, no, it's not. It's my I'm-still-listening expression."

"Well, perhaps I shouldn't have simplified like that."

"Really? Oh, I'll simplify it for you, if you want it simple."
"Don't say nothing. I hate you to say nothing."

"It's very strange to see you."
"Stranger not to, isn't it?"
"No, I usually *don't* see you."
"You do look a bit different. What's been happening to you?"
"That makes me look so different? You tell me what the difference is and I'll tell you what did it. Am I taller, shorter, fatter, wider?"
"No, it's very subtle."
"Something subtle? Shall I be serious? I missed you."

"I went to see a friend of ours who left her husband. She's very clever, she's very beautiful, and she's very successful. And she's extremely courageous and self-disciplined. And she's got lots of money. And she looks terrible."
"How long has she been on her own?"
"Two months."
"She'll look worse."
"Not only does she earn this huge amount of money in an interesting job, but she had a lot of money, so that there are no problems of that sort."
"She have children?"
"She has two children."
"A cautionary visit."
"Well, if she can't do it, well . . . really. She's just been terribly ill, she's moved house, she's just got divorced, and her children are kicking up from being wretched and . . . I couldn't begin. I couldn't begin."

"You don't want him to give her up though, do you? You don't want to say, 'If you don't give her up, I'm going to sleep in the other room. You can either fuck me or you can fuck her. Take your choice.'"
"No. No. I think that she's really an important part of his life, and it would not only be mad but selfish."
"Selfish on your part?"
"Yes."

"Really? Is that your point of view? If it is, then you can marry me. That's a lovely point of view—I've never run into it before. A woman saying, 'It would be selfish for me to ask my husband to give up his girlfriend.'"

"I think it would though."

"Usually people think it's selfish of the man to want her and to have her, not selfish of the woman to ask him to give her up."

"A point of view that is reasonable and right doesn't come naturally. That was my first response. But it is what I think . . . I can see that I've behaved very stupidly with my husband, but maybe it's because I don't know what I've done wrong. He has had to put up with years of me being terribly depressed and lonely. I don't think it was entirely surprising—I was alone so much and he was away so much and working so hard. I didn't have other affairs, because I always thought he was vulnerable and had to be protected."

"He doesn't sound that vulnerable to me."

"So he's safely in a hospital room. You think the tootsie's over there?"

"'Tootsie' is such a wonderful word."

"I thought you might like it. You're getting your little vacation finally."

"Well, I think I've given him an unduly bad press. He has many, many qualities. But the truth of the matter is that I haven't slept so well for a long time. I woke up this morning feeling absolutely normal."

"Did you listen to the record I gave you?"

"No. I had to hide it."

"Why do you have to hide it?"

"Because it would be unusual for me to buy a record. I don't often do it."

"What are you going to do with it?"

"Well, I'll play it in the evening when I'm alone."

"What are you going to do if it's found? Salt and pepper it and eat it?"

"I did buy records, but I did get so upset for a while that—well, that's history."

"What? Did you have fights about that too?"

"Yes."

"Did you really?"

"Yes."

"That's not necessary."

"No."

"You look lovely. That's a nice outfit. Is it on inside out?"

"No. I have lots of clothes with seams on the outside. You never noticed. It's terribly smart. Suggests that you're somewhat anarchic."

"Well, you look lovely but you sound awfully tired. And you're getting skinny again. Don't you take vitamins and all the rest of those things?"

"Intermittently I do. It's that I haven't eaten for three days. I'm so busy."

"Too busy."

"Yeah. I'm sitting in this room trying to type, and this little one comes in and first of all she does a pee on the carpet. And then she goes out and she cries some more and then she comes in again. Then she shuffles several pages around, then she takes the telephone off the hook, and then she comes up to me and she does a crap all over my sofa. Then I have to go off to work and make sycophantic noises at my boss for eight hours."

"And the husband?"

"It's easier when I don't see you. One makes an adjustment and places one's distractions elsewhere—and just forgets, you know? You don't get involved in this terrible comparing. I've wanted very much to explain to you what's been going on in my head. But I feel that perhaps I'm abusing you, and I don't want to do that. One thing that I want is to stop having to explain all that shit to you. I will if you ask me but I'd rather not talk about it."

"Talk about it. I like to know what's going on in your head. I'm very fond of your head."

"I just had my mother for the weekend. And he just disappeared. I had my mother entirely on my own for the weekend. And I haven't slept well for nights. And I think about you a great deal. And tomorrow I have to have lunch with my mother-in-law, which is a slightly grueling experience—she's a woman who can really criticize. She can be so hellishly unpleasant that one tries to keep things out of her way. And the nanny is restive. They all hop around from one house to another, the nannies, comparing employers, and ours becomes very restive. And you know what a cervix is?"

"I think so."

"Such a silly word, 'cervix.' Well, I've got a lump on mine. I have to go have a test or something. And my husband says I've ruined his sex life. He says, 'You're so heavy, everything is so serious, awful, there's no joy, no fun, no humor in anything'—and it's true, I think. I think he exaggerates grossly, but it's truish. I don't enjoy sex at all. It's all rather lonely and hard. But it's like this, life, isn't it?"

"Why don't you do your husband a favor and try to come?"

"I don't want to."

"Do it. Just let yourself do it. It's thought to be better than arguing."

"I get so angry with him."

"Don't get angry. He's your husband. He's fucking you. Let him."

"You mean try harder."

"No. Yes. Just *do* it."

"Those things are not under one's conscious control."

"Yes, they are. Just be a whore for half an hour. It won't kill you."

"Whores don't come. They certainly don't want to."

"*Play* the whore. Don't be so serious about it."

"That's his problem—*he's* so serious about it. He's one of these people who think women should have multiple orgasms and everybody should come together. Well, this is all perfectly normal, and what happens among young people, because it's so easy. But as soon as you've acquired a history and a few resentments—oh, there's *so* much antagonism between us. And why *is* it that one just loses interest utterly in someone sexually?"

"Why don't you ask me why it snows?"

"But it is a reason for leaving him, isn't it?"

"That isn't the reason you're leaving him, if you're even leaving him."

"No. But if I come right down to it, that's what lies underneath it all. He couldn't bear my losing interest in him."

*

"How are you?"

"Oh, busy and angry, as usual."

"You look tired."

"Well, it's not surprising, is it? I've got mascara, I'm afraid, running down my face."

"What are you angry about?"

"I had this terrible scene with my husband. Yesterday. Because it was Valentine's Day and you have to have a scene. Somebody had said to him that he isn't the right husband for me because I really like to be spoiled, and of course I got very indignant—but sometimes I wonder."

"Well, maybe because it was Valentine's Day I woke up in the middle of the night and I had the terrific sensation of your hand on my cock. Now that I think about it, it might have been my hand. But it wasn't—it was yours."

"It was no one's—it was a dream."

"Yes—called 'Be My Valentine.' How did I get so hooked on you?"

"I think it's that you spend all day in this room. Sitting in this room, you don't have any new experience."

"I have you."

"I'm just the same as everything else."

"Oh no you're not. You're lovely."

"Really? Do you think so? I feel a bit ropey, actually. I feel a lot older."

"How long is it now?"

"Us? About a year and a half. I usually don't do anything for more than two years. I mean jobs and things. I don't really know anything about you, you know? Oh, I know a bit about you. From reading your books. But not a lot. It's difficult to know somebody in one room. We might as well be holed up in an attic like the Frank family."

"Well, that's what we're stuck with."

"I suppose. This is life."

"There is no other."

"Why don't you give me a drink?"

"You're near tears, aren't you?"

"Am I? I feel so urgently the need for privacy. I've been longing to sleep alone for as long as I can remember. No, that's an exaggeration. But at the end of the day, when I'm really tired and it's another emotional battle . . . And not only that, but the distraction of somebody else sleeping beside me. We have a very big bed, but not big enough. It's just so sad, isn't it? I mean he has so many wonderful qualities— May I have that drink, please? I'm not terribly stable today. I find it absolutely intolerable that he should say to me, 'I've given up so much for you and it's not worth it.' It's *so* painful. And he said that twice in the last couple of weeks. *Why* can't it get better? We get on so *well!* And actually I do care for him. I'd miss him horribly if I weren't there. There's so much I like about him. . . . Anyway, I shouldn't go on with you like this."

"Why not?"

"Oh, I don't know what I want."

"What you want is not to be in this situation any longer."

"Is that what I want? Is that it?"

"Do you think it would help to see a psychiatrist? Because what I still don't know is what I want. If somebody said to me, 'Look, your husband will stop fooling around, and he will treat you with great respect, and deference, and he'll be utterly charming, but you won't feel different sexually, you're not going to feel any sexual interest, and you're going to have to put up with—' "

"Do you feel any interest in anyone?"

"Now, or ever?"

"Both."

"I used to really enjoy it."

"And now? You don't want to make love to me, do you?"

"I don't want to make love to anybody. At all. I don't know the answer to this. I don't think there's anything wrong with me sexually in general. But there certainly is at the moment. I've even got to the stage where it actually hurts."

"The answer to your question about seeing a psychiatrist is yes."

"Somebody good is difficult to find."

"Are you going to do that on the sly, or openly? And if you do it openly, why are you going to say you're doing it?"

"The only reason I wouldn't do it openly is because later it might emerge that I was unfit to be a mother. That I was neurotic and therefore it would be much better if the child were with her father."

"No court would hear it."

"But I don't want to go to court—I just want things to be *different*."

"You know what I'm doing on Tuesday? I'm going to see a solicitor."

"About getting divorced?"

"Well, not really about that. Just to find out what's up. I'll probably arrive here in a very heightened state."

"Good. It'll be interesting."

"What happens when he asks you how you got that bruise on your thigh?"

"He already did."

"Oh. And?"

"I told the truth. I always tell the truth. That way you never get caught in a lie."

"What did you say?"

"I said, 'I got this bruise in a torrid embrace with an unemployed writer in a walk-up flat in Notting Hill.'"

"And?"

"It sounds silly and everybody laughs."

"And you maintain the illusion that you're an honest woman."

"Absolutely."

"You're trembling. Are you ill?"

"I'm excited."

"Do I look horrible?"

"We'll pour some whiskey down you."

"If I start to go through this divorce business, I'm going to have to behave quite impeccably. But I don't think I'm going to do it."

"Then don't do it."

"I don't know what my intentions are. It was rather a strain telling all these things to some lawyer. What I found offensive is that he had some very attractive young girl lawyer there as well. I nearly said she must go and then I thought we better not start off like that. I decided that I wasn't going to go into any confessions or anything. But there are certain things you cannot avoid, like 'Has your husband committed adultery?'"

"What did you say?"

"I said yes. He has for years. Well, if you put up with someone's adultery for six months, you condone it. And it can no longer be a cause in itself. They were quite curious to know why I put up with it. So I said, forget that, it's really this: he has this wonderful setup where he can do exactly what he likes, and I have discovered that this is a terribly unusual setup, and if I can't get something like that going on my side, I think I might as well call it a day. And this girl was shocked that I was being so frivolous. But it's very difficult to discuss these things. You don't really want to talk to them about it."

"But you have to."

"You know, once upon a time when I lived in the country, and before I spent a lot of time in the city, I felt simple and I wished to be simple. But that dies if you struggle a lot. I used to be a lot of fun."

"I enjoy you now."

"I'm kind of grieving today over the fact that we don't have any kind of sexual life. I mean, whatever sexual life we have is not what *I* want."

"You tell the lawyers?"

"That? No, of course not. He's very keen on sex, but from my point of view, the way it's all worked out, there's nothing in it."

"You told me. You endure it."

"Well, not even that anymore. I've decided to give it up."

"So that's going to bring the end about even if the lawyers don't."

"I know. But it just seemed too stupid. Funnily enough, oddly enough, I think there's something to be said for . . ."

"Celibacy?"

"I wasn't going to say that, though I think that's also true. It's much better for working—I have a lot more ideas. And feel much more in control of myself. And have much more access to all the things I want to think about. And am not so terribly distracted as I was. What happens, I think, is that you sort of close down shop, sexually. You go into hibernation. I don't know because I haven't done it before. It's not really natural to me. I used to be sexually quite arrogant because it was all so easy."

"Once upon a time."

"Yeah."

I AM Czechoslovakian girl, graduate of Russian literature. I emigrated to U.S.A. in 1968 after the Russian tanks come. I lived in U.S.A. for six years, in Upper East Side, and now I come back."

"Welcome."

"I fell hopelessly in love with my new home in '68. Everything in America was new—I had to learn many things and I had to be fast. I studied acting but I did not go any further than to bikini test for Paramount. So I went into fashion but I was not so happy with that job, so I would like to write book now. This is why I come to see you."

"I'm glad you did, though I don't know if I can help."

"When I arrived in U.S.A. I worked at first for television producer and lived in his town house as live-in baby-sitter. I thought this is America. When I left this house I found myself apartment in East Side. I found that my body was out of the usual. They invited me for modeling. They put me in silk robe embroiled with gold. I look down at what he is doing and I saw his big big penis and he was waiting if I look for the penis or if I keep myself busy with modeling robe. I did not go for the penis, so he ask for my girlfriend. It was clear to me that I will have to make life at my own."

"How did you do that?"

"The man who I was meeting got me new apartment in celebrity building. Across from live beautiful black model. I saw the beautiful black man taking out her garbage. I will always run just to stay next to them in the elevator. Actor who live in that building also take me visit to his girlfriend. He will make love to the two of us and then make climaxed only the other

478

girl. I was despaired. The man was doing that to me everywhere. Some of my girlfriend become prostitutes. They will come home in the morning with pocketbook full of hundred-dollar bills. I succeed to get job as a bra model. They put at me black Valentino dress on I did model. I kept the dress and start to visit bars in the Hotel Pierre and Plaza. What are men like? Will they like me?"

"Did they?"

"Men like me too much. I started to hate my body. I will tight my big breast under the clothes, I will go to take voice and speech lessons just to loose my accent. As I found out the accent was doing that to me too. But there was still my off-white complexion left. I started to hate money. Anything I dream about was love. I think I will go to the Sigmund Freud doctor."

"You got therapy."

"No. I become party girl. The man took me to show business party, call girls party, United Nation party. I become jet-setter. I will fly to Acapulco and beautifully wasted my time. I run in fifty-four-year-old Belgian millionaire and for two years we entertain our self as what the money can buy and where ever in beautiful place its can take you. You know the mentality; he will go in bed with half of the disco but always leave with me. I started to do the same, as I felt I was woman and it was time of women's liberation. Fulfillment to me was trip to Monte Carlo, Regine's disco, five beautiful lovers calling my apartment in Fifth Avenue, Parke-Bernet, couturier clothes, French restaurants, et cetera. My life was quite meaningless but it was always better than to marry poor man, live in Brooklyn, and have three children. All over I felt it was all the time the same. Only the decorations changed. With the bill being served to my boyfriend. We both started to dream about foreign places and foreign people. As everybody who watched me started to talk about his airplane and take out his money or credit cards. I became very curious about the sex and I start to experimentize at my own, as I saw everybody to do that. I got myself the best the Manhattan can offer to me. I end up in hospital with the emotional illness."

"For how long?"

"Two months. I come out. Living the flashy life, I always

keep study. I become professional apartment decorator, I went to school to become fashion designer, I took French cooking courses, finishing school for young ladies. I work with discipline. And as the miracles are often achieved with the discipline it happen with me."

"And the discipline—that's the happy end of the story?"

"No. No, no. In Regine's disco in Monte Carlo I met beautiful stranger and I let myself to fall hopelessly in love with him. He was Arab. I live with him one year in style in Paris, where I go to French classes and he marry me. I went to live with him Kuwait. There was a price for a thousand and one nights. I kept fainting all over the place. Bang, and I was just right at the floor. He turned into the hard, intelligent, brutal man. Then the Palestinian raped me, they told me that my husband was paid to marry me. They took me into the Embassy, they told me that my husband was Communist and they offer me to sign contract for two hundred thousand dollars. I found the connection between the ambassador to the United Nations who I kept meeting at the Upper East Side parties. They follow me. Communists. I run up to the Czechoslovakian Embassy. They already know everything. I was set up. They said, 'You go to U.S.A. and work for us. You go and beat the Jews.'"

"That doesn't entirely surprise me."

"They took me to police station and beat criminal in front of me until I fainted. I ran to the United Nations, the committee for human rights. They said, we cannot do anything for you. It is criminal intent to the United States security."

"I don't follow you."

"They said, you are very important political witness. I remember all this years being outsider in the society and now there was not even law for me."

"And what are you asking of me?"

"Please, I love Kafka and I studied Freud. And I love and deeply respect Jewish people. I admire their intelligence. I am looking for somebody who will read and help me with my book."

"Your book is about what?"

"There was not in the history published book about prostitute written by prostitute. I need to found somebody who will help me to get published. I will be so glad if it could be you."

Y ou think Jews in England try harder?"

"I do."

"But it's not hard to try harder in England."

"Nonsense. Really, your picture of the English is very different from mine."

"The lowest production rate per capita in the world is in England."

"You're talking about industrial workers. And they're very smart. Why should they work? But people who actually have something to gain by working in this country, they work. And I've seen them do it."

"And the Jews work even harder than these people."

"No. I just said they tried harder than I did."

"Do you have a Jewish woman friend?"

"No. Obviously not a close one, or I could think of her. I'm trying to think of a less close one. I've had [*laughing*] close Jewish men friends."

"Which do you prefer?"

"I don't wish to talk about this."

"But I want to know. Which do you prefer?"

"For fondling, the uncircumcised. It's interesting to move the sheath over the head."

"And for fucking?"

"You can't ask this of a nicely brought-up English female."

"For fucking."

"The circumcised."

"Why?"

"It's like having it naked."

"The naked penis."

"I guess."

"Honestly, I swear to you that it's true. I never masturbated until I was twenty-seven."

"Poor you."

"Close your eyes."

"Uh-oh."

"Close 'em."

"I am not going to be tied up."

"My dear friend, who here ever suggested tying you up this early in the game?"

"I've read about it in books."

"So?"

"Writers write those books."

"Close your eyes."

"If I must."

"Let's see how much attention you've been paying. Describe this room."

"To begin with, it's far too small for two people to conduct a love affair in."

"Can't we find a house with a bed in it?"

"No. We can't. I've thought about it. I have friends with houses with beds in them but I don't see how we could. There are cleaning ladies, nannies, children—"

"Then this little room without a bed will have to do, won't it?"

"It does have two nice French windows looking out on a green lawn and a flowering tree. In keeping with the room's functional austerity, the windows have neither shades nor curtains, so that the people in the houses across the garden, I am quite certain, can clearly see everything that is going on."

"Mostly what they see is someone typing. Sometimes they see him reading. Anything more interesting they deserve."

"There is a very comfortable black leather chair in which a woman who should be back at work is sitting. Wearing two rubber bands around his wrist, bending and twisting the paper clips with which he constantly fidgets while he listens to the woman complain about her marriage, is a man in a leather desk chair. His desk, about three by five, consists of a gray metallic pedestal and a pale Formica top whose surface is not as orderly as his compulsiveness would lead you to expect, though he seems to know which uneven pile of papers is unfinished manuscript and which is a stack of unanswered letters and which contain the clippings about Israel that he cuts from the London papers to prove to her that the British are anti-Semitic. The typewriter, on a typing desk placed at right angles to the writing desk, is an IBM Correcting Selectric Two. Black and serious. A Prestige Pica Seventy-two golf ball."

"Very good."

"Bookshelves built into the wall behind the desk. Much complaining about shoddy British workmanship while construction was under way. Books: *Heine's Jewish Comedy* by Prawer, *The Jew as Pariah* by Hannah Arendt, *White Nights* by Menachem Begin—on and on. Entirely too many books about Jews, by Jews, for Jews. A dusty, torn Japanese paper globe suspended over the desk, property of previous tenant. Two chrome architect lamps, or whatever they're called, one for each desk. Two Dimplex heating units, white. Commercial carpet, steel blue. One plastic mat for back exercises and adultery. Various London literary weeklies stacked beside Roberts radio tuned to Radio Three on cheap glass-and-bamboo coffee table. Paris edition of *Herald Tribune* open and folded back to sports page. One extra-large wicker wastebasket stuffed with *Herald Tribune* back issues, discarded work sheets, torn manuscript pages; also several Spud-U-Like cardboard containers for baked potatoes with ratatouille filling, signifying lunch is as Spartan as everything else. Plaster floral ornamentation on ceiling molding the sole voluptuous detail."

"That all?"

"Unfortunately. Now you close your eyes."

"Okay."

"Let's see how much attention *you've* been paying."

"Go ahead."

"Describe me."

"I made such a fuss about what they're going to do with the baby if there's anything wrong with it. I wanted a doctor who would bump it off. I found several. I just went to these doctors

and said, what would you do if there was something seriously
wrong with the baby. Obviously they're not going to bump off
a child who looks healthy just because you're afraid it might be
brain damaged. But a spina bifida child or a mongol or certain
very gross obvious problems. And I know what I'm talking
about. I talked to four doctors. What was interesting at the
time and why I was particularly upset about it was because
there were two cases, just before I was due. One was where a
guy did murder a child and he was convicted of it. Of murder.
There was tremendous controversy. All over the papers. He
was recognized to be a fanatically devoted, decent man. He'd
brought up a handicapped child himself, so though he had
killed it he was left off. But he had done it. He hadn't intervened
and he hadn't given the child enough nourishment. But it takes
ages if you're going to starve them. You have to really beat
their heads in if you're going to be serious about it. You can
murder them or you can let them die. And the awful thing is
that babies who have something seriously wrong with them are
often very strong—otherwise they'd have died in the womb or
been aborted. The other case was when a woman with a mongol child had to give it up and somebody adopted it after she'd
tried to murder it. There are lots of creeps who want to raise
handicapped children."

"You're not one."

"Are you? You don't even want to raise a healthy child. The
first doctor I went to, a very decent man, he said he agreed to
my attitude but he wouldn't risk his career for it. And that's
that. One of them said that of course he agreed with me and I
shouldn't worry. Babies could easily be disposed of by shoving
surgical swabs down their throats until they choked. So I said I
thought that was rather excessive, there must be kinder ways
of murdering babies. The nicest man and the best doctor said
yes, and he clearly would have done something terribly painful
for himself and difficult—oh, I did worry about it a lot. And
there was something else I'd found out, which was sustaining.
Which is that if you're a woman and you commit any crime
within six weeks of giving birth, you almost certainly will not
even go to court about it. Because there's a dispensation in law
that women in that period, and even within a year of giving
birth—well, they consider that you're slightly off your head.

So you could murder it and you'd get away with it, I think. You'd have to be damn careful, but I do think you would get away with it."

"You're not saying much. You hardly do, you know, when I'm here."

"I'm listening. I listen. I'm an écouteur—an audiophiliac. I'm a talk fetishist."

"Ummm. It *is* erotic, you just sitting there listening."

"Not so odd, really."

"It isn't, is it?"

"We used to have the television in the bedroom and everybody used to come and watch it in this huge double bed we have. It was the beginning of so many destructive alliances. For the sake of the community we took it out of the bedroom. At least three couples found each other watching telly on our double bed."

"Sounds like a nice idea."

"No, it wasn't very helpful."

"Last Sunday you said, 'I have to go home because he'll get curious.' Why do you care if he gets curious?"

"Because I have to tell lies and I don't like doing it. I have to preserve some sense of truth without actually getting caught, and it's extremely irritating. Tedious. It is. I have plenty of other plans to make without having to construct a hundred little red herrings."

"It's very cozy with you on a snowy day. Lying just like this and all the snow going round the trees—quite wonderful."

Undressing him. "This is a new belt."

After he comes. Softly. "Are you all right?"

"Sweet girl."

"What are you thinking?"

"No thoughts. Isn't that nice?"

"It's sublime."

*

"Do you honestly have thoughts about jumping out a window?"

"Oh yes."

"A lot?"

"Frequently."

"And what stops you?"

"It isn't that I want to die, it's that I want to live—to live better. I want life to be better, so I realize I better stay in it for a while longer."

"There was a crime prevention officer at home. *And* my husband. So they held me up a bit."

"Are you okay?"

"Yes, I am. May I sit down, please?"

"Yes, you sit down right there, miss."

"I was very surprised to find these two men at home."

"I like 'crime prevention officer.'"

"I know. How about that. But he didn't have my crime in mind. There's been a rape in our road. Next door, in fact. So I was worried about our house, which is full of windows. And we have this very attractive young girl, our nanny. So the police came around to see me. A very handsome young police officer, out of uniform, came to see me. He wanted to have a chat."

"What's a crime prevention officer?"

"He wants to prevent crime. He wants to prevent, in particular, the crime of anybody breaking into our house. Because it's not properly fortified."

"But Banham's does this."

"But I had them to do it. They did such a bad job that I can get in myself."

"And rape yourself."

"I've got other things to do when I'm at home. So that's why I'm late. It took me aback."

"So how did you get out?"

"Well, it was really quite difficult, because my husband was expecting that I'd come home from work and stay and have tea with the baby."

"So what did you say?"

"I said I was going out."

"And he said?"

"Where to? And I said, I'm not going to tell you. But in a very friendly way. And—so I went. And here I am."

"Irritated with me because you had to go through all that to get here."

"I'm not."

"Okay."

"I don't think I'm irritated."

"Well, let's find out."

"Did you get my letter?"

"Yes, I did. It was wonderful. I tore it up. I thought that would be the perfect thing to do."

"It's five o'clock. Time you Gentiles start drinking, isn't it?"

"I think so."

"Very impressive."

"What?"

"You with your hair up."

"It doesn't suit me."

"It suits *me*."

"Why aren't you happy with your wife? Why isn't it enough?"

"Why isn't your husband enough?"

"I told you a great deal about him. I want to hear about you. I've told you plenty about myself. I want to know why she isn't enough."

"You're asking the wrong question."

"What's the right question?"

"I don't know."

"Why am I here?"

"Because I followed temptation where it led me. I do that now that I'm older."

"All of this sounds like a popular song."

"That's why they're popular."

"Why are you so anxious to avoid wounding her?"

"Why should I want to wound her?"

"I didn't mean that you would or you should. But since you don't seem free to do anything . . ."

"What's free? You?"

"Freeish. Free-er."

"Nonsense."

"But if you care about somebody enough to want to protect her . . . I just wonder why she should be in such a vulnerable position."

"You're being euphemistic."

"I'm not."

"Then I don't understand."

"I would have thought that she would keep your attention, more of your attention, than she seems to have. And it seems odd that she hasn't. But then people say the same of me, I suppose. I mean, about my husband."

"Perhaps we should give this conversation up."

"Why, when there are things about you I want to know?"

"Perhaps it works better if only one participant in an adulterous affair complains about domestic dissatisfactions. If both go at it, it's unlikely there'd be time for the thing itself."

"So your dissatisfactions are out of bounds. Except your dissatisfactions with England and Englishness."

"Isn't it possible that domestic dissatisfaction—as distinct from cultural displacement—has nothing to do with having fallen in love with you? Isn't it possible that I'm not as burdened by all that as you are and consequently have less to say about it? Isn't it possible that my predicament lies elsewhere?"

"It's cultural displacement that's driven you into this—is that what you're telling me?"

"Maybe something like that."

"Could you be a little more specific, please?"

"As they say in an idiom more succinct than our own, *Il faut coucher avec sa dictionnaire.*"

"So our story isn't a love story, really—it's a cultural story. That's the one that interests you."

"That one always interests me."

"That explains the Gentile women, does it? You fall in love for the anthropology."

"Could be worse. There are other ways of addressing anthropological differences, you know. There's the old standby hatred. There's xenophobia, violence, murder, there's genocide—"

"So, you're kind of the Albert Schweitzer of cross-cultural fucking."

Laughing. "Well, not *so* saintly. The Malinowski will do."

I WAS a little Czech girl and I came to your hotel and you wanted me to go up to your room to get some books to help you to carry. It was ten o'clock in the morning. They were very rude. They treated me like a whore and then you made a scene. Then I took you across the Charles Bridge. And you taught me all those colloquial words. We had dinner in your hotel. You didn't particularly care about me, because when I came to your hotel you were sitting and drinking something. I was about twenty-one, twenty-two. I'm much older now."

"What's the name of that park, at the top of Prague, where we sat?"

"I don't know. We didn't go there. It must have been someone else."

"No, no one else. I particularly *did* care for you."

"You telephoned me once to invite me to an orgy. Remember? And I said I could only watch. And you said, no, you have to participate. So I wasn't brave enough to go."

"You didn't miss anything."

"You were followed all the time and when we sat in a restaurant this chap sat with us and we just couldn't take it. Working in the American Library wasn't a very clever thing for me to do. My professor got me the job. He said, almost as a joke, it would be nice for all of us, because we could get books and we can't go there. We all thought I'd be sitting in a library and working with books and reading. Which for two years it was. It was a great job, fantastic job, but in the end it started to be difficult. I had to decide whether I work for Secret Service or go. I'm not supposed to talk about it still."

"You're in London. It's okay. Talk."

"How I got the job, I went to see the cultural attaché. And he said, 'Oh, I'd be interested in you because you studied literature and so on.' He was a very nice man. Of Czech origin. So I liked him and he liked me, and he gave me a job, no trouble. But then you have to go to the Czech organization, who either give it to you or not. It organizes all employees for any foreign work, which in reality is a branch of Secret Service. Which I didn't know. I was just a stupid little girl and I was very excited about the job. I thought it would be great, I'll be in contact, it's exactly what I studied. And I had some nice friends, and I was popular, but the more I was popular with Americans, the more I was in trouble. This organization, they let me work for two years and then they call me back and they said, 'Oh, we're sure you like your job, also you have much more money in that job than anywhere else and lots of other perks.' And then they count on your not being brave enough to leave but staying and working for them. And also it's very difficult to leave because after that nobody will employ me as a teacher. First they give me a piece of paper to sign, saying that this discussion we were about to have was a state secret and that if I ever tell anybody about it, I can be put in prison. I could be put in prison anyway because I talk to my girlfriends, to several people, because I was so scared. I was informed that this discussion is under paragraph such and such and it's a state secret. And if I reveal it to anybody, including my own family, I can be prosecuted and in prison up to seven years. I said, 'What do you want me to do?' and they said they won't tell me until I sign. So I said, 'I can't sign anything I don't know about.' So they said, 'Do you want a few days to decide?' And I said, 'No, I can tell you straightaway. I can't do it, I don't want to do it.' So they said, 'You'll have to find yourself another job. Because it's no future for you in the library.' They didn't fire me, they said I'd have to find another job. They didn't do anything to me, they just said there was no future for me and that I eventually had to leave. I went back to work and I didn't tell anybody. On top of it, the Americans then did the same thing. Told me that they were very interested in me. And the same thing, I refused as well. They didn't want me to sign something, they just asked me to work for them. I said no, I didn't want to do it. So by that time, my situation started to be absolutely awful. On both sides. They both were interested in me because I speak the languages. I speak German as well. So probably I would be suitable for them. I was quite good at translating. I always enjoyed literature and translated stories for Czech newspapers. So since then I started being not very welcome from both of them. I left very soon afterwards. I left and I was forgotten. Fortunately I found a teaching job. For another two years I did that—then I married. He came to Czechoslovakia and he married me. In between I was in love with an American professor who was very serious but I was not permitted to see him—the Czechs wouldn't let me go out and he lived in Toronto. And also he was getting divorced and didn't know what to do and I was very upset about men who don't know what they want to do. So I married this stupid Englishman who at least knew he wanted me. 1978. It was absolutely silly because he was an easygoing Englishman who all he likes is the football and cricket. He's this type who will go to pubs—I had quite an interesting half year seeing horses and dogs and pubs. I can't blame him, I can only blame myself."

"You married him to get out."

"I don't know, because I was longing for something nice, something . . . And I didn't even like him by the time I was leaving Czechoslovakia because I hadn't seen him all year. It took me over a year to get out. To sort all my papers, because, you know, you must have hundreds of papers, you have to pay for your education. When I came to England he was so upset when I was crying, and I was miserable, and I couldn't cope. I just couldn't cope, it was so difficult. And he started to hate me. I was supposed to be very happy that he rescued me from a dreadful, awful country. And I wasn't. I was miserable and awful and missing all my friends. You probably never met certain English people, because you always move in circles that are different—they're interesting, educated people. But if you get among ordinary people, who may be quite nice, but you just talk a different language . . . You just have nothing in common. It was so awful for me to try to live here and to try to get various jobs, and then you mention that you just arrived in England, and nobody wants you. So that was very difficult. I did all possible jobs, typing and selling books at Foyle's—I was thrown out on the third day because the manager was unbearable and I talked back, which you don't do in this country. So I was sacked. But I was still myself. I was still like a Czech. Please, I don't feel like telling you my life story. I told you already in Prague."

"Then it was a different story."

"You should tell me your life story. It's more interesting."

"It's not. Go on."

"He was not a bad man—but I was somebody straight from Czechoslovakia, straight from—well, I always had a rather nice life there, an easy life, apart from those few times I was bothered by the Secret Service. But they didn't do me any harm. They just asked me if I would work for them, I said no, and I think they more or less let me alone. But I was frightened just that they were there. I actually first met them when I met you. When I was caught with you in the hotel, they called me straight when you left for the airport. And wanted to ask me lots of questions about you. I was absolutely terrified then. I was very scared. My hands were trembling. They asked me what I was doing in the hotel with you. And how did I come to get to know you. And if I slept with you. Imagine, I was only twenty-one. They just took me to their offices. To this building. Suddenly they were on my doorstep, showed me the badge, and took me away. I said to them, 'I met him, I spoke to him, I liked him, that's all.' They questioned me not very long, about an hour. One was sort of threatening and one was nice. You know, they have these roles. This was my first time. You always hear about these people in Czechoslovakia, but you never meet them. But this was *me*, and I was sitting there, not knowing what was going to happen to me. I was too young to realize that they can't really do much to me. Now I'm not scared when I see them but at the time I was. You know, I felt dreadful because all I did was go to your room and you said could I help you with some books. That's how they know who I was—because they took my identity card, took my name and address and everything, and apparently just when you left . . . and I was very fond of you, I don't know, there was something nice about you, I liked you very much, in fact. At first I didn't but then you walked across the Charles Bridge, I was sort of— it was just a very nice thing for me to go with somebody whose book I read. One of them said, 'You better tell us everything because we know everything anyway.' To which I answered, 'If you know everything, why do you ask it? Why do you ask me when you know?' They didn't ask me anything about you. They mainly were interested in whether I slept with you. Maybe they thought that somebody who writes a book like this must be a sex maniac. They take any small bit about anybody. So you caused it all—you have to buy me a drink."

"How did it end with the English husband?"

"I saw this advertisement, that they want guides who speak languages. And I went for an interview and it was a Greek, this guy, with dark eyes, a nice man. English people, I hated them at that time, because they are so polite, but just when I would open my mouth and they would hear my foreign accent, I had no chance. And I couldn't prove that I was rather intelligent, because they couldn't care less. Because he was a Greek he said he didn't like the English either and he gave me the job straightaway. So I was delighted, I was absolutely thrilled that finally after one year I got something to do and make a bit of money. I told him I was married and I wanted to do just a few tours because I couldn't do it all the time. And he agreed, this manager, it was okay, I could do just a few tours. So I came home and I said to William that I took it, and he said, 'Well, you decided you want the job?' And I said, 'I do,' and he said, 'Well, pack up your things and get out of my flat.' So I did and that was that. It wasn't much fun because it was about eleven o'clock at night. And I was sitting on my cases out in the street. On the one hand I was very happy because I was out of something I didn't want to be. But it wasn't much fun, because a Czech girl sitting on her cases eleven o'clock at night in London . . . Well, I telephoned a girlfriend who was Czech and who also had a difficult experience here, but she emigrated in 1968, when the Russians invaded our country, she didn't speak the language, so she understood. She said, 'Oh, I expected this telephone call for a long time. Stay there,' and she and her boyfriend came and picked me up. And put me up for a few days. So I was very lucky. Then I just arranged to see the manager and told him I had nowhere to go, so I arranged to work all through the season. And I did so, sleeping in various hotels, every night in a different bed. I got stubborn. I could have packed it up and go home. And start all over again.

But there was something in me—I went through this, I bought a flat, and then I fell in love with someone whom I loved very much but he was married. So that was the saddest thing for me. It only finished recently. It just didn't work. In the beginning it was very beautiful. He very much wanted both. He had two children. He was forty-five. He was very clever and interesting and nice. He was one of the managers of my company. Quite important job. For about a year he was totally in love with me. But it went all wrong because he started to be scared. You know, in England they so very much are in love with their little house—and the *garden*. And wife. And he has kids. I didn't want to marry. I just wanted to be with him. I just wanted him to love me. I could feel how I was losing, because his wife started to say, 'I'm going to destroy you.' At the beginning he said to me that they were sort of separated. Then it was awful, it really was. I nearly went the wrong way. But I actually made it work. Though she started to be so worried that she would lose her husband and all her money. But money was not what I cared for. I wanted him. But what was tragic was that I started slowly to see how I was losing. Because I didn't want to fight. I wanted him to love me because he loved me, not because I would trick him into it. She was clever, she used every technique against me. She knew about me. I even saw her a couple of times. She just came to see me. To talk to me. To say that she was going to destroy us. But I was very strong, because I didn't care. I didn't have anything anyhow. I'm thirty-two, and when you get to this age you discover . . ."

"Discover what? What have you discovered?"

"I always was trying to be more or less like other people and worried what they think about me. Now I know I'm different. I want to be myself. I want somebody who's going to love me, whom I'm going to love. I'm not necessarily going to be married to someone, I just want . . . But people here, or people anywhere, have rules. I hate Czechoslovakia because it has very set rules. You can't breathe. I don't particularly like England because it has another set of rules. Of little houses and little vegetable gardens, and all their life is to get something like that. I can't be like that. You know, that man made me welcome. Because he is very much interested in the war and

East Europe. And he knew a lot about it. He wasn't like the majority of people here, who are typically English and don't know much about the outside world. He knew what I was like and we could talk about a lot of things. It was wonderful. I felt totally different, I enjoyed being here. That's why I was so hurt, because I'm back being a—well, now again, I have my distance. I hate my distance. Because I was educated I more belong to the class that I don't have the money to be in. I have much more in common with these people than with the people I belong to because of money. I'm misplaced. Totally."

YOU got thinner."

"No, you've just grown used again to somebody heavier."

"Well, I've got much fatter."

"Have you? It's nice to see you."

"I wish you could have come skiing. I hurt my knee so badly on Thursday that I spent two days lying on the sofa. But it's still a wonderful thing to do. It's so peaceful. Going up the hill very quietly on the lift. And a lot of snow so you couldn't see very well. Just the hiss of your skis."

"Did you have any new thoughts?"

"Thoughts? No. You can't think on the slopes. It's too frightening and too exciting. I had the most thoughtless time. Our friends had an existentialist nephew of twenty-two visiting. Telling us all about why we didn't exist. Or did. It was a little too much. We said, 'Look, we're sorry, but we've read all this too. Leave us alone. We don't want to sit here suffering all the time—we want to go skiing.' You've been with me on a lot of mountains."

"Me?"

"Yes. While riding the T-bar."

"Me and the hiss."

"That's right."

"I want some lunch, actually."

"I can give you bits and pieces of things."

"Can you?"

"We'll see if we can put something together for you. Everything all right at home?"

"Yes, it is. It's fine."

"Nothing better for a marriage than an old boyfriend on the side."

"Is that what you think?"

"You want to play reality shift?"

"Maybe."

"My mother taught me never to sit with my cunt exposed."

"And your legs over a gentleman's shoulders."

"She never told me that. I don't think she had any idea I'd go in for that."

"It's called Jack Daniel's. Smell it."

"Ummm. It does smell good."

"I'll tell you an experience that was shocking. To smell this woman's scent on my baby. And the final irony is that it used to be a scent I wore when I was much younger."

"He likes it."

"He doesn't even know that's why he likes it so much. I got tired of it and stopped wearing it, and then it became very popular. It's screamingly popular. It's called Fiji. These things have a scarcity value. If you can smell it in every shop, then it doesn't have et cetera et cetera. But *he* gave it to me."

"I feel as though I don't have a cunt. I left my cunt behind today. I don't want to be reminded about it."

"Okay."

"You want me to go?"

"Hardly. You're near tears again today."

"I do feel a bit teary, yes. Can I have something to eat?"

"Well, there are some strawberries, and some melons, and there's some bread, and there's wine, and there's marijuana."

"Can I have a little of each, please?"

"You don't also have to fuck when your mother's there, do you? Can't you at least get out of that?"

"No. I have to do everything. Fucking, sucking. Everything. Cooking. There are all these substances in and out of people's mouths. It does sometimes feel that way. I have to make everything right and happy. A barrel of fun."

"It's hard to provide fun."

"It certainly is."

"Maybe you should just become a hooker."

"Oh, I don't think I'd be a very good hooker."

"You'd be a marvelous hooker."

"Yes? What kind of business would I have? I don't think I fit into the general whatever it is, you know, that people have about hookers."

"Are you kidding?"

"I'd have to be a kind of matron type, wouldn't I?"

"Oh, I see—in the sense of people who want discipline. The la-di-da accent and the cool gaze."

"Yes. Who want to have a respectable schoolmistress show them how."

"Yes, you might be able to make money that way."

"Ummm. I would like the money. It's a thought."

"Suppose I were to die and a biographer were to go through my notes and come upon your name. He asks, 'Did you know him?' Would you talk?"

"Depends how intelligent he was. If it were someone really serious, yes, I might talk to him. I might say, 'You're going to have to let me see everything in his notebooks before I decide whether to talk to you.'"

" 'He liked you quite a bit, I can tell you that. Can you tell me something about him?' "

"Why are you doing this?"

"I'm curious. 'I want to get this right and you can help me. I have a lot to lose if I get it wrong, and so does he. And so do you. He was big on candor, so why not help me get it right?' "

"If I thought the man was just an idiot, I wouldn't talk to him, because he'd get it even further wrong. What would be the point?"

"Take the best case, not the worst."

"Yeah, well, I might talk to him."

"What would you tell him?"

" 'He didn't write any of his books. They were written by a series of mistresses. I wrote the last two and a half. And even those notes he took down in his hand are my dictation.' "

" 'Look, miss, you're very sweet and pretty, and maybe we

can have lunch sometime and you can charm me like this again. But you're not telling me the truth. What kind of affair did you have with him?'"

"'Very occasional.'"

"'Was he in love with you?'"

"'I don't know the answer to that.' What he'd really want to know is what you were really like. What I thought you were really like. I'd be quite good on that."

"Would you?"

"Yes."

"What's the answer?"

"Well, there's no short answer."

"'You were going to tell me what he was like.'"

"'I'm not going to tell you. Even if I did, you'd get it wrong in the book.'"

"'What was he like to you?'"

"'He was very nice.'"

"'Nice? That isn't what I've heard. What was he like?'"

"'A tall, thin man with a cheap watch.'"

"'Did you want to marry him?'"

"This is a very handy device to get me to reveal myself, isn't it? But I ain't talking. It has to be Leon Edel or I'm not saying a thing."

"I find it bloody embarrassing to think that you might be clutching yourself with one hand and the telephone with the other. You don't do that."

"Not with you, toots."

"I'm glad to hear it. I don't think that's quite on."

"It's been done."

"Oh, I know. I know it's commonly done. Giving good phone."

"You told me I give good phone."

"Yes. But I don't necessarily give as good as I get."

"You remember me."

"Yes, it's coming back slowly."

"Okay. Take your time."

*

"What can I do for you today?"

"I would like a drink."

"It's got beautiful out."

"Is it? I wasn't noticing."

"You don't look too cheerful."

"We went to dinner on Saturday night. And—I love dancing."

"I didn't know that."

"Disco dancing. I'm really very good at it. I think I'm unusually good at it. I don't very often like to do it because I think it's a form of sexual display. And it's very confusing when you're making sexual displays all over the place. I think it's terribly sexy—and I don't know quite what to do about that. So I have to be quite drunk to do it. And also, this is true, I've never quite enjoyed disco dancing with my husband. Although he's extremely fit and well built and graceful, it's never struck me the right way. And he's always known this even though I've tried to disguise it. And also there's only one nightclub that we belong to and I think it's very dull and middle-aged. I mean very very middle-aged. It's people taking whores there. I say this because it's necessary to understand the story. But the fact of the story is that we went to a dinner party with old friends, all rather laid back and left wing. Hangovers from the late sixties. People who never really grew up—most of them never married or had children. There was a very attractive young girl sitting next to my husband. She looked a little bit like my husband's girlfriend. The long and short of it is that he took her off to a nightclub. Pissed off in the middle of dinner, not just after pudding, and he sort of excluded me from the invitation in an extremely subtle way. He pissed off well before the end of the evening with one of the guests! Against the will of everybody there."

"Were you embarrassed?"

"No, I wasn't embarrassed—I can't afford to be embarrassed. I wanted to be very embarrassed, if you know what I mean."

"I know what you mean. Was there a man there for you?"

"Well, some were unattached. It was sort of a mixed bag. So I got very upset. Though you must at one level, I think, admire the style and the will. And he looked so utterly charming doing it. Couldn't wait to go dancing, he was so bored with all this stuff."

"Did he fuck her?"

"Don't think so, but I didn't ask."

"And may I ask what you think about all this?"

"I got terribly upset, the most awful feelings. We had the most awful scene when he came home."

"What time?"

"About three-thirty."

"He fucked her. And what then—did he fuck you too?"

"No, certainly not. This is his answer: 'You don't like dancing with me. You don't fancy me. Don't be hypocritical about it. Don't demand from me things that you don't give yourself.' We had a long conversation, of course, very serious."

"How angry were you?"

"I was absolutely furious. But why *should* he be tied to somebody, you know . . ."

"Why should you for that matter?"

"I'm terribly angry with him. But it's true that I'm not in a position to get angry—that's the awful part. It's very difficult, I must say. How does one deal with these things? I have absolutely no feeling for him at all—at all. Yet this terrible jealousy I feel—what is it? What's the message, doctor?"

"My sweet girl, the message is that you have a choice, you have an option, but one that's unacceptable to you."

"What's that?"

"Guess."

"He always does these things when I'm so defenseless. When I'm on top of the world he behaves beautifully. But as soon as it looks as though I'm going to be without a job, or I have a new baby—"

"Or you don't have a lover."

"Or whatever—but what can I do? I could take the view that I'm onto a very good thing, that he can do whatever he likes as long as he behaves nicely—"

"And pays the bills."

"And pays the bills."

"Perhaps you could reach that arrangement. You're very good at articulating the terms of things aloud."

"Can I ask you something? Why shouldn't they go out

dancing? And it actually probably was only dancing, and if it wasn't, so what? Why shouldn't he? What is wrong about that?"

"You know something, you're hypnotized by bad behavior. You think it's stylish."

"Please answer me. I'm telling you what he says. Just tell me what's wrong with that. That's his position."

"You say, 'I don't know what's wrong with that—it's probably great, but I don't want it.'"

"Do I then say, 'Look, I don't care what your needs are, I want you to stay at home. And not leave me to go out with strange women'?"

"That's right."

"'I don't care if you're frustrated and wasted. You just stay at home.'"

"There's another way of doing it, of course."

"What's that?"

"It's called going back to the lawyer. It's called getting a divorce so he can go off and dance his fucking heart out every night of the week, only without humiliating you."

"I have this fantasy every other day."

"You are too young to be afraid to leave."

"Why am I so afraid? It's not because I don't want to."

"You *do* want to. That's why you're afraid."

"If I'd said that I want to come—I didn't actually want to go—but I had the chance of saying I want to come."

"Why should you? 'I want to come too.' No. What are you, an extra child?"

"He was trying to persuade all of us to go, and all of us were saying no, no, no. That girl wouldn't look me in the eye when she left. She said goodbye to everybody except me. So she knew it wasn't right."

"He's tamed you again. You were out of his control about three or four months ago, but he's tamed you again."

"Why can't it just get better?"

"It never gets better. It's like a play. They never get better, either. If you want to leave at the interval of a play, leave, because it's not going to get any better."

"But I don't know what I want."

"I've already told you a hundred times. You don't want to be in this mess. And that's why you have been marginally farting around with me."

"It's true that that's what made me feel free to, as you put it, fart around with you."

"Marginally."

"When we met, when I said to you I want distraction, that's what my motive was. And it was."

"Well, you've had the distraction, for whatever it's been worth, and now you have progressed to the next step. It always comes after distraction. It's known as taking your life in hand."

"I *could* go to a lawyer again. And the more predatory the better."

"Since I happen not to be in your husband's shoes, I agree."

"But what they would then get up to against *me*—and I say 'they' because it wouldn't be just him, it would be him and his huge mother."

"Who's not so nuts about you to begin with."

"Well, she's not only that, she's vicious. She isn't just a miserable spouse, she's naturally vicious. And she's absolutely obsessed with her grandchild. She said to me the other day, 'You do realize that people can sue for access to their grand-children.'"

"You should have kicked her right in the ass."

"It isn't my way."

"But it is your way to go to a lawyer again; that fits in exactly with your logical mind and your realism."

"Yes, but why am I so paralyzed?"

"You're terrified."

"I'm not terrified of him."

"No, of being alone and penniless."

"Why shouldn't someone be terrified, someone who's seen in her own family what I have? I have seen financial insecurity and I have been *marked* by it. Do you still think it would help to see a psychoanalyst? Because what I don't know is what I want."

"So you say and say."

"And he has a big hang-up about sexual power, my husband. It's a real problem. That's why it went—because of his obsession with sexual power. Looking around at what you might call all our middle-class friends, they accept the limitations of their sex life."

"He doesn't want to accept it."

"Well, I did."

"Some few do."

"He's so strange."

"He sounds rather typical to me."

"A typical man?"

"No, typical of a man like himself. Penetrate and withdraw. Penetrate and withdraw. He may be extraordinary in some ways but he's not strange."

"Why are all these friends relatively content while I'm so miserable?"

"How do you know they're content? You don't know anything until you see the position of their feet in the bed."

"Thank you, doctor."

"I'm not your doctor. I'm your friend. Your admirer."

"You see, it's been a difficult time for you to come back here and visit. I should have warned you."

"I would have come anyway."

"I went down for the weekend to see my mother, who's much better. But I sat there as if anesthetized. As if someone had injected me with some—some aging drug. You know, something that will take the spirit out of you. Even she commented on it. I just didn't do anything. My God, I've been through so much with that woman, terrible things that I've handled, years and years of ghastliness which I've managed to deal with since my father's death. And she finally seemed so much better and I was miserable."

"When the patient recovers the nurse falls ill."

"Yeah, something of that. I remember thinking that in order for me and my sisters to be sane, it's essential for her spirit to be broken and for her to be written off. I remember thinking it's a family conspiracy. My uncles and aunts felt the same: she's got to go."

"Those are ghastly feelings."

"With all the weight of difficulties I'm contending with here, then to go down there—and always to go down there by myself. I don't like that because I know my husband is having a good time in London, and it's painful that he won't come, that a certain kind of decency is dead, that he ought to support me more in it in a conventional way. Sitting there with my mother I felt as though I were waiting to die. She was in good form, she was doing well, and she was getting me down so terribly. Sometimes when one's in a bad situation, life seems over and you're just waiting for the time to be used up. Did you ever have that feeling?"

"Sure."

"With your father?"

"No, not with him. My old father still lives at the boil. He's got an opinion about everything and often it's not mine. I sometimes have to suppress being a fourteen-year-old with my father. Rather than waiting to die, sitting with my father I sometimes feel as though I'm waiting for life to begin. This last summer he got all riled up when one of my brother's kids decided to marry a Puerto Rican. Since he can't hide his feelings and usually doesn't try, he got the kid riled up, and then my brother got angry and he called me, and so I got into the car and drove down from Connecticut to New Jersey. When I got there he started in with *me* about it. I listened for about half an hour and then I said that maybe he needed a little history lesson. I said, '*Your* father, at the turn of the century, had three choices. One, he could have stayed in Jewish Galicia with Grandma. And had he stayed, what would have happened? To him, to her, to you, me, Sandy, mother—to all of us? Okay, that's number one: ashes, all of us. Number two. He could have gone to Palestine. You and Sandy would have fought the Arabs in 1948 and even if one or the other of you didn't actually get killed, somebody would have lost a finger, an arm, a foot, for sure. In 1967, I would have fought in the Six Day War, and at the least have caught a little shrapnel. Let's say in the head, losing the sight in one eye. In Lebanon your two grandchildren would have fought and, well, to be conservative, let's assume only one of them got killed. That's Palestine. The third choice he had was to come to America. Which he did. And the worst thing that can happen in America? Your grandson marries a Puerto Rican. You live in Poland and take the consequences of being a Polish Jew, or you live in Israel and take the consequences of being an Israeli Jew, or you live

in America and take the consequences of being an American
Jew. Tell me which you prefer. Tell me, Herm.' 'Okay,' he said,
'you're right—you win! I'll shut up!' I was delighted. I had
him outfoxed and wouldn't let him go either, not quite yet.
'And now you know what I'm going to do?' I said. 'I'm going
out to Brooklyn to talk to the girl's mother. I'm sure she's
down crying on her knees too, giving her rosary beads a real
workout. I'm going out to Brooklyn to tell her the same goddamn thing I told you. "You want to live in Puerto Rico, your
daughter marries a nice Puerto Rican boy all right, but you all
have to live in Puerto Rico. You want to live in Brooklyn, the
worst that happens is that your daughter marries a Jew, but
you get to live in Brooklyn. Take your choice." ' Well, this starts
my father right up again. 'What kind of comparison is that?
What do you mean, "the worst that can happen"? The woman
ought to be tickled to death who her daughter's marrying.'
'Sure,' I said, 'she is—tickled to death just about as much as
you are.' "

"How did it end? What happened?"

"The marriage took place in St. Patrick's Cathedral. With a
rabbi in attendance. Just to be sure they didn't try to slip us a
fast one."

"What a carry-on! Why do they all magnify these things so
much?"

"Why do you all try to minimize them so much? In England, whenever I'm in a public place, a restaurant, a party, the
theater, and someone happens to mention the word 'Jew,' I
notice that the voice always drops just a little."

"Does it really?"

"The way most people say 'shit' in public, you all say 'Jew.'
Jews included."

"I really think that only you would notice a thing like that."

"That doesn't mean it isn't so."

"God, you are your father's son, aren't you?"

"Whose should I be instead?"

"Well, it's just all a bit of a surprise, after reading your
books."

"Is it? Read 'em again."

*

"Why does everybody around here hate Israel so much? Can you explain that to me? I have an argument every time I go out now. And I come home in a fury and can't sleep all night. I am allied, in one way or another, with the planet's two greatest scourges, Israel and America. Let's grant that Israel is a terrible country—"

"But I won't."

"But let's grant it. Still, there are many countries that are far more terrible. Yet the hostility to Israel is almost universal among the people I meet."

"I have never been able to understand it myself. It seems to me one of the most curious freaks of modern history. Because it's just an article of faith among left and left of center, isn't it?"

"But why?"

"I simply don't understand it."

"Do you ever ask people?"

"Yes, often."

"And what do they say? Because of the way they treat Arabs. That is the greatest crime in all of human history."

"Oh, sure, that's what they say. I don't believe a word of it. I think it's one of the most extraordinary pieces of hypocrisy in human history."

"Do they know Arabs?"

"Of course they don't. In English high culture, you could say it's because of this Foreign Office fantasy about Arabs, and Lawrence of Arabia, all this, coupled with a serious knowledge of Arab interests, and families with all sorts of contacts with sheikhs and who still get watches for Christmas and all that rubbish. It's a kind of feudal thing which the British quite like. You know, our boys and their boys. But that's sort of establishment —the actual antagonism comes from the so-called intelligentsia of this country."

"And what do you think is at the root of it?"

"I don't think it's anti-Semitism."

"No?"

"Not in the main, no. It's just the fashionable left. They're very depressing. I can only come to the conclusion that some people are so wedded to certain unrealistic ideas of human justice and human rights that they can't make concessions to necessity of any kind. In other words, if you're an Israeli you must live by the highest standards and therefore you can't do anything really, just go back and turn the other cheek, like J.C. said. But also it seems to me an unspoken corollary that you criticize most harshly the people who actually behave best, or the least badly. It's quite banal, isn't it? These hotheaded people disapprove selectively and most strongly of the least reprehensible things. It's just unreal, isn't it? I think it has to do with the last gasp of romantic hatred of the twentieth century. But it's not really as strong in this country as you may think."

"You think not."

"I'm sure not."

"Well, I'd feel much better if that's true. About this country, and about you too."

Laughter.

"I'm not anti-Israel. I loathe Arabs. We had them crapping on the pavement around our house, putting up property prices, and all the rest of it, the way the Jews would never do."

"We never crap on pavements. Putting property prices up is something else."

"Well, I think the Israelis have got into a very, very difficult position, and there's nothing really they can do, and they could be a lot nastier than they are. I think there are lots of reprehensible incidents, some of which we hear about. But that's the nature of the game. Look what happens in Northern Ireland. The torture of some particular individual, the shelling of a particular family of small children—nobody wishes as a matter of policy for disgusting incidents to take place. But perhaps they don't always regret them as much as they should."

"I never hear about Northern Ireland when I'm out on the town here. I hear only about Nazi Israel and Fascist America."

"Well, you don't hear that from me. People in this country who have any sense at all, who are people of any kind of discrimination and judgment, are not anti-Israel and don't believe that America is the Great Satan."

"These are people on the right."

"I would think on the whole they tend to be. Centrist types too."

"Is that what you are?"

"I'm nothing. I don't know anything about politics. Though

certainly I know all the opinions. As if *everyone* doesn't know every last argument on either side of every issue and has to hear them again and again and again."

"That happened last night—some genius 'batting on,' as you say, about the sainted Sandinistas. And about the torture chambers the U.S. supports in El Salvador, Chile, and Guatemala. Supported by '*your* president,' he told me, 'by *your* tax dollars.' I said that I had no brief to make for El Salvador, Chile, and Guatemala, let alone for 'my' president, but since he was listing Latin American regimes which brutally crush any dissenting voice, I wonder how he could fail to mention Cuba. I said that because it is not a regime supported by the U.S., that doesn't make life any more pleasant for those who are imprisoned and tortured there. 'Cuba is strongly allied to Nicaragua,' I said. 'I would go so far as to say that this alliance goes unquestioned by the Cuban and Nicaraguan people, and unchallenged by the press that's permitted in both countries, whereas the alliance between Chile and us is openly attacked by opposition politicians, journalists, and academics in Fascist America. But leaving these differences aside,' I said, 'do you feel it is as reprehensible for Nicaragua to be allied to a country where people are imprisoned and tortured for their ideas as it is for the U.S. to be allied to such a country?'"

"And?"

"What do you think? 'Your president is going to blow up the world! What are *you* doing to stop him? What about your blacks? What are *you* doing for your blacks?'"

"Where were you having dinner, in a pre-school nursery?"

"No, no, London's highest literary circles, my dear. Over dessert I defended dropping the bomb on Hiroshima *and* Nagasaki."

"You took that bait, *too?*"

"I defended Harry Truman against war crimes charges until one a.m."

"*Why?*"

"Because being a Jew and being an American in this country of yours is making me into a very contentious fellow. I'd forgotten about both, really. Then I moved to England and started attending smart dinner parties."

I'M having trouble with the tenants—I think they're taking drugs.' 'Do you want me to come?' I ask. 'No. I have a friend staying with me. Andrew. It's okay.' She meets me at the airport. I bring her a Laura Ashley dress. Perfume. She kisses me tenderly. There's dinner for me. Then the door opens by itself. A six-foot black man. Shoes for two hundred dollars. A gold ring. A gold necklace. 'This is Andrew.' 'What is the function of Andrew?' 'Can he live in the spare room? He has nowhere to go.' 'I don't think there is any future together here with Andrew. He can go to a thirty-nine-dollar motel.' 'You think Andrew could have dinner?' 'It's my first night back, but okay.' If he was white I would have said no, but you can't tell a black person, straight into his nose, no, you can't have dinner here. Then I see some of my condoms are missing. Olina is having trouble with the IUD and I am using condoms. We're going to the theater. 'Can Andrew come with us?' 'Do you think he'd enjoy it?' I ask. 'He's half illiterate.' He comes to the theater. I notice at the theater that she's leaning toward him. I separate them and pull her to me. Coming home I start speaking in Czech. I say, 'Listen, this Andrew has to leave the house.' She says, 'It's very impolite to speak Czech.' 'He's a tenant—fuck it.' To Andrew I say, 'You have to leave tomorrow.' He comes down the next day and tells me, 'You pushed a button too much.' She says, 'I love him. I want to marry him.' To have someone fucking in your bed for four weeks! And to have my Olina lying into my eyes! I was close to buying a shotgun. Not a rifle but a shotgun. Wait for the man and shoot him into the trousers. I had a mild heart attack. Terrible chest pains and I'm in the hospital for a week. My lawyer laughs.

'You have a joint account with your wife?' But I trusted her as a Czech girl, not as an American bitch. It's that nigger that does it. I don't say 'black person,' I say 'nigger.' This girl, educated in a Catholic family, she was frigid. She went to bed with me in a long nightdress. Never had an orgasm. I'm not so young but I used to be a very good worker. Unfortunately, I never got anywhere. Impossible. But he gives her an orgasm on his black prick. It wouldn't be hard to give Olina something to smoke and then stick it in. A real Slavonic character is Olina. He's a typical pimp type. An unsuccessful operator. Has a four-thousand-dollar Hasselblad camera, a truck—and that's it. Has nothing. Does little odd jobs. Doesn't know how to spell, writes like a child. This half-illiterate black guy lives with that beautiful girl in a motel about thirty miles from the center of the city. In one room with a shower, in a motel. Black guy doesn't work. Lives off her unemployment benefits. She was fired. The productivity of her work dropped because all the ladies took part in the soap opera of her life. She cried a lot and they fired her. She looks bloody awful. She suffers a great deal. She wants to divorce me because she says that she loves that man. You know how women are. Suddenly she felt the terrible desire to be somebody else. The speed with which this gentle aristocratic Czech lady was pushing for a divorce! A hard-hearted, proud person is Olina. Good. Fine. I couldn't kiss ever again the mouth that sucked that long black prick. Only she has too much love for that black guy. He's unable to take that, especially if there's no money forthcoming. He's too primitive. He doesn't understand it. He'll leave her. She will return to Prague because she will have nowhere else to go. But this is the Soviet Union she will be dealing with, not a washed-up old emigré like me—never again will she be able to go to America. Authorities will always be worried that she is a spy. All because of his long black prick! He did not fuck her the way you fucked her, for her stories. He fucked her for fucking. You are more interested in listening than in fucking, and Olina is not that interesting to listen to. She is even less interesting to listen to than to fuck."

"I never fucked Olina."

"You're lying to me, my friend."

"She's lying to you, if it's she who told you."

"You fucked her four times. In New York. When we were all such good friends after I arrived from Prague."

"Not even once, Ivan."

"Other men listen patiently as part of the seduction leading up to the fuck. That is why men usually talk to women—to get them in bed. *You* get them in bed to talk to them. Other men let them begin their story, then when they believe they have been sufficiently attentive, they gently press the moving mouth down on the erection. Olina told me about you. She repeated it a couple of times. She said, 'Why does he keep asking these irritating questions? It is not emotionally conventional to ask so many questions. Do all Americans do this?'"

"Ivan, enough of whatever this is. None of it is true."

"With the nigger it's his prick and with the Jew it's his questions. You are a treacherous bastard who cannot resist a narrative even from the wife of his refugee friend. The stronger the narrative impulse in her, the more captivated you are. And all of this, I must tell you, limits you not only as a friend but as a novelist."

"So my books stink too."

"Play dumb if you like, but you know the truth. You only enter into life to keep the conversation going. Even sex is really at the edge. You are not driven by eros—you are not driven by anything. Only by this boyish curiosity. Only by this gee-whiz naïveté. Here are people—women—who do not live life as material but live it soulfully. And for you the more soulful the better. You like it best when they are in posttraumatic shock trying to recover their lives, like Olina fresh from Prague. You like it best when these soulful women can't actually tell their own tales but struggle for access to their story. That is the erotica of it for you. The exotica too. Every woman a fuck, every fuck a Scheherazade. They have not been able to gain access to their story and in the telling of their story there is a kind of compulsion to complete the life—and there is much pathos in this. Of course it is stirring; just the wash of their sound, the quality of intimate conversation, to you is stirring. What is stirring is not necessarily in the stories but in their urge to *make*, the stories. The undevelopedness, the unplottedness, what is merely latent, that is actuality, you are right. Life before the narrative takes over *is* life. They try to fill with their words the enormous chasm between the act itself and the narrativizing of it. And you listen and rush to write it down and then you ruin it with your rotten fictionalizing."

"How so exactly?"

"Yes, you *would* expect me to help you perfect your lousy art, you *would* want to talk about literature, you shitface, after having helped yourself to my wife!"

"Cast it in the form of an insult if that makes it more fun. In your eyes, as a writer, what *do* I do wrong? Tell me. You've never wanted to before and you know how much I respect your taste. I've picked up a lot from the talks we've had."

"You insist on playing dumb. Even *this* you banally fictionalize. You are not even sweating. Maybe you should have been a wonderful actor instead of a terrible novelist who will never understand the power of a narrative that *remains* latent. You don't know how to leave *anything* alone. Just to give voice to the woman is never enough for you. You will not just drown in her cuntliness. You must always submerge and distort her in your hero's stupid, artificial *plot*."

"So that's my vice and ruination—blatant instead of latent. The blatant American. Look—listen to me, *please*: the reason I'm not sweating is because none of this is so. I'm an *awful* actor. When I'm guilty I can outsweat Nixon. Believe me, either it's your paranoia or Olina's vindictiveness that's convinced you I fucked her. You're the ones who, if I may say so, are banally, blatantly fictionalizing. Her leaving you like this is obviously killing you. It's awful. I know how much you've lost already. Things haven't worked out for you here professionally —and now this, losing her. But don't extend your sense of betrayal to me. It's not justified. I hate to remind you, but I've been one of your supporters here."

"You were staring at her ever since the first time we all met."

"She's very beautiful, she's young, so I stared. But staring isn't fucking in my book."

"So why my Olina now tells me that four times you fucked her is only vindictively to drive me even more insane."

"Something like that seems to be happening, yes."

"You shitface! You lying, pampered American shitface!"

"Calm down—*sit* down! You're going to give yourself an-other heart attack—and there is no reason for it."

"Don't worry, don't worry, little American boy, I'm not going to shoot a shotgun into your trousers."

"Good, because there's no cause to."

"No, you I'll shoot into the ears!"

THIS is the situation. Zuckerman, my character, dies. His young biographer is having lunch with somebody, and he's talking about his difficulties getting started with the book. He's found a tremendous lack of objectivity in people's responses to Zuckerman. Everybody gives him a different story. There are two nightmares for a biographer, he says. One is that everybody gives you the same story, and the other is that everybody gives you a different story. If everybody gives you the same story, then the subject has made himself into a myth, he's rigidified himself, but you can sort of crack at it with an ice pick and break it down. It's much harder when everybody gives you a different story. You may be closer that way to a portrait of a multiple personality, but it's also awfully confusing. All right. You be the biographer and I'll be the friend. The biographer is still at the point, after having done a lot of research, where he's not even sure he wants to go through with it. Do I want to write this life? What's the real interest in this life? He doesn't just want to retell the story of Zuckerman's boring Newark. What interests him is the terrible ambiguity of the 'I,' the way a writer makes a myth of himself and, particularly, *why*. What started it? Where do they come from, all these improvisations on a self? By now the biographer is already somewhat angry with Zuckerman and is trying to overcome it."

"Why is he angry with him?"

"Because of his sense of insignificance and having to establish himself in relation to the subject. He's begun to turn against Zuckerman, to resent him, because he has this responsibility to him. We all need a mode in which to write—this biographer seems to need either hostility or awe, and so he oscillates from

one to the other. He was, in fact, moved by wading through all
the childhood stuff. You're back thirty-five years and the
writer is unguarded by any sense of self-consciousness. He's
not writing for any audience. It's the writer before the audience sets in. You see this slightly repulsive embryonic writer in
his letters, trying out on one or two people, and in private, the
voice with which he's going to try to capture the attention of
the larger audience. And all the false steps. The falseness in the
voice moves you more than anything else. You see the writer
becoming more and more manipulative, slier and craftier and
underhanded. Now this biographer—you—he's already written the biography of E. I. Lonoff. He wouldn't have undertaken Zuckerman's biography, but since Zuckerman only lived
to be forty-four, he figures he can do it in two years. Lonoff
drove him nuts. Lonoff destroyed everything, and it took him
five years to do a hundred and eighty-five pages. None of the
people in Lonoff's life would give him anything. Zuckerman
died suddenly and so he didn't have a chance to destroy anything. The Lonoff book turned out to be a critical biography,
Between Worlds, The Life of E. I. Lonoff. The tentative title of
the Zuckerman book is *Improvisations on a Self*, and he started
off thinking it was going to be easy. People say to him, 'Why
are you wasting your time on a minor writer?' But he knows
he's going to make money on this book. There's a lot of curiosity about Zuckerman. The fucking particularly. People want
to know the dirt. It's going to be Book-of-the-Month Club.
First serial rights to *Vanity Fair.* His wife, too, thinks he ought
to be doing a major writer, but he says to her, 'We want to
have a baby, we need a bigger apartment. I can do Zuckerman
in two years. I need a hundred thousand bucks if we're going
to buy a bigger co-op and there's no other writer I can do this
fast for that kind of dough. He was forty-four years old, only
four books, and the literary criticism isn't that difficult. It's the
dream biography—the author died young, he led a juicy life
with lots of women, he outraged popular opinion, he had an
instant audience, and he made a lot of money. Also, he's a serious writer whose books are readable and I can go to town on
the autobiographical issue. It's really the biography every biographer wants to write because the *issue* is biography. I wasted
five fucking years on E. I. Lonoff and in the end I came up

with his critical biography and nobody read it. It won some obscure prize.' 'But ten years from now,' the wife says, 'nobody's even going to read Zuckerman's books.' 'That's right,' he says, 'the only book they're going to read is mine.'"

"And what is it you expect me to do?"

"Play reality shift."

"Must I? I almost think I'd rather fuck."

"Please, I'm stuck. Help me."

"Oh, okay."

"You're the biographer. *You're* stuck. You're flooded by now with impressions and information and you have no idea where to go. You've been following every lead, trying just to go with the tide, and you feel tremendously unbalanced. That's why you ask me to have lunch with you."

"Who are you?"

"I am myself."

"How—?"

"Don't ask me how. I'll worry about how."

"Is this really the book you want to be writing? Because it doesn't seem to me like a very good idea, to have, in the same narrative, you *and* Zuckerman—"

"Who knows? We'll find out. Look—we're at lunch. I say to you, 'But, Fred, Bill, Joe, whatever your name is, you met Zuckerman yourself. Start from there. During the Lonoff biography you saw him about five times.'"

"'Three times. I have notes. At that point I liked him but he intimidated me.'"

"Good. 'How?'"

"'He somehow made me feel like an earnest graduate student. And I'm not really earnest, though I do present myself in an earnest way.'"

"'But *he* was earnest.'"

"'Yeah, but I guess my earnestness brought out his sardonic side.'"

"Wonderful. I love you."

"No you don't—you love *this*."

"'Did he talk to you about Lonoff?'"

"'Yes. He was really cordial. He gave me his letters. I don't know if he gave me all of them—he probably didn't. Now I'll find out. He had some imagination for my difficulties.'"

" 'Which were?' "

" 'Writing about this absolutely private man. And he gave me some good advice about writing. He was very lucid about writing.' "

"Who are you talking about?"

"Guess."

" 'What did he say?' "

" 'Well, I was in a crazy state when I was working on that book. Can you imagine? Five years. And Hope Lonoff and the children wouldn't talk to me. Wouldn't *see* me. They suppress the story of his every human exchange as though this fastidious hunger artist, whose high and rigid principles denied him so much of the pleasure of appetite and elemental life, in secret had the remissive history of Jean Genet. It would have been comical, all their obstruction, if it hadn't made my life hell. The self-imprisoning scrupulosity, the block against contaminating experience that all but strangled his art they monumentalize into his pious memorial. All that timidity, disguised as "discretion," about a man's contradictions and pagan urges. The fear of desanctification and the dread of shame. As though it's *purity* that's the heart of a writer's nature. Heaven help such a writer! As though Joyce hadn't sniffed filthily at Nora's underpants. As though in Dostoyevsky's soul, Svidrigailov never whispered. *Caprice* is at the heart of a writer's nature. Exploration, fixation, isolation, venom, fetishism, austerity, levity, perplexity, childishness, *et cetera*. The nose in the seam of the undergarment—*that's* the writer's nature. *Im*purity. But these Lonoffs—such a suffocating investment in temperance, in *dignity*, of all damn things. As though the man wasn't an American novelist but was ambassador to the Holy See! . . .' Isn't that enough for now?"

"Absolutely not. No! You're cookin'. You're on fire! You're dazzling! Go on, go on."

"But that would not be my position at all, of course. I'd *side* with the Lonoffs. I happen to believe *strongly* in privacy."

"Who cares? This is exquisite. *Go on.*"

" 'And then all the things that Lonoff himself destroyed. Lonoff was so paternal—I had to work through all my father shit with him. My wife wouldn't believe that. She kept telling me, "Come on, just type it up and hand it in. What's your problem?" I showed Zuckerman a chapter. I was so embarrassed, because I hate to show people things that are messy and unfinished. He read it and he said, "It's all here somewhere. But there are two things you're really going to have to do here. You can't do it right away. You're going to have to put this away for a while." ' "

" 'What were the two things?' "

" 'He said, "You have to write and you have to think." ' "

" 'And that was helpful to you? You didn't know that?' "

" 'It was helpful. The most helpful things are the most obvious things. Coming from someone else and said in a certain tone. He sort of brought me back down to earth. You work on the life of Lonoff long enough and there's a sense of this rarefied being. A kind of piety crept into my approach, which I couldn't stand. And Zuckerman was great, because as a young man he'd had the same feelings. He was very funny about it. He gave me a sort of license to transgress. Zuckerman was the great sanctioner. Not that I wanted to slash Lonoff to pieces. But I had to feel that I *wasn't* an earnest graduate student, that I *didn't* have to have this phony nobility I had about Lonoff, revering him and so on. Zuckerman told me how, when he visited Lonoff in his early twenties, Lonoff had said to him, "You're not so nice as you look." Zuckerman said to me, "I'm going to repeat to you what Lonoff said to me." And it was the most liberating thing he could have told me.' "

" 'How so?' "

" 'It liberated me from my scruples.' "

"Oh, sweetheart—why do you look so sad saying that?"

"Because *you* have no scruples and I just know what I'm in for."

"I have no scruples but I do love you terribly."

"You only do if I play reality shift."

"You were wonderful. *You* should be the writer, you know."

"Nope. Never. Couldn't."

"Why not?"

"Not a bad enough fellow. Insufficiently aggressive. Insufficiently ruthless. Insufficiently capricious, venomous, childish, *et cetera*. My scruples."

"But maybe you're not as nice as you look either."
"I'm afraid I am. It's grotesque. I'm English. I'm even nicer."

"I had a little adventure on Sunday. I was walking in Chelsea
with my Israeli friend Aharon Appelfeld and his son Itzak. We
were just off St. Leonard's Terrace, heading up toward the
King's Road. We were on the left side of the street and coming
along on the right side were two men in their thirties or early
forties, who looked like professional men, nicely dressed in
sweaters and slacks, out for a stroll. As they were approaching
us, they began to cross over to our side of the street and I noticed that one of them, wearing a green sweater, was mumbling out loud, or repeating something out loud, and all the
while glaring at me. I couldn't make out what he was saying—
he was sort of half saying it to himself—but he kept it up even
as they passed us and continued down the street. I turned to
look after them just as he happened to turn to look after us,
and he was still at it. I couldn't figure it out exactly, though I
had a hunch. I shouted at him, 'What's bothering you?' At first
he just glared back at me. Then he gestured at his own clothes
and he shouted, 'You don't even dress right!' I got confused
by that. My pullover sweater happened to be dark brown while
his was green, but otherwise we were dressed almost exactly
alike. Though I did have my beard, of course, and it is getting
scruffy and needs a trim. So—what he'd seen, you see, was a
bearded, spectacled, darkish man dressed more or less like himself, talking animatedly to a smallish, bald middle-aged man
wearing a sports jacket and a sport shirt and to a dark-haired
boy of eighteen, both of whom had been listening and laughing
as they all three walked along the quiet, civilized streets of
Chelsea on a beautiful Sunday afternoon at the end of the summer almost, I might add, as though they owned the place. He
answered, 'You don't even dress right,' and just stood there
glaring at me, full of fury. And then I knew for sure what it
was. I could have killed him. If I'd had a gun I would have shot
him. Not because I was that enraged for myself—it was because
who I happened to be walking with was a dear friend whose
mother had been killed by the Nazis and who had himself
spent part of his childhood in a concentration camp. I thought,
'No, this won't do,' and I walked a couple of steps toward him

and, in my best American accent, I said, 'Why don't you go fuck yourself?' He looked back at me for a second or two, but then he just turned and stormed away. I have to tell you, if there was going to be a brawl, I was counting very heavily on Itzak, Aharon's son, a big strong boy who does lots of push-ups every morning, but it turned out that the English gentleman wasn't looking for a fight. He was just furious, that's all, the mere *sight* of me on the quiet, civilized streets of Chelsea had simply driven him up the wall. The fury was in his stride, on his face, it was in every breath he drew. The whole thing left me very agitated—and a little puzzled. I couldn't understand what he'd meant by telling me that I wasn't even dressed right. Aharon couldn't figure it out either and Itzak was just amused. He's an Israeli-born kid and he'd never actually witnessed an anti-Semitic incident before. To this boy from Jerusalem the man had just seemed ludicrous. But I come from Newark and I kept puzzling over the damn thing, and then it dawned on me: the reason my clothes just like his were wrong was *because* they were just like his. What with my beard and my looks and my gesticulations, I should have been wearing a caftan and a black felt hat. I should have been wrapped in a prayer shawl. I shouldn't have been in clothes like his *at all*. Well, that afternoon Aharon took the train back to Oxford, where he was staying with Itzak, and that evening we had a few people over for dinner and I told them this story. I was still full of what had happened and also I thought that his remark about my clothes was kind of interesting for having seemed, at first, so enigmatic. Actually, to run into an anti-Semite on a London street didn't seem to me so amazing—that could happen anywhere. No, what amazed me was that every last person at that dinner was convinced that I *hadn't* run into an anti-Semite. They were all amused by me, by how I had, characteristically, misconstrued the meaning of his behavior. He was just eccentric, they told me, crazy—'mad' is the euphemistic Englishism—he was just some kind of lunatic, and the incident was utterly without meaning. Except for its proving, once again, what a paranoid I am on this subject. I said, 'But what activated his "madness"? What about me in particular set him off?' But they all just laughed and explained to me again how nuts I am and, I tell you, never have I felt more misplaced in *any* country than I

did listening to all these intelligent and decent people going
on and on denying what was staring them right in the face. I
remember the first year I was here, I was watching television
one night and there was a commercial for little cigars, cigarillos, whatever they're called. It showed the final moments of a
performance of a play featuring Dickens's Fagin, a Fagin complete with the enormous hooked nose and disheveled mop of
greasy white hair. The curtain comes down, Fagin takes his
bows—and then the actor is back in his dressing room, in front
of his mirror, pulling off the hooked nose and the ugly wig and
scrubbing himself back to normal with cold cream. Underneath the makeup there is, lo and behold, a fair-haired, handsome, youngish middle-aged, rather upper-class English actor.
To relax after the performance he lights up one of these little
cigarillos, contentedly he puffs away at it, talking about the flavor and the aroma and so on, and then he leans very intimately
into the camera and he holds up the cigarillo and suddenly, in
a thick, Faginy, Yiddish accent and with an insinuating leer on
his face, he says, 'And, best of all, they're *cheap*.' Well, being
characteristically myself, I was a little taken aback by this. I
happened to be home alone at the time and since I felt the urge,
suddenly, to ask somebody a few questions about this place
where I was now trying to live in peace, I telephoned an old
friend of mine, an English Jew up in Hampstead and I said,
'Do you know what I just saw on television?' But when I told
him, he laughed too. 'Don't worry,' he said to me, 'you'll get
used to it.'"

"You really are boiling, aren't you?"

"Well, the insinuation that *I'm* the one who's behaving badly
by taking exception to these insults does piss me off a little,
yes. 'Oh, why do you Jews make such a fuss about being Jewish?' But is it we who are making the fuss? Do you believe that
too, my dear?"

"I wouldn't dare."

"You asked me what lay behind the British distaste for Jews
—those were your words. I think actually it *is* snobbery. And
I'll tell you what makes me think so—because it's not felt
about those Jews who are part of the aristocratic establishment
or upper-middle-class establishment."

"But Jews have the same snobbery about Jews themselves."

"Yes. But I'm just trying to explain something to you. That the general perception of Jews is of, I think—this may not be right—I think it's of Jews who are not like that, who haven't become part of British culture in the sense that they have been here for centuries, like the Waly-Cohens, who are very rich—"

"So it's money."

"It is with the aristocracy generally. You can't *be* upper class without money."

"If you make it through into the upper class, then you are relieved of certain distasteful stigmas."

"I'm trying to tell you something interesting and you're being quite resentful."

"No I'm not. I'm not. I'm listening."

"They aren't just rich. These certain families, like the Samuelses and to a certain extent the Sieffs and the Seligmanns and the Montefiores, and plenty of others, they are not only acceptable, they are smack in the middle of British culture: they own land, they captain cricket teams, they master the fox-hounds, they get into the House of Lords—you know, the whole bit. Just the same as anybody else in that kind of way of life. What people hold against certain Jewish manifestations is that these are downmarket carry-ons. This may sound very stupid to you, but I'm sure if I put it better, and more subtly—"

"You're talking about ethnic behavior. It doesn't go here. But what about the Italians in London, the Italians, the Greeks—do their downmarket carry-ons excite the same disgust?"

"No. Because Italians and Greeks aren't prominent in other ways in English life. There's no doubt about it, the Jews achieve in disproportion to their numbers and therefore they attract attention."

"Is that distasteful as well?"

"No, not in itself. But it makes people quite twitchy."

"So behaving upmarket isn't really more helpful, finally, than behaving downmarket, where a Jew is concerned. Unless he has ten million pounds and captains the cricket team, virtually *any* manifestation of social behavior on the part of the Jew is going to elicit an enormous amount of sensitivity. Make people 'twitchy.'"

"Well, no, I don't think that's true. People don't feel like that about them. If you look into certain worlds, if you look into the world of art dealing that is carried on by a collection of aristocratic Jewish owners—but this is clearly a dangerous subject with you. You are getting more and more resentful with every word I say, and so I am saying no more."

"Can you explain to the court why you hate women?"

"But I don't hate them."

"If you do not hate women, why have you defamed and denigrated them in your books? Why have you abused them in your work *and* in your life?"

"I have not abused them in either."

"We have heard testimony from expert witnesses, expert witnesses who have pointed to chapter and verse to support their every judgment. And yet you are trying, are you, to tell this court that these authorities with unimpeachable professional standards, testifying under oath in a court of law, are either mistaken or lying? May I ask you, sir—what have you ever done that has been of *service* to women?"

"And why do you, may I ask, take the depiction of one woman as a depiction of all women? Why do you imagine that your expert witnesses might not themselves be contradicted by a different gang of expert witnesses? Why—?"

"You are out of order! It is not for you to interrogate the court but to answer the questions of the court. You are charged with sexism, misogyny, woman abuse, slander of women, denigration of women, defamation of women, and ruthless seduction, crimes all carrying the most severe penalties. People like you are not treated kindly if found guilty, and for good reason. You are one with the mass of men who have caused women great suffering and extreme humiliation—humiliation from which they are only now being delivered, thanks to the untiring work of courts such as this one. Why did you publish books that cause women suffering? Didn't you think that those writings could be used against us by our enemies?"

"I can only reply that this self-styled equal-rights democracy of yours has aims and objectives that are not mine as a writer."

"Please, the court is not eager to hear once again a discussion of literature from you. The women in your work are all vicious stereotypes. Was *that* your aim as a writer?"

"Many people have read the work otherwise."

"Why did you portray Mrs. Portnoy as a hysteric? Why did you portray Lucy Nelson as a psychopath? Why did you portray Maureen Tarnopol as a liar and a cheat? Does this not defame and denigrate women? Why do you depict women as shrews, if not to malign them?"

"Why did Shakespeare? You refer to women as though every woman is a person to be extolled."

"You dare to compare yourself to Shakespeare?"

"I am only—"

"Next you will be comparing yourself to Margaret Atwood and Alice Walker! Let us go into your background. You were once a university professor."

"I was."

"As a university professor, you engaged in sexual practices with your female students."

"That humiliates women too?"

"Does it not? They were honored, were they, to be chosen? How many times did you forcibly induce your students to fornicate with you, a professor acting in loco parentis."

"There was no need to exert force."

"Only because of the power to influence and control implicit in the relationship."

"Of course there is the possibility of abuse—there as everywhere. On the other hand, you may do your own sex a disservice when you postulate intelligent young women as lacking the courage to be desirable—as having no aggression, no imagination, no daring, no adventurousness, and no perversity. For an education in the temptation to brutal sensuality that springs up spontaneously between youth and maturity, for a lesson on the torrents of feeling that flow just the other side of the taboo, you might do well to study the erotic liaisons depicted by a French writer named Colette."

"A counterrevolutionary voluptuary named Colette! A traitor bent on pleasure named Colette! How many students did you abuse and exploit in this way?"

"Three. I had love affairs, over the years, with three—"

"First you patronize us with a lecture on literature; now are we to have a lecture on *love*? From *you*? Be careful, sir, how far you go with your insulting ironies. The court may feel

obliged to have patience with such behavior but, I must warn
you, the vast, indignant television audience that watches these
trials is not bound by the legal niceties that obtain here. You
were an adulterer, were you not?"

"Still am."

"With the wives of friends?"

"Sometimes. More often with the wives of strangers, like
you."

"And with whom was the treachery more perversely enjoyable? Whom did you delight most in sadistically betraying,
friends whose wives you ruthlessly seduced or strangers whose
wives you ruthlessly seduced?"

"Oh, you *are* a wonderful girl! You *are* clever! You *are* beautiful!"

"Your Honor, I must ask the court to instruct this *man* that
I am not a 'girl'!"

"Come over here, prosecutor, would you please—"

"Your Honor, I *beg* you, the defendant is *blatantly*—"

"I want to ask your expert opinion about this—this—"

"Help, help, he's exploiting me, he's degrading me, he's de-
faming me, he's attempting with this grotesque display of
phallic—"

"You delicious, brilliant, lovely—"

"He's maligning me, Your Honor—in a court of law!"

"No, no, this is fucking, sweetheart—I'm fucking you in a
court of law."

"Your Honor, the television—this is pornography!"

M Y mother's a very smart, foxy woman, who did very well for herself, in what she wanted to do. Wealthy marriages. I guess she wanted me to follow in her footsteps. I didn't fall into that mold, I haven't lived up to her expectations. It's just as simple as that, really. I would call her a typically smart Jewish girl who came from a very coarse background of immigrant stock. As she said, she always had her eye on the ball, which was money. She made her trade-offs, which were considerable. And she settled herself first in England, which was a disaster. She didn't fit in with the English at all. Among other things, her table manners were bad, she didn't have the breeding. She married a man from a very wealthy English Jewish background. She was married to him for about five years. It started out as a loving marriage but it disintegrated very quickly. Her in-laws were very averse to his marrying a poor Jewish girl."

"Your father. Where'd she meet *him*?"

"He was married five times. He always married ladies. My mother was the exception. He always married genteel women who couldn't fight back. He was very good at spending money himself. He didn't want to work. He had some money from his family. His father was a very stern WASP lawyer and used to ask him every day, 'What have you done to justify your existence?' He left St. Louis, rejected everything that his father stood for, and came East. To tell you the truth, I don't know very much about him. He disappeared when I was about one. But I know that he was a very, very shrewd guy. That marriage sounds as though it was totally loveless, the whole thing. Each was sizing up the other for how much money do you have. My stepfather was like having a grandfather. When he died, he was nearly ninety. He was very sweet, but it wasn't a father, it wasn't the real thing."

"What was he like?"

"He met this woman—while he was married to his first wife—who was really no more than a high-class prostitute. She finagled a meeting in Central Park on horseback. He always regretted that. He said, 'If I hadn't been on my goddamn horse I would have saved a lot of money.' And a lot of heartache. She came after him full-scale. She was a lot younger and she said, 'I don't want to remain your mistress, I want to be married.' And his wife offered him to come back. She said, 'I'll take you back, Bernard,' but he said no, he'd made up his mind. And then on the honeymoon cruise, she would leave him in the stateroom and was slipping into other men's rooms. Every tutor that came in for the kids would become her lover. The humiliation was horrendous, and he was a gentleman of the old school. Yale graduate, revered surgeon. He'd never encountered anything like that in his life before, and it devastated him. Also, she tried to kill him in his sleep—she drugged him and she tried to hold a pillow over his head. She was a criminal."

"What happened?"

"She's in a madhouse now."

"How did he get rid of her?"

"Divorced her. All in the papers. Aerial views of the house. Big scandal. Terrible. They never forgot it in Bedford. They were always suspicious of my mother. What was this nice, intelligent man doing with another vulgar self-seeker? They thought she was a replacement, another facsimile of her. But he didn't know how to cope with someone like this. She'd come from Akron, the first destroyer, very bloozy and blowsy and feisty, and there was no way he could cope with her."

"How come you never told me all this?"

"I wanted to forget about my money-mad mother. I wanted to forget my missing father. I didn't want to carry on, like the college girls in the dormitory, endlessly and boringly about my family. I was above that. I wanted to carry on endlessly about 'The Blood of the Walsungs' and 'Michael Kohlhaas' and 'In the Ravine.'"

"And how are you now? How are you? What's been the fate of the smartest girl in the seminar?"

"I can't seem to communicate to people, that's how I am."

"You?"

"It's very frightening to me but I don't seem to remember the past. I really only vaguely remember you. I had shock therapy but that made it worse. That's when I was in the first hospital, about eight treatments. It was very pleasant, actually. They give you sodium pentothal. You're out. You don't know anything. After you come around you just feel groggy. They stopped giving them to me because they really didn't do that much. About twice a week. I wasn't frightened. I thought it was the answer. What I'm waiting for to happen is some kind of energy to come back. That's what's frightening. I just don't feel it. I try to remember things but I can only remember part of them. It comes back at times, but it's very frightening. You don't know what's going on. Things don't penetrate too much. I want so much to talk to people but I can't seem to do it. When I speak to people it's kind of a downer not to be able to talk to anyone, or answer anyone's questions, or use anything. I have to make a tremendous effort—like right now, with you. I don't know how to get around it, though. I feel so damn uncomfortable around people. I guess most of my life I've felt terrible around people. Excuse me, Philip, do you have an ashtray?"

"Are you on drugs?"

"Because I was so depressed they gave me a combination of drugs. They said there would be no problem with that, and that in the past the two drugs never worked against each other. What happened is that I had a very bad reaction. I became extremely paranoid. I had to be hospitalized. And I was going crazy. I really went off the wall. When they took me down for the tests I thought they were taking me to a torture chamber. I still swear to God that someone came into my room, and they had a paper, and they said, 'Will you please sign this paper that says you beat your mother to death.' I went into fits. 'How can you ask me to sign such a paper—how dare you!' Well, none of this, I'm told, happened. I swore to God that it happened, I really believed it. The doctor said they'd never seen such a reaction. That was in September. And I'm on an antipsychotic drug right now. To prevent a paranoid experience. I don't take as much as they want me to take but I take a fair amount. I mean I'm down to quite a little. Though sometimes I still get very afraid in crowds."

"But what did you in like this? How can this be? You were fine when I knew you. Intellectually stubborn and very shrewd-looking and boldly aloof for a kid, and you had great flair in those uncompromising black outfits. Very Hamletish. Beautifully imperfect too, with the student pallor and that chipped tooth and those tired eyes. Or does all that now sound to you like a description of your burden?"

"That's what you said to me ten years ago. The first time you took me to dinner in that restaurant on Third Avenue. Le Moal."

"I remember the dinner but not what we said."

"You wished me luck. You said I'd need it."

"Why?"

"Because some people might find me irresistible. I was so wild with nerves it was one of the few things I even heard. *That* I remember."

"I wasn't too calm myself."

"I couldn't have known that then. You were my teacher."

"That's why I wasn't too calm. You were something, silently slinking into class with all that disheveled hair and then laying down the law on Kafka. I remember those A students all reading Kafka's *Letter to His Father* and explaining exactly how 'Metamorphosis' and *The Trial* derived from his relationship to his father. 'No,' you said wearily, 'it's just the other way around. His idea of his relationship to his father derives from "Metamorphosis" and *The Trial*.' Set them up with that and then delivered your haymaker. 'By the time a novelist worth his salt is thirty-six, he's no longer translating experience into a fable—he's imposing his fable onto experience.' Not too many nineteen-year-olds say such things, not within my hearing, anyway. Elegant performances given by you in that class. You were already somebody."

"Was I already crazy?"

"No. No. No, absolutely not. Don't you impose a fable on *your* experience. High-strung, of course, but to me you seemed astonishingly *poised*."

"Maybe you were also crazy."

"And maybe I wasn't. You wrote me a note, in that first class of mine you took. 'I pray for only one thing every night, and that is to be a good writer.'"

"Is that how the little vixen went about it?"

"It was young—so what? You *were* young. But that note was you: direct and straight. Tell me again what happened. What did this to you? Make me understand the shock treatments and the hospitals. I just can't."

"The old old story—deceived by life. I had a fatal attraction to hypnotic womanizers and I went batty."

"Is that an accusation?"

"Only if you feel like taking it as one. No, with you it was fresh—so fresh I was hypnotized by *me*. There I was, on weekends, still snuggling up in my Doctor Dentons under the covers in my bedroom in Bedford, with my ballet shoes in the closet from when I was ten, and then, Monday afternoons, total abandon in some anonymous bed in some anonymous room on some anonymous floor in some anonymous Hilton. And so intimate, it made my head spin—the only familiar thing in that entire hotel was our flesh. I suppose you *could* call it basic training. And it *was* scary. For months I went sleepless. When you said 'love' it gave me terrible gastritis. But it was exciting, all right. The fatherly lover who listened. Somebody who is disillusioned involved with somebody who is innocent—educational all around. At least nobody in that Hilton was into murder."

"You fell for the boys who shoot to kill."

"Yes, sex merchants, basically. The libido mob. Couldn't resist them. Didn't know how to flirt with them. Didn't know how to handle them at all. That's something we failed to cover in that seminar. And, of course, I was catnip for the ones who wanted me who I didn't want. What was driving me crazy was that there was always somebody running after me passionately, calling me up on the phone, and coming after me, and swamping me with invitations; you know—drowning me, basically. And at the same time there was the absentee lover, who was gone and not interested, or playing a lot of games with me, and I went a little bit crazy, kind of nuts. It happens. It was all right at the beginning, but the mistake was that it happened over and over and over and I couldn't seem to get out of it. And that's been my nemesis. That's been the whole thing."

"Didn't you have any affairs that weren't fraught—that were pleasant?"

"Sort of."

"What happened to those?"

"I got bored."

I'M much fatter."

"A bit. Not quite the matron yet."

"I was even fatter. I've started to lose it."

"What is it, a protest you're making against something?"

"I don't worry about anything anymore. I'm not anxious anymore."

"Since I disappeared."

"I don't know what it's since. But I think what keeps me thin is undue anxiety."

"And how's that go down on the home front—does he like 'em nice and fat? I like 'em the way you used to be, thin and neurotic."

"Well, things are much better. I don't know how permanent it is. But what happened since you've been gone was a shift in the balance of power. In my favor. And it's been very slow and painful. It was very bad up until three weeks ago, but he's just slowly begun to behave much better to me. Don't ask me why. But I can't spend the whole rest of my life being so bored, apart from everything else. I go into a panic about it which ends with making an appointment with a good solicitor. It seems to me that I keep going into rehearsals. Very tiring. You don't know if this is going to be just a dreary pattern, just a little marital misery that you go through from time to time, or whether, on the other hand, they are steps into the abyss, the kind you study about in history. What happens in history is that it's dotted with disasters, and when you study history, you go from one disaster and you look forward to the next, and you have steps into the abyss, and there are dates and concepts, you learn those, and then you pass the exam. The trouble with life is you don't really know if this is a downward process. The trouble with life is you don't really know what's going on at all."

"'How do you know such things? You've never been here before. How come you think you know about these things?' And I said, 'What the hell are you talking about? I've been thinking about these things for twenty years. I've been thinking about these things for as long as I could think. Why shouldn't I know about them? And, what's more, I thought I was here to talk. Why shouldn't I have some views on it?' They said, well, that's fine, but why shouldn't I be nervous for a year?—that's the message, that you sit around being timorous. And I said, 'I *am* nervous. I don't want to expose myself,' and then they said, 'Well, we're angry with you about that as well.'"

"What is this 'we'—they take a vote?"

"No, that is burlesque. But it comes out very clearly. They are a little family and I'm the new girl. And they're not sure they want a new mate in the family."

"And it's all so transparent?"

"Yeah. Crass. So I got very angry, and then one of them said something really silly. 'I can warm to Wilfred, I'm sure if I could understand his vulnerability I'd learn to love him, but I can't figure out his vulnerability, so I can't care for him.' And I said, 'Are you suggesting, is it an assumption of yours, that if you spot someone's vulnerability you ipso facto care for them?' —I didn't say 'ipso facto'—and she said, 'Well, yes. Why do you want to know?' And I said, 'Well, I'm just curious to know what the assumptions are around here. Because that's why I've had difficulty talking about myself. Because I don't know what you all think and how it all works and so forth.' At this point, the analyst, who's very sensible, chipped in and did support me, but they were angry with me yet again. She said, 'But what's wrong?' And I said, 'Look, at the worst extreme, this kind of language, which covers up certain kinds of assumptions, is nothing but psychobabble.' 'Are you accusing us of psychobabble, blah blah blah?'"

"How many are there?"

"Eight to ten. They're supposedly professional people. It makes me angry. I just have gone six or seven times. I'm not going again. It's worth it to me as copy—I like to hear them talk about themselves. But they're angry with me because I'm too clever. It did give me the most wonderful charge, this group, for about a month. One is even a novelist. Well, would-be sort of. A woman. She was the one who I had most to learn from, who was most interesting, and who most disliked me. She was most articulate, she spoke beautifully, it was fun to listen to her, and she couldn't bear somebody else also speaking well. It's stupid of her because the way she speaks well is quite different from the way I do. There's this solicitor fellow called Wilfred. There is a guy who works for the Festival Hall. There's a woman who has a lot of expensive jewelry and a Louis Vuitton bag, which means—"

"She doesn't know anything."

"Yes. What else? At least two of them were training to be psychotherapists."

"The first day you must have been nervous."

"I wasn't at all nervous."

"And you got into the room and there they all were and you said, 'Hello, I'm the new girl.'"

"No, no. I was the first there. They all turn up late. They're all just awful. It's just like being late for family dinner. They all sort of trickle in. And they spend an awful lot of time staring at the floor not saying anything. Which given that it's quite expensive is quite annoying. I don't know what they think they're doing. And a lot of them clearly make sacrifices to go."

"What was your maiden speech?"

"I don't remember. But it was probably a sort of well-disposed sensible question. I always knew what they were going to say in the end, but I thought I better not let on to that, so I just asked leading questions, like a barrister. Obviously somebody felt that she never got any attention in life and this is why everything was so unfair and horrible, and so I said, 'Are you the only child in the family?' These are the kind of acceptable questions. And this can get on to whether or not you're used to dividing attention. But they're hopeless. They don't get anywhere. I felt like saying I don't think they can deal with any real problem that I might have, I don't think they have the sense to do it."

"But aren't they supposed to deal with the problem of you and not with your problems?"

"I suppose. Who knows? I thought it would make me understand in practice why relations at work are so difficult and why I hate my job so, a crappy job with stupid people ordering me about. Somebody in this group started accusing me of thinking I was a clever girl. And that's exactly a problem I have. And I was longing to hear more about all that. Although I find it hurtful as well."

"But you *are* a clever girl. I love you for being a clever girl. Where's the problem? Who are these people? I'll go over and punch 'em all right in the nose."

"Of course they're going to be envious because I *am* cleverer than them and what the *fuck* are they going to do about it? You know the conclusion I came to?"

"What?"

"I came to the conclusion that I ought to be more drastic."

"I've just seen my daughter performing in her Nativity play. The Nativity is something we have about the birth of Jesus."

"Is that what it is?"

"Yes."

"When did that happen? I probably was paying no attention. I missed the newspaper several days last week."

"Well, it was actually quite a long time ago. And they've read a lot into it. I wish you could have seen it. It was so funny. It really was funny. It was in the drawing room. With a grand piano and a marble fireplace. My daughter was so funny. She's such a little card. She was a queen, as in the king. She had to bring gifts. We got to talking about it one day and I said, 'What are the gifts?' and she said, 'Well, there's gold, fuckincense, and myrrh.'"

"Did you correct her?"

"I didn't, actually. I just said, 'Which are you giving?' and she said, 'I'm giving gold,' and I thought, 'Fine, she doesn't have to mention it probably.' I'm afraid I have to go back to this scene of Christian triumphalism quite soon."

"I'm going to have a birthday this year again."

"Not again."

"Yes. No way round it. Subtract nineteen thirty-three from

nineteen eighty-four, and there's no way around it—it's fifty-one."

"Of course you could totally ignore it. Why do you take it so hard?"

"You, who's pissing and moaning about being thirty-four?"

"I know why *I* take it so hard. I'm asking why you take it so hard."

"Because life will be over soon, that's why. I'll be dead."

"One of the unfair things about adultery, when you compare the lover to the spouse, the lover is never seen in those awful dreary circumstances, arguing about the vegetables, or burning toast, or forgetting to ring up for something, or putting upon someone or being put upon. All that stuff, I think, people deliberately keep out of affairs. I'm generalizing from tiny, tiny experience, almost none. But I think they do. Because if they didn't it would be so unrestful. Unless you like two sets of domestic conflict, and you could go from one to the other."

"Yes, with the lover everyday life recedes. Emma Bovary disease. In the woman's first flush of passion, every lover is Rodolphe. The lover who makes her cry to herself, 'I have a lover! I have a lover!' 'A kind of permanent seduction,' Flaubert calls it."

"My handbook, that book."

"What's your favorite part?"

"Oh, the brutal stuff, of course. When she runs to Rodolphe in the end for the money, when she pleads for three thousand francs to save her and he says, 'I haven't got it, dear lady.' "

"You should read a little aloud to your daughter each night at bedtime. Flaubert's a good girls' guide to men."

" 'I haven't got it, dear lady.' Delicious."

"I used to tell my students that you don't need three men to go through what she does. One will usually fill the bill, as Rodolphe, then Léon, then Charles Bovary. First the rapture and the passion. All the voluptuous sins of the flesh. In his bondage. Swept away. After the torrid scene up at his château, combing your hair with his comb—and so on. Unbearable love with the perfect man who does everything beautifully. Then, with time, the fantastical lover erodes into the workaday lover, the practical lover—becomes a Léon, a rube after all. The tyranny of the actual begins."

"What's a rube?"

"A hick. A provincial. Sweet enough, attractive enough, but not exactly a man of valor, sublime in all things and knowing all. A little foolish, you know. A little flawed. A little stupid. Still ardent, sometimes charming, but, if the truth be known, in his soul a bit of a clerk. And then, with marriage or without —though marriage will always speed things along—he who was a Rodolphe and has become Léon is transformed into Bovary. He puts on weight. He cleans his teeth with his tongue. He makes gulping sounds when he swallows his soup. He's clumsy, he's ignorant, he's coarse, even his back is irritating to look at. This merely gets on your nerves at first; in the end it drives you nuts. The prince who saved you from your boring existence is now the slob at the core of the boring existence. Dull, dull, dull. And then the catastrophe. Somehow or other, whatever his work, he fucks up colossally on the job. Like poor Charles with Hippolyte. He sets out to do the equivalent of removing a bunion and gives somebody gangrene. The once perfect man is a despicable failure. You could kill him. Actuality has triumphed over the dream."

"And which are you to me, do you think?"

"At this moment? I'd say somewhere between a Rodolphe and a Léon. And slipping. No? On the slide to Bovary."

"Yes." Laughing. "That's just about right."

"Yes, somewhere between desire and disillusionment on the long plummet to death."

"I've never seen such a thoroughgoing exploitation of sado-masochism in my life. Bacon's portraits look like nothing so much as what you want to do to your enemy."

"How dramatic."

"But there are people, aren't there, who you don't actually want to do violence to—you just want to smear their faces like paint."

"You're more aggressive than I am."

"Why do all these Slavs come to see you?"

"Czechs aren't Slavs."

"Well, why do you see all these Czechs and Slavs?"

"Why they come to me and why I see them are different questions."

"Why do you see them?"

"I like them."

"Better than the English."

"Wouldn't you?"

"Why? Because they suffer so much? Are you *that* in love with suffering?"

"I'm interested in it. Isn't everyone?"

"Hardly. Most people prefer to avert their gaze."

"Well, I'm counterphobic and I stare. Displaced persons have things to tell you. Sometimes you can even lend a hand."

"A soft spot for victims—is that from being Jewish too?"

"Is it? There are plenty of Jews who couldn't care less. I don't think of myself as a Jewish victim, you know. Quite the contrary."

"But that's it, though—you're of the little pocket of Jews born in this century who miraculously escaped the horror, who somehow have lived unharmed in an amazing moment of affluence and security. So those who didn't escape, Jewish or not, have this fascination for you."

"They hold no fascination for you?"

"I'm curious, but I don't go out of my way to cultivate them. I would never think of going to any of those countries for a holiday, while spending two weeks in a place where everybody is oppressed and miserable is your idea of a good time. How did you get onto that?"

"It was accidental. I'd finished a book and I was traveling. It was '71. We drove from Vienna to Prague. After just the first half hour of walking around that place, I thought, 'There's something here for me.' I had a publisher there, who'd published my first book years before. I went to the publishing house the next morning and introduced myself and the director and his staff toasted me with slivovitz at ten a.m. Then I went to lunch with one of the editors, who told me that the director was a swine. I began to get the idea. A thousand stories later I was there alone for a few weeks one spring and I got corralled on the street by the police. Over the years I'd got used, each spring, to being followed everywhere by the cops, especially when I went to see writer friends, but these were polite plainclothesmen who kept their distance. This time—it was '75—two police in uniforms came directly up to me on the street and asked to see my papers. I showed them my passport, my visa, my hotel identification card, but they said that wasn't enough, I had to come with them to the police station. I began to shout, alternately in English and in my high school French, that I wanted to see the ambassador at the American Embassy. I was only a few feet from the trolley stop and I started shouting at the people standing there that I was being harassed for no reason by the police and I demanded to be taken to the American Embassy. One of the cops meanwhile went up the street and there was my plainclothesman, in his blue raincoat, and the two of them talked for a while, and then the uniformed cop came back and said I had to go to the police station—he spoke in Czech, but I got his drift all right. I still refused to move and just kept shouting. This went on for about fifteen minutes. Each time I said no the cop would go back up to the plainclothesman for instructions and then come back and insist that I had to go to the station. A young German couple by the trolley stop had come up close to see what was happening. They spoke English to me, and I said, 'Will you stay here until this is settled?' I told them my name and where I was staying and to call the American ambassador if I got dragged away. Eventually the cops got so frustrated that they *both* went up to the end of the block to talk to the plainclothesman. Just then a trolley pulled up at the stop. I thought, 'Why wait to be arrested?' I hopped on the trolley and it started away. I was in a terrific sweat by then and my heart was pounding, and two stops down I jumped off the trolley and ran across a bridge and got a trolley going in the opposite direction. I took it to God knows where and jumped off next when I saw a phone kiosk. I telephoned one of my Czech friends and told him what had happened. He laughed. He said, 'They only wanted to harass you. They only wanted to scare you.' I allowed as though they had. He assured me that nothing further would happen to me if I went back to my hotel—and I went back and nothing did. Except that after that I was never able to get a visa to Czechoslovakia again. The evening after I left Prague, they picked up my friend, the one I'd phoned, took him from his house, and questioned him all night at the police station. He wrote later to tell me that all they wanted to talk about was me and my annual visits. They kept asking him, 'Why does he come to Czechoslovakia all the time?' And he said, 'Haven't you read his book? If you read more, you would know. He comes to Czechoslovakia for the girls.'"

"And is that so?"

"No. I went to Czechoslovakia for the jokes. I come to England for the girls."

"Everyone I keep meeting these days—I remember you at Oxford, they say, you wore transparent blouses and no bra on."

"So you're an ex-extrovert."

"Yes! And it's all true. Everybody used to disapprove of me because I had my hair dyed red and exposed my breasts."

"Well, I haven't seen your breasts exposed around here for a long time."

"That's true. But I'm not friends with them anymore."

"Do you think I overestimate you?"

"No."

"You think I have you right."

"Well, I am clever. I have no sense of intellectual fashion but I'm still quite clever."

"So what do you think I should write about, if you're so clever?"

"*Not me.*"

"You've come for your lesson."

"Yep."

"Did you do your homework?"

"I'm not sure."

"Okay. Let's lock up here before we start any of that stuff."

"I'd rather you didn't call me anything today. The nameless one."

"How about Nobody?"

"No, that's too definite."

"If you called a character Nobody, I wonder where it would land you. There was a character called Nobody."

"I would think you'd need more ideas than that to begin a book."

"That's more than I usually begin with. Nobody went to Heathrow Airport. Nobody boarded a plane. Where did Nobody go?"

"Nobody went to France. Why did Nobody go to France?"

"Because Nobody likes it."

"Then Nobody meets Somebody. The other character is Somebody. Nobody and Somebody became lovers."

"And?"

"Let me give you a drink."

"I'd love a drink. I feel very much between things."

"Which things?"

"You and the deep blue sea."

"You're looking very well. You're looking quite different."

Laughs. "You always tell me that."

"What time do you have to get back to work?"

"I think I should get back sometime in the afternoon."

"That's one of the nicest things that's been done to me all week."

"I liked it too."

"He doesn't really understand why I don't do any work. But he's determined to think well of me and to like me. Because he's a nice man. The other day I was going to spend the entire day not working—I was going to come here as a matter of fact. I was going to spend the day behaving quite disgracefully. I said to him, 'I'll be gone all day, out of the office, mainly for the purposes of self-advancement.' And he was so upset. He wanted me to tell him a nice lie, you know. Can you imagine this man? He's very good-looking. And he's a Christian. He's a terribly decent man. He always has this slightly conciliatory, appeasing look. He knows that I behave so badly at work."

"Do you behave so badly?"

"Well, in a sense. I just pissed off today. I've done nothing since about half past twelve. And there are certainly things for me to do. I mean, by ordinary standards they are paying me to

do some things. Do you ever feel like getting a job? It's very
nice really, seeing all those people every day, and they all say
wonderful things. They're often very funny. You might actually enjoy it more than this."

"It's all very harassing—endless demanding phone calls, stu-
pid domestic chores, and boring people who give you a hard
time to work with if you just show them a single weakness."
"You look so fucking tired."
"I know. But what can *I do*?"
"I don't know, sweetheart. Run away."

"There's something in this cigarette."
"Yes."
"Somebody slipped me a Mickey."
"Uh-huh. Me too."
"You're slightly swimming."
"I'm slightly sinking."
"Swimming before my eyes."

"You're very official today."
"I'm in a terrible mood. I'm feeling terrible at the moment."
"Well, at least you haven't lost your looks."
"Haven't I?"
"Nope. The fight's still in you."
"It comes and goes."
"When the fight's still in you, you look pretty good."
"It's funny, that sensation that you're losing it, it's very
odd."
"Losing what, the fight or the looks?"
"Both. I think they're all connected."
"You mustn't lose the fight."
"It's not entirely in one's control, I don't think."

"You might not think so, but I really did do some quite remarkable things as a teenager, things which were very unusual.
The last thing I did, being Mummy's good girl, was to get all
those scholarships when I was sixteen to Oxford and Cambridge. Most people can't get them at eighteen. And it was English, which is the most difficult subject because there are

thousands and thousands of applicants. Anyway, it just *was* clever. Or, at any rate, somehow this performance could be forced out of me. Actually I enjoyed that, I enjoyed those exams—I could do all those things, I was good at them. That's what's perplexing me so about now. Why do I find it so difficult *now*?"

"Why *do* you?"

"I guess because so much of my married life has been so bad for me. I just operate on one cylinder these days, as opposed to three or four, or however many other people have functioning. Even a small thing, like doing something slightly difficult rather well for only a few hours, has such a devastating effect upon my morale. It's really something, when I think of myself at sixteen."

"Why don't you step over here and give me a kiss?"

"I don't want to. I'm not feeling at all good. I'm not feeling terribly communicative. I've had enough of this new shrink. I don't think this stuff is for me. Actually I think they're all quite creepy. I think they perv off a bit on—"

"Perv off?"

"Oh, awful schoolgirl slang. I think they take a perverted interest in, and pleasure in—that's what it means. I'm not going there anymore. It upsets me too much, really."

"How many times did you see him, about ten?"

"About that."

"And when did you stop?"

"Today, actually. I just called up and canceled. I have to go to see him or write to him that I don't want to go."

"But why? Where was he leading you that you didn't like? Or did you just think that he was stupid?"

"I didn't think I'd heard anything that I hadn't thought of a million, million times before. Not one single thing that was new."

"What did he make of our deceiving your husband like this?"

"I never talk to him about you."

"Never? Then he wasn't getting the full story, was he, of these last four years?"

"You've simply distracted me from the central concerns of my life."

"Oh? I was *intended* as a distraction all right, but it didn't work out that way, you know. Because I became a temptation: a source of fantasy in the beginning, a source of possibility after that, and then, eventually, a disappointment."

"Is that how you see yourself?"

"In your life, yes. That's how I think you experience it."

"Why?"

"Why do you experience it that way or why do I think that?"

"Either. It's the same, actually. You can only tell me what you think; therefore whether you tell me the objective truth or what you think, it's all the same."

"But that *is* what happened to you. I saw you. I watched you. I saw the color in your face. I felt you tremble. You used to tremble when you came here, remember? Hide from the shrink whatever you like but that's what used to happen."

"He's not the kind of man you can tell anything to, really."

"Then he's really in the right job."

"He was awful. I'd tell my cleaning lady more than I'd tell him."

"You're looking kind of cheery, honey."

"I'm doing much better."

"How are you doing? You seem a bit sad."

"This little shit upset me. They're very good at upsetting people. A lot of them are really rather unpleasant. The unpleasant ones, who are always young men, very young men, they have a specialty—a lot of them are public school boys— they have a horrible line with women, particularly women who show any sign of hesitancy, they just like to tear into them."

"They tore into you."

"They would have. I walked out. I came here. Here I am again."

"I do have some kind of courage, which I'm always feeling myself lacking, because I've just had two perfectly ghastly nights. All-night rows."

"Why the hell are you still having these rows?"

"Because neither of us can accept what we recognize. Though sometimes it does seem that we're entering new territory, and we did seem to be, because he was actually talking about moving out. I was saying that would be quite a good idea. And he didn't like that very much, so . . . I mean all this kind of practical discussion seems slightly different from the mutual recrimination. But it does of course degenerate into a quarrel. But *I* can't move out. Because I would have to spend all my time trying to get injunctions to get him to pay the rent on whatever I'd found. I can in theory, but in practice, no. You see, as long as we're still fighting, I think he thinks if only he can get it right somehow, he can have everything, he can have his girlfriend, and the outdated wife . . . oh, it's all kind of hopelessly vague."

"We'll move on to another subject then."

"Please. Immediately."

"I listen to you a lot, you know."

"Too much. Why do you?"

"What is it?"

"I'm thinking that I still love you."

"Really? Despite?"

"Despite."

"It's beneath you to stay in a marriage because you think you can't get another job and this way you have a meal ticket."

"A meal ticket is not beneath anybody."

"It's beneath *you*."

"If the marriage is so clearly over, why don't you go? I no longer understand."

"I don't want to."

"There is your dignity, you know."

"That won't exist without an income."

"Clever but not true. Just the opposite is true."

"I have a check for you."

"That's terribly nice of you. It really is. But I can't take it."

"Why don't you just cash it? Put it in your bank. Hide it at your office. Just don't deposit it in your joint account."

"We don't have a joint account. He's not so foolish. It's terribly nice. Can I frame it?"

"No. And don't mislay it."

"Can I put it in my Bible?"

"No, you can put it in your bank for a rainy day."

"It's terribly nice of you."

"Why don't you think about it, before you throw it away? You can do whatever you like with it—just don't mislay it."

Sets it down. "Thank you very much."

"Well, it would be best if you took it."

"Either you're a guilty secret, which makes me deceitful in a very important argument in which I am demanding honesty and plain dealing. Or if things do degenerate, I think it'll be easier if it's true to say that I've had absolutely nothing to do with you for an extremely long time. And finally, if I end up living on my own, I ought to be emotionally freer than I am. With you."

"Okay. I will miss you. I'll miss you a lot."

"I'll often think about you too."

"It's a damn shame about you and me."

"Do you know that poem of Marvell's?"

"Which poem?"

" 'It was begotten by desire upon impossibility.' That poem."

"I thought it was 'despair'—'begotten by despair.' "

"It is. It was. Both."

How are you?"

"I'm all right. I'm about to go in today."

"I thought you would be. What do you know? Anything new?"

"No. I'm going to have a CAT scan this morning. It's quite a heavy day."

"I see. And the CAT scan will tell you what?"

"How much longer. No—if the CAT scan shows tumors, then it's all bad news, the drugs aren't working, and if it doesn't show anything, I still have to have surgery to see what's going on. They'll read it to me on Monday. And so . . . I don't know what to say. I feel all right. How are you?"

"I'm okay. So—this is a big weekend."

"It was all supposed to happen on Good Friday, but I thought that was loading the symbols."

"Yes, it's not good literature. It's not even good life."

"I don't know. Every time I do this I have to get this strength out of somewhere. It's like draining a swamp. I don't know where to get it. Maybe it's like the reverse of draining. What would it be? Making a swamp?"

"Are you able to write anything?"

"Not a lot. Narrative crumbles under the weight of these endless stories."

"You writing these endless stories down?"

"No, I'm not. I don't function from one sentence to the next. No, I've been doing yoga. Some macrobiotic. And I've just been trying to live with what joy there is. You know, this kind of indefiniteness is very disconcerting."

"How's your support system going?"

"Great. Even my father phoned from wherever the hell he lives now."

"So it's not so great."

"No, they *are* great. All my ex-men are being very nice. Look, just a *call* from my father makes cancer worth it. I could do with a hand from you, though. Are you ever coming back to America?"

"I'll be in New York in a month. I'll see you the day I get there."

"Good. What's up over there? What's your life in London like?"

"Not much different from what it was like when we were criminals on Eighty-first Street."

"Still writing, are you?"

"Yep."

"I thought you'd give that up, with any luck."

"No. In my room with my typewriter all day, and social and cultural events in the evening, and it's all opaque and English to me. I'm off to a cultural event tonight. I was to a social event last night."

"The social events are called dinner parties."

"Yes. The trouble with dinner parties is that I get seated next to other men's wives."

"Of course."

"You know something about other men's wives?"

"They're boring."

"They are not as interesting as you when you were another man's wife."

"Who was there?"

"Too boring."

"And where's my book?"

"What book?"

"The book with me in it. I like that one."

"My dear, you are going to have to do something interesting that I can stick in there."

"I am. I'm probably dying."

"You don't know that."

"I'll know Monday."

"I'll phone Monday to find out what the score is. What your score is—okay? Look, you'll find the strength somewhere. And now I'm going to stop before I utter still more platitudes."

"Yes, I know a platitude when I hear one."

"Me too. 'Bye."

"Goodbye."

"Hello."

Singingly. "Yes, hello."

"What's up?"

"Well—a miracle. Yeah, it's a miracle."

"Tell me about the miracle."

"It's a miracle. The CAT scan showed no trace of pathology. Which means that in three months this thing that I was told was incredibly virulent, and I had a thirty to fifty percent chance of it being okay, and if it wasn't okay I'd be gone within a year, seems to be responding at lickety-split speed to this stuff. And the doctor's very pleased and he seems to think that the prognosis is now changed. So it's a fucking relief."

"Yeah, I'll say."

"Strange, very strange, because it's so fast. There's not a trace of it. I still have to be opened up in June to make sure that what the CAT scan can see is the same as what you'd get from a test tube inspection, but—you know, the thing could recur but not with these drugs. I think at worst it means that if I could have these drugs for the rest of my life I could have a life. But they don't even think that. They just think that I should finish this course of treatment and then just hope that it doesn't recur. It very often doesn't. I think everybody is very surprised. If you looked at my CAT scan now and anybody else's, from that evidence I have no longer got cancer. So it's amazing, eh?"

"Pretty good. You did all right."

"I did all right."

"Did you think you had it in you?"

"Noooooo."

"That's called a pardon from the governor."

"It certainly is."

"But who is the governor?"

"I don't know. But clearly I have to stay on his good side for a while. It doesn't mean that this is all a nightmare which is past. It just means that there is much pressure removed."

"Now the CAT scan, that's your entire body?"

"No, it goes from my groin to my heart. And the doctor said that if there was any tumor anywhere else there would have been something, a fluid, a shadow, in that area, which is the area where it starts. There is this thing called the preferred path of these cancers. You know about that?"

"That's in your notes, not mine."

"Well, the next place this thing would have gone is the liver. It doesn't go to the brain."

"The Preferred Path."

"Yeah. A title. But I'll wait on that, I think."

"Look, this is all terrific. I didn't know what I was going to hear when I phoned you. This is extraordinary news."

"Quite a day, though. I told them not to tell me but in fact the technician rushed out and told the person I was with that it was clean and there was nothing and it was all wonderful. That made me very nervous."

"Well, yes—your character hasn't changed in all this."

"I'm very happy that I haven't gone into a large depression. I thought there might be something hideous in my nature that would make me weep at the news."

"You're entitled to any reaction. There is no preferred path of emotion. This is great news. I'll just say goodbye to you then. There's nothing more to say, is there?"

"You mean, that's it?"

"Absolutely. Now that you're well . . ."

Laughing. "Exactly, I knew you'd feel like that. . . . No, I really don't think so. I think we must be friends again now, old friends. Anyway, I'm not completely out of the woods, so you can still be a little nice to me."

"And when you *are* completely out of the woods?"

"Then you can return to normal."

"I had such a lovely dream about you."

"You did, really?"

"I had the most wonderful dream about you. The essence of you, my dear."

"Speak a little louder."

"How can I speak louder? It's hard to say these things."

"Oh, so that's why your voice is so soft. Well, pull yourself together and say them. You've been through worse. What happened to us in your dream? Anything that didn't in days of yore?"

"Oh, yes."

"Really? That *must* have been some dream. I was quite in love with you."

"Were you?"

"Oh, yes."

"Well, that helps. It's wonderful to hear your voice. I can't tell you how lovely this dream was, and I wish you'd had it too."

"Well, write it out and send it to me. I might be able to stick it in the book about you."

"Don't be silly. I'm not going to lay myself on the line."

"You sound shaky."

"I have chemotherapy today."

"That's why I called."

"Then I have this god-awful operation. And I just feel, because I feel fine and I'm getting on with my life, that they're going to give me some little yank back to the . . ."

"It's not going to happen."

"The aftereffects are pretty grim."

"As grim as when you began?"

"Much worse."

"Why does it get worse?"

"Because the poison's inside you."

"But by Sunday you're yourself?"

"Not really anymore. It takes till Tuesday or Wednesday."

"When do you leave the hospital?"

"Tomorrow morning. They just throw you out. Then I come home and I sleep for fourteen hours straight."

"And then on, say, Saturday how do you feel?"

"Like you have very bad flu. Up and in bed. Up and in bed. And then I get on with life, such as it is."

"And how do you look? Are you wan, are you thin?"

"I wish I were thin. I look bursting with health. And I have no hair. Otherwise I look great."

"You have no hair—you have a wig?"

"No, I don't have a wig. I have all these god-awful babush-
kas."

"The hair is going to grow back?"

"Yes, but it needs a little encouragement. It gets whapped
once a month."

"Listen. You are feeling well and you are well-looking and
those things must point to something."

"Yes, it points to the fact that I'm not going to go immediately. There's a possibility that there'll be tiny little cells still in
there that the CAT scan didn't pick up. Unfortunately that'll
mean another six months of this stuff. I'm dreading that. And
of course the worst nightmare is that there's a surprise for the
doctors when they open me up, and they see the whole thing
is full of tumors."

"Can that possibly be?"

"I don't think so. But how could any of this possibly be?"

"No answer."

"I may be bald but I'm not even forty. I really don't think I
should die."

"You won't."

"That's what you said in the dream too."

"Well, I can't be wrong twice in twenty-four hours."

"Say that again."

"I can't be wrong."

"Again."

"You're not going to die."

"One last time."

"You're not going to die. You're going to live."

"All right. Thank you. 'Bye."

WELL, I've missed you too. I was thinking of coming over to see you, if you would see me."

"Oh, really? What about your lying? What about my being a guilty secret that keeps you from being honest?"

"Oh, well, I'm not sure."

"You're not sure about what?"

"I think I've been changing a lot."

"Are you learning to be a liar?"

"I wouldn't say that."

"Tell me the truth."

"What truth?"

"What are you trying to say?"

"I'm simply saying that I was thinking of coming round to see you."

"But you had all those principles about plain dealing."

"It's not a question of principles. It's a question of how relationships work. Isn't it?"

"I don't know. You tell me."

"Well, I think so. I think certain relationships . . . you know, you're not free to tell lies or conceal the truth—whatever the reasons, they're ultimately boring but they're there."

"But I thought you were not free to tell lies."

"That's right, that's what I thought I wasn't."

"Aren't you?"

"Well, I'm not so sure."

"I don't understand."

"Well, I don't really either. But I think I've been changing —I don't want to go into this."

"You might as well."

"No, no, I mustn't."

"Well, look, darling, of course I want to see you—but what have all these months without you been about then?"

"Well, you might well ask. I suppose I seem very capricious, or something. But probably I shouldn't come anyway."

"I think you wanted to try something. You tried it. I don't think you're capricious at all."

"I don't really want to talk about it. But it's not silly."

"What happens now? Are you bound to tell the truth?"

"Yes, and I'll bring a couple of gossip columnists and a fingerprint man."

"I'm confused."

"Yes. But I'm sure you've had relationships like this yourself, though, in which the balance of power changes radically for one reason or another. And the whole thing has changed."

"So what's happened? You better tell me."

"No, I don't want you ever again to be confused by my domestic life."

"I wasn't confused in the old days. I'm confused now."

"No, no, you shouldn't be confused now. You should just ignore the whole thing. Really, it would be much better. If I spend my entire time telling you about my domestic life and leaning on you and all that, it's hopeless."

"Is that what you were doing, leaning on me?"

"Yes."

"And now?"

"I don't want to lean on anybody, you know. Not because I disapprove of it or anything like that. Just because I'm like a tadpole whose legs are emerging. A tadpole of thirty-six. Sad, isn't it?"

"But if questioned under oath, what are you going to say?"

"What do you mean under oath? In court? Well, listen [*laughing*], I would not lie in court, I must admit."

"Then you oughtn't to come."

"I might lie in court in some circumstances. But not necessarily."

"Do we know what those circumstances are?"

"No."

"Then maybe you oughtn't come. I'd love to see you. I'm dying to see you. I'm really very confused by you at this moment."

"Sorry. I don't want to be tiresome."

"Don't be silly. But I'm telling you I'm confused by you. Of course I missed you. Terribly this afternoon, in fact."

"What do you miss?"

Laughter.

"Oh, come on. I don't want any dirty talk."

"I'm afraid some of it would be dirty talk."

"Well, I suppose that has its place."

"Yes, well, then come around. Sure, come around, my little liar."

ARE you interested in politics because you're a Pole or because you're interested in politics?"

"I think mostly by being a Pole. It came from a feeling of being quite desperate about our situation. And finding ways to make it better. One has to get involved. I'm not very active in the underground—because I cannot find a place for myself. Because I'm not a Catholic and the Polish underground is mainly Catholic. I was born a Catholic but I'm no longer a Catholic. Even the Jews in the underground accept the Polish church, which I cannot do. Because I think they keep the Polish people with the mentality of the Middle Ages. And I think it's also because of the church that our situation is economically and politically what it is. It is a very backward force. Both my parents are long dead, long ago, and though they were born Catholics, they were not practicing. They sent me to have my first Communion."

"What are you, about thirty?"

"Me? Thirty-three. I left my faith in the secondary school. It didn't interest me anymore. It didn't give anything. No inspiration. It was just going to church and listening to sermons which were not inspiring."

"What do you remember about your childhood and adolescence?"

"My father suffered oppression—a lot. He was a director of a coal mine. In Silesia. Before the war—and after the war he had a lot of assets in this coal mine, and under the Communists, of course, he lost everything. And the Communists moved him to another position because he didn't want to join the Party. He died of a heart attack. I came to the university after '68. I was still in a secondary school when '68 happened. I studied English philology. Can you tell?"

"Yes. Oh, yes."

"English culture, English history, language, and so on and so forth. A very nice thing happened to me yesterday. A nasty thing happened before, then a nice one. It was rush hour. I went to Charing Cross station. Hundreds of people going past me, and I felt very unsecure. I bought the ticket. And then I couldn't find my way to the platform. I mean I knew where the platforms were but I couldn't find the right platform. I didn't know how people find out such things. I couldn't find any information center. I was lost in the crowd and people were in such a hurry. And I approached the gateman. He was barring the door because one train was leaving, and beside me was a very hysterical woman trying to get past the barrier, and he was trying to push her out. Somehow I managed to ask him humbly where the platform for Greenwich was and he said, 'Look at the board, lady.' And I thought, 'What kind of board? My God.' Then finally, yes, there was a board—there were all sorts of signs and I couldn't find the solution to the signs. Finally I calmed down a bit and found the right train, the right hour, and the platform. I was slightly relieved. But I am still in this terrible crowd—people were pushing me because I was standing in the middle of their way to the platform. And probably the panic must have been in my eyes, because I thought I behaved quite normally. I kept walking to the platform and I showed the ticket to the man in the booth, who collects it or, I don't know, *checks* the ticket. And I showed it to him, then put it back in my purse, and he grabbed me—he leaned out of his booth and he grabbed me. And he shook me and said, 'Cheer up!' I was shocked."

"You must have looked terribly despondent. You must have been despondent about more than that."

"Yes. It was just terrible. But I loved this man. He was very nice. It never happened to me before that somebody reacted to me in this way. And one more thing happened to me, two hours before. I went up the escalator in one of the undergrounds, and many people went, and I wasn't in a hurry, and a lot of people were passing me. And I noticed a friend of mine passing me in a hurry, and before I managed to react—I hadn't seen the man for ten years—he was somewhere up the stairs where I couldn't catch him. I stood there looking."

"That happened earlier."

"Yes."

"So you were already upset and frustrated by this."

"Yes. Also. Things are strange."

"He was a Pole."

"No. He's American. He was my lover. Ten years ago." Laughing. "Imagine passing him."

"Your lover in America?"

"No. In Poland. He came to Poland, twice. He thought himself a poet and he wanted to find his 'roots.'"

"He was a Polish American?"

"No. An American Jew."

"You mean his Jewish roots?"

"Probably."

"So that did disturb you a little."

"It was so strange, don't you think?"

"Yes. On the other hand, you're like a tinderbox. You know what that means?"

"Uh-uh."

"It isn't hard to make you explode. Or go off. You happen to be suffering the human predicament times ten. Anybody who spends, as they say, two weeks in another town, is always a little susceptible but you're even more so. Here. *Tinder.* 'Any dry or flammable substance that readily takes fire from a spark and burns or smolders.' A tinderbox is a box containing tinder. Get it?"

"The tinderbox gets it, yes. At home I'm using the same dictionary. I use it for translation. It takes most of my time, translation. When I get back from the office, and take care of some house duties, and when I put my daughter to bed, I sit down to the translation. Three hours." Laughing. "To make my life more meaningful. I want to use my life properly, to some good cause."

"We all try to do that, you know. Even privileged Westerners."

"I got this strange thing that I knew you already when I met you two days ago at the party."

"Maybe we understand each other. However, yours is a different fate from mine. I don't envy you."

"Yes, the Communists want to make life easier for everybody, so that's why they torture us. That *is* different."

"What are you laughing at now?"

"At you, of course."

"Well, why not?"

"I have so little experience with Jewish people. I don't know anything about anti-Semitism. By the time I got around to being born, there were no more Jews left in my country. I couldn't even recognize a Jew. I wasn't aware of different facial characteristics. I don't know why. Because I read literature, I read descriptions, but somehow, no experience in the streets. It happened in Long Island the first time. My husband and I were a year in America, before we had my daughter. He was studying. We were on the train to Manhattan, and there were a lot of people going to work. And at one station the Jews got onto the train."

"How did you know that?"

"My husband said, 'Look, those people are Jewish. If you want to know how Jews look like, look at them.' "

"They weren't religious Jews."

"No, no, no. Executives. With briefcases."

"Jews with briefcases."

"Yeah. Strange? No."

"No. Stranger today are Jews with sidelocks. What did you see, aside from their briefcases?"

"Hair like yours. Clothes like yours—no." Laughing. "Later on I started noticing the features."

"But you'd had this lover, searching for his roots. Didn't you take a good look at him?"

"He didn't look that Jewish. But now when I try to remember, yes, he did have some features. But it somehow didn't strike me as something different. Look, I guess I must leave now."

Kisses her. She laughs. "What is it, sentimentality?"

"No, just pity." Both laughing. "Anyway, I'm kissing your sentences, not you. I'm kissing your English."

"I kill you. I come here with a bomb."

"I'm like the Communists. I'm just trying to make your life easier."

"You're just trying to make my sentences more *complicated*."

"Of course—also to find out why you go around spying on Jews."

"You better tell me what's upsetting you so. I cannot come home from my studio every day and sit down to dinners like this night after night. You don't speak. You don't respond to anything I say. And you look awful."

"I don't sleep."

"Why don't you? Tell me."

"I don't know."

"What's bothering you?"

"It's nothing to do with you."

"That's no reason not to tell me. It *does* have to do with me, doesn't it?"

"I want to know—no, I don't, I don't want to know!"

"Oh, here we go. What *is* it?"

"You do not go off to your studio to work—you go off to your studio to fuck! You are having an affair with someone in your studio!"

"Oh, do I? Am I?"

Bursting into tears. "Yes!"

"The only woman in my studio is the woman in my novel, unfortunately. It would be nicer with company but it doesn't work that way."

"Not your novel—your notebook! You left it out of your briefcase and I picked it up and stupidly—and now I wish I never had! I *knew* not to open that—I knew it would be awful!"

"You are working yourself into a state over nothing, you know."

"Am I?"

"Well, what do you think? You happen to have read some notes—"

"Not 'notes'—conversations with this woman!"

"Who is imaginary."

"How can she be imaginary when she knows all these things *you* couldn't possibly know? She is someone who comes to your studio and she is why you have been so distracted and totally uninterested in me now for months. When I speak to you, you're barely able to stay awake. When *she* speaks to you, it's all so wonderful that you have to write it down, every wonderful word. She so much as opens her *mouth* and you're an 'écouteur—an audiophiliac.' God, what pretentious crap!"

"She could well be why I have been uninterested in everything for months—and then again the book I'm writing may be why I have been interested in nothing else for months."

"You do—you do—" Crying bitterly.

"Do what?"

"You love her more than you ever loved me!"

"*Because she doesn't exist.* If you didn't exist I'd love you like that too. I can't believe that we are having this argument."

"We're having it because you are lying!"

"Really, this is too stupid."

"I suppose talking to Rosalie Nichols in the hospital was imaginary, too. But you *did* talk to her in the hospital, you *told* me you talked to her in the hospital!"

"I did. And wrote down some of what we said to each other —and more that we didn't say I made up, and where the real exchange ends and the invented one begins I can't even remember anymore. Her situation was awful, she was being so gallant, and I didn't want to forget it. Some of what's there is accurate reporting and it inspires what I would hope is accurate imagining. My Czech friend Ivan, crazy as he may be, never accused me of sleeping with Olina; we had no such falling out after she left him—did you read that part?"

"I read it all! I already had on my coat and, *stupidly, stupidly*, I sat back down and read the whole thing! Oh, it's so much better *not* to know!"

"Well, I don't believe this soap opera, really. You must dramatize everything."

"It's you who dramatizes, who has to have this one because she's the voice of *Mitteleuropa* and that one because she sounds so fucking well born—"

"Look, this is simply too corny. I refuse to explain myself. I refuse to have this argument with you, of all people. I refuse to remind you that the sounds people make hold a certain appeal for me, and maybe this is a notebook about *that*. I have imagined a love affair—I do it all the time. Not the way most men ordinarily do, while clutching at their dicks, but because that is my *work*."

"But I've *read* those chapters, the manuscript chapters you gave me to read about the English woman—and this is *not* that English woman, this is the *model* for that woman, this is *the real woman!* Don't pretend they are one and the same!"

"I don't. One is a figure sketched in conversation in a notebook, the other is a major character entangled in the plot of an intricate book. I have been imagining myself, outside of my novel, having a love affair with a character inside my novel. If Tolstoy had imagined himself in love with Anna Karenina, had Hardy imagined himself in an affair with Tess—look, I follow my leads where they take me—ah, the hell with it. What do you propose, that I police myself? That I don't follow through on this sort of impulse for fear—for fear of *what*? Enlightened prurient opinion? Well, not by you and not by anyone will I be censored like that!"

"Oh, the self-righteousness of the liar caught with his pants down! Don't be so fucking self-righteous, and don't scream at me—I cannot be screamed at! You are caught and you are trying to confuse me!"

"I am trying to straighten you out! I gave you the example of Ivan and Olina. When Olina ran off with that black guy, we *did* have lunch together, Ivan and I, and he *did* tell me all about what had happened, but he did *not* go on to accuse me of having betrayed him with his wife. I never did betray him with his wife, never was accused of betraying him with his wife, *except in that notebook you read*. I portray myself as implicated because it is not enough just to be present. That's not the way I go about it. To compromise some 'character' doesn't get me where I want to be. What heats things up is compromising me. It kind of makes the indictment juicier, besmirching myself. As is proved, if you still doubt me, by this fucking argument."

"But the Polish woman you *did* meet at Diana's party. You told me that. You had to tell me when she called you here."

"And? So?"

"You had an affair with her too."

"Did I? Too? She was only here a week."

"So—that week. You had to have an affair because of the overwhelming enchantment of her accent! And who is the little American loony? Where does *she* fit in?"

"Control yourself. *Think.*"

"*She* thinks—go argue with her!"

"Who is 'she' this time?"

Crying. "Your thirty-six-year-old."

"Let's get the notebook, okay? Let's sit down here and go over it. I will, if I have to, explain to you, line by line, if I have to, what I have been up to, as best I understand it. I will tell you which bits are out of conversations I have had with any number of people—including Rosalie Nichols and that Polish woman *and* 'the little American loony'—and those that are not, which happen to be the preponderance of what you read. A lot goes back to the affair, before I ever met you, with Rosalie. When she turned up with her husband upstairs on Eighty-first Street, they were moving *from* England. Did it never occur to you that she might be the English woman whose England— *and* whose marriage—I was drawing on in what you read? Look, I don't mind your reading it. I wouldn't have left it lying around if I worried about your reading it. I carry it back and forth between here and the studio because sometimes I sit in the bedroom, as you know, sit in the bedroom chair at the end of the day, while you are asleep in bed, and make up little conversations between myself and this woman. And other women too. Maybe to the degree that I carry on like this in the bedroom where you are sleeping, maybe to that degree I am guilty of a sort of perverse betrayal. But then I am not the only man who thinks about imaginary women while in the bedroom with the woman he regularly sleeps with. There may even be women who behave just as impurely in their bedrooms with the men they regularly sleep with. The difference is that what I impurely imagine, I am impelled to develop and write down. A mitigating circumstance: my work, my livelihood. In my imagination I am unfaithful to everybody, by the way, not just to you. Look, think of it as an act of mourning, because it is that too—a lament of sorts for a life I did lead before you. I don't any longer, I actually happen to live as married men were once supposed to—but allow me to miss the old ways just a little. Such longings aren't entirely unnatural, you know. Please, if coming upon my notebook has caused you all this misery, I am sorry and I wish it hadn't. But I do have to say, what you are confronting me with is a naively perfect paranoid misreading."

"So, except insofar as I'm supposed to believe that she's based on an English woman you had an affair with in New York a hundred years ago, she doesn't exist, other than in your imagination."

"And in yours."

"And you never had an affair with Olina. I'm to believe that too. Otherwise I'm not only paranoid but, even worse, philistinely naive."

"Ivan was broken enough, he'd lost enough—Olina was all he had. Not only did I not but he never even accused me of it. Nor did he ever tell me what a lousy writer I am. Phone him in New York and ask him. Phone Olina—ask *her*."

"Explain to me if you will, then, how you happen to know all these things about English life that this English woman who doesn't exist tells you in your studio while you are conducting this affair with her in your head."

"Because I've been living here awhile and I sometimes pay attention. Because I learned a little from Rosalie. Because it's my business to seem to know more than I do. This woman is simply the repository of all that."

"But the conversations are so *intimate*."

"I see where that might be maddening. Of course I understand how this might drive you just a little nuts. But intimacy is interesting too—it's a subject too."

"Postcoital intimacy. That's the subject."

"Is it? I hadn't thought of it precisely that way."

"Well, please do. That serenity. That talk. That's the whole mood. You're more intimate with her than you are with me."

"That isn't true."

"Lately it is."

"Well, these things wax and wane—detachment and tenderness, incredible tenderness and then incredible inaccessibility, that's the pattern with people who've stuck together as long as we have. What I'm thinking about with her isn't that. It's the love that exists *because* it's compartmentalized. The stolen moment that can't be sustained."

"It's sustained in that notebook."

"You know, I ought really to interpret your jealousy as a terrific tribute to my persuasiveness."

"And I suppose I ought to interpret what I've read here as a measure of my terrific failure. Whether I believe she exists or whether I believe she doesn't exist, certainly the love for her exists, the desire for her *to* exist exists. And that is even more wounding. The whole notebook is nothing more than an attempt to escape the marriage and me."

"And if it were? If it is? Where have *you* been? The attempt to escape the marriage is an ingredient of marriage. In some I've seen it's the vital principle that keeps it going. I wrote these things out, not to wound *you*, but partly, I think, to trace down the logic of that—the *illogic* of that. It's too bad you can't read it that way."

"How would you read it if *I* was charged up with desire for somebody who is everything *you're* not?"

"You really cannot allow yourself to be crushed like this over a situation that is invented."

"Can't I? Can't I? Oh, you're right. It isn't fair, I'm sure. It's just, you have been so remote . . . terribly remote."

"If so, that's something else."

"No, no. It's the same thing. You wouldn't have an imaginary friend, you wouldn't need an imaginary friend . . . And are you going to publish that notebook? The novel and then the notebook, the tragic lament for the life you once led? Is that the plan?"

"I don't know."

"Don't you? Is that why the sections are interspliced like that, with all that Czechoslovak mirroring of everything, because you don't know?"

"It's occurred to me. I'm not sure what it adds up to, if anything. But of course I've thought of it."

"To publish it as it is?"

"I said I don't know. There's something to be said for being shed of all the expository fat, but I haven't begun to think it through. I don't really know what it is I've got. A portrait of what? Up till now I have been fiddling with it on the side and mostly worrying about the novel."

"Well, maybe you should, you know, think it through. Because what you've got a portrait of is adulterous love, and, consequently, it might be advisable to take your name out—don't you think? 'Philip, do you have an ashtray?' You would change that to 'Nathan,' would you not? If it were ever to be published?"

"Would I? No. It's not Nathan Zuckerman—it's not meant to be Zuckerman. The *novel* is Zuckerman. The notebook is me."

"You just told me it's not you."

"No, I told you it is me, imagining. It's the story of an *imagination* in love."

"But if one day it should be published more or less as it is, liberated from exposition et cetera, people aren't going to know that it's just a little story of an imagination in love, any more than I did."

"They generally don't, so what difference does that make? I write fiction and I'm told it's autobiography, I write autobiography and I'm told it's fiction, so since I'm so dim and they're so smart, let *them* decide what it is or it isn't."

"Yes, I can see where that might be a lot of fun for you and your readers, letting them decide—but what about me?"

"You'll have to decide as well, if you insist on not believing what this actually is."

"I meant, what about humiliating me?"

"How could you be humiliated by something that's *not so?* It is *not* myself. It is *far* from myself—it's play, it's a game, it is an *impersonation* of myself! Me *ventriloquizing* myself. Or maybe it's more easily gasped the other way around—everything here is falsified *except* me. Maybe it's *both*. But both ways or either way, what it adds up to, honey, is *homo ludens!*"

"*But who would know that, aside from us?*"

"Look, I cannot and do not live in the world of discretion, not as a writer, anyway. I would prefer to, I assure you—it would make life easier. But discretion is, unfortunately, not for novelists. Neither is shame. *Feeling* shame is automatic in me, inescapable, it may even be *good*; it's yielding to shame that's the serious crime."

"But who is even talking about shame? All it would require is your having that wretched American girl say, '*Nathan*, do you have an ashtray?' All it would require is that, in three or four places, and none of this would be a problem for anyone. Where are you going?"

"Out! Somebody telling me what to write happens to drive me absolutely nuts, so I am going out!"

"Don't. Don't go alone! I'll come with you."

"But we cannot continue this fight on the street. It has gone far enough. It is *over*. I simply cannot be hounded like this for something I have written, particularly by you. Darling, this is writing, that is all it is!"

"But published *as* it is—"

"Jesus Christ, *is* this Eastern fucking Europe? I will not be put in that position! That is *too* absurd! I won't have it! You cannot stop me from writing what I write for a simple and ridiculous pathological reason—because I cannot stop myself! I write what I write the way I write it, and if and when it should ever happen, I will publish what I publish however I want to publish and I'm not going to start worrying at this late date what people misunderstand or get wrong!"

"Or get right."

"We are talking about a notebook, a blueprint, a diagram, and not about human beings!"

"But you are a human being, whether you like it or not! And so am I! And so is she!"

"She's not, she's *words*—and try as I will, I cannot fuck words! I'm going out—alone!"

ELLO? Hello?"

"Hello."

". . . Hello."

"It's me."

"I know. I recognize your voice."

"I certainly recognize yours."

"How are you?"

"How am I? I'm okay. How are you? That's what I was calling about."

"I'm fine. I've been trying to call you. But I didn't know where to reach you. I tried your number. Your old number is not operative."

"In what country were you trying to call me?"

"Your studio in England."

"I'm not there anymore. I'm living in America for good now. Look, how are you?"

"I'm very well. I've been thinking so much about you. Ever since I read your book I haven't known whether to call or not. I thought about it a lot."

"I'll bet you did. I thought about it too. I thought about its effect on your marriage."

"Oh, well, he didn't read it."

Laughing. "Wonderful. Of course. All that worrying for nothing. How are you anyway? Tell me."

"I'm fine, aren't I? I don't know where to begin really."

"Did you wonder why I didn't call you?"

"No, I didn't. I just thought it was a decision. The last time we'd spoken, I don't think everybody was very happy. You made it very clear you had to go your way. I thought, yes, you have to go your way and I suppose I have to go mine. And that was a couple of years ago. So I went my way and you went yours."

"Yes."

"Well, I'm very glad you called because I've missed you such a lot. For a long time I didn't call because you said you didn't want to see me because it wasn't a love affair any longer. So I—"

"No, no. You said you didn't want to see *me*. You said you couldn't take any more of this guilty secret stuff."

"Did I?"

"Yes. Many times. You know I have a good memory."

"Goodness, do you! I was astonished. And in that way you betrayed yourself, because two people said, 'I heard you in that book.' To me."

"Really?"

"Yes, exactly my voice."

"Who said that?"

"I do have friends who read literature and who also listen to me."

"Well, you have a distinctive delivery. I was in love with you for twenty reasons but that was one of them. For me, it was a long, wonderful, finally very sad, important—"

"I would say the same."

"I don't think anyone's ever been quite so appreciated before. I was nuts about you."

"Oh."

"Did you know?"

"I . . . oh, dear. . . ."

"Don't turn English."

"Well, I was thinking . . ."

"You were thinking what?"

"Why it didn't happen. As it does in the book. One of the reasons was that you were away so much, particularly at the beginning. And it stayed in the world of fantasy. It stayed like a dream, really. It was so enclosed."

"You've been on my mind so much."

"Well, I've been thinking about you too."

"Shall I start the 'Remember that afternoon we' stuff?"

"Yes! Yes!" Laughing. "I'm not young anymore, by the way.

When I met you I was still young. When you get to be thirty-eight it's suddenly all over. You know what I mean. It's not all all over but some of it's all over."

"The glow gone?"

"Oh, that was gone probably around the age of nineteen. I'll be thirty-nine any minute. I'm thinking of having a party in the dinosaur hall of the Natural History Museum."

"That's a lovely place. That's a very good idea."

"I just mean I think I'm turning that corner of thinking of myself quite differently. You know, when you absolutely don't think of yourself as a girl, you don't . . . I don't know, it's hard to put quickly, but that transition, which is so difficult for women, is one that I've begun. I'm sure you've heard about it."

"I didn't call before because I didn't want to disturb your life again. Are you still living together?"

"Yes. Are you?"

"Yes."

"We get on much better."

"Maybe I had something to do with it."

"Oh, I would think so. One of the reasons that I didn't call you again, though I didn't think I should anyway, was that I didn't realize that I was pregnant when I last saw you. I have another child."

"Oh, my. Do you?"

"Yes. And I find that's very ironic. Given the book. And of course it's a boy. So there we are. He's a very nice boy."

"Whose boy is it?"

"It's, it's my husband's . . . it is."

"Okay. I had to ask."

"He asked too."

"Are you sure? That it's his?"

"Absolutely certain."

"Well, ironies abound. You had the son all right but not by my character and not in my book. I imagined it but he did it. That's the difference between us; that's why you live with him and not me."

"Yes. That's life for you. Always slightly askew fiction."

"So you're the mother of two."

"Yup."

"You said that sadly."

"Ah well, I just think the phrase has some sad connotations. But they're lovely children. I've kind of been very busy these days counting my blessings."

"And so you and your husband are just hitting it off now?"

"Well, doing the decent thing, you know? I keep wondering where the big problem is these days. Obviously there are the intractable problems. Loneliness—I feel terribly lonely, I get quite bored sometimes at my job. But still, short of the big ones, there's nothing wrong."

"Do you have a lover?"

"No. No, I don't. Listen, I was astonished to see this character so terribly passive. I had simply no idea. Insofar as it's me . . ."

"Insofar as it's you, insofar, it's pretty much you."

"Well, I'm not like that anymore." Laughing. "I'm a positive person now."

"Are you, really? Thank God that happened after I wrote about you. Positive people in books put me to sleep."

"But the passivity—it was terrifying. To me that's a portrait of somebody who's in deep trouble. Somebody who's absolutely out of the ordinary swim of life. Don't you think?"

"Well, at a certain point the writing did take over and alter things."

"I can see where it came from, however. A friend of mine, just a few weeks ago, he'd finished the book and he asked me just how many times I'd had lunch with you. He said, 'There's a character in this book that's extraordinarily like you.' My husband was sitting right there. I said something noncommittal. I don't know what I said."

"You said, 'I don't eat lunch.'"

"I didn't really know how to say anything tremendously clever at that point. The other thing that troubled me is why, why do you *do* that? Why do you take life like that? And especially considering that you wanted secrecy—and our relationship was *distorted* by secrecy, by your almost paranoid efforts to keep the whole thing hidden. For the sake of your wife. Why did you then write a book which she, I'm sure, can't help but think is based on a real person? Why?"

"Because it's what I do. It wasn't paranoia. It was never paranoia. It was protecting somebody from something she couldn't be expected to be happy about. Besides, she thinks the real person is Rosalie Nichols."

"Oh, of course. Of yesteryear."

"Yes. Who did live upstairs like the woman in the book."

"Well, I know all that. We talked about her. She was at Oxford with me."

"I know."

"How funny. And what does Rosalie Nichols think?"

"It fooled her too. She said, 'All the time I thought you loved me for my body when in fact it was only for my sentences.'"

"I knew she would say that to you. I knew that would happen, I just knew she would think it was herself. She's having a fine time, I'll bet. And I also expect to be *told* by someone or other, sooner or later, that it's her."

"That'll be original, won't it?"

"Not only do you steal my words, you've given them to someone else."

"You want to be angry about that too?"

"I don't like it much."

"Would you have liked it better if I'd included in a footnote your name and address?"

"All of it's difficult. Angry, yes. I *was* angry. I thought if I was in your wife's position I'd know immediately that he'd been being consumed by somebody else for a very long time. And it seemed to me a complete reversal of everything you said. All the deformities imposed on our time together were pointless, because you'd done this anyway."

"Well, I wasn't worried about me—I had Rosalie as my beard. I thought it was going to be worse for you."

"It could have been. In fact, who knows? It could well be in the future."

"And you have another child, which comes as—well, not a blow . . . but . . . well, a blow, yes. I did love you terribly."

"I think you may be idealizing me from afar. I'd think that by this time the reality would be unable to compare, if not with what you now remember, with what you wrote. The one you loved so terribly may not be unfictional little me."

"It was you. I couldn't have written about her that way if it hadn't been for you. I don't know if I ever told you how much or if I even knew how much *until* I wrote the book. There were certain necessary restraints all around. We had an awfully good time, even locked up in that terrible room. But I wasn't just living with you in those few hours—I had a life with you when I was writing. I had an imaginary life with you when you weren't there. It was all very strong."

"But you *can't*. You *can't* have an imaginary life and a real life simultaneously like that. And it was probably the imaginary life you had with me and the real life you had with her. Listen, you can't take down everything someone says like that."

"But I did. I do."

"Well, I felt quite angry about it. Rather like those native people who don't want their photographs taken; it takes something away from their souls."

"I'm sure you were angry."

"Very angry, yes."

"When did you get over it?"

"I probably haven't got over it."

"I've missed talking to you."

"And taking down what I say."

"Of course."

"But, you know . . . I've missed talking to *you*. I've missed talking to you so badly. I talk to you sometimes in my head."

"I talk to you too."

"I don't think Freshfield was at all a good name for me. You should have consulted me about that."

"It comes by way of an English poem. 'Tomorrow to fresh woods and pastures new.'"

"I realized that. But it wasn't all right. It was too easy."

"You haven't lost your bite."

"Our experience with the anti-Semitic woman in the restaurant—all the English reviewers said it was impossible in every detail."

"Yes." Laughing. "I thought you might come forward to defend me."

Laughing. "They thought it was too much a feat of imagination."

"Yes. They should go out to eat more often."

"So should we have."

"Well, we tried but that broad put us in our place. After that, I wasn't going out with you again, not in a Christian country I wasn't."

"Is that why you're living back in America? Is that why you've given up coming here—because the place is too Christian for you? That's what it sounds like from your book."

"My book's a book. I left for lots of reasons. Our parting was one."

"Yes, but in the novel it's England that I sort of stand for. Isn't it? I've been thinking about it. I sort of turned you into a foreigner here. Made you realize that England is not for you."

"Everything made me realize that. Did you turn me into a foreigner? I see what you're saying, but actually you cut both ways. Listening to you sometimes did make me feel an outsider but an outsider who, through you, was a little of an insider too. I learned from you. It isn't that you eluded me; it's that you made clear to me how much everything eluded me. Before I knew you I thought something of the place was getting through. But the more I knew you the more I felt as though I were spending half of each year in twelfth-century China. In the end I didn't understand anything."

"How could you expect to, all day hiding out in a little room without even a bed in it? Now that you're back, do you understand everything there?"

"I understand something. I take long walks in New York, and every once in a while I stop and find I'm smiling. I hear myself saying aloud, 'Home.'"

"So you're one of those people who careen around the New York streets talking to themselves. I've seen them there. I thought they were crazy."

"No, just all back from their service in England. Walking the streets I do see something I was missing terribly. Something I was longing for. It didn't occur to me, at least not in any blatant way, until I was back a few months."

"What's that?"

"Jews."

"We've got some of them in England, you know."

"Jews with force, I'm talking about. Jews with appetite. Jews without shame. Complaining Jews who get under your skin.

Brash Jews who eat with their elbows on the table. Unaccommodating Jews, full of anger, insult, argument, and impudence. New York's the real obstreperous Zion, whether Ariel Sharon knows it or not."

"So England *was* too Christian for you."

"Tel Aviv's too Christian compared to this place. After London even Ed Koch looks good."

"Who's he?"

"The Jewish mayor my liberal friends hate. Not me. I watch him waving his arms on television, I hear that singsong, self-satisfied ethnic squawk, and I lean forward and kiss the set. The other day I was driving to Jersey to see my father, and coming out of the Lincoln Tunnel, the guy in the next car called me an asshole. He rolls down the window and he says, 'You fuckin' asshole, you!' I didn't even know what I'd done wrong. I just smiled. I told him, 'Force the issue, man. Pour it on.' All that truculence. All that wholehearted, unapologetic pugnacity—absolutely rejuvenating. When I see everybody everywhere pushing to be first, I begin to remember what it means to be human."

"So you've returned to the bosom of the tribe."

"Yes, I have. Isn't that odd?"

"Not very. The one who has gone home. You've read the *Odyssey*."

"I see. Another little epic of exile and return. With you as who? As Nausicaä? Calypso?"

"As Homer. I have been thinking about writing a book about *you*."

"Charge ahead."

"And do you know what it would be called? This is not the object of the enterprise. It's the very subject of the book. *Kiss and Tell*. Can you imagine how terrible this could be?"

"For whom?"

"For *you*."

"Do what you like."

"That's not the way I think. You know that I object greatly to writing down exactly what people said. I object greatly to this taking people's lives and putting them into fiction. And then being a famous author who resents critics for saying that he doesn't make things up."

"Because you had a baby doesn't mean I didn't make up a baby; because you're you doesn't mean I didn't make *you* up."

"I also exist."

"Also. You also exist and also I made you up. 'Also' is a good word to remember. You also don't exist as only you."

"I certainly don't anymore."

"You never did. As I made you up, you *never* existed."

"Then who was that in your studio with my legs over your shoulders? Please, no more of this highbrow nonsense. I'm English and I don't even hear it. What's wonderful about English culture is that we're either too damn sensible or too damn stupid to listen to that stuff. All I began to say is that I have very muddled, complex feelings about the whole business of self-exposure and the different kinds of betrayal, and what all these things amount to."

"Betrayal is an overpowering charge, don't you think? There was no contract drawn up stating that in matters pertaining to you I would forswear my profession. I am a thief and a thief is not to be trusted."

"Not even by his moll?"

"However visible you may be feeling, you weren't identified in that book or made overly identifiable. However much you may have served as a model, the great British public happens to be ignorant of it and you only have not to tell them for them to remain ignorant."

"Don't bristle so. I didn't just say to you my feelings were simple about all this—I said they were complex. And they are. What it comes down to is that a woman comes to a man to chat a little, and all the man is really thinking about is his typewriter. You love your typewriter more than you could ever love any woman."

"I don't think that was so with you. I believe I loved you both equally."

"Well, I happen to know that whenever you feel agitated and ambivalent, then you do indeed have something to write about. And it—*my* book—is all about kissing and telling, because if I were to write this book I would be doing that. I haven't described it at all well to you."

"You have."

"Should I write it?"

"I'm not the one to say no, especially as I may do another about you."

"You wouldn't. You're not. You aren't, are you?"

Laughing. "Yes, of course I will. This'll be part of it."

"Well, I'd be amazed. I would call that scraping the barrel, really."

"Don't underestimate yourself. You're a great barrel. For me you were."

"Was I? Oh, I felt so angry. I was angry for months. Although I was very torn, really, because as soon as I read it, I also couldn't be angry."

"Why was that?"

"Because it was so, so tender . . . I think. Unless I got it wrong."

"No. I thought there were some things you'd like. Things I planted just for you to be amused by."

"Oh, there were. I didn't miss them. It was very strange reading it, absolutely strange. Because I was in no doubt which of it was addressed to me. I may have been wrong but I felt no doubt. And which bits of it were not, particularly."

"I'm sure you didn't miss any of it. But that was our life, I thought, as it might have been. Our life also."

"I saw. I saw. It's such a strange story."

"I know. No one would believe it."

PATRIMONY

A True Story

For our family,
the living and the dead

1

Well, What Do You Think?

M Y father had lost most of the sight in his right eye by the time he'd reached eighty-six, but otherwise he seemed in phenomenal health for a man his age when he came down with what the Florida doctor diagnosed, incorrectly, as Bell's palsy, a viral infection that causes paralysis, usually temporary, to one side of the face.

The paralysis appeared, out of nowhere, the day after he had flown from New Jersey to West Palm Beach to spend the winter months sharing a sublet apartment with a retired book-keeper of seventy, Lillian Beloff, who lived upstairs from him in Elizabeth and with whom he had become romantically in-volved a year after my mother died in 1981. At the West Palm airport, he had been feeling so fit that he hadn't even bothered with a porter (whom, besides, he would have had to tip) and carried his own luggage from the baggage area all the way out to the taxi stand. Then the next morning, in the bathroom mirror, he saw that half his face was no longer his. What had looked like him the day before now looked like nobody—the lower lid of the bad eye bagged downward, revealing the lid's inner lining, the cheek on that side had gone slack and lifeless as though beneath the bone had been filleted, and his lips were no longer straight but drawn down diagonally across his face.

With his hand he pushed the right cheek back to where it had been the night before, holding it there for the count of ten. He did this repeatedly that morning—and every day there-after—but when he let go, it wouldn't stay. He tried to tell himself that he had lain the wrong way in bed, that his skin was simply furrowed from sleep, but what he believed was that he'd had a stroke. His father had been crippled by a stroke back in the early 1940s, and once he'd become an old man himself, he said to me several times, "I don't want to go the way he did. I don't want to lie there like that. That's my worst fear." He told me how he used to stop off to see his father at the hospital early in the morning on the way downtown to the

office and again on his way home at night. Twice a day he lit
cigarettes and stuck them in his father's mouth for him and in
the evening he sat beside the bed and read to him from the
Yiddish paper. Immobilized and helpless, with only his cigarettes to soothe him, Sender Roth lingered for almost a year,
and until a second stroke finished him off late one night in 1940,
my father, twice each day, sat and watched him die.

The doctor who told my father that he had Bell's palsy assured him that in a short time most, if not all, of the facial
paralysis would be gone. And within days of his getting this
prognosis, it was confirmed for him by three different people,
in just his section of the vast condominium development,
who'd had the same ailment and recovered. One of them had
had to wait for nearly four months, but eventually the paralysis
went away as mysteriously as it had come.

His didn't go away.

He soon couldn't hear out of his right ear. The Florida doctor examined the ear and measured the hearing loss, but told
him it had nothing to do with the Bell's palsy. It was just something that happened with age—he had probably been losing
the hearing in the right ear as gradually as he had lost the sight
in the right eye and only now had noticed it. This time when
my father asked how much longer the doctor thought he'd
have to wait before the Bell's palsy disappeared, the doctor told
him that in cases that continued as long as his had, it sometimes never disappeared. Look, count your blessings, the doctor said; except for a blind eye, a deaf ear, and a half-paralyzed
face, he was as healthy as a man twenty years younger.

When I phoned each Sunday, I could hear that as a consequence of the drooping mouth, his speech had become slurred
and difficult to follow—he sounded at times like someone fresh
from the dental chair whose novocaine hadn't worn off; when
I flew to Florida to see him, I was startled to find him looking
as though he might not be able to speak at all.

"Well," he said, in the lobby of my hotel, where I was meeting
Lil and him for dinner, "what do you think?" Those were his
first words, even as I bent over to kiss him. He was sunk down
beside Lil in a tapestried love seat, but his face was aimed
straight up at me so that I could see what had happened. Over
the last year he had intermittently been wearing a black patch

over his blind eye to prevent the light and the wind from irritating it, and what with the eye patch, the cheek, the mouth, and the fact that he had lost a lot of weight, he seemed to me gruesomely transformed—in the five weeks since I'd last seen him in Elizabeth—into an enfeebled old man. It was hard to believe that only some six years earlier, the winter after my mother's death, when he was sharing the Bal Harbour apartment of his old friend Bill Weber, he'd had no difficulty convincing the wealthy widows in the building—who'd immediately begun to swarm with interest around the gregarious new widower in the fresh seersucker jacket and pastel trousers —that he had only just reached seventy, even though we had all gathered together to mark his eightieth birthday the summer before in my house in Connecticut.

At dinner in the hotel I began to understand how much of a handicap the Bell's palsy was, in addition to being disfiguring. He could now drink successfully only by using a straw; otherwise the liquid ran out the paralyzed half of his mouth. And eating was a bite-by-bite effort, laden with frustration and embarrassment. Reluctantly he agreed, after spotting his tie with his soup, to allow Lil to wrap a napkin around his neck—there was already a napkin across his lap, more or less protecting his trousers. Occasionally Lil reached over with her own napkin and, to his disgruntlement, removed a piece of food that had slipped out of his mouth and adhered to his chin without his knowing it. Several times she reminded him to put less food on his fork and to try, with each bite, to take into his mouth a little less than he was accustomed to. "Yeah," he mumbled, staring disconsolately into his plate, "yeah, sure," and after two or three bites he forgot. It was because eating had become a depressing ordeal that he had lost all this weight and looked so pathetically undernourished.

What made everything still more difficult was that cataracts in both his eyes had thickened in recent months, so that even the sight in his one good eye had grown blurry. For several years my ophthalmologist in New York, David Krohn, had been following the progress of my father's cataracts and dealing with his deteriorating vision, and when, in March, my father returned to New Jersey from his unhappy stay in Florida, he went to New York to urge David to remove the cataract from the good eye; because he was powerless to do anything about the Bell's palsy, he was particularly eager that some action be taken toward restoring his sight. But late in the afternoon following my father's visit, David phoned to say that he was reluctant to operate on the eye until further tests had determined the cause of the facial paralysis and the hearing loss. He wasn't convinced that it was Bell's palsy.

He was right not to be. Harold Wasserman, my father's New Jersey physician, had arranged locally for the MRI scan that David ordered, and when Harold received the report from the lab, he called me early that evening to give me the results. My father had a brain tumor, "a massive tumor," Harold called it, and though with MRI pictures one couldn't distinguish between a benign and a malignant tumor, Harold said, "Either way, those tumors kill you." The next step was to consult with a neurosurgeon, to determine precisely the kind of tumor it was and what, if anything, might be done. "I'm not optimistic," Harold said, "and neither should you be."

I managed to get my father to the neurosurgeon without telling him what the MRI had already disclosed. I lied and said that the tests showed nothing, but that David, being extra cautious, wanted to get one last opinion on the facial paralysis before he went ahead with the cataract removal. In the meantime, I arranged for the MRI pictures to be sent to the Essex House Hotel in New York. Claire Bloom and I were temporarily living there while we were looking for an apartment—we were planning to find a place in Manhattan after ten years of dividing our lives between her house in London and mine in Connecticut.

In fact, only about a week before the MRI pictures of my father's brain, along with the radiologist's report, were delivered to the hotel in an oversized envelope, Claire had returned to London to see her daughter and to look after repairs on her house and to meet with her accountant over a long-standing negotiation with the British tax authorities. She had been yearning terribly for London, and the month's visit was designed not merely to let her attend to practical matters but to take the edge off her homesickness. I suppose that if my father's tumor had been discovered earlier, when Claire was with me, my preoccupation with him would not have been so all-consuming, and—at least in the evenings—I might have been less likely to become as depressed about his illness as I did on my own. Yet even at the time it seemed to me that Claire's absence—along with the fact that in a hotel, feeling transient and homeless, I was finding it impossible to write—was a peculiarly opportune fortuity: with no other responsibilities, I could attend entirely to him.

Being by myself also allowed me to be as emotional as I felt, without having to put up a manly or mature or philosophical front. Alone, when I felt like crying I cried, and I never felt more like it than when I removed from the envelope the series of pictures of his brain—and not because I could readily identify the tumor invading the brain but simply because it *was* his brain, my father's brain, what prompted him to think the blunt way he thought, speak the emphatic way he spoke, reason the emotional way he reasoned, decide the impulsive way he decided. This was the tissue that had manufactured his set of endless worries and sustained for more than eight decades his stubborn self-discipline, the source of everything that had so frustrated me as his adolescent son, the thing that had ruled our fate back when he was all-powerful and determining our purpose, and now it was being compressed and displaced and destroyed because of "a large mass predominantly located within the region of the right cerebellopontine angles and prepontine cisterns. There is extension of the mass into the right cavernous sinus with encasement of the carotid artery . . ." I didn't know where to find the cerebellopontine angles or prepontine cisterns, but reading in the radiologist's report that the carotid artery was encased in the tumor was, for me, as good as reading his death sentence. "There is also apparent destruction of the right petrous apex. There is significant posterior displacement and compression of the pons and right cerebellar peduncle by this mass . . ."

I was alone and without inhibition, and so, while the pictures of his brain, photographed from every angle, lay spread across the hotel bed, I made no effort to fight back anything. Maybe the impact wasn't quite what it would have been had I been holding that brain in the palms of my hands, but it was along those lines. God's will erupted out of a burning bush and, no less miraculously, Herman Roth's had issued forth all these years from this bulbous organ. I had seen my father's brain, and everything and nothing was revealed. A mystery scarcely short of divine, the brain, even in the case of a retired insurance man with an eighth-grade education from Newark's Thirteenth Avenue School.

My nephew Seth drove my father up to Millburn to see the neurosurgeon, Dr. Meyerson, in his suburban office. I had arranged for my father to see him there rather than at Newark's University Hospital because I thought the mere location of the doctor's hospital office, which I had been told was in the oncology wing, would signal to him that he had a cancer, when no such diagnosis had been made and he didn't even know yet that he had the tumor. This way he wouldn't be frightened out of his skin, at least for a while.

And when I spoke to Dr. Meyerson on the phone later that day, he told me that a tumor like my father's, located in front of the brain stem, was benign about ninety-five percent of the time. According to Meyerson, the tumor could have been growing there for as long as ten years; but the recent onset of facial paralysis and deafness in the right ear suggested that "in a relatively short time," as he put it, "it'll get much worse." It was still possible, however, to remove it surgically. He told me that seventy-five percent of those operated on survive and are better, ten percent die on the table, and another fifteen percent either die shortly afterward or are left worse.

"If he survives," I asked, "what is the convalescence like?"

"It's difficult. He'd be in a convalescent home for a month —maybe as long as two or three months."

"It's hell, in other words."

"It's rough," he said, "but do nothing and it could be rougher."

I wasn't about to give Meyerson's news to my father on the phone, and so the next morning, when I called at around nine, I said I was going to come over to Elizabeth to see him.

"So, it's that bad," he said.

"Let me drive over and we'll sit down and talk about it."

"Do I have cancer?" he asked me.

"No, you don't have cancer."

"What is it then?"

"Be patient for another hour and I'll be there and tell you exactly what the situation is."

"I want to know now."

"I'll only be an hour—less than an hour," I said, convinced that it was better for him to have to wait, however frightened he was, than to tell him flat out on the phone and have him sitting alone, in shock, until I arrived.

It was probably no wonder, given the task I was about to perform, that when I got off the turnpike in Elizabeth, I missed the fork in the exit road that would have taken me into North Avenue and directly to my father's apartment building a few blocks away. Instead, I wound up on a stretch of New Jersey highway that, a mile or two on, passed right alongside the cemetery where my mother had been buried seven years before. I didn't believe there was anything mystical about how I'd got there, but it was amazing nonetheless to see where the twenty-minute drive from Manhattan had landed me.

I had been to the cemetery only twice, first on the day of her funeral in 1981 and the following year, when I took my father out to see her stone. Both times we had driven from Elizabeth proper and not from Manhattan, and so I hadn't known that the cemetery could even be reached by the turnpike. And had I actually been driving over to find the cemetery that day, I more than likely would have lost my way in the complex of turnoffs to Newark Airport, Port Newark, Port Elizabeth, and back to downtown Newark. Though I wasn't searching for that cemetery either consciously or unconsciously, on the morning when I was to tell my father of the brain tumor that would kill him, I had flawlessly traveled the straightest possible route from my Manhattan hotel to my mother's grave and the grave site beside hers where he was to be buried.

I hadn't wanted to leave my father waiting any longer than was absolutely necessary, yet having arrived where I had, I was unable to continue on by as though nothing unusual had happened. I didn't expect to learn anything new by going off and standing at the foot of my mother's grave that morning; I didn't expect to be comforted or strengthened by her memory or better prepared somehow to help my father through his affliction; nor did I figure I'd be weakened substantially seeing his plot beside hers. The accident of a wrong turn had brought me there, and all I did by getting out of the car and entering the cemetery to find her grave was to bow to its impelling force. My mother and the other dead had been brought here by the impelling force of what was, after all, a more unlikely accident—having once lived.

I find that while visiting a grave one has thoughts that are more or less anybody's thoughts and, leaving aside the matter of eloquence, don't differ much from Hamlet's contemplating the skull of Yorick. There seems little to be thought or said that isn't a variant of "he hath borne me on his back a thousand times." At a cemetery you are generally reminded of just how narrow and banal your thinking is on this subject. Oh, you can try talking to the dead if you feel that'll help; you can begin, as I did that morning, by saying, "Well, Ma . . ." but it's hard not to know—if you even get beyond a first sentence —that you might as well be conversing with the column of vertebrae hanging in the osteopath's office. You can make them promises, catch them up on the news, ask for their understanding, their forgiveness, for their love—or you can take the other, the active approach, you can pull weeds, tidy the gravel, finger the letters carved in the tombstone; you can even get down and place your hands directly above their remains— touching the ground, *their* ground, you can shut your eyes and remember what they were like when they were still with you. But nothing is altered by these recollections, except that the dead seem even more distant and out of reach than they did when you were driving in the car ten minutes earlier. If there's no one in the cemetery to observe you, you can do some pretty crazy things to make the dead seem something other than dead. But even if you succeed and get yourself worked up enough *to feel their presence*, you still walk away without them. What cemeteries prove, at least to people like me, is not that the dead are present but that they are gone. They are gone and, as yet, we aren't. This is fundamental and, however unacceptable, grasped easily enough.

2

Mommy, Mommy, Where Are You, Mommy?

M Y father's retirement pension from Metropolitan Life provided him with more than enough to live on in the modest no-frills style that seemed to him natural and sufficient for someone who grew up in near-poverty, worked slavishly for some forty years to give his family a secure, if simple, home life, and lacked the slightest interest in conspicuous consumption, ostentation, or luxury. In addition to the pension he'd been receiving now for twenty-three years, he drew Social Security income and the interest on his accumulated wealth— some eighty thousand dollars' worth of savings accounts, CDs, and municipal bonds. Despite his solid financial situation, however, in advanced old age he had become annoyingly tight about spending anything on himself. Though he did not hesitate to give generous gifts to his two grandsons whenever they needed money, he was continually saving inconsequential sums that deprived him of things he himself liked or needed.

Among the more distressing economies was his refusal to buy his own *New York Times*. He worshiped that paper and loved to spend the morning reading it through, but now, instead of buying his own, he waited all day long to have a copy passed on to him by somebody in his building who had been feckless enough to fork over the thirty-five cents for it. He'd also given up buying the *Star-Ledger*, a fifteen-cent daily that, along with the defunct *Newark News*, he had read ever since I was a child and it was called the *Newark Star-Eagle*. He also refused to retain, on a weekly basis, the cleaning woman who used to help my mother with the apartment and the laundry. The woman now came one day a month, and he cleaned the apartment himself the rest of the time. "What else do I have to do?" he asked. But as he was nearly blind in one eye and had a cataract thickening in the other and was no longer as agile as he liked to imagine, no matter how hard he worked the job he did do was awful. The bathroom smelled, the carpets were dirty, and few of the appliances in the kitchen could have passed muster with a health inspector who hadn't been bribed.

It was a comfortably furnished, rather ordinary three-room apartment, decorated with neither flair nor bad taste. The living room carpet was a pleasant avocado green and the furniture there mostly antique reproductions, and on the walls were two large reproductions (chosen for my parents nearly forty years back by my brother, who had been to art school) of Gauguin landscapes framed in wormwood as well as an expressionistic portrait that my brother had painted of my father in his early seventies. There were thriving plants by the row of windows that faced a quiet, tree-lined, residential street to the south; there were photos in every room—of children, grandchildren, daughters-in-law, nephews, nieces—and the few books on the shelves in the dining area were either by me or on Jewish subjects. Aside from the lamps, which were a little glitzily ornate and surprisingly uncharacteristic of my mother's prim, everything-in-its-place aesthetic, it was a warm, welcoming apartment whose gleaming appearance—at least when my mother was still alive—was somewhat in contrast to the depressing lobby and hallways of the thirty-year-old building, which were uninvitingly bare and growing slightly dilapidated.

Ever since my father had been alone, when I was visiting, I'd sometimes wind up, after having used the toilet, scouring the sink, cleaning the soap dish, and rinsing out the toothbrush glass before I returned to sit with him in the living room. He insisted on washing his underclothes and his socks in the bathroom rather than parting with the few quarters that it cost to use the washer/dryer in the basement laundry room; every time I came to see him, there were his grayish, misshapen things draped over wire hangers on the shower rod and the towel racks. Though he prided himself on being nattily dressed and always enjoyed putting on a nicely tailored new sports jacket or a three-piece Hickey-Freeman suit (enjoyed it particularly when he'd bought it at an end-of-season sale), he had taken to cutting corners on whatever wasn't visible to anyone else. His pajamas and handkerchiefs, like his underwear and socks, looked as though they hadn't been replaced since my mother's death.

When I got to his apartment that morning—after the inad-

vertent visit to my mother's grave—I quickly excused myself
and went off to the toilet. First I'd missed a turnoff, and now
in the bathroom I was taking another few minutes to rehearse
for a final time the best way to tell him about the tumor. While
I stood over the bowl, his undergarments hung all around me
like remnants strung out by a farmer to scare the birds away.
On the open shelves above the toilet, where there was an as-
sortment of prescription drugs, as well as his Polident, Vaseline,
and Ascriptin, his boxes of tissues, Q-tips, and absorbent cotton, I spotted the shaving mug that had once been my grandfather's; in it my father kept his razor and a tube of shaving
cream. The mug was pale blue porcelain; a delicate floral design enclosed a wide white panel at the front, and inside the
panel the name "S. Roth" and the date "1912" were inscribed
in faded gold Gothic lettering. The mug was our one family
heirloom as far as I knew, aside from a handful of antique snapshots the only thing tangible that anyone had cared to save
from the immigrant years in Newark. I had been intrigued by
it ever since my grandfather had died a month short of my sev-
enth birthday and it made its way into our Newark bathroom,
back when my father was still shaving with a bristle brush and
shaving soap.

Sender Roth had been a remote, mysterious presence to me
as a small boy, an elongated man with an undersized head—
the forebear whom my own skeleton most resembles—and
about whom all I knew was that he smoked all day long, spoke
only Yiddish, and wasn't much given to fondling the American
grandchildren when we all showed up with our parents on
Sundays. After his death, the shaving mug in our bathroom
brought him much more fully to life for me, not as a grandfather but, even more interestingly then, as an ordinary man
among men, a customer of a barbershop where his mug was
kept on a shelf with the mugs of the other neighborhood immigrants. It reassured me as a child to think that in that household where, according to all reports, there was never a penny
to spare, a dime was set aside every week for him to go to the
barbershop and get his Sabbath shave.

My grandfather Roth had studied to be a rabbi in Polish
Galicia, in a small town not far from Lemberg, but when he arrived in America alone in 1897, without his wife and his three

sons (my uncles Charlie, Morris, and Ed), he took a job in a hat factory to earn the money to bring his family over and worked there more or less most of his life. There were seven children born between 1890 and 1914, six sons and a daughter, and all but the last two of the boys and the one girl left school after the eighth grade to find jobs to help support the family. The shaving mug inscribed "S. Roth" had seemed to free my grandfather—if only momentarily, if only for those few minutes he quietly sat being shaved in the barber's chair late on a Friday afternoon—from the dour exigencies that had trapped him and that, I imagined, accounted for his austere, uncommunicative nature. His mug emitted the aura of an archaeological find, an artifact signaling an unexpected level of cultural refinement, an astonishing superfluity in an otherwise cramped and obstructed existence—in our ordinary little Newark bathroom, it had the impact on me of a Greek vase depicting the mythic origins of the race.

By 1988 what amazed me about it was that my father hadn't thrown it out or given it away. Over the years, when it was within his power, he had gotten rid of just about everything "useless" to which any of us might have been thought to have a sentimental attachment. Though these seizures of largess were, on the whole, admirably motivated, they sometimes lacked sensitivity to innate property rights. So eager was he to answer the need (real or imagined) of the recipient that he did not always think about the effect of his impulsiveness on the unwitting donor.

My two-volume stamp collection, for instance, studiously acquired by me throughout my late grade school years—a collection partially inspired by the example of the country's most famous philatelist, Franklin Delano Roosevelt, and underwritten with virtually all my riches—he gave away to a greatnephew of his the year I went off to college. I didn't know this until ten years later, when I was thinking of drawing on my scholarly discoveries as a boy stamp collector for an episode in a piece of fiction and went down to my parents' house in Moorestown to get the albums out of the attic. It was only after I had searched thoroughly, but in vain, through the cartons I'd stored there that my mother reluctantly—and not until we were off alone together—explained how they had come to disappear. She assured me that she had tried to stop him, that she had told him that my stamps weren't his to dispose of, but he wouldn't listen. He told her that I was grown up, away at college, didn't "use" the stamps anymore, whereas Chickie, his great-nephew, could bring them with him to school, et cetera, et cetera, et cetera. I suppose I could have found out if any part of my collection even existed any longer by contacting Chickie—a relative who was virtually a stranger to me and by then a young married man—but I decided to let the whole thing drop. I was terrifically irritated to hear what he had done —and, when I remembered how much of my childhood had gone into that collection, genuinely pained—but as it was so long ago that he had done it and as I had rather more difficult problems to deal with (I was in the midst of an acrimonious marital separation) I said nothing to him. And even if I had been inclined to, it would have been no easier for me to criticize him to his face at twenty-eight than it had been at eighteen or eight, since his most blatantly thoughtless acts were invariably ignited by this spontaneous impulse to support, to assist, to rescue, to save, prompted by the conviction that what he was doing—giving away my stamps, for example—was generous, helpful, and morally or educationally efficacious.

I believe another motive was operating in him—one harder to fathom and name—when we came back from burying my mother in May of 1981, and even as the apartment began filling up with family and friends, he disappeared into the bedroom and started emptying her bureau drawers and sorting through the clothes in her closet. I was still at the door with my brother, welcoming the mourners who'd followed us back from the cemetery, and so I wouldn't right off have known what he was up to had not my mother's sister Millie rushed out of the bedroom and down the hallway calling for help. "You better go in there and do something, darling," she whispered into my ear; "your father's throwing everything out."

Not even my opening the bedroom door and coming into the room and firmly saying, "Dad, what are you doing?" did anything to slow him down. The bed was already strewn with dresses, coats, skirts, and blouses pulled from the closet, and he was now busily chucking things from a corner of her lowest bureau drawer into a plastic garbage bag. I put my hand on his shoulder and gripped it forcefully. "People are here for you," I said; "they want to see you, to talk to you—" "What good is this stuff anymore? It's no good to me hanging here. This stuff can go to Jewish relief—it's in mint condition—" "Stop, please —just stop. There's time for all this later. We'll do it together later. Stop throwing things out," I said. "Pull yourself together. Go into the living room where you're needed."

But he *was* pulled together. He didn't appear to be either in a daze or in the throes of a hysterical fit—he was simply doing what he had done all his life: the next difficult job. Thirty minutes before, we had buried her body; now to dispose of her things.

I ushered him out of the bedroom, and once among the guests who had come to offer condolences, he immediately began talking away, assuring everyone that he was fine. I returned to the bedroom to remove from the garbage bag the pile of mementos that he'd already discarded and that my mother had neatly and carefully saved over the years—among them, in a tiny brown envelope, my Phi Beta Kappa key, which she had coveted, a collection of programs to family graduation exercises, birthday cards from my brother and me, a handful of telegrams announcing good news, clippings friends had sent her about me and my books, specially prized snapshots of her two grandsons as small boys. They were all items for which my father could imagine no function now that she who had treasured them was gone, the sentimental keepsakes of someone whose sentiments had been snuffed out forever two nights earlier at a seafood restaurant where, as was their custom, they had gone with friends for Sunday night dinner. My mother had just been served clam chowder, a favorite dish of hers; to everyone's surprise she had announced, "I don't want this soup"; and those were her last words—a moment later she was dead of a massive coronary.

It was my father's primitivism that stunned me. Standing all alone emptying her drawers and her closets, he seemed driven by some instinct that might be natural to a wild beast or an aboriginal tribesman but ran counter to just about every mourning rite that had evolved in civilized societies to mitigate the sense of loss among those who survive the death of a loved one. Yet there was also something almost admirable in this pitilessly realistic determination to acknowledge, instantaneously, that he was now an old man living alone and that symbolic relics were no substitute for the real companion of fifty-five years. It seemed to me that it was not out of fear of her things and their ghostlike power that he wanted to rid the apartment of them without delay—to bury *them* now, too—but because he refused to sidestep the most brutal of all facts.

Never in his life, as far as I knew, had he been one to try to elude the force of a dreadful blow, and yet, as I later learned, on the evening of her death he had fled from her corpse. This occurred not at the restaurant, where she had in fact died, but at the hospital, where she was declared dead after the paramedics had worked in vain to revive her on the ambulance ride from the restaurant to the emergency room. At the hospital, they pushed her stretcher into a cubicle of its own, and when my father, who had followed the ambulance in his car, went in by himself to look at her, he could not stand to see what he saw and so he ran. It was months before he could speak about this to anyone; and when he did, it wasn't to me or to my brother but to Claire, who, as a woman, could grant him the womanly absolution he required to begin to shed his shame.

Though he wasn't himself equipped to account for why he'd run away like that, I wondered if it hadn't something to do with his realizing that he might have contributed to the heart attack by pushing my mother that afternoon to walk beyond her endurance. She had been suffering for some time from severe shortness of breath and, unknown to me, from angina; during the previous winter there had also been a long siege of arthritic pain that had demoralized her terribly. That winter she'd had all she could do just to sit up comfortably in a chair, but on the day she died, because the May weather was so beautiful and she was finally out of doors getting some exercise, they'd walked as far as the drugstore, three very long city blocks away, and then, because he insisted it would be good for her, they'd also walked all the way home. According to Aunt Millie—whom my mother had phoned before they went out for the evening—by the time they'd reached the drugstore, she was already hopelessly exhausted. "I didn't think I could get back," she'd reported to my aunt, but instead of calling a taxi or waiting for a bus, they had rested a little on a nearby bench, and then he'd got her up on her feet for the return trek. "You know your father," my aunt had said to me. "He told her she could do it." She had spent the rest of the afternoon on the bed, trying to recover enough strength to go out to dinner.

As it happened, only an hour or so before they'd left for their walk, I'd made my customary Sunday call from England and told her playfully that I expected her to go a mile with me down the country road outside my house when she and my father came to visit that summer. She replied, "I don't know if it'll be a mile, dear, but I'll try." She was sounding bright and confident for the first time in months and could well have gone off that afternoon hoping to begin to prepare herself for our summer stroll.

In fact, when I arrived back in America the next day and took a taxi from Kennedy directly over to Elizabeth, my father's first words to me were "Well, she won't be taking that walk, Phil." He was in her reclining chair, his body decrepit, his face battered-looking and drained of all life. I thought (not incorrectly, as it turned out), "This is what he will look like when *he* is dead." My brother, Sandy, and his wife, Helen, had arrived earlier in the day from Chicago and were at the apartment when I got there. Sandy had already been to the funeral home to arrange for the burial the next day. Before he'd gone, my father had spoken on the phone to the elderly funeral director, a man with whom my mother had attended Elizabeth's Battin High around the end of the First World War. My father, in tears, had told him, "Take care of her body, take good care of it, Higgins," then for the rest of the day he went on weeping, there in that chair in which she would stretch out after supper and try to get some relief from her arthritis while they watched the news together. "She ordered New England clam chowder," he told me as I knelt beside him, still in my coat and holding his hand, "and I ordered Manhattan. When it came she said, 'I don't want this soup.' I said, 'Take mine—we'll switch,' but she was gone. Just slumped forward. Didn't even fall. Made no trouble for anyone. The way she always did everything."

Over and over again he recounted for me the pure prosaicness of the seconds preceding her extinction, while all the while I was thinking, "What are we going to do with this old guy?" To have ministered to my mother's needs, had she been the elderly survivor of their marriage, would have seemed manageable and natural enough; it was she who was the repository of our family past, the historian of our childhood and growing up, and, as I now realized, it was she around whose quietly efficient presence the family had continued to cohere in the decades since my brother and I had left home. My father was a more difficult personality, far less seductive and less malleable, too: bluntly resisting points of view that diverged only slightly from his own reigning biases was, in fact, one of his most rigorously unthinking activities. Still kneeling before him with his hand in mine, I understood just how much we were going to have to help him—what I couldn't understand was how we were going to get through to him.

His obsessive stubbornness—his stubborn obsessiveness—had very nearly driven my mother to a breakdown in her final years: since his retirement at the age of sixty-three, her once spirited, housewifely independence had been all but extinguished by his anxious, overbearing bossiness. For years he had believed he was married to perfection, and for years he wasn't far wrong—my mother was one of those devoted daughters of Jewish immigrants who raised housekeeping in America to a great art. (Don't talk to anyone in my family about cleaning—we saw cleaning in its heyday.) But then my father retired from one of the Metropolitan Life's big South Jersey offices, where he'd been managing a staff of fifty-two people, and the efficient, clear-cut division of labor that had done so much to define their marriage as a success gradually began to be obliterated—by him. He had nothing to do and she had everything to do—and that wouldn't do. "You know what I am now?" he told me sadly on his sixty-fifth birthday. "I'm Bessie's husband." And by neither temperament nor training was he suited to be that alone. So, after a couple of years of volunteer work—stints at the V.A. Hospital in East Orange, with Jewish relief groups and the Red Cross—and even of working as an underling for a friend who owned a hardware store, he settled down to become Bessie's boss—only my mother happened not to need a boss, having been her own since her single-handed establishment of a first-class domestic-management and mothering company back in 1927, when my brother was born.

Just the summer before her death, during a weekend visit to
Connecticut, when we two were alone having a cup of tea in
the kitchen, she had announced that she was thinking of getting a divorce. To hear the word "divorce" from my mother's
lips astonished me almost as much as it would have if she had
uttered an obscenity. But then the inmost intertwining of
mother and father's life together, the difficulties and disap-
pointments and enduring strains, remain mysterious, really,
forever, perhaps particularly if you grew up as a good boy in a
secure, well-ordered home—and simultaneously as a good
girl. People don't always realize what good girls we grew up
as, too, the little sons suckled and gurgled by mothers as adroit
as my own in the skills of nurturing domesticity. For a very
long and impressionable time the male who's not around all
day remains much more remote and mythological than the palpable woman of wizardly proficiency anchored firmly, during
the decades when I was young, in the odorous kitchen where
her jurisdiction was absolute and her authority divine. "But,
Ma," I said, "it's late for a divorce, no? You're seventy-six." But
she was crying quite pitifully already. That astonished me too.
"He doesn't listen to what I say," she said. "He interrupts all
the time to talk about something else. When we're out, that's
the worst. Then he won't let me speak at all. If I start to, he
just shuts me up. In front of everyone. As though I don't
exist." "Tell him not to do it," I said. "It wouldn't make any
difference." "Then tell him a second time and if it still doesn't
work, get up and say 'I'm going home.' And go." "Oh, darling,
I couldn't. No, I couldn't embarrass him like that. Not with
company." "But you tell me he embarrasses you when you're
with company." "That's different. He's not like me. He
couldn't take it, Philip. He would crumple up. It would kill
him."

Three months after her death, in August 1981, I came down
from Connecticut to take him to the Jewish Federation Plaza
in West Orange, where we were to look at the living accom-
modations for retired and elderly people. The Plaza had been
recommended to us by an old Newark friend of my brother's,
a New Jersey attorney on the Federation's board of directors.
He had said he might be able to help my father get an apart-

ment without too long a delay, if my father was interested. The
Plaza residents lived in two- and three-room apartments of
their own, but the round of life itself was strongly communal:
each evening they ate together in a dining room where their
meals were prepared for them, and they had easy access to all
the group activities at the flourishing Y next door. West Orange
was still one of Newark's pleasant suburbs, and the Plaza, as
it was described to me, was situated back on a green hillside
overlooking a main thoroughfare, a few minutes' walk from a
shopping center and also from the Temple B'nai Abraham,
which, like the Y, had been transplanted from decaying Newark
and served the elderly as a cultural center as well as a synagogue. In all, the Plaza struck me as a place where he would
not lack for companionship, and I was hoping that after we
had looked around, the idea of moving might appeal to him. I
was afraid that if he tried much longer to hang on by himself in
the Elizabeth apartment, he might literally die there of loneliness. His meals, when he even sat down and ate them, seemed
to consist mostly of boiled hot dogs and Heinz baked beans,
and when I phoned in the middle of the day I often found him
asleep or in tears.

It was clear to me when I arrived at the apartment that day
that he had been sitting there crying by himself. He could have
been crying since he'd got up; for all I knew, he could have been
crying all night long. He'd spent a few weeks with us in Connecticut in June and then again in July and had seemed in that
time to have gotten on top of the worst of his grief, but now
that he was back in the apartment without my mother, he was
hopelessly bereft all over again. Though outside it was a beautiful August day, he was sitting there with the shades down and
no lights on. I noticed that his clothes, while clean, didn't
quite match, as if getting out of bed he'd pulled on whatever
came to hand first. When I asked what he'd had for breakfast,
he answered, "Nothing. Something. I don't remember."

"I've got a present for you." I turned on a light and showed
him my plastic shopping bag. "Just what you always wanted.
Close your eyes."

To my surprise he obeyed, like a child awaiting a gift, though
with no discernible look of anticipation lighting up his face.

"Here." I produced from the bag a toilet bowl brush and a

bottle of Lysol that I'd bought at the local general store before leaving Connecticut three hours earlier. I'd also brought a bottle of 2 milligram Valium. The idea was to get him off the 5 milligram tablets that I'd got for him after her death to help him sleep. "Come on," I said. "I'm going to teach you something you never learned at Thirteenth Avenue School."

He followed me into the bathroom, where several pairs of his big boxer shorts were hanging out to dry on a couple of wire hangers, and there I showed him how to clean the bowl with the brush.

"If you insist on being your own cleaning woman—" I began, but he cut me off abruptly.

"What do I need to pay somebody when I can do it myself? I get up at five and I begin vacuuming. I swore, I swore to myself when she died that I was going to keep this place the way Mother did." Those words alone got him crying again.

In the living room I gave him the new bottle of 2 milligram Valium and told him that if he needed it, he should now take one of these at night and pour the others down the drain. With this he didn't argue, though he was someone who previously would balk at the thought of taking even an aspirin. I was not so lucky when I reminded him that we were due at the Jewish Federation Plaza at one o'clock. He told me, dismissively, that he wasn't interested. "The hell with it," he said. "I'm fine right here. Everything is fine."

"Is it?"

"The hell with it, Phil—I don't want to go."

"Look, this isn't the way the game is played, you know. You're not being fair. Instead of treating me like a member of your family, do me a favor and pretend you're still the manager of an insurance office. If somebody came to you at the Metropolitan with a proposal that he thought might be of help to you, you'd at least let the guy make his case. You'd sit back and hear him out, and then you'd think it over and come up with your decision. You certainly wouldn't say, after inviting him to talk to you, 'The hell with it,' and not even listen. I'm proposing to you only that we go up and look at the place, as we agreed we would a week ago. It is not a nursing home and it is not an old people's home or anything resembling one—it's a new apartment complex that people are lining up to get into and that's designed to make life comfortable and companionable for, among other people, men and women in your fix. It may be for you and it may not be for you, but there's no way for us to find out if you don't cooperate. Please, act like an insurance manager instead of whatever it is you *are* acting like, and maybe we can get something accomplished today."

It not only worked, my speech—it worked dramatically. "Okay!" he said with great decisiveness, and shot energetically up off the sofa. "Let's go."

I couldn't remember ever in my life persuading him to do something he didn't want to do. I wasn't sure that I'd ever before been so foolish as to try.

"That's more like it," I said. "Maybe you want to go in first and do something about your socks. You've got two different colors on. And I don't know if that checked shirt goes with those plaid trousers. You might want to change out of one or the other."

"Jesus," he said, looking down at his outfit, "where am I?"

Though it was, as advertised, set back on a nice lawn at the top of a rise overlooking Northfield Avenue, the complex itself was not as homey and inviting as I'd hoped. The Federation Plaza was new and in excellent repair but looked more institutional than residential, a cross between a small college dormitory and a minimum-security prison. We were to be meeting with a woman named Isabel Berkowitz, a resident who had volunteered to show us around. We had her apartment number, but as the approach to the building was a maze of walkways, I stopped two very elderly women who were talking together on the main path leading down to Northfield Avenue and asked if they could direct us to Isabel Berkowitz's.

"My name is Berkowitz, also," one of them answered. She spoke with a Yiddish accent that, along with her dress and her manner, made her appear to have more in common with my grandparents' generation than with my mother and father and their friends. I was pretty sure my father was thinking the same thing—that he wasn't the kind of old person these old people were and, what's more, he didn't belong here. "I'm the other Berkowitz!" she told us cheerily.

"Berkowitz from where?" my father asked her.

"Where else? Newark."

It was only a matter of seconds before he discovered that he had known her late husband, who had owned Central Paper Supply on Central Avenue, that she, in turn, had known his friend Feiner's brother, and so on.

In his apartment he had been sullen and angry, driving up to West Orange he'd been silent and grim, but he had only to come on someone who had known someone he had known in Newark to become blissfully self-forgetful—talkative, energetic, gregarious, very much the forceful insurance man whose years in Newark as an agent and assistant manager had familiarized him with nearly every Jewish family in the city.

Unmindful by now not only of his woes but even of what we were there for, he named for this other Mrs. Berkowitz all the shopkeepers whose businesses abutted her husband's Central Avenue store some forty years back.

I stood by till he had finished exhibiting to them his perfect memory and then I asked the old woman once again if she could tell us how to get to where we wanted to go. It turned out that she couldn't. When she tried, she became befuddled, all at once wholly unable to focus her mind. "Look," she said, after working hard to collect her thoughts, "I'm a pumpkin head—I'll *show* you where she lives."

The other woman didn't speak, and as they led us to the doorway opening onto Isabel Berkowitz's corridor, I saw that she was a stroke victim. My father noticed, too, and once again, without his even having to tell me, I heard him insisting that he wasn't this kind of old person. "True," I thought, "but given the kind of old person you are, what is going to become of you all alone?"

The Mrs. Berkowitz we were looking for was—to my relief —a quick-witted, lively, attractive woman who looked ten years younger than her seventy years. Her two-room apartment, though a bit cube-like, was bright with sunlight and the walls were hung with lots of little paintings she'd collected over the years. There was even one she'd painted herself, a colorful still-life, and framed alongside it were samples of her embroidery. She seemed delighted to see us, and immediately offered us something cold to drink, and within only five minutes of meeting her, when we two were momentarily alone again, my father turned to me and said, "She's some girl!" Though Isabel, who'd begun her career as a Brooklyn nurse and eventually became a public health administrator in New York, may have been a touch more worldly than my mother, her mixture of outgoing vitality and good-natured gentility reminded me very much of what my mother had been like when I was growing up. The resemblance could even have been what prompted my father—while we were waiting out in the corridor for Isabel to lock up her apartment and take us on a tour of the place—to announce spontaneously, as though all his troubles were over, "I love her! She's terrific!"

Isabel told us that she had moved in when the Plaza first opened in October and that she was still having trouble "adjusting." It was a big change from her old life. She and her late husband—a vigorous, self-made man with a c.v. much like my father's—had lived in a spacious apartment in Jersey City with a view out to the Statue of Liberty. But she had decided to give it up and move to the Plaza because she had had a bad time with her health recently and because she wanted to be near the Berkowitzes.

My father surprised me by saying, "Yes, they're a wonderful family." He'd given no indication till that moment that he knew Isabel's Berkowitzes as *well* as the other woman's Berkowitzes. But then maybe he was only trying to ingratiate himself with a woman toward whom he seemed drawn by an undisguisable, surprisingly headlong tug of feeling.

As we were walking down the corridor, Isabel Berkowitz said to me, "So you're Philip Roth. Thank you for all the laughs." Turning to my father, she said, "Your son's got quite a sense of humor."

"The jokes," I told her, "originate with him."

"Yes?" She smiled and said to my father, "Tell me a joke, Herman."

She knew her man. "You hear the one about the two Jewish fellas . . . You hear the one about the fella who wakes up in the morning . . . You hear the one about the guy in Florida who gets sick . . ."

I hadn't seen him so animated in years, let alone since my mother's death. In fact, so busy was he presenting his Jewish joke repertoire, he barely bothered to look at the facilities that

Isabel was beginning to show us. We walked through the dining hall, which was clean and simple, a large room that looked just like a school cafeteria; we peered through an open door into the kitchen, where the equipment was all shining and spotless and a heavyset black woman sat at a long table methodically cutting wedges of lettuce for several hundred dinner salads; we crossed over from the Plaza to the Y and looked into rooms where meetings were in progress and card games were going on, and though I kept hoping for him to begin to respond, if only with a little curiosity, to the life around him, and for him to see in it—if not necessarily now, in the days to come—a way out of his loneliness, his attention was riveted on Isabel, for whom he was now recounting stories, not entirely unfamiliar to me, about his childhood in immigrant Newark.

A day camp was in session at the Y, and when we went to look at the gym, there were some thirty little children sitting in a circle on the gymnasium floor, listening to their two counselors explain a new game. "Aren't our Jewish children beautiful?" Isabel said; but if she was trying to get him to see what was in front of his eyes, it didn't work—without even looking where she pointed, he continued describing Newark in 1912.

Only at the office of the director of the Y did the reminiscing momentarily abate while he told the director and his assistant there that the director of the Elizabeth Y, where he was a morning regular several times a week, was no damn good: the Elizabeth director never came into the health club to talk to the men, he had no idea what was going on with them, and, my father told them all bluntly, he himself didn't get along with the man at all. "I don't even bother with him. I organized the Roth Raiders, my special little group of *alte kockers*, and we have a good time on our own. The hell with him." "You're the kind of person we need here," the director replied, but the veiled invitation elicited no response. In the corridor outside the director's office, we ran into Bleiberg, the president of the Plaza social organization, a man of about seventy-five suffering from multiple sclerosis. Isabel introduced us. "Bleiberg. Bleiberg. I remember you, Bleiberg," my father told him. "You were a jeweler on Green Street." Bleiberg had indeed been a jeweler on Newark's Green Street. "How do you like living here, Mr. Bleiberg?" I asked. "I love it," Bleiberg said, while my father said, "Sure, Green Street. I'll tell you who else was on Green Street," and did just that.

When we were back in the car later, I suggested that we drive up the road to look at the shopping center, where there was a bookstore and a bank and a coffee shop and where, Isabel had told us, Plaza residents sometimes went for lunch. Afterward, I said, we could drive over to see the new B'nai Abraham.

"There's nothing to see," he said.

"But don't you want to take a look at the temple? You go in Elizabeth to Friday night services."

"Let's go home."

"Well," I said, after I'd turned down Northfield Avenue, in the opposite direction from the shopping center and the temple, "what did you make of it?"

"Nothing."

"Nothing at all?"

"Not for me."

"Well, you could be right. Though that's a first impression. Let it sink in a little. I hope you're going to take Isabel up on her invitation."

Isabel had suggested as we were leaving that he come back in a few days and together they go to one of the movies that were shown at the Y a couple of evenings each week. "I'll bring the popcorn," she'd said with a charming smile. The prospect had seemed to entice him at the moment and he'd taken her phone number and said he would call, but now, as though her proposal had been utterly preposterous, he told me, "Come on, I'm not driving all the way up here to go to the movies."

A calendar of the Y social activities for August and September, given him by the director, had slipped out of his hand and onto the floor of the car, but when we got back to Elizabeth, he didn't even bother to pick it up. For that matter, neither did I. Inside the apartment I went around raising the shades to let the light in while he went to the bathroom. Over the sound of his stream in the toilet bowl, I heard him crying, "Mommy, Mommy, where are you, Mommy?"

He spent his first winter as a widower just north of Miami Beach in Bal Harbour, sharing the condominium apartment of his old friend Bill Weber. When I was growing up, Bill and his late wife Leah had lived not far from our Leslie Street apartment just across the Newark line in Irvington. In the early 1940s, along with their younger son, Herbie, who was my brother's age, they'd shared a small summer cottage at the Jersey shore with us and two other families, all of them friends of my parents going back to before the war. Bill had installed and serviced oil furnaces and may have been the only close family friend who was a skilled laborer as opposed to a salesman or a shopkeeper and who came home from work filthy at the end of the day. As a young Marine in World War I, Bill had been stationed at Guantánamo in Cuba, where he'd played the trumpet in the Marine band, and now, in his middle eighties, a little hard of hearing but otherwise quite fit, he maintained that he heard the tunes that he used to play with the Marine band being played inside his teeth. "That's not possible," my father told him categorically. "Herman, I hear it," Bill said. "I'm hearing it now." "You can't be." "I *am*. It's like in my mouth a radio is playing." I had flown from London to Florida to visit my father, and the three of us were sitting in their little kitchen, eating the bologna sandwiches that my father had prepared for lunch. "What do you hear exactly?" I asked Bill. "Tonight? 'The Marine Hymn,'" he said. "'From the halls of Montezuma . . .'" he began singing. "You're imagining it," my father insisted. "Herman, it's as real as your Philip sitting in this kitchen."

My father appeared to me to have recovered all his old force and zest during his several months in Florida, and he looked wonderfully rejuvenated. Some years back, as a result of surgery, he'd lost the musculature in his midsection and developed a stomach, but otherwise he was, for his age, a most fit-looking man of medium height whose spontaneous, unassuming virility and spirited decency had made him instantaneously appealing to the widows around. He had been impressively strong through the arms and the chest when he was young, and a little of that solidity was still discernible in his upper torso, particularly so with this resurgence of vitality. Though he could be bluntly outspoken and dominate a conversation with his boiling anti-Republican diatribes, he happened to be an agreeable-looking person as well, and the mundane forthrightness his appearance exuded registered on all sorts of people as real charm. If he'd had the leisure for it, or the instinct, or the need, he might even have been handsome in an anonymous sort of way, but "handsome" was no asset where he'd fought his battles, and long ago he had settled upon looks people trusted rather than envied or praised. Now, of course, his hair was very thin and had only a touch of brown left in it; and his face, though unlined, had slackened along the jawline into the pronounced family dewlap; and his ears seemed somehow to have been tugged a bit, like taffy, and lengthened. Only his eyes, really, remained "beautiful," and you never would have known that unless you happened to be nearby when he slipped off his glasses for a moment. Then you would have seen how much gray there was in those eyes, and that there was even some green there—up close you would have seen how gentle and untroubled those eyes were, as though they alone had existed since 1901 beyond the reverberations of that crude, imperfect, homemade dynamo whose stubborn output had driven him through the obstacle course just about everything had been.

His Florida recovery may have owed something to his having found in Bill Weber a fairly good stand-in for my mother —a good-natured, even-tempered, untroublesome partner whose faults and failings he could correct unceasingly. I caught him improving Bill virtually the moment I arrived in Bal Harbour. When I got off the elevator on their floor, there were my father and Bill heading down the hallway together some twenty feet in front of me. Instead of calling out to them, I followed silently behind, listening while my father berated Bill for his social shortcomings. "Ask her to a movie, ask her out to dinner—don't just sit home night after night." "I don't want to take her out, Herman. I don't want to take anybody out." "You're antisocial." "If that's what you call it, okay, I am." "You live like a hermit." "Okay." "*Not* okay. You've got to mix more with people. There are women around here who are dying for companionship. I'm not talking about women with hang-ups. Not all of them want to possess you. Not all of them want to sink their teeth into you." "I don't want a woman. There's nothing I can do for a woman. I'm eighty-six years old, Herman." "C'mon, for Christ's sake, I'm not talking about that. I'm talking about eating a pleasant meal with somebody, socializing with people like a human being." "You're good at it, I'm not. I'll stay home." "I don't understand you, Bill. I don't understand why you fight me like this when all I'm trying to do is to help you out."

The evening I arrived, a musical program was to be performed by four residents of the condominium who had formed a chamber ensemble earlier in the season. The elderly Russian-born violinist, the ensemble leader, was said to be "Vienna-trained" by the people my father had introduced me to at the pool that afternoon. They had told me that if I liked music I should be sure to come; the concert was to take place following the weekly meeting of the Galahad Hall Social Club and would be attended by nearly all those in Galahad Hall who were ambulatory and even, as I would see, by some in wheelchairs and on walkers who were accompanied by their nurses. There was entertainment or a slide show or a lecture every week, refreshments were served, and I was assured that I would have a good time.

After our dinner of hot dogs and beans—prepared by my father while Bill neatly set three places at the table—my father told Bill to put on a jacket and a pair of shoes and come along with us to "the musicale." All Bill wanted was to stay upstairs and watch the pro basketball game on television, but as my father wouldn't let up about Bill's failure to mix with people, his failure to make friends, his failure to go out in the evening and have a good time, Bill gave in and agreed that he would come after the music for the refreshments. But "after" wasn't good enough, and ten minutes later, when my father still wouldn't leave him alone, Bill pulled a jacket out of the closet and put on a pair of shoes, and we took the elevator to the social hall in back of the lobby, where the meeting was already under way.

As the three of us came through the door, the chairwoman of the Matzoh Fund, which collected donations for Passover provisions for the Jewish poor in South Miami Beach, was announcing the grand total raised during the Matzoh Fund drive. The chairwoman looked down at her notes while she spoke causing several people around the room to shout, "Can't hear you! We can't hear you, Belle!" When she looked up, a little puzzled by the ruckus, a man at the end of the back row, who must have been her husband, put a hand to the side of his mouth and called to her, "Pretend you're talking to me, honey —holler." Everyone laughed, Belle loudest of all, and then in a good strong voice she announced that the fund had reached its goal of two thousand dollars, or the equivalent of about ten dollars from each person in the building, and the audience applauded.

I noticed two rows in front of us the people I'd met at the pool with my father that afternoon—the retired bathing suit manufacturer and his wife, the retired coffee and tea importer and his wife, and the recently widowed woman who years ago had been a New York buyer and was my father's choice as a mate for Bill Weber. All of them turned and waved hello as we slid into seats behind them. Our three seats in the last of the fifteen or so rows were virtually the only ones left in the house. Four music stands and four bridge chairs had been arranged in a little semicircle at the front, and off to the far side, near the door, was a long table set up for coffee. The refreshments were already there, the plates stacked high with cookies and slices of cake covered with Saran Wrap.

When the Matzoh Fund report was concluded, the club's president congratulated the chairwoman on the success of the drive. He was a dapper, suntanned man of about seventy—a passionate golfer, I'd been told that afternoon—who after his retirement as a successful leather goods and luggage manufac- turer, had taken a desk at Merrill Lynch and made a second fortune managing his own money. He said, "Ladies and gentle- men. Before the music begins, I want to tell you that a few moments ago a young man walked in and I'd like to introduce him to you. Young man, will you stand?"

I was just a year short of my fiftieth birthday but he was pointing my way and I stood.

"Ladies and gentlemen, this is Philip Roth the author, the son of Herman Roth."

They applauded, neither more nor less than they had for the Matzoh Fund, and after acknowledging the reception with a wave, I sat down.

But the president said, "Mr. Philip Roth, may I ask you a question?"

I smiled at him and, coming halfway to my feet, replied, "Oh, no questions, really. I'm just a guest."

"Just one question. Can you tell us a little bit about your father?"

"I can assure you," I said, putting a hand on his shoulder, "just ask my father and he'll tell you everything you want to know. Maybe even more."

My father got a kick out of that and so did his friends in front of us. The retired bathing suit manufacturer turned around in his seat and said to him, "The kid's got your number, Herm." At the pool earlier in the day, he had jokingly referred to my father as "the condo commander," but then, while my father was in swimming, he had confided to me, "Your dad's a real human being—he's the one here who gives spirit to everybody else."

"One more question—" the president said.

I interrupted him: "Oh, you don't have to ask me questions. I just came down to enjoy the music. Let the music begin!" And I got another round of applause and sat down again.

Bill, who was seated to one side of me, winked at me and whispered proudly, "That's telling 'em."

"You know me, Bill—always with the common touch."

"My Philip," Bill said, and he took my hand and sat there holding it in his even as the musicians appeared with their instruments, took their seats, and began tuning up. Bill wasn't holding my hand because he thought I was still seven but because he had known me since I was seven and he had a right to hold my hand, however old I'd become in the interim.

Over the next thirty minutes or so I came to understand—as I never entirely had when the performer was Perlman or Yo-Yo Ma—just how much muscular labor goes into playing a stringed instrument. In the middle of only the first movement I wondered if it was really a good idea for the viola player to go on. He was probably close to eighty, a large, heavyset man with a stern, expressionless face, and as the music heated up, that face grew paler and paler and I could see him beginning to pant. The performance was as alarming as it was heroic, as though these four aging people were trying to push free a car that was mired in the mud, and though the music didn't always sound like a Haydn string quartet, at the end of the first movement everyone applauded enthusiastically and some of the friends of the musicians shouted "Bravo! Bravo!" and half the

audience got up and began to make their way toward the refreshment table.

"No, no!" the club president called out, jumping from the
front row and turning to face the crowd. "Please, there's
more!" The musicians, having mopped their faces and turned
to a fresh page of the score, waited patiently until everyone was
seated and quiet again. They weren't too many bars into the
second movement, however, before the purses began clicking
open and shut and couples began quietly gabbing together.
Directly in front of me, a nicely dressed old woman who had a
cane at her feet and a neatly stacked pile of bills on her lap was
discreetly writing out checks and then clipping each check to
the appropriate bill and putting it in an envelope. She had even
brought along a roll of stamps. It was better than paying her
bills upstairs alone.

Bill, with my hand still in his, inclined his head to my ear
and whispered, "This stuff isn't for this audience, Philip."

"You may be right," I told him.

"A little Victor Herbert," he whispered, "a little Gershwin—a clarinet, an oboe, a French horn. This way all you hear
is the screeching of the violin."

Twice more, at the end of a movement, many in the audience thought that it was over, and twice more, those who were
headed for the coffee and cake had to be reprimanded and made
to return to their seats, and when the spirited finale finally
came, and it *was* over, really and truly over for good, they were
up on their feet to give a standing ovation that I interpreted as
a means of congratulating themselves for their endurance as
much as the musicians for their physical fortitude. There had
been something sort of good-natured and self-disciplined about
the way they'd gone back to their chairs and sat there that reminded me of people sitting through the prayers in the synagogue when I was a kid—when, after the reading of the Torah,
the thing still went on and on, and people had no idea what
anyone was reading but they sat there nicely *out of respect.* Of
course, there were always a few in the synagogue who sat there
on and on because they couldn't get enough of it, but that
didn't look to have been the case at the musicale in Galahad
Hall.

The club president was going from one musician to the

other, shaking each player's hand—the violist could barely lift his head by then, let alone a hand, and I continued to wonder if something medical ought not to be done for him—and then the president turned to the audience and waved both arms high in the air, bidding us to clap even louder. "That's it, ladies and gentlemen. Every artist, I don't care who he is, needs to know if you like him or not. Let's let them know how we feel!"

"Bravo! Bravo!" The applause had turned into a rhythmic pounding with wild overtones of a kind you couldn't have imagined emanating from this temperate crowd, but their relief at being sprung was that great. The applause was loudest from those who had bounded out of their seats and were already lined up two deep in front of the refreshment table. "Bravo!"

On it went until, in a triumphant voice, the president announced above the tumult, "Ladies and gentlemen! Ladies and gentlemen! Good news! The artists are going to give you an encore!"

I thought there would be a riot. I thought plates would go sailing through the air from the direction of the refreshment table. I thought somebody might just walk up and put a foot through the cello. But no, these were decent people who had lived a long time, who had known and endured their share of grief before, Jewish people who had been born back when cultivation still had, even for untutored Jews, its religious clout, and so their deference to anyone who picked up a bow and a fiddle—as opposed to a bow and an arrow—was simply insurmountable. Agonizing as the prospect was, they kept their misery to themselves and returned yet again to their seats, many bearing coffee cups and cake plates, which they balanced on their knees or placed at their feet, while the first violinist's wife, a petite white-haired woman who had been sitting in the first row, stepped energetically out of the audience and sat down at a piano that was off to the side of the quartet. As the violist, the cellist, and the second violinist looked on in exhaustion, the first violinist, a man of the most remarkable stamina for his years, joined his wife in a duet by Fritz Kreisler. The violinist smiled at her whenever their eyes met, and this led several of the women around me to turn to each other and whisper admiringly, "He's looking at his wife."

My father had slept through most of the Haydn, but when the rousing encore was over, he popped up with everyone else and said, "Beautiful. Beautiful."

"Herman," Bill said to him, slowly rising from the seat beside me, "you were bored to death."

"Well, I'm not a music lover. But that doesn't mean it wasn't beautiful."

"It *wasn't* beautiful, Herman," Bill said unhappily. "It was awful. Jack Benny played better. I'm going upstairs."

"Jesus, Bill. Again? To sit with your ice cream and the television? Estelle is here," he said, pointing to where the ex-buyer could be seen talking animatedly to the first violinist's wife, who was at the piano still, playing something that nobody was listening to. The audience didn't dare to listen. They hadn't even applauded the encore for fear that it would unleash yet another one. "Talk to Estelle, will you?" my father begged Bill.

"Herman, I'm going upstairs."

"Bill, you're a grown man, you're eighty-six years old—you can talk to a woman."

But Bill, waving goodbye to me, headed for the refreshment table to get a piece of cake to take away in a napkin and have with his ice cream while he watched the game.

"What am I going to do with that guy?" my father asked me as we pushed into the throng at the refreshment table.

"Why not nothing?" I suggested airily. "Why not let him be?"

"So he can die on the vine of loneliness? So he can sit there every night by himself? Absolutely not!"

He had found Bill to help and he had found women to court, and the liaisons with these women, the sexual particulars of which I couldn't determine, seemed as much the cause as the result of his rejuvenation. In just my first few days there I took me for drinks at the homes of three wealthy Jewish widows ranging in age from sixty-five to seventy-five, all of them quite polished and attractive and, according to my father, eager to press on with their relationship. Walking to their condominiums he would tell me about the businesses their husbands had established, how many children they had and what businesses the children had succeeded in, the state of their health, the tragedies in their lives, how much their apartments

were worth, and then on the way back home he would ask,
"Well . . . what did you think?" Each time I answered, altogether truthfully, "She seemed very nice. I liked her." He'd
then reply, "She wants me to go on a cruise with her next fall,"
or "You know what she tells me? Her apartment is twice what
she needs. She rattles around there all by herself. . . ."
"And?" I would ask. "And nothing. Me, I just listen, I don't
say nothin'. Phil, it's too soon. . . ." And here he would
burst into tears, and though he didn't sob with the alarming
abandon of those first months after my mother's death, the
emotional flow was still considerable. "I didn't know how sick
she was," he told me. "If I had had any idea . . ." "Nobody
knew," I assured him. "There's nothing anybody could have
done." "Oh, Bessie," he cried, "Bessie, Bessie, I didn't know,
I didn't realize. . . ." Later, the two of us would go to dinner
together, and after he'd drunk a vodka Gibson with his shrimp
cocktail, I would suggest to him that it would be no crime if
he went on a cruise in the fall with Cora B. or if he decided
next winter to share the apartment of Blanche K., and he, in
turn, would recount for me exemplary stories illustrating my
mother's modesty, humility, loyalty, bravery, efficiency, depend-
ability . . . and then we would walk back to the apartment,
where Bill was watching television in his undershorts, and
my father would start giving it to him for sitting all night by
himself.

3

Will I Be a Zombie?

So, having arrived at his apartment from my mother's grave, I'd gone into the toilet, where, while eyeing my grandfather's shaving mug, I'd rehearsed my lines for the fiftieth time; then I'd come back out into the living room and looked at him slumped down in a corner of the sofa waiting for the verdict. Lil waited in the other corner of the sofa. She said to me, "Philip, do you want me to go?"

"Of course not."

"Herman," she said to him, "do you want me to stay?" But he didn't even hear her. And from then on Lil was so silent she might as well not have been there.

"Well," he said slowly, in a very gloomy voice, "what's the sad news?"

I sat in the chair across from him, my heart pounding as though I were the one about to be told something terrible. "You have a serious problem," I began, "but it can be dealt with. You have a tumor in your head. Dr. Meyerson says that given the location, the chances are ninety-five percent that it's benign." I had intended, like Meyerson, to be candid and describe it as large, but I couldn't. That there was a tumor seemed enough for him to take in. Not that he had registered any shock as yet—he sat there emotionless, waiting for me to go on. "It's pressing on the facial nerve, and that's what's caused the paralysis." Meyerson had told me that it was wrapped *around* the facial nerve, but I couldn't say that either. My evasiveness reminded me of his on the night my mother had died. At midnight London time, he had told me that my mother had had a serious heart attack and that I'd better make arrangements to fly home because they didn't know if she was going to survive. "It doesn't look good, Phil," he said; but an hour later, when I phoned back to tell him my flight plans for the next morning, he began to cry and revealed that she had actually died in the restaurant where they had had dinner a few hours earlier.

"It's not Bell's palsy," he said.

"No. It's a tumor. But it's not malignant, and it's operable. He can operate, if we want him to. Dr. Meyerson wants to speak to you about an operation. I think it's a good idea to go back and talk to him now that we know what's up. I think that all of us should sit down together in his office and see if an operation is feasible. Finally, it's going to be your decision." I added, feebly, "Meyerson says that it's a routine operation." Meyerson had indeed used that phrase at the close of our phone conversation the day before—and I had thought, "Sure it is—routine for *you*."

"Will my face get better if he operates?"

"No. There just won't be any more deterioration."

"So, this is the way I'm going to be."

"I'm afraid so." Two minutes and I had learned to talk like a surgeon.

"I see," he said, and then he fell silent and then he was lost, alone and lost, and I wouldn't have been surprised if, right then, he had died. His eyes were looking out to nowhere, onto nothing, like someone who had just been fatally shot. He was gone like that for about a minute. Then, having absorbed the blow, he was back in the midst of the struggle, estimating the scale of his loss. "And my hearing?"

"What the tumor has damaged can't be retrieved. The operation, as I understand it, will prevent anything further from happening." Unless the operation were itself to make something "further" happen . . . but I didn't go into that. I would let Meyerson apprise him of the risks, as well as of the size of the tumor and the encasement of the facial nerve.

"Will it grow back?" he asked.

"I don't know. I wouldn't think so, but you'll have to ask the doctor. We'll make up a list of questions. You'll write them down and you'll take them with you, and then you can ask the doctor everything you want to know."

"Will I be a zombie?"

"I don't think Meyerson would propose the operation if he thought that could possibly be the outcome." But could it not be? Of the fifteen percent who Meyerson allowed were worse after the surgery, weren't they zombies or close enough to what my father meant by a zombie?

"Where is it?" he asked.

"In front of the brain stem. That's at the base of the skull. The doctor will show you where exactly. I want you to write down all your questions so you can go over everything with him on Monday. I've made an appointment for us to see him and to talk this thing through with him on Monday."

Of all things, he smiled, a wry half-smile really, that worldly-wise, heartbroken smile that says, *But of course.*

He put his hand to the base of his skull and, feeling nothing unusual there, smiled again. "Well, everybody leaves this earth in a different way."

"And," I replied, "everybody lives on it in a different way. Everybody's battle is different and the battle never ends. It's going to be an ordeal, but if the surgery seems to all of us the right way to proceed, then two months from now we're going to be sitting right here talking and you're not going to have that thing inside you pressing on those nerves."

It was wretched being unable to believe my own words but I did not know what else to say. I thought, "Two months from now he'll be in a convalescent home, barely able to lift a spoon to feed himself his cereal; two months from now he'll be a zombie in a bed somewhere, fed intravenously, whom I sit helplessly beside just the way he once sat with his father; two months from now he'll be in the cemetery where I wound up this morning."

In the meantime, he had gone off to the bathroom, and when he came out, trying with his hand to hide a large, damp urine stain on the inside of his trouser leg, he was talking about his appendectomy in 1944, when, against heavy odds, he had survived a dreadful bout with peritonitis. He was remembering how I had nearly died of a burst appendix and peritonitis in 1968. Then he was back in 1942, recalling my hernia operation at age nine—how he had taken me to see the family doctor after I had been in distress on a Sunday drive with the family. It was the second time in a month we had been to the doctor about my discomfort. "I told the doctor, I insisted, 'This boy is not a complainer, there must be something wrong,' and they told us there was nothing wrong, but I insisted and insisted and eventually they found out I was right. I told Dr. Ira, he should rest in peace—you remember our doctor, Ira

Flax?" "Of course I do. I was nuts about him." "I said to him, 'Ira, this is a frisky boy who loves to run and play ball and if there is something wrong with him, I want it fixed.' I'll never forget him coming down those stairs in the Beth Israel Hospital the night that you were born. Three in the morning. The main staircase of the hospital. Ira was in his white gown. I said to him, 'What is it, Ira, Phyllis or Philip?' and he said, 'It's Philip, Herman. Another boy.' I'll never forget that. And my brother Charlie dying in my arms. Such a handsome man, all that energy, four children, and he died in my arms, my older brother I worshiped. And my Milton, my brother Milton—remember Milton?" "No," I said, "Milton died the year before I was born. That's how I got my middle name." "Milton," he said, "nineteen years old, a brilliant student, the shining light of the family, his senior year at Newark College of Engineering . . ." On and on, remembering the illnesses, the operations, the fevers, the transfusions, the recoveries, the comas, the vigils, the deaths, the burials—his mind, in its habitual way, working to detach him from the agonizing isolation of a man at the edge of oblivion and to connect his brain tumor to a larger history, to place his suffering in a context where he was no longer someone alone with an affliction peculiarly and horribly his own but a member of a clan whose trials he knew and accepted and had no choice but to share.

In this way did he manage to domesticate his terror and eat his lunch and that night, as he reported to me the next morning on the telephone, to get six continuous hours of sleep before waking in a sweat at 5:00 A.M.

I was not so lucky. I couldn't find *any* context to diminish my forebodings. The thought of his undergoing an operation as awful as that at the age of eighty-six was unbearable. And if he even made it successfully through the surgery, the prospect of the recovery—and if something *should* go wrong during the surgery . . . I couldn't sleep for six continuous minutes, and early the next morning, after sitting up in bed for several hours trying to read, I phoned my friend C. H. Huvelle, who until his retirement from practice a few years back had, as our family doctor in Connecticut, helped me through some physical difficulties of my own. I told C.H. about the brain tumor and the proposed operation.

"Look," he said, after hearing me out, "this is the way it stacks up. If he dies on the table, well, he will have died at eighty-six, which isn't the worst age to die at. If he lives and the operation is a success, which the guy says happens seventy-five percent of the time, good. The only bad result, as far as I see it, is if he suffers a further neurological deficit as a result of the surgery. Not the likeliest outcome, but it's possible and you have to calculate it in."

"I also have to calculate in what happens if we don't do anything. The brain surgeon assures me that it's going to get worse in a very short time. I take it that he means what you mean by further neurological deficit."

"That's what he means. Lots of things could go wrong."

"So," I said, "it could be agony either way. Operating could initiate one kind of horror and not operating another kind of horror."

"But operating," he said, "is more likely to yield something in the end that amounts to a *reprieve* from all-out horror."

"But I don't want to put him through this surgery for no good reason. It would be murder to come back from this kind of operation at forty; at eighty-six, it's unthinkable—isn't it?"

"Philip, get a second opinion, and then if you want to, call me back and we can talk it through some more. Just remember: you can't prevent your father from dying and you may not be able to prevent him from suffering. I've seen hundreds of people go through this with their parents. You were spared it with your mother and she was spared it, too. With him, it doesn't look like it's going to be so easy."

At about ten, after having tried a walk in Central Park to get myself to think about something else, I phoned my father for the second time that morning. "Zombie"—a word I don't suppose I'd heard since, as children, my brother and I used to go to see horror movies at the Rex Theater in Irvington—kept conjuring up the most hideous medical scenarios, and when I got back to the hotel, as disconcerted as when I'd left for the park, I phoned to ask if he wanted to go for a ride. I kept imagining him in the apartment, sitting in the corner of the sofa, with the radio off and the shades drawn—and when I did, it simply made no sense for me to be strolling around New York, or having lunch with a friend, or sitting in a movie theater in order to forget for a few hours my father and that massive tumor of his, over there together in Elizabeth, keeping each other company.

No, he didn't want to go for a ride.

But it was a beautiful spring day. We could drive up to the Orange Mountains. We could go to Grunings for lunch.

No, he was better off at home.

I said I would come over and we could take a walk.

He didn't want to go for a walk.

I said I'd buy some lox and bagels and drive over and have lunch with him and Lil at the apartment. Was Lil around?

She was upstairs.

Well, tell her to come down and we'll have lunch together.

It wasn't necessary.

"Maybe not for you," I thought, "but it is for me," and so I went out and bought lox, bagels, and cream cheese in a Sixth Avenue deli and then got the car and drove over to Jersey.

This time when I left the turnpike, I concentrated on my driving to be sure that I didn't mistakenly get onto the road to the cemetery. There was nothing to be gained by making a habit of that, though I wasn't sorry that the day before I had taken the wrong turn. I couldn't have explained what good it had done—it hadn't been a comfort or consolation; if anything it had only confirmed my sense of his doom—but I was still glad that I had wound up there. I wondered if my satisfaction didn't come down to the fact that the cemetery visit was *narratively* right: paradoxically, it had the feel of an event *not* entirely random and unpredictable and, in that way at least, offered a sort of strange relief from the impact of all that was frighteningly unforeseen.

When I got there, he was sitting as I had imagined, alone on the sofa, pitifully dejected-looking. The shades *were* drawn, the radio music *wasn't* on, and it appeared as though he hadn't even bothered to borrow yesterday's newspaper from one of his spendthrift neighbors. As I began to unpack the food I'd brought, he told me he wasn't hungry; when I suggested that instead of eating right away, we go out and take a walk, he made a noise to indicate that he didn't want to.

"Where's Lil?" I asked, turning on a lamp at about eleven in the morning.

"Upstairs."

"Don't you want to see her?"

He shrugged: he didn't care either way.

I hoped they hadn't argued, though I wouldn't have put it past him, even at the time of his greatest need, to go to work, first thing, on one or more of those many failings of hers that it had become his mission to eradicate. She ate too much and was overweight; she was cheap and wouldn't part with a dime; she talked for hours on the phone with a sister of hers he couldn't stand; she was always running somewhere—to this flea market to buy crap, to that flea market to buy crap; she took stupid risks with money he told her to stick into CDs; she didn't drive a car to his satisfaction. . . . The list was long, maybe even endless, though of course, at the beginning of their affair, it had been for him as it is for all of us. In '82 and '83, when he was off for his second and third winters as a widower in Florida and she was still holding down her job in New Jersey, he had sent her a letter daily, by and large a miscellany of little news bulletins about his waking hours composed in fragments over the course of the day. They were sprightly, playful, conspicuously loving, shyly sexual, unashamedly romantic letters embellished on occasion with upbeat doggerel (both plagiarized and invented) and adorned with stick-figure drawings of the two of them holding hands, hugging and kissing, or lying side-by-side in bed, letters beginning "Sweet Lilums" and "Hello Baby" and "Dearest, dear Lil"—"a continus stream," as he, at once proudly and little self-mockingly, described his correspondence to her, "of preaching, philosuphy, poems, and art." And tenderness. "I hope," he wrote, "that winter is not harsh, please take care going to and from work. . . ." "Without you this is another dull day. . . ." "Here's my hand to hold real tight. . . ." and directly beneath, a third grader's drawing of a hand. "Think of you all day. . . ." "I saw the smile on your pretty face, when I called, also the happiness in your voice, well, I must confess, I smiled also. . . ." "The song the man is singing on the radio is 'Are you lonesome tonight?' Are you? I was. . . ." Into a single, ordinary envelope, he stuffed, for her, Xeroxed copies of the first pages of the sheet music for "Love Somebody," "Love Makes the World Go 'Round," "Love Is a Many-Splendored Thing," "L-O-V-E," and "Where Do I Begin" from the movie *Love Story*. In precise detail he reported daily what he'd eaten, at what time he'd swum and for how long, where he'd walked and how far, whom he'd played cards and kibitzed with, exactly how many days were left before he saw her again, even what he wore. "All dressed in white, Shoes, socks, trousers, and shirt. As for a Jacket, lets see. Either the red and white one you say you don't care for or the black and white. Well sweety I don't have you here to make the choice so will have to make the momentous decision myself. Tried them both on the red and white one looks best on me. But decided on the other because I will be sitting most of the time, and it is a lighter weight, so that's that. . . ." Several times each week he begged her to believe (apparently she didn't) that the wealthy, charming widows he'd met his first winter in Florida were now only platonic friends he saw very occasionally (which was only a shade away from the truth), that she and she alone was his "pretty lady," and, too, he kept her briefed on the day-by-day struggle to broaden Bill Weber's horizons. "Bill is a strictly Jewish meat and potatoes man, can't even get him to go out for Chinese. . . ." "Finally convinced Bill to go out for Chinese food. . . ." There was absolutely nothing he didn't want to tell her then. She had been perfect then, even her flaws were beautiful. Yes, back then her physical proportions were characterized in rather more flattering terms than he would have used to describe them now. "She's like that painter," he had told me, "you know who I mean. . . ." I hadn't met Lil as yet, but I took a guess. "Rubens?" "That's the one," he said. "Well, *zaftig* is nice, too," I said. "Philip," he said shyly, "I'm doing things I haven't done since I was a boy." "We should all be so lucky," I told him.

But it wasn't her weight that had determined Lil's fate so much as her docility, a patient, bovine tolerance (or, for all I know, a saintly genius) for being poked and prodded about her shortcomings. There were times, to be sure, when the criticism became too much even for her, and after a bitter flare-up that took him completely by surprise, she retreated upstairs and didn't return for a day or even two. Then, thinking to himself, "Hell, I've got hundreds of women, I don't need her," he got on the phone to one or another of the widows down in Bal

Harbour. There was also Isabel Berkowitz, up at the Jewish Federation Plaza, who had sometimes come to visit him when Lil was off on one of her biannual package tours with her sister, and whom he spoke with on the phone every week (and whenever he and Lil were on the outs). But the fact was that these women he phoned were wealthier and more worldly than Lil, women accustomed, as the widows of successful businessmen, to living somewhat more expansively than she ever had and capable of inspiring in my father rather more social admiration—in short, women less malleable than the woman he had settled on and ones whose faults he might not necessarily have got away with correcting a hundred times a day.

Lil, until her retirement—which my father had talked her into, somewhat against her better judgment—had worked in the office of an auto supply house that happened to be owned by one of my boyhood friends, Lenny Lonoff, whose family had lived just across the street from us when we were grade school kids. Lil had moved into my father's apartment building shortly after the death of her husband—and a year after the death of my mother—and lived there with one of her two stepsons, Kenny, whose financial acumen didn't entirely meet my father's standards. Not only didn't my father approve of how Kenny went about his business but he didn't like the way Lenny Lonoff ran the auto supply house either. When he told Lil as much, instead of retorting that he didn't know what he was talking about or that she didn't need his opinion, she sat and she listened and didn't talk back, and as I see it, this forbearance may perhaps have had more to do with what seduced him than did the Rubenesque amplitude that he soon came to see as a result of her continuing to eat much too much despite his relentless upbraiding of her, meal by meal, course by course, helping by helping. Eating was her only revenge, and like the tumor, it was something he could not stop, no matter how he railed against it.

He could never understand that a capacity for renunciation and iron self-discipline like his own was extraordinary and not an endowment shared by all. He figured if a man with all his handicaps and limitations had it in him, then anybody did. All that was required was willpower—as if willpower grew on trees. His unswerving dutifulness toward those for whom he was

responsible seemed to compel him to respond to what he perceived as their failings as viscerally as he did to what he took—
and not necessarily mistakenly—to be their needs. And because
his was a peremptory personality and because buried deep inside him was an unalloyed nugget of prehistoric ignorance as
well, he had no idea just how unproductive, how maddening,
even, at times, how cruel his admonishing could be. He would
have told you that you can lead a horse to water and you *can*
make him drink—you just hock him and hock him and hock
him until he comes to his senses and does it. (Hock: a Yid-
dishism that in this context means to badger, to bludgeon, to
hammer with warnings and edicts and pleas—in short, to drill
a hole in somebody's head with words.)

After he and Lil got to West Palm Beach one December, my
father wrote a letter to my brother, covering both sides of two
sheets of white tablet paper with his laborious scrawl. Sandy
had cautioned him, for the sake of domestic peace, to try to be
a little less critical of Lil, particularly about her eating, once
they were alone together in Florida. Sandy added that he might
want to take it easy, too, on Jonathan, Sandy's younger son,
who was just then beginning to make the first real money of
his life as a sales rep for Kodak and whom my father, in weekly
phone calls and in letters, was advising, with the usual relentlessness, to save and not spend.

Dear Sandy
I think there are two type's of (among people) Philosphies. People
who care, and those that dont, People who *do* and people who Procrastinate and never *do* or *help*.

I came home from the office and did not feel well, you and Phil
were very young. Mother made dinner. I did not sit down to eat, instead I went into the liveing room. Within the hour Dr. Weiss was in
the house, mother called him. This was the scenario. he asked me what
was wrong. I told him, I had a pain over my heart, after examination,
he told me he could not detect anything wrong with me. He then
asked me what I did in excess. I told him the only thing I could think
of I smoke a lot, He said how about cutting it down to three instead
of 24 a day. I said why not none and within the week my pain disappeared I cut out smokeing completely. *Mother cared, Dr. Weiss advised,
I listened*, There are many advisers in this world, also people who *care*
and *do*, and people who listen, In many instances lives are safed, and
there are also overindulgers, those who smoke to much and drink to

much, take drugs, and also are impulsive eaters. In each case all these conditions can cause sickness and sometimes even worse.

You wanted a house. I went at once and got you the money to buy it. Why? because I cared. Phil needed an operation for Hernia, I took him to the Dr. and he was operated on. Same with mother after she suffered for 27 years. Why because I cared and I am a doer. Did her parents care, I guess so, but I felt the pain of both and did, *I did not procrastinate.* I tell Jon and *hock him.* I use all kind of Cliches , 'Like,' a fool and his money are soon parted) (A Penny saved is a penny earned) (someday there will be an old man dependent on you.) and when he asked who, I tell him its you.) etc I dont tell him once, I keep telling or Hocking, why, because he forgets, like a compulsive drinker, or drug taker, etc. Why do I continue, hocking? I realize its a pain in the ass, but if its people I *care for* I will try to cure, even if they object or wont $\frac{\text{diceplin}}{\text{disaplin}}$ themselves I including myself. I have many battles with my concience, but I fight my wronge thoughts. *I care,* for people in *my way.*

Please excuse the spelling and writing. I was never a good writer but now its worse, I don't *see so good*

> The Hocker, Misnomer
> it should be the carer
> Love
> Dad.

I will always continue to
Hock and Care. Thats me
to people I care
      for

"Did you and Lil have a fight?" I asked when I walked in and saw him by himself.

"She's never around anyway, so what difference does it make? She runs here, she runs there. When she was sick, I took care of her, I waited on her hand and foot. The hell with her. Let her go. I'm fine. I don't need anyone."

"It's not my business to butt in," I said, "but is this really a good time to start an argument?"

"I don't argue with anybody," he told me. "I never argue. If I tell her something, I only tell it to her for her own good. If she doesn't want to listen, the hell with her."

"Look, put on a sweater and put on your walking shoes, and I'm going to phone Lil, and if she wants to come along, we're all going out for a walk. It's a beautiful day and you can't sit around inside like this, with the shades drawn and so on."

"I'm fine inside."

I then spoke four words to him, four words that I'd never uttered to him before in my life. "Do as I say," I told him. "Put on a sweater and your walking shoes."

And they worked, those four words. I am fifty-five, he is almost eighty-seven, and the year is 1988: "Do as I say," I tell him—and he does it. The end of one era, the dawn of another.

While he went to the closet and put on a bright red sweater and his white Adidas, I phoned Lil and asked if she'd like to take a walk with us.

"Your father's going for a walk?" she said. "Really?"

"He is. Come and join us."

"I suggest we go out for a walk, that it'll do him good, and he jumps down my throat. I don't mean to criticize but that's the truth, Philip. You're the only one he listens to."

I laughed. "And that may not last too long either."

"I'll be right down," she said.

The three of us walked together to the drugstore three blocks away, past the old apartment buildings and the new condominiums that were going up where the last of Elizabeth's opulent Victorian houses had once stood. It was the same walk on which my mother had overextended herself on the day she died. Lil held him by one arm and I by the other, since walking had become very uncertain for him because of his poor vision. Only a few months earlier he had been patiently waiting for the cataract on his good eye to ripen so that it could be removed. Now, instead of looking forward to the minor surgery that would restore his vision and with it—he confidently assumed —his robust independence, he was contemplating an operation on his head that could kill him.

As we walked he began to reminisce in a very rambling way. "My memory is no good anymore," he explained.

But that wasn't exactly true. The sequence was often random and the focus sometimes blurry, but then, the logic of his recollections could always be a little elusive, even in the best of times. He certainly had no difficulty remembering the names of people dead now twenty, thirty, and forty years, or where they had lived, to whom they were related, and what they had said to him or he to them on occasions not necessarily that remarkable.

Through my father's mother's line we had belonged to a vast family network that had eventually organized into a family association in 1939, at the outbreak of the European war. While I was growing up, the association had consisted of some eighty families in and around Newark and some seventy families in and around Boston. There was an annual convention and an annual summer outing, a family newspaper that was printed quarterly, a family song, a family seal, and family stationery; a current roster of names and addresses of every family member was sent out to everyone each year, a Happy Day Fund looked after the ill and the convalescing, and an Education Fund assisted children of the family with their college tuition. In 1943, Herman Roth had become the fifth family member and the second of his brothers to be elected president. His first vice president had been Harold Chaban of Roxbury, Massachusetts. Harold Chaban was the son of Max Chaban and Ida Flaschner —Harold's uncle was Uncle Sam Flaschner, the family pioneer in America. His second vice president was Herman Goldstein, who lived in New York. Goldstein was a hatter like Sender Roth, loved to play cards with Liebowitz, and had married Bertha, the niece who had lived with the family on Rutgers Street when she came over with her sister Celia from the old country in 1913. His assistant treasurer had been his wife, Bess —my mother—his assistant secretary had been his sister-in-law Byrdine, Bernie's wife, his assistant historian had been his younger sister, Betty. . . . All this was recounted to Lil and me as we began our walk down North Broad Street.

"Our family association," he said, "back in those years, was one of the largest and strongest associations of its kind in the United States." It was the very tone in which he used to tell me as a boy that Metropolitan Life was "the largest financial institution in the world." We may have been ordinary people, but our affiliations were not without grandeur.

Out of nowhere, he said, "Used to be only Jews around this part of Elizabeth when Mother and I moved from Newark. Not when she was growing up here, of course. It was Irishmen, then. All Catholics. No more. Spanish, Korean, Chinese, black. The face of America is changing every day."

"That's true," I said. "A friend of mine calls Fourteenth Street in Manhattan the Fifth Avenue of the Third World."

"When my father sold the house on Rutgers Street," he said, "he sold it to an Italian family."

"Did he? How much did he get? What year was that?"

"I was born 1901, they moved to Rutgers Street 1902, we lived there fourteen years, so it must have been sold in 1916. Six thousand dollars, that's what he got for it. The Italian paid him in nickels, dimes, and quarters. It took a week to count it."

As we approached Salem Avenue, he gestured toward the apartment building on the corner. "That's where Millie used to live."

I knew that, of course; she and her husband, Joe Komisar, and my cousin Ann had moved there years ago, when I was in college. Millie was one of my mother's two younger sisters; she had died at seventy-eight only a few months earlier, and by pointing to her building he had been pointing not to where she used to live but to where she who no longer lived lived no longer. She and Joe were buried on one side of my mother, and my father's plot was on the other side. That's where Millie lived now.

"My father," he said, as we approached the drugstore to which my mother had taken the last long walk of her life, "my father had to beat my older brother Ed to prevent him from marrying a worldly woman. Had to beat him."

My Uncle Ed had been a bruiser with a short fuse who used to take me to football games when I was a child. His big hands and his broken nose and his rough, argumentative nature would thrill me for an hour or two, and I loved him, but I was always glad, at the end of a day's outing, that he was my cousin Florence's father. "You never told me that," I said. "Grandpa beat him?"

"Had to. Saved him. Saved him from that woman."

"How old was Ed?"

"Twenty-three."

He'd first told me that story when I was sixteen and in my last year of high school. I don't remember why he told it, but it was at dinner, near the end of the meal, and I had jumped up from the table in a rage and then bolted from the room when I'd heard him conclude, "They don't have that kind of discipline anymore." My mother had come into my bedroom to try to get me to go back to eat my dessert; she had begged me to forgive him for whatever he had said that offended me so. "Please, dear, do it for me. Your father is not an educated man. . . ." But I had been adamant and refused to return to spoon down Jell-O across the table from somebody who considered beating the love for a woman out of a twenty-three-year-old man—even one as pigheaded as my Uncle Ed—a praiseworthy form of discipline.

No doubt he had forgotten that incident and so, actually, had I, until the moment, thirty-nine years later, when for some obscure reason he had chosen to tell this story to me again.

But there was no rage now against the storyteller. It was I, in fact, who now said to him, philosophically, "Well, they don't have that kind of discipline anymore."

"No. My brother Bernie, he should rest in peace, you know what he said to me when I told him not to marry Byrdine Bloch? Of course I was proved right, because after twenty years of marriage and two beautiful children, he wound up getting that terrible divorce that tore the family apart. But when I cautioned him about Byrdine, when I told him, 'Bernie, she looks old enough to be your mother—is that really what you want?' you know what he said to me, an older brother who was trying only to warn him? 'Mind your own goddamn business.' We didn't talk for months."

"That was when?" I asked.

"That? That must be . . . 1927. I married Mother in February and Bernie married Byrdine in July."

"I didn't realize that you were both married in the same year," I said.

We were walking back now the way we'd come. He was silent for a while. Then, as though having glimpsed the solution to some intractable problem after a long and arduous effort, he began to say, "Yes . . . yes . . ."

"Yes what?" I asked.

"I've been alive a long time."

"You're the insurance man, you know the statistics. On the actuarial charts you have achieved a great age."

"Where is the tumor?" he asked for the second time in two days.

"In front of the brain stem. At the base of the skull."

"Have you seen the pictures?"

I didn't want him to think that too much had been going on without his knowledge and so I lied. "I couldn't read them if I had," I said. "Look, it's operable—remember that." But that was what he couldn't forget, and dreaded most. "If we all decide that's the course to follow, then he'll go in and get it out, and after a brief convalescence, you'll be yourself again."

"It would be nice to have a few more years," he said.

"You'll get them," I said.

I drove over again on Sunday morning and he had a set of sherry glasses ready for me to take away, each glass individually wrapped in a page of the previous week's Sunday *Star-Ledger* and all of them wedged bulkily together in a shoebox. He never used them, he said, he didn't need them, and he wanted Claire and me to enjoy them in the country.

Ever since my mother's death, each time he came to stay with us in Connecticut he had something with him in a paper bag or a shopping bag or in the little plaid valise that he carried alongside him during the three-hour car ride with the local driver we sent down to Elizabeth to get him. Unlike the sherry glasses, it was usually a present for him and my mother from me, or from Claire and me, that now, years later, he was returning as though what they had been given had only been on loan or left there in storage. "Here are those napkins." "What napkins?" "From Ireland." Ireland? That would have been 1960, the year of my Guggenheim. My then wife and I had stopped in Ireland on the way home, to walk around Joyce's Dublin. "There's a tablecloth, too," he added, "from Spain." 1971. Gaudí's Barcelona. Or, "Here are the place mats. I don't think Mother used them twice. For her, they were special, for company only." "Here are the steak knives" and "Here is the flower vase" and "Here are the coffee mugs," and in the beginning, when I resisted, explaining to him, "But they're yours, they were gifts," he would reply, with no idea that there might be a grain of insult lurking in all this unburdening, "What the hell do I need them for? Look at this clock. A beautiful clock that somebody gave us. Must have cost a fortune. What good is it to me?"

The clock had cost about two hundred dollars in Hungary in 1973. I had given it to my mother, a little porcelain clock with a floral design of the kind she liked that I bought for her in an antique shop in Budapest, on my way home one spring from visiting friends in Prague. But I took it back silently. Little by little I took everything back, struck each time by how inconsequential to him was the sentimental value—even the material value—of things intended to betoken the love of those he most cherished. Strange, I would think, to find that particular blank spot in a man on whom the claims of family were so emotionally tyrannical—or maybe not strange at all: how could mere keepsakes encapsulate for him the overpowering force of blood bonds? Item by item, I took it all back like a well-trained refund clerk in a first-rate department store, but wondering if perhaps what he was thinking, while he wrapped these gifts in old newspaper and stuffed them in cartons of every description, was that this way we wouldn't have too many of his possessions to bother about after the funeral. He could be a pitiless realist, but I wasn't his offspring for nothing, and I could be pretty realistic, too.

This time, instead of silently accepting the goods being returned, I reminded him that I was still a transient in a New York hotel, didn't know when I'd next be in Connecticut, and would just as soon have him hold on to the glasses.

"Take them," he insisted. "I want to get rid of them."

"Dad," I said, setting the shoebox on the breakfront, where I assumed the glasses had been stored all these years, "these glasses are the least of our worries."

But rushing around the apartment looking for the next thing to get rid of, finding the glasses, packing them in newspaper, finding the shoebox—for a moment this had given the day a purpose, provided some little release for all that was brutally thwarted. Now there was nothing for him but to be frightened again. I was sorry, suddenly, for not having let him have his way and just taken the damn things back to the hotel. But I was getting frazzled, too.

"I've been like that all my life," he said, dropping unhappily onto his spot on the sofa.

"Like what?"

"Impulsive."

I was unused to hearing this kind of self-criticism from him, and I wondered if it was such a wonderful development. At the age of eighty-six, with a massive tumor in his head, better to continue wearing, at either side of his bridle, those blinders that had kept him pulling his load straight ahead all his life.

"I wouldn't worry about it," I said. "It isn't as if you're only impulsive. You can be cautious and prudent, too. You oscillate. People do."

But he was being gnawed at by something and wouldn't be consoled.

"What are you thinking?" I asked.

"I gave my tefillin away. I got rid of my tefillin."

"Why?"

"They were sitting in the drawer."

Tefillin are the two small leather boxes containing brief Biblical extracts that an Orthodox Jew fastens to himself by narrow thongs—one box strapped to the forehead, the other to the left arm—during his weekday morning prayers. Back when my father was an overworked insurance man, being a Jew for him hadn't had much to do with formal worship, and like most of the first-generation American fathers in our neighborhood, he visited the nearby synagogue only on the High Holidays and, when it was necessary, as a mourner. And at home there were really no rituals he observed. Since his retirement, however, and particularly in the last decade of my mother's life, they had begun to attend services together mostly every Friday night, and though he still didn't go so far as to lay tefillin in the morning, his Judaism was more pointedly focused on the synagogue and the service and the rabbi than it had been at any time since his childhood.

The temple was a hundred or so yards down the road on a little side street off North Broad, in an old house that was rented by the small congregation of elderly, local people, who were barely able to meet the upkeep costs. To my surprise—and perhaps because they couldn't afford anyone else—the cantor wasn't even a Jew but a Bulgarian who worked for a New York auction house during the week and for this little conclave of Elizabeth Jews on their sabbath. After the service was over, he sometimes entertained them with songs from

Yentl and *Fiddler on the Roof.* My father loved the Bulgarian's deep voice and considered him a buddy; he also thought highly of the yeshiva student who came over from New York to lead their services on the weekend, a twenty-three-year-old whom my father called "Rabbi" most respectfully and spoke of as something of a sage.

However humble their manifestations, these yearnings for a formalized religion in his old age were inspired by something far from hypocrisy or conventional decorum; in fact, the consolation that he seemed to derive from going to synagogue regularly—the sense of unity it bestowed on his long life and the communion with his own mother and father he told me he felt there—made his "getting rid" of the tefillin one of the more enigmatic instances of his lifelong habit of relinquishing, rather than saving, the treasured objects of the past. Given the link of sentiment that Jewish belief now seemed to furnish between the isolation of old age and the striving, populous life that was all but gone, I could have imagined him, instead of parting with his tefillin, rediscovering in the mere contemplation of them something of their ancient fetishistic power.

But my imagining this old man meditatively fondling his long-neglected tefillin was so much sentimental kitsch, really, a scene out of some Jewish parody of *Wild Strawberries.* How my father actually disposed of the tefillin reveals an imagination altogether bolder and more mysterious, inspired by a personalized symbolic mythology as eccentric as Beckett's or Gogol's.

"Who'd you give the tefillin to?" I asked him.

"Who? Nobody."

"You threw them out? In the trash?"

"No, no, of course I didn't."

"You gave them to the synagogue?" I didn't know what you did do with tefillin when you no longer wanted or needed them, but surely, I thought, there would be a religious policy for discarding them, overseen by the synagogue.

"You know the Y?" he said to me.

"Sure."

"Three, four mornings a week when I could still drive over there, I'd swim, kibitz, I'd watch the card game. . . ."

"And?"

"Well, that's where I went. The Y. . . . I took the tefillin in a paper bag. The locker room was empty, I left them. . . . In one of the lockers."

The halting way he revealed the details, the bafflement he himself seemed to feel looking back now on this original plot he'd devised for their disposal, prompted me to wait a little before asking anything further.

"I'm curious," I finally said. "How come you didn't go to the rabbi? Ask him to take them off your hands."

He shrugged and I realized that he hadn't wanted the rabbi to know what he was up to, for fear of what the twenty-three-year-old whom he so respected would think of a Jew who was ditching his tefillin. Or was I wrong about that, too? Maybe he'd never even thought of the rabbi, as perhaps the shrug was meant to indicate—maybe it was just revealed to him in a flash, the knowledge that in that secret place where Jewish men stood unashamedly naked before one another, he could lay his tefillin to rest without worry; the understanding that where his tefillin would come to no harm, where they would not be profaned or desecrated, where they might even be resanctified, was in the midst of those familiar Jewish bellies and balls. Perhaps what the act signified was not his shame before the young rabbi-in-training but a declaration that the men's locker room at the local YMHA was closer to the core of the Judaism he lived by than the rabbi's study at the synagogue—that nothing would have been *more* artificial than going with the tefillin to the rabbi, even if the rabbi had been a hundred with a beard down to the ground. Yes, the locker room of the Y, where they undressed, they schvitzed, they stank, where, as men among men, familiar with every nook and cranny of their worn-down, old, ill-shapen bodies, they kibitzed and told their dirty jokes, and where, once upon a time, they'd made their deals—that was their temple and where they remained Jews.

I didn't ask why he hadn't turned them over to me. I didn't ask why, instead of giving back to me all those napkins and tablecloths and place mats, he hadn't given me the tefillin instead. I wouldn't have prayed with them, but I might well have cherished them, especially after his death. But how was he to know that? He probably thought I would have scoffed at the very idea of his handing on his tefillin to me—and forty years earlier he would have been right.

I didn't ask because I realized that to do so was truly to place the two of us back inside that corny scenario I couldn't seem to cut myself loose from. Somewhat improbably, where his tefillin were concerned, it was I whose imagination kept running to the predictably maudlin while his had the integrity of a genuinely anomalous talent, compelled by the elemental feeling that can lend ritualistic intensity to even the goofiest act.

"Well," I said, when it was clear that he had no more to tell me, "one of your pals there must have got a big surprise when he came up from the pool. He must have thought a miracle had happened. There he had left his shower clogs in the bottom of his locker and, lo and behold, they'd been turned into tefillin. An argument not only for the existence of God but for the existence of a God most bountiful."

He didn't as much as smile at what I'd said—maybe because he didn't get it, or maybe because he did. "No," he replied, in all seriousness, "the locker was empty."

"When did you do this?"

"In November. A couple days before we went to Florida."

So—he had more than likely been thinking *this*: "If I die in Florida, if I never come back . . . no, the tefillin must not wind up in the garbage."

"Then, November thirtieth, we flew to West Palm. I carried my suitcases from the baggage place all the way to the taxi stand—that's how good I felt. And the next morning, my first morning in Florida, I woke up and this had happened in my sleep." Yet again he was pushing the fallen cheek up with his fingertips to see if this time it would stay. "I look in the mirror, I see my face, and I knew my life would never be the same. Come here," he said, "come to the bedroom."

I followed him down the corridor from the living room, past the blown-up photographs of my brother's sons, taken some twenty-five years ago, when they were little children vacationing on Fire Island. Why he hadn't thought to give Seth or Jonathan the tefillin was easier to understand than why he hadn't thought to pass them on to me. My nephews, raised in a secular ethos, with no knowledge of Judaism, were Jews in name alone; my father, like my mother, adored them, worried about them, praised them, lavished on them gifts of money—and a good deal more advice than they wished to hear—but he knew better than to expect them to know what the tefillin were, let alone to want to own them.

As for my brother, my father probably imagined that Sandy would have been as unreceptive as I to such a bequest, though my guess is that Sandy might have been touched by that memento, not because of its religious significance but as a solid piece of our past, as something that he remembered, as I did, seeing neatly stored for years and years in a velvet bag in a drawer of the dining room breakfront in the apartment where we had grown up. But our father, being our father, couldn't have been expected to understand that. He understood, like the rest of us, only what he understood, though that he understood fiercely.

I could no longer enter my father's bedroom without remembering the night just after my mother's death—and after I had arrived from London that afternoon—when I had slept with him in his double bed. Sandy and Helen had gone to sleep at Sandy's suburban house in Englewood Cliffs, where Seth and Jon, now young working men, were still living but which Sandy planned to sell shortly, since his job had already relocated him in Chicago.

In May 1981, at seventy-nine, my father was in excellent health and impressively vigorous, but twenty-four hours after his wife died in that seafood restaurant, he looked almost as bad as he did now disfigured by the tumor. That first night together, before bed, I had given him 5 milligrams of Valium and a glass of warm milk to wash the tablet down. He disapproved of tranquilizers and sleeping pills, criticized vehemently anyone who relied on either—instead of on willpower the way he did—but beginning that night and for the next few weeks, he accepted the Valium without any questions when I said it would help him to sleep (though later, perhaps to ease his conscience, he referred to the drug he'd taken as Dramamine). We took turns in the bathroom and then, in our pajamas, we lay down side by side in the bed where he had slept with my mother two nights before, the only bed in the apartment. After turning off the light, I reached out and took his hand and held it as you would the hand of a child who is frightened of the dark. He sobbed for a minute or two—then I heard the broken, heavy breathing of someone very deeply asleep, and I turned over to try to get some rest myself.

Thirty minutes later, having taken no Valium, I was lying there wide awake, when, on the night table beside me, the phone rang. I grabbed it so that my father's sleep wouldn't be disturbed and heard someone laughing at the other end. "Who is this?" I asked, but the answer was more crazy laughter. I hung up, uncertain whether the call was a fluke wrong number or deliberate, the work of some ghoul who followed the obituary pages in the local paper (where my mother's death had been reported that morning) and then phoned the families of the dead at night to get his kicks. When the phone rang again less than a minute later—the luminescent clock radio still showed eleven-twenty—I knew it was no innocent wrong number. There again was the vicious laugh of one who has triumphed over an enemy, the gleeful sadism of a victorious avenger.

After putting down the receiver, I got out of bed and ran to the living room extension to take the receiver there off the hook before the phone rang a third time. I left it like that until around six the next morning, when I got up and stole back into the living room to replace it so that my father wouldn't ask any questions. I was in the bathroom when it rang around seven. My father answered. When I came out and asked who had phoned so early, he said angrily, "No one," but it was clear enough what had happened. "Who was it?" I repeated, and this time he described the laughing he'd heard. "Sounds like some screwball," I told him, without mentioning the calls I'd taken the night before. "It's Wilkins," he replied. "Who's Wilkins?" "From across the street." "How do you know it's him?" "I know, all right." "What's he got against you?" I asked. "He's a fascist dog. A real Jew-hater. He lives alone. Not a friend in the world. Just that mutt. Loves only Mr. Ray-gun and Plastic Nancy and that filthy mutt of his. Put Ray-gun stickers all over the laundry room. *Our* laundry room. Doesn't ask— just comes over here and does it." "So you told him not to." "I saw them, and sure, I told him not to. And the next day he puts up more. When I saw what he'd done, I tore 'em down. I phoned him. I told him that wasn't what this laundry room was for. It was for people to wash their clothes in peace and not for political campaigning." "What else did you tell him?" "I told him what I thought of Mr. Ray-gun. I told him, in case he hadn't heard, just what Jews have suffered for two thousand years." "You're sure it's him?" "It's Wilkins, all right. I'll get him," he said, half to himself, "I'll get the son of a bitch." "Dad, don't bother—from the sound of it, they got him. You know what a punishment it is for a man to laugh at somebody else's grief? Forget him. Let's just get ready now—we've got a big day."

We buried my mother at noon, he began emptying out her bedroom closet and her bureau drawers around one, and by ten-thirty we were back in the double bed—and at eleven-twenty, while my father slept and I lay there wide awake once again, wondering what was going to become of him and wondering where my mother was, the phone rang. The laughing began as soon as I picked it up. I listened for a long time with the phone held tightly to my ear. And then, when the caller had neither stopped laughing nor hung up, I said softly—doing my best, by cupping the mouthpiece, not to wake my father— "Wilkins, pull this shit one more time, *once* more, and I will be over at your door with my ax. I've got a big ax, Wilkins, and I know where you live. I will beat your door down with my ax and then I am going to come in and split you up the middle like a log. Do you have a dog, by any chance? I'm going to turn your doggy into sausage, Wilkins. With just my ax to help me, I will then shove him up your ass and down your throat until you and Fido are one. Call my father one more time, day or night, *ever again*, and your head, you crazy, sick, psychotic ghoul, your fucking head, when I am finished with it . . ."

My heart was pumping blood as though for ten people and my pajamas were soaked through with the perspiration of someone who has lain all night in a malarial fever and, at the other end, the phone was dead.

In the bedroom—where the mahogany bedroom suite no longer gleamed with polish as it had when my mother was in charge of the housekeeping, where instead you could now initial the dust coating the upper surfaces—my father showed me, in the middle of the top bureau drawer, the little metal box where he kept his will, his insurance policy, and his savings books. There was also a record of his CDs and municipals. "All my papers," he said. "And here—the key to my safe deposit box."

"Okay," I said.

"I did what you told me," he said. "I made all my savings accounts joint with Sandy."

He took out the savings books—there were four of them—to show me where my brother's name now appeared beneath his as the account owner. Flipping through the savings books, I saw that the savings added up to about fifty thousand dollars; the CDs and municipals came to another thirty thousand—they, too, were to be left to my brother.

"The ten-thousand-dollar insurance policy goes to you," he said. "I know what you told me, but that I had to do—I wasn't going to leave you nothing."

"Fine," I said.

When I was visiting him in Florida some two or three years after my mother's death, the subject of his will had come up and I had told him to leave all his money to Sandy to split, as he wished, between his two kids and himself. I told him that I didn't need any money and that what Seth and Jonathan got could make a big difference to them if the money was divided two ways, or three at the most. I had meant it when I said it, I had confirmed it in a letter to him afterward, and I hadn't thought about his will since.

But now with his death anything but remote, being told by him that he had gone ahead and, on the basis of my request, substantially eliminated me as one of his heirs elicited an unforeseen response: I felt repudiated—and the fact that his eliminating me from the will had been my own doing did not at all mitigate this feeling of having been cast out by him. I had made a generous gesture that was also, I suppose, of a piece with the assertions of equality and self-reliance that I had been making to my father since early adolescence. Admittedly, it was also a characteristic attempt to take the moral high ground within the family, to define myself in my fifties, as I had in college and graduate school and later as a young writer, as a son to whom material considerations were largely negligible—and I felt crushed for having done it: naive and foolish and crushed.

To my great dismay, standing with him over his last will and testament, I discovered that I wanted my share of the financial surplus that, against all odds, had been accumulated over a lifetime by this obdurate, resolute father of mine. I wanted the money because it was his money and I was his son and I had a right to my share, and I wanted it because it was, if not an authentic chunk of his hard-working hide, something like the embodiment of all that he had overcome or outlasted. It was what he had to give me, it was what he had wanted to give me, it was due me by custom and tradition, and why couldn't I have kept my mouth shut and allowed what was only natural to prevail?

Didn't I think I deserved it? Did I consider my brother and his children more deserving inheritors than I, perhaps because my brother, by having given him grandchildren, was more legitimately a father's heir than was the son who had been childless? Was I a younger brother who suddenly had become unable to assert his claim against the seniority of someone who had been there first? Or, to the contrary, was I a younger brother who felt that he had encroached too much upon an older brother's prerogatives already? Just where had this impulse to cast off my right of inheritance come from, and how could it have so easily overwhelmed expectations that I now belatedly discovered a son was *entitled* to have?

But this had happened to me more than once in my life: I had refused to allow convention to determine my conduct, only to learn, after I'd gone my own way, that my bedrock feelings were sometimes more conventional than my sense of unswerving moral imperative.

During the walk we took that afternoon, in which I steered my father very slowly twice around the block, I was not able to tell him, however much I wanted to—and however efficaciously humbling a confession of error might have been—that I would like him to reassign to me the share of his estate that he had originally bequeathed to me in his will. For one thing, because several years back my brother had had to provide his signature to gain access to the joint savings accounts, he already knew of the changes, and it did not seem worth even the thirty or forty thousand dollars to establish the conditions for a family feud or the eruption of poisonous feeling that is notoriously associated with the last-minute adjustment of an inheritance. And there was my pride—if you like, the hubris. In short, for something like the reasons that had probably contributed to my telling him to leave the money to others in the first place, I now found myself unable to renounce my instructions.

So much for learning from one's mistakes. "Let it be," I thought. "It's almost worth the dough to be able to savor, yet again, the comedy of your own automatic brand of elevated stupidity."

But if it was too late—or for me just too difficult—to lay claim to my original share of the money, I knew what it was I wanted in its place. But I then discovered myself unable to ask for *that*. Not directly, anyhow. Self-reliant to the last! Independent to the end! The son perpetually protesting his autonomy! *I don't need anything.*

"Tell me about Grandpa's shaving mug," I said. "I was looking at it in your bathroom. Where was his barbershop? Do you remember?"

"Of course I remember. Bank Street. Below Wallace Place, where the German hospital used to be, on the corner of Wallace Place and Bank Street. There was a barber on Bank Street and when I was a little boy we used to go around and get my hair cut and my father would get a shave. The mug had 'S. Roth' and a whaddyacallit on it, a date, and they kept it for him in this barbershop."

"How'd you come to get it?"

"How did I get it? That's a good question. Let me remember. I don't think I did. No. I didn't. I took it from my brother Ed. Yes. When we moved from Rutgers Street, Pop took it with him to Hunterdon Street and went to the barber on Johnson Avenue and Avon Avenue and then Ed took it after Pop died and I took it from him. I think it was the only thing that was ever left to me. And it wasn't even left to me. I took it."

"You wanted it," I said.

"I wanted it," he told me with a laugh, "since I was a little boy."

"Want to know something?" I said. "I did, too."

He smiled at me with the half of his mouth that could still

move. "Remember when we came to visit you in Rome, me
and Mother, when you took me for a shave?"

"That's right. On Via Giulia, in that tiny barbershop. That
may have been the best of that whole year for me," I said,
thinking of the marital battles that erupted daily in the small
apartment, around the corner from Via Giulia, on Via di Sant'
Eligio, that I shared unhappily with an unhappy wife when we
were living in Italy on my thirty-two-hundred-dollar Guggenheim. "I'd go down the street for a shave in the afternoon after
I'd finished writing. My big luxury. The barber was Guglielmo.
He wanted to talk all the time about Caryl Chessman. He
prided himself on his English. Every time I came in, 'Happy
birthday, Maestro, Fourth of July.' Hot towels, big shaving
brush, straightedge razor, slapped silly with witch hazel to top
it off, and all for the equivalent of about fifteen cents. 1960," I
said. "You would have been only a couple of years older than I
am now."

"I used to go get a shave with Bill Eisenstadt, he should rest
in peace. Remember Bill?"

"Of course. Bill and Lil and their son, Howie."

"A barber on Clinton Place, right around the corner from
the high school. Cost a quarter. You leave it to Bill to find the
last quarter shave in Newark."

From Bill Eisenstadt he went on to invoke Abe Bloch and
Max Feld and Sam Kaye and J. M. Cohen, the totemic male figures out of my earliest childhood, insurance men with him at
the Metropolitan, pinochle players in our kitchen on Friday
nights, companions, with their wives and kids, on the Memorial Day picnics up at the South Mountain Reservation—the
veteran foot soldiers with whom he had gone out collecting
door-to-door on Newark's benighted "colored debit," coming
home long after dark with his clothes smelling sourly of cheap
cooking oil. "There would be colored families," he now told
me, "still paying premiums twenty, thirty years after the death
of the insured. Three cents a week. That's what we collected."
"How come they kept paying?" "They never said anything to
the agent. Somebody died and they never mentioned it. The
insurance man came round and they paid him." "Amazing," I
said, though it was by no means the first time that I was hearing
his stories of the eerie evenings collecting pennies from the

poorest of Newark's poor, stories from thirty-eight years with the Metropolitan, with Bill and Abe and Sam and J. M. Cohen, all of them, as he reminded me several times, long gone.

And of the few friends alive there wasn't much good news to report, either. "Louie Chesler is in a hospital, pissing blood. Ida Singer is almost blind. Milton Singer can't walk; he's in a wheelchair. Turro—remember Dick Turro?—he has cancer, poor guy. Bill Weber doesn't even know who I am when I call up. 'Herman, Herman who? I don't know any Herman.' He's living with Frankie now but Frankie says they're going to have to put him in a home."

Thus he managed not to dwell entirely on his tumor, speaking instead of the old dead and the dying and those of his friends who would have been better off dead.

The next day I drove to Elizabeth to pick my father up and take him over to University Hospital on Springfield Avenue in Newark; he was to consult there about an operation with the brain surgeon, Dr. Meyerson. Lil and he were immediately at loggerheads when I asked the best way to get to Meyerson's office. It turned out that Lil was talking about how to get to Meyerson's office in Millburn, where she had gone with my father the first time he'd been to see Meyerson, and he was talking about how to drive to Meyerson's hospital office, where, unknown to Lil, this second appointment had been scheduled. In the car he managed to keep the disagreement simmering for some time after the confusion had been resolved.

He only quieted down about it when I turned up from Elizabeth Avenue toward Bergen Street and began to drive through the most desolate streets of black Newark. What in my childhood had been the busy shopping thoroughfares of a lower-middle-class, mostly Jewish neighborhood were now almost entirely burned out or boarded up or torn down. The only ones about seemed to be unemployed black men—at any rate, black men standing together on the street corners, seemingly with nothing to do. It was not a scene conducive to alleviating the gloom of three people on their way to consult with a brain surgeon, and yet the rest of the way to the hospital, my father forgot the encounter awaiting him there and, instead, reminisced in his random fashion about who had lived and worked where when he was a boy before the First World War and on these streets immigrant Jews and their families were doing what they could to survive and flourish.

"Mr. Tibor lived there. I suppose he was a Hungarian. He made my birthday suit and he made the pants too short. And I couldn't go to my graduation."

"Because the pants were too short?" I asked.

"The suit was useless. That's where Al Schorr's family lived. My God, that's still standing. Remember Al?"

"Sure. How could I forget Al and that voice of his."

"Yeah, well, he had that croaking voice all his life. Rasping like that and deep. Had it when he was a little kid. Al was thrown out of his class. And so he came to my class and I made him treasurer, class treasurer. I was the president. On graduation day we had some money left over, so we went downtown to spend it."

"I see," I said, " 'money left over.' When the guys go into the banks with the masks and the guns that's what they usually say to the teller. They say, 'Excuse me, do you happen to have any money left over?' "

My words managed to lighten up his gloom by about a milliwatt. "Well," my father said, "Al was a great guy. He didn't do it with a gun. He did it with a laugh. He did everything with a laugh. He worked with me until we fired him. I got him in the insurance business. Every job Al ever had I got him. But he was stealing money and he says, 'Hey,' he says, 'hey, they're after me, Herman, the police are after me.' 'Well,' I says, 'here's five dollars, go to the sweat baths in New York.' And I gave him five dollars and he went to New York. And he come back, then he paid the company off and I got him a job with Louie Chesler. He sold. I told him, if he ever stole from Louie, I said, I'd shoot him. He worked for the Shuberts in Newark. The theater. He used to pick the tickets, that the people would tear in half, off the ground. He would put them together, put 'em in a box, and steal the money. His mother had to pay up, I don't know, two, three thousand dollars. His teacher threw him out of his class, that's how we became friends. He looked around the classroom the first day in eighth grade—you know what a *pishka* is," he said to me suddenly, interrupting his story.

"Of course I know. A collection box. Where do you think I was raised, in Montana?"

"Well, Al looked around the classroom and he said to his teacher, in that gravel-pit voice, 'If they paint this room I'll put a dime in the *pishka*.' And *she* didn't know what *pishka* meant and she threw him out of the room. And so he came into my room, and I sized him up, and I made him treasurer. I was president. Thirteenth Avenue School. God, there it is, my school."

Meyerson, who David Krohn had assured me was reputed to be among the best brain surgeons in Jersey, was a plain, plumpish fellow in his early forties, gentle and extremely amiable right off the bat. When he had settled in behind his desk, he looked across to where I was sitting and asked what questions I had. I pointed to my father, looking awfully glum in a chair between Lil, whom the doctor had called "Mrs. Roth," and Meyerson's chief nurse who, we were told, customarily sat in on preoperative consultations. "My father has the questions," I said. "Go ahead, Dad. Ask Dr. Meyerson everything you want to know."

All those questions about the operation that he had been asking me during the last several days, I had told him to write down and bring with him for the consultation. He'd written them in pencil, laboriously laid them out in that artlessly sprawling, yokel handwriting, capitalizing most of the nouns but spelling all except one or two words correctly. He'd showed me the list before we left the house and I had thought, "I want this list. The list and the shaving mug will do it."

My father removed the piece of lined paper from his pocket and unfolded it on his lap. "One," he began. "What's the procedure?" He looked up at Meyerson. "Pardon my ignorance, Doctor."

Meyerson reached behind him and, from a shelf with half a dozen medical texts carelessly flopped over at one end, took down a small painted plastic model of the brain and the skull. Turning it in his hand and pointing with a pencil, he explained where the tumor was situated and where it was pressing into the brain. He showed us, on the back wall of the skull, where he could cut through to go in to remove it. "We'll just lift the brain a little here and take out what's growing underneath it."

The thought of his "lifting" my father's brain staggered me. I hadn't believed you could do such a thing to a brain without inviting disaster. And for all I knew, you couldn't.

"What do you use to go in there?" my father asked. "General Electric or Black and Decker?"

He had been looking so ancient and so vanquished that I was surprised by his mordancy and the objective courage it seemed to attest to.

The doctor's reply demonstrated his own quiet objectivity. "Surgical companies make the tools."

My father returned to the next prepared question. "Two. Will it grow back?"

"Eventually it might," Meyerson said. And now it was he who was mildly, mordantly ironic. "Maybe in ten or fifteen years we'll have to do it again."

My father registered the point wryly with a single, slow nod. "Three," he said, returning to his list again. "How much pain is there?"

"No, there isn't much pain," Meyerson told him. "You'll be pretty sick afterward. You'll have a high fever. You'll be very weak."

Meyerson's nurse, a slight, peppy middle-aged woman wearing ordinary street clothes, no less pleasant and genial a person than the doctor, put her hand sympathetically on my father's and said, "We'll try to get you up and sitting five or six days later."

In response, my father simply mumbled, "Oh boy." Five or six days unable to lift himself off the bed gave him the picture, if he hadn't got it already.

He didn't give out, however, but proceeded to his fourth question. "How long does the operation take?"

"Anywhere," Meyerson replied, "from eight to ten hours."

He managed to take that in without flinching, which was better than I did. Eight to ten hours, then five to six days, and what would he be worth after that? After the impoverished childhood and the limited education, after the failure of the shoe store and of the frozen-food business, after the struggle to gain a managerial role in the teeth of the Metropolitan's Jewish quotas, after the premature deaths of so many loved ones—brothers Morris, Charlie, and Milton in the 1920s and '30s, his young niece Jeanette and his young nephew David and his beloved sister-in-law Ethel in the 1940s—after all that he had weathered and survived without bitterness or brokenness or despair, wasn't eight to ten hours of brain surgery really asking too much? Isn't there a limit?

The answer is yes, yes absolutely, yes to the thousandth degree—this *was* asking too much. To "Isn't there a limit?" the answer is no.

"Most of the operating time," Meyerson explained, "is spent getting in through the skull. It depends then on the kind of tumor I find. In that area, ninety-five percent, ninety-eight percent are benign. There isn't much bleeding generally. If there is—because of the nature of the tumor—that can slow things up a little."

On he went, the stoical father whom I had never admired more in his life. "Five. Will I have to learn to walk again afterward?"

"Yes," Meyerson said. And just when I had thought that *I* had the picture, I realized that not by any means had I grasped as yet the awfulness of this thing. "Yes," Meyerson said, "you probably will."

There were another five questions written down on the piece of paper but even my father had heard enough. Pushing the list back into his pocket, he looked directly at Meyerson and said, "I've got a problem."

"You do," Meyerson agreed.

This time we drove through the ruins of Newark in silence. He had nothing more to ask, his childhood recollections were spent, he did not even have it in him to improve Lil—there was only that final exchange in Meyerson's office for all of us to think about and think about. Meyerson had agreed that we should now solicit a second neurosurgical opinion, but assuming as he did that the second doctor confirmed his judgment and we decided to go ahead with surgery at University Hospital, he advised us to have it sooner rather than later and to set up a tentative appointment for the operation on the first open date in his calendar. It turned out to be the anniversary of my mother's death seven years earlier.

At the apartment Lil went into the kitchenette to prepare some Campbell's soup for lunch. My father went in after her to get the dishes to set the dining room table, and I sat in the living room trying to envision how Meyerson was going to lift my father's brain without damaging it. "There must be ways," I thought.

Lil was apparently using the manual opener screwed to the wall beside the sink, because I heard my father telling her, "Hold the can from the bottom. You're not holding it from the bottom."

"I know how to open a can of soup," she said.

"But you're not holding it right."

"Herman, let me be. I *am* holding it right."

"Why can't you just do what I ask you when I ask you? It *isn't* right. Hold it from the *bottom*."

And from the other room I had all I could do not to shout, "You're on the brink of a catastrophe, you idiot—let her open the can any fucking way she wants!" though I was also telling myself, "Of course. How to open a soup can. What else is there to think about? What else is there that matters? This is what's kept him going for eighty-six years and what, if anything, is going to get him through now. Hold it from the bottom, Lil—he knows what he's saying."

Admittedly, he went overboard about how she was heating up—or failing to heat up—the soup. After setting our three places at the table, he returned to the kitchenette and stood next to her over the saucepan. She kept insisting the soup wasn't hot yet and he kept insisting it had to be—it didn't take all day to heat up a can of vegetable soup. This exchange was repeated four times, until his patience—if that is the word—ran out and he pulled the pot off the burner and, leaving Lil empty-handed at the stove, came into the dining room and poured the soup into the bowls and onto the place mats and over the table. Maybe because of his bad eyes, he didn't see the extent of the mess he'd made.

The soup was cold. Nobody said so. He probably didn't even notice.

Halfway through the silent meal he said, matter-of-factly, "This is the last chapter," but kept spooning soup into his lopsided mouth until his bowl was empty and his shirt looked as though he had been painting with the soup.

As I was leaving to go back to New York, he went into the bedroom and returned with a small package for me. A couple of brown paper bags had been savagely twisted about to accommodate the contents and then bound together with varying lengths of Scotch tape, most of which were coiled up on themselves like strands of DNA. I spotted the wrapping as his handiwork and I recognized his penmanship as well—with a Magic Marker he had written in uneven block letters across the top fold of the wrapping, "From a Father To a Son."

"Here," he said. "Take this home."

Downstairs in the car I tore off all the wrappings and found my grandfather's shaving mug.

4

I Have to Start Living Again

FROM the hotel later that afternoon I phoned Claire in London and my brother in Chicago and recounted what had happened at Meyerson's office, gave them the tentative date for the surgery, and told them about the plan to get a second opinion. But that evening, after having been out alone for a bowl of pasta I couldn't eat and then watching the Mets as though baseball were a game I couldn't fathom, I found that I was afraid to try to go to sleep without talking to someone and being consoled, if only by a presence at the other end of the line.

I phoned my friend Joanna Clark, who I figured might still be awake. Joanna was a Pole who had married an American, come to Princeton to live, succumbed to drink, divorced, collapsed, recovered, and, probably of all my friends, had endured the most torment over the course of her life. She could also be funny about the two of us. "I pollute you with fumes, I shower you with murky stories, I make foolish jokes in my broken English, and, really, you only want to have a little Eastern European chat. Well, nothing comes free. Some Poles are crazykins and I am one—harmless, I believe." At the very beginning of the war, in September 1939, her father had been killed by German artillery. "I don't remember my father at all," she had told me one evening when I'd stopped off in Princeton for dinner. I was on my regular trip up to New York from Philadelphia, where I was teaching at the University of Pennsylvania. In those years Joanna was usually already half-drunk when she picked me up in her car at the Junction train station, and her babble while driving—about Gombrowicz, Witkiewicz, Schulz, Konwicki—was alarmingly mythomaniacal, brilliantly eccentric, terrifically informative, and, to me, not unalluring. She was dour and sober-sounding about her father, however, as we wove back along the road into Princeton. "He was shot in the trench. Defending Warsaw. In fact, he was carried by his Jewish lieutenant. He was in a trench and he got it. He didn't die right away. He died in the hospital of a wound." "How old was he?" "He was very young. He was thirty-seven." "And so you have no recollection of him." "I was a baby. No, none. Except what I was told."

I looked up her number and dialed at just about the time I used to get her worrying, compulsive phone calls in the old days, back when, even after she'd hid her address book from herself so she wouldn't start phoning people, she fell victim to that mad telephonitis that goes together with drinking and dialed whosever number she could still remember. All I wanted was her ear—having fatherless, courageous, rejuvenated Joanna just listening to me might provide whatever it was *I* now needed at eleven-thirty at night to face putting my own father, at eighty-six, through a ten-hour operation, five lifeless days in bed, three or four months of convalescence, and all of it with no real certainty that it would do him a damn bit of good.

Eighty-six. Eighty-six kept coming in like a knell. I suppose in phoning Joanna I was conceding that even I knew you couldn't have a father forever.

She *was* still awake when I phoned, up waiting for a call from one of her "pigeons"—that's how she referred to the recovering addicts she looked after. At a local recovery program, whose meetings she attended regularly, she'd become surrogate mother to some five or six young girls trying to kick drugs. The girl she was waiting to hear from was moving out on a deadbeat boyfriend, who the night before, when she'd told him she was leaving, had bloodied her nose with one punch.

"Well," I said, "I've been involved in some unpleasantness myself. I'm another of your pigeons."

"What is it, Philip?"

"My father is ill."

"Oh, I'm sorry."

"He's facing a very bleak prospect. He has a big brain tumor. The doctor says it's been growing anywhere from five to ten years. They tell me he's going to be in desperate shape in a very short time. They're going to have to try to get it out. It's a terrible operation."

"Does he want it?"

"Want? No. But the alternative is to let it grow and take the consequences, and that could be grotesque. The problem is that for an eighty-six-year-old man, even if he survives—and the doctor claims they survive three times out of four—the recovery will be a nightmare. He'll never be himself again, though maybe he can be something close to himself."

"So much closer," Joanna said, "than with that thing in his head."

"With the thing he's doomed. It's a helluva choice, but there is no choice."

"With the end of life it always gets that way."

"He's been remarkable. I don't mean in some unusual way, I mean in his own mundane, bullheaded way. His strength amazes me. But what fuels the strength is what makes the situation so awful: the last thing he wants to do is to die."

"It makes you sit and cry," Joanna said.

"Well, I don't cry all the time—mostly I seem to sit in this hotel and do absolutely nothing. Then I think, 'Why am I sitting here when he's over there?' and I drive to Elizabeth and take him for a walk. Tomorrow is going to be the first day that he's really alone. But I don't have it in me to go over again. I need a day off."

"He needs to be alone once in a while, too," she said.

"So there it is," I said. "Anybody's helplessness is difficult, a child's, a friend's, but the helplessness of an old person who once had such vigor . . ."

"Especially of a father."

"Yes. He's fought such a long"—and the adjective that came to me was not one I'd ever thought to associate with his efforts, however much I'd always respected his gumption— "long, long distinguished battle." The word's utter aptness took me by surprise.

"What's good," Joanna said, "is that he has this choice, that he is involved with the choice."

"The choice isn't real, however. The alternative is unacceptable. The choice would be to jump out of the window."

"And you admire that in him, that jumping out of a window for him is an impossible act."

"Admire it and envy it. When I was on the bottom last year, I thought about jumping every day."

"I remember. I had my own stupid times when I thought it was a solution."

"Not him. He doesn't even have it as a fantasy solution. I was over there today to get him to the doctor. I had to drive him across poor, poor, poor old Newark. He knows every street corner. Where buildings are destroyed, he remembers the buildings that were there. You mustn't forget anything— that's the inscription on his coat of arms. To be alive, to him, is to be made of memory—to him if a man's not made of memory, he's made of nothing. 'See those steps, 1917 I was sitting on that stoop with Al Borak—you remember Al Borak? He had the furniture store—I was sitting there with Al the day America went into the war. It was springtime, April or May, I forget. There's where your great-aunt had the candy store. That's where my brother Morris had his first shoe store. Gee, is that still there?' he says. On and on. We passed his school, Thirteenth Avenue School, where he was the teacher's favorite. 'My teacher, she loved me. "Herman," she said—' On he goes all the way across the city."

"Well, life."

"You can say that again. We get to the hospital and he says, 'What a blessing for the city of Newark when they built this hospital.' So he's thinking not about his tumor but about the city of Newark. *He's* the bard of Newark. That really rich Newark stuff isn't my story—it's his."

"He's a good citizen."

"I drive him around, I sit with him, I eat with him, and all the time I'm thinking that the real work, the invisible, huge job that he did all his life, that that whole generation of Jews did, was making themselves American. The *best* citizens. Europe stopped with him."

"Oh, not entirely. He hasn't given up Europe entirely," she said. "The Europe in him is his survivorship. These are people who will never give up. But they are better than Europe, too. There was gratitude in them and idealism. That basic decency."

That was why I'd called Joanna—that was what she shared with my father and what I prized in both of them: survivorship, survivorhood, survivalism.

"Did I ever tell you what happened when he was mugged a couple of years ago? He could have got himself killed."

"No. Tell me."

"A black kid about fourteen approached him with a gun on

a side street leading to their little temple. It was the middle of
the afternoon. My father had been at the temple office helping
them with mailing or something and he was coming home.
The black kids prey on the elderly Jews in his neighborhood
even in broad daylight. They bicycle in from Newark, he tells
me, take their money, laugh, and go home. 'Get in the bushes,'
he tells my father. 'I'm not getting in any bushes,' my father
says. 'You can have whatever you want, and you don't need
that piece to get it. You can put the piece away.' The kid lowers
the gun and my father gives him his wallet. 'Take all the money,'
my father says, 'but if the wallet's of no value to you, I wouldn't
mind it back.' The kid takes the money, gives back the wallet,
and he runs. And you know what my father does? He calls
across the street, 'How much did you get?' And the kid is
obedient—he *counts* it for him. 'Twenty-three dollars,' the kid
says. 'Good,' my father tells him—'now don't go out and spend
it on crap.'"

Joanna laughed. "Well, he's not guilty, your father. Of
course he treats him like a son. He knows that the Jews in Bia-
lystok were not responsible for the New England slave trade."

"It's that—it's more. He doesn't experience powerlessness
in the usual way."

"Yes, he's oblivious to it," she said. "He won't give in to it.
It makes for terrific insensitivity but also for terrific guts."

"Yes, what goes into survival isn't always pretty. He got a
lot of mileage out of never recognizing the differences among
people. All my life I have been trying to tell him that people
are different one from the other. My mother understood this
in a way that he didn't. Couldn't. This is what I used to long
for in him, some of her forbearance and tolerance, this simple
recognition that people are different and that the difference is
legitimate. But he couldn't grasp it. They all had to work the
same way, want the same way, be dutiful in the same way, and
whoever did it different was *meshugge*—crazy."

"I understand what *meshugge* is, Philip, even if I am a Pole."

"Of course he's not the first person to have such thoughts.
But he had his own particular Jewish style of insisting on his
absolutely totalistic notions of what is good and what is right,
and as a kid it really used to get me down. Everybody has to
do it exactly the same way. The way he does it."

"Well, you are relentless, too, you know. It's in you, too, a certain relentlessness that you got from him. You, too, are not always so tactful when you think you are right."

"So Claire tells me."

"You've forgiven him. You've forgiven him that relentlessness and that tactlessness, that wanting to make everybody over in the same mold. All children pay a price, and the forgiveness entails forgiveness also for the price you paid. You talk about him in a very reconciled way."

"I should hope so. Since my mother died, I've got awfully close to him. It would have been easier the other way."

"It wouldn't. The death of a parent, it's horrible. When my mother died," she said, "I had no idea that I would feel that way. Half, or more, of life goes. You feel poorer, you know: somebody who knew me all those years . . ."

"I sat with him and with the neurosurgeon today, said to be the best in New Jersey, a very kind fellow about forty, forty-five years old, a puffy, genial Jewish boy, got good grades, not very athletic—to look at him, I wouldn't trust him to carve my Thanksgiving turkey." I told her how the doctor had asked me if I had any questions and I had told him that my father had the questions, and how my father had sat there reading the list of questions, and how the doctor had showed him, on the model of the brain, the crazy thing he was going to do. "He is going to chop his head open, pick his brain up, and cut away inside his skull with a laser, with a beam of light—and I thought, 'I know where people's weaknesses come from, we all know that, but where is the source of the strength? Where does the strength come from in two men facing this situation this way?'"

"From self-esteem," she said. "They think well of themselves."

"Is that it? I don't know. I'm sure this is all very elementary but it's got me stumped tonight. You don't need surreal art, you know. This is surreal to me. Those two men sitting there, facing what they were facing."

"And where is Claire?" Joanna asked.

"In London. At home. She gets upset when I call. She's said she wants to come back to help but I told her to stay put and do what she has to do there. In a way it's actually better alone, moping about by myself, rather than having her here to drag

down, too. I'd just drive back from Jersey and sit and stare at
her—better to sit and stare by myself. It's better to be concentrated on what has to be done. Though all the concentration
isn't so wonderful either. I can't read, God knows I can't write
—I can't even watch a stupid baseball game. I absolutely cannot think. I can't do a thing."

"You don't have to. That's also your father," she said,
laughing at me now. "You don't have to work all the time."

"It'll be strange and lonely without him. And who understood that?"

"Well, you don't have to understand everything, either."

"I don't understand anything."

I took a shower later, repeating those words. I clipped my
toenails, sitting at the edge of the bed—the first thing in days
I'd been able to concentrate on other than him—repeating
those words. Four words again, very, very basic stuff, but that
night, after Joanna had done me the favor of hearing me out,
it sounded like all the wisdom in the world to me. I didn't
understand anything. As I'd driven back to Manhattan that
afternoon with my grandfather's shaving mug clutched in one
hand, certainly nothing could have been clearer to me than
how little I knew. It wasn't that I hadn't understood that the
connection to him was convoluted and deep—what I hadn't
known was how deep deep can be.

I slept fitfully till four in the morning, then I turned on the
light, got out of bed, and looked at the pictures of his brain
again, understanding nothing about that either.

Had it been the MRI of Yorick's brain that Hamlet had
been looking at, even he might have been speechless.

A few days later we got the second opinion, and my father preferred it to the first. Vallo Benjamin, a neurosurgeon at NYU
Hospital in Manhattan, had agreed to fit us in at the request of
David Krohn, who had described him to me as "world-class."
Benjamin was an authoritative, worldly man of about my age,
a smartly dressed, dark-eyed foreigner, virilely good-looking in
the forthright school of Picasso, whom he resembled. He listened to the medical history my father recounted, asked if he
got headaches or dizzy spells, then touched the point of a pin
to the two sides of my father's face to determine how much

feeling he'd lost on the bad side. Benjamin looked to be scrutinizing him very carefully as my father answered all the questions, asked his own questions, and waited to hear if a stay of execution might be granted and his sentence lifted, leaving him free to feel as though he were forty again. "I feel like forty" was something he'd told everyone, even on days when it wasn't true, until just a few months back.

Benjamin stuck the MRI pictures of the brain up on the lighted screen behind his desk and told me to come around and take a look at them with him. My father sat docilely beside Lil, holding in his hand his piece of paper with the list of questions, while the doctor, speaking so softly that only I could hear, traced a finger over the pictures to show me the extensiveness of the tumor. Strictly speaking, he said, it wasn't a brain tumor. Probably it had begun as a tumor on a facial nerve and grown to where now it was not only pushing against the brain stem but extruding through the bone at the back of the nose. Meyerson had estimated that it would take eight to ten hours to operate and had called the operation routine. Now I was told that it would more likely take thirteen or fourteen hours and that the operation involved working where all the arteries and nerves are massed together—"tricky terrain," the doctor said. "Are you telling me it's impossible?" I asked him. "Not at all," he snapped back, as though I had impugned his expertise. "It can be done, of course."

When we sat back down, my father said to Benjamin, "Doctor, I have a friend in the building. His brother-in-law had a tumor like this and they radiated it. Used radiation and it went away. I'm not saying that would solve everything, be permanent. But if I could just have another couple of years . . ."

"Mr. Roth," he replied, very gently, "I don't know if radiation would be effective until I know the kind of tumor we're dealing with. To know that, I need, in addition to these pictures, a CAT scan to give us a picture of the skull as well as the situation with the brain. I then need a biopsy of the tumor. Yours could be one of three kinds of tumors, and only after a biopsy can I determine which it is and what to suggest to you, sir."

"I see," replied my father glumly.

"The biopsy is done with a needle," the doctor told him.

"It's a procedure that takes no more than an hour. I would recommend that you come into the hospital overnight so that we can watch you afterward. You would go home the next day."

"Where do you stick the needle?" my father asked, his tone indicating that nobody was going to torture him without explaining beforehand.

My father's unembellished style and the fight that was obviously still in him despite his age and all he was up against seemed somewhat to beguile the sophisticated neurosurgeon and even to touch some chord of personal sympathy. Several times, in recounting the history of his illness, my father had veered off into an anecdote out of his Newark childhood some seventy-five years earlier, a narrative whose subterranean message appeared to be that he had learned to be realistic on Rutgers Street and was prepared for whatever befell him now. He and life went way, way back together, and he wanted Benjamin to know that too.

To each story—whether about standing up to the Irish ruffians from "down neck" in Newark or working after school in his cousin's blacksmith shop—the doctor listened with nearly as much curiosity as impatience, and he kindly waited to steer him back to the business at hand until my father had illustrated his point. Then he explained to him in detail how the needle would be inserted up through the roof of the mouth, the tissue removed from the tumor with the needle, and so on, step by step.

"And radiation?" my father asked again, a little desperately this time.

"The biopsy will determine if it is the kind of tumor that responds to radiation. There is always a chance, though given the size of your tumor and the length of time you probably have had it, not a great one."

"Understand," my father said, "I'm talking about just another three or four years . . ."

The doctor nodded; he understood very well. The original request for a couple more years had, in a matter of minutes, been extended to three or four, I noticed. My father was obviously coming to trust and even to imbue with a certain divine might this doctor who was at once so much more patrician and potent-looking than *haimisher*, heavyset Dr. Meyerson, who had proposed to do rather more than stick a needle up through the roof of his mouth. It occurred to me that if we were all to sit and talk together in Benjamin's office for another day or two, my father would eventually overcome his fear of calling down even worse misery upon himself by appearing sinfully greedy and proclaim to this doctor what had to be in his heart, which was that he wanted not just three or four years more, but to tackle the whole damn thing all over again: "I raised myself up out of the immigrant streets without even a high school education, I never knuckled under, never broke the law, never lost my courage or said 'I quit.' I was a faithful husband, a loyal American, a proud Jew, I gave two wonderful boys every opportunity I myself never had, and what I am demanding is only what I deserve—another eighty-six years! Why," he would ask him, "should a man die at all?" And of course, he would have been right to ask. It's a good question.

"A needle," my father was saying, "sticking a needle—is that safe?"

"Generally it's a very safe procedure," the doctor told him. "You'll feel nothing. You will have a general anesthetic. Afterward, for two or three days, your mouth will be quite sore but that will go away."

"And then," my father said, "if it's the right tumor, radiation . . . ?"

The doctor raised his two hands in a sign of helplessness, looking for the first time not like a world-class neurosurgeon but a bargaining businessman in an Oriental bazaar. "It's not wholly impossible and I can't rule it out entirely, but right now I don't know."

"What are the effects of radiation?" my father asked.

"If you were a young person, you might be affected about thirty years later."

"But one thing is certain, if I understand correctly—you don't want to operate."

"I wouldn't and I couldn't. I have to know first exactly what I'd find inside."

When we left the doctor's office, I suggested that instead of his going directly home, we take the elevator downstairs to the hospital cafeteria and, while the consultation was fresh in our minds, go over what the doctor had said.

We found a table for four—with us also was my nephew Seth, who lives in Jersey City with his wife and who had driven Lil and my father from Elizabeth and was going to drive them back. Seth had sat out in the waiting room during the consultation, and partly for his information but mainly to be sure that my father hadn't misunderstood, in the cafeteria I went over everything again, emphasizing that though the doctor had left open the possibility of the tumor being susceptible to treatment by radiation, that wasn't the likely eventuality.

"I like this man," my father said when I had finished. "I'm impressed by this man. The other guy just wanted to go in and cut. This man wants all the information first. I'm impressed by him. Weren't you?" he asked Lil. "Impressed by him?"

"Yes," Lil said. "He seemed very nice."

"Were you, Phil?"

"Yes. I'm sure he's an excellent doctor. David assured me he was."

"That's right. And he said wait. What is he?" my father asked me. "A Jew?"

"I believe so. I think a Persian Jew."

"Good-looking man," my father said.

There were crowds outside the elevator on the main floor, and pushing through the busy hospital lobby, I held him by one arm while Seth took the other. "I have to start living again," my father suddenly told me. "I can't hole up in that apartment anymore. I can't be a hermit."

"Absolutely," I said.

"I have to go back to the Y. The cantor from the synagogue came to see me—did I tell you? Two men from the synagogue and the cantor. They'd heard about the tumor. They said they'll drive me every day to the Y."

"Good. Go."

"I didn't know I had so many friends," he said.

"A reprieve," I thought, "and let him enjoy it. Enjoy it yourself," I thought, "if only till the next decision has to be made tomorrow." And so that night I managed to watch the Mets game with some pleasure, concentrating, like any ordinary run-of-the-mill escapist, on Darling's three-hitter and McReynolds's home run rather than on my father and the tumor that was still there inside his head despite the Mets' victory, blindly, massively there, and that, if left there, would in the end be as merciless as a blind mass of anything on the march.

Two years earlier, on October 14, 1986, I unfortunately had to be in London while the Mets were playing Houston in game five of the play-offs. It was eleven-fifteen London time when I phoned him in Elizabeth, and my father was ecstatic. I'd got him to take an interest in the Mets only that spring, when he was laid low for about a month by a debilitating malaise that nobody could diagnose and that probably had had something to do with the brain tumor. His strength deserted him almost completely, he had no appetite for food, and sometimes when he got up to walk he listed from side to side. I'd flown back from London to find out what was wrong, and during the weeks I'd stayed on in New York, I had tried to divert his attention from this unexplained illness by getting him interested in the Mets, who were on the way to winning the pennant. I would come over some evenings for dinner and watch the game with him, and when I went out to a couple of games at Shea Stadium, I'd told him to keep his eyes open and see if he could spot me in the stands. By the time I left his symptoms had all but disappeared and he was nearly fit again, and also very much a fan—and a fan for the first time, really, since I was a small boy and he used to take my brother and me out to Ruppert Stadium in Newark to see the old Triple-A Newark Bears play a Sunday doubleheader against our rivals from across the marshes, the Jersey City Giants.

When I wound up in London during the playoffs, I phoned him each night to find out about the games. I loved his exuberant descriptions.

"Mets won," he told me as though it had been a triumph for him as well. "Twelfth inning. A helluva game. Gooden against Ryan. Strawberry hit a home run. Then they tied it. *Helluva* game."

"Whoa. Slow down," I said. "When did Strawberry hit the home run?"

"In the sixth. They won in the twelfth. Backman hits a ball too hot for the third baseman. Couldn't hold on to it. He got on first. Then the pitcher for the Houston Astronauts threw a wild pitch to first and he went to second. So there was no

sense pitching to Hernandez and he put him on. Then Carter
came up. He is 0 for twenty-two or twenty-three. And he hit
the ball back up the middle, Backman scored, and that was it.
Mets won two to one."

"Great. How long ago did it end?" I asked.

"About half an hour ago. Hey, did you hear about your
friend Wiesel?"

"Yeah, somebody told me about it." The novelist Elie
Wiesel, whom I had known slightly years ago, had won the
Nobel Peace Prize that day.

"A hundred and twenty thousand bucks, plus the honor,"
my father said. "So this year he's the third Jew to win one."

"Is that right? Who are the other two?"

"This guy Cohen and this Italian-Jewish girl named Levy-
something."

"Well," I said, "it's a great day for the Jews and a great day
for the Mets. Mets two, Houston one—Jews three, Gentiles
nothing. Now they're going down to Houston, right? And
play tomorrow?"

"Right. They just have to win one," he said.

"Well," I said, "stranger things have happened than losing
two in a row."

"No," he said, "they can't drop two, they're too good. Today was a *helluva* game."

"If it goes to seven they'll have to face Scott again," I said.

"Phil, they'll beat him. First of all, he's pitching for the second time after three days' rest. Or is it four days' rest? There was
the rain-out, then today, Wednesday—it'll be three days' rest."

"Okay," I said, "you say they'll beat him, I believe you. I'll
speak to you tomorrow. And congratulations on Wiesel. You
Jews ought to be proud."

"Ah, cut that crap out, will ya?" he said, but he was laughing
when he hung up.

And laughing when I called the next night. "Well, what happened?" I said.

"It's still on. You wouldn't believe it. Thirteenth inning."

"My God."

"They were behind three one in the ninth but it's now the
thirteenth inning and it's tied score. I'm watching it now. I
didn't even eat."

"One game's closer than the other," I said.

"It's beautiful," he said.

"Well, I'm going to sleep," I said. "It's eleven-thirty here. I figured it would be over by now because they started at three."

"No. It's two out in the top of the thirteenth inning."

"Who's pitching for the Mets?"

"McDowell is pitching and Anderson is pitching for the Houstons."

"Well, I'm going to have to go to sleep," I said.

But at midnight, after having brushed my teeth and gone to bed, I got out of bed and came down to the kitchen to call him again. I wasn't just calling because of the Mets. "What happened?" I asked him.

"Phil? Oh, my God, it's *unbelievable*."

"Still playing?"

"The Mets went ahead four three just after you hung up. Strawberry—and I think Dykstra got him around. And then this guy hit a home run in the Houston bottom of the fourteenth. And now it's the top of the fifteenth. It's four four and there's some fat Mexican pitching."

"Oh, yeah, that very attractive fellow."

"The Mets have got this very young shortstop up, who can only strike out. . . . No—pop-up. He popped up. Well, that isn't a strikeout. Hey, I'm giving you this pitch by pitch to London, it's going to cost you a fortune."

But pitch by pitch I was enjoying it enormously, maybe even more than if I had been there. "Go ahead, Herm. I'm a rich man. Pitch by pitch. Who's up?"

"They got Hernandez and Carter coming up. It's been an unbelievable game, but it was three nothing going into the ninth. The Mets had only got two hits. You know something? It's almost time for the Red Sox to get started. That's supposed to start at eight o'clock and here it is seven already. Upps, Keith struck out."

"He struck out? This game's going to go on all night."

He laughed loudly. "I think so."

"Okay. I'll give you a ring tomorrow to see what happened. Here's hopin'."

"Don't you worry, they'll win. You just get some sleep," he said.

At seven the next morning his time—noon London time—he phoned to tell me the results.

"Phil?"

"Yes."

"It's Dad. You've never seen anything like it. Mets won in the sixteenth."

"Great. I was going to phone you a little later."

"I only just got up. I knew you'd be wondering. They were down three in the ninth. Did I tell you this last night, about the ninth?"

"Don't worry. Tell me everything."

"Get this. They get three runs in the ninth. They go ahead four three. That pitcher is in there."

"Kerfeld, for Houston?"

"No. For the Mets. I can never think of his name."

"McDowell."

"No. The other guy."

"Orosco."

"Yeah, Morosco. The Mets go ahead four three. Then Houston gets a home run, ties it up four four. In the sixteenth inning the Mets get three runs. They go ahead seven four. Houston gets up. Guy gets on base and the next guy gets a home run. Seven six. And then Kevin Bass strikes out and they won the game seven six."

"So they won the series."

"They won the series."

"How'd the Mets get the three runs?"

"Dykstra. I'm telling you! After Morosco gave up the runs in the sixteenth, Hernandez came out to the mound—I just read this in the paper—and you know what he said to him? 'If you throw another fastball, I'll kill you.'"

"I wonder if he would have."

"*I* would have," my father said, laughing, and sounding as though whatever had floored him in the spring was a fluke and he was going to live a thousand years.

Our reprieve lasted about twenty-four hours. Then the brain tumor took charge again.

For the next month and a half nothing happened and nothing was done—none of us knew what exactly *to* do. Since the first neurosurgeon had said that the tumor would not respond to radiation and the second had indicated that the chances radiation would help were small, the biopsy began to seem an ordeal that we had no business forcing on him, particularly as I had learned by asking around that it could be very painful and, given where the needle was to be blindly inserted, not without some risk. And if the result was only to present us with the option we already dreaded—an operation that could leave him worse off rather than better—what was gained by subjecting him to it?

To make things more difficult, only a few days after our consultation Dr. Benjamin left America for over a month to lecture in Europe, and there was no way that I could air my doubts with him until his return on June 20. He had given us the name of someone to whom he was willing to entrust the biopsy, but though my father went back over to New York to see that doctor—this time accompanied by my brother, who had flown in from Chicago for a week to be with him and to spell me a little—we all felt there were too many unanswered questions to proceed before Dr. Benjamin's return, if at all.

And my father was hardly equipped to make the decision to go ahead on his own. He'd conducted himself gallantly with the two brain surgeons, but now, caught in the vise of their differing proposals, he succumbed to a wild helplessness. He began to say things to me that didn't make much sense, and then for longer periods said nothing or suddenly, unprovoked, lashed out at Lil so uncontrollably that even he was startled afterward by his vehemence and meekly apologized. Apologizing to Lil would not have seemed like an unfortunate development had it not signaled demoralization rather than remorse. He repeated to me, to my brother, to everyone, that he didn't want a biopsy or an operation through the back of his head or the roof of his mouth—all he wanted was what he had wanted from the start: to be able to see his food and to read his paper and, as he put it, to "navigate" on his own. Why couldn't they just remove the cataract from his good eye and give him back his sight? I found a draft of a letter to the ophthalmologist on the dining room table one day when I came over for lunch: "Dear Dr. Krohn, I want my sight back. I want my eye fixed. That's what I want. Herman Roth"

Of course, as the days passed and he dangled impotently in despair, I could not forget that Dr. Meyerson, who had never struck me as a fool, had warned us that things were going to get worse "in a relatively short time" unless something was done. Meyerson had told us that to remove the tumor he would go in through the back of the skull and take eight to ten hours to get it out, and Benjamin had told us that to remove the tumor he would go up through an incision in the roof of the mouth—following something like the route of the biopsy needle—and extract it in thirteen or fourteen hours, and my father was telling me that the one prospect was as horrifying as the other and that submitting to either was unthinkable. "All I want is my sight back. I want to see!"

In bed I'd think, "Listen to him. Listen to what he is saying. He is telling you what he wants and it's very simple. He wants his eye fixed. He's not a child—he's made it through eighty-six years on his own kind of wisdom, so honor that wisdom and just give him what it is he wants." But then, in the next minute, it would seem to me that by yielding to his unrealistic appraisal of the crisis I was only trying to evade the hard choice . . . and so around again I went, unconvinced that there was any reward commensurate with the risks involved in surgery, yet conscious that if nothing was done, *in a relatively short time* his condition could deteriorate horribly.

One morning, after my brother had flown back to Chicago, I made a call to Palm Beach, to Sandy Kuvin, a doctor cousin of ours. Over the years, at my request, he had been checking in on my father when my father was vacationing in Florida, and he had given us sensible advice about such health problems as had cropped up for my father down there. Sandy was a couple of years older than I, a father of three college kids and a vigorous supporter of Israel, who spent nearly half his working year at a medical research clinic in Jerusalem for which he'd raised the endowment and which was named for him. I'd made a tour of the place with one of his staff the last time I'd been in Jerusalem. We'd all grown up in the same part of Newark, we'd gone to the same high school in the forties, and though he and I had only met up again recently—when I began visiting my father in Florida each winter—our annual evening together at a local restaurant and our afternoons at his airy house on a Palm Beach inlet had been friendly and enjoyable, each of us getting a kick out of seeing how far the other fellow had traveled from the halls of Weequahic High.

After I explained the situation and described to him my indecision, Sandy said to me, "He's an old man, Philip—he's lived a long life and by now that tumor is growing pretty slowly. In ten years or so it's caused no more damage than the hearing loss in one ear and the facial paralysis on one side of his face. Maybe some of his headaches come from it, and it may be that when he walks some of his uncertainty isn't just from the bad vision but from this thing pressing on the eighth nerve. But the damage hasn't been ruinous and it may never be."

"But the damage you speak of has all happened in the last six months. What's going to happen in the next six months?"

"Nobody knows. Maybe nothing," he said, "and maybe everything. If he wants his vision, give him his vision, and if he has it for as little as a month before he dies, well, he will at least have had what he wanted for a month. Maybe he'll be lucky and have it for longer."

"That's what I've been thinking—when I'm not thinking the opposite. Doc, will you do me a favor? Will you telephone him? Don't let on that we spoke. Call him out of the blue and let him tell you his story and then tell him what you told me— that it's growing slowly and to forget it. Because he's really headed for the bottom if something doesn't lift him soon. He might just keel over and call it quits out of sheer emotional agony."

Within half an hour my father phoned me, sounding vigorous and full of bounce, as though wholly reempowered. Chinning himself up on life *again*.

"Guess who just invited me to his daughter's wedding in December?"

"Who?"

"Sandy Kuvin called from Palm Beach. You know what he said? I told him what's happening and he said, 'Herman, forget it. You've had it for ten years and the pace that it's growing at is so slow that you can have it for another ten years before it does any more harm.' Kuvin told me I could be killed by ten other things before the tumor gets any larger." With something that sounded like real delight, he enumerated for me the potential killers. "I could get a heart attack, I could get a stroke, I could get cancer—before that thing kills me, a hundred other things could finish me off."

I had to laugh. "Well, that's great news."

"Kuvin says forget it and get on with my life."

"Did he? Then maybe that's what you ought to do."

"His Michelle, his daughter, is getting married on—here, I wrote it down—on Tuesday, December 27, 1988. At their house. Eleven-thirty A.M. He wants you to come to the wedding, too. With me and Lil."

December was seven months off. Did that or did that not constitute "a relatively short time"? "If you go, I'll go," I said.

"Phil, I want my eyesight back. I want Dr. Krohn to fix my eye. Enough farting around with this other thing."

5

Maybe Ingrid
Can Look After Me for Good

B UT a week after Benjamin returned from Europe, my
father went in for the biopsy, not as a prelude to surgery—
by that time we were all firmly decided against surgery—but
on the possibility, however slight, that the biopsy would disclose a type of tumor that radiation could shrink. I didn't see
how, in good conscience, we could simply ignore the tumor
until we were sure there was nothing to treat it other than
the butchery that was unacceptable to all of us. I dreaded the
thought that the needle that was to be stuck up through the
roof of his mouth could damage something inside his skull,
but I allowed myself to be convinced by Benjamin that Dr.
Persky, who would perform the procedure, was as skilled a
practitioner as we could find.

The super of his building drove my father and Lil over to
Manhattan to the hospital, where I met them and, after an interminable bureaucratic delay, got him registered and up to his
room. There he was given some supper; to my surprise, he was
able to absorb himself completely in the meal. Then Lil left,
and I took him down to be interviewed by a young resident to
whom he told the history of his illness as well as several brief
anecdotes out of his childhood. Back in his room we got the
pajamas out of his overnight case, and after he had been to the
bathroom I helped him into the bed. He was exhausted, and
his face, with the patch off the blind eye on the drooping side,
looked dreadful. Yet he seemed, if anything, less dejected than
he'd been during the period when nothing was being done.
There was a new ordeal to face, and facing ordeals did not allow for hopelessness. It called forth instead that amalgam of
defiance and resignation with which he had learned to confront the humiliations of old age.

At the registration desk downstairs, he had been told that it
cost $3.50 a day to watch the TV set in the room and he had
refused to pay it. When I saw him on the bed staring at the

ceiling with the one working eye, I told him that I would pay
for it. "Come on," I said. "I'm a sport—I'll blow you to a
night's television."

"Three and a half dollars for television? They're out of their
minds."

"We can watch the ball game. The Mets are playing the
Reds."

"Not for three fifty," he replied adamantly. "The hell with it."

"It beats lying on your bed like that, worrying about tomorrow."

"I'm not worrying. I don't allow myself the luxury. You go
home."

"It's only seven. You can watch *MacNeil/Lehrer*."

"Don't worry about me. I'm fine. You get something to eat
and go home to the hotel and watch the Mets."

In the chair beside his bed I began to read the late edition of
the *Post*. "You want me to read you the news?" I asked.

"No."

"We should have thought to bring a radio. You could have
listened to the game on the radio."

"I don't need a radio."

Fifteen minutes later he had fallen asleep and within an hour
it looked as though he might well be out for the night, and
this before the nurse had even given him the sleeping pill that
I had asked the resident to order for him. His teeth were lying
on the bedside table where he'd left them. I put them into the
plastic dish the hospital provided for dentures and, capping it,
put the dish away in the table drawer. These teeth were new
ones, made for the lower right side of his mouth. Because of
the facial disfigurement, the dentist was having a lot of trouble
fitting them precisely; only two days earlier, out taking a walk
with me, my father had yanked them from his mouth—"These
goddamn things! Too many teeth!"—but then when he had
them in his hand he didn't know what to do with them. We
were crossing North Broad Street at the time and the light was
about to turn against us. "Here," I'd said, "give them to me,"
and I took the dentures and stuck them in my pocket. To my
astonishment, having them in my own hand was utterly satisfying. Far from feeling squeamish or repelled, as I continued
along, guiding him by one arm up onto the curb, I was amused

by the rightness of it, as though we'd now officially become partners in a comical duo—as though I'd assumed the role of straight man to a clown whose ill-fitting false teeth invariably brought the house down, a joke on a par with Durante's nose or Eddie Cantor's eyes. By taking the dentures, slimy saliva and all, and dumping them in my pocket, I had, quite inadvertently, stepped across the divide of physical estrangement that, not so unnaturally, had opened up between us once I'd stopped being a boy.

I waited beside the bed for another few minutes, and then, as he still gave no sign of awakening, I quietly left him. At the nurse's desk I stopped to find out when he was due to go down to the operating room the next day. Then from a telephone booth at the end of the corridor I phoned my brother in Chicago.

"I hope we're not doing this just to be doing something," I said. "I get that feeling, ever so slightly."

"How is he?"

"Well, this, like everything, he's going to meet head-on. Won't put up with any distraction. They charge three and a half bucks to watch the TV in the room and he told the poor overworked bastard down at the registration office that it was highway robbery."

My brother laughed. "He is a stubborn prick, all right."

"Yeah, well, in the circumstances it may not turn out to be such a bad thing to be a stubborn prick. I'll speak to you tomorrow when he comes up from the operating room. He goes down around noon."

"First Avenue and Thirtieth Street," I told the driver the next day. "University Hospital."

"Good-looking broad you came out of that hotel with," the driver said as we started crosstown. Just before hailing the cab, I'd been talking under the hotel canopy to the wife of an old friend, whom I'd run into as I was leaving the Essex House on the way downtown to the hospital.

"Yes?"

"You jump her bones?" he asked me.

"Pardon?"

"You fuck her?"

In the rearview mirror I saw a pair of green eyes whose truc-
ulent glare was even more startling than the question. If I
hadn't already lost time talking out in front of the hotel, I
would have decided against entrusting my life to those eyes and
got out of the cab, but as I wanted to be sure to be at the hospital to see my father before he went in to the operating room,
I said, "As a matter of fact, no. One of my friends does. She's
his wife."

"What difference does that make? He'd fuck your wife."

"No, this particular friend wouldn't, though I understand it
happens." I understood because I'd done it myself on a few
occasions but, unlike the driver, I wasn't putting all my cards
on the table right off. We had a ways to go yet.

"It happens all the time, buddy," he told me.

I didn't think cutting him was a good idea, so I replied,
lightly enough, "Well, it's good to talk to a realist."

He answered me with undisguised contempt. "Is that what
they call it?"

Registering for the first time the buildings out the window,
I realized that he had turned in the wrong direction on Park
and was driving uptown. "Hey!" I said and reminded him
where we were going.

To correct his error he decided to proceed all the way east to
the F.D.R. Drive and then "shoot" south. This entailed going
even farther in the wrong direction to get onto the drive.

I'd allowed myself far more time than was necessary to get
to the hospital by eleven-thirty, but now, because of a tie-up at
the entrance to the drive, it was already after eleven before the
taxi had even begun to edge toward the heavy flow of south-
bound traffic.

"You a doctor?" he asked, fixing me, I saw in the mirror,
with that warlike look.

"Yes," I said.

"What kind?"

"Take a guess."

"Head," he said.

"That's right."

"Psychiatrist," he said.

"That's right."

"At University Hospital."

"No, up in Connecticut."

"You head of the clinic?"

"Do I look like the head of the clinic?"

"Yeah," he said authoritatively.

"No," I said, "just one of the staff doctors. I'm content with that."

"You're smart—you don't go chasing the buck."

I found myself studying him as though I were indeed a professional whose interest exceeded that of an ordinary, transient passenger's. The man was a mastodon, and though the taxi was a full-size sedan, he overflowed his half of the front seat and rose to a fraction of an inch of the ceiling—and in his hands the wheel was a tiny infant, an infant he was throttling. Of his face all I could see in the mirror were those eyes, which looked as though, when they jumped out of his head, they'd be as capable as his hands of ending your life. His aura was even more menacing than his opening remark had suggested, and I didn't like the idea of "shooting" down the drive with him, especially since it was clear—and not only from his having turned the wrong way almost right off—that his attention was targeted on something more compelling than taking me where I wanted to go.

"You know something, Doc," he said, swinging suddenly, with no lack of daring, into the fast lane going south, "my old man's in his grave now without his four front teeth. I knocked 'em out of his fucking mouth for him."

"You didn't like him."

"He was a shit-heel and a failure and he wanted me to fail, too. Misery loves company. He used to get my older brother to beat me up on the street. My older brother beat me up and my old man never stopped him. So one day when I was twenty I went up to him and knocked his fucking teeth out and I said, 'You know what that's for? For never protecting me against Bobby.' I didn't go to his funeral even. But a lot of children don't go to their parents' funeral, do they?" In a voice all at once hollowly, defensively hangdog, he added, "I'm not the first."

In the mirror the eyes that hid nothing brutal or bellicose were waiting on my response.

"You're not the first," I assured him.

"My mother is no better," he said, and "mother" he expectorated, as though it were not a word but something putrid that he'd bit into. "She called me up crying that he was dead and I said, 'Yeah, go ahead, cry for the great hero.' And I told her what a stupid bastard she was."

"You had a rough time of it, didn't you?"

The purity of the paranoia that flared up in those eyes made me think, *light bouncing off the blade of a knife*. But he had me wrong if he believed I was an ironist of the sort who, like his father, needed to go to his grave minus four front teeth. I was a psychiatrist, I did not stoop to judgments, and that, fortunately, seemed to sink in soon enough. He was by no means stupid but, boy, was he lacking in trust. By having failed to protect him from Bobby, his late father had unleashed upon the world one very skeptical younger son.

"Yeah," he replied in a sad voice, "you can call it rough." But butting the air with his head, he added angrily, "I survived."

"You sure have."

Then he astonished me. I would have been no more surprised had he raised a teacup from the seat beside him and, with his pinky pointing politely, daintily taken a little sip. "Doc, I'm insecure."

"You?" Incredulous, I let him have it. "What the hell are you talking about? You knocked your father's teeth down his throat, you told your mother off when she was in tears—this is your cab you're driving, isn't it?"

"Yeah. I got two."

"*Two*—why, you're as secure as they come."

"Am I?" this violent bastard asked me.

"Seems so to me."

"You're good to me, Doc—I'm taking a buck off the fare. You shouldn't have to pay for my mistake." Swinging from the drive onto Thirty-fourth Street, he grew still more magnanimous. "I'm turning the meter off right now and taking another buck off the top."

"If you like. That's very kind of you."

I wondered if I hadn't overdone it. I looked in the mirror expecting to find that he was ready to kill me for calling him kind. But no, he *liked* it. This guy is human, I thought, in the worst sense of the word.

In front of the hospital, when I hopped out of the cab, I was a good psychiatrist and gave him the only advice I thought he could actually follow. "Keep punchin'," I told him.

"Hey, you too, Doc," he said, and the face, which I now saw was that of a man-baby, of an over-fleshed, hard-drinking, rancorous infant age forty, had dissolved into a surfeited smile, indicating that, on just my first professional outing, a positive transference had been effected. He actually did it, I realized, annihilated the father. He is of the primal horde of sons who, as Freud liked to surmise, have it in them to nullify the father by force—who hate and fear him and, after overcoming him, honor him by devouring him. And I'm from the horde that can't throw a punch. We aren't like that and we can't do it, to our fathers or to anyone else. We're the sons appalled by violence, with no capacity for inflicting physical pain, useless at beating and clubbing, unfit to pulverize even the most deserving enemy, though not necessarily without turbulence, temper, even ferocity. We have teeth as the cannibals do, but they are there, imbedded in our jaws, the better to help us articulate. When we lay waste, when we efface, it isn't with raging fists or ruthless schemes or insane sprawling violence but with our words, our brains, with mentality, with all the stuff that produced the poignant abyss between our fathers and us and that they themselves broke their backs to give us. Encouraging us to be so smart and such *yeshiva buchers*, they little knew how they were equipping us to leave them isolated and uncomprehending in the face of all our forceful babble.

I suppose it was the fear of this drastic outdistancing of my father that had caused me, in my first years of college, to feel as though I were something like his double or his medium, emotionally to imagine that I was there at college in his behalf and that it wasn't just I who was being educated but he whom I was delivering from ignorance as well. Just the opposite was happening, of course: every book I underlined and marginally notated, every course I took and paper I wrote was expanding the mental divide that had been growing wider and wider between us since I had prematurely entered high school at twelve, just about the age when he had left school for good to help support his immigrant parents and all their children. Yet for many months there was nothing my reasonable self could do to shake off the sense of merging with him that overcame me in the library and in the classroom and at my dormitory desk, the impassioned, if crazy, conviction that I was somehow inhabited by him and quickening his intellect right along with mine.

When I reached my father's hospital room, it was empty. There was nothing of his on the bedside table, and in the closet I saw that his clothes, his robe, and his little suitcase were gone. Most frightening to see was the bare mattress, stripped of all its bedding. I rushed back down the hall to the nurse's desk, thinking, "*It's over, it's over, he's been spared the worst,*" and there, to my enormous relief, I learned that he had simply been taken to the operating room a few minutes earlier. I'd missed him because of the extended session with my own patient, the parricidal driver. He was not dead. "*But if they stick the needle in the wrong place, if they blind him, if they paralyze the rest of his face . . .*"

It was nearly five when they brought him down from the recovery room and into a room for four postoperative cases, where he was hooked up to the monitoring machines and where a nurse was on duty round the clock. I sat beside his bed until visiting hours were over, watching with wonder as his pulse maintained itself at a steady rate of sixty beats a minute. Around the room the other patients fresh from surgery were registering drastically fluctuating blood pressure readings while his remained virtually fixed at 155 over 78. I couldn't, of course, interpret the EKG pattern flickering steadily across the screen, but it didn't seem to me to be signaling anything erratic or arrhythmical. He was still, systemically, a marvel and therefore fated to be spared nothing.

They had given him ice to suck on to ease the pain inside his mouth. I kept feeding it to him and replenishing the bowl. His mouth hurt so much he could hardly talk. And when he finally had something to say, he made it short and sweet.

"How do you feel now?" I asked after he'd been up from the recovery room for about an hour.

The voice was weak, the tone grim, the message unambiguous. "I wish I were dead."

He did not complain again.

In the bed across the way there was a very frail old Oriental

man with a tube inserted directly into his throat. He'd had in-
testinal surgery and kept gagging wretchedly and trying to
hawk up phlegm. His daughter, a rather pretty little woman of
about forty, terrifically efficient and concentrated entirely on
her father, silently went about doing what she could to make
him comfortable, but it did not seem possible to alleviate his
misery. Though his face remained expressionless, every few
minutes we heard him struggling with the tube as if he were
about to choke to death.

When I got to the hospital the next morning, I said to my
father, "How did you sleep?"

"No good. The Chinaman kept everybody up."

In a chair beside his bed the old man, sitting now, was struggling with the tube, and his daughter was already there silently
ministering to him.

"The mouth?" I asked.

He shook his head to indicate that his mouth still felt awful.

The nurse said that the doctor had decided that my father
was in too much distress to leave that day. He also hadn't urinated and they couldn't let him go home until he had. My
father told me that he hadn't moved his bowels either, and he
kept getting out of the bed to go to the toilet and try. Each
time I would guide him to the bathroom and then stand outside the door, waiting there in case he needed help. From time
to time, the Oriental woman and I looked at each other tending
our fathers and smiled.

Lil came to visit; Seth came with his wife, Ruth; Sandy and
Helen phoned him from Chicago; Claire, who was back from
London, phoned him from Connecticut; Jonathan phoned
him from where he was working out on the road; and then,
late in the day, while I was helping him to eat what he could of
his watery, unappetizing supper, Dr. Benjamin appeared, tailored splendidly and radiating all the self-assurance that one
would hope to see in one's neurosurgeon. He was accompanied by a crisp-looking administrative aide in a tie and a white
shirt, who exercised his duty with military precision. By comparison, my father, slumped in front of his supper tray, his food-
stained hospital gown ineptly tied at the back, his teeth out
and half his face down the drain, looked like a small old lady—
and the small old lady he looked like was his mother, Bertha

Zahnstecher Roth, as I remembered her in the hospital near the end of her life. I recalled very clearly being home from college and standing beside her bed while *he* was feeding *her* and she was mumbling to him in Yiddish.

Benjamin gave us the results of the biopsy. The tumor was an extremely rare type formed out of a kind of cartilaginous material, "a little like your fingernail," he told my father. It was benign but not susceptible to radiation. He proposed to remove it surgically in two operations, each about seven or eight hours long. The first time he would go in through the mouth to extract part of the bulk that way and then, some months later, he would go in through the back of the head to extract the rest.

Probably it hadn't been tactically possible for him, but I wished that the doctor could have taken me aside to apprise me of all this first. It was a lot to tell an old man whose strength, that evening, you could have measured in teaspoons. After the doctor had spoken his piece, my father looked for a long time at the tray on which they'd served him another dinner of cold consommé and yogurt and a chocolate drink and Jell-O and a Popsicle. It was impossible to guess from his lost, unfocused gaze what, if anything, he was thinking about. I was thinking of the fingernail that had been aggrandizing the hollows of his skull for a decade, the material as obdurate and gristly as he was, that had cracked open the bone behind his nose and, with a stubborn, unrelenting force just like his, had pushed tusklike through into the cavities of his face.

When finally my father seemed to remember Benjamin's presence, he looked up and said to him, "Well, Doctor, I've got a lot of people waiting for me on the other side," and with his head jutting out toward the bowl, he dropped his spoon into the Jell-O and resumed the attempt to eat something.

I walked out into the corridor with the doctor and his aide. "I don't see how he could survive two operations like that," I said.

"Your father is a strong man," the doctor replied.

"A strong eighty-six-year-old man. Maybe enough is enough."

"The tumor is at a critical point. You can expect him to have serious trouble within a year."

"With what?"

"Probably with swallowing," he said, and that, of course, evoked a horrible picture, but not much worse than envisioning him recovering not from one eight-hour operation on his head but now from two. The doctor said, "Anything can happen, really."

"We'll have to think it all through," I said.

We shook hands, but as he and his aide started away, he turned back to offer a gentle reminder. "Mr. Roth, once something happens, it may be too late to help him."

"Maybe it's already too late," I replied.

By the next morning he still hadn't urinated, and as he didn't look forward to being catheterized any more than anyone else does, I told him to go into the toilet and turn the water on in the sink and sit there until something happened. He went in three times, and the last time, after twenty minutes, he came out and said it had worked. He made it work.

After I had helped him get into his street clothes, I went off to phone my brother and tell him we were about to check out of the hospital and drive up to the Connecticut house, where Claire and I had moved for the summer. "Well, now we know for sure that there's nothing to do," I said to my brother. "Two operations are out of the question. You should see what he looks like just from this."

As I packed my father's suitcase with his shaving things, the old man across the way was still choking on the tube in his throat and the daughter was still silently moving about trying to make him comfortable. I went up to say goodbye to her.

"Your father better?" she asked, her English heavily accented and hard to make out.

"For now," I replied.

"Your father is a brave man," she said.

"So is yours," I said. "Old age is no picnic, is it?"

She smiled and shook my hand, probably having failed to understand what I said.

Outside the hospital, as I was leading him very slowly across the parking lot to my car, he said to me, rather like a child who'd been promised a reward for taking some terrible medicine, "*Now* can I have my eye fixed?"

*

He was to stay in an upstairs bedroom where the windows
looked out on the apple trees and the ash trees and the maples.
The room had a wood-burning stove in it and a bright-colored
North African rug, and it was a room he said that he always
loved to sleep in during the years when he'd come to visit with
my mother and later, after her death, when he and Lil came up
a couple of times each summer for a weekend with us in the
country. I got him upstairs to take a nap after lunch. That
morning Claire had made a big pot of vegetable soup for him
for the next few days and had cut some flowers in the garden
to liven up his room, but it turned out that he still couldn't take
anything warm in his mouth and was so worn out from the
two-hour drive up from the hospital that he'd just sat staring
into the soup bowl, unable to respond to her attempts to make
him feel at home.

In his room he immediately fell asleep on top of the bed-
spread; however, when I came to check on him about twenty
minutes later, I saw, as I passed the partially open door of the
bathroom next to his bedroom, that he was sitting on the toilet holding his head in his hands. On the way up we'd had to
stop twice at gas stations when he thought he might have to
use a rest room.

"You all right?" I called.

"It's okay, it's okay," he said, but when I tried afterward to
get him to take a little stroll around the grounds with me, he
said he was afraid to walk outside in case he needed to go to the
toilet. He still hadn't moved his bowels, and he asked me to
drive over to buy some prune juice at the general store to see if
that would help. He was dreadfully down, mentally and physically depleted, though once, when I happened to be in the hall
outside the living room, where he sat, shrunken-looking, in the
easy chair in front of the fireplace, I heard him muttering something that turned out not to be about his own misery at all.
"That poor Chinaman," he was saying.

The next morning he was stronger at breakfast and was even
able to drink some tepid tea and to tolerate in his mouth about
half of the bowl of oatmeal that Claire had prepared for him and
cooled with some milk. I went up to his bedroom while they
were talking at the table—patiently Claire listened as he told
her, and not for the first time either, what a saint his mother

had been, cooking for eight, nine, and ten people, taking in immigrant relatives who arrived penniless at their door, scrubbing the outside wooden staircase on her knees . . . I intended to air his room, make the bed for him, and collect the soiled things from his hospital suitcase and take them over to the laundry that afternoon with our week's wash. But when I pulled back the top sheet of his bed, I saw that the bottom sheet was stained with his blood and so was the seat of his fresh pajamas. I threw his pajamas into the laundry hamper, got him a clean pair of my own, and then stripped the bed and made it up fresh. Where his midsection would lie, I stretched a double thickness of heavy bath towels across the width of the bed to prevent him from staining the bottom sheet again. I was alarmed by the evidence of so much rectal bleeding and didn't know how to account for it. I wondered if he did.

I had no chance to find out, because immediately after he had finished talking to Claire—while cleaning up the breakfast dishes, she'd heard the details of the bankruptcy of the little shoe store he'd opened up with my mother after their marriage —he took the newspaper from the day before and went up again to the bathroom. He'd had a glass of prune juice before retiring and another at breakfast, but when I called in to him some twenty minutes later to ask if he was all right, he replied glumly, like somebody at the Off-Track Betting parlor instead of on the toilet, "No luck."

"It'll happen," I called back.

"Four days," he said, mournfully.

"The biopsy, the anesthetic, lying in the bed—everything's thrown your system off. Another day or two of regular meals, a little exercise, and you'll be fine. How about coming outside? Seth and Ruth will be here any minute. Walk over with me to my studio and you can sit on the porch while I answer my mail."

"In a little while."

He didn't emerge for another half hour, and then looking so thoroughly defeated that it wasn't necessary to ask anything. Downstairs he said no to a walk and sank down in the living room easy chair again. I sat on the sofa with the *Times* and offered to read to him about Dukakis and Bush. "Bush," he said disgustedly, "and his boss, Mr. Ray-gun. You know what he learned to do in eight years, Mr. Ray-gun? Sleep and salute.

The greatest saluter in the country. I never saw a better
saluter." I began to read to him from the front page of the
Times, but he interrupted to tell me that he had left his teeth
upstairs and that he didn't want "the children" to see him
without them. So I set down the paper and went upstairs to
get them from the shelf beside the toilet, where he'd put them
while he was trying in vain to move his bowels. Under the tap,
I rinsed the teeth of the remains of his breakfast and then carried them downstairs, thinking, "His teeth, his eyes, his face,
his bowels, his rectum, his brain . . ." and there was plenty
more left. It could be worse and it would be worse, much worse,
but this was still a pretty healthy lot of misery for the beginning of an end. It probably wouldn't even have been inappropriate for that poor Chinaman lying in his bed and choking on
his tube to think, in passing, about my father, "That poor Jew."

We had lunch in the summer room, just off the kitchen, a
rustic, big, barnlike room with a stone floor that originally had
been the woodshed of the old farmhouse. One side of the
room was now all sliding glass doors and looked off to the
lawn, the stone walls, and the meadows and fields that opened
out in front of the house. In the past I used to set him up there
in a wicker chair facing the view, and in warm weather he could
sit all morning contentedly reading the daily *Times*, the news
about Israel first and then the articles about the Reagan administration that enabled him to stoke up his hatred of the
president for the rest of the day.

Now, with Seth and Ruth visiting for lunch, and all of us
making light conversation, and the luminous day as seductive as
a summer's day gets, he was utterly isolated within a body that
had become a terrifying escape-proof enclosure, the holding
pen in a slaughterhouse.

Near the end of lunch he pushed back his chair and started
toward the steps to the kitchen. It was the third time during the
meal that he had got up to leave the table, and I got up with
him to help him upstairs. He wouldn't let me help, however,
and since I figured he was setting off to try yet again to move
his bowels, I didn't want to embarrass him by insisting.

We were drinking our coffee when it occurred to me that he

was still gone. I quietly left the table and, while the others were talking, slipped into the house, certain that he was dead.

He wasn't, though he might well have been wishing that he were.

I smelled the shit halfway up the stairs to the second floor. When I got to his bathroom, the door was ajar, and on the floor of the corridor outside the bathroom were his dungarees and his undershorts. Standing inside the bathroom door was my father, completely naked, just out of the shower and dripping wet. The smell was overwhelming.

At the sight of me he came close to bursting into tears. In a voice as forlorn as any I had ever heard, from him or anyone, he told me what it hadn't been difficult to surmise. "I beshat myself," he said.

The shit was everywhere, smeared underfoot on the bathmat, running over the toilet bowl edge and, at the foot of the bowl, in a pile on the floor. It was splattered across the glass of the shower stall from which he'd just emerged, and the clothes discarded in the hallway were clotted with it. It was on the corner of the towel he had started to dry himself with. In this smallish bathroom, which was ordinarily mine, he had done his best to extricate himself from his mess alone, but as he was nearly blind and just up out of a hospital bed, in undressing himself and getting into the shower he had managed to spread the shit over everything. I saw that it was even on the tips of the bristles of my toothbrush hanging in the holder over the sink.

"It's okay," I said, "it's okay, everything is going to be okay."

I reached into the shower stall and turned the water back on and fiddled with the taps until it was the right temperature. Taking the towel out of his hand, I helped him back under the shower.

"Take the soap and start from scratch," I said, and while he obediently began again to soap his body all over, I gathered his clothes and the towels and the bathmat together in a heap and went down the hall to the linen closet and got a pillowcase to dump them in. I also found a fresh bath towel for him. Then I got him out of the shower and took him straight into the hallway where the floor was still clean, and wrapped him up in the towel and began to dry him. "You made a valiant effort," I said, "but I'm afraid it was a no-win situation."

"I beshat myself," he said, and this time he dissolved in tears.

I got him into his bedroom, where he sat on the edge of the bed and continued to towel himself while I went off and got a terry-cloth robe of mine. When he was dry I helped him into the robe and then pulled back the top sheet of the bed and told him to get in and take a nap.

"Don't tell the children," he said, looking up at me from the bed with his one sighted eye.

"I won't tell anyone," I said. "I'll say you're taking a rest."

"Don't tell Claire."

"Nobody," I said. "Don't worry about it. It could have happened to anyone. Just forget about it and get a good rest."

I lowered the shades to darken the room and closed the door behind me.

The bathroom looked as though some spiteful thug had left his calling card after having robbed the house. As my father was tended to and he was what counted, I would just as soon have nailed the door shut and forgotten that bathroom forever. "It's like writing a book," I thought—"I have no idea where to begin." But I stepped gingerly across the floor and reached out and threw open the window, which was a start. Then I went down the back stairway to the kitchen, and keeping out of sight of Seth and Ruth and Claire, who were still in the summer room talking, I got a bucket, a brush, and a box of Spic and Span from the cabinet under the sink and two rolls of paper towels and came back upstairs to the bathroom.

Where his shit lay in front of the toilet bowl in what was more or less a contiguous mass, it was easiest to get rid of. Just scoop it up and flush it away. And the shower door and the windowsill and the sink and the soap dish and the light fixtures and the towel bars were no problem. Lots of paper towels and lots of soap. But where it had lodged in the narrow, uneven crevices of the floor, between the wide old chestnut planks, I had my work cut out for me. The scrub brush seemed only to make things worse, and eventually I took down my toothbrush and, dipping it in and out of the bucket of hot sudsy water, proceeded inch by inch, from wall to wall, one crevice at a time, until the floor was as clean as I could get it. After some fifteen minutes on my knees, I decided that flecks and particles down so deep that I still couldn't reach them we would simply all live with. I removed the curtain from the window, even though it looked to be clean, and shoved it in the pillowcase with all the other soiled things, and then I went into Claire's bathroom and got some eau de cologne, which I sprinkled freely over the swabbed and scoured room, flicking it off my fingertips like holy water. I set up a small summer fan in one corner and got it going, and I went back to Claire's bathroom and washed my arms and my hands and my face. There was a little shit in my hair, so I washed that out, too.

I tiptoed back into the bedroom where he was asleep, still breathing, still living, still with me—yet another setback outlasted by this man whom I had known unendingly as my father. I felt awful about his heroic, hapless struggle to cleanse himself before I had got up to the bathroom and about the shame of it, the disgrace he felt himself to be, and yet now that it was over and he was so deep in sleep, I thought I couldn't have asked anything more for myself before he died—this, too, was right and as it should be. You clean up your father's shit because it has to be cleaned up, but in the aftermath of cleaning it up, everything that's there to feel is felt as it never was before. It wasn't the first time that I'd understood this either: once you sidestep disgust and ignore nausea and plunge past those phobias that are fortified like taboos, there's an awful lot of life to cherish.

Though maybe once is enough, I added, addressing myself mentally to the sleeping brain squeezed in by the cartilaginous tumor; if I have to do this every day, I may not wind up feeling quite so thrilled.

I carried the stinking pillowcase downstairs and put it into a black garbage bag which I tied shut, and I carried the bag out to the car and dumped it in the trunk to take to the laundry. And *why* this was right and as it should be couldn't have been plainer to me, now that the job was done. So *that* was the patrimony. And not because cleaning it up was symbolic of something else but because it wasn't, because it was nothing less or more than the lived reality that it was.

There was my patrimony: not the money, not the tefillin, not the shaving mug, but the shit.

*

I helped him bathe the next night. That morning, making up
his bed, I had again found blood stains on his pajama trousers
and on the layer of bath towels covering the bottom sheet, and
when I'd asked if he was aware of all that blood, he told me
that it was what happened when he didn't take a sitz bath
before going to sleep. "But if that's all it is, you can bathe in
the front bathroom," I said. "You should have told me. You
don't have to take a shower."

"I need Epsom salts."

I drove to the drugstore in the next town to get a box of
Epsom salts, and that evening I drew him a bath and stirred
a handful into the water. I sat on the edge of the tub while
the water ran, testing the temperature with my fingers—my
mother, I remembered, used to test it with her elbow. He sat
waiting on the lowered toilet seat in my red terry-cloth robe.
When the tub was full, I put the rubberized shower mat on the
tub floor to guard against his taking a fall getting in and out.
Then I offered my arm, but he wouldn't let me help him even
when I insisted. Instead, he made me stand aside, and by
kneeling and swiveling about, he managed to get one leg into
the water and then the other and, once inside, to circle around
slowly on his knees until he was facing the front.

"That's a complicated maneuver," I said.

"I do this all alone at night."

"Well, I'll just sit here. In case you need me."

"Ah, it feels good," he said, pushing water over his chest
with his two hands. Weakly at first, then more vigorously, he
began to flex his knees and I could see the muscles working in
his thin shanks. I looked at his penis. I don't believe I'd seen it
since I was a small boy, and back then I used to think it was
quite big. It turned out that I had been right. It was thick and
substantial and the one bodily part that didn't look at all old.
It looked pretty serviceable. Stouter around, I noticed, than
my own. "Good for him," I thought. "If it gave some pleasure
to him and my mother, all the better." I looked at it intently, as
though for the very first time, and waited on the thoughts. But
there weren't any more, except my reminding myself to fix it
in my memory for when he was dead. It might prevent him

from becoming ethereally attenuated as the years went by. "I must remember accurately," I told myself, "remember everything accurately so that when he is gone I can re-create the father who created me." *You must not forget anything.*

He was kicking his legs forcefully up and down now, rather like a baby playing in the water, but there was nothing of a baby's delight in his grimly set half-face. He seemed in deadly earnest about this bath, as though, like nearly everything of late, it, too, must be undertaken with the utmost determination.

I washed his back for him, and while I was noticing how pale his body had become, he said, "That happened to me one other time in my life."

I understood what he was alluding to and just kept soaping away with the cloth, as though scrubbing at him like this might renew some of the vigor.

"It was after I was transferred to South Jersey," he told me. "I just took over the Maple Shade district. I had forty men down there. Big office. Twelve secretaries. I got a phone call in the middle of the night that there was somebody in the office —somebody, they said, broke into the office. I got out of bed, and before I could make it to the toilet, the same thing happened. Must have been the fear."

"Here," I said, and gave him the soap and the washcloth and sat back on the lowered toilet seat while he gently washed his backside. Then with a hand on each side of his buttocks he held his cheeks apart. "The doctor told me to do this," he said.

"Fine," I said. "It's a good idea. Take your time."

In 1956, at exactly my age, my father had been entrusted by Metropolitan Life with an office of forty agents, assistant managers, and ordinary representatives and a secretarial staff of twelve. He was a manager who drove his employees as unsparingly as he drove himself, and the transfer to the Maple Shade district had been his third promotion since 1948, when he'd been elevated from an assistant manager in Newark. What these promotions meant was that he was given responsibility for a larger office with a greater potential for increasing his income but in even worse shape and doing less business than the previous office, which he had rescued from its difficulties and whipped into one of the most productive in the territory. For him advancement was generally a kind of demotion as well, and the struggle was perpetually uphill.

As I sat watching him let the warm water soothe the rectal fissures that he had told me caused his bleeding, I was thinking that the Metropolitan Life Insurance Company could never sufficiently have recognized what it was they had in Herman Roth. They had rewarded him with a decent enough pension on his retirement twenty-three years before, and during his working life he had received numerous plaques and scrolls and lapel buttons attesting to his achievement. Scores of managers must, of course, have worked as hard and with no less success, but of the thousand Metropolitan district managers scattered around the country there simply could not have been another who, on being notified in the middle of the night that his office had been broken into, had—to use his word—"beshat" himself out of fear. For that kind of fealty, the company should have beatified Herman Roth, as the Church beatifies martyrs who suffer for its cause.

And had I, as his son, received devotion any less primitive and slavish? Not always the most enlightened devotion—indeed, devotion from which I already wanted to be disentangled by the time I was sixteen and feeling myself beginning to be disfigured by it, but devotion that I now found gratifying to be able to requite somewhat by sitting on the lid of the toilet overseeing him as he kicked his legs up and down like a baby in a bassinet.

You can say that it doesn't mean much for a son to be tenderly protective of a father once the father is powerless and nearly destroyed. I can only reply that I felt as protective of his vulnerability (as an emotional family man vulnerable to family friction, as a breadwinner vulnerable to financial uncertainty, as a rough-hewn son of Jewish immigrants vulnerable to social prejudice) when I was still at home and he was powerfully healthy and driving me crazy with advice that was useless and strictures that were pointless and reasoning that caused me, all alone in my room, to smack my forehead and howl in despair. This was exactly the discrepancy that had made repudiating his authority such an oppressive conflict, as laden with grief as it was with scorn. He wasn't just any father, he was *the* father, with everything there is to hate in a father and everything there is to love.

The next day, when Lil phoned from Elizabeth to ask how he was doing, I overheard him saying to her, "Philip is like a mother to me."

I was surprised. I would have thought he'd say "like a father to me," but his description was, in fact, more discriminating than my commonplace expectations while at the same time much more flagrant, unblinking, and enviably, unself-consciously blunt. Yes, he was always teaching me something, not the conventional American dad stuff, not the school stuff or the sports stuff or the Prince Charming stuff, but something coarser than could be accommodated by my predictably vainglorious boyhood yearnings for a judicious, dignified father to replace the undereducated father who I found myself half-ashamed of at the very same time that his assailability, particularly as a target of anti-Semitic discrimination, quickened my solidarity with him and hardened my hatred of his belittlers: he taught me the vernacular. He *was* the vernacular, unpoetic and expressive and point-blank, with all the vernacular's glaring limitations and all its durable force.

Anti-Semitism had, in fact, been the subject of a brief exchange, only the previous fall, between John Creedon, the president and C.E.O. of Metropolitan Life, and me as a result of an autobiographical piece that I'd published in the *New York Times Book Review* in October. The piece, which, as "Safe at Home," became the opening chapter of *The Facts*, described my Newark neighborhood as a protective sanctuary for the Jewish children who grew up there during the thirties and forties, when I for one had felt menaced, as an American, by the Germans and the Japanese and, though only a child, "was not unaware," as a Jew, "of the power to intimidate that emanated from the highest and lowest reaches of gentile America."

It was an allusion that I'd made there to the corporate discrimination practiced by Metropolitan Life in those years that was singled out by John Creedon in his letter. After reminding me that he had met my father several years earlier, Creedon went on to tell me that my father had said nothing to him on

that occasion about any such discrimination; and he was certainly confident, Creedon continued, that no discrimination of
any sort existed at the Metropolitan today. What had actually
prompted him to write, he said, was a letter, taking exception
to my *Times* piece, from an old associate of his, a retired M.D.
who had been an officer of the company in the 1940s. Along
with his own letter, Creedon enclosed the correspondence I
had unwittingly instigated between the two of them.

The doctor's letter to Creedon devoted three paragraphs to
refuting my characterization of the Metropolitan as discriminatory during the thirties and forties. He told Creedon that he
was "shocked" that Philip Roth should believe this and, as
evidence to the contrary, noted that "one of the best known
senior officers of the Metropolitan was a Jew, Louis I. Dublin,
world-famous for his public health and statistical pronounce-
ments in the name of Metropolitan," and that another Jew, Lee
Frankel, was "a senior officer and virtually the right-hand man
of Haley Fisk," the company president. "I suppose," he went
on, "Mr. Roth will say in his defense that these are his childhood impressions and perhaps he is just reflecting comments
and attitudes expressed at home about the Company. I wish
there were some way to try to correct these impressions."

In Creedon's reply to the doctor he mentioned having invited my father to come to the home office to have lunch with
him some years back, after having run into my brother at a
Chicago dinner party and been told about our father's career
at the Metropolitan, his starting out as a lowly agent for them
and ending up the district manager of a sizable office. Creedon
described my father as an interesting person and added that
if the views he'd once held about the Metropolitan's religious
bias were accurately reported in his son's autobiography, they
had clearly changed since.

If the doctor was shocked that I should think that a great
American insurance company had ever discriminated against
Jews, I was myself not a little surprised that two of that company's eminent executives, whose letters were otherwise wholly
well-meaning, should find this simple historical fact had still to
be denied in the late 1980s, even to themselves. However, had
there been nothing more annoying in these letters than this
unlikely innocence, I probably would have responded with a

cordial note saying that I had reason to hold a different opinion, and ended it there. What rankled me and goaded me on was that they were both determined to blame an unflattering perception of their company on my father, on unsubstantiated "attitudes" and "views" of his rather than on the company's prior practices.

I phoned my father after getting these letters and said to him, "Hey, you were wrong all those years about the Metropolitan. They loved Jews. Couldn't promote them fast enough. All that other stuff was just Jew paranoia."

I read him the letter that the doctor had written to John Creedon in response to my piece.

When I was finished, he began to laugh a little sardonically.

"Well, what do you think?" I said.

"The guy's wet behind the ears. What's his name again?"

I told him.

"Sure Dublin was a Jew," he said. "So was my boss, Peter-freund. But for a Jew to advance in that company like a Christian? In those days? Come on. You could count the Jews in the home office and you wouldn't need your whole hand."

I spent the next few afternoons in the archives of the American Jewish Committee on East Fifty-sixth Street. I'd been directed there by one of the officers of the B'nai Brith Anti-Defamation League, when I'd phoned the A.D.L. to ask where I might do research on discrimination in the insurance industry. After I'd compiled pages of notes drawn from articles published over the years in the *New York Times*, from memos of the Civil Rights Section of the A.J.C., and from various books and periodicals, I composed a two-and-a-half-page letter to John Creedon, providing documentation for those "attitudes" of my father's which he and the doctor had been so quick to discredit.

December 10, 1987

Dear Mr. Creedon:

. . . I'm sure, as you suggest in your letter, that the availability of executive opportunities to minority groups has vastly expanded at the Metropolitan since the 1930s and 1940s, the period I was writing about in my autobiographical essay. Since the passage of the Fair Employment Practice Act in 1951, there has, of course, been steady and successful pressure on business and industries previously discriminatory, to recruit, hire, and promote to managerial and executive positions members of minority groups. Nonetheless, as late as the 1960s, the federal government—according to a *New York Times* article of March 20, 1966—had to start "a quiet but seemingly firm campaign against alleged religious discrimination in insurance companies." "The aim," the story said, "is to open executive positions to Jews and Roman Catholics, as well as to Negroes and other racial minorities, in companies where the top jobs may be reserved for Anglo-Saxon Protestants."

I went on to quote from an investigation into the insurance industry published in 1966 by New York State Attorney General Louis Lefkowitz and from a study made in 1960, while my father happened still to be working for the Metropolitan, which indicated that in the home offices of the seven major life insurance companies the proportion of Jewish executives was about three and a half percent of the combined seven companies and that two thirds of those were confined, like Louis I. Dublin, largely to statistical work or employed as actuaries, physicians, attorneys, or accountants. I ended by saying, "In the light of what all these findings reveal about discriminatory practices in the history of the major American insurance companies . . . I wonder why it should be my father's 'views' that you hope have changed: the historical facts do not allow for a revision of his views. What's been called for has been a revision of insurance company policy as regards minority groups, and this, in fact, has occurred in response to federal law and government inquiries."

I sent a copy to Creedon and, when I saw him next, gave a copy to my father.

After he read it, he didn't seem to know what to make of what I had done.

"How do you find all this stuff?" he asked me.

"The archives at the American Jewish Committee. I spent a couple of afternoons there."

"He's an awfully nice fellow, Mr. Creedon. He had me to the home office for lunch, you know."

"I know."

"He sent a limousine over here to take me to the home office that day."

"Look, I'm sure he's a nice fellow. There are just a couple of little holes in his sense of history."

"Well, you laid it out for him, all right."

"Well, I didn't like what he wrote about you—that he hoped *you'd* changed *your* mind. Screw that."

"They've been awfully good to me, the Metropolitan. You know how much pension I've received since I retired? I figured it out here just last week. Well over a quarter of a million dollars."

"That's peanuts. You're worth twice that."

"With an eighth-grade education? Am I?" He laughed. "I had nothing, absolutely nothing. Mother and I were flat broke and they hired me. It's a wonder what happened to a man like me."

"The hell it is. You worked. You sweated blood for them. You have a history and so do they. The difference is that you own up to yours, you say you were 'nothing,' but they don't like to admit to theirs, if those letters are any indication."

"They don't like the truth. What's so unusual about that? Do me a favor, will you? After this," he said, holding up my letter, "that's enough."

Well, *this* was new—my father expressing chagrin over something I had written. In my Zuckerman novels, I had given Nathan Zuckerman a father who could not stand his writer son's depiction of Jewish characters, whereas fate had given me a fiercely loyal and devoted father who had never found a thing in my books to criticize—what enraged *him* were the Jews who attacked my books as anti-Semitic and self-hating. No, what made my father nervous wasn't what I wrote about Jews but, as it turned out, what I had now written about Gentiles —about Gentiles to Gentiles, and to Gentiles who had been his bosses.

"I don't think they're going to tamper with your pension because of my letter—if that's what's worrying you."

"Nothing's worrying me," he said.

"I certainly didn't mean to upset you. Quite the contrary."

"I'm not upset. But just don't send 'em another one."

And yet, at my father's funeral, my cousin Ann told me that when she and her husband, Peter, had been visiting him one evening, he had gone to his files and taken out the letter to show it proudly to Peter, who was his lawyer. To me he never mentioned it again, nor did I receive a reply from anyone at the Metropolitan.

*

He was with us in Connecticut for a week after the biopsy, and by the time he was ready to return to Elizabeth there was very little pain in his mouth and he was able to eat again with appetite; he had gained back the few pounds that he'd lost in the hospital and even recovered enough strength to take a short walk with me after breakfast and again in the afternoon. Every morning he came into the kitchen saying, "Slept like a top," and in the evening, after dinner, he sat across from Claire with his coffee, and long after I had slipped away to read or to watch the ball game, he was still in the kitchen narrating his stories to her about the family and their fortunes in America. They were tedious stories, to anyone who had grown up outside the family largely pointless stories, and, one would have assumed, by now tremendously repetitious even to him (this one died, this one married, this one lost his money, this one lost his wife, this one, thank God, finally did okay). Yet he recited them night after night, with no less freshness than Yul Brynner singing "'Tis a Puzzlement" in *The King and I* for the four thousandth time. Every night at the kitchen table Claire sat and listened, drooping with boredom but by no means unimpressed by the urgency with which this meandering saga unfolded or by the hypnotic hold that the mundane destiny of an ordinary immigrant family seemed still to have on him in his eighty-seventh year. How his late brother Charlie, who'd died in 1936, married Fanny Spitzer in 1912; how, after Fanny died fourteen years later, Charlie married Sophie Lasker; how Sophie was a mother to Milton, Rhoda, Kenny, and Jeanette; how, in 1942, only twenty-eight years old, Jeanette died; how his brother Morris, the go-getting, prosperous brother who died at twenty-nine, had a shoelace factory down on Pacific Street, where my grandfather used to put tips on the shoelaces; how Morris had two houses and four garages; how when he died he left his fortune behind to a spendthrift wife, who after Morris's death bought a Velie. "You ever hear of the Velie automobile? Look it up. V-e-l-i-e. It was a big roadster. Everything went, Ella sold everything. Then she got married again. She married a guy and he impregnated her and she thought she had a lump in her stomach. And this guy was an Army captain, and he took all her money, Morris's fortune, and he went to Germany, he

made her buy leather—but her father, Uncle Klein, said they
had to pay the money to an American bank and he wouldn't
give up the bill of lading. Uncle Klein used to have a five-and-
ten-cent store on the corner of Avon Avenue—no, Clinton
Avenue, Clinton and Hunterdon Street—" It was his Deuter-
onomy, the history of his Israel, and ever since his retirement,
whether he was on a Caribbean cruise or in a Florida hotel
lobby or in a doctor's waiting room, very few who wound up
sitting across from him for any length of time didn't get at
least the abridged version of his sacred text. Gentiles whom he
had sometimes run into in his travels with my mother had been
known to pick themselves up and move off in mid-sentence,
and even on those occasions when my mother dared to explain
to him why a perfect stranger might not be interested in Charlie's Belmont Avenue shoe store or Morris's motion picture
theater next door to the shoelace factory on Pacific Street, he
never seemed to get the idea, or to want to. All the privation
and rebuilding and regeneration, all those *people*, all that *dying*,
all their *work*—how could anyone fail to be moved and even,
ultimately, to be as awestruck as he was by how, in America,
our Roths had persevered and endured?

At the end of the week I drove him home to Elizabeth, stopping first in Manhattan to take him to the ophthalmologist.
We had decided that there was nothing to do now but forget
the tumor and proceed with the eye operation. He was to have
a preoperative examination that afternoon and was scheduled
to go back into the hospital at the beginning of July, after the
holiday weekend, for the removal of the cataract. My brother
was flying in to see him through that.

As he was ninety percent blind in the right eye, the operation on the other eye was going to render him virtually sight-
less, the doctor told us, for perhaps as long as three or four
weeks. We had very little time to find somebody to look after
him during his convalescence, but fortunately, after only a day
or two of phoning around, I discovered that my brother's former housekeeper, Ingrid Burlin, who for five years had helped
Sandy raise his two boys after his first wife died of cancer in
1971, was just completing a job with a Manhattan family. Ingrid
was willing to begin working for us the day he got home from
the cataract operation and to continue on until he left with Lil

in December for their four months in West Palm Beach (if the
tumor spared him for West Palm Beach). Ingrid was now in
her forties, an exceedingly good-natured, intelligent, and reliable woman to whom both my mother and my father had
grown very close during the years she'd been with my brother,
and it seemed a piece of astonishing good luck that she should
be available to look after him at just this moment. Ingrid was
to come in on the bus from Manhattan for eight hours a day,
five or six days a week, to cook for him, shop for him, keep the
apartment clean for him, and, what afforded us the most relief,
keep him company all day while he was housebound. Since
Sandy and I knew that our father wasn't about to dip into his
CDs or his savings accounts in order to pay Ingrid's salary, we
agreed to divide the cost between us and to reimburse ourselves from the bequest after his death. There was enough
money there to pay Ingrid for three years, if, as was unlikely,
he remained alive that long.

On the drive down, when I saw that his spirits had begun to
plummet now that the week with us was over and everything
loomed up just as overwhelmingly as it had before, I reminded
him that Ingrid's presence was going to make a big difference
—as was the cataract operation. What with Ingrid around the
house and his sight restored, he would be far less dependent
on Lil, and perhaps the tension between them that his illness
had exacerbated would become manageable again.

But saying that got him going in a way I hadn't foreseen.
"Suddenly she's a Jew," he said to me. "I had to drag her to
services. Till she knew me she never went at all. Lil didn't even
know where the synagogue *was*. But the Friday before my operation she left me to go to services. I told her, 'Even a dog
stands by his master. People buy a dog for companionship, and
you run away from me!'"

"Well," I said, "a dog might not have been the best example.
I can see where she might not feel flattered by the comparison."

But he was in no mood to be either amused or mollified. He
was, rather, in the mood to hate, now that he was headed
home. I wondered if some of what he expressed might not be
veiled hatred of me for taking him home. Or maybe he was furious over that question he had not bothered to ask Dr. Benjamin or Dr. Meyerson or me, the writer son, because he knew

that none of us, even with all our schooling, our degrees, our smooth sentences and clever words, could make any more sense of it than he did. Why should a man die? It was enough to put anybody in a rage, that question. He was indispensable, goddamnit, if no longer to others then to himself. So why should he die? Someone with brains answer that!

"She doesn't do anything right," he told me.

"Who does?"

"Mother did. Mother did everything right."

"Well, that made her pretty much the only one in the world then. Maybe you better get off Lil's back."

"Look, there are plenty of women down in Florida who I could move in with. They're crazy about my company."

I couldn't be cruel enough, a moment earlier, to remind him that my mother, who may have looked to be doing everything right when he was away at the office ten and twelve hours a day, hadn't seemed so perfect to him during the last years of her life. Nor could I remind him now that the Bal Harbour women whom he'd wowed in 1981—back when he'd appeared in the condominium pool, freshly widowered, doing fifteen minutes of his methodical, slow breaststroke every noon and then, in his trunks and his robe, sitting in the sun telling "the girls" the jokes from the Elizabeth Y—might not be so crazy for the company of the man he was in 1988.

He didn't need me to remind him, anyway; it occurred to him spontaneously a second or two later and made him even angrier than before, this time ostensibly at Lil's sister, not a great favorite of his (nor he of hers, from what I surmised).

"Why doesn't she marry *her*?" he demanded. "They're on the phone sixteen hours a day—why doesn't she marry her sister and get it over with!"

But the one Lil had once wanted to marry was my father. Only he was married, if not to my mother any longer, to their marriage. Some time ago, in a mellower mood, he'd said to me, "I sometimes think that Mother sent Lil to me." I was surprised by this dreaminess, which was so very uncharacteristic, but as I didn't see where it did any harm—I wondered, even, if it might not be just the lullaby to soothe his conscience and diminish a little the shame and guilt perpetuating his fidelity to a corpse—I said, "Who knows? Maybe she did." He'd seemed to be trying to find a way not so much to loving Lil whole-heartedly (even he was too experienced to expect that) as to granting her a position of equality in his distinctive clan, with what was to him its unparalleled history. He had always been wonderfully attentive and devoted to any friend who was ill, and probably never came closer to being a loving husband than when he supported Lil, over the period of a year, through two mastectomies and afterward helped nurse her back to health. But only as his patient did she get anywhere near being a darling wife; and once *he* began to falter, once he became increasingly needy himself, she was doomed by being imperfect never to achieve the status of Bess Roth, whom he now exalted, along with his mother, as a paragon of womanhood. With Lil, once the romantic infatuation had waned, he lived out the less censored version of what he had done with my mother, particularly toward the end.

Temporarily worn down by the rush of rage, he soon let his head slump forward and fell asleep. When he awoke, on Route 684, the object of his fury was drivers and driving. Somebody changed lanes in front of me, he said disgustedly, "What the hell is that guy doing?" Somebody whizzed past me on my left, he cried, "Doesn't anybody observe the fifty-five-mile limit anymore?" Then: "These goddamn trucks!" Then: "Smoking! She's got a baby in the car and she's smoking!"

"Take it easy," I said.

"Now they've got the telephones. There's a brilliant invention. They drive and they talk on the telephone! Maybe Ingrid can help out Abe," he suddenly said to me.

"What? What are you talking about?"

"Maybe Ingrid can help out Abe," he repeated. "Abe lives with a terrible bitch."

Abe was a ninety-three-year-old neighbor with whom my father tried to take a daily constitutional when the weather was good. Abe appeared to be quite alert and moved with an amazingly upright, confident gait for a man that old, though when he and my father went off in the afternoon to take their turn around the block, they linked arms to be sure that neither of them tripped on the cracked cement of the local sidewalks. "The halt and the blind" my father called the pair of them, wryly. Sometimes they went down North Broad Street as far as the drugstore, sometimes they accompanied each other to the barbershop, and one day when I drove over, they'd just come back from going to vote together in the mayoral primary. The results of the primary were a foregone conclusion, my father told me, but voting had given him and Abe something to do. And whenever they returned from wherever they had been and Abe went on to his own apartment, my father invariably said, "Five minutes from now he'll forget he saw me."

The day I'd gone over to tell him about the tumor, Abe had called just after I'd broken the bad news, while my father was compressed down in a corner of the sofa contemplating what he was in for. I got up and answered the phone and there was Abe on the other end, a real zing in his sprightly voice. "Hello, Herman?" "No, Philip," I said. "Your father want to take a walk?" "He wants to sit and talk now, Abe. Maybe he'll go out later." Barely ten minutes had passed when the phone rang again. "Your father want to take a walk?" "No, Abe, not right now, I'm afraid." And after I'd hung up for the second time, I left the receiver off the hook just as I had the night before my mother's funeral, when Wilkins, another neighbor, was trying to spook my father with his crazy laugh.

"What's Ingrid's number in New York? I'm going to talk to her about Abe."

"Dad, leave Abe as he is, okay? For the time being let's have Ingrid help just you."

"Once I get this damn eye fixed—! If I could see, I could go to the bank, I could go to the dentist, I wouldn't need anybody."

"Well, you're going to have it fixed in a couple of weeks. David Krohn moved heaven and earth to get you scheduled as soon as possible. It's why we're going to see him today."

"When Aunt Millie died, Ann called me and I just broke down and wept on the phone with her for half an hour. Did I tell you that?"

Ann, you remember, was the daughter of my mother's younger sister Millie.

"I wept for half an hour," he said. "And you know who I realize I was weeping for? Mother. When she died, I ran around the hospital shouting, 'Where's my wife? What are you doing for my wife?' I didn't have time to cry, I was so angry. But when I heard Millie died, that was the last part of Mother, and I cried like a baby."

We were entering Manhattan from the West Side Highway when he awakened from sleeping for the third time and, resigned and sounding rather sheepish, said, "Maybe Ingrid can look after me for good."

"That's possible, too," I said.

6

They Fought Because They Were Fighters, and They Fought Because They Were Jews

---

J UST about a year passed before he began, all at once, to lose his equilibrium. In the meantime, he'd had the cataract removed—restoring to his left eye practically 20/20 vision— and he and Lil had gone to Florida for their usual stay of four months. In December, in Palm Beach, they even attended the wedding that Sandy Kuvin had invited him to the previous spring, back when the brain surgeon had told me that unless we okayed the operation, in a relatively short time he'd be much worse off—back when I thought that he'd never see Florida again.

When he returned to Elizabeth at the end of March and I went over to welcome him home, I saw that his condition had already worsened since I'd visited him in Florida the month before. His head was beginning to hurt him practically every day, the facial paralysis seemed to have got worse, causing his speech to thicken now nearly to the point of unintelligibility, and he had become alarmingly unsteady on his feet. Late one night, a few weeks after coming home, when he got out of bed to go to the bathroom, he lost his balance (or momentarily blacked out) and fell. He was on the bathroom floor some ten minutes before Lil woke up and heard him calling. He came away with nothing worse than some badly bruised ribs, but the damage to his morale was enormous.

At about this time, a friend told me about a living will, a legal document that—in its own phraseology—enables you to declare in advance that in the event of extreme physical or mental disability from which there's no reasonable expectation of recovery, you refuse any sort of life-support system. The signer designates who will make the necessary medical treatment decisions if he or she is incapable of doing so. I called my lawyer

to ask if living wills were valid in New Jersey, and when she
said yes, I instructed her to draw up two living wills, one for
my father and another for me.

The next week I drove over to New Jersey to have dinner
with my father, Lil, and Ingrid, who was working as his housekeeper again now that he was home—she'd begun the previous July, just after he'd had the cataract removed. I brought
with me my own living will, signed and notarized at a local
luncheonette that afternoon, and the living will that had been
prepared by my lawyer for him, which assigned the power to
make medical decisions—if he was not able—to my brother and
me. I was hoping that if I showed him that I'd had a living will
drawn up for myself, signing his might seem to him not so much
portentous as commonsensical, something any adult ought to
do regardless of age or physical condition.

But when I got there and discovered how depressed he still
was as a result of the bathroom fall, I found it was even harder
for me to talk about the living will than it had been to tell him
about the brain tumor the year before. In fact, I couldn't do
it. Ingrid had prepared a big turkey dinner and I had brought
some wine and we sat a long time at the dining table, where,
instead of explaining what a living will was and why I wanted
him to have one, I tried to get his mind as far from death as I
could by telling him about a book that I'd just finished reading.
I'd picked it up while browsing in a Judaica store on upper
Broadway when I'd been out taking a walk a few days before.
It was called *The Jewish Boxers' Hall of Fame*—old archive photographs and chapter-long biographies of thirty-nine boxers, a
number of them world champions or "title claimants" who
had been active in the ring when my father was young. As a
boy, along with my brother, I had been taken by him to the
Thursday night fights at Newark's Laurel Garden, and though
I for one no longer had an interest in the sport, he still enjoyed
enormously watching boxing on television. I asked him how
many of the old-time Jewish fighters he thought he could
name.

"Well," he said, "there was Abe Attell."

"That's right," I said. "You were just a little kid when Attell
was featherweight champ."

"Was I? I thought I saw him fight. There was what's-his-name, the big lug . . . Levinsky—Battling Levinsky. He was champ—right?"

"Light heavyweight champ."

"Benny Leonard, of course. Ruby Goldstein. He became a referee."

"So did Leonard. He dropped dead refereeing a fight at the old St. Nick's Arena. Remember that?"

"No, I don't. But there was Lew Tendler. He finally opened a restaurant. I used to go to it, in Philadelphia. A steak house. They were terrific characters. They were poor boys, just like the colored, that made the grade in boxing. Most of them wasted their money, they died poor men. The only one who I think made money was Tendler. I remember the era very vividly of Tendler, Attell, and Leonard. Barney Ross. He was a helluva fighter. I saw him fight in Newark. There was Bummy Davis— he was a Jew. There was Slapsie Maxie Rosenbloom. Sure, I remember them."

"Did you know," I said, "that Slapsie Maxie fought another Jew for the light heavyweight title?" I'd learned this myself only the night before, skimming through an appendix to the *Hall of Fame* book titled "Jews Who Fought Other Jews for the World Title." The list, a longer one than I would have expected, came just before the appendix listing "Lester Bromberg's 10 Great Jewish American Boxers of All Time." "He fought a guy named Abie Bain," I said.

"Sure. Abie Bain," my father said, "he was a nut from Jersey here—Newark, Hillside, around these parts. And he was a bum. They were all bums. You know how it was: these kids grew up, they had a tough life, the slums, no money, and they always had an adversary. The Christian religion was an adversary. They fought two battles. They fought because they were fighters, and they fought because they were Jews. They'd put two guys in the ring, an Italian and a Jew, an Irishman and a Jew, and they fought like they meant it, they fought to hurt. There was always a certain amount of hatred in it. Trying to show who was superior."

This line of thinking led him to remember a childhood friend, Charlie Raskus, who, after he left the neighborhood, became a killer for the kingpin Newark mobster Longie Zwillman.

"Charlie was no good even as a kid," my father said.

"How so?" I asked.

"He tied his teacher to her desk in grade school."

"No kidding."

"Sure. They threw him out and put him in an ungraded school and he wound up killing people for Longie. They were a bad bunch, Charlie and his friends. They were all Jewish boys around the Third Ward. The Polocks used to kill the Jews who had beards, in the Third Ward I'm saying, not just in the old country, and so the Jewish boys started a gang—it had a name but it doesn't come to me right away—and they'd kill the Polocks. I mean personally kill them. They were all no good. My father used to call them 'Yiddische bums.'"

"What happened to Charlie Raskus?"

"He's dead. He died. Natural causes. He wasn't that old. Even the bastards die," my father said. "That's about the only good thing you can say for death—it gets the sons of bitches, too."

About ten-thirty, after we'd caught the Mets score on the news and he seemed, at least for the moment, to have been distracted from his gloom, I took the living wills, his and mine, which I'd carried rather officially with me in something I rarely ever use—my ancient briefcase—and drove with them back to New York, thinking maybe it was a mistake to force him to face the most bitter of all possibilities. "Enough," I thought, and went home, where, unable to sleep, I passed the night studying, in Appendix V, the won-and-lost records of some fifty Jewish world champions and contenders, including Jersey's own Abie Bain, who'd won forty-eight—thirty-one by knockout—lost eleven, and, strangely, according to this book, had thirty-one no decisions.

Early the next morning, however, before he'd begun to have a chance to be worn down by worrying, I telephoned my father and launched into my spiel: I told him how my lawyer had suggested that I ought to have a living will, how she had explained its function to me, how I had said it sounded like a good idea and had asked her, as she was preparing one for me, to draw up one for him as well. I said, "Let me read you mine. Listen." And of course, his reaction was nothing like what I'd feared it would be.

How could I have forgotten that I was dealing with somebody who'd spent a lifetime talking to people about the thing they least wanted to think about? When I was a small boy and would go with him to his office on a Saturday morning, he used to tell me, "Life insurance is the hardest thing in the world to sell. You know why? Because the only way the customer can win is if he dies." He was an old and knowledgeable expert in these contracts dealing with death, more used to them by far than I was, and as I slowly read him each sentence over the phone, he responded as matter-of-factly as if I were reading the fine-print boilerplate prose off an insurance policy.

" 'Measures of artificial life support in the face of impending death,' " I read, " 'that I specifically refuse are: (a) Electrical or mechanical resuscitation of my heart when it has stopped beating.' "

"Uh-huh," he said.

" '(b) Nasogastric tube feeding'—that's feeding through the nose—'when I am paralyzed or unable to take nourishment by mouth.' "

"Uh-huh, yeah."

" '(c) Mechanical respiration when I am no longer able to sustain my own breathing.' "

"Uh-huh."

I continued on through to where my brother and I were named as the people who should make his medical decisions for him if he became unable to do so. Then I said, "So? How does it strike you?"

"Send it over and I'll sign."

And that was it. Instead of feeling like the insurance man's son, I felt like an insurance man myself, one who'd just sold his first policy to a customer who could win only if he died.

When Claire and I went for dinner on a May Friday a few weeks later, the focus of the evening, as far as I knew, was to be Ingrid's wonderful bouillabaisse, a dish my father liked to eat but couldn't for the life of him pronounce. For convenience's sake, he had come to call it "*ballaboosteh*," a workable and witty enough approximation since that is the Yiddish encomium for "housewife" or "homemaker," and it seemed to encapsulate both the heartiness of the fare that Ingrid was cooking up for us and the soothing managerial role she had quickly come to play in the household.

Despite his now having to hold his arms out to balance himself against the walls of the apartment when he moved from room to room—and having to take only the tiniest steps so as to keep from falling—Ingrid's presence had enormously alleviated his sense of vulnerability and thus (contrary to my naive expectations) enabled him to *increase* his criticism of Lil. I didn't think that it was possible for him to ferret out still more things that were wrong with her, but for Lil's imperfections, even with only one good eye, his vision was microscopic.

"She can't even buy a cantaloupe," he told me in disgust on the phone one morning, and because I had by then heard just about enough on the general subject of what Lil could not do, I answered, "Look, a cantaloupe is a hard thing to buy— maybe the hardest thing there is to buy, when you stop to think about it. A cantaloupe isn't an apple, you know, where you can tell from the outside what's going on inside. I'd rather buy a car than a cantaloupe—I'd rather buy a *house* than a cantaloupe. If one time in ten I come away from the store with a decent cantaloupe, I consider myself lucky. I smell it, sniff it, press both ends with my thumb, I smell another one, press down again with my thumb—eight, nine, ten cantaloupes I can go through like this before finally I settle on one and I take it home and we cut it open for dinner and the thing is tasteless and hard as a rock. I'll tell you about making a mistake with a cantaloupe: *we all do it.* We weren't *made* to buy cantaloupe. Do me a favor, Herm, get off the woman's ass, because it isn't just Lil's weakness buying a shitty cantaloupe: *it's a human weakness.* She is being persecuted by you for something that maybe one percent of the human population is able to do right—and even with half of them it's probably guesswork."

"Well," he said uncertainly, taken aback a bit by my thoroughness, "the cantaloupe is the least of it . . ." but for the time being he had no more complaints to make to me about Lil.

On the Friday evening we joined my father, Lil, Ingrid, and Seth and Ruth for dinner in Elizabeth, our centerpiece turned out to be not the bouillabaisse but a guest whose presence I hadn't known about beforehand. A little surprisingly, when our guest sat down at the table, he told me that he had already had his dinner at home with his wife. It seemed that he had been invited, like a medieval bard or a strolling player, to tell his story to us while *we* ate our dinner—to tell it particularly to me.

He was Walter Herrmann, a survivor of two concentration camps who had come to Newark in 1947, speaking only German; fresh from Auschwitz and only twenty-two, he had somehow found a little money somewhere and, with a partner, bought a small grocery store just down Chancellor Avenue from my high school. From there he had gone on to buy the whole building, then the building next door, and so on, until eventually he sold off his extensive Newark holdings in the mid-fifties—just before the bottom began to fall out of the property market there—went into furs—his family's business in Germany before the war—and became a very rich man. My father knew him from the Elizabeth Y; they used to play cards there when my father could still drive his car and was going to the Y three or four times a week. He had invited him to meet me because Walter was writing a book about his wartime experience. This was not the first time my father had put an aspiring author in touch with me. It did not matter to him, either, when I told him that there was absolutely nothing I could do for somebody who was writing, say, about home mortgages or annuity funds; he would then press me for the office telephone number of my editor friends Aaron Asher or David Rieff and, bypassing me, deal directly with them. Some years back, one of the manuscripts by a friend of his that he sent to Aaron, a book about the real-estate business, went on to be published successfully by Harper & Row, Aaron's house at the time. My father received a finder's fee, and Aaron took the two of us out to lunch in Manhattan. After that there was no stopping him, if there ever had been.

While we were all having a drink in the living room before dinner—on his arrival, Walter had presented my father with a bottle of champagne—I remembered that my father had mentioned this friend of his to me a few weeks back when I told him on the phone that my Hunter literature class had just been reading a book about Auschwitz—Tadeusz Borowski's *This*

Way for the Gas, Ladies and Gentlemen—and another about Treblinka—Gitta Sereny's *Into That Darkness*. My duties, over the years, as a university professor were always a little shadowy to him, and every once in a while he would ask me what exactly it was I taught in my classes and I would try to explain. After I told him about the two concentration camp books, he said, "I have a friend from the Y who was in Auschwitz. He's writing a book himself. Wonderful man." "Is he?" "Maybe you can help him." "I have all I can do helping myself with my own books." "But you could give him some tips." "Dad, I don't have any. There are no tips." "What about Aaron Asher?" "What about him?" "Has he moved again? Is he still at that place?" "Grove? Yes." "Gimme his number again." "Has your friend even finished his book?" "I told you—he's writing it." "Why don't you wait then and call up Aaron when the book is done."

That was the last I heard of Walter and the book until he turned up at the bouillabaisse dinner, where my father was instructing him, "Show him, show him your number, Walter."

We were at the table by then, and as Ingrid was seated between my father and Walter (who had drawn a spare chair up directly beside me) and happened just then to be explaining to Claire and Ruth, across the table, what went into her bouillabaisse, it was necessary for my father to speak *over* their conversation. "Show him your number!" he called again to his friend.

Since it was a warmish night and Walter was wearing a short-sleeved shirt—his light sports jacket he'd already removed and draped over the back of his chair—he had only to rotate his wrist a little for me to be able to read the numerals on his forearm. As he did so, he said to my father, "He's seen this before, I'm sure."

True. My sister-in-law's parents were Holocaust survivors, I knew survivors in Israel, and of course, it wasn't unusual to see camp numerals on the arms of all sorts of people one came across in New York. I had also been seated among at least a dozen survivors the year before during the weeks I had attended the trial in Jerusalem of John Demjanjuk, the Treblinka guard known as Ivan the Terrible. Probably the survivor whose number had had the greatest impact on me when I saw it was the Italian writer Primo Levi. In 1986, I had traveled to

Turin to do a long interview with him for the *New York Times*, and over the course of the four days together we had become mysteriously close friends—so close that when my time came to leave, Primo said, "I don't know which of us is the younger brother and which is the older brother," and we embraced emotionally as though we might never meet again. It turned out that we never did. We had spoken at length about Auschwitz, about his twelve months there as a young man and the two grave books he'd written about the camps, and this had become the heart of the interview. It was published in the *Times*'s Sunday book section just six months before Primo Levi committed suicide by jumping from the top of the deep stairwell in his Turin apartment building—the same stairwell whose five flights of steps I had mounted with such anticipation every day I went there for our talks. I wondered if Primo Levi and Walter Herrmann could possibly have met at Auschwitz. They would have been about the same age and able to understand each other in German—thinking that it might improve his chances of surviving, Primo had worked hard at Auschwitz to learn the language of the Master Race. In what way did Walter account for *his* survival? What had *he* learned? However amateurish or simply written the book, I expected something like that to be its subject.

Walter held what I took to be a manuscript in a large manila envelope on his lap. During the meal he spoke steadily into my ear, about his bourgeois childhood in Berlin, the dancing classes, the Latin studies, about his mother, who had miraculously survived the war, and his father, whom the Nazis had murdered; he spoke about his boyhood reading—"Heine," he said, kissing the tips of his fingers in appreciation—and let me know how much he had loved the works of Franz Werfel. Then he told me how he had been able to hide for several years in Berlin before the Nazis caught up with him and sent him first to Belsen and then to Auschwitz only months before the war ended.

"In Berlin?" I asked. "How could you hide in Berlin?"

"Women. With women. I was the only man left in Berlin. I was eighteen, nineteen. All the German men were in the Army and all the Jewish men were gone. I was hidden by women." He smiled impishly. "My book is not a book like Elie Wiesel writes or Samuel Pisar. Elie Wiesel is to me a genius. I couldn't write such a tragic book. Until the camps, I had a very happy war."

Walter opened the envelope on his lap and what he withdrew was not the manuscript of his book—not that quite yet—but first something on the order of the credentials entitling him to write his book. On the linen tablecloth, beside my bouillabaisse bowl, he placed a small, worn piece of what looked like discolored parchment. It was a much-handled, much-folded identification paper that the Germans had issued to him in the late thirties. I saw that like every other Jewish male in the Third Reich, Walter Herrmann had been given by the Aryan authorities the middle name "Israel." A photograph in one corner of the document showed a boy in his late teens, slender, full-lipped, darkish, vaguely Tartar-looking, and no Adonis. A resemblance to the man on my right was still there, even though the picture was about fifty years old. But where today, in his mid-sixties, Walter seemed no less confident than any other respectable, wealthy Jersey businessman, the boy he had been back then looked like someone who would have been far more comfortable off in a corner reading Franz Werfel than as the only male left for the women of Berlin.

The black hair that grew low on his forehead in the photograph and was styled in what looked like a pompadour had fallen out a week after the war; he had lost it overnight, he said, when he came down with typhus and nearly died following the camp's liberation. This story, which he had told about himself barely a minute or two after having been introduced to the family in the living room, was my first indication that Walter was not one of those survivors who prefer to keep their memories submerged.

He had an additional certificate of validation to produce before we got to the manuscript. This, as he explained to me, was the outer wrapping of a pack of cigarette papers, on the inside of which he had penciled a tiny letter from Auschwitz to his mother. She had been in hiding somewhere in Germany, and for such a letter to have reached her would have taken some doing. Yet clearly she had got it, saved it, and brought it with her to America, for here it was in New Jersey in 1989, what could have been a son's last words in 1944.

"Pass 'em around," my father told me, and so Walter's Third Reich ID card and his two-inch-wide Auschwitz letter went from me to Claire, then from Claire to Seth and Ruth, who were born, respectively, in 1957 and 1961 and who seemed as bemused by the two documents as they were by the loquacious stranger with the number on his arm. They passed them on to Lil, who said of the picture, "Walter, you look like a real *yeshiva bucher*," and she passed them on to my father, who said, "I saw it at the Y," and he passed them on to practical-minded Ingrid, who examined each document altogether neutrally, as though what she held in her hand had been handed over to her as identification for a check to be cashed. Finally the two documents were returned to their owner, who slipped them back in the envelope and extracted next still not the pages of manuscript but a series of recent Polaroid photographs of his grandchildren at one of their birthday parties. These, too, made their way around the table, and only then did he withdraw from the envelope, in a transparent plastic folder, some half dozen sample pages from his book and hand them to me.

"I work on a Macintosh," he told me. "You?"

"Still a typewriter," I said.

Though I could tell that Claire was less than captivated by Walter's personality—in the car on the way home, when I asked what she'd made of Walter, she described him as a lurid exhibitionist—she alone at the table had been following my conversation with him. My father, a ringmaster intent on talking simultaneously to everyone, was able only to tune in and out on Walter and me, and the others were no more interested in Walter than he was in them. I myself didn't know what to make of him, whether he was as forward about his Auschwitz past with everyone he met or whether what looked to Claire to be exhibitionism hadn't perhaps been galvanized a little by my father's promise of assistance from the writer son who gave his college classes books to read about the concentration camps.

"I wrote it in German," he explained as I removed the pages from the folder. "The translation I made myself. But my German by now is not that good and my English when I write is only so-so. I am giving it to my daughter to fix the English for me." Speaking softly to me alone, he said, "I don't know what my daughter will think. She does not know how I survived in Berlin. This isn't the way a child thinks of a parent. She is a married woman, of course; but, still, a father . . ."

This is what I read. *My member was enormous once again and we had only finished. . . . My fountain of juice flowed into her delicious hole. . . . Her lips descended upon my swollen prick. . . . Oh, do that to me again, she said, oh beloved, again. . . . Her dress fell, revealing to me tits more magnificent than Barbara's and bigger than Helen's. . . . I came. . . . She came. . . . It was a delirium.*

And meanwhile, I thought, there was a Holocaust going on.

"Well, Phil, what do you think?" my father asked me. At the table everyone was looking my way, though no one as earnestly as Walter.

"Haven't finished," I said.

She was starved for a man as only a woman of thirty-five can be in wartime. She bathed me in her tub. While the water drained I leaned back. As though it were a ten-course meal, she fell upon my penis. My son, she said, my son. I had never been devoured like this before. Only Katrina had come close to this. Look at it, she said, it is a wonder! I came again. She came again. I came again.

On and on.

When I had finished all the pages, I silently returned them to the folder. Walter said, "This is only a sample."

"There's more."

"Much more. Could it be published?"

"You should finish before you worry about publication."

"I *am* finished. It only needs my daughter to edit the English."

"What about Asher?" my father said to me.

I shrugged. Walter, of course, wouldn't have dreamed of showing these pages to my father, nor did it occur to my father to ask to read them. All he wanted to do was to help a Jewish victim of Hitler and a friend from the Y.

My shrug, I saw, had irritated my father—and puzzled him, too. Was I or was I not interested in books about the Holocaust?

"Give it to *me*, Walter," he said. "I'll take care of it with Aaron Asher. What about David Rieff?" my father said to me.

"Yes," I said, "there's always David."

"Do I have his phone number?" my father asked. "Is it the old number?"

"The old number."

"So—what *do* you think?" my father asked again, no longer hiding his exasperation.

I made a gesture with my two hands that didn't mean a thing, accompanied by an agreeable smile.

"Your son is not a man to commit himself," Walter said politely to my father.

"Yeah . . ." he mumbled disgustedly and went back to his *ballaboosteh.*

On the phone just two days later, my father said, "I'm going to send you some mail. Walter was here this afternoon. He has something for you."

"Dad, no more pages, please, from the book."

"It's the coat he told you about. He left a photograph and the information. He wants me to mail it to you."

After dessert, Walter had told Claire and me that he had the perfect coat for a movie star: "Made for this year's winter collection—so special only a few women in the world could carry it off. A full-length sable, the softest, most weightless sable you've ever seen, and a wonderful shawl collar of summer ermine. I could restyle it for Miss Bloom and it would be gorgeous." It should sell, by all rights, for well over a hundred thousand, Walter told us, but he would talk to his son and they would come up with an interesting proposition. "So special, these furs," he added, "that only two such coats were ever made." "I'll take both," I told him. "I'm afraid that only one is left," Walter replied.

His humorless ardor about giving away, at rock-bottom, this full-length summer ermine and sable coat, the last one in the world and just what we needed, made me think of that chapter in *Survival in Auschwitz* in which Primo Levi describes the forbidden bartering and bargaining among the prisoners; a ration of bread was the most common unit of currency, but everything from a ragged shred of a shirt to the gold teeth in one's mouth was being continuously traded in the corner of the camp farthest from the S.S. barracks. Could not Walter, as a young man, have been among the most brazen of those

Auschwitz traders, or was the capitalist zeal something he'd picked up when he got to America? I said to my father, "Your friend isn't easily discouraged."

"You know he's been to Israel forty-five times?"

"What's he selling to them?" I asked.

"You're a wise guy."

"So's Walter, if you don't mind my saying so. This is one very mischievous Jew. Jewish mischief, thank God, survived the camps too. Guess what his book's about."

"I'm going to mail you the picture of the coat."

"Keep it and buy it for Lil. I said his book—guess what it's about."

"Well, it's about his incarceration."

"No, no," I said.

"It's about his days in Germany."

"It's pornography. Did you know that?"

"I don't know anything. I didn't read any of it."

"It's all about fucking. Every page. He makes me look like a piker."

"Yeah? No kidding." He sounded, for the moment, a little stunned.

"That's why I didn't say anything when you asked me. I was sitting there having dinner with you all, and he gives me this thing, and it's pornography." I was laughing now, and my father joined in.

"And he just left about half an hour ago," my father said.

"Yeah, well, this one sucked me, this one fucked me, I had the biggest cock in Nazi Germany."

We were still laughing when my father said, "Maybe it'll be a best-seller like *Portnoy*."

"Of course. A pornographic best-seller about the Holocaust."

"Guess so."

"Well, that'll be a first," I said.

"His daughter is editing it," my father said.

"She's going to be in for a big surprise."

He was still laughing a little when he said, "I bought that cane today."

"What kind of cane?"

"Sandy wanted me to buy it. With four prongs on it."

"And have you tried it?"

"Yeah. I don't like it because you become accustomed to it. I don't want to become dependent on it."

"You used it when you took your walk? It helped?"

"Yeah, sure. It helped. I don't have to hold on to Abe. Because he's beginning to sag a little himself."

"What do you boys talk about on those walks?"

"We get talking about old times. The old comedians. The Howard Brothers. Lou Holtz. Cantor. Benny. And we sing songs together. Abe likes that. You remember Lou Holtz? He used to say, 'Vas you dere, Chollie?'"

"Is that who said that? I've often wondered. I always say it to Claire but I never knew who the comedian was. He's before my time, Lou Holtz. Vas you dere, Chollie?"

"Sure. We talk about Harry Lauder. Then I sing a song to him about Harry Lauder, and Abe joins in. That's how we walk up and down every day. Abe loved Harry Lauder. The Scotch comedian. I used to watch him when I went to the Palace in Newark. He used to come out and sing this one song. I forget it now that I have to remember. He used to come out with a bent cane and he used to sing this Scottish song. Abe loves that song. He always sings it. It was all clean fun."

"Well, there's the difference for you between old Newark and old Berlin."

"Yeah. Poor Walter."

"Don't feel too sorry for poor Walter. He can take care of himself. He's had some fun in his time."

"Yeah? You believe that stuff? You believe all those things there?"

"Don't you?"

"Who knows? Maybe he's just writing a book."

Our family plans to celebrate his birthday in Connecticut—as we'd done each August since my mother's death eight years back —had to be canceled when, as the summer wore on, his health deteriorated still further. Even with the new four-pronged cane it was now downright dangerous for him to try to move about the apartment on his own, let alone to walk outside anymore. The arm-in-arm sing-alongs with Abe abruptly came to an end and then, intermittently, he began to develop trouble when he swallowed, coughing and choking particularly hard while trying to get down liquids. He associated these difficulties with a lingering cold when, in fact, the enlarging tumor had begun to interfere with the part of the brain that controls the swallowing mechanism.

Unlike my father, I wasn't unprepared for this, since, a little more than a year before, Dr. Benjamin had warned me—after I'd said no at the hospital to the brain surgery—that the swallowing was likely to be affected next. I got in touch with Dr. Wasserman to ask what, if anything, could be done for him. Some tests were ordered and they confirmed that he had begun to aspirate what he ate and was in danger of contracting bronchial pneumonia by this taking of food or drink into his lungs through his windpipe. "It would be better," Harold Wasserman suggested to me, "if he didn't eat." When I asked—startled by his words—what that could possibly mean, Harold explained how the danger of pneumonia could be circumvented by inserting a tube into my father's stomach and feeding him that way. A gastrostomy, it was called. "And what does he do with his saliva?" I asked. "Spits it out," I was told. "It can also be cleaned out with a machine."

Now comes the pay-off, I thought, the consequences of having decided against the operation. "It's beginning to get horrible," I told my brother and for the next few weeks he and I let our father go along blaming his new problem on the cold; until the difficulty got dramatically worse—and we were assured that it would soon enough—we would not depress him further by explaining to him the real source of his trouble. He seemed himself to sense that something serious was up, however, because when I asked on the phone if eating had gotten any easier, he began to deny that it had ever become hard. "It's just that I can't drink sweet liquids," "It's just if the food is too hot," and so on. "I bring up phlegm," he said, "because of my cold. I'm not having any operation on my throat." "Nobody's proposing an operation. But you do seem to have a little swallowing problem." "I don't. I'm fine."

In the meantime, it was summer, and in the Connecticut hills I'd take a fast four-mile walk early each morning, while it was still cool, and in the late afternoon, after another day's work on a novel I had just about finished, I'd go for a thirty-minute swim in the pool. Despite my worries about my father, I hadn't felt healthier in years, and nearing the end of the revisions of *Deception*, the new novel, was the sweet relief that finishing a book always is. But early in August, when I went to take my afternoon swim one day, something unexpected happened, only this time not to my father but to me—after just one easy lap, my head was splitting, my heart was pounding madly, and I could barely catch my breath. Clinging to the edge of the pool, I told myself, "It's anxiety. What are you so anxious about?"—the sort of question that people in physical trouble had the sense not to bother about before the advent of the psychosomologists. What lay in store for my father had debilitated more than just my morale: I felt dreadful, I told myself, because his months and months of misery with the brain tumor were to culminate now in having a feeding tube inserted permanently into his stomach.

My diagnosis was wrong. I felt dreadful after only one lap because over the course of fifty-six years virtually every major artery to my heart had become eighty to a hundred percent occluded and I was not far from a huge heart attack. Twenty-four hours after I climbed out of the swimming pool, gasping for air, I was saved from the heart attack—and from preceding my father to the grave—and he was spared having to bury me —by an emergency quintuple bypass operation.

At 2:00 A.M. on the night before the surgery, when the symptoms took an alarming turn and some half-dozen interns, residents, and nurses began circling busily around the instruments monitoring my worsening condition, a call went out to the surgeon to see if he wanted to change his plans and operate immediately. I realized that never had I been more at one with my father than I was at that moment: not since college, when I used to smuggle him secretly into class with me, the intellectual homunculus for whose development I felt as responsible as I did for my own, had our lives been, if not identical, so intermeshed and spookily interchangeable. Helpless at the center of this little medical hubbub, I confronted, with a clarifying shock, the inevitability in which, for him, every second of existence was awash now.

The difference, of course, was that *after* the surgery I felt reborn—at once reborn and as though I had given birth. My heart, which for any number of years prior to the operation, had apparently been performing on as little as twenty percent of its normal blood supply, was being permeated by all the blood it could want. I would smile to myself in the hospital bed at night, envisioning my heart as a tiny infant suckling itself on this blood coursing unobstructed now through the newly attached arteries borrowed from my leg. This, I thought, is what the thrill must be like nursing one's own infant—the strident, drumlike, postoperative heartbeat was not mine but *its.* So that the night nurse couldn't hear, I whispered to that baby, just under my breath, "Suck, yes, suck, suck away, it's yours, all yours, for you . . ." and never in my life had I been happier.

I don't know how much of that recurrent fantasy and its accompanying litany was a consequence of the euphoria of having had my life saved and how much was the lingering aftereffect of five hours under heavy anesthesia, but during those first few nights, when the pain in my chest wall made continuous sleep impossible, the thought that I was giving suck to my own newborn heart provided hours of the most intense pleasure, sessions during which I did not have to use any imagination at all to feel myself androgynously partaking of the most delirious maternal joy. It strikes me now, looking back, that in the exuberant reveries of those first postoperative nights, I was as near to being the double of my own nurturing mother as, during the anxious, uncertain hours on the eve of the bypass, I had come to feeling myself *transposed*, interchangeable with— even a sacrificial proxy for—my failing father, choking on his mortality at the dinner table. I was never a heart patient alone in that bed: I was a family of four.

I had hoped to keep the news from my father until I was entirely recovered—or for good, if that seemed warranted—but it was impossible. On the Thursday evening before the operation —just a few hours before I took the bad turn—I had phoned him from my bed in the coronary care unit and, pretending that I was home in Connecticut, told him that I had been asked, at the last minute, to fill in at a literary conference for a writer who'd become ill and that I'd be away in New Haven all weekend, probably unable to get to a phone until I was back on Sunday evening. "How much they paying you?" he asked. "Ten thousand bucks," I said, picking a somewhat inflated figure out of the air, one that was bound to please him and—I thought rightly—to distract him from asking anything further. "Good," he said, but with the implication that it was no more than I deserved. Just some sixty or so hours after the operation, on Sunday evening, I phoned again, explaining that if my voice was weak, it was from having talked all weekend at the conference. "They pay you?" "You bet. In singles. Gave it to me in a wheelbarrow." "Well," he replied, laughing, "that was a profitable weekend."

For the next few days, I continued to convince him on the phone each morning that I was leading my regular life—until, that is, the hospital public affairs office rang my room one afternoon to tell me that they had just had calls from the *News* and the *Post* asking for details about me. Though the public affairs officer assured me that she had given them no information, she wanted to let me know that there was likely to be something in the papers anyway. For fear of what might happen if my father, frail and vulnerable as he now was, came unsuspecting upon the news in a gossip column the next day—or got it from someone telephoning to talk to him about what they'd just read about me in the paper—I summoned up all my strength and telephoned New Jersey.

When I told him that I had had a successful coronary bypass operation (I skipped the quintuple part for the time being), he couldn't get his bearings momentarily.

"But who have I been talking to?"

I explained that it had been me, myself, phoning him, just as I was doing now, from my hospital bed. I assured him that I was coming along excellently and told him that the surgeon expected me to be home by the end of a week.

To my surprise then, he got angry. "Remember when you were in college and Mother had the operation and we didn't tell you? Remember what you said when you found out?"

"I don't, no."

"You said, 'Are we a family or aren't we a family?' You got on your high horse. You said, 'Don't ever try to "spare" me again.' You gave us a real tongue-lashing."

"Look, you're none the worse for not having had to sweat it out while I was in the operating room."

"How long were you in the operating room?"

Lopping off a couple of hours, I told him. "And you didn't need that wait," I said. "You've got enough to deal with right now."

"That's not for you to decide."

"Herm, I decided it," I said with a laugh, trying to lighten things up.

But he remained serious—even ominous. "Well, don't do it again," he warned me, as though all of life still lay before us.

Each day and each night while I was in the hospital, and during the first few weeks when I was slowly convalescing at home, I prayed directly to him. "Don't die. Don't die until I get my strength back. Don't die until I can do it right. Don't die while I'm helpless." Sometimes on the phone from the hospital I had to restrain myself from saying it to him out loud. I believe now that he understood what it was I was silently asking of him.

"How are *you* feeling?" I'd ask him. "Me?" he replied—"I'm great. I gave Abe a ninety-fourth birthday party. Ingrid made a pork roll and parsleyed potatoes. Seth and Ruth came, Rita, Abe, Ingrid, me, and Lil. We had a good time. Abe can eat, God bless him. He can walk and he can eat and the next day he even remembered the party."

Some six weeks later, when I was able to travel over to see him, he surprised me again, though this time by being almost childishly apologetic. I couldn't figure out what had him so chagrined, partly because I myself was so dismayed at the changes that had taken place in him since only the last time I'd been there. I would say it was as though a year had passed if I couldn't just as easily have said, looking at him, that it was a lifetime. He who had given Abe a ninety-fourth birthday party had himself become one of the aged whose age is incalculable, little more than a shrunken thing with a crushed face, wearing a black eye patch and sitting completely inert, almost unrecognizable now, even to me. From the way he was propped up in his usual spot at the end of the sofa, it seemed unlikely that he could get himself moving from there without being lifted onto his feet. A toe that had been painfully broken the month before —he'd blacked out in the bathroom and fallen again—was only just beginning to heal. I saw later that even with the aid of his brand-new walker, he could barely locomote himself, by himself, further than a foot or two.

On the bureau across from the sofa was the enlargement of the fifty-two-year-old snapshot, taken with a box camera at the Jersey shore, that my brother and I also had framed and situated prominently in our houses. We are posing in our bathing suits, one Roth directly behind the other, in the yard outside the Bradley Beach rooming house where our family rented a bedroom and kitchen privileges for a month each summer. This is August of 1937. We are four, nine, and thirty-six. The three of us rise upward to form a V, my two tiny sandals its pointed base, and the width of my father's solid shoulders—between which Sandy's pixyish bright face is exactly centered—the letter's two impressive serifs. Yes, V for Victory is written all over that picture: for Victory, for Vacation, for upright, unbent Verticality! There we are, the male line, unimpaired and happy, ascending from nascency to maturity!

To unite into a single image the robust solidity of the man in the picture with that strickenness on the sofa was and was not an impossibility. Trying with all my mental strength to join the two fathers and make them one was a bewildering, even hellish job. And yet I suddenly did feel (or made myself feel) that I could perfectly well remember (or make myself think I remembered) the very moment when that picture had been taken, over half a century before. I could even believe (or make myself believe) that our lives only seemed to have filtered through time, that everything was actually happening simultaneously, that I was as much back in Bradley with him towering over me as here in Elizabeth with him all but broken at my feet.

"What is it?" I asked when I realized that, merely from seeing me, he was upset enough to cry. "Dad—I'm fine now," I said. "You can tell that. Look at me. *Look*. Dad, what's the matter?"

"I should have been there," he told me in a breaking voice, the words barely words now because of what the paralysis had made of his mouth. "I should have been there!" he repeated, this time with fury.

He meant by my side at the hospital.

*

He died three weeks later. During a twelve-hour ordeal that began just before midnight on October 24, 1989, and ended just after noon the next day, he fought for every breath with an awesome eruption, a final display, of his lifelong obstinate tenacity. It was something to see.

Early on the morning of his death, when I arrived at the hospital emergency room to which he had been rushed from his bedroom at home, I was confronted by an attending physician prepared to take "extraordinary measures" and to put him on a breathing machine. Without it there was no hope, though, needless to say—the doctor added—the machine wasn't going to reverse the progress of the tumor, which appeared to have begun to attack his respiratory function. The doctor also informed me that, by law, once my father had been hooked up to the machine he would not be disconnected, unless he could once again sustain breathing on his own. A decision had to be made immediately and, since my brother was still en route by plane from Chicago, by me alone.

And I, who had explained to my father the provisions of the living will and got him to sign it, didn't know what to do. How could I say no to the machine if it meant that he needn't continue to endure this agonizing battle to breathe? How could I take it on myself to decide that my father should be finished with life, life which is ours to know just once? Far from invoking the living will, I was nearly on the verge of ignoring it and saying, "Anything! Anything!"

I asked the doctor to leave me alone with my father, or as alone as he and I could be in the middle of the emergency room bustle. As I sat there and watched him struggle to go on living, I tried to focus on what the tumor had done with him already. This wasn't difficult, given that he looked on that stretcher as though by then he'd been through a hundred rounds with Joe Louis. I thought about the misery that was sure to come, provided he could even be kept alive on a respirator. I saw it all, all, and yet I had to sit there for a very long time before I leaned as close to him as I could get and, with my lips to his sunken, ruined face, found it in me finally to whisper, "Dad, I'm going to have to let you go." He'd been unconscious for several hours and couldn't hear me, but, shocked, amazed, and weeping, I repeated it to him again and then again, until I believed it myself.

After that, all I could do was to follow his stretcher up to the room where they put him and sit by the bedside. Dying is work and he was a worker. Dying is horrible and my father was dying. I held his hand, which at least still felt like his hand; I stroked his forehead, which at least still looked like his forehead; and I said to him all sorts of things that he could no longer register. Luckily, there wasn't anything I told him that morning that he didn't already know.

Later in the day, at the bottom of a bureau drawer in my father's bedroom, my brother came upon a shallow box containing two neatly folded prayer shawls. These he hadn't parted with. These he hadn't ferreted off to the Y locker room or given away to one of his great-nephews. The older tallis I took home with me and we buried him in the other. When the mortician, at the house, asked us to pick out a suit for him, I said to my brother, "A suit? He's not going to the office. No, no suit—it's senseless." He should be buried in a shroud, I said, thinking that was how his parents had been buried and how Jews were buried traditionally. But as I said it I wondered if a shroud was any less senseless—he wasn't Orthodox and his sons weren't religious at all—and if it wasn't perhaps pretentiously literary and a little hysterically sanctimonious as well. I thought how bizarrely out-of-character an urban earthling like my insurance-man father, a sturdy man rooted all his life in everydayness, would look in a shroud even while I understood that that was the idea. But as nobody opposed me and as I hadn't the audacity to say, "Bury him naked," we used the shroud of our ancestors to clothe his corpse.

I dreamed I was standing on a pier in a shadowy group of unescorted children who may or may not have been waiting to be evacuated. The pier was down in Port Newark, but the Port Newark of some fifty years ago, where I had been taken by my father and my Uncle Ed to see the ships anchored in the bay that opened in the distance to the Statue of Liberty and the Atlantic. It was always a surprise to me, as a small child, to be reminded that Newark was a coastal city, since the port was beyond the swamplands, on the far side of the new Newark airstrip and remote from life in the neighborhoods. To be taken down to the harbor and on to the wharves to look up at the ships and out beyond to the bay was to be put in touch momentarily with a geographical vastness that you couldn't imagine while playing stoop ball with your little pals on our cozy, clannish street of two-and-a-half-family houses.

In the dream, a boat, a medium-size, heavily armored, battle-gray boat, some sort of old American warship stripped of its armaments and wholly disabled, floated imperceptibly toward the shore. I was expecting my father to be on the ship, somehow to be among the crew, but there was no life on board and no sign anywhere of anyone in command. The dead-silent picture, a portrait of the aftermath of a disaster, was frightening and eerie: a ghostly hulk of a ship, cleared by some catastrophe of all living things, aiming toward the shore with only the current to guide it, and we on the pier who may or may not have been children gathered together to be evacuated. The mood was heartbreaking in exactly the way it had been when I was twelve and, only weeks before the triumph of V-E Day, President Roosevelt died of a cerebral hemorrhage. Draped in black bunting, the train moving F.D.R.'s casket up from Washington to Hyde Park had passed with lumbering solemnity through the bereaved crowd squeezed in beside the tracks downtown— during those silent seconds on its journey north, consecrating even workaday Newark. Ultimately the dream became unbearable and I woke up, despondent and frightened and sad— whereupon I understood that it wasn't that my father was aboard the ship but that my father *was* the ship. And to be evacuated was physiologically just that: to be expelled, to be ejected, to be born.

I lay awake until dawn. The dream had disturbed my sleep only hours before the morning at the end of July when my father was to have the second MRI of his brain. Dr. Benjamin had ordered the pictures after I had asked Harold Wasserman to consult Benjamin about my father's swallowing problem. I phoned him after he got home from the MRI and when I asked, "How did it go?" he replied, "Old people, young people, healthy-looking people, sick-looking people—and everybody there has something inside them."

To have dreamed of my father's death on the eve of that second MRI wasn't at all remarkable, nor, really, was the incarnation that the dream had worked upon his body. I lay in bed till it was light, thinking of all the family history compressed into that snippet of silent dream-film: just about every major theme of his life was encapsulated there, everything of significance to both of us, starting with his immigrant parents' transatlantic crossing in steerage, extending to his grueling campaign to get ahead, the battle to make good against so many obstructive forces—as a poor boy robbed of serious schooling, as a Jewish working man in the Gentile insurance colossus—and ending with his transformation, by the brain tumor, into an enfeebled wreck.

The defunct warship drifting blindly into shore . . . this is not a picture of my father, at the end of his life, that my wide-awake mind, with its resistance to plaintive metaphor and poeticized analogy, was ever likely to have licensed. Rather, it was sleep that, in its wisdom, kindly delivered up to me this childishly simple vision so rich with truth and crystallized my own pain so aptly in the figure of a small, fatherless evacuee on the Newark docks, as stunned and bereft as the entire nation had once been at the passing of a heroic president.

Then, one night some six weeks later, at around 4:00 A.M., he came in a hooded white shroud to reproach me. He said, "I should have been dressed in a suit. You did the wrong thing." I awakened screaming. All that peered out from the shroud was the displeasure in his dead face. And his only words were a rebuke: I had dressed him for eternity in the wrong clothes.

In the morning I realized that he had been alluding to this book, which, in keeping with the unseemliness of my profession, I had been writing all the while he was ill and dying. The dream was telling me that, if not in my books or in my life, at least in my dreams I would live perennially as his little son, with the conscience of a little son, just as he would remain alive there not only as my father but as *the* father, sitting in judgment on whatever I do.

You must not forget anything.

CHRONOLOGY

NOTE ON THE TEXTS

NOTES

Chronology

Born Philip Roth on March 19 in Newark, New Jersey, second child of Herman Roth and Bess Finkel. (Bess Finkel, the second child of five, was born in 1904 in Elizabeth, New Jersey, to Philip and Dora Finkel, Jewish immigrants from near Kiev. Herman Roth was born in 1901 in Newark, New Jersey, the middle child of seven born to Sender and Bertha Roth, Jewish immigrants from Polish Galicia. They were married in Newark on February 21, 1926, and shortly afterward opened a small family-run shoe store. Their son Sanford ["Sandy"] was born December 26, 1927. Following the bankruptcy of the shoe store and a briefly held position as city marshal, Herman Roth took a job as agent with the Newark district office of the Metropolitan Life Insurance Company, and would remain with the company until his retirement as district manager in 1966.) Family moves into second-floor flat of two-and-a-half-family house (with five-room apartments on each of the first two floors and a three-room apartment on the top floor) at 81 Summit Avenue in Newark. Summit Avenue was a lower-middle-class residential street in the Weequahic section, a twenty-minute bus ride from commercial downtown Newark and less than a block from Chancellor Avenue School and from Weequahic High School, then considered the state's best academic public high school. These were the two schools that Sandy and Philip attended. Between 1910 and 1920, Weequahic had been developed as a new city neighborhood at the southwest corner of Newark, some three miles from the edge of industrial Newark and from the international shipping facilities at Port Newark on Newark Bay. In the first half of the twentieth century Newark was a prosperous working-class city of approximately 420,000, the majority of its citizens of German, Italian, Slavic, and Irish extraction. Blacks and Jews composed two of the smallest groups in the city. From the 1930s to the 1950s, the Jews lived mainly in the predominantly Jewish Weequahic section.

1938   Philip enters kindergarten at Chancellor Avenue School in January.

1942   Roth family moves to second-floor flat of two-and-a-half-family house at 359 Leslie Street, three blocks west of Summit Avenue, still within the Weequahic neighborhood but nearer to semi-industrial boundary with Irvington.

1946   Philip graduates from elementary school in January, having skipped a year. Brother graduates from high school and chooses to enter U.S. Navy for two years rather than be drafted into the peacetime army.

1947   Family moves to first-floor flat of two-and-a-half-family house at 385 Leslie Street, just a few doors from commercial Chancellor Avenue, the neighborhood's main artery. Philip turns from reading sports fiction by John R. Tunis and adventure fiction by Howard Pease to reading the left-leaning historical novels of Howard Fast.

1948   Brother is discharged from navy and, with the aid of G.I. Bill, enrolls as commercial art student at Pratt Institute, Brooklyn. Philip takes strong interest in politics during the four-way U.S. presidential election in which the Republican Dewey loses to the Democrat Truman despite a segregationist Dixiecrat Party and a left-wing Progressive Party drawing away traditionally Democratic voters.

1950   Graduates from high school in January. Works as stock clerk at S. Klein department store in downtown Newark. Reads Thomas Wolfe; discovers Sherwood Anderson, Ring Lardner, Erskine Caldwell, and Theodore Dreiser. In September enters Newark College of Rutgers as pre-law student while continuing to live at home. (Newark Rutgers was at this time a newly formed college housed in two small converted downtown buildings, one formerly a bank, the other formerly a brewery.)

1951   Still a pre-law student, transfers in September to Bucknell University in Lewisburg, Pennsylvania. Brother graduates from Pratt Institute and moves to New York City to work for advertising agency. Parents move to Moorestown, New Jersey, approximately seventy miles southwest of Newark; father takes job as manager of Metropolitan Life's south Jersey district after having previously managed several north Jersey district offices.

1952   Roth decides to study English literature. With two friends, founds Bucknell literary magazine, *Et Cetera*, and becomes its first editor. Writes first short stories. Strongly influenced in his literary studies by English professor Mildred Martin, under whose tutelage he reads extensively, and with whom he will maintain lifelong friendship.

1954   Is elected to Phi Beta Kappa and graduates from Bucknell magna cum laude in English. Accepts scholarship to study English at the University of Chicago graduate school, beginning in September. Reads Saul Bellow's *The Adventures of Augie March*, and under its influence explores Chicago.

1955   In June receives M.A. with Honors in English. In September, rather than wait to be drafted, enlists in U.S. Army for two years. Suffers spinal injury during basic training at Fort Dix. In November, is assigned to Public Information Office at Walter Reed Army Hospital, Washington, D.C. Begins to write short stories "The Conversion of the Jews" and "Epstein." *Epoch*, a Cornell University literary quarterly, publishes "The Contest for Aaron Gold," which is reprinted in Martha Foley's *Best American Short Stories 1956*.

1956   Is hospitalized in June for complications from spinal injury. After two-month hospital stay receives honorable discharge for medical reasons and a disability pension. In September returns to University of Chicago as instructor in the liberal arts college, teaching freshman composition. Begins course work for Ph.D. but drops out after one term. Meets Ted Solotaroff, who is also a graduate student, and they become friends.

1957   Publishes in *Commentary* "You Can't Tell a Man by the Song He Sings." Writes novella "Goodbye, Columbus." Meets Saul Bellow at University of Chicago when Bellow is a classroom guest of Roth's friend and colleague, the writer Richard Stern. Begins to review movies and television for *The New Republic* after magazine publishes "Positive Thinking on Pennsylvania Avenue," a humor piece satirizing President Eisenhower's religious beliefs.

1958   Publishes "The Conversion of the Jews" and "Epstein" in *The Paris Review*; "Epstein" wins *Paris Review* Aga Khan Prize, presented to Roth in Paris in July. Spends first summer abroad, mainly in Paris. Houghton Mifflin awards Roth the Houghton Mifflin Literary Fellowship to publish the novella and five stories in one volume; George Starbuck, a poet and friend from Chicago, is his editor. Resigns from teaching position at University of Chicago. Moves to two-room basement apartment on Manhattan's Lower East Side. Becomes friendly with *Paris Review* editors George Plimpton and Robert Silvers and *Commentary* editor Martin Greenberg.

1959   Marries Margaret Martinson Williams. Publishes "Defender of the Faith" in *The New Yorker*, causing consternation among Jewish organizations and rabbis who attack magazine and condemn author as anti-Semitic; story collected in *Goodbye, Columbus* and included in *Best American Short Stories 1960* and *Prize Stories 1960: The O. Henry Awards*, where it wins second prize. *Goodbye, Columbus* is published in May. Roth receives Guggenheim fellowship and award from the American Academy of Arts and Letters. *Goodbye, Columbus* gains highly favorable reviews from Bellow, Alfred Kazin, Leslie Fiedler, and Irving Howe; influential rabbis denounce Roth in their sermons as "a self-hating Jew." Roth and wife leave U.S. to spend seven months in Italy, where he works on his first novel, *Letting Go*; he meets William Styron, who is living in Rome and who becomes a lifelong friend. Styron introduces Roth to his publisher, Donald Klopfer of Random House; when George Starbuck leaves Houghton Mifflin, Roth moves to Random House.

1960   *Goodbye, Columbus and Five Short Stories* wins National Book Award. The collection also wins Daroff Award of the Jewish Book Council of America. Roth returns to America to teach at the Writers' Workshop of the University of Iowa, Iowa City. Meets drama professor Howard Stein (later dean of the Columbia University Drama School), who becomes lifelong friend. Continues working on *Letting Go*. Travels in Midwest. Participates in *Esquire* magazine symposium at Stanford University; his speech "Writing American Fiction," published in *Commentary* in March 1961, is widely discussed. After a speaking engagement in Oregon, meets Bernard Malamud, whose fiction he admires.

1962   After two years at Iowa, accepts two-year position as writer-in-residence at Princeton. Separates from Margaret Roth. Moves to New York City and commutes to Princeton classes. (Lives at various Manhattan locations until 1970.) Meets Princeton sociologist Melvin Tumin, a Newark native who becomes a friend. Random House publishes *Letting Go*.

1963   Receives Ford Foundation grant to write plays in affiliation with American Place Theater in New York. Is legally separated from Margaret Roth. Becomes close friend of Aaron Asher, a University of Chicago graduate and editor at Meridian Books, original paperback publisher of *Goodbye, Columbus*. In June takes part in American Jewish Congress symposium in Tel Aviv, Israel, along with American writers Leslie Fiedler, Max Lerner, and literary critic David Boroff. Travels in Israel for a month.

1964   Teaches at State University of New York at Stony Brook, Long Island. Reviews plays by James Baldwin, LeRoi Jones, and Edward Albee for newly founded *New York Review of Books*. Spends a month at Yaddo, writers' retreat in Saratoga Springs, New York, that provides free room and board. (Will work at Yaddo for several months at a time throughout the 1960s.) Meets and establishes friendships there with novelist Alison Lurie and painter Julius Goldstein.

1965   Begins to teach comparative literature at University of Pennsylvania one semester each year more or less annually until the mid-1970s. Meets professor Joel Conarroe, who becomes a close friend. Begins work on *When She Was Good* after abandoning another novel, begun in 1962.

1966   Publishes section of *When She Was Good* in *Harper's*. Is increasingly troubled by Vietnam War and in ensuing years takes part in marches and demonstrations against it.

1967   Publishes *When She Was Good*. Begins work on *Portnoy's Complaint*, of which he publishes excerpts in *Esquire, Partisan Review*, and *New American Review*, where Ted Solotaroff is editor.

1968   Margaret Roth dies in an automobile accident. Roth spends two months at Yaddo completing *Portnoy's Complaint*.

1969   *Portnoy's Complaint* published in February. Within weeks becomes number-one fiction bestseller and a widely discussed cultural phenomenon. Roth makes no public appearances and retreats for several months to Yaddo. Rents house in Woodstock, New York, and meets the painter Philip Guston, who lives nearby. They remain close friends and see each other regularly until Guston's death in 1980. Renews friendship with Bernard Malamud, who like Roth is serving as a member of The Corporation of Yaddo.

1970   Spends March traveling in Thailand, Burma, Cambodia, and Hong Kong. Begins work on *My Life as a Man* and publishes excerpt in *Modern Occasions.* Is elected to National Institute of Arts and Letters and is its youngest member. Commutes to his classes at University of Pennsylvania and lives mainly in Woodstock until 1972.

1971   Excerpts of *Our Gang*, satire of the Nixon administration, appear in *New York Review of Books* and *Modern Occasions;* the book is published by Random House in the fall. Continues work on *My Life as a Man*; writes *The Breast* and *The Great American Novel.* Begins teaching a Kafka course at University of Pennsylvania.

1972   *The Breast*, first book of three featuring protagonist David Kepesh, published by Holt, Rinehart, Winston, where Aaron Asher is his editor. Roth buys old farmhouse and forty acres in northwest Connecticut, one hundred miles from New York City, and moves there from Woodstock. In May travels to Venice, Vienna, and, for the first time, Prague. Meets his translators there, Luba and Rudolph Pilar, and they describe to him the impact of the political situation on Czech writers. In U.S., arranges to meet exiled Czech editor Antonin Liehm in New York; attends Liehm's weekly classes in Czech history, literature, and film at College of Staten Island, City University of New York. Through friendship with Liehm meets numerous Czech exiles, including film directors Ivan Passer and Jiří Weiss, who become friends. Is elected to the American Academy of Arts and Sciences.

1973   Publishes *The Great American Novel* and the essay "Looking at Kafka" in *New American Review.* Returns to Prague and meets novelists Milan Kundera, Ivan Klíma, Ludvik Vaculik, the poet Miroslav Holub, and other writers blacklisted and persecuted by the Soviet-backed

Communist regime; becomes friendly with Rita Klímová, a blacklisted translator and academic, who will serve as Czechoslovakia's first ambassador to U.S. following the 1989 "Velvet Revolution." (Will make annual spring trips to Prague to visit his writer friends until he is denied an entry visa in 1977.) Writes "Country Report" on Czechoslovakia for American PEN. Proposes paperback series, "Writers from the Other Europe," to Penguin Books USA; becomes general editor of the series, selecting titles, commissioning introductions, and overseeing publication of Eastern European writers relatively unknown to American readers. Beginning in 1974, series publishes fiction by Polish writers Jerzy Andrzejewski, Tadeusz Borowski, Tadeusz Konwicki, Witold Gombrowicz, and Bruno Schulz; Hungarian writers György Konrád and Géza Csáth; Yugoslav writer Danilo Kiš; and Czech writers Bohumil Hrabal, Milan Kundera, and Ludvik Vaculik; series ends in 1989. "Watergate Edition" of *Our Gang* published, which includes a new preface by Roth.

1974   Roth publishes *My Life as a Man*. Visits Budapest as well as Prague and meets Budapest writers through Hungarian PEN and the *Hungarian Quarterly*. In Prague meets Vaclav Havel. Through friend Professor Zdenek Strybyrny, visits and becomes friend of the niece of Franz Kafka, Vera Saudkova, who shows him Kafka family photographs and family belongings; subsequently becomes friendly in London with Marianne Steiner, daughter of Kafka's sister Valli. Also through Strybyrny meets the widow of Jiří Weil; upon his return to America arranges for translation and publication of Weil's novel *Life with a Star* as well as publication of several Weil short stories in *American Poetry Review*, for which he provides an introduction. In Princeton meets Joanna Rostropowicz Clark, wife of friend Blair Clark; she becomes close friend and introduces Roth to contemporary Polish writing and to Polish writers visiting America, including Konwicki and Kazimierz Brandys. Publishes "Imagining Jews" in *New York Review of Books*; essay prompts letter from university professor, editor, writer, and former Jesuit Jack Miles. Correspondence ensues and the two establish a lasting intellectual friendship. In New York, meets teacher, editor, author, and journalist Bernard Avishai; they quickly establish a strong intellectual bond and become lifelong friends.

1975   Aaron Asher leaves Holt and becomes editor in chief at
        Farrar, Straus and Giroux; Roth moves to FSG with Asher
        for publication of *Reading Myself and Others*, a collection
        of interviews and critical essays. Meets British actress
        Claire Bloom.

1976   Interviews Isaac Bashevis Singer about Bruno Schulz for
        New York Times Book Review article to coincide with pub-
        lication of Schulz's *Street of Crocodiles* in "Writers from
        the Other Europe" series. Moves with Claire Bloom to
        London, where they live six to seven months a year for
        the next twelve years. Spends the remaining months in
        Connecticut, where Bloom joins him when she is not act-
        ing in films, television, or stage productions. In London
        resumes an old friendship with British critic A. Alvarez
        and, a few years later, begins a friendship with American
        writer Michael Herr (author of *Dispatches*, which Roth
        admires) and with the American painter R. B. Kitaj. Also
        meets critic and biographer Hermione Lee, who becomes
        a friend, as does novelist Edna O'Brien. Begins regular
        visits to France to see Milan Kundera and another new
        friend, French writer-critic Alain Finkielkraut. Visits Israel
        for the first time since 1963 and returns there regularly,
        keeping a journal that eventually provides ideas and ma-
        terial for novels *The Counterlife* and *Operation Shylock*.
        Meets the writer Aharon Appelfeld in Jerusalem and they
        become close friends.

1977   Publishes *The Professor of Desire*, second book of Kepesh
        trilogy. Beginning in 1977 and continuing over the next
        few years, writes series of TV dramas for Claire Bloom:
        adaptations of *The Name-Day Party*, a short story by
        Chekhov; *Journey into the Whirlwind*, the gulag autobi-
        ography of Eugenia Ginzburg; and, with David Plante,
        It Isn't Fair, Plante's memoir of Jean Rhys. At request
        of Chichester Festival director, modernizes the David
        Magarshack translation of Chekhov's *The Cherry Orchard*
        for Claire Bloom's 1981 performance at the festival as
        Madame Ranyevskaya.

1979   *The Ghost Writer*, first novel featuring novelist Nathan
        Zuckerman as protagonist, is published in its entirety in
        The New Yorker, then published by Farrar, Straus and
        Giroux. Bucknell awards Roth his first honorary degree;
        eventually receives honorary degrees from Amherst,

Brown, Columbia, Dartmouth, Harvard, Pennsylvania, and Rutgers, among others.

1980   *A Philip Roth Reader* published, edited by Martin Green. Milan and Vera Kundera visit Connecticut on first trip to U.S.; Roth introduces Kundera to friend and *New Yorker* editor Veronica Geng, who also becomes Kundera's editor at the magazine. Conversation with Milan Kundera, in London and Connecticut, published in *New York Times Book Review*.

1981   Mother dies of a sudden heart attack in Elizabeth, New Jersey. *Zuckerman Unbound* published.

1982   Corresponds with Judith Thurman after reading her biography of Isak Dinesen, and they begin a friendship.

1983   Roth's physician and Litchfield County neighbor, Dr. C. H. Huvelle, retires from his Connecticut practice and the two become close friends.

1984   *The Anatomy Lesson* published. Aaron Asher leaves FSG and David Rieff becomes Roth's editor; the two soon become close friends. Conversation with Edna O'Brien in London published in *New York Times Book Review*. With BBC director Tristram Powell, adapts *The Ghost Writer* for television drama, featuring Claire Bloom; program is aired in U.S. and U.K. Meets University of Connecticut professor Ross Miller and the two forge strong literary friendship.

1985   *Zuckerman Bound*, a compilation of *The Ghost Writer*, *Zuckerman Unbound*, *The Anatomy Lesson*, with epilogue *The Prague Orgy*, published. Adapts *The Prague Orgy* for a British television production that is never realized.

1986   Spends several days in Turin with Primo Levi. Conversation with Levi published in *New York Times Book Review*, which also asks that Roth write a memoir about Bernard Malamud upon Malamud's death at age 72. *The Counterlife* published; wins National Book Critics Circle Award for fiction that year.

1987   Corresponds with exiled Romanian writer Norman Manea, who is living in Berlin, and encourages him to come to live in U.S; Manea arrives the next year, and the two become close friends.

1988 *The Facts* published. Travels to Jerusalem for Aharon Appelfeld interview, which is published in *New York Times Book Review*. In Jerusalem, attends daily the trial of Ivan Demjanjuk, the alleged Treblinka guard "Ivan the Terrible." Returns to America to live year-round. Becomes Distinguished Professor of Literature at Hunter College of the City University of New York, where he will teach one semester each year until 1991.

1989 Father dies of brain tumor after yearlong illness. David Rieff leaves Farrar, Straus. For the first time since 1970, acquires a literary agent, Andrew Wylie of Wylie, Aitken, and Stone. Leaves FSG for Simon and Schuster. Writes a memoir of Philip Guston which is published in *Vanity Fair* and subsequently reprinted in Guston catalogs.

1990 Travels to post-Communist Prague for conversation with Ivan Klíma, published in *New York Review of Books*. *Deception* published by Simon and Schuster. Roth marries Claire Bloom in New York.

1991 *Patrimony* published; wins National Book Critics Circle Award for biography. Renews strong friendship with Saul Bellow.

1992 Reads from *Patrimony* for nationwide reading tour, extending into 1993. Publishes brief profile of Norman Manea in *New York Times Book Review*.

1993 *Operation Shylock* published; wins PEN/Faulkner Award for fiction. Separates from Claire Bloom. Writes *Dr. Huvelle: A Biographical Sketch*, which he publishes privately as a 34-page booklet for local distribution.

1994 Divorces Claire Bloom.

1995 Returns to Houghton Mifflin, where John Sterling is his editor. *Sabbath's Theater* is published and wins National Book Award for fiction.

1997 John Sterling leaves Houghton Mifflin and Wendy Strothman becomes Roth's editor. *American Pastoral*, first book of the "American trilogy," is published and wins Pulitzer Prize for fiction.

1998 *I Married a Communist*, the second book of the trilogy, is published and wins Ambassador Book Award of the English-Speaking Union. In October Roth attends three-day international literary program honoring his work in Aix-en-Provence. In November receives National Medal of Arts at the White House.

2000 Publishes *The Human Stain*, final book of American trilogy, which wins PEN/Faulkner Award in U.S., the W. H. Smith Award in the U.K., and the Prix Medicis for the best foreign book of the year in France. Publishes "Rereading Saul Bellow" in *The New Yorker*.

2001 Publishes *The Dying Animal*, final book of the Kepesh trilogy, and *Shop Talk*, a collection of interviews with and essays on Primo Levi, Aharon Appelfeld, I. B. Singer, Edna O'Brien, Milan Kundera, Ivan Klíma, Philip Guston, Bernard Malamud, and Saul Bellow, and an exchange with Mary McCarthy. Receives highest award of the American Academy of Arts and Letters, the Gold Medal in fiction, given every six years "for the entire work of the recipient," previously awarded to Willa Cather, Edith Wharton, John Dos Passos, William Faulkner, Saul Bellow, and Isaac Bashevis Singer, among others. Is awarded the Edward McDowell Medal; William Styron, chair of the selection committee, remarks at the presentation ceremony that Roth "has caused to be lodged in our collective consciousness a small, select company of human beings who are as arrestingly alive and as fully realized as any in modern fiction."

2002 Wins the National Book Foundation's Medal for Distinguished Contribution to American Letters.

2003 Receives honorary degrees at Harvard University and University of Pennsylvania. Roth's work now appears in 31 languages.

2004 Publishes novel *The Plot Against America*, which becomes a bestseller and wins the W. H. Smith Award for best book of the year in the U.K.; Roth is the first writer in the 46-year history of the prize to win it twice.

2005 *The Plot Against America* wins the Society of American Historians' James Fenimore Cooper Prize as the outstanding historical novel on an American theme for 2003–04. On October 23, Roth's childhood home at 81 Summit Avenue in Newark is marked with a plaque as a historic landmark and the nearby intersection is named Philip Roth Plaza.

2006   Publishes *Everyman* in May. Becomes fourth recipient of
        PEN's highest writing honor, the PEN/Nabokov Award.
        Receives Power of the Press Award from the New Jersey
        Library Association for Newark *Star-Ledger* eulogy to
        his close friend, Newark librarian and city historian
        Charles Cummings.

2007   Receives PEN/Faulkner Award for *Everyman*, the first
        author to be given the award three times. Wins the inau-
        gural PEN/Saul Bellow Award for Achievement in Amer-
        ican Fiction and Italy's first Grinzane-Masters Award, an
        award dedicated to the grand masters of literature. *Exit
        Ghost* is published.

2008   Roth's 75th birthday is marked by a celebration of his life
        and work at Columbia University. *Indignation* is published.

Note on the Texts

This volume contains Philip Roth's books *The Counterlife* (1986), *The Facts* (1988), *Deception* (1990), and *Patrimony* (1991).

The Counterlife was published in New York by Farrar, Straus & Giroux in 1986 and in England by Jonathan Cape the following year. A limited edition of the novel was published in 1986 by the Franklin Library, which contained a short introduction by Roth; in the present volume, this introduction is included in the Notes. The text printed here of *The Counterlife* is taken from the 1986 Farrar, Straus & Giroux edition.

Excerpts from *The Facts* began appearing in periodicals in 1987, when versions of chapters of the book were published in *The New York Times*, *Atlantic*, and *Vanity Fair*. *The Facts* was brought out by Farrar, Straus & Giroux in New York in 1988 and by Jonathan Cape in England in 1989; the 1988 Farrar, Straus & Giroux edition of *The Facts* contains the text printed here.

Deception was published by Simon & Schuster in New York and by Jonathan Cape in England in 1990. A pre-publication excerpt from the novel had appeared in *Esquire*. The 1990 Simon & Schuster edition of *Deception* contains the text printed here.

In January 1991, a little more than a year after the death of Roth's father, *Patrimony* was published by Simon & Schuster; Jonathan Cape brought out an English edition of the memoir in 1991. Entitled "The Last Days of Herman Roth," a version of the book's final chapter was featured in *The New York Times Magazine* late in 1990. The text printed here is taken from the 1991 Simon & Schuster edition of *Patrimony*.

This volume presents the texts of the original printings chosen for inclusion here, but it does not attempt to reproduce nontextual features of their typographic design. The texts are presented without change, except for the correction of typographical errors. Spelling, punctuation, and capitalization are often expressive features and are not altered, even when inconsistent or irregular. The following is a list of typographical errors corrected, cited by page and line number: 48.1, again.; 76.11, so?'; 117.38, Zuzkerman; 295.5, along; 325.31, ring-a-lievo; 365.13, thown; 474.23, with—"; 475.20, Hill."; 530.27–28, 'Metamorphosis'; 541.15, Well.; 586.6, 1942; 625.36, lonsome.

Notes

In the notes below, the reference numbers denote page and line of this volume (the line count includes chapter headings). Biblical quotations are keyed to the King James Version. Quotations from Shakespeare are keyed to *The Riverside Shakespeare*, ed. G. Blakemore Evans (Boston: Houghton Mifflin, 1974).

1.1   THE COUNTERLIFE]   A limited edition of the novel published by the Franklin Library contained the following prefatory note by Roth:

> This book was not conceived in a flash. It didn't develop a brain—and with a brain a sense of itself and its dimensions—until it was almost fully grown. It just picked up and went striding off and, reluctantly but obediently, I followed after, recording in my notebook, when I could, my impressions of its mindless wanderings. With increasing frustration and uncertainty, I wondered if it could ever come to understand where it was going and why, but for several years I nonetheless hung back, allowing the novel to proceed every which way, and thinking that since it was not my first offspring but my fifteenth, I was sufficiently practiced to be able to prevent it from getting away entirely if it should begin running amok.
>
> Here is a small sample of the notes that I made while I followed the book along a narrative road that I myself had never seen or taken before. You who have not yet read *The Counterlife* may complain that my notes are inconclusive, underdeveloped thoughts, teasingly opaque and intellectually truncated—that since you are as yet without knowledge of the finished work, these notes are actually more puzzling than illuminating. I agree. I too was someone who, when he read these notes, had not yet read *The Counterlife*, and so I know exactly how you feel.
>
> *The closest we can come to the truth about reality is in the fictions we create about it.*
>
> *Life can go this way or life can go that way. The alternative, the alternative to the alternative, etc.*
>
> *People tell themselves stories. Why? What kind?*
>
> *Characters who set out to change their stories.*
>
> *Anything can happen—and that is precisely what happens: anything.*

Radical change is the law of life.

A series of fictive propositions about what it would be like IF.

Like a series of propositions in a scientific demonstration. If we mix this with this, then what happens? What happens if you mix the same elements into some other context?

A series of equations. If Henry, then what? Title: If/Then.

A fullish exploration of the imagining of the alternatives to one's existence.

Everyone invents a fictitious character for himself some time or other.

Your original reading is repeatedly challenged and you are released as much as you want to be, as far as you wish to be. To some degree you are released, to some degree you are held.

You have to adjust to new information that is seemingly contradictory. Sometimes several different things are going on, contending for your belief. You finish the book with a question.

"The author is a barbaric god who revels in human sacrifice." Genet.

A novel that undermines itself. The Counterbook.

The quote about the author as "barbaric god" is taken from Jean-Paul Sartre's book *Saint Genet* (1952), an excerpt of which appears in the introduction to an English translation of Jean Genet's novel *Our Lady of the Flowers* (1944).

6.26   *the underside . . . career*]   Dixie Dugan was the heroine of the popular novel *Show Girl* (1928) by J. P. McEvoy, which became the basis of a long-running newspaper comic strip by McEvoy and illustrator John H. Striebel, as well as a Broadway musical and movies. Starting out as a showgirl, Dixie worked more wholesome jobs for most of the run of the strip.

8.10   *the museum*]   The Metropolitan Museum of Art.

8.14   "*Lay, . . . bed . . .*"]   From Dylan's 1969 hit single "Lay Lady Lay."

8.32   *Asbury Park*]   Seaside resort on the Jersey Shore, fifty miles from Newark.

14.18   Chancellor Avenue]   Principal commercial street in Newark's Weequahic section.

19.10   Largo . . . *Xerxes*,"] Popular instrumental piece from *Xerxes* (1738), opera by German-born composer George Frederick Handel (1685–1759).

25.27   Mel Tormé] Jazz singer, songwriter, and actor (b. 1925) nick-named "The Velvet Fog."

33.14   Olympic Park] Amusement park in Irvington, New Jersey, not far from Newark.

33.16   Wendell Willkie] American politician (1892–1944), Republican candidate for president in 1940.

36.9–10   Collins Avenue] In Miami Beach.

36.24   UJA] United Jewish Appeal.

37.11–12   to recast . . . date] An update of Babel's phrase "glasses on your nose and autumn in your heart." See "How Things Were Done in Odessa," a story from *Odessa Stories* (1931), in which Reb Arye-Leib tells the narrator to "forget for a while that you have glasses on your nose and autumn in your heart. Forget that you pick fights from behind your desk and stutter when you are out in the world! Imagine for a moment that you pick fights in town squares and stutter only among papers."

38.3   *Tristan and Isolde*] The adulterous love affair between the Cornish knight Tristan and the Irish princess Isolde has been the subject of literary adaptations since the Middle Ages, most famously the three-act opera (1865) whose music and libretto were written by German composer Richard Wagner (1813–1883).

39.25   Donahue] Nationally syndicated talk-show hosted by the television personality Phil Donahue (b. 1935).

42.12–13   or perhaps . . . Richard the Third] In his rise to become king, Richard III, in Shakespeare's play (1591), seduces Anne of Neville after killing her husband and her father. In a soliloquy he boasts: "Was ever woman in this humor woo'd? / Was ever woman in this humor won? / I'll have her, but I will not keep her long" (I.ii.227–29).

49.11   Theodor Herzl] Hungarian-born political leader, lawyer, and writer (1860–1904), founder of modern Zionism.

52.15–16   General Moshe Dayan] Israeli military commander and states-man (1915–1981), popular with American Jews for his military exploits.

52.19   Mogen David] Literally, "the shield of David," the Star of David, Israeli national symbol.

52.25–26   Menachem Begin . . . Golda's] Polish-born Israeli politician Menachem Begin (1913–1992) Israeli Prime Minister from 1977 to 1983; Golda

Meir (1898–1978), Israeli Prime Minister (1969–74) who had lived in the United States from 1906 to 1921.

52.33   Abba Eban]   South African–born, Cambridge-educated Israeli diplomat and government minister (1915–2002) who served as foreign minister, 1966–74.

55.26   cheder]   Hebrew: children's school.

55.27   *payess*]   Yiddish: sidelocks.

58.27   Dizengoff Street]   Central boulevard in Tel Aviv, named for its first mayor.

60.23   Sayings of Chairman Arafat]   A play on the title of the Chinese collection of quotations from Mao Zedong (also known in the West as *The Little Red Book*), with Mao's name being replaced by that of Palestinian leader Yasser Arafat (1929–2004).

60.31   W11]   The postal code for the Notting Hill and Holland Park areas of West London.

66.34   man who runs Libya]   Muammar al-Qaddafi (b. 1942), dictator of Libya since seizing power in a 1969 coup.

68.32   made aliyah]   Immigrated to Israel (*aliyah* is a Hebrew word meaning "ascent").

73.13   Daniel Barenboim]   Argentine-born Israeli pianist and conductor (b. 1942).

74.12   Moonie]   Widely used derogatory term to describe members of the Unification Church, led by its Korean founder, Sun Myung Moon (b. 1920).

79.13   Shalom aleichem."]   A Hebrew greeting meaning "Peace be upon you."

79.29   shnorring]   Yiddish: begging.

81.18   chazan]   Hebrew: cantor.

81.39   minyan]   Literally "number" in Hebrew: a quorum of ten adult Jewish males to conduct public prayers, as required by Jewish law.

83.20   mitzvah]   Hebrew: a good deed.

86.24   Habitat of Larry Holmes]   Boxer Larry Holmes (b. 1949), the "Easton Assassin," was a heavyweight boxing champion.

93.36   Sacco-Vanzettian eloquence]   Nicola Sacco (1891–1927) and Bartolomeo Vanzetti (1888–1927) were anarchist Italian immigrants convicted of murder and armed robbery in 1920 and executed in 1927 despite international protests that their guilt had not been proven. To their supporters, the broken English with which they defended themselves came across as a kind of eloquence.

100.29–31   Chekhov's . . . Three.]   "One must not put a loaded rifle on the stage if no one is thinking of firing it," Chekhov wrote in an 1889 letter. S. Shchukin's *Memoirs* (1911) quotes Chekhov as remarking, "If you say in the first chapter that there is a rifle hanging on a wall, in the second or third chapter it absolutely must go off."

101.14–15   the Zuckerman differences . . . Agamemnon's?]   Agamemnon, the son of King Atreus of Mycenae, commanded the Greek forces in the Trojan War. The history of his family (the House of Atreus) is replete with incidents of rape, incest, and murder among its members.

102.16   Shema Yisrael]   In Judaism, the prayer beginning "Shema Yisrael, Adonai Eloheinu, Adonai Echad" ("Hear, O Israel: The Lord our God, the Lord is One"). It is recited twice daily, in the morning and evening.

102.17   lay tefillin]   Tefillin, or phylacteries, are two black leather boxes containing Biblical verses attached to leather straps. They are fastened to the left arm and to the forehead by adult Jewish males when they recite their morning prayers.

105.7   Nineveh]   Assyrian city that is castigated in the Bible for its decadence.

107.16–17   Harpo Marx . . . hardly mute]   Comedian and actor Arthur Marx (1888–1964), known as Harpo, was the silent one of the three Marx Brothers.

111.15   Judah Maccabee]   The second-century-B.C.E. Jewish leader Judah Macabee led a revolt against the repressive king Antiochus IV Epiphanes, the ruler of the Hellenistic Seleucid Empire. After Judah Maccabee's forces drove their enemies out of Jerusalem, the Jewish Temple in the city was rededicated in 165 B.C.E., an event commemorated by the festival of Chanukah.

111.16   Bar Kochba against the Romans]   Simeon Bar Kochba led an unsuccessful Jewish revolt against the Romans (132–35 C.E.).

113.1   Sadat . . . back]   Egyptian president Anwar Sadat had made an official trip to Israel in November 1977, the first state visit by an Arab leader to Israel since its foundation in 1948.

113.11–12   I have read . . . Thoreau]   Both Gandhi and Thoreau advocated civil disobedience in their writings.

115.39   *Judenrein*]   German: cleansed of Jews.

116.7   *Ich bin ein Berliner*] "I am a Berliner": declaration of John F. Kennedy in a speech delivered at West Berlin's City Hall on June 26, 1963.

117.30–31   Mailer. . . killing?] Norman Mailer often wrote about criminals, most notably in "The White Negro" (1957), *An American Dream* (1965), and *The Executioner's Song* (1979), based on the execution in Utah of convicted murderer Gary Gilmore. In 1981, Mailer helped win the release of a convicted murderer, Jack Henry Abbott (1944–2002), whose writings from prison he had come to admire. While out on parole in New York City, Abbott fatally stabbed a 22-year-old man in a restaurant after an argument.

124.5   "Inner Sanctum,"] *Inner Sanctum Mysteries*, a national radio show that ran from 1941 to 1952; each episode began with the creaking of a door.

124.14–15   'Duffy's . . . This?'] *Duffy's Tavern* (1940–52), radio comedy set in a family bar on Manhattan's Third Avenue; *Can You Top This?* (1940–1954), radio (and later television) comedy show in which listeners were invited to submit jokes that a panel of four comedians—Joe Laurie, Jr., Harry Hershfield, Peter Donald, and "Senator" Ed Ford—would then try to "top," as measured by an applause meter in the studio.

124.16   WJZ and WOR] A.M. radio stations originating in Baltimore and New York City, respectively, that could be heard all over the East Coast.

124.18–19   Ruppert . . . Bears] The New York Yankees' minor-league farm team, the Newark Bears, played in Ruppert Stadium in Newark's Ironbound section.

127.22   Myshkin motives] The dreamy idealist Prince Myshkin, protagonist of Fyodor Dostoevsky's novel *The Idiot* (1868), suffers from epilepsy and is thought to be innocent and mentally disabled.

132.6–7   faster than a Paganini Caprice] The Italian violinist and composer Niccolò Paganini (1782–1840) played at great speed and wrote technically demanding showpieces to show off his virtuosity.

153.10   *bucher*] Yiddish: student at a rabbinical school (yeshiva).

155.21–22   a little Eichmann] An officer in the SS, Adolf Eichmann (1906–1962) headed the Jewish Department of the Reich Main Security Office, 1939–45, and played a major role in organizing the deportation of European Jews to extermination camps. He was captured in Argentina by Israeli agents on May 11, 1960, and taken to Israel, where he was tried for war crimes in 1961 and hanged on May 31, 1962.

157.16   Brooke Shields] Child actress and model (b. 1965), star of Louis Malle's controversial film *Pretty Baby* (1978), in which she played a young girl growing up in a turn-of-the-century New Orleans brothel.

159.35   schmatta] Yiddish: rag.

166.36   Satan . . . Budd] In Herman Melville's novella *Billy Budd,
Sailor*, posthumously published in 1924, a beautiful and innocent young sailor
has been impressed into the Royal Navy during the Napoleonic Wars. While
serving on board the HMS *Bellipotent*, he is falsely accused of mutinous behavior by an Iago-like officer whom he accidentally kills during a confrontation. Too inarticulate to defend himself, he is court-martialed and hanged at
sea.

167.25   T. S. Eliot's poem] "Burbank with a Baedeker: Bleistein with a
Cigar," in Eliot's *Poems* (1920), which offers an anti-Semitic portrait of Blei-
stein: "But this or such was Bleistein's way: / A saggy bending of the knees /
And elbows, with the palms turned out, / Chicago Semite Viennese."

176.23   *Tel Quel*] Influential literary journal founded in Paris in 1960 by
the French critics Phillipe Sollers and Marcelin Pleynet.

177.20–21   "'And as . . . health?'"] Friedrich Nietzsche, from the essay
Nietzsche contra Wagner, published posthumously in 1895.

178.17–18   'Twere profanation . . . Donne."] Lines 7–8 of "A Valedic-
tion Forbidding Mourning" (1633) by the English poet John Donne (1572–
1631).

189.32   *salto mortale*] Italian: mortal leap.

196.15–17   Henry Miller . . . 'cunt.'] While an expatriate in Paris, American novelist Henry Miller (1891–1980) wrote candidly about sex in novels such
as *Tropic of Cancer* (1934), which along with his other books was banned from
the United States for decades.

204.36   Neil Simon] Playwright and screenwriter (b. 1927), author of
The Odd Couple (1965) and more than thirty other comedies for the stage as
well as more than twenty screenplays.

204.36–37   Hegel's unhappy consciousness] A stage in the evolution of
self-consciousness as outlined in the *Phenomenology of Spirit* (1807) by German philosopher Georg Wilhelm Friedrich Hegel (1770–1831).

205.13   Chaim Weizmann] Zionist statesman (1874–1952), the first president (1949–1952) of Israel.

226.13–14   like Garbo . . . furniture.] Swedish-born movie star Greta
Garbo (1905–1990) played the title role in *Queen Christina* (1933). Traveling
incognito, the queen spends the night in an inn with her Spanish lover. In a
famous scene, she caresses the furniture and other items in their room at the
inn so as to memorize them. "In the future, in my memory," she says, "I shall
live a great deal in this room."

228.36–38   Lady Byron . . . writings]   Lady Anne Isabella Noel Byron (1792–1860) was the divorced wife of the English poet George Gordon, Lord Byron (and mother of their daughter Ada), who destroyed some of Byron's manuscripts after his death. Lady Isabel Burton (1831–1896), writer and wife of the explorer and diplomat Sir Richard Burton (1821–1890). They traveled together and collaborated on a translation of *A Thousand and One Nights*. After her husband's death, she destroyed some of his personal papers, including writings dealing with sexuality.

233.7   *deus ex machina*]   Latin: God in the machine; a term in ancient drama indicating the sudden appearance and intervention of a god late in the play to resolve a seemingly intractable plot dilemma.

236.6   Buñuel]   Spanish director Luis Buñuel (1900–1983), whose many films include *Viridiana* (1961), *The Exterminating Angel* (1962), and *The Milky Way* (1969).

236.15–16   Like Mayerling . . . Vetsera]   Archduke Rudolph, crown prince of Austria (1858–1889), and his mistress, Baroness Marie Vetsera (1871–1889), died in an apparent love suicide pact at Mayerling, the royal hunting lodge.

243.8   V & A]   London's Victoria & Albert Museum.

243.20   the Sixth,"]   I.e., the Sixth Form, the two years of secondary school for British students aged 16 to 18.

246.24   rowing eights]   Eight-man racing sculls.

247.13   Kurtz]   Deranged ivory trader in Joseph Conrad's novella *Heart of Darkness* (1902).

250.28   "Keep Death Off the Road,"]   Postwar public-safety slogan of Britain's Ministry of Transport.

251.12–16   Sheraton . . . Chippendale]   English furniture designers Thomas Sheraton (1751–1806) and Thomas Chippendale (1718–1779).

253.39–254.3   They've done . . . *Bowl*]   The BBC aired a four-part adaptation of James's 1896 novel *The Spoils of Poynton* in 1970 and a six-part adaptation of his 1904 novel *The Golden Bowl* in 1972.

256.5–8   ancient yews . . . Gray]   Eighteenth-century English poet Thomas Gray's "Elegy Written in a Country Churchyard" (1751) refers to the "yew-tree's shade" in its fourth stanza.

256.32–33   visionary feelings . . . Wordsworth]   For example, "Lines Composed a Few Miles Above Tintern Abey" (1798), lines 93–102: "And I have felt / A presence that disturbs me with the joy / Of elevated thoughts; / a sense sublime / Of something far more deeply interfused, / Whose dwelling is the light of setting suns, / And the round ocean and the living air, / And the blue sky, and in the mind of man; / A motion and a spirit, that impels / All thinking things, all objects of all thought, / And rolls through all things."

257.32–33   portraits of horses . . . sub-Stubbs] English artist George Stubbs (1724–1806) was acclaimed for his paintings of horses.

263.28   John Buchan] Scottish novelist, biographer, historian, and statesman (1875–1940) best known for his thrillers, particularly *The Thirty-Nine Steps* (1915).

265.31   the Moor . . . Desdemona] The Moor Othello, and his young Venetian wife, Desdemona, in Shakespeare's *Othello* (1603).

270.34   Kierkegaard?] Danish philosopher and religious thinker Søren Kierkegaard (1813–1855), author of *Either/Or: A Fragment of Life* (1843) and *Fear and Trembling* (1843).

271.14–15   like Gulliver] In Part I of Jonathan Swift's *Gulliver's Travels* (1726), Lemuel Gulliver travels to the island of Lilliput, inhabited by tiny humans less than six inches tall.

271.37–38   like the character . . . off.'] Olga, the oldest of the three Prozorov sisters, opens Chekhov's 1901 play by recalling, "Father died just a year ago, on this very day."

274.28   *Gentleman's Agreement*] Film (1947) starring Gregory Peck (in the role of a journalist who poses as a Jew to research anti-Semitism) and directed by Elia Kazan, based on Laura Z. Hobson's novel (1941).

297.1   Grossinger's] Popular Jewish resort in the "Borscht Belt" in New York's Catskill Mountains.

297.10–11   Disraeli or Lord Weidenfeld] Benjamin Disraeli (1804–1881), novelist and Conservative prime minister, was a Sephardic Jew who was baptized in the Church of England in 1817; a Jew born in Vienna, George, Baron Weidenfeld (b. 1919) is a publisher and philanthropist.

299.24–25   When Balzac died . . . deathbed] While on his deathbed, French novelist Honoré de Balzac (1799–1850) is reputed to have asked his doctor to send for Horace Bianchon, the fictional doctor who cares for many of the characters in Balzac's monumental cycle of novels, *La comédie humaine*.

301.17–18   Homo Ludens] Latin: man the player. The phrase was popularized after it served as the title of a 1938 book about the role of play in human affairs by the Dutch historian and social theorist, Johan Huizinga (1872–1945).

302.26   Schweiz] German: Switzerland.

302.27   Constable's England] Painter John Constable (1776–1837) was the greatest English landscape painter of his generation.

THE FACTS

309.33–34   between exhibitionistic . . . Salingerism] Norman Mailer (see note 117.30–31) reveled in public exposure and even ran for mayor of New York City in 1969; American novelist and short-story writer J. D. Salinger (b. 1919) is famously reclusive and for nearly six decades has lived entirely out of the public eye.

317.19   *Hear, O Israel, the family is God, the family is one.*]   See note 102.16.

318.25   *balabusta*] Yiddish: homemaker.

319.1   their Gonerils . . . Cordelias] Lear's three daughters in Shakespeare's *King Lear* (1608).

320.17   William Buckley] William F. Buckley, Jr. (1925–2008), author, editor, host of the public-affairs television program *Firing Line*, and conservative polemicist who founded the magazine *National Review* in 1955.

320.17–18   MacNeil–Lehrer] Public-television news program, named for its co-anchors Robert MacNeil (b. 1931) and Jim Lehrer (b. 1934).

322.6   CORREGIDOR FALLS] The island of Corregidor in Manila Bay fell to the Japanese on May 6, 1942, in what was a major Japanese victory in the early months of U.S. involvement in World War II.

324.20–21   our family's Bernard Baruch] American Jewish financier and philanthropist (1870–1965), adviser to several presidents including Franklin D. Roosevelt.

325.12   blackout shades] Heavy black window coverings that prevented light from escaping from inside buildings. They were installed along the Eastern seaboard to prevent ships from being silhouetted against the coastline, thereby becoming more vulnerable to German submarine attack.

325.31   ring-a-levio] Children's game in which one team's players hide and the other team tries to capture them.

330.11   Jewish National Fund] Organization founded in 1901 to buy land for Jewish settlement in Palestine.

331.16–17   Galicia and Polish Russia] Galicia was a region in the southeastern part of present-day Poland and the southwestern part of present-day Ukraine; "Polish Russia" describes the large part of Poland annexed by Russia in the late eighteenth century. Both areas once had significant populations of Jews.

332.6   Seabees] Common name for the United States Naval Construction Battalions.

333.1–2   Meyer Lansky's . . . Avenue] Meyer Lansky (1902–1983) was a Russian-born Jewish gangster who helped organized a national crime syndicate in the 1930s. In later years he and his wife lived in Miami Beach.

335.12   S. Klein's] Discount department store in downtown Newark.

335.27   Ironbound district] Working-class neighborhood east of downtown Newark, so called because it is bounded on the west by Pennsylvania Railroad tracks.

335.36–38   brotherhood . . . Symphony,"] Title song (music by Earl Robinson, lyrics by Abel Meeropol, under the pseudonym Lewis Allen) sung by Frank Sinatra for the Oscar-winning film *The House I Live In* (1945), a short film that spoke out against anti-Semitism and promoted racial tolerance. Tony Martin's "Tenement Symphony," written for the Marx Brothers' film *The Big Store* (1941), is a sentimental song about ethnic harmony in the city ("The Cohens and the Kellys / The Campbells and Vermicellis / All form a part of my tenement symphony").

337.13   GI Bill] Officially called the Servicemen's Readjustment Act (1944), the GI Bill guaranteed access to college education and provided tuition funding for returning veterans.

337.31–32   *Winesburg, Ohio . . . Brooklyn*] Respectively, the collection of related short stories (1919) by Sherwood Anderson, the novel *A Portrait of the Artist as a Young Man* (1916) by James Joyce, and the short story (1935) by Thomas Wolfe.

338.4–5   despite the presence of Einstein . . . pilgrimage] During his long tenure (1933–55) at Princeton University's Institute for Advanced Study, Einstein lived in town at 112 Mercer Street.

338.13   Four Freedoms] President Roosevelt named "four essential human freedoms" in his State of the Union address of January 6, 1941: freedom of speech; freedom of worship; freedom from want; and freedom from fear.

338.14   DAR] Daughters of the American Revolution, conservative women's organization that limits its membership to descendants of individuals who participated in the American War of Independence.

338.14   Henry Wallace] Henry Wallace (1888–1965), Vice-President (1941–45) of the United States and Progressive candidate for President in 1948.

338.27   Stan Lomax and Bill Stern] The sports broadcasters Stan Lomax (1899–1987) and Bill Stern (1907–1971).

338.33–34   Longy Zwillman and the Newark mob] Jewish gangster

Abner "Longy" Zwillman (1889–1959) was known as the "Al Capone of New Jersey."

342.30–31   unoutlandish little college town . . . Allyson]   Bandleader Kay Kyser (1905–1985) was a popular radio, television, and movie personality; he was "The Ol' Professor" on his program *Kay Kyser's Kollege of Musical Knowledge*. Actress June Allyson (1917–2006) was cast in wholesome roles in movies such as *Good News* (1947), a musical comedy set at the fictional Tait University in the 1920s.

344.34–36   by Budd Schulberg's novel . . . Glick]   Schulberg's *What Makes Sammy Run?* (1941) recounted the rise of Sammy Glick from his impoverished Lower East Side roots to success as a cunning Hollywood producer.

348.17   *Guys and Dolls*]   Broadway musical (1950; music and lyrics by Frank Loesser) about the colorful adventures of small-time gamblers, based on the stories of Damon Runyon.

350.10–11   inspired . . . Ross]   English essayists Joseph Addison (1672–1719) and Richard Steele (1672–1729) were the major contributors to the London daily periodical *The Spectator*, which they published 1711–12 (Addison briefly revived it in 1714); their urbane, polished prose style is a model of elegant essay-writing. Harold Ross (1892–1951), founding editor of *The New Yorker*, edited the magazine from 1925 until his death.

350.12   Mike Todd]   Broadway and Hollywood producer (1909–1958) known for his flamboyant large-cast movie productions such as *Around the World in 80 Days* (1956).

350.29   Plato's Retreat]   Private sex club that opened in 1977 in the basement of New York's Ansonia Hotel. Fitted out with a disco, saunas, and a swimming pool with waterfalls, the club promoted orgiastic sex among its members.

350.33–34   Jerry Rubin . . . lawyer]   Led by Abbie Hoffman (1936–1989) and Jerry Rubin (1938–1994), the Yippies were a group of satirists and provocateurs whose stunts included the founding of the Youth International Party. Both were members of the "Chicago Eight," a group charged with conspiracy to incite a riot during the 1968 Democratic National Convention in Chicago. They were represented in federal court by attorney William Kunstler (1919–1995), a New York defense attorney who specialized in representing political radicals.

350.34–36   Tuli Kupferberg . . . *Arts*]   Tuli Kupferberg (b. 1923), poet who in 1964 co-founded the satiric rock band The Fugs with poet and peace-activist Ed Sanders (b. 1939). *Fuck You/A Magazine of the Arts*, "Edited,

Published & Printed by Ed Sanders at a Secret location in the Lower East Side, New York City, USA," was launched in 1962.

350.36–37 *Oh, Calcutta!*] *Oh, Calcutta!* (1969), provocative theatrical review featuring nudity created by English writer and theater critic Kenneth Tynan (1929–1980) and produced by Hillard Elkins (b. 1929). It enjoyed long runs in an Off-Broadway production in New York and in London.

350.37–38 Al Goldstein . . . Norman Mailer] Al Goldstein (b. 1936) started the sex tabloid *Screw* in 1968; Allen Ginsberg (1926–1997), Beat poet whose poem "Howl" (1956) was the subject of a widely publicized obscenity trial; outspoken political activist Bella Abzug (1920-1998) served in the U.S. House of Representatives from 1970 to 1976; comedian Lenny Bruce (1925–1966) was arrested numerous times on obscenity charges; Norman Mailer, see notes 117.30–31 and 309.33–34.

351.21–22 "Let's start . . . fearlessly obscene . . ." . . . E. E. Cummings] From the opening of an untitled poem from *No Thanks* (1935) by American poet E. E. Cummings (1894–1962): "let's start a magazine // to hell with literature / we want something redblooded // lousy with pure / reeking with stark / and fearlessly obscene."

351.27 William Shawn's . . . *Yorker*] Succeeding Harold Ross in 1952, William Shawn (1907–1992) was the editor of the *New Yorker* for thirty-five years.

352.18 Antioch] Socially progressive liberal-arts college in Yellow Springs, Ohio (now defunct).

353.15 Cynewulf to *Mrs. Dalloway*] I.e., the central tradition of English literature as it was taught to undergraduates though survey and other courses. Cynewulf was an Anglo-Saxon poet about whom little is definitively known; *Mrs. Dalloway* is Virginia Woolf's modernist novel, published in 1925.

353.20–21 Thomas Wolfe's . . . Dublin] Thomas Wolfe set fiction in his hometown of Asheville, North Carolina; James Joyce made similar use of Dublin, Ireland.

354.14–15 the young Capote] The early works of writer Truman Capote (1924–1984) include a series of short stories published in the 1940s and the novel *Other Voices, Other Rooms* (1948).

355.13 New York paper *P.M.*] Leftist daily tabloid (1940–48) spearheaded by its publisher and editor Ralph Ingersoll (1900–1984); it did not run advertisements and published work by prominent writers and journalists such as I. F. Stone, its Washington correspondent.

357.14 McCarthy hearings] Joseph McCarthy (1908–1957), Republican senator from Wisconsin, chaired a Senate subcommittee investigating purported Communist influence in government.

357.37–38 'So we beat on . . . the past.'] From the final lines of F. Scott Fitzgerald's *The Great Gatsby* (1925).

358.1 white bucks] Casual shoes that, along with khaki trousers, oxford shirt, and crewneck Shetland sweater, were an essential component of the clean-cut "Collegiate" style of the 1950s.

361.13 "The Fight at Finnsburgh,"] Surviving fragment of an Old English epic poem.

361.24–25 "the golden . . . Byzantium"] See the final stanza of "Sailing to Byzantium" (1927) by William Butler Yeats (1865–1939): "Once out of nature I shall never take / My bodily form from any natural thing, / But such a form as Grecian goldsmiths make / Of hammered gold and gold enameling / To keep a drowsy Emperor awake; / Or set upon a golden bough to sing / To lords and ladies of Byzantium / Of what is past, or passing, or to come."

369.23–24 (". . . they were drunken . . . Wolfe)] From Wolfe's novel *Of Time and the River* (1935).

370.26 *volkisch*] German: of the folk, a key term in the vocabulary of Nazi propaganda.

370.31–33 a friend of Andy Hardy's . . . Carpenter.] Andy Hardy (played by Mickey Rooney) was an all-American boy in a successful series of movie comedies that included *You're Only Young Once* (1937) and *Love Finds Andy Hardy* (1938); June Allyson, see note 342.30–31; Carleton Carpenter (b. 1926), similarly wholesome actor and songwriter.

371.1 Ingmar Bergman] Swedish film director Ingmar Bergman (1918–2007) specialized in searching psychological dramas such as *Persona* (1966).

372.30 *shagitz*] Yiddish: Gentile man.

373.16 Chicago's Hyde Park] Where the University of Chicago is located.

373.20–21 Max . . . sociologist] Max Horkheimer (1895–1973), German-Jewish philosopher and sociologist who, with his colleague Theodor Adorno (1903–1969), was the guiding intellectual force behind the Marxist-inflected Frankfurt School of social theory.

374.5 IC] Illinois Central, the Chicago-area commuter-rail system.

379.14–15 Othello's tales . . . shoulders] See *Othello*, I.iii.142–44, in which Othello recounts telling Desdemona tales of his travels among "the Cannibals that each other eat, / The Anthropophagi, and men whose heads / Do grow beneath their shoulders."

379.32 *Swann's Way*] First volume (1913) of Marcel Proust's seven-volume novel, *A la recherche du temps perdu* (*In Search of Lost Time*).

380.37–38   like the defendants at Nuremberg] After the end of World
War II, Nazi political and military leaders were tried for war crimes by a tribunal convened in the Bavarian city of Nuremberg.

381.2–4   benighted American life . . . Dreiser] Realist depictions of
American poverty and desperation were characteristic of novels such as Anderson's *Poor White* (1920) and Dreiser's *An American Tragedy* (1925).

381.11   parfit Jewish knight] A "parfit [perfect] gentil knyght" is how
Chaucer describes the Knight in the General Prologue to *The Canterbury Tales*
(c. 1387).

381.23   D&C] Dilation and curettage, a common gynecological procedure that can be used as an early-term abortion technique.

394.25–26   Times Square . . . *Live!*] Based on the story of Barbara
Graham (1923–1955), the 1958 melodrama *I Want to Live* starred Susan Hayward (1917–1975) as a convicted murderer facing execution.

395.36   Reader, I married her.] Cf. Charlotte Brontë's *Jane Eyre*, ch. 38,
when Jane announces that she has become the wife of Mr. Rochester:
"Reader, I married him."

397.7   *The Wings of the Dove*] Novel (1902) by Henry James.

397.11   Isabel Archer] Heroine of James's *The Portrait of a Lady* (1881).
The American expatriate Gilbert Osmond (397.14) is her self-absorbed husband in a loveless marriage.

399.2–3   S. J. . . . Salinger] Humorist S. J. Perelman (1904–1979), nov-
elist Irwin Shaw (1913–1984), comic writer Arthur Kober (1900–1975), and
J. D. Salinger (see note, 309.33–34) were all frequent contributors to *The
New Yorker*.

402.8   *shammes*] Yiddish (derived from Hebrew): servant; the caretaker
of a synagogue.

402.13   *minyan*] See note 81.39.

402.33   *shul*] Yiddish: synagogue.

403.24–25   Broadway . . . Aleichem] The stories of Yiddish writer
Sholem Aleichem (1859–1916) were adapted by Arnold Perl into the play
Tevya and His Daughters (1958), which in turn became the basis for the hit
Broadway musical *Fiddler on the Roof* (1964).

404.7   Anti-Defamation League] B'nai B'rith Anti-Defamation League,
organization founded in 1913 to combat prejudice and discrimination against
Jews.

404.39–405.1   another set . . . *Exodus*] Leon Uris (1924–2003) was a writer of best-selling historical novels, many with Jewish themes. The subject of *Exodus* (1958) is the founding of the State of Israel in 1948.

422.18   Kennedy . . . McCarthy's candidacy]   Before his assassination in June 1968 Kennedy and Minnesota senator Eugene McCarthy (1916–2005) were rival antiwar candidates for the Democratic presidential nomination.

431.22   pre-chic Barneys]   Before its reinvention as an upscale clothing store, Barneys was a discount retailer.

432.5–7   I watched Mayor Daley's police . . . conventioneers]   Long-time Chicago mayor Richard Daley (1902–1976) called in the police to sub-due thousands of antiwar demonstrators (including Yippies: see note 350.33–34) who mounted protests during the 1968 Democratic National Convention. A government-sponsored independent commission later called the response to the demonstrations a "police riot."

436.33   a young James Jones]   American novelist (1921–1977) best known for his books about American military life, particularly his first novel, *From Here to Eternity* (1951).

446.38   *shicker*]   Yiddish: drunkard.

454.33   amid the alien corn]   See John Keats, "Ode to a Nightingale" (1819), stanza 7: "Perhaps the self-same song that found a path / Through the sad heart of Ruth, when, sick for home, / She stood in tears amid the alien corn."

457.6–7   Randomness . . . *Ulysses*."]   The stream-of-consciousness tech-nique used in James Joyce's novel *Ulysses* (1922) allows for the random thoughts of its protagonist Leopold Bloom, as well as other chance intru-sions, to find their way into the narrative.

DECEPTION

473.31–32   holed up . . . Frank family]   The Jewish teenager Anne Frank (1929–1945) wrote nearly all of her world-famous diary while she and her fam-ily hid from the Nazis in an Amsterdam attic from July 1942 to August 1944, when they were betrayed to the SS security police.

478.2   in 1968 after the Russian tanks]   On August 21, 1968, Warsaw Pact troops invaded Czechoslovakia to quash the "Prague Spring" movement championed by Alexander Dubček (1921–1992), who upon his appointment as the first secretary of the Czechoslovak Communist Party in January 1968 had begun instituting reforms in accord with a vision of "socialism with a human face."

479.26   Regine's disco]   Nightclub and jet-set haunt on New York's Park Avenue as well as other chic locales worldwide.

479.27   Parke-Bernet]   High-end auction house.

483.14–16   *Heine's Jewish Comedy* . . . Begin]   *Heine's Jewish Comedy: A Study of His Portraits of Jews and Judaism* (1983) by literary biographer S. S. Prawer, *The Jew as Pariah: Jewish Identity and Politics in the Modern Age*, which collects essays from the 1940s by German-American political philosopher Hannah Arendt, and *White Nights: The Story of a Prisoner in Russia* (1957) by Menachem Begin, later Israeli prime minister.

483.23   Radio Three]   BBC station featuring cultural programming, especially classical music.

486.27   Banham's]   English security company.

488.28–29   *Il faut . . . dictionnaire.*]   French: one must sleep with one's dictionary.

488.38   Albert Schweitzer]   Physician, theologian, and musician Albert Schweitzer (1875–1965) founded a hospital in Lambaréné (in present-day Gabon, Africa) and spent most of his life working there. He was awarded the Nobel Peace Prize in 1952. He became an emblem of humanitarian values.

488.40   Malinowski]   Bronislaw Malinowski, Polish-born anthropologist (1884–1942), author of *The Sexual Life of Savages in North-western Melanesia* (1929), a book often referred to simply as *The Sexual Life of Savages*.

499.22   Leon Edel]   Biographer and literary critic (1907–1997) best known for his five-volume life of Henry James.

507.26   Lawrence of Arabia]   British military officer T. E. Lawrence (1888–1935) fought with the Arabs during their revolt against the Ottoman Empire. Known as "Lawrence of Arabia," he became a controversial figure because of his close identification with the Arab cause. He wrote a romantic version of his life in the bestseller *The Seven Pillars of Wisdom: A Triumph* (1922).

512.32   Scheherezade]   Legendary Persian queen and storyteller in the classic *The Book of One Thousand and One Nights*. Every day the king would marry a new virgin and behead the old wife. Scheherazade tells clever stories to divert the king and stay alive.

518.14   the remissive history of Jean Genet]   French novelist and playwright (1910–1986) whose early career as a petty criminal and prostitute was the basis for books such as *The Miracle of the Rose* (1946) and *The Thief's Journal* (1949).

518.22   Nora's]   Nora Barnacle, Joyce's wife.

518.23–24   Svidrigailov]   Enigmatic sensualist and villain in Dostoevsky's novel *Crime and Punishment* (1866).

522.6   Dickens's Fagin]   A rapacious Jewish criminal in *Oliver Twist* by
English novelist Charles Dickens (1812–1870).

523.6   Waley-Cohens]   Jewish family whose members include Sir Bernard
Waley-Cohen (1919–1991), Lord Mayor of London in 1960.

523.15–17   the Samuelses . . . Montefiores]   Prominent Jewish merchant-
banking families in Britain.

525.11–12   Next you . . . Walker!]   Canadian writer Margaret Atwood
(b. 1939), author of *The Handmaid's Tale* (1985), and African-American writer
Alice Walker (b. 1944), author of *The Color Purple* (1982).

525.32–33   the erotic liaisons . . . Colette]   French novelist (1873–1954),
author of *Sido* (1929), *Gigi* (1945), and the pseudonymously published "Clau-
dine" tetralogy, wrote candidly about sex and erotic relationships.

528.37   'The Blood of the Walsungs']   German novelist Thomas Mann's
1905 novella about brother-sister incest in a wealthy Jewish family.

528.37   'Michael Kohlhaas']   Novella (1810) by German writer Heinrich
von Kleist, recounting a horse trader's campaign of violence against a local
nobleman after his horses are confiscated.

528.37–38   'In the Ravine.']   Long story by Anton Chekhov published in
1900.

530.24–25   Kafka's *Letter* . . . *Trial*]   The agonized letter Franz Kafka
wrote to his father in 1919 was posthumously published as a short book.
Kafka's novella *The Metamorphosis* (1915) tells the story of Gregor Samsa, who
wakes up one morning to discover that he has been transformed into a monstrous bug; in *The Trial* (published posthumously in 1925), the clerk Josef K.
is subjected to a mysterious trial for an unspecified crime that is never
resolved.

538.30–31   Bacon's portraits . . . enemy.]   The portraits of Anglo-Irish
painter Francis Bacon (1909–1992) are characterized by grotesquely distorted
features.

541.36   character called Nobody]   In Homer's *Odyssey*, Odysseus calls
himself "Nobody" as part of a ruse to escape from the cave where the man-
eating Cyclops holds him captive.

547.23–27   poem of Marvell's . . . Both.]:   See the opening of "The De-
finition of Love" (1650–52) by English poet Andrew Marvel (1621–1678): "My
Love is of a birth as rare / As 'tis for object strange and high; / It was
begotten by despair / Upon Impossibility."

563.39   *Mitteleuropa*]   German term for Central Europe.

568.34   *homo ludens*]   See note 301.17–18.

573.27–28   "Tomorrow . . . new."]   Milton, *Lycidas* (1638), final line.

577.3–4   Ariel Sharon]   Right-wing Israeli military and political leader (b. 1928).

577.26   Nausicaä? Calypso?]   In Homer's *Odyssey*, Odysseus was ship-wrecked for seven years on the island of the nymph Calypso. Although she was in love with him and promised him immortality if he remained on the island, he yearned to return home to his wife Penelope. The gods intervened on his behalf and ordered Calypso to let him go. When he reached the land of the Phaeacians by raft, he was taken by the young princess Nausicaä to her father, who provided him with ships on which to sail home.

PATRIMONY

592.8–9   Hamlet's . . . Yorick]   See *Hamlet* V.i.

592.10–11   "he hath . . . times."]   Hamlet speaking of Yorick to his friend, Horatio, at *Hamlet* V.i.185–86.

595.39   Lemberg]   Present day Lviv, Ukraine.

598.19   Phi Beta Kappa key]   Prestigious academic honor society based on undergraduate achievement; its inductees receive a key to indicate membership.

608.30   *alte kockers*]   Literally "old shitters" in Yiddish: old-timers, old farts.

614.28–29   Perlman or Yo-Yo Ma]   Virtuoso musicians who enjoy world-wide fame: violinist Itzhak Perlman (b. 1945) and cellist Yo-Yo Ma (b. 1955).

615.19–20   a little Victor Herbert . . . a little Gershwin]   Victor Herbert (1859–1924), composer of light opera and popular music; George Gershwin (1898–1937), composer of works in both the classical and popular repertoire, most familiarly *Rhapsody in Blue* (1924) and the opera *Porgy and Bess* (1935).

616.37   Fritz Kreisler]   Austrian-born American violinist and composer (1875–1962).

617.9   Jack Benny played better]   Comedian Jack Benny (1894–1974) often told jokes with a violin tucked under his arm as a prop. He played the violin for laughs as well.

624.6   Grunings]   Ice-cream parlor in the village of South Orange, NJ.

625.36   "Are you lonesome tonight?"]   Popular song first published in 1926 by Lou Handman and Roy Turk; it was a hit for Elvis Presley, among others.

626.28   "Rubens?" . . . *zaftig*] Yiddish: full-figured; an apt description of the women in the paintings of Flemish Baroque artist Peter Paul Rubens (1577–1640).

634.30   Gaudí's Barcelona] The buildings of Catalan architect Antonio Gaudí (1852–1926), marked by their striking and idiosyncratic sculpted forms, pervade Barcelona.

637.1   *Yentl . . . Roof*] *Yentl* (1983), movie musical starring Barbra Streisand adapted from the I. B. Singer story "Yentl, the Yeshiva Boy"; *Fiddler on the Roof*, see note 403.24–25.

637.23   *Wild Strawberries*] Film (1957) directed by Ingmar Bergman about an old man revisiting the scenes of his youth.

637.26   Beckett's or Gogol's] Irish playwright and novelist Samuel Beckett (1906–1989), whose seminal late-modernist works include the play *Waiting for Godot*, first staged in 1953, and the novel trilogy *Molloy* (1951), *Malone Dies* (1951), and *The Unnameable* (1953); Russian writer Nikolai Gogol (1809–1852), author of *Dead Souls* (1842).

646.11   Caryl Chessman] Caryl Chessman (1921–1960), convicted of rape and kidnapping charges in California, was on death row for twelve years before being executed. He wrote four books while in prison, and his case became an international cause célèbre for anti-death penalty advocates.

654.30–31   Gombrowicz . . . Konwicki] Polish novelists: Witold Gombrowicz (1904–1969), author of *Ferdydurke* (1937) and *Trans-Atlantyk* (1953); Stanislaw Witkiewicz (1885–1939), author of *Insatiability* (1930) and plays such as *The Madman and the Nun* (1925); Bruno Schulz (1892–1942), author of the books of stories *The Street of Crocodiles* (1933) and *Sanatorium Under the Sign of the Hourglass* (1937) and whose career was cut short when he was murdered by the Nazis in 1942; Tadeusz Konwicki (b. 1926), author of *A Dreambook for Our Time* (1963) and *A Minor Apocalypse* (1979). English translations of *Ferdydurke*, *The Street of Crocodiles*, *Sanatorium Under the Sign of the Hourglass*, and *A Dreambook for Our Time* were included in Penguin's "Writers from the Other Europe" series, of which Roth was general editor.

662.19   "down neck"] Working-class Newark neighborhood.

662.40   *haimisher*] Yiddish: homey, in the sense of "*haimisher mensch*," an unpretentious man who is easy to be around.

666.8–9   Elie Wiesel] Romanian-born Jewish writer (b. 1928), author of more than forty books, most notably *Night* (1958), an account of his experiences surviving the Holocaust. He was awarded the Nobel Peace Prize in 1986.

666.14–15   This guy Cohen . . . Levy-something.] American biochemist

Stanley Cohen (b. 1922) and Italian neurobiologist Rita Levi-Montalcini (b. 1909) shared the 1986 Nobel Prize in Medicine.

675.3–5   false teeth . . . eyes] Jimmy Durante, American variety entertainer (1893–1980) who sang comic and sentimental songs while accompanying himself on the piano; he was famed for his large nose. Singer and actor Eddie Cantor (1882–1964) was called "Banjo Eyes" because of the size and expressiveness of his eyes.

679.25   *yeshiva buchers*] See note 153.10.

698.17–18   Yul Brynner . . . four thousandth time.]   "A Puzzlement" is a song from the musical *The King and I* (1951), music by Richard Rodgers (1902–1979) and lyrics by Oscar Hammerstein II (1895–1960). Russian-born actor Yul Brynner (1920–1985) played the King of Siam in the play's successful Broadway run, a movie adaptation, and several revivals; after his 4,500th performance as the king, he was given a special Tony Award.

698.34   Velie] A brand of luxury automobiles manufactured by the Velie Motors Corporation of Moline, Illinois, from 1908 to 1929.

707.7   old St. Nick's Arena] St. Nicholas Arena, located on West 66th Street in Manhattan, began holding boxing matches in 1906 and was an important boxing venue until its closing in 1962.

711.40   Tadeusz Borowski's] Polish writer and journalist Tadeusz Borowski (1922–1951) survived both the Auschwitz and Dachau concentration camps.

712.2   Gitta Sereny's *Into That Darkness*]   *Into That Darkness: From Mercy Killing to Mass Murder* (1974), by Austrian-born journalist and biographer Gitta Sereny (b. 1923), is an extensive psychological and moral study of Franz Stangl (1908–1971), commandant of the Nazi extermination camps at Sobibór and Treblinka.

712.37   John Demjanjuk] Ukrainian-born John Demjanjuk (b. 1920) immigrated to the United States after World War II and became an American citizen. After allegations arose that he had been "Ivan the Terrible," an especially brutal guard at the Treblinka extermination camp, he was stripped of his American citizenship by an Ohio district court and was extradited in February 1986 to Israel, where he was tried for war crimes. Found guilty and sentenced to death, he won a reversal of his conviction on appeal when evidence from the Soviet Union cast doubt on his identification as Ivan the Terrible. He returned to the United States, where his citizenship was restored in 1998. The U.S. government then sought again to strip him of his citizenship because, having failed to reveal that he had been a guard at three Nazi concentration camps (an allegation Demjanjuk denied), he had sought citizenship under false pretenses. His citizenship was revoked in 2004 when a circuit-court panel declared that there was clear and convincing evidence that he had been a concentration-camp guard, and he was later ordered deported to Ukraine, although most likely he will remain in the United States until he dies.

712.40   Primo Levi] Italian writer and chemist Primo Levi (1919–1987) wrote about his experiences in Auschwitz and his various ordeals after he was liberated.

713.29   Heine] German-Jewish writer Heinrich Heine (1797–1856), one of Germany's major nineteenth-century romantic poets.

713.31   Franz Werfel] Czech-born novelist, poet, and playwright (1890–1945) who wrote in German. He is best known for his novel *The Song of Bernadette* (1941).

713.40–714.1   Not a book . . . Samuel Pisar] Elie Wiesel, see note 666.8–9; Samuel Pisar (b. 1929), Polish-born American lawyer and Holocaust survivor, author of the memoir *Of Blood and Hope* (1979).

THE LIBRARY OF AMERICA SERIES

The Library of America fosters appreciation and pride in America's literary heritage by publishing, and keeping permanently in print, authoritative editions of America's best and most significant writing. An independent nonprofit organization, it was founded in 1979 with seed money from the National Endowment for the Humanities and the Ford Foundation.

This book is set in 10 point Linotron Galliard,
a face designed for photocomposition by Matthew Carter
and based on the sixteenth-century face Granjon. The paper
is acid-free lightweight opaque and meets the requirements
for permanence of the American National Standards Institute.
The binding material is Brillianta, a woven rayon cloth made
by Van Heek-Scholco Textielfabrieken, Holland. Compo-
sition by Dedicated Business Services. Printing by
Malloy Incorporated. Binding by Dekker Book-
binding. Designed by Bruce Campbell.